A Treasury of
ANIMAL STORIES

A Treasury of
ANIMAL STORIES

Selected and With a Foreword by
E. LOUISE MALLY

CASTLE BOOKS

Published by
CASTLE BOOKS
A division of Book Sales, Inc.
P.O. Box 7100
Edison, NJ 08818-7100

Published by arrangement with Citadel Press, an imprint of the
Carol Publishing Group, 600 Madison Avenue, New York, NY 10022.

ISBN 0-7858-0213-4

Printed in the United States of America

Acknowledgments

For arrangements made with various authors, their representatives, and publishing houses whereby certain copyrighted material was permitted to be reprinted, and for the courtesy extended by them, the following acknowledgments are gratefully made:

Mrs. George Bambridge. The story "Conversion of St. Wilfrid" from *Rewards and Fairies* by Rudyard Kipling. Reprinted by permission of Mrs. G. Bambridge and Doubleday, Doran & Co. Copyrighted 1909–1910 by Rudyard Kipling and 1936 by Mrs. Bambridge.

Brandt & Brandt. The four stories: "The Honk Honk Breed" from *Arizona Nights* by Stewart Edward White, copyright, 1907, by Doubleday, Doran & Co., copyright, 1935, by Stewart Edward White. "For My Lady" by Albert R. Wetjen, copyright, 1932, by Crowell-Collier Publishing Company. "The Stuff of Dreams" by Helen Dore Boylston, copyright, 1937, by The Atlantic Monthly Company. "King of the Cats" by Stephen Vincent Benét from *Selected Works of Stephen Vincent Benét*, published by Farrar & Rinehart, Inc. "King of the Cats" copyright, 1929, by Stephen Vincent Benét.

Mrs. John Keith Butler. The story "Whippitsnapper."

Jacques Chambrun, Inc. The story "Wild Goat's Kid" by Liam O'Flaherty.

Dodd, Mead & Company. The story "Riquet" from *The Amethyst Ring* by Anatole France, and "Oracle of the Dog" from *The Incredulity of Father Brown* by G. K. Chesterton. Reprinted by permission of Dodd, Mead & Company, Inc.

Doubleday, Doran & Company, Inc. The two stories: "The Friendly Rat" from *The Book of a Naturalist* by W. H. Hudson, copyright, 1919, by Doubleday, Doran & Company, Inc., and "Mehitabel's Extensive Past" from *Archy and Mehitabel*, by Don

v

Marquis, copyright, 1927–30, by Doubleday, Doran & Company, Inc.

E. P. Dutton & Co., Inc. The story "Miss Holloway's Goat" from *Horse in the Moon* by Luigi Pirandello, translated from the Italian by Samuel Putnam, published and copyrighted by E. P. Dutton & Co., Inc., New York.

Harcourt, Brace & Company, The poems: "The Naming of Cats" and "The Song of the Jellicles" from *Old Possum's Book of Practical Cats,* copyright, 1939, by T. S. Eliot. By permission of Harcourt, Brace & Company, Inc.

Harper & Brothers. The three stories: "Æpyornis Island" from *Thirty Strange Stories* by H. G. Wells, "Madame Jolicoeur's Cat" from *From the South of France* by Thomas A. Janvier, and "Urban & Suburban Rat" from *Fables for the Frivolous* by Guy Wetmore Carryl. Reprinted by permission of Harper & Brothers.

Alfred A. Knopf, Inc. The two stories: "A Tent in Agony" from *Midnight Sketches* by Stephen Crane, copyright, 1926, by Alfred A. Knopf, Inc., and "Lady Into Fox," by David Garnett, copyright, 1923, by Alfred A. Knopf, Inc. Reprinted by permission of Alfred A. Knopf, Inc.

The Macmillan Company. The stories: "Hey Diddle, Diddle, The Cat" from *Up Hill, Down Dale* by Eden Phillpots. "Kashtanka" from *The Cook's Wedding & Other Stories* by Anton Chekhov, translated by C. Garnett. "For the Love of a Man" from *The Call of the Wild* by Jack London. "A Sailor's Yarn" from *A Mainsail Haul* by John Masefield. By permission of The Macmillan Company, publishers.

Harold Matson. The two stories: "The Backbreaker's Bride" by Henry Williamson, and "Mary" from *Presenting Moonshine* by John Collier.

The New Yorker. The story "A Cat in the Family" by Winifred Williams. By permission of *The New Yorker,* copyright, 1944, The F-R. Publishing Corporation.

G. P. Putnam's Sons. The story "Northward" from *The Way of the Wild* by Herbert Ravenel Sass, copyright, 1925, by Mr. Sass. Courtesy of G. P. Putnam's Sons.

Charles Scribner's Sons. The two stories: "Kerfol" from *Zingu and Other Stories* by Edith Wharton, copyright, 1916, by Charles Scribner's Sons; copyright, 1944, by E. P. de C. Tyler, and *The Rubáiyát of a Persian Kitten* by Oliver Herford, copyright, 1904, by Oliver Herford.

Mr. James Thurber. For "The Wood Duck."

Viking Press, Inc. The two stories: "The Gift" from *The Red Pony* by John Steinbeck, copyright, 1938, by John Steinbeck, and "Sredni Vashtar" from *The Short Stories of Saki* (H. H. Munro). Reprinted by permission of The Viking Press, New York.

Table of Contents

Introduction

FROM THE TIME when primitive man drew incredibly alive pictures of bison and cruder pictures of men with animal masks on the walls of the caves in southern France, man has been aware of his special kinship with animals. Primitive man thought of special animals as his ancestors—different animals being the ancestors of different tribes or groupings within the tribe—and had a special, magic relation to them; modern man knows that in terms of evolution he is related, even though ever so distantly, to the most uncomplicated piece of unicellular life, and that man himself is actually a highly complex animal.

I think part of man's interest in animals is based on that relationship, though the animal lover may know little of the beliefs of his ancestors. The men who created the mediaeval tales about the faithful dog, the faithful warhorse, the faithful falcon admittedly continued to accept certain superstitions about animals and their relationship to man: the witch's cat, which was the servant of the devil being one example. But he did not think of the faithful dog or horse or falcon having any special, magic relation to man, and certainly in his philosophy, man had no scientific relationship to beasts: man was of a completely different species and had been created separately from all other life. Nevertheless, man could not help recognizing in animals those admirable traits which he looked for in the best of human beings.

Man recognized and recognizes specific traits in animals which also belong to human beings, and frequently he finds them there in intensified form. That is not to say that animals are better or in any way more important than human beings. Men are not only more complicated, but are more capable of pain and delight, and infinitely more capable of change than any animal. Animals cannot do a fraction of the things that man can do. But what animals can do, they frequently do so much better, because they do it instinctively and simply and easily. Primitive man knew this and wanted to believe he had a special relationship with animals, in part so that he could acquire some of their abilities: he wanted the swiftness of the stag or the fierceness of the bear, or the very strange power which the snake has. Many of us, I suspect, are fascinated by animals because of this same specialisation, though we have lost any hope of acquiring their characteristics by any magic means. A cat, to my perhaps prejudiced eyes, is more graceful than the greatest dancer, and frequently gayer and more full of that aliveness which is perhaps the most attractive quality in any human being than any except the most fascinating men and women ever are.

There are other reasons why we are interested in animals. The old nursery rhyme with its moral:

> " 'Why did the lamb love Mary so?'
>   The eager children cried.
>   ' 'Cause Mary loved the lamb, you know,'
>   The teacher then replied"

can be reversed. It is very easy to love animals because they love us so quickly, and for such unimportant reasons—because we feed them, and scratch them behind the ears, and keep them comfortable. Anyone can be loved by an animal if he will go to the slightest trouble to win an animal's affection. That is not anything of which we need be particularly proud, but perhaps, in a complicated world, it is just as well to be able to have a few good things easily. And the love of our pets is very comfortable and heart warming.

Yet the fact that man is interested in animals would be no reason for the assembling of 600 pages of animal stories if those stories were not also good literature. Fortunately, this very interest in animals of which we have been speaking has resulted in the writing of a great many wonderful tales. I have tried to choose all the best that I know, and there are here, accordingly, all sorts of stories about all sorts of animals. There are stories about whales and seals, and chickens and falcons, and rats and monkeys, and of course about dogs and cats and horses. *Northwind* and *For my Lady* are stories of action; *Sredni Vashtar* and *A Vendetta* are stories of cruelty and revenge; *The Conversion of St. Wilfred* and *Hey Diddle, Diddle, the Cat and* . . . are frankly sentimental; *Whippetsnapper* is silly. And there are all manner of stories in between. But they are all good, and some of them are superlative of their kind. And that is why I have included them. I have also wished to give something of a historical sampling of the literature about animals, though most of the stories in this book are modern or comparatively modern. But the criterion has always been: is this a good story, and will it interest the man who likes animals and wants to read about them?

A very few of these stories are about animals only as animals symbolize specific qualities in men. One only, *The Crocodile*, depends upon an animal for its plot, but otherwise is not an animal story.

A word about the modernisation of Chaucer's *Chanticleer and Pertelote* and the liberties of form I have taken with it. I have in many cases used assonance and half rhymes, and I have also used far more run-on lines than is characteristic of Chaucer's work. I have done this because I have tried, whenever possible, to use Chaucer's own words rather than to shift for the sake of rhyme and formal accuracy—though I have had to re-rhyme and change the wording often enough too. But I think I have in large degree preserved the feeling and the charm of the original fable.

I cannot here thank all my many friends who have suggested animal stories to me, but I do wish to acknowledge my indebtedness to them.

E. Louise Mally

A Treasury of
ANIMAL STORIES

How Saint Francis Preached to the Birds

The thirteenth century saint, who has been called the only true Christian since Jesus, embraced the whole universe in his love. The animals were members of one community with him; he called the wolf "brother" and preached to the birds. And according to the beautiful old legend, the birds listened. . . .

THAT humble servant of Jesus Christ, Saint Francis, shortly after his conversion, having already gathered together many companions and received them into the Order, fell into deep thought and into grave doubt as to what he should do—whether he should devote himself wholly to prayer, or whether, indeed, he should sometimes preach; and on this subject he greatly desired to the will of God. And forasmuch as the Saintly Humility which was in him would not let him trust to himself or to his own prayers alone, he strove to seek out the Divine will through the prayers of others; hence he called Brother Maximus, and spake to him thus: "Go to Sister Clara and tell her from me that she, with certain of her most spiritual companions, shall pray devoutly to God that it may please Him to reveal to me whether it is better that I should devote myself to preaching, or merely to prayer. And then go to Brother Sylvester and say the same words." This was that same Master Sylvester who had seen a golden cross come forth from the mouth of Saint Francis, which was as high as the heavens and as broad as the confines of the globe. And such were the devotion and the sanctity of this same Brother Sylvester, that whatsoever he asked of God, even that same he obtained, and his prayer was granted, and many times he spake with God; and yet Saint Francis also had great piety.

Brother Maximus went forth, and according to the command of

Saint Francis he fulfilled his errand first to Saint Clara and then to Brother Sylvester; who, when he had received it, incontinently fell to praying, and praying he heard the Divine voice, and turning to Brother Maximus he said: "Thus saith the Lord, which you shall repeat to Brother Francis—that God did not call him unto this state for himself alone, but that he might reap a harvest of souls, and many through him shall be saved." Having this answer, Brother Maximus returned to Saint Clara to know that which she had obtained of God. And she made answer that she and her Companions had had from God the selfsame answer which Brother Sylvester had had.

With this Brother Maximus returned to Saint Francis; and Saint Francis received him with the utmost Affection, washing his feet and laying the cloth for him to dine. And after eating, Saint Francis called Brother Maximus into the thick wood; and there he knelt before him, and drawing down his Cowl over his face, he crossed his arms and asked him, saying, "What does my Lord and Master Jesus Christ command me to do?" Brother Maximus made answer: "Both to Brother Sylvester and to Sister Clara, with her Sisters, Christ has replied and made manifest that it is His will that you shall go forth into the world to preach; forasmuch as He did not call you for yourself alone, but even also for the salvation of others." And then Saint Francis, when that he had heard this answer and learned therefrom the will of Jesus Christ, rose up with the greatest fervour, saying, "Let us go forth in the name of God."

And he took for his Companions Brother Maximus and Brother Andrew, holy men both; and going forth filled with the things of the Spirit, without considering their road or their way, they came to a Castle, which is called Savurniano, and Saint Francis began to preach; and he first commanded the Swallows, which were singing, to keep silence so long as until he should have preached; and the Swallows obeyed him; and he preached in this place with such fervour that all the men and the women in that Castle, from devotion, would have followed after him and forsaken the Castle; but Saint Francis forbade them, saying, "Be not in haste, and depart not, and I will order all things which you are to do for the salvation of your soul." And then he created the Third Order, for the Universal Salvation of all men; and thus leaving many consoled and well disposed to penitence, he departed from thence and came to Cannajo and Bevagno.

And passing on his way with the selfsame fervour, he raised his eyes and saw certain trees by the roadside in which were an infinite multitude of birds; at which Saint Francis marveled greatly, and said to his Companions, "Await me here in the road, and I will go and preach to my Sisters the birds." And he entered the field and began to preach to the birds which were on the ground; and suddenly those which were in the trees came down to him, and as many as there were they all stood quietly until Saint Francis had done preaching; and even then they did not depart until such time as he had given them his blessing; and according to the later recital of Brother Maximus to Brother James of Massa, Saint Francis, moving among them, touched them with his cape, but not one moved.

The substance of Saint Francis' sermon was this: "My Sisters the birds, ye are greatly beholden unto God your Creator, and always and in every place it is your duty to praise Him, forasmuch as He hath given you freedom to fly in every place; also hath He given you raiment twofold and threefold almost, because He preserved your Seed in the ark of Noah, that your race might never be less. Again, ye are bounden to Him for the element of the air, which He has deputed unto you; moreover, you sow not, neither do you reap, and God feeds you, and gives you the streams and fountains for your thirst; He gives you mountains and valleys for your refuge; tall trees wherein to make your nests; and inasmuch as you neither spin nor weave, God clothes you, you and your children; hence ye should love your Creator greatly, Who gives you such great benefits, and therefore beware, my Sisters, of the sin of ingratitude, and ever strive to praise God."

Saint Francis, saying these words to them, all those birds, as many as there were, began to ope their beaks and stretch forth their necks and spread their wings and reverently to bow their heads even to the earth, and by their acts and their songs to set forth that the Holy Father gave them the utmost delight; and Saint Francis rejoiced with them, pleased and marveling much to see so vast a multitude of birds, and their most beautiful variety, their attention and familiarity; for the which things in them he devoutly praised the Creator.

Finally, his preaching ended, Saint Francis made them the sign of the Cross and gave them leave to depart; and then all those birds rose into the air with wondrous songs; and then, according to the Cross which Saint Francis had made them, they divided into four parts; and the one part flew towards the east, and the other towards the west, and the one part towards the south, and the other towards the north, and each band went away singing marvelous songs; signifying by this how that Saint Francis, the Ensign of the Cross of Christ, had come to preach to them, and had made the sign of the Cross over them, according to which they had scattered to the four quarters of the globe.

Thus the preaching of the Cross of Christ renewed by Saint Francis was by him and his Brethren borne throughout the whole world; which Brethren, even as the birds, possessed nothing of this world's goods, but committed their life to the sole and only providence of God.

From the Navaho

The American Indian, like most primitives, believes animals to be so completely a part of his life that, in his legends and poetry, it is often difficult to tell whether he is speaking of an actual animal or of himself in his magic incarnation as that animal. Certainly the blackbird in "Hunting Song" is the human singer.

. . . The Turquoise Horse of Johano-ai is no actual horse, but is the glorified abstraction of the horses that are part of the Navaho's culture. . . .

HUNTING SONG

Comes the deer to my singing,
Comes the deer to my song,
Comes the deer to my singing.

He, the blackbird, he am I,
Bird beloved of the wild deer,
Comes the deer to my singing.

From the Mountain Black,
From the summit,
Down the trail, coming, coming now,
Comes the deer to my singing.

Through the blossoms,
Through the flowers, coming, coming now,
Comes the deer to my singing.

Through the flower dew-drops,
Coming, coming now,
Comes the deer to my singing.

Through the pollen, flower pollen,
          Coming, coming now,
          Comes the deer to my singing.

Starting with his left fore-foot,
Stamping, turns the frightened deer,
          Comes the deer to my singing.

Quarry mine, blessed am I
In the luck of the chase.
          Comes the deer to my singing.

          Comes the deer to my singing,
          Comes the deer to my song,
          Comes the deer to my singing.
                    Translated by Natalie Curtis

SONG OF THE HORSE

          How joyous his neigh!
Lo, the Turquoise Horse of Johano-ai,
          How joyous his neigh!
There on precious hides outspread standeth he;
          How joyous his neigh!
There on tips of fair fresh flowers feedeth he;
          How joyous his neigh!
There of mingled waters holy drinketh he;
          How joyous his neigh!
There he spurneth dust of glittering grains;
          How joyous his neigh!
There his offspring may grow and thrive for evermore;
          How joyous his neigh!
                    Translated by Natalie Curtis

Tale of the Gypsy Horse

by DONN BYRNE

"I can quite understand the trainer who, pointing to Manifesto, said that if he ever found a woman with a shape like that, he'd marry her. So out of my heart through my lips came the cry: 'Och, asthore!' which is, in our Gaelic, 'Oh, my dear!'"

The essence of all men's love for a high bred animal is, I think, in this half paragraph, and were there no other cause to include this excerpt from "Destiny Bay," by the author of "Messer Marco Polo," I would include it for the sake of those two sentences. But this is also the story of a very exciting horse race, and it is full of the lilt that those born to the Irish tongue alone know how to give to their writings.

O saddle me my milk white steed,
Go and fetch me my pony, O!
That I may ride and seek my bride,
Who is gone with the raggle-taggle gypsies, O!

ANON.

I THOUGHT first of the old lady's face, in the candlelight of the dinner table at Destiny Bay, as some fine precious coin, a spade guinea perhaps, well and truly minted. How old she was I could not venture to guess, but I knew well that when she was young men's heads must have turned as she passed. Age had boldened the features much, the proud nose and definite chin. Her hair was grey, vitally grey, like a grey wave curling in to crash on the sands of Destiny. And I knew that in another woman that hair would be white as scutched flax. When she spoke, the thought of the spade guinea came to me again, so rich and golden was her voice.

"Lady Clontarf," said my uncle Valentine, "this is Kerry, Hector's boy."

"May I call you Kerry? I am so old a woman and you are so much a boy. Also I knew your father. He was of that great line of soldiers who read their Bibles in their tents, and go into battle with a prayer in their hearts. I always seem to have known," she said, "that he would fondle no grey beard."

"Madame," I said, "what should I be but Kerry to my father's friends!"

It seemed to me that I must know her because of her proud high face, and her eyes of a great lady, but the title of Clontarf made little impress on my brain. Our Irish titles have become so hawked and shopworn that the most hallowed names in Ireland may be borne by a porter brewer or former soap boiler. O'Conor Don and MacCarthy More mean so much more to us than the Duke of This or the Marquis of There, now the politics have so muddled chivalry. We may resent the presentation of this title or that to a foreigner, but what can you do? The loyalty of the Northern Irishman to the Crown is a loyalty of head and not of heart. Out of our Northern country came the United Men, if you remember. But for whom should our hearts beat faster? The Stuarts were never fond of us, and the Prince of Orange came over to us, talked a deal about liberty, was with us at a few battles, and went off to grow asparagus in England. It is so long since O'Neill and O'Donnell sailed for Spain!

Who Lady Clontarf was I did not know. My uncle Valentine is so offhand in his presentations. Were you to come on him closeted with a heavenly visitant he would just say: "Kerry, the Angel Gabriel." Though as to what his Angelicness was doing with my uncle Valentine, you would be left to surmise. My uncle Valentine will tell you just as much as he feels you ought to know and no more —a quality that stood my uncle in good stead in the days when he raced and bred horses for racing. I did know one thing: Lady Clontarf was not Irish. There is a feeling of kindness between all us Irish that we recognise without speaking. One felt courtesy, gravity, dignity in her, but not that quality that makes your troubles another Irish person's troubles, if only for the instant. Nor was she English. One felt her spiritual roots went too deep for that. Nor had she that brilliant armour of the Latin. Her speech was the ordinary speech of a gentlewoman, unaccented. Yet that remark about knowing my father would never fondle a grey beard!

Who she was and all about her I knew I would find out later from my dear aunt Jenepher. But about the old drawing-room of Destiny there was a strange air of formality. My uncle Valentine is most courteous, but to-night he was courtly. He was like some Hungarian or Russian noble welcoming an empress. There was an air of deference about my dear aunt Jenepher that informed me that Lady Clontarf was very great indeed. Whom my aunt Jenepher likes is lovable, and whom she respects is clean and great. But the most extraordinary part of the setting was our butler James Carabine. He looked as if royalty were present, and I began to say to myself: "By damn, but royalty is! Lady Clontarf is only a racing name. I know that there's a queen or princess in Germany who's held by the Jacobites to be Queen of England. Can it be herself that's in it? It sounds impossible, but sure there's nothing impossible where my uncle Valentine's concerned."

At dinner the talk turned on racing, and my uncle Valentine inveighed bitterly against the new innovations on the track; the starting gate, and the new seat introduced by certain American jockeys, the crouch now recognised as orthodox in flat-racing. As to the value of the starting gate my uncle was open to conviction. He recognised how unfairly the apprentice was treated by the crack jockey with the old method of the flag, but he dilated on his favourite theme: that machinery was the curse of man. All these innovations—

"But it isn't an innovation, sir. The Romans used it."

"You're a liar!" said my uncle Valentine.

My uncle Valentine, or any other Irishman for the matter of that, only means that he doesn't believe you. There is a wide difference.

"I think I'm right, sir. The Romans used it for their chariot races. They dropped the barrier instead of raising it." A tag of my classics came back to me, as tags will. "*Repagula submittuntur*, Pausanias writes."

"Pausanias, begob!" My uncle Valentine was visibly impressed.

But as to the new seat he was adamant. I told him competent

judges had placed it about seven pounds' advantage to the horse.

"There is only one place on a horse's back for a saddle," said my uncle Valentine. "The shorter your leathers, Kerry, the less you know about your mount. You are only aware whether or not he is willing. With the ordinary seat, you know whether he is lazy, and can make proper use of your spur. You can stick to his head and help him."

"Races are won with that seat, sir."

"Be damned to that!" said my uncle Valentine. "If the horse is good enough, he'll win with the rider facing his tail."

"But we are boring you, Madame," I said, "with our country talk of horses."

"There are three things that are never boring to see: a swift swimmer swimming, a young girl dancing, and a young horse running. And three things that are never tiring to speak of: God, and love, and the racing of horses."

"A *kushto jukel* is also *rinkeno, mi pen*," suddenly spoke our butler, James Carabine.

"*Dabla*, James Carabine, you *roker* like a *didakai*. A *jukel* to catch *kanangre!*" And Lady Clontarf laughed. "What in all the *tem* is as *dinkeno* as a *kushti-dikin grai?*"

"A *tatsheno jukel, mi pen*, like Rory Bosville's," James Carabine evidently stood his ground, "that *noshered* the Waterloo Cup through *wafro bok!*"

"*Avali!* You are right, James Carabine." And then she must have seen my astonished face, for she laughed, that small golden laughter that was like the ringing of an acolyte's bell. "Are you surprised to hear me speak the *tawlo tshib*, the black language, Kerry? I am a gypsy woman."

"Lady Clontarf, Mister Kerry," said James Carabine, "is saying there is nothing in the world like a fine horse. I told her a fine greyhound is a good thing too. Like Rory Bosville's, that should have won the Waterloo Cup in Princess Dagmar's year."

"Lady Clontarf wants to talk to you about a horse, Kerry," said my uncle Valentine. "So if you would like us to go into the gunroom, Jenepher, instead of the withdrawing room while you play—"

"May I not hear about the horse too?" asked my aunt Jenepher.

"My very, very dear," said the gypsy lady to my blind aunt

Jenepher, "I would wish you to, for where you are sitting, there a blessing will be."

My uncle Valentine had given up race horses for as long as I can remember. Except with Limerick Pride, he had never had any luck, and so he had quitted racing as an owner, and gone in for harness ponies, of which, it is admitted, he bred and showed the finest of their class. My own two chasers, while winning many good Irish races, were not quite up to Aintree form, but in the last year I happened to buy, for a couple of hundred guineas, a handicap horse that had failed signally as a three-year-old in classic races, and of which a fashionable stable wanted to get rid. It was Ducks and Drakes, by Drake's Drum out of Little Duck, a beautifully shaped, dark grey horse, rather short in the neck, but the English stable was convinced he was a hack. However, as often happens, with a change of trainers and jockeys, Ducks and Drakes became a different horse and won five good races, giving me so much in hand that I was able to purchase for a matter of nine hundred guineas a colt I was optimistic about, a son of Saint Simon's. Both horses were in training with Robinson at the Curragh. And now it occurred to me that the gypsy lady wanted to buy one or the other of them. I decided beforehand that it would be across my dead body.

"Would you be surprised," asked my uncle Valentine, "to hear that Lady Clontarf has a horse she expects to win the Derby with?"

"I should be delighted, sir, if she did," I answered warily. There were a hundred people who had hopes of their nominations in the greatest of races.

"Kerry," the gypsy lady said quietly, "I think I will win." She had a way of clearing the air with her voice, with her eyes. What was a vague hope now became an issue.

"What is the horse, Madame?"

"It is as yet unnamed, and has never run as a two-year-old. It is a son of Irlandais, who has sired many winners on the Continent, and who broke down sixteen years ago in preparation for the Derby and was sold to one of the Festetics. Its dam is Iseult III, who won the Prix de Diane four years ago."

"I know so little about Continental horses," I explained.

"The strain is great-hearted, and with the dam, strong as an oak tree. I am a gypsy woman, and I know a horse, and I am an old, studious woman," she said, and she looked at her beautiful, unringed golden hands, as if she were embarrassed, speaking of something we, not Romanies, could hardly understand, "and I think I know propitious hours and days."

"Where is he now, Madame?"

"He is at Dax, in the Basse-Pyrénées, with Romany folk."

"Here's the whole thing in a nutshell, Kerry: Lady Clontarf wants her colt trained in Ireland. Do you think the old stables of your grandfather are still good?"

"The best in Ireland, sir, but sure there's no horse been trained there for forty years, barring jumpers."

"Are the gallops good?"

"Sure, you know yourself, sir, how good they are. But you couldn't train without a trainer, and stable boys—"

"We'll come to that," said my uncle Valentine. "Tell me, what odds will you get against an unknown, untried horse in the winter books?"

I thought for an instant. It had been an exceptionally good year for two-year-olds, the big English breeders' stakes having been bitterly contested. Lord Shere had a good horse; Mr. Paris a dangerous colt. I should say there were fifteen good colts, if they wintered well, two with outstanding chances.

"I should say you could really write your own ticket. The ring will be only too glad to get money. There's so much up on Sir James and Toison d'Or."

"To win a quarter-million pounds?" asked my uncle Valentine.

"It would have to be done very carefully, sir, here and there, in ponies and fifties and hundreds, but I think between four and five thousand pounds would do it."

"Now if this horse of Lady Clontarf's wins the Two Thousand and the Derby, and the Saint Leger—"

Something in my face must have shown a lively distaste for the company of lunatics, for James Carabine spoke quietly from the door by which he was standing.

"Will your young Honour be easy, and listen to your uncle and my lady."

My uncle Valentine is most grandiose, and though he has lived in epic times, a giant among giants, his schemes are too big for practical business days. And I was beginning to think that the gypsy lady, for all her beauty and dignity, was but an old woman crazed by gambling and tarot cards, but James Carabine is so wise, so beautifully sane, facing all events, spiritual and material, foursquare to the wind.

"—what would he command in stud fees?" continued quietly my uncle Valentine.

"If he did this tremendous triple thing, sir, five hundred guineas would not be exorbitant."

"I am not asking you out of idle curiosity, Kerry, or for information," said my uncle Valentine. "I merely wish to know if the ordinary brain arrives at these conclusions of mine; if they are, to use a word, of Mr. Thackeray's, apparent."

"I quite understand, sir," I said politely.

"And now," said my uncle Valentine, "whom would you suggest to come to Destiny Bay as trainer?"

"None of the big trainers will leave their stables to come here, sir. And the small ones I don't know sufficiently. If Sir Arthur Pollexfen were still training, and not so old—"

"Sir Arthur Pollexfen is not old," said my uncle Valentine. "He cannot be more than seventy-two or seventy-three."

"But at that age you cannot expect a man to turn out at five in the morning and oversee gallops."

"How little you know Mayo men," said my uncle Valentine. "And Sir Arthur with all his triumphs never won a Derby. He will come."

"Even at that, sir, how are you going to get a crack jockey? Most big owners have first or second call on them. And the great free lances, you cannot engage one of those and ensure secrecy."

"That," said my uncle Valentitne, "is already arranged. Lady Clontarf has a Gitano, or Spanish gypsy in whom her confidence is boundless. And now," said my uncle Valentine, "we come to the really diplomatic part of the proceeding. Trial horses are needed, so that I am commissioned to approach you with delicacy and ask you if you will bring up your two excellent horses Ducks and Drakes and the Saint Simon colt and help train Lady Clontarf's horse. I don't see why you should object."

To bring up the two darlings of my heart, and put them under the care of a trainer who had won the Gold Cup at Ascot fifty years before, and hadn't run a horse for twelve years, and have them ridden by this Gitano or Spanish gypsy, as my uncle called him; to have them used as trial horses to this colt which might not be good enough for a starter's hack. Ah, no! Not damned likely. I hardened my heart against the pleading gaze of James Carabine.

"Will you or won't you?" roared my uncle diplomatically.

My aunt Jenepher laid down the lace she was making, and reaching across, her fingers caught my sleeve and ran down to my hand, and her hand caught mine.

"Kerry will," she said.

So that was decided.

"Kerry," said my uncle Valentine, "will you see Lady Clontarf home?"

I was rather surprised. I had thought she was staying with us. And I was a bit bothered, for it is not hospitality to allow the visitor to Destiny to put up at the local pub. But James Carabine whispered: " 'Tis on the downs she's staying, Master Kerry, in her own great van with four horses." It was difficult to believe that the tall graceful lady in the golden and red Spanish shawl, with the quiet speech of our own people, was a roaming gypsy, with the whole world as her home.

"Good night, Jenepher. Good night, Valentine. *Boshto dok*, good luck, James Carabine!"

"*Boshto dok, mi pen*. Good luck, sister."

We went out into the October night of the full moon—the hunter's moon—and away from the great fire of turf and bogwood in our drawing-room the night was vital with an electric cold. One could sense the film of ice in the bogs, and the drumming of snipe's wings, disturbed by some roving dog, come to our ears. So bright was the moon that each whitewashed apple tree stood out clear in the orchard, and as we took the road toward Grey River, we could see a barentine offshore, with sails of polished silver—some boat from Bilbao probably, making for the Clyde, in the daytime a scrubby ore carrier but to-night a ship out of some old sea story, as of Magellan, or our own Saint Brendan:

"*Feach air muir lionadh gealach buidhe mar ór,*" she quoted in Gaelic; "See on the filling sea the full moon yellow as gold. . . . It is full moon and full tide, Kerry; if you make a wish, it will come true."

"I wish you success in the Derby, Madame."

Ahead of us down the road moved a little group to the sound of fiddle and mouth organ. It was the Romany body-guard ready to protect their chieftainess on her way home.

"You mean that, I know, but you dislike the idea. Why?"

"Madame," I said, "if you can read my thoughts as easily as that, it's no more impertinent to speak than think. I have heard a lot about a great colt to-night, and of his chance for the greatest race in the world, and that warms my heart. But I have heard more about money, and that chills me."

"I am so old, Kerry, that the glory of winning the Derby means little to me. Do you know how old I am? I am six years short of an hundred old."

"Then the less—" I began, and stopped short, and could have chucked myself over the cliff for my unpardonable discourtesy.

"Then the less reason for my wanting money," the old lady said. "Is not that so?"

"Exactly, Madame."

"Kerry," she said, "does my name mean anything to you?"

"It has bothered me all evening. Lady Clontarf, I am so sorry my father's son should appear to you so rude and ignorant a lout."

"Mifanwy, Countess Clontarf and Kincora."

I gaped like an idiot. "The line of great Brian Boru. But I thought—"

"Did you really ever think of it, Kerry?"

"Not really, Madame," I said. "It's so long ago, so wonderful. It's like that old city they speak of in the country tales, under Ownaglass, the grey river, with its spires and great squares. It seems to me to have vanished like that, in rolling clouds of thunder."

"The last O'Neill has vanished, and the last Plantagenet. But great Brian's strain remains. When I married my lord," she said quietly, "it was in a troubled time. Our ears had not forgotten the musketry of Waterloo, and England was still shaken by fear of the Emperor, and poor Ireland was hurt and wounded. As you know, Kerry, no peer of the older faith sat in College Green. It is no new thing to ennoble, and steal an ancient name. Pitt and Napoleon passed their leisure hours at it. So that of O'Briens, Kerry, sirred and lorded, there are a score, but my lord was Earl of Clontarf and Kincora since before the English came.

"If my lord was of the great blood of Kincora, myself was not lacking in blood. We Romanies are old, Kerry, so old that no man knows our beginning, but that we came from the uplands of India centuries before history. We are a strong, vital race, and we remain with our language, our own customs, our own laws until this day. And to certain families of us, the Romanies all over the world do reverence, as to our own, the old Lovells. There are three Lovells, Kerry, the *dinelo* or foolish Lovells, the *gozvero* or cunning Lovells, and the *puro* Lovells, the old Lovells. I am of the old Lovells. My father was the great Mairik Lovell. So you see I am of great stock too."

"Dear Madame, one has only to see you to know that."

"My lord had a small place left him near the Village of Swords, and it was near there I met him. He wished to buy a horse from my father Mairik, a stallion my father had brought all the way from the Nejd in Arabia. My lord could not buy that horse. But when I married my lord, it was part of my dowry, that and two handfuls of uncut Russian emeralds, and a chest of gold coins, Russian and Indian and Turkish coins, all gold. So I did not come empty-handed to my lord."

"Madame, do you wish to tell me this?"

"I wish to tell it to you, Kerry, because I want you for a friend to my little people, the sons of my son's son. You must know everything about friends to understand them.

"My lord was rich only in himself and in his ancestry. But with the great Arab stallion and the emeralds and the gold coins we were well. We did a foolish thing, Kerry; we went to London. My lord wished it, and his wishes were my wishes, although something told me we should not have gone. In London I made my lord sell the great Arab. He did not wish to, because it came with me, nor did I wish to, because my father had loved it so, but I made him sell it. All the Selim horses of to-day are descended from him, Sheykh Selim.

"My lord loved horses, Kerry. He knew horses, but he had no luck. Newmarket Heath is a bad spot for those out of luck. And my lord grew worried. When one is worried, Kerry, the heart contracts a little,—is it not so? Or don't you know yet? Also another thing bothered my lord. He was with English people, and English people have their codes and ordinances. They are good people, Kerry, very honest. They go to churches, and like sad songs, but whether they believe in God, or whether they have hearts or have no hearts, I do not know. Each thing they do by rote and custom, and they are curious in this: they will make excuses for a man who has done a great crime, but no excuses for a man who neglects a trivial thing. An eccentricity of dress is not forgiven. An eccentric is an outsider. So that English are not good for Irish folk.

"My own people," she said proudly, "are simple people, kindly and loyal as your family know. A marriage to them is a deep thing, not the selfish love of one person for another, but involving many factors. A man will say: Mifanwy Lovell's father saved my honour once. What can I do for Mifanwy Lovell and Mifanwy Lovell's man? And the Lovells said when we were married: Brothers, the *gawjo rai*, the foreign gentleman, may not understand the gypsy way, that our sorrows are his sorrows, and our joys his, but we understand that his fights are our fights, and his interests the interests of the Lovell Clan.

"My people were always about my lord, and my lord hated it. In our London house in the morning, there were always gypsies waiting to tell my lord of a great fight coming off quietly on Epsom Downs, which it might interest him to see, or of a good horse to be bought cheaply, or some news of a dog soon to run in a coursing match for a great stake, and of the dog's excellences or his defects. They wanted no money. They only wished to do him a kindness. But my lord was embarrassed, until he began to loathe the sight of a gypsy neckerchief. Also, in the race courses, in the betting ring where my lord would be, a gypsy would pay hard-earned entrance money to tell my lord quietly of something they had noticed that morning in the gallops, or horses to be avoided in betting, or of neglected horses which would win. All kindnesses to my lord. But my lord was with fashionable English folk, who do not understand one's having a strange friend. Their uplifted eyebrows made my lord ashamed of the poor Romanies. These things are things you might laugh at, with laughter like sunshine, but there would be clouds in your heart.

"The end came at Ascot, Kerry, where the young queen was, and the Belgian king, and the great nobles of the court. Into the paddock came one of the greatest of gypsies, Tyso Herne, who had gone before my marriage with a great draft of Norman trotting horses to Mexico, and came back with a squadron of ponies, suitable for polo. Tyso was a vast man, a *pawni Romany*, a fair gypsy. His hair was red, and his moustache was long and curling, like a Hungarian pandour's. He had a flaunting *diklo* of fine yellow silk about his neck, and the buttons on his coat were gold Indian mohurs, and on his bell-shaped trousers were braids of silver bells, and the spurs on his Wellingtons were fine silver, and his hands were covered with rings, Kerry, with stones in them such as even the young queen did not have. It was not vulgar ostentation. It was just that Tyso felt rich and merry, and no stone on his hand was as fine as his heart.

"When he saw me he let a roar out of him that was like the roar of the ring when the horses are coming in to the stretch.

" 'Before God,' he shouted, 'it's Mifanwy Lovell.' And, though I am not a small woman, Kerry, he tossed me in the air, and caught me in the air. And he laughed and kissed me, and I laughed and kissed him, so happy was I to see great Tyso once more, safe from over the sea.

" 'Go get your *rom, mi tshai*, your husband, my lass, and we'll go to the *kitshima* and have a jeraboam of Champagne wine.' "

"But I saw my lord walk off with thunder in his face, and all the English folk staring and some women laughing. So I said: 'I will go with you alone, Tyso.' For Tyso Herne had been my father's best friend and my mother's cousin, and had held me as a baby, and no matter how he looked, or who laughed, he was well come for me.

"Of what my lord said, and of what I said in rebuttal, we will not speak. One says foolish things in anger, but, foolish or not, they leave scars. For out of the mouth come things forgotten, things one thinks dead. But before the end of the meeting, I went to Tyso Herne's van. He was braiding a whip with fingers light as a woman's, and when he saw me he spoke quietly.

" 'Is all well with thee, Mifanwy?'

" 'Nothing is well with me, father's friend.'

"And so I went back to my people, and I never saw my lord any more."

We had gone along until in the distance I could see the gypsy fire, and turning the headland we saw the light on Farewell Point. A white flash; a second's rest; a red flash; three seconds occulation; then white and red again. There is something heartening and brave in Farewell Light. Ireland keeps watch over her share of the Atlantic sea.

"When I left my lord, I was with child, and when I was delivered of him, and the child weaned and strong, I sent him to my lord, for every man wants his man child, and every family its heir. But when he was four and twenty he came back to me, for the roving gypsy blood and the fighting Irish blood were too much for him. He was never Earl of Clontarf. He died while my lord still lived. He married a Herne, a grandchild of Tyso, a brave golden girl. And he got killed charging in the Balkan Wars.

"Niall's wife—my son's name was Niall—understood, and when young Niall was old enough, we sent him to my lord. My lord was old at this time, older than his years, and very poor. But of my share of money he would have nothing. My lord died when Niall's Niall was at school, so the little lad became Earl of Clontarf and Kincora. I saw to it he had sufficient money, but he married no rich woman. He married a poor Irish girl, and by her had two children, Niall and Alick. He was interested in horses, and rode well, my English friends tell me. But mounted on a brute in the Punchestown races, he made a mistake at the stone wall. He did not know the horse very well. So he let it have its head at the stone wall. It threw its head up, took the jump by the roots, and so Niall's Niall was killed. His wife, the little Irish girl, turned her face away from life and died.

"The boys are fifteen and thirteen now, and soon they will go into the world. I want them to have a fair chance, and it is for this reason I wish them to have money. I have been rich and then poor, and then very rich and again poor, and rich again and now poor. But if this venture succeeds, the boys will be all right."

"Ye-s," I said.

"You don't seem very enthusiastic, Kerry."

"We have a saying," I told her, "that money won from a book-maker is only lent."

"If you were down on a race meeting and on the last race of the last day you won a little, what would you say?"

"I'd say I only got a little of my own back."

"Then we only get a little of our own back over the losses of a thousand years."

We had come now to the encampment. Around the great fire were tall swarthy men with coloured neckchiefs, who seemed more reserved, cleaner than the English gypsy. They rose quietly as the gypsy lady came. The great spotted Dalmatian dogs rose too. In the half light the picketed horses could be seen, quiet as trees.

"This is the Younger of Destiny Bay," said the old lady, "who is kind enough to be our friend."

"*Sa shan, rai!*" they spoke with quiet courtesy. "How are you, sir?"

Lady Clontarf's maid hurried forward with a wrap, scolding, and speaking English with beautiful courtesy. "You are dreadful, sister. You go walking the roads at night like a courting girl in spring. Gentleman, you are wrong to keep the *rawnee* out, and she an old woman and not well."

"Supplistia," Lady Clontarf chided, "you have no more manners than a growling dog."

"I am the *rawnee's* watchdog," the girl answered.

"Madame, your maid is right. I will go now."

"Kerry," she stopped me, "will you be friends with my little people?"

"I will be their true friend," I promised, and I kissed her hand.

"God bless you!" she said. And "*kushto bok, rai!*" the gypsies wished me. "Good luck, sir!" And I left the camp for my people's house. The hunter's moon was dropping toward the edge of the world, and the light on Farewell Point flashed seaward its white and red, and as I walked along, I noticed that a wind from Ireland had sprung up, and the Bilbao boat was bowling along nor'east on the starboard tack. It seemed to me an augury.

In those days, before my aunt Jenepher's marriage to Patrick Herne, the work of Destiny Bay was divided in this manner: my dear aunt Jenepher was, as was right, supreme in the house. My uncle Valentine planned and superintended the breeding of the harness ponies, and sheep, and black Dexter cattle which made Destiny Bay so feared at the Dublin Horse Show and at the Bath and West. My own work was the farms. To me fell the task of preparing the stables and training grounds for Lady Clontarf's and my own horses. It was a relief and an adventure to give up thinking of turnips, wheat, barley, and seeds, and to examine the downs for training ground. In my great-grandfather's time, in pre-Union days, many a winner at the Curragh had been bred and trained at Destiny Bay. The soil of the downs is chalky, and the matted roots of the woven herbage have a certain give in them in the driest weather. I found out my great-grandfather's mile and a half, and two miles and a half with a turn and shorter gallops of various gradients. My grandfather had used them as a young man, but mainly for hunters, horses which he sold for the great Spanish and Austrian regiments. But to my delight the stables were as good as ever. Covered with reed thatch, they required few repairs. The floors were of chalk, and the boxes beautifully ventilated. There were also great tanks for rainwater, which is of all water the best for horses in training. There were also a few stalls for restless horses. I was worried a little about lighting, but my uncle Valentine told me that Sir Arthur Pollexfen allowed no artificial lights where he trained. Horses went to bed with the fowls and got up at cockcrow.

My own horses I got from Robinson without hurting his feelings. "It's this way, Robinson," I told him. "We're trying to do a crazy thing at Destiny, and I'm not bringing them to another trainer. I'm bringing another trainer there. I can tell you no more."

"Not another word, Mr. Kerry. Bring them back when you want to. I'm sorry to say good-bye to the wee colt. But I wish you luck."

We bought three more horses, and a horse for Ann-Dolly. So that with the six we had a rattling good little stable. When I saw Sir Arthur Pollexfen, my heart sank a little, for he seemed so much out of a former century. Small, ruddy-cheeked, with the white hair of a bishop, and a bishop's courtesy, I never thought he could run a stable. I thought, perhaps, he had grown too old and had been thinking for a long time now of the Place whither he was going, and that we had brought him back from his thoughts and he had

left his vitality behind. His own servant came with him to Destiny
Bay, and though we wished to have him in the house with us, yet
he preferred to stay in a cottage by the stables. I don't know what
there was about his clothes, but they were all of an antique though
a beautiful cut. He never wore riding breeches but trousers of a
bluish cloth and strapped beneath his varnished boots. A flowered
waistcoat with a satin stock, a short covert coat, a grey bowler hat
and gloves. Always there was a freshly cut flower in his buttonhole,
which his servant got every evening from the greenhouses at Destiny
Bay, and kept overnight in a glass of water into which the least drop
of whiskey had been poured. I mention this as extraordinary, as most
racing men will not wear flowers. They believe flowers bring bad
luck, though how the superstition arose I cannot tell. His evening
trousers also buckled under his shoes, or rather half Wellingtons,
such as army men wear, and though there was never a crease in them
there was never a wrinkle. He would never drink port after dinner
when the ladies had left, but a little whiskey punch which James
Carabine would compose for him. Compared to the hard shrewd-
eyed trainers I knew, this bland, soft-spoken old gentleman filled
me with misgiving.

I got a different idea of the old man the first morning I went out
to the gallops. The sun had hardly risen when the old gentleman appeared, as beautifully turned out as though he were entering the
Show Ring at Ballsbridge. His servant held his horse, a big grey,
while he swung into the saddle as light as a boy. His hack was
feeling good that morning, and he and I went off toward the training ground at a swinging canter, the old gentleman half standing in
his stirrups, with a light firm grip of his knees, riding as Cossacks
do, his red terrier galloping behind him. When we settled down to
walk he told me the pedigree of his horse, descended through
Matchem and Whalebone from Oliver Cromwell's great charger
The White Turk, or Place's White Turk, as it was called from the
Lord Protector's stud manager. To hear him follow the intricacies
of breeding was a revelation. Then I understood what a great horseman he was. On the training ground he was like a marshal commanding an army, such respect did every one accord him. The lads
perched on the horses' withers, his head man, the grooms, all watched
the apple-ruddy face, while he said little or nothing. He must have

had eyes in the back of his head, though. For when a colt we had brought from Mr. Gubbins, a son of Galtee More's, started lashing out and the lad up seemed like taking a toss, the old man's voice came low and sharp: "Don't fall off, boy." And the boy did not fall off. The red terrier watched the trials with a keen eye, and I believe honestly that he knew as much about horses as any one of us and certainly more than any of us about his owner. When my lovely Ducks and Drakes went out at the lad's call to beat the field by two lengths over five furlongs, the dog looked up at Sir Arthur and Sir Arthur looked back at the dog, and what they thought toward each other, God knoweth.

I expected when we rode away that the old gentleman would have some word to say about my horses, but coming home, his remarks were of the country. "Your Derry is a beautiful country, young Mister Kerry," he said, "though it would be treason to say that in my own country of Mayo." Of my horses not a syllable.

He could be the most silent man I have ever known, though giving the illusion of keeping up a conversation. You could talk to him, and he would smile, and nod at the proper times, as though he were devouring every word you said. In the end you thought you had a very interesting conversation. But as to whether he had even heard you, you were never sure. On the other hand when he wished to speak, he spoke to the point and beautifully. Our bishop, on one of his pastoral visitations, if that be the term, stayed at Destiny Bay, and because my uncle Cosimo is a bishop too, and because he felt he ought to do something for our souls he remonstrated with us for starting our stable. My uncle Valentine was livid, but said nothing, for no guest must be contradicted in Destiny Bay.

"For surely, Sir Valentine, no man of breeding can mingle with the rogues, cut-purses and their womenfolk who infest race courses, drunkards, bawds and common gamblers, without lowering himself to some extent to their level," his Lordship purred. "Yourself, one of the wardens of Irish chivalry, must give an example to the common people."

"Your Lordship," broke in old Sir Arthur Pollexfen, "is egregiously misinformed. In all periods of the world's history, eminent personages have concerned themselves with the racing of horses. We read of Philip of Macedon, that while campaigning in Asia

Minor, a courier brought him news of two events, of the birth of his
son Alexander and of the winning, by his favourite horse, of the
chief race at Athens, and we may reasonably infer that his joy over
the winning of the race was equal to if not greater than that over
the birth of Alexander. In the life of Charles the Second, the traits
which do most credit to that careless monarch are his notable and
gentlemanly death and his affection for his great race horse Old
Rowley. Your Lordship is, I am sure," said Sir Arthur, more blandly
than any ecclesiastic could, "too sound a Greek scholar not to remember the epigrams of Maecius and Philodemus, which show what
interest these antique poets took in the racing of horses. And coming
to present times, your Lordship must have heard that his Majesty
(whom God preserve!) has won two Derbies, once with the leased
horse Minoru, and again with his own great Persimmon. The premier
peer of Scotland, the Duke of Hamilton, Duke of Chastellerault
in France, Duke of Brandon in England, hereditary prince of Baden,
is prouder of his fine mare Eau de Vie than of all his titles. As to
the Irish families, the Persses of Galway, the Dawsons of Dublin,
and my own, the Pollexfens of Mayo, have always been interested
in the breeding and racing of horses. And none of these—my punch,
if you please, James Carabine!—are, as your Lordship puts it,
drunkards, bawds, and common gamblers. I fear your Lordship has
been reading—" and he cocked his eye, bright as a wren's, at the
bishop, "religious publications of the sensational and morbid type."

It was all I could do to keep from leaping on the table and giving
three loud cheers for the County of Mayo.

Now, on those occasions, none too rare, when my uncle Valentine and I differed on questions of agricultural economy, or of
national polity, or of mere faith and morals, he poured torrents of
invective over my head, which mattered little. But when he was
really aroused to bitterness he called me "modern." And by modern
my uncle Valentine meant the quality inherent in brown buttoned
boots, in white waistcoats worn with dinner jackets, in nasty little
motor cars—in fine, those things before which the angels of God
recoil in horror. While I am not modern in that sense, I am modern
in this, that I like to see folk getting on with things. Of Lady Clontarf
and of Irlandais colt, I heard no more. On the morning after seeing

her home I called over to the caravan but it was no longer there. There was hardly a trace of it. I found a broken fern and a slip of oaktree, the gypsy patteran. But what it betokened or whither it pointed I could not tell. I had gone to no end of trouble in getting the stables and training grounds ready, and Sir Arthur Pollexfen had been brought out of his retirement in the County of Mayo. But still no word of the horse. I could see my uncle Valentine and Sir Arthur taking their disappointment bravely, if it never arrived, and murmuring some courteous platitude, out of the reign of good Queen Victoria, that it was a lady's privilege to change her mind. That might console them in their philosophy, but it would only make me hot with rage. For to me there is no sex in people of standards. They do not let one another down.

Then one evening the horse arrived.

It arrived at sundown in a large van drawn by four horses, a van belonging evidently to some circus. It was yellow and covered with paintings of nymphs being wooed by swains, in clothes hardly fitted to agricultural pursuits: of lions of terrifying aspect being put through their paces by a trainer of an aspect still more terrifying: of an Indian gentleman with a vast turban and a small loincloth playing a penny whistle to a snake that would have put the heart crosswise in Saint Patrick himself; of a most adipose lady in tights swinging from a ring while the husband and seven sons hung on to her like bees in a swarm. Floridly painted over the van was "Arsène Bombaudiac, Prop., Bayonne." The whole added no dignity to Destiny Bay, and if some sorceress had disclosed to Mr. Bombaudiac of Bayonne that he was about to lose a van by fire at low tide on the beach of Destiny in Ireland within forty-eight hours—The driver was a burly gypsy, while two of the most utter scoundrels I have ever laid eyes on sat beside him on the wide seat.

"Do you speak English?" I asked the driver.

"Yes, sir," he answered, "I am a Petulengro."

"Which of these two beauties beside you is the jockey?"

"Neither, sir. These two are just gypsy fighting men. The jockey is inside with the horse."

My uncle Valentine came down stroking his great red beard. He seemed fascinated by the pictures on the van. "What your poor aunt Jenepher, Kerry," he said, "misses by being blind!"

"What she is spared, sir! Boy," I called one of the servants, "go get Sir Arthur Pollexfen. Where do you come from?" I asked the driver.

"From Dax, sir, in the South of France."

"You're a liar," I said. "Your horses are half-bred Clydesdale. There's no team like that in the South of France."

"We came to Dieppe with an *attelage basque*, six yoked oxen. But I was told they would not be allowed in England, so I telegraphed our chief, Piramus Petulengro, to have a team at Newhaven. So I am not a liar, sir."

"I am sorry."

"Sir, that is all right."

Sir Arthur Pollexfen came down from where he had been speaking to my aunt Jenepher. I could see he was tremendously excited, because he walked more slowly than was usual, spoke with more deliberation. He winced a little as he saw the van. But he was of the old heroic school. He said nothing.

"I think, Sir Valentine," he said, "we might have the horse out."

"Ay, we might as well know the worst," said my uncle Valentine.

A man jumped from the box, and swung the crossbar up. The door opened and into the road stepped a small man in dark clothes. Never on this green earth of God's have I seen such dignity. He was dressed in dark clothes with a wide dark hat, and his face was brown as soil. White starched cuffs covered half of his hands. He took off his hat and bowed first to my uncle Valentine, then to Sir Arthur, and to myself last. His hair was plastered down on his forehead, and the impression you got was of an ugly rugged face, with piercing black eyes. He seemed to say: "Laugh, if you dare!" But laughter was the furthest thing from us, such tremendous masculinity did the small man have. He looked at us searchingly, and I had the feeling that if he didn't like us, for two pins he would have the bar across the van door again and be off with the horse. Then he turned and spoke gutturally to some one inside.

A boy as rugged as himself, in a Basque cap and with a Basque sash, led first a small donkey round as a barrel out of the outrageous van. One of the gypsies took it, and the next moment the boy led out the Irlandais colt.

He came out confidently, quietly, approaching gentlemen as a gentleman, a beautiful brown horse, small, standing perfectly. I had just one glance at the sound strong legs and the firm ribs, before his head caught my eye. The graceful neck, the beautiful small muzzle, the gallant eyes. In every inch of him you could see breeding. While Sir Arthur was examining his hocks, and my uncle Valentine was standing weightily considering strength of lungs and heart, my own heart went out to the lovely eyes that seemed to ask: "Are these folk friends?"

Now I think you could parade the Queen of Sheba in the show ring before me without extracting more than an offhand compliment out of me, but there is something about a gallant thoroughbred that makes me sing. I can quite understand the trainer who, pointing to Manifesto, said that if he ever found a woman with a shape like that, he'd marry her. So out of my heart through my lips came the cry: *"Och, asthore!"* which is, in our Gaelic, "Oh, my dear!"

The Spanish jockey, whose brown face was rugged and impassive as a Pyrenee, looked at me, and broke into a wide, understanding smile.

"Si, si Señor," he uttered, *"si, si!"*

Never did a winter pass so merrily, so advantageously at Destiny Bay. Usually there is fun enough with the hunting, but with a racing stable in winter there is always anxiety. Is there a suspicion of a cough in the stables? Is the ground too hard for gallops? Will snow come and hold the gallops up for a week? Fortunately we are right on the edge of the great Atlantic drift, and you can catch at times the mild amazing atmosphere of the Caribbean. While Scotland sleeps beneath its coverlet of snow, and England shivers in its ghastly fog, we on the northeast seaboard of Ireland go through a winter that is short as a midsummer night in Lofoden. The trees have hardly put off their gold and brown until we perceive their cheeping green. And one soft day we say: "Soon on that bank will be the fairy gold of the primrose." And behold, while you are looking the primrose is there!

Each morning at sun-up, the first string of horses were out. Quietly as a general officer reviewing a parade old Sir Arthur sat on his grey horse, his red dog beside him, while Geraghty, his head man, galloped about with his instructions. Hares bolted from their forms in the grass. The sun rolled away the mists from the blue mountains of Donegal. At the starting gate, which Sir Arthur had set up, the red-faced Irish boys steered their mounts from a walk toward the tapes. A pull at the lever and they were off. The old man seemed to notice everything. "Go easy, boy, don't force that horse!" His low voice would carry across the downs. "Don't lag there, Murphy, ride him!" And when the gallop was done, he would trot across to the horses, his red dog trotting beside him, asking how Sarsfield went. Did Ducks and Drakes seem interested? Did Rustum go up to his bit? Then they were off at a slow walk toward their sand bath, where they rolled like dogs. Then the sponging and the rubbing, and the fresh hay in the managers kept as clean as a hospital. At eleven the second string came out. At half-past three the lads were called to their horses, and a quarter of an hour's light walking was given to them. At four, Sir Arthur made his "stables," questioning the lads in each detail as to how the horses had fed, running his hand over their legs to feel for any heat in the joints that might betoken trouble.

Small as our stable was, I doubt if there was one in Great Britain and Ireland to compare with it in each fitting and necessity for training a race horse. Sir Arthur pinned his faith to old black tartar oats, of about forty-two pounds to the bushel, bran mashes with a little linseed, and sweet old meadow hay.

The Irlandais colt went beautifully. The Spanish jockey's small brother, Joselito, usually rode it, while the jockey's self, whose name we were told was Frasco, Frasco Moreno—usually called, he told us, Don Frasco—looked on. He constituted himself a sort of sub-trainer for the colt, allowing none else to attend to its feeding. The small donkey was its invariable stable companion, and had to be led out to exercise with it. The donkey belonged to Joselito. Don Frasco rode many trials on other horses. He might appear small standing, but on horseback he seemed a large man, so straight did he sit in the saddle. The little boys rode with a fairly short stirrup, but the gitano scorned anything but the traditional seat. He never seemed to move on a horse. Yet he could do what he liked with it.

The Irlandais colt was at last named Romany Baw, or "gypsy friend" in English, as James Carabine explained to us, and Lady Clontarf's colours registered, quartered red and gold. When the winter lists came out, we saw the horse quoted at a hundred to one, and later at the call over of the Victoria Club, saw that price offered but not taken. My uncle Valentine made a journey to Dublin, to arrange for Lady Clontarf's commission being placed, putting it in the hands of a Derry man who had become big in the affairs of Tattersall's. What he himself and Sir Arthur Pollexfen and the jockey had on I do not know, but he arranged to place an hundred pounds of mine, and fifty of Ann-Dolly's. As the months went by, the odds crept down gradually to thirty-three to one, stood there for a while and went out to fifty. Meanwhile Sir James became a sensational favourite at fives, and Toison d'Or varied between tens and one hundred to eight. Some news of a great trial of Lord Shire's horse had leaked out which accounted for the ridiculously short price. But no word did or could get out about Lady Clontarf's colt. The two gypsy fighters from Dax patrolled Destiny Bay, and God help any poor tipster or wretched newspaper tout who tried to plumb the mysteries of training. I honestly believe a bar of iron and a bog hole would have been his end.

The most fascinating figure in this crazy world was the gypsy jockey. To see him talk to Sir Arthur Pollexfen was a phenomenon. Sir Arthur would speak in English and the gypsy answer in Spanish, neither knowing a word of the other's language, yet each perfectly understanding the other. I must say that this only referred to how a horse ran, or how Romany Baw was feeding and feeling. As to more complicated problems, Ann-Dolly was called in, to translate his Spanish.

"Ask him," said Sir Arthur, "has he ever ridden in France?"

"*Oiga, Frasco,*" and Ann-Dolly would burst into a torrent of gutturals.

"*Si, si, Doña Anna.*"

"Ask him has he got his clearance from the Jockey Club of France?"

"*Seguro, Don Arturo!*" And out of his capacious pocket he extracted the French Jockey Club's "character." They made a picture I will never forget, the old horseman ageing so gently, the vivid boyish beauty of Ann-Dolly, and the overpowering dignity and manliness of the jockey. Always, except when he was riding or working at his anvil,—for he was our smith too—he wore the dark clothes, which evidently some village tailor of the Pyrenees made for him—the very short coat, the trousers tubed like cigarettes, his stiff shirt with the vast cuffs. He never wore a collar, nor a neckerchief. Always his back was flat as the side of a house.

When he worked at the anvil, with his young ruffian of a brother at the bellows, he sang. He had shakes and grace notes enough to make a thrush quit. Ann-Dolly translated one of his songs for us.

> No tengo padre ni madre . .
> Que desgraciado soy yo!
> Soy como el arbol solo
> Que echas frutas y no echa flor . . .

"He sings he has no father or mother. How out of luck he is! He is like a lonely tree, which bears the fruit and not the flower."

"God bless my soul, Kerry," my uncle was shocked. "The little man is homesick."

"No, no!" Ann-Dolly protested. "He is very happy. That is why he sings a sad song."

One of the reasons of the little man's happiness was the discovery of our national game of handball. He strolled over to the Irish Village and discovered the court back of the Inniskillen Dragoon, that most notable of rural pubs. He was tremendously excited, and getting some gypsy to translate for him, challenged the local champion for the stake of a barrel of porter. He made the local champion look like a carthorse in the Grand National. When it was told to me I couldn't believe it. Ann-Dolly explained to me that the great game of Basque country was *pelota*.

"But don't they play *pelota* with a basket?"

"Real *pelota* is *à mains nues*, 'with the hands naked.' "

"You mean Irish handball," I told her.

I regret that the population of Destiny made rather a good thing out of Don Frasco's prowess on the court, going from village to village, and betting on a certain win. The end was a match between Mick Tierney, the Portrush Jarvey and the jockey. The match was billed for the champion of Ulster, and Don Frasco was put down on the card, to explain his lack of English, as Danny Frask, the Glenties Miracle, the Glenties being a district of Donegal where Erse is the native speech. The match was poor, the Portrush Jarvey, after the first game, standing and watching the ball hiss past him with his eyes on his cheek bones. All Donegal seemed to have turned out for the fray. When the contest was over, a big Glenties man pushed his way toward the jockey.

"Dublin and London and New York are prime cities," he chanted, "but Glenties is truly magnificent. *Kir do lauv anshin, a railt na hooee*, 'Put your hand there, Star of the North.' "

"*No entiendo, señor*," said Don Frasco. And with that the fight began.

James Carabine was quick enough to get the jockey out of the court before he was lynched. But Destiny Bay men, gypsies, fishers, citizens of Derry, bookmakers and their clerks and the fighting tribes of Donegal went to it with a vengeance. Indeed, according to experts, nothing like it, for spirit or results, had been seen since or before the Prentice Boys had chased King James (to whom God give his deserts!) from Derry Walls. The removal of the stunned and wounded from the courts drew the attention of the police, for the fight was continued in grim silence. But on the entrance of half a dozen peelers commanded by a huge sergeant, Joselito, the jockey's young brother, covered himself with glory. Leaping on the reserved seats, he brought his right hand over hard and true to the sergeant's jaw, and the sergeant was out for half an hour. Joselito was arrested, but the case was laughed out of court. The idea of a minuscule jockey who could ride at ninety pounds knocking out six foot three of Royal Irish Constabulary was too much. Nothing was found on him but his bare hands, a packet of cigarettes and thirty sovereigns he had won over the match. But I knew better. I decided to prove him with hard questions.

"Ask him in Romany, James Carabine, what he had wrapped around that horseshoe he threw away."

"He says: 'Tow, Mister Kerry.' "

"Get me my riding crop," I said; "I'll take him behind the stables." And the training camp lost its best lightweight jockey for ten days, the saddle suddenly becoming repulsive to him. I believe he slept on his face.

But the one who was really wild about the affair was Ann-Dolly. She came across from Spanish Men's Rest flaming with anger.

"Because a Spanish wins, there is fighting, there is anger. If an

Irish wins, there is joy, there is drinking. Oh, shame of sportsman-
ship!"

"Oh, shut your gab, Ann-Dolly," I told her. "They didn't know
he was a Spanish, as you call it."

"What did they think he was if not a Spanish? Tell me. I demand
it of you."

"They thought he was Welsh."

"Oh, in that case . . ." said Ann-Dolly, completely mollified. *Ipsa
hibernis hiberniora!*

I wouldn't have you think that all was beer and skittles, as the
English say, in training Romany Baw for the Derby. As spring
came closer, the face of the old trainer showed signs of strain. The
Lincoln Handicap was run and the Grand National passed, and
suddenly flat-racing was on us. And now not the Kohinoor was
watched more carefully than the Derby horse. We had a spanking
trial on a course as nearly approaching the Two Thousand Guineas
route as Destiny Downs would allow, and when Romany Baw flew
past us, beating Ducks and Drakes who had picked him up at the
mile for the uphill dash, and Sir Arthur clicked his watch, I saw his
tense face relax.

"He ran well," said the old man.

"He'll walk in," said my uncle Valentine.

My uncle Valentine and Jenico and Ann-Dolly were going
across to Newmarket Heath for the big race, but the spring of the
year is the time that the farmer must stay by his land, and nurse it
like a child. All farewells, even for a week, are sad, and I was loath
to see the horses go into the races. Romany Baw had a regular summer bloom on him and his companion, the donkey, was corpulent as
an alderman. Ducks and Drakes looked rough and backward, but
that didn't matter.

"You've got the best-looking horse in the United Kingdom," I
told Sir Arthur.

"Thank you, Kerry," the old man was pleased. "And as to Ducks
and Drakes, looks aren't everything."

"Sure, I know that," I told him.

"I wouldn't be rash," he told me, "but I'd have a little on both.
That is, if they go to the post fit and well."

I put in the days as well as I could, getting ready for the Spring Show at Dublin. But my heart and my thoughts were with my people and the horses at Newmarket. I could see my uncle Valentine's deep bow with his hat in his hand as they passed the Roman ditch at Newmarket, giving that squat wall the reverence that racing men have accorded it since races were run there, though why, none know. A letter from Ann-Dolly apprised me that the horses had made a good crossing and that Romany Baw was well—"and you mustn't think, my dear, that your colt is not as much and more to us than the Derby horse, no, Kerry, not for one moment. Lady Clontarf is here, in her caravan, and oh, Kerry, she looks ill. Only her burning spirit keeps her frail body alive. Jenico and I are going down to Eastbourne to see the little Earl and his brother . . . You will get this letter, cousin, on the morning of the race. . . ."

At noon that day I could stand it no longer so I had James Carabine put the trotter in the dogcart. "There are some things I want in Derry," I told myself, "and I may as well get them to-day as tomorrow." And we went spinning toward Derry Walls. Ducks and Drakes' race was the two-thirty. And after lunch I looked at reapers I might be wanting in July until the time of the race. I went along to the club, and had hardly entered it when I saw the boy putting up the telegram on the notice board.

1, *Ducks and Drakes*, an hundred to eight; 2, Geneva, four to six; 3, *Ally Sloper*, three to one. "That's that!" I said. Another telegram gave the betting for the Two Thousand: Threes, *Sir James*; seven to two, *Toison d'or*; eights, *Ca' Canny, Greek Singer, Germanicus*; tens, six or seven horses; twenty to one any other. No word in the betting of the gypsy horse, and I wondered had anything happened. Surely a horse looking as well as he did must have attracted backers' attention. And as I was worrying the result came in, *Romany Baw*, first; *Sir James*, second, *Toison d'Or*, third.

"Kerry," somebody called.

"I haven't a minute," I shouted. Neither I had, for James Carabine was outside, waiting to hear the result. When I told him he said: "There's a lot due to you, Mister Kerry, in laying out those gallops." "Be damned to that!" I said, but I was pleased all the same.

I was on tenterhooks until I got the papers describing the race. Ducks and Drakes' win was dismissed summarily, as that of an Irish outsider, and the jockey, Flory Cantillon (Frasco could not manage the weight), was credited with a clever win of two lengths. But the account of Romany Baw's race filled me with indignation. According to it, the winner got away well, but the favourites were hampered at the start and either could have beaten the Irish trained horse, only that they just didn't. The race was won by half a length, a head separating second and third, and most of the account was given to how the favourites chased the lucky outsider, and in a few more strides would have caught him. There were a few dirty backhanders given at Romany's jockey, who, they said, would be more at home in a circus than on a modern race track. He sat like a rider of a century back, they described it, more like an exponent of the old manège than a modern jockey, and even while the others were thundering at his horse's hindquarters he never moved his seat or used his whip. The experts' judgment of the race was that the Irish colt was forward in a backward field, and that Romany would be lost on Epsom Downs, especially with its "postillion rider."

But the newspaper criticisms of the jockey and his mount did not seem to bother my uncle Valentine or the trainer or the jockey's self. They came back elated; even the round white donkey had a humorous happy look in his full Latin eye.

"Did he go well?" I asked.

"He trotted it," said my uncle Valentine.

"But the accounts read, sir," I protested, "that the favourites would have caught him in another couple of strides."

"Of course they would," said my uncle Valentine, "at the pace he was going," he added.

"I see," said I.

"You see nothing," said my uncle Valentine. "But if you had seen the race you might talk. The horse is a picture. It goes so sweetly that you wouldn't think it was going at all. And as for the gypsy jockey—"

"The papers say he's antiquated."

"He's seven pounds better than Flory Cantillon," said my uncle Valentine.

I whistled. Cantillon is our best Irish jockey, and his retaining fees are enormous, and justified. "They said he was nearly caught napping—"

"Napping be damned!" exploded my uncle Valentine. "This Spanish gypsy is the finest judge of pace I ever saw. He knew he had the race won, and he never bothered."

"If the horse is as good as that, and you have as high an opinion of the rider, well, sir, I won a hatful over the Newmarket meeting, and as the price hasn't gone below twenties for the Derby, I'm going after the Ring. There's many a bookmaker will wish he'd stuck to his father's old-clothes business."

"I wouldn't, Kerry," said my uncle Valentine. "I'm not sure I wouldn't hedge a bit of what I have on, if I were you."

I was still with amazement.

"I saw Mifanwy Clontarf," said my uncle Valentine, "and only God and herself and myself and now you, know how ill that woman is."

"But ill or not ill, she won't scratch the horse."

"She won't," said my uncle Valentine, and his emphasis on 'she' chilled me to the heart. "You're forgetting, Kerry," he said very quietly, "the Derby Rule."

Of the Derby itself on Epsom Downs, everybody knows. It is supposed to be the greatest test of a three-year-old in the world, though old William Day used to hold it was easy. The course may have been easy for Lord George Bentinck's famous and unbeaten mare Crucifix, when she won the Oaks in 1840, but most winners over the full course justify their victory in other races. The course starts up a heartbreaking hill, and swinging around the top, comes down again toward Tattenham Corner. If a horse waits to steady itself coming down it is beaten. The famous Fred Archer (whose tortured soul God rest!) used to take Tattenham Corner with one leg over the rails. The straight is uphill. A mile and a half of the trickiest, most heartbreaking ground in the world. Such is Epsom. Its turf has been consecrated by the hoofs of great horses since James I established there a race for the Silver Bell: by Cromwell's great Coffin Mare; by the Arabs, Godolphin and Darby; by the great bay, Malton; by the prodigious Eclipse; by Diomed, son of Florizel, who went to America. . . .

Over the Derby what sums are wagered no man knows. On it is won the Calcutta Sweepstake, a prize of which makes a man rich for life, and the Stock Exchange sweep, and other sweeps innumerable. Some one has ventured the belief that on it annually are five million of pounds sterling, and whether he is millions short, or millions over none knows. Because betting is illegal.

There are curious customs in regard to it, as this: that when the result is sent over the ticker to clubs, in case of a dead heat, the word "dead heat" must come first, because within recent years a trusted lawyer, wagering trust funds on a certain horse, was waiting by the tape to read the result, and seeing another horse's name come up, went away forthwith and blew his brains out. Had he been less volatile he would have seen his own fancy's name follow that, with "dead heat" after it and been to this day rich and respected. So now, for the protection of such, "dead heat" comes first. A dead heat in the Derby is as rare a thing as there is in the world, but still you can't be too cautious. But the quaintest rule of the Derby is this: that if the nominator of a horse for the Derby Stakes dies, his horse is automatically scratched. There is a legend to the effect that an heir-at-law purposed to kill the owner of an entry, and to run a prime favourite crookedly, and that on hearing this the Stewards of the Jockey Club made the rule. Perhaps it has a more prosaic reason. The Jockey Club may have considered that when a man died, in the trouble of fixing his estates, forfeits would not be paid, and that it was best for all concerned to have the entry scratched. How it came about does not matter, it exists. Whether it is good in law is not certain. Racing folk will quarrel with His Majesty's Lord Justices of Appeal, with the Privy Council, but they will not quarrel with the Jockey Club. Whether it is good in fact is indisputable, for certain owners can tell stories of narrow escapes from racing gangs, in those old days before the Turf was cleaner than the Church, when attempts were made to noble favourites, when jockeys had not the wings of angels under their silken jackets, when harsh words were spoken about trainers—very, very long ago. There it is, good or bad, the Derby Rule!

As to our bets on the race, they didn't matter. It was just bad luck. But to see the old lady's quarter million of pounds and more go down the pike was a tragedy. We had seen so much of shabby great names that I trembled for young Clontarf and his brother.

Armenian and Greek families of doubtful antecedents were always on the lookout for a title for their daughters, and crooked businesses always needed directors of title to catch gulls, so much in the United Kingdom do the poor trust their peers. The boys would not be exactly poor, because the horse, whether or not it ran in the Derby, would be worth a good round sum. If it were as good as my uncle Valentine said, it would win the Leger and the Gold Cup at Ascot. But even with these triumphs it wouldn't be a Derby winner. And the Derby means so much. There are so many people in England who remember dates by the Derby winner's names, as "I was married in *Bend Or's* year," or "the *Achilles* was lost in the China seas, let me see when,—that was in *Sainfoin's* year." Also I wasn't sure that the Spanish gypsy would stay to ride him at Doncaster, or return for Ascot. I found him one day standing on the cliffs of Destiny and looking long at the sea, and I knew what that meant. And perhaps Romany Baw would not run for another jockey as he ran for him.

I could not think that Death could be so cruel as to come between us and triumph. In Destiny we have a friendliness for the Change which most folk dread. One of our songs says:

"When Mother Death in her warm arms shall embrace me,
Low lull me to sleep with sweet Erin-go-bragh—"

We look upon it as a kind friend who comes when one is tired and twisted with pain, and says: "Listen, *avourneen*, soon the dawn will come, and the tide is on the ebb. We must be going." And we trust him to take us, by a short road or a long road to a place of birds and bees, of which even lovely Destiny is but a clumsy seeming. He could not be such a poor sportsman as to come before the aged gallant lady had won her last gamble. And poor Sir Arthur, who had come out of his old age in Mayo to win a Derby! It would break his heart. And the great horse, it would be so hard on him. Nothing will convince me that a thoroughbred does not know a great race when he runs one. The streaming competitors, the crackle of silk, the roar as they come into the straight, and the sense of the jockey calling on the great heart that the writer of Job knew so well. "The glory of his nostril is terrible," says the greatest of poets. "He pauseth in the valley and rejoiceth in his strength: he goeth on

to meet the armed men." Your intellectual will claim that the thoroughbred is an artificial brainless animal evolved by men for their
amusement. Your intellectual, here again, is a liar.

Spring came in blue and gold. Blue of sea and fields and trees;
gold of sun and sand and buttercup. Blue of wild hyacinth and
bluebell; gold of primrose and laburnum tree. The old gypsy lady
was with her caravan near Bordeaux, and from the occasional letter
my uncle Valentine got, and from the few words he dropped to
me, she was just holding her own. May drowsed by with the cheeping of the little life in the hedgerows. The laburnum floated in a
cloud of gold and each day Romany Baw grew stronger. When
his blankets were stripped from him he looked a mass of fighting
muscle under a covering of satin, and his eye showed that his heart
was fighting too. Old Sir Arthur looked at him a few days before
we were to go to England, and he turned to me.

"Kerry," he said, very quietly.

"Yes, Sir Arthur."

"All my life I have been breeding and training horses, and it
just goes to show," he told me, "that goodness of God that he let
me handle this great horse before I died."

The morning before we left my uncle Valentine received a letter
which I could see moved him. He swore a little as he does when
moved and stroked his vast red beard and looked fiercely at nothing
at all.

"Is it bad news, sir?" I asked.

He didn't answer me directly. "Lady Clontarf is coming to the
Derby," he told me.

Then it was my turn to swear a little. It seemed to me to be but
little short of maniacal to risk a Channel crossing and the treacherous
English climate in her stage of health. If she should die on the way
or on the downs, then all her planning and our work was for nothing. Why could she not have remained in the soft French air, hus-
banding her share of life until the event was past!

"She comes of ancient, violent blood," thundered my uncle Valentine, "and where should she be but present when her people or
her horses go forth to battle?"

"You are right, sir," I said.

The epithet of "flaming" which the English apply to their June was in this year of grace well deserved. The rhododendrons were bursting into great fountains of scarlet, and near the swans the cygnets paddled, unbelievably small. The larks fluttered in the air above the downs, singing so gallantly that when you heard the trill of the nightingale in the thicket giving his noontime song, you felt inclined to say: "Be damned to that Italian bird; my money's on the wee fellow!" All through Surrey the green walls of spring rose high and thick, and then suddenly coming, as we came, through Leatherhead and topping the hill, in the distance the black colony of the downs showed like a thundercloud. At a quarter mile away, the clamour came to you, like the vibration when great bells have been struck.

The stands and enclosures were packed so thickly that one wondered how movement was possible, how people could enjoy themselves, close as herrings. My uncle Valentine had brought his beautiful harness ponies across from Ireland, "to encourage English interest in the Irish horse" he explained it, but with his beautifully cut clothes, his grey high hat, it seemed to me that more people looked at him as we spun along the road than looked at the horses. Behind us sat James Carabine, with his face brown as autumn and the gold rings in his thickened ears. We got out near the paddock and Carabine took the ribbons. My uncle Valentine said quietly to him: "Find out how things are, James Carabine." And I knew he was referring to the gypsy lady. Her caravan was somewhere on the Downs guarded by her gypsies, but my uncle had been there the first day of the meeting, and on Monday night, at the National Sporting, some of the gypsies had waited for him coming out and given him news. I asked him how she was, but all his answer was: "It's in the Hands of God."

Along the track toward the grand stand we made our way. On the railings across the track the bookmakers were proclaiming their market: "I'll give fives the field. I'll give nine to one bar two. I'll give twenty to one bar five. Outsiders! Outsiders! Fives *Sir James*. Seven to one *Toison d'Or*. Nines *Honey Bee*. Nines *Welsh Melody*. Ten to one the gypsy horse."

"It runs all right," said my uncle Valentine, "up to now."

"Twenty to one *Maureen Roe!* Twenties *Asclepiades!* Twenty-five *Rifle Ranger*. Here thirty-three to one *Rifle Ranger, Monk of Sussex*, or *Presumptuous*—"

"Gentlemen, I am here to plead with you not to back the favourite. In this small envelope you will find the number of the winner. For the contemptible sum of two shillings or half a dollar, you may amass a fortune. Who gave the winner of last year's Derby?" a tipster was calling. "Who gave the winner of the Oaks? Who gave the winner of the Steward's Cup?"

"All right, guv'nor, I'll bite. 'Oo the 'ell did?"

Opposite the grand stand the band of the Salvation Army was blaring the music of "Work, for the Night is Coming." Gypsy girls were going around *dukkering* or telling fortune. "Ah, gentleman, you've a lucky face. Cross the poor gypsy's hand with silver—"

"You better cut along and see your horse saddled," said my uncle Valentine. Ducks and Drakes was in the Ranmore Plate and with the penalty he received after Newmarket, Frasco could ride him. As I went toward the paddock I saw the numbers go up, and I saw we were drawn third, which I think is best of all on the tricky Epsom five-furlough dash. I got there in time to see the gypsy swing into the saddle in the green silk jacket and orange cap, and Sir Arthur giving him his orders. "Keep back of the Fusilier," he pointed to the horse, "and then come out. Hit him once if you have to, and no more."

"*Si, si, Don Arturo!*" And he grinned at me.

"Kerry, read this," said the old trainer, and he gave me a newspaper, "and tell me before the race," his voice was trembling a little, "if there's truth in it."

I pushed the paper into my pocket and went back to the box where my uncle Valentine and Jenico and Ann-Dolly were. "What price my horse," I asked in Tattersall's. "Sixes, Mister MacFarlane." "I'll take six hundred to an hundred twice." As I moved away there was a rush to back it. It tumbled in five minutes to five to two.

"And I thought I'd get tens," I said to my uncle Valentine, "with the Fusilier and Bonny Hortense in the race. I wonder who's been backing it."

"I have," said Ann-Dolly. "I got twelves."

"You might have the decency to wait until the owner gets on," I said bitterly. And as I watched the tapes went up. It was a beautiful start. Everything except those on the outside seemed to have a chance as they raced for the rails. I could distinguish the green jacket but vaguely until they came to Tattenham Corner, when I could see Fusilier pull out, and Bonny Hortense follow. But back of Fusilier, racing quietly beside the filly, was the jacket green.

"I wish he'd go up," I said.

"The favourite wins," they were shouting. And a woman in the box next us began to clap her hands calling: "Fusilier's won. Fusilier wins it!"

"You're a damn fool, woman," said Ann-Dolly. "Ducks and Drakes has it." And as she spoke, I could see Frasco hunch forward slightly and dust his mount's neck with his whip. He crept past the hard-pressed Fusilier to win by half a length.

In my joy I nearly forgot the newspaper, and I glanced at it rapidly. My heart sank. "Gypsy Owner Dying as Horse runs in Derby," I read, and reading down it I felt furious. Where the man got his information from I don't know, but he drew a picturesque account of the old gypsy lady on her deathbed on the Downs as Romany Baw was waiting in his stall. The account was written the evening before, and "it is improbable she will last the night," it ended. I gave it to my uncle Valentine, who had been strangely silent over my win.

"What shall I say to Sir Arthur Pollexfen?"

"Say she's ill, but it's all rot she's dying."

I noticed as I went to the paddock a murmur among the race-goers. The attention of all had been drawn to the gypsy horse by its jockey having won the Ranmore Plate. Everywhere I heard questions being asked as to whether she were dead. Sir James had hardened to fours. And on the heath I heard a woman proffer a sovereign to a bookmaker on Romany Baw, and he said: "That horse don't run, lady." I forgot my own little triumph in the tragedy of the scratching of the great horse.

In the paddock Sir Arthur was standing watching the lads leading the horses around. Twenty-seven entries, glossy as silk, muscled like athletes of old Greece, ready to run for the Derby stakes. The jockeys, with their hard wizened faces, stood talking to trainers and owners, saying nothing about the race, all already having been said, but just putting in the time until the order came to go to the

gate. I moved across to the old Irish trainer and the gypsy jockey.
Sir Arthur was saying nothing, but his hand trembled as he took a
pinch of snuff from his old-fashioned silver horn. The gypsy jockey
stood erect, with his overcoat over his silk. It was a heart-rending
five minutes standing there beside them, waiting for the message that
they were not to go.

My uncle Valentine was standing with a couple of the Stewards.
A small race official was explaining something to them. They nodded
him away. There was another minute's conversation and my uncle
came toward us. The old trainer was fumbling pitifully with his
silver snuff horn, trying to find the pocket in which to put it.

"It's queer," said my uncle Valentine, "but nobody seems to
know where Lady Clontarf is. She's not in her caravan."

"So—" questioned the old trainer.

"So you run," said my uncle Valentine. "The horse comes under
starter's orders. You may have an objection, Arthur, but you run."

The old man put on youth and grandeur before my eyes. He stood
erect. With an eye like an eagle's he looked around the paddock.

"Leg up, boy!" he snapped at Frasco.

"Here, give me your coat." I helped throw the golden-and-red
shirted figure into the saddle. Then the head lad led the horse out.

We moved down the track and into the stand, and the parade
began. Lord Shire's great horse, and the French hope Toison d'Or;
the brown colt owned by the richest merchant in the world, and the
little horse owned by the Leicester butcher, who served in his own
shop; the horse owned by the peer of last year's making; and the bay
filly owned by the first baroness in England. They went down
past the stand, and turning breezed off at a gallop back, to cross the
Downs toward the starting gate, and as they went with each went
some one's heart. All eyes seemed turned on the gypsy horse, with
his rider erect as a Life Guardsman. As Frasco raised his whip to his
cap in the direction of our box, I heard in one of the neighbouring
boxes a man say: "But that horse's owner is dead!"

"Is that so, Uncle Valentine?" asked Ann-Dolly. There were
tears in her eyes. "Is that true?"

"Nothing is true until you see it yourself," parried my uncle
Valentine. And as she seemed to be about to cry openly,—"Don't
you see the horse running?" he said. "Don't you know the rule?"

But his eyes were riveted through his glasses on the starting gate. I could see deep furrows of anxiety on his bronze brow. In the distance, over the crowd's heads, over the bookmaker's banners, over the tents, we could see the dancing horses at the tape, the gay colours of the riders moving here and there in an intricate pattern, the massed hundreds of black figures at the start. Near us, across the rails, some religious zealots let fly little balloons carrying banners reminding us that doom was waiting. Their band broke into a lugubrious hymn, while nasal voices took it up. In the silence of the crowded Downs, breathless for the start, the religious demonstration seemed startlingly trivial. The line of horses, formed for the gate, broke, and wheeled. My uncle snapped his fingers in vexation.

"Why can't the fool get them away?"

Then out of a seeming inextricable maze, the line formed suddenly and advanced on the tapes. And the heavy silence exploded into a low roar like growling thunder. Each man shouted: "They're off!" The Derby had started.

It seemed like a river of satin, with iridescent foam, pouring, against all nature, uphill. And for one instant you could distinguish nothing. You looked to see if your horse had got away well, had not been kicked or cut into at the start, and as you were disentangling them, the banks of gorse shut them from your view, and when you saw them again they were racing for the turn of the hill. The erect figure of the jockey caught my eye before his colours did.

"He's lying fifth," I told my uncle Valentine.

"He's running well," my uncle remarked quietly.

They swung around the top of the hill, appearing above the rails and gorse, like something tremendously artificial, like some theatrical illusion, as of a boat going across the stage. There were three horses grouped together, then a black horse—Esterhazy's fine colt—then Romany Baw, then after that a stretching line of horses. Something came out of the pack at the top of the hill, and passed the gypsy horse and the fourth.

"Toison d'Or is going up," Jenico told me.

But the gallant French colt's bolt was flown. He fell back, and now one of the leaders dropped back. And Romany was fourth as they started downhill for Tattenham Corner. "How slow they go!" I thought.

"What a pace!" said Jenico, his watch in his hand.

At Tattenham Corner the butcher's lovely little horse was beaten, and a sort of moan came from the rails where the poor people stood. Above the religious band's outrageous nasal tones, the ring began roaring: "Sir James! Sir James has it. Twenty to one bar St. James!" As they came flying up the stretch I could see the favourite going along, like some bird flying low, his jockey hunched like an ape on his withers. Beside him raced an outsider, a French-bred horse owned by Kazoutlian, an Armenian banker. Close to his heels came the gypsy horse on the inside, Frasco sitting as though the horse were standing still. Before him raced the favourite and the rank outsider.

"It's all over," I said. "He can't get through. And he can't pull around. Luck of the game!"

And then the rider on the Armenian's horse tried his last effort. He brought his whip high in the air. My uncle Valentine thundered a great oath.

"Look, Kerry!" His fingers gripped my shoulder.

I knew, when I saw the French horse throw his head up, that he was going to swerve at the whip, but I never expected Frasco's mad rush. He seemed to jump the opening, and land the horse past Sir James.

"The favourite's beat!" went up the cry of dismay.

Romany Baw, with Frasco forward on his neck, passed the winning post first by a clear length.

Then a sort of stunned silence fell on the Derby crowd. Nobody knew what would happen. If, as the rumour went around, the owner was dead, then the second automatically won. All eyes were on the horse as the trainer led him into the paddock, followed by second and third. All eyes turned from the horse toward the notice board as the numbers went up: 17, 1, 26. All folk were waiting for the red objection signal. The owner of the second led his horse in, the burly Yorkshire peer. An old gnarled man, with a face like a walnut, Kazoutlian's self, led in the third.

"I say, Kerry," Jenico called quietly, "something's up near the paddock."

I turned and noticed a milling mob down the course on our right. The mounted policemen set off at a trot toward the commotion. Then cheering went into the air like a peal of bells.

Down the course came all the gypsies, all the gypsies in the world, it seemed to me. Big-striding, black men with gold earrings and coloured neckerchiefs, and staves in their hands. And gypsy women, a-jingle with coins, dancing. Their tambourines jangled, as they danced forward in a strange East Indian rhythm. There was a loud order barked by the police officer, and the men stood by to let them pass. And the stolid English police began cheering too. It seemed to me that even the little trees of the Downs were cheering, and in an instant I cheered too.

For back of an escort of mounted gypsies, big foreign men with moustaches, saddleless on their shaggy mounts, came a gypsy cart with its cover down, drawn by four prancing horses. A wild-looking gypsy man was holding the reins. On the cart, for all to see, seated in a great armchair, propped up by cushions, was Lady Clontarf. Her head was laid back on a pillow, and her eyes were closed, as if the strain of appearing had been too much for her. Her little maid was crouched at her feet.

For an instant we saw her, and noticed the aged beauty of her face, noticed the peace like twilight on it. There was an order from a big Roumanian gypsy and the Romany people made a lane. The driver stood up on his perch and manœuvring his long snakelike whip in the air, made it crack like a musket. The horses broke into a gallop, and the gypsy cart went over the turfed course toward Tattenham Corner, passed it, and went up the hill and disappeared over the Surrey downs. All the world was cheering.

"Come in here," said my uncle Valentine, and he took me into the cool beauty of our little church of Saint Columba's-in-Paganry. "Now what do you think of that?" And he pointed out a brass tablet on the wall.

"In Memory of Mifanwy, Countess of Clontarf and Kincora," I read. Then came the dates of her birth and death, "and who is buried after the Romany manner, no man knows where." And then came the strange text, "In death she was not divided."

"But surely," I objected, "the quotation is: 'In death they were not divided.'"

"It may be," said my uncle Valentine, "or it may not be. But as the living of Saint Columba's-in-Paganry is in my gift, surely to

God!" he broke out, "a man can have a text the way he wants it in his own Church."

This was arguable, but something more serious caught my eye.

"See, sir," I said, "the date of her death is wrong. She died on the evening of Derby Day, June the second. And here it is given as June the first."

"She did not die on the evening of Derby Day. She died on the First."

"Then," I said, "when she rode down the course on her gypsy cart," and a little chill came over me, "she was—"

"As a herring, Kerry, as a gutted herring," my uncle Valentine said.

"Then the rule was really infringed, and the horse should not have won."

"Wasn't he the best horse there?"

"Undoubtedly, sir, but as to the betting."

"The bookmakers lost less than they would have lost on the favourite."

"But the backers of the favourite."

"The small backer in the silver ring is paid on the first past the post, so they'd have lost, anyway. At any rate, they all should have lost. They backed their opinion as to which was the best horse, and it wasn't."

"But damn it all, sir! and God forgive me for swearing in this holy place—there's the Derby Rule."

" 'The letter killeth,' Kerry," quoted my uncle gravely, even piously. " 'The letter killeth.' "

Kerfol

by EDITH WHARTON

*Many times animals have taken the place, for lonely
men and women, of the human companionship that is
denied them. In this strange story of an unhappy marriage, five dogs repay human love with that faith of
which they are themselves the symbol.*

"**Y**OU ought to buy it," said my host; "it's just the place for
a solitary-minded devil like you. And it would be rather
worth while to own the most romantic house in Brittany. The present people are dead broke, and it's going for a song—you ought to
buy it."

It was not with the least idea of living up to the character my
friend Lanrivain ascribed to me (as a matter of fact, under my
unsociable exterior I have always had secret yearnings for domesticity) that I took his hint one autumn afternoon and went to
Kerfol. My friend was motoring over to Quimper on business: he
dropped me on the way, at a cross-road on a heath, and said: "First
turn to the right and second to the left. Then straight ahead till you
see an avenue. If you meet any peasants, don't ask your way. They
don't understand French, and they would pretend they did and mix
you up. I'll be back for you here by sunset—and don't forget the
tombs in the chapel."

I followed Lanrivain's directions with the hesitation occasioned
by the usual difficulty of remembering whether he had said the first
turn to the right and second to the left, or the contrary. If I had
met a peasant I should certainly have asked, and probably been sent
astray; but I had the desert landscape to myself, and so stumbled on
the right turn and walked across the heath till I came to an avenue. It
was so unlike any other avenue I have ever seen that I instantly knew

it must be *the* avenue. The grey-trunked trees sprang up straight to a great height and then interwove their pale-grey branches in a long tunnel through which the autumn light fell faintly. I know most trees by name, but I haven't to this day been able to decide what those trees were. They had the tall curve of elms, the tenuity of poplars, the ashen colour of olives under a rainy sky; and they stretched ahead of me for half a mile or more without a break in their arch. If ever I saw an avenue that unmistakably led to something, it was the avenue at Kerfol. My heart beat a little as I began to walk down it.

Presently the trees ended and I came to a fortified gate in a long wall. Between me and the wall was an open space of grass, with other grey avenues radiating from it. Behind the wall were tall slate roofs mossed with silver, a chapel belfry, the top of a keep. A moat filled with wild shrubs and brambles surrounded the place; the drawbridge had been replaced by a stone arch, and the portcullis by an iron gate. I stood for a long time on the hither side of the moat, gazing about me, and letting the influence of the place sink in. I said to myself: "If I wait long enough, the guardian will turn up and show me the tombs—" and I rather hoped he wouldn't turn up too soon.

I sat down on a stone and lit a cigarette. As soon as I had done it, it struck me as a puerile and portentous thing to do, with that great blind house looking down at me, and all the empty avenues converging on me. It may have been the depth of the silence that made me so conscious of my gesture. The squeak of my match sounded as loud as the scraping of a brake, and I almost fancied I heard it fall when I tossed it onto the grass. But there was more than that: a sense of irrelevance, of littleness, of futile bravado, in sitting there puffing my cigarette smoke into the face of such a past.

I knew nothing of the history of Kerfol—I was new to Brittany, and Lanrivain had never mentioned the name to me till the day before—but one couldn't as much as glance at that pile without feeling in it a long accumulation of history. What kind of history I was not prepared to guess: perhaps only that sheer weight of many associated lives and deaths which gives a majesty to all old houses. But the aspect of Kerfol suggested something more—a perspective of stern and cruel memories stretching away, like its own grey avenues, into a blur of darkness.

Certainly no house had ever more completely and finally broken with the present. As it stood there, lifting its proud roofs and gables to the sky, it might have been its own funeral monument. "Tombs in the chapel? The whole place is a tomb!" I reflected. I hoped more and more that the guardian would not come. The details of the place, however striking, would seem trivial compared with its collective impressiveness; and I wanted only to sit there and be penetrated by the weight of its silence.

"It's the very place for you!" Lanrivain had said; and I was overcome by the almost blasphemous frivolity of suggesting to any living being that Kerfol was the place for him. "Is it possible that any one could *not* see—?" I wondered. I did not finish the thought: what I meant was undefinable. I stood up and wandered toward the gate. I was beginning to want to know more; not to *see* more—I was by now so sure it was not a question of seeing—but to feel more: feel all the place had to communicate. "But to get in one will have to rout out the keeper," I thought reluctantly, and hesitated. Finally I crossed the bridge and tried the iron gate. It yielded, and I walked through the tunnel formed by the thickness of the *chemin de ronde*. At the farther end, a wooden barricade had been laid across the entrance, and beyond it was a court enclosed in noble architecture. The main building faced me; and I now saw that one half was a mere ruined front, with gaping windows through which the wild growths of the moat and the trees of the park were visible. The rest of the house was still in its robust beauty. One end abutted on the round tower, the other on the small traceried chapel, and in an angle of the building stood a graceful well-head crowned with mossy urns. A few roses grew against the walls, and on an upper window-sill I remember noticing a pot of fuchsias.

My sense of the pressure of the invisible began to yield to my architectural interest. The building was so fine that I felt a desire to explore it for its own sake. I looked about the court, wondering in which corner the guardian lodged. Then I pushed open the barrier and went in. As I did so, a dog barred my way. He was such a remarkably beautiful little dog that for a moment he made me forget the splendid place he was defending. I was not sure of his breed at the time, but have since learned that it was Chinese, and that he was of a rare variety called the "Sleeve-dog." He was very small and golden brown, with large brown eyes and a ruffled throat: he looked like a large tawny chrysanthemum. I said to myself: "These little beasts always snap and scream, and somebody will be out in a minute."

The little animal stood before me, forbidding, almost menacing: there was anger in his large brown eyes. But he made no sound, he came no nearer. Instead, as I advanced, he gradually fell back, and I noticed that another dog, a vague rough brindled thing, had limped up on a lame leg. "There'll be a hubbub now," I thought; for at the same moment a third dog, a long-haired white mongrel, slipped out of a doorway and joined the others. All three stood looking at me with grave eyes; but not a sound came from them. As I advanced they continued to fall back on muffled paws, still watching me. "At a given point, they'll all charge at my ankles: it's one of the jokes that dogs who live together put up on one," I thought. I was not alarmed, for they were neither large nor formidable. But they let me wander about the court as I pleased, following me at a little distance—always the same distance—and always keeping their eyes on me. Presently I looked across at the ruined façade, and saw that in one of its empty window-frames another dog stood: a white pointer with one brown ear. He was an old grave dog, much more experienced than the others; and he seemed to be observing me with a deeper intentness.

"I'll hear from *him*," I said to myself; but he stood in the window-frame, against the trees of the park, and continued to watch me without moving. I stared back at him for a time, to see if the sense that he was being watched would not rouse him. Half the width of the court lay between us, and we gazed at each other silently across it. But he did not stir, and at last I turned away. Behind me I found the rest of the pack, with a newcomer added: a small black greyhound with pale agate-coloured eyes. He was shivering a little, and his expression was more timid than that of the others. I noticed that he kept a little behind them. And still there was not a sound.

I stood there for fully five minutes, the circle about me—waiting, as they seemed to be waiting. At last I went up to the little golden-brown dog and stooped to pat him. As I did so, I heard myself give a nervous laugh. The little dog did not start, or growl, or take his eyes from me—he simply slipped back about a yard, and then paused and continued to look at me. "Oh, hang it!" I exclaimed, and walked across the court toward the well.

As I advanced, the dogs separated and slid away into different corners of the court. I examined the urns on the well, tried a locked door or two, and looked up and down the dumb façade; then I faced about toward the chapel. When I turned I perceived that all the dogs had disappeared except the old pointer, who still watched me from the window. It was rather a relief to be rid of that cloud of witnesses; and I began to look about me for a way to the back of the house. "Perhaps there'll be somebody in the garden," I thought. I found a way across the moat, scrambled over a wall smothered in brambles, and got into the garden. A few lean hydrangeas and geraniums pined in the flower-beds, and the ancient house looked down on them indifferently. Its garden side was plainer and severer than the other: the long granite front, with its few windows and steep roof, looked like a fortress-prison. I walked around the farther wing, went up some disjointed steps, and entered the deep twilight of a narrow and incredibly old box-walk. The walk was just wide enough for one person to slip through, and its branches met overhead. It was like the ghost of a box-walk, its lustrous green all turning to the shadowy greyness of the avenues. I walked on and on, the branches hitting me in the face and springing back with a dry rattle; and at length I came out on the grassy top of the *chemin de ronde*. I walked along it to the gate-tower, looking down into the court, which was just below me. Not a human being was in sight; and neither were the dogs. I found a flight of steps in the thickness of the wall and went down them; and when I emerged again into the court, there stood the circle of dogs, the golden-brown one a little ahead of the others, the black greyhound shivering in the rear.

"Oh, hang it—you uncomfortable beasts, you!" I exclaimed, my voice startling me with a sudden echo. The dogs stood motionless, watching me. I knew by this time that they would not try to prevent my approaching the house, and the knowledge left me free to examine them. I had a feeling that they must be horribly cowed to be so silent and inert. Yet they did not look hungry or ill-treated. Their coats were smooth and they were not thin, except the shivering greyhound. It was more as if they had lived a long time with people who never spoke to them or looked at them: as though the silence of the place had gradually benumbed their busy inquisitive natures. And this strange passivity, this almost human lassitude, seemed to me sadder than the misery of starved and beaten animals. I should have liked to rouse them for a minute, to coax them into a game or a scamper; but the longer I looked into their fixed and weary eyes the more preposterous the idea became. With the windows of that house looking down on us, how could I have imagined such a thing? The dogs knew better: *they* knew what the house would tolerate and what it would not. I even fancied that they knew what was passing through my mind, and pitied me for my frivolity. But even that feeling probably reached them through a thick fog of listlessness. I had an idea that their distance from me was as nothing to my remoteness from them. The impression they produced was that of having in common one memory so deep and dark that nothing that had happened since was worth either a growl or a wag.

"I say," I broke out abruptly, addressing myself to the dumb circle, "do you know what you look like, the whole lot of you? You look as if you'd seen a ghost—that's how you look! I wonder if there *is* a ghost here, and nobody but you left for it to appear to?" The dogs continued to gaze at me without moving. . . .

It was dark when I saw Lanrivain's motor lamps at the cross-roads —and I wasn't exactly sorry to see them. I had the sense of having escaped from the loneliest place in the whole world, and of not liking loneliness—to that degree—as much as I had imagined I should. My friend had brought his solicitor back from Quimper for the night, and seated beside a fat and affable stranger I felt no inclination to talk of Kerfol. . . .

But that evening, when Lanrivain and the solicitor were closeted in the study, Madame de Lanrivain began to question me in the drawing-room.

"Well—are you going to buy Kerfol?" she asked, tilting up her gay chin from her embroidery.

"I haven't decided yet. The fact is, I couldn't get into the house,"

I said, as if I had simply postponed my decision, and meant to go back for another look.

"You couldn't get in? Why, what happened? The family are mad to sell the place, and the old guardian has orders—"

"Very likely. But the old guardian wasn't there."

"What a pity! He must have gone to market. But his daughter—?"

"There was nobody about. At least I saw no one."

"How extraordinary! Literally nobody?"

"Nobody but a lot of dogs—a whole pack of them—who seemed to have the place to themselves."

Madame de Lanrivain let the embroidery slip to her knee and folded her hands on it. For several minutes she looked at me thoughtfully.

"A pack of dogs—you *saw* them?"

"Saw them? I saw nothing else!"

"How many?" She dropped her voice a little. "I've always wondered—"

I looked at her with surprise: I had supposed the place to be familiar to her. "Have you never been to Kerfol?" I asked.

"Oh, yes: often. But never on that day."

"What day?"

"I'd quite forgotten—and so had Hervé, I'm sure. If we'd remembered, we never should have sent you to-day—but then, after all, one doesn't half believe that sort of thing, does one?"

"What sort of thing?" I asked, involuntarily sinking my voice to the level of hers. Inwardly I was thinking: "I *knew* there was something . . ."

Madame de Lanrivain cleared her throat and produced a reassuring smile. "Didn't Hervé tell you the story of Kerfol? An ancestor of his was mixed up in it. You know every Breton house has its ghost-story; and some of them are rather unpleasant."

"Yes—but those dogs?"

"Well, those dogs are the ghosts of Kerfol. At least, the peasant say there's one day in the year when a lot of dogs appear there; and that day the keeper and his daughter go off to Morlaix and get drunk. The women in Brittany drink dreadfully." She stopped to match a silk; then she lifted her charming inquisitive Parisian face. "Did you *really* see a lot of dogs? There isn't one at Kerfol," she said.

II

Lanrivain, the next day, hunted out a shabby calf volume from
the back of an upper shelf of his library.

"Yes—here it is. What does it call itself? *A History of the Assizes
of the Duchy of Brittany. Quimper*, 1702. The book was written
about a hundred years later than the Kerfol affair; but I believe
the account is transcribed pretty literally from the judicial records.
Anyhow, it's queer reading. And there's a Hervé de Lanrivain
mixed up in it—not exactly *my* style, as you'll see. But then he's only
a collateral. Here, take the book up to bed with you. I don't exactly
remember the details; but after you've read it I'll bet anything you'll
leave your light burning all night!"

I left my light burning all night, as he had predicted; but it was
chiefly because, till near dawn, I was absorbed in my reading. The
account of the trial of Anne de Cornault, wife of the lord of Kerfol,
was long and closely printed. It was, as my friend had said, probably an almost literal transcription of what took place in the court-
room; and the trial lasted nearly a month. Besides, the type of the
book was very bad. . . .

At first I thought of translating the old record. But it is full of
wearisome repetitions, and the main lines of the story are forever
straying off into side issues. So I have tried to disentangle it, and
give it here in a simpler form. At times, however, I have reverted to
the text because no other words could have conveyed so exactly the
sense of what I felt at Kerfol; and nowhere have I added anything
of my own.

III

It was in the year 16— that Yves de Cornault, lord of the domain
of Kerfol, went to the *pardon* of Locronan to perform his religious
duties. He was a rich and powerful noble, then in his sixty-second
year, but hale and sturdy, a great horseman and hunter and a pious
man. So all his neighbours attested. In appearance he was short and
broad, with a swarthy face, legs slightly bowed from the saddle, a
hanging nose and broad hands with black hairs on them. He had
married young and lost his wife and son soon after, and since then

had lived alone at Kerfol. Twice a year he went to Morlaix, where he had a handsome house by the river, and spent a week or ten days there; and occasionally he rode to Rennes on business. Witnesses were found to declare that during these absences he led a life different from the one he was known to lead at Kerfol, where he busied himself with his estate, attended mass daily, and found his only amusement in hunting the wild boar and water-fowl. But these rumours are not particularly relevant, and it is certain that among people of his own class in the neighbourhood he passed for a stern and even austere man, observant of his religious obligations, and keeping strictly to himself. There was no talk of any familiarity with the women on his estate, though at that time the nobility were very free with their peasants. Some people said he had never looked at a woman since his wife's death; but such things are hard to prove, and the evidence on this point was not worth much.

Well, in his sixty-second year, Yves de Cornault went to the *pardon* at Locronan, and saw there a young lady of Douarnenez, who had ridden over pillion behind her father to do her duty to the saint. Her name was Anne de Barrigan, and she came of good old Breton stock, but much less great and powerful than that of Yves de Cornault; and her father had squandered his fortune at cards, and lived almost like a peasant in his little granite manor on the moors. . . . I have said I would add nothing of my own to this bald statement of a strange case; but I must interrupt myself here to describe the young lady who rode up to the lych-gate of Locronan at the very moment when the Baron de Cornault was also dismounting there. I take my description from a faded drawing in red crayon, sober and truthful enough to be by a late pupil of the Clouets, which hangs in Lanrivain's study, and is said to be a portrait of Anne de Barrigan. It is unsigned and has no mark of identity but the initials A. B., and the date 16—, the year after her marriage. It represents a young woman with a small oval face, almost pointed, yet wide enough for a full mouth with a tender depression at the corners. The nose is small, and the eyebrows are set rather high, far apart, and as lightly pencilled as the eyebrows in a Chinese painting. The forehead is high and serious, and the hair, which one feels to be fine and thick and fair, is drawn off it and lies close like a cap. The eyes are neither large nor small, hazel probably, with a look at once shy and steady. A pair of beautiful long hands are crossed below the lady's breast. . . .

The chaplain of Kerfol, and other witnesses, averred that when the Baron came back from Locronan he jumped from his horse, ordered another to be instantly saddled, called to a young page to come with him, and rode away that same evening to the south. His steward followed the next morning with coffers laden on a pair of pack mules. The following week Yves de Cornault rode back to Kerfol, sent for his vassals and tenants, and told them he was to be married at All Saints to Anne de Barrigan of Douarnenez. And on All Saints' Day the marriage took place.

As to the next few years, the evidence on both sides seems to show that they passed happily for the couple. No one was found to say that Yves de Cornault had been unkind to his wife, and it was plain to all that he was content with his bargain. Indeed, it was admitted by the chaplain and other witnesses for the prosecution that the young lady had a softening influence on her husband, and that he became less exacting with his tenants, less harsh to peasants and dependents, and less subject to the fits of gloomy silence which had darkened his widowhood. As to his wife, the only grievance her champions could call up in her behalf was that Kerfol was a lonely place, and that when her husband was away on business at Rennes or Morlaix—whither she was never taken—she was not allowed so much as to walk in the park unaccompanied. But no one asserted that she was unhappy, though one servant-woman said she had surprised her crying, and had heard her say that she was a woman accursed to have no child, and nothing in life to call her own. But that was a natural enough feeling in a wife attached to her husband; and certainly it must have been a great grief to Yves de Cornault that she bore no son. Yet he never made her feel her childlessness as a reproach—she admits this in her evidence—but seemed to try to make her forget it by showering gifts and favours on her. Rich though he was, he had never been openhanded; but nothing was too fine for his wife, in the way of silks or gems or linen, or whatever else she fancied. Every wandering merchant was welcome at Kerfol, and when the master was called away he never came back without bringing his wife a handsome present—something curious and particular—from Morlaix or Rennes or Quimper. One of the waiting-women gave, in cross-examination, an interesting list of one year's gifts, which I copy. From Morlaix, a carved ivory junk, with Chinamen at the oars, that a strange sailor had brought back as a votive offering for Notre Dame de la Clarté, above Ploumanac'h; from Quimper, an embroidered gown, worked by the nuns of the Assumption; from Rennes, a silver rose that opened and showed an amber Virgin with a crown of garnets; from Morlaix, again, a length of Damascus velvet shot with gold, bought of a Jew from Syria; and for Michaelmas that same year, from Rennes, a necklet or bracelet of round stones—emeralds and pearls and rubies—strung like beads on a fine gold chain. This was the present that pleased the lady best, the woman said. Later on, as it happened, it was produced at the trial, and appears to have struck the Judges and the public as a curious and valuable jewel.

The very same winter, the Baron absented himself again, this time as far as Bordeaux, and on his return he brought his wife something even odder and prettier than the bracelet. It was a winter evening when he rode up to Kerfol and, walking into the hall, found her sitting by the hearth, her chin on her hand, looking into the fire. He carried a velvet box in his hand and, setting it down. lifted the lid and let out a little golden-brown dog.

Anne de Cornault exclaimed with pleasure as the little creature bounded toward her. "Oh, it looks like a bird or a butterfly!" she cried as she picked it up; and the dog put its paws on her shoulders and looked at her with eyes "like a Christian's." After that she would never have it out of her sight, and petted and talked to it as if it had been a child—as indeed it was the nearest thing to a child she was to know. Yves de Cornault was much pleased with his purchase. The dog had been brought to him by a sailor from an East India merchantman, and the sailor had bought it of a pilgrim in a bazaar at Jaffa, who had stolen it from a nobleman's wife in China: a perfectly permissible thing to do, since the pilgrim was a Christian and the nobleman a heathen doomed to hell-fire. Yves de Cornault had paid a long price for the dog, for they were beginning to be in demand at the French court, and the sailor knew he had got hold of a good thing; but Anne's pleasure was so great that, to see her laugh and play with the little animal, her husband would doubtless have given twice the sum.

So far, all the evidence is at one, and the narrative plain sailing; but now the steering becomes difficult. I will try to keep as nearly as possible to Anne's own statements; though toward the end, poor thing . . .

Well, to go back. The very year after the little brown dog was brought to Kerfol, Yves de Cornault, one winter night, was found dead at the head of a narrow flight of stairs leading down from his wife's rooms to a door opening on the court. It was his wife who found him and gave the alarm, so distracted, poor wretch, with fear and horror—for his blood was all over her—that at first the roused household could not make out what she was saying, and thought she had suddenly gone mad. But there, sure enough, at the top of the stairs lay her husband, stone dead, and head foremost, the blood from his wounds dripping down to the steps below him. He had been dreadfully scratched and gashed about the face and throat, as if with curious pointed weapons; and one of his legs had a deep tear in it which had cut an artery, and probably caused his death. But how did he come there, and who had murdered him?

His wife declared that she had been asleep in her bed, and hearing his cry had rushed out to find him lying on the stairs; but this was immediately questioned. In the first place, it was proved that from her room she could not have heard the struggle on the stairs, owing to the thickness of the walls and the length of the intervening passage; then it was evident that she had not been in bed and asleep, since she was dressed when she roused the house, and her bed had not been slept in. Moreover, the door at the bottom of the stairs was ajar, and it was noticed by the chaplain (an observant man) that the dress she wore was stained with blood about the knees, and that there were traces of small blood-stained hands low down on the stair-case walls, so that it was conjectured that she had really been at the postern-door when her husband fell and, feeling her way up to him in the darkness on her hands and knees, had been stained by his blood dripping down on her. Of course it was argued on the other side that the blood-marks on her dress might have been caused by her kneeling down by her husband when she rushed out of her room; but there was the open door below, and the fact that the finger-marks in the staircase all pointed upward.

The accused held to her statement for the first two days, in spite of its improbability; but on the third day word was brought to her that Hervé de Lanrivain, a young nobleman of the neighbourhood, had been arrested for complicity in the crime. Two or three witnesses thereupon came forward to say that it was known throughout the country that Lanrivain had formerly been on good terms with the lady of Cornault; but that he had been absent from Brittany for over a year, and people had ceased to associate their names. The witnesses who made this statement were not of a very reputable sort. One was an old herb-gatherer suspected of witchcraft, another a drunken clerk from a neighbouring parish, the third a half-witted shepherd who could be made to say anything; and it was clear that the prosecution was not satisfied with its case, and would have liked to find more definite proof of Lanrivain's complicity than the statement of the herb-gatherer, who swore to having seen him climbing the wall of the park on the night of the murder. One way of patching out incomplete proofs in those days was to put some sort of pressure, moral or physical, on the accused person. It is not clear what pressure was put on Anne de Cornault; but on the third day, when she was brought in court, she "appeared weak and wandering," and after being encouraged to collect herself and speak the truth, on her honour and the wounds of her Blessed Redeemer, she confessed that she had in fact gone down the stairs to speak with Hervé de Lanrivain (who denied everything), and had been surprised there by the sound of her husband's fall. That was better; and the prosecution rubbed its hands with satisfaction. The satisfaction increased when various dependents living at Kerfol were induced to say—with apparent sincerity—that during the year or two preceding his death their master had once more grown uncertain and irascible, and subject to the fits of brooding silence which his household had learned to dread before his second marriage. This seemed to show that things had not been going well at Kerfol; though no one could be found to say that there had been any signs of open disagreement between husband and wife.

Anne de Cornault, when questioned as to her reason for going down at night to open the door to Hervé de Lanrivain, made an answer which must have sent a smile around the court. She said it was because she was lonely and wanted to talk with the young man. Was this the only reason? she was asked; and replied: "Yes, by the Cross over your Lordships' heads." "But why at midnight?" the court asked. "Because I could see him in no other way." I can see the exchange of glances across the ermine collars under the Crucifix.

Anne de Cornault, further questioned, said that her married life had been extremely lonely: "desolate" was the word she used. It was true that her husband seldom spoke harshly to her; but there were days when he did not speak at all. It was true that he had never struck or threatened her; but he kept her like a prisoner at Kerfol, and when he rode away to Morlaix or Quimper or Rennes he set so close a watch on her that she could not pick a flower in the garden without having a waiting-woman at her heels. "I am no Queen, to need such honours," she once said to him; and he had answered that a man who has a treasure does not leave the key in the lock when he goes out. "Then take me with you," she urged; but to this he said that towns were pernicious places, and young wives better off at their own firesides.

"But what did you want to say to Hervé de Lanrivain?" the court asked; and she answered: "To ask him to take me away."

"Ah—you confess that you went down to him with adulterous thoughts?"

"No."

"Then why did you want him to take you away?"

"Because I was afraid for my life."

"Of whom were you afraid?"

"Of my husband."

"Why were you afraid of your husband?"

"Because he had strangled my little dog."

Another smile must have passed around the court-room: in days when any nobleman had a right to hang his peasants—and most of them exercised it—pinching a pet animal's wind-pipe was nothing to make a fuss about.

At this point one of the Judges, who appears to have had a certain sympathy for the accused, suggested that she should be allowed to explain herself in her own way; and she thereupon made the following statement.

The first years of her marriage had been lonely; but her husband had not been unkind to her. If she had had a child she would not have been unhappy; but the days were long, and it rained too much.

It was true that her husband, whenever he went away and left her, brought her a handsome present on his return; but this did not make up for the loneliness. At least nothing had, till he brought her the little brown dog from the East: after that she was much less unhappy. Her husband seemed pleased that she was so fond of the dog; he gave her leave to put her jewelled bracelet around its neck, and to keep it always with her.

One day she had fallen asleep in her room, with the dog at her feet, as his habit was. Her feet were bare and resting on his back. Suddenly she was waked by her husband: he stood beside her, smiling not unkindly.

"You look like my great-grandmother, Juliane de Cornault, lying in the chapel with her feet on a little dog," he said.

The analogy sent a chill through her, but she laughed and answered: "Well, when I am dead you must put me beside her, carved in marble, with my dog at my feet."

"Oho—we'll wait and see," he said, laughing also, but with his black brows close together. "The dog is the emblem of fidelity."

"And do you doubt my right to lie with mine at my feet?"

"When I'm in doubt I find out," he answered. "I am an old man," he added, "and people say I make you lead a lonely life. But I swear you shall have your monument if you earn it."

"And I swear to be faithful," she returned, "if only for the sake of having my little dog at my feet."

Not long afterward he went on business to the Quimper Assizes; and while he was away his aunt, the widow of a great nobleman of the duchy, came to spend a night at Kerfol on her way to the *pardon* of Ste. Barbe. She was a woman of piety and consequence, and much respected by Yves de Cornault, and when she proposed to Anne to go with her to Ste. Barbe no one could object, and even the chaplain declared himself in favour of the pilgrimage. So Anne set out for Ste. Barbe, and there for the first time she talked with Hervé de Lanrivain. He had come once or twice to Kerfol with his father, but she had never before exchanged a dozen words with him. They did not talk for more than five minutes now: it was under the chestnuts, as the procession was coming out of the chapel. He said: "I pity you," and she was surprised, for she had not supposed that any one thought her an object of pity. He added: "Call for me when you need me," and she smiled a little, but was glad afterward, and thought often of the meeting.

She confessed to having seen him three times afterward: not more. How or where she would not say—one had the impression that she feared to implicate some one. Their meetings had been rare and brief; and at the last he had told her that he was starting the next day for a foreign country, on a mission which was not without peril and might keep him for many months absent. He asked her for a remembrance, and she had none to give him but the collar about the little dog's neck. She was sorry afterward that she had given it, but he was so unhappy at going that she had not had the courage to refuse.

Her husband was away at the time. When he returned a few days later he picked up the animal to pet it, and noticed that its collar was missing. His wife told him that the dog had lost it in the undergrowth of the park, and that she and her maids had hunted a whole day for it. It was true, she explained to the court, that she had made the maids search for the necklet—they all believed the dog had lost it in the park. . . .

Her husband made no comment, and that evening at supper he was in his usual mood, between good and bad: you could never tell which. He talked a good deal, describing what he had seen and done at Rennes; but now and then he stopped and looked hard at her, and when she went to bed she found her little dog strangled on her pillow. The little thing was dead, but still warm; she stooped to lift it, and her distress turned to horror when she discovered that it had been strangled by twisting twice round its throat the necklet she had given to Lanrivain.

The next morning at dawn she buried the dog in the garden, and hid the necklet in her breast. She said nothing to her husband, then or later, and he said nothing to her; but that day he had a peasant hanged for stealing a faggot in the park, and the next day he nearly beat to death a young horse he was breaking.

Winter set in, and the short days passed, and the long nights, one by one; and she heard nothing of Hervé de Lanrivain. It might be that her husband had killed him; or merely that he had been robbed of the necklet. Day after day by the hearth among the spinning maids, night after night alone on her bed, she wondered and trembled. Sometimes at table her husband looked across at her and smiled; and then she felt sure that Lanrivain was dead. She dared not try to get news of him, for she was sure her husband would find out if she did: she had an idea that he could find out anything. Even when a witch-woman who was a noted seer, and could show you the whole world in her crystal, came to the castle for a night's shelter, and the maids flocked to her, Anne held back.

The winter was long and black and rainy. One day, in Yves de Cornault's absence, some gypsies came to Kerfol with a troop of performing dogs. Anne bought the smallest and cleverest, a white dog with a feathery coat and one blue and one brown eye. It seemed to have been ill-treated by the gypsies, and clung to her plaintively when she took it from them. That evening her husband came back, and when she went to bed she found the dog strangled on her pillow.

After that she said to herself that she would never have another dog; but one bitter cold evening a poor lean greyhound was found whining at the castle-gate, and she took him in and forbade the maids to speak of him to her husband. She hid him in a room that no one went to, smuggled food to him from her own plate, made him a warm bed to lie on and petted him like a child.

Yves de Cornault came home, and the next day she found the greyhound strangled on her pillow. She wept in secret, but said nothing, and resolved that even if she met a dog dying of hunger she would never bring him into the castle; but one day she found a young sheep-dog, a brindled puppy with good blue eyes, lying with a broken leg in the snow of the park. Yves de Cornault was at Rennes, and she brought the dog in, warmed and fed it, tied up its leg and hid it in the castle till her husband's return. The day before, she gave it to a peasant woman who lived a long way off, and paid her handsomely to care for it and say nothing; but that night she heard a whining and scratching at her door, and when she opened it the lame puppy, drenched and shivering, jumped upon her with little sobbing barks. She hid him in her bed, and the next morning was about to have him taken back to the peasant woman when she heard her husband ride into the court. She shut the dog in a chest, and went down to receive him. An hour or two later, when she returned to her room, the puppy lay strangled on her pillow. . . .

After that she dared not make a pet of any other dog; and her loneliness became almost unendurable. Sometimes, when she crossed the court of the castle, and thought no one was looking, she stopped to pat the old pointer at the gate. But one day as she was caressing him her husband came out of the chapel; and the next day the old dog was gone. . . .

This curious narrative was not told in one sitting of the court, or received without impatience and incredulous comment. It was plain that the Judges were surprised by its puerility, and that it did not help the accused in the eyes of the public. It was an odd tale, certainly; but what did it prove? That Yves de Cornault disliked dogs, and that his wife, to gratify her own fancy, persistently ignored this dislike. As for pleading this trivial disagreement as an excuse for her relations—whatever their nature—with her supposed accomplice, the argument was so absurd that her own lawyer manifestly regretted having let her make use of it, and tried several times to cut short her story. But she went on to the end, with a kind of hypnotized insistence, as though the scenes she evoked were so real to her that she had forgotten where she was and imagined herself to be reliving them.

At length the Judge who had previously shown a certain kindness to her said (leaning forward a little, one may suppose, from his row of dozing colleagues): "Then you would have us believe that you murdered your husband because he would not let you keep a pet dog?"

"I did not murder my husband."

"Who did, then? Hervé de Lanrivain?"

"No."

"Who then? Can you tell us?"

"Yes, I can tell you. The dogs—" At that point she was carried out of the court in a swoon.

.   .   .   .

It was evident that her lawyer tried to get her to abandon this line of defense. Possibly her explanation, whatever it was, had seemed convincing when she poured it out to him in the heat of their first private colloquy; but now that it was exposed to the cold daylight of judicial scrutiny, and the banter of the town, he was thoroughly ashamed of it, and would have sacrificed her without a scruple to save his professional reputation. But the obstinate Judge —who perhaps, after all, was more inquisitive than kindly—evidently wanted to hear the story out, and she was ordered, the next day, to continue her deposition.

She said that after the disappearance of the old watch-dog nothing particular happened for a month or two. Her husband was much as usual: she did not remember any special incident. But one evening a pedlar woman came to the castle and was selling trinkets to the maids. She had no heart for trinkets, but she stood looking on while the women made their choice. And then, she did not know how, but the pedlar coaxed her into buying for herself a pear-shaped pomander with a strong scent in it—she had once seen something of the kind on a gypsy woman. She had no desire for the pomander, and did not know why she had bought it. The pedlar said that whoever wore it had the power to read the future; but she did not really believe that, or care much either. However, she bought the thing and took it up to her room, where she sat turning it about in her hand. Then the strange scent attracted her and she began to wonder what kind of spice was in the box. She opened it and found a grey bean rolled in a strip of paper; and on the paper she saw a sign she knew, and a message from Hervé de Lanrivain, saying that he was at home again and would be at the door in the court that night after the moon had set. . . .

She burned the paper and sat down to think. It was nightfall, and her husband was at home. . . . She had no way of warning Lanrivain, and there was nothing to do but to wait. . . .

At this point I fancy the drowsy court-room beginning to wake up. Even to the oldest hand on the bench there must have been a certain relish in picturing the feelings of a woman on receiving such a message at nightfall from a man living twenty miles away, to whom she had no means of sending a warning. . . .

She was not a clever woman, I imagine; and as the first result of her cogitation she appears to have made the mistake of being, that evening, too kind to her husband. She could not ply him with wine, according to the traditional expedient, for though he drank heavily at times he had a strong head; and when he drank beyond its strength it was because he chose to, and not because a woman coaxed him. Not his wife, at any rate—she was an old story by now. As I read

the case, I fancy there was no feeling for her left in him but the
hatred occasioned by his supposed dishonour.

At any rate, she tried to call up her old graces; but early in the
evening he complained of pains and fever, and left the hall to go up
to the closet where he sometimes slept. His servant carried him a
cup of hot wine, and brought back word that he was sleeping and
not to be disturbed; and an hour later, when Anne lifted the tapestry
and listened at his door, she heard his loud regular breathing. She
thought it might be a feint, and stayed a long time barefooted in
the passage, her ear to the crack; but the breathing went on too
steadily and naturally to be other than that of a man in a sound
sleep. She crept back to her room reassured, and stood in the window watching the moon set through the trees of the park. The sky
was misty and starless, and after the moon went down the night was
black as pitch. She knew the time had come, and stole along the
passage, past her husband's door—where she stopped again to listen
to his breathing—to the top of the stairs. There she paused a moment, and assured herself that no one was following her; then she
began to go down the stairs in the darkness. They were so steep
and winding that she had to go very slowly, for fear of stumbling.
Her one thought was to get the door unbolted, tell Lanrivain to
make his escape, and hasten back to her room. She had tried the bolt
earlier in the evening, and managed to put a little grease on it; but
nevertheless, when she drew it, it gave a squeak . . . not loud, but
it made her heart stop; and the next minute, overhead, she heard a
noise. . . .

"What noise?" the prosecution interposed.

"My husband's voice calling out my name and cursing me."

"What did you hear after that?"

"A terrible scream and a fall."

"Where was Hervé de Lanrivain at this time?"

"He was standing outside in the court. I just made him out in
the darkness. I told him for God's sake to go, and then I pushed the
door shut."

"What did you do next?"

"I stood at the foot of the stairs and listened."

"What did you hear?"

"I heard dogs snarling and panting." (Visible discouragement of the bench, boredom of the public, and exasperation of the lawyer for the defense. Dogs again—! But the inquisitive Judge insisted.)

"What dogs?"

She bent her head and spoke so low that she had to be told to repeat her answer: "I don't know."

"How do you mean—you don't know?"

"I don't know what dogs. . . ."

The Judge again intervened: "Try to tell us exactly what happened. How long did you remain at the foot of the stairs?"

"Only a few minutes."

"And what was going on meanwhile overhead?"

"The dogs kept on snarling and panting. Once or twice he cried out. I think he moaned once. Then he was quiet."

"Then what happened?"

"Then I heard a sound like the noise of a pack when the wolf is thrown to them—gulping and lapping."

(There was a groan of disgust and repulsion through the court, and another attempted intervention by the distracted lawyer. But the inquisitive Judge was still inquisitive.)

"And all the while you did not go up?"

"Yes—I went up then—to drive them off."

"The dogs?"

"Yes."

"Well—?"

"When I got there it was quite dark. I found my husband's flint and steel and struck a spark. I saw him lying there. He was dead."

"And the dogs?"

"The dogs were gone."

"Gone—where to?"

"I don't know. There was no way out—and there were no dogs at Kerfol."

She straightened herself to her full height, threw her arms above her head, and fell down on the stone floor with a long scream. There was a moment of confusion in the court-room. Some one on the bench was heard to say: "This is clearly a case for the ecclesiastical authorities"—and the prisoner's lawyer doubtless jumped at the suggestion.

After this, the trial loses itself in a maze of cross-questioning and squabbling. Every witness who was called corroborated Anne de Cornault's statement that there were no dogs at Kerfol: had been none for several months. The master of the house had taken a dislike to dogs, there was no denying it. But, on the other hand, at the inquest, there had been long and bitter discussions as to the nature of the dead man's wounds. One of the surgeons called in had spoken of marks that looked like bites. The suggestion of witchcraft was revived, and the opposing lawyers hurled tomes of necromancy at each other.

At last Anne de Cornault was brought back into court—at the instance of the same Judge—and asked if she knew where the dogs she spoke of could have come from. On the body of her Redeemer she swore that she did not. Then the Judge put his final question: "If the dogs you think you heard had been known to you, do you think you would have recognized them by their barking?"

"Yes."

"Did you recognize them?"

"Yes."

"What dogs do you take them to have been?"

"My dead dogs," she said in a whisper. . . . She was taken out of court, not to reappear there again. There was some kind of ecclesiastical investigation, and the end of the business was that the Judges disagreed with each other, and with the ecclesiastical committee, and that Anne de Cornault was finally handed over to the keeping of her husband's family, who shut her up in the keep of Kerfol, where she is said to have died many years later, a harmless mad-woman.

So ends her story. As for that of Hervé de Lanrivain, I had only to apply to his collateral descendant for its subsequent details. The evidence against the young man being insufficient, and his family influence in the duchy considerable, he was set free, and left soon afterward for Paris. He was probably in no mood for a worldly life, and he appears to have come almost immediately under the influence of the famous M. Arnauld d'Andilly and the gentlemen of Port Royal. A year or two later he was received into their Order, and without achieving any particular distinction he followed its good and evil fortunes till his death some twenty years later. Lanrivain showed me a portrait of him by a pupil of Philippe de Champaigne:

sad eyes, an impulsive mouth and a narrow brow. Poor Hervé de Lanrivain: it was a grey ending. Yet as I looked at his stiff and sallow effigy, in the dark dress of the Jansenists, I almost found myself envying his fate. After all, in the course of his life two great things had happened to him: he had loved romantically, and he must have talked with Pascal. . . .

The Wood Duck

by JAMES THURBER

A wood duck that adopted a road side stand. This is Thurber in a serious mood, and yet very definitely Thurber.

MR. KREPP, our vegetable man, had told us we might find some cider out the New Milford road a way—we would come to a sign saying "Morris Plains Farm" and that would be the place. So we got into the car and drove down the concrete New Milford road, which is black in the center with the dropped oil of a million cars. It's a main-trunk highway; you can go fifty miles an hour on it except where warning signs limit you to forty or, near towns, thirty-five, but nobody ever pays any attention to these signs. Even then, in November, dozens of cars flashed past us with a high, ominous whine, their tires roaring rubberly on the concrete. We found Morris Plains Farm without any trouble. There was a big white house to the left of the highway; only a few yards off the road a small barn had been made into a roadside stand, with a dirt driveway curving up to the front of it. A spare, red-cheeked man stood in the midst of baskets and barrels of red apples and glass jugs of red cider. He was waiting on a man and a woman. I turned into the driveway—and put the brakes on hard. I had seen, just in time, a duck.

It was a small, trim duck, and even I, who know nothing about wild fowl, knew that this was no barnyard duck, this was a wild duck. He was all alone. There was no other bird of any kind around, not even a chicken. He was immensely solitary. With none of the awkward waddling of a domestic duck, he kept walking busily around in the driveway, now and then billing up water from a dirty

70

puddle in the middle of the drive. His obvious contentment, his apparently perfect adjustment to his surroundings, struck me as something of a marvel. I got out of the car and spoke about it to a man who had driven up behind me in a rattly sedan. He wore a leather jacket and high, hard boots, and I figured he would know what kind of duck this was. He did. "That's a wood duck," he said. "It dropped in here about two weeks ago, Len says, and's been here ever since."

The proprietor of the stand, in whose direction my informant had nodded as he spoke, helped his customers load a basket of apples into their car and walked over to us. The duck stepped, with a little flutter of its wings, into the dirty puddle, took a small, unconcerned swim, and got out again, ruffling its feathers. "It's rather an odd place for a wood duck, isn't it?" asked my wife. Len grinned and nodded; we all watched the duck. "He's a banded duck," said Len. "There's a band on his leg. The state game commission sends out a lot of 'em. This'n lighted here two weeks ago—it was on a Saturday—and he's been around ever since." "It's funny he wouldn't be frightened away, with all the cars going by and all the people driving in," I said. Len chuckled. "He seems to like it here," he said. The duck wandered over to some sparse grass at the edge of the road, aimlessly, but with an air of settled satisfaction. "He's tame as anything," said Len. "I guess they get tame when them fellows band 'em." The man in the leather jacket said, " 'Course they haven't let you shoot wood duck for a long while and that might make 'em tame, too." "Still," said my wife (we forgot about the cider for the moment), "it's strange he would stay here, right on the road almost." "Sometimes," said Len, reflectively, "he goes round back o' the barn. But mostly he's here in the drive." "But don't they," she asked, "let them loose in the woods after they're banded? I mean, aren't they supposed to stock up the forests?" "I guess they're supposed to," said Len, chuckling again, "but 'pears this'n didn't want to."

An old Ford truck lurched into the driveway and two men in the seat hailed the proprietor. They were hunters, big, warmly dressed, heavily shod men. In the back of the truck was a large bird dog. He was an old pointer and he wore an expression of remote disdain for the world of roadside commerce. He took no notice of the duck. The two hunters said something to Len about cider, and

I was just about to chime in with my order when the accident happened. A car went by the stand at fifty miles an hour, leaving something scurrying in its wake. It was the duck, turning over and over on the concrete. He turned over and over swiftly, but lifelessly, like a thrown feather duster, and then he lay still. "My God," I cried, "they've killed your duck, Len!" The accident gave me a quick feeling of anguished intimacy with the bereaved man. "Oh, now," he wailed. "Now, that's awful!" None of us for a moment moved. Then the two hunters walked toward the road, slowly, self-consciously, a little embarrassed in the face of this quick incongruous ending of a wild fowl's life in the middle of a concrete highway. The pointer stood up, looked after the hunters, raised his ears briefly, and then lay down again.

It was the man in the leather jacket finally who walked out to the duck and tried to pick it up. As he did so, the duck stood up. He looked about him like a person who has been abruptly wakened and doesn't know where he is. He didn't ruffle his feathers. "Oh, he isn't quite *dead!*" said my wife. I knew how she felt. We were going to have to see the duck die; somebody would have to kill him, finish him off. Len stood beside us. My wife took hold of his arm. The man in the leather jacket knelt down, stretched out a hand, and the duck moved slightly away. Just then, out from behind the barn, limped a setter dog, a lean white setter dog with black spots. His right back leg was useless and he kept it off the ground. He stopped when he saw the duck in the road and gave it a point, putting his head out, lifting his front leg, maintaining a wavering, marvellous balance on two legs. He was like a drunken man drawing a bead with a gun. This new menace, this anticlimax, was too much. I think I yelled.

What happened next happened as fast as the automobile accident. The setter made his run, a limping, wobbly run, and he was in between the men and the bird before they saw him. The duck flew, got somehow off the ground a foot or two, and tumbled into the grass of the field across the road, the dog after him. It seemed crazy, but the duck could fly—a little, anyway. "Here, here," said Len, weakly. The hunters shouted, I shouted, my wife screamed. "He'll kill him! He'll *kill* him!" The duck flew a few yards again, the dog at his tail. The dog's third plunge brought his nose almost to the duck's tail, and then one of the hunters tackled the animal and pulled him down and knelt in the grass, holding him. We all breathed easier. My wife let go Len's arm.

Len started across the road after the duck, who was fluttering slowly, waveringly, but with a definite purpose, toward a wood that fringed the far side of the field. The bird was dazed, but a sure, atavistic urge was guiding him; he was going home. One of the hunters joined Len in his pursuit. The other came back across the road, dragging the indignant setter; the man in the leather jacket walked beside them. We all watched Len and his companion reach the edge of the wood and stand there, looking; they had followed the duck through the grass slowly, so as not to alarm him; he had been alarmed enough. "He'll never come back," said my wife. Len and the hunter finally turned and came back through the grass. The duck had got away from them. We walked out to meet them at the edge of the concrete. Cars began to whiz by in both directions. I realized, with wonder, that all the time the duck, and the hunters, and the setter were milling around in the road, not one had passed. It was as if traffic had been held up so that our little drama could go on. "He couldn't o' been much hurt," said Len. "Likely just grazed and pulled along in the wind of the car. Them fellows don't look out for anything. It's a sin." My wife had a question for him. "Does your dog always chase the duck?" she asked. "Oh, that ain't my dog," said Len. "He just comes around." The hunter who had been holding the setter now let him go, and he slunk away. The pointer, I noticed, lay with his eyes closed. "But doesn't the duck mind the dog?" persisted my wife. "Oh, he minds him," said Len. "But the dog's never really hurt him none yet. There's always somebody around."

We drove away with a great deal to talk about (I almost forgot the cider). I explained the irony, I think I explained the profound symbolism, of a wild duck's becoming attached to a roadside stand. My wife strove simply to understand the duck's viewpoint. She didn't get anywhere. I knew even then, in the back of my mind, what would happen. We decided, after a cocktail, to drive back to the place and find out if the duck had returned. My wife hoped it wouldn't be there, on account of the life it led in the driveway; I hoped it wouldn't because I felt that would be, somehow, too pat an ending. Night was falling when we started off again for Morris Plains Farm. It was a five-mile drive and I had to put my bright lights on before we got there. The barn door was closed for the night. We didn't see the duck anywhere. The only thing to do was to go up to the house and inquire. I knocked on the door and a young man opened it. "Is—is the proprietor here?" I asked. He said no, he had gone to Waterbury. "We wanted to know," my wife said, "whether the duck came back." "What?" he asked, a little startled, I thought. Then, "Oh, the duck. I saw him around the driveway when my father drove off." He stared at us, waiting. I thanked him and started back to the car. My wife lingered, explaining, for a moment. "He thinks we're crazy," she said, when she got into the car. We drove on a little distance. "Well," I said, "he's back." "I'm glad he is, in a way," said my wife. "I hated to think of him all alone out there in the woods."

The Gift

by JOHN STEINBECK

Published only eight years ago, this story has already become a classic, and may outlive most of John Steinbeck's other writing, excepting, always, "The Grapes of Wrath."

AT daybreak Billy Buck emerged from the bunkhouse and stood for a moment on the porch looking up at the sky. He was a broad, bandy-legged little man with a walrus mustache, with square hands, puffed and muscled on the palms. His eyes were a contemplative, watery grey and the hair which protruded from under his Stetson hat was spiky and weathered. Billy was still stuffing his shirt into his blue jeans as he stood on the porch. He unbuckled his belt and tightened it again. The belt showed, by the worn shiny places opposite each hole, the gradual increase of Billy's middle over a period of years. When he had seen to the weather, Billy cleared each nostril by holding its mate closed with his forefinger and blowing fiercely. Then he walked down to the barn, rubbing his hands together. He curried and brushed two saddle horses in the stalls, talking quietly to them all the time; and he had hardly finished when the iron triangle started ringing at the ranch house. Billy stuck the brush and currycomb together and laid them on the rail, and went up to breakfast. His action had been so deliberate and yet so wasteless of time that he came to the house while Mrs. Tiflin was still ringing the triangle. She nodded her grey head to him and withdrew into the kitchen. Billy Buck sat down on the steps, because he was a cowhand, and it wouldn't be fitting that he should go first into the dining-room. He heard Mr. Tiflin in the house, stamping his feet into his boots.

The high jangling note of the triangle put the boy Jody in motion. He was only a little boy, ten years old, with hair like dusty yellow grass and with shy polite grey eyes, and with a mouth that worked when he thought. The triangle picked him up out of sleep. It didn't occur to him to disobey the harsh note. He never had: no one he knew ever had. He brushed the tangled hair out of his eyes and skinned his nightgown off. In a moment he was dressed—blue chambray shirt and overalls. It was late in the summer, so of course there were no shoes to bother with. In the kitchen he waited until his mother got from in front of the sink and went back to the stove. Then he washed himself and brushed back his wet hair with his fingers. His mother turned sharply on him as he left the sink. Jody looked shyly away.

"I've got to cut your hair before long," his mother said. "Breakfast's on the table. Go on in, so Billy can come."

Jody sat at the long table which was covered with white oilcloth washed through to the fabric in some places. The fried eggs lay in rows on their platter. Jody took three eggs on his plate and followed with three thick slices of crisp bacon. He carefully scraped a spot of blood from one of the egg yolks.

Billy Buck clumped in. "That won't hurt you," Billy explained. "That's only a sign the rooster leaves."

Jody's tall stern father came in then and Jody knew from the noise on the floor that he was wearing boots, but he looked under the table anyway, to make sure. His father turned off the oil lamp over the table, for plenty of morning light now came through the windows.

Jody did not ask where his father and Billy Buck were riding that day, but he wished he might go along. His father was a disciplinarian. Jody obeyed him in everything without questions of any kind. Now, Carl Tiflin sat down and reached for the egg platter.

"Got the cows ready to go, Billy?" he asked.

"In the lower corral," Billy said. "I could just as well take them in alone."

"Sure you could. But a man needs company. Besides your throat gets pretty dry." Carl Tiflin was jovial this morning.

Jody's mother put her head in the door. "What time do you think to be back, Carl?"

"I can't tell. I've got to see some men in Salinas. Might be gone till dark."

The eggs and coffee and big biscuits disappeared rapidly. Jody followed the two men out of the house. He watched them mount their horses and drive six old milk cows out of the corral and start over the hill toward Salinas. They were going to sell the old cows to the butcher.

When they had disappeared over the crown of the ridge Jody walked up the hill in back of the house. The dogs trotted around the house corner hunching their shoulders and grinning horribly with pleasure. Jody patted their heads—Doubletree Mutt with the big thick tail and yellow eyes, and Smasher, the shepherd, who had killed a coyote and lost an ear in doing it. Smasher's one good ear stood up higher than a collie's ear should. Billy Buck said that always happened. After the frenzied greeting the dogs lowered their noses to the ground in a business-like way and went ahead, looking back now and then to make sure that the boy was coming. They walked up through the chicken yard and saw the quail eating with the chickens. Smasher chased the chickens a little to keep in practice in case there should ever be sheep to herd. Jody continued on through the large vegetable patch where the green corn was higher than his head. The cow-pumpkins were green and small yet. He went on to the sagebrush line where the cold spring ran out of its pipe and fell into a round wooden tub. He leaned over and drank close to the green mossy wood where the water tasted best. Then he turned and looked back on the ranch, on the low, whitewashed house girded with red geraniums, and on the long bunkhouse by the cypress tree where Billy Buck lived alone. Jody could see the great black kettle under the cypress tree. That was where the pigs were scalded. The sun was coming over the ridge now, glaring on the whitewash of the houses and barns, making the wet grass blaze softly. Behind him, in the tall sagebrush, the birds were scampering on the ground, making a great noise among the dry leaves; the squirrels piped shrilly on the side-hills. Jody looked along at the farm buildings. He felt an uncertainty in the air, a feeling of change and of loss and of the gain of new and unfamiliar things. Over the hillside two big black buzzards sailed low to the ground and their shadows slipped smoothly and quickly ahead of them. Some animal had died in the vicinity. Jody knew it. It might be a cow or it might be the remains of a rabbit. The buzzards overlooked nothing. Jody hated them as all decent things hate them, but they could not be hurt because they made away with carrion.

After a while the boy sauntered down hill again. The dogs had long ago given him up and gone into the brush to do things in their own way. Back through the vegetable garden he went, and he paused for a moment to smash a green muskmelon with his heel, but he was not happy about it. It was a bad thing to do, he knew perfectly well. He kicked dirt over the ruined melon to conceal it.

Back at the house his mother bent over his rough hands, inspecting his fingers and nails. It did little good to start him clean to school for too many things could happen on the way. She sighed over the black cracks on his fingers, and then gave him his books and his lunch and started him on the mile walk to school. She noticed that his mouth was working a good deal this morning.

Jody started his journey. He filled his pockets with little pieces of white quartz that lay in the road, and every so often he took a shot at a bird or at some rabbit that had stayed sunning itself in the road too long. At the crossroads over the bridge he met two friends and the three of them walked to school together, making ridiculous strides and being rather silly. School had just opened two weeks before. There was still a spirit of revolt among the pupils.

It was four o'clock in the afternoon when Jody topped the hill and looked down on the ranch again. He looked for the saddle horses, but the corral was empty. His father was not back yet. He went slowly, then, toward the afternoon chores. At the ranch house, he found his mother sitting on the porch, mending socks.

"There's two doughnuts in the kitchen for you," she said. Jody slid to the kitchen, and returned with half of one of the doughnuts already eaten and his mouth full. His mother asked him what he had learned in school that day, but she didn't listen to his doughnut-muffled answer. She interrupted, "Jody, tonight see you fill the wood-box clear full. Last night you crossed the sticks and it wasn't only about half full. Lay the sticks flat tonight. And Jody, some of the hens are hiding eggs, or else the dogs are eating them. Look about in the grass and see if you can find any nests."

Jody, still eating, went out and did his chores. He saw the quail come down to eat with the chickens when he threw out the grain. For some reason his father was proud to have them come. He never allowed any shooting near the house for fear the quail might go away.

When the wood-box was full, Jody took his twenty-two rifle up to the cold spring at the brush line. He drank again and then aimed the gun at all manner of things, at rocks, at birds on the wing, at the big black pig kettle under the cypress tree, but he didn't shoot for he had no cartridges and wouldn't have until he was twelve. If his father had seen him aim the rifle in the direction of the house he would have put the cartridges off another year. Jody remembered this and did not point the rifle down the hill again. Two years was enough to wait for cartridges. Nearly all of his father's presents were given with reservations which hampered their value somewhat. It was good discipline.

The supper waited until dark for his father to return. When at last he came in with Billy Buck, Jody could smell the delicious brandy on their breaths. Inwardly he rejoiced, for his father sometimes talked to him when he smelled of brandy, sometimes even told things he had done in the wild days when he was a boy.

After supper, Jody sat by the fireplace and his shy polite eyes sought the room corners, and he waited for his father to tell what it was he contained, for Jody knew he had news of some sort. But he was disappointed. His father pointed a stern finger at him.

"You'd better go to bed, Jody. I'm going to need you in the morning."

That wasn't so bad. Jody liked to do the things he had to do as long as they weren't routine things. He looked at the floor and his mouth worked out a question before he spoke it. "What are we going to do in the morning, kill a pig?" he asked softly.

"Never you mind. You better get to bed."

When the door was closed behind him, Jody heard his father and Billy Buck chuckling and he knew it was a joke of some kind. And later, when he lay in bed, trying to make words out of the murmurs in the other room, he heard his father protest, "But, Ruth, I didn't give much for him."

Jody heard the hoot-owls hunting mice down by the barn, and he heard a fruit tree limb tap-tapping against the house. A cow was lowing when he went to sleep.

When the triangle sounded in the morning, Jody dressed more quickly even than usual. In the kitchen, while he washed his face and combed back his hair, his mother addressed him irritably. "Don't you go out until you get a good breakfast in you."

He went into the dining-room and sat at the long white table. He took a steaming hotcake from the platter, arranged two fried eggs on it, covered them with another hotcake and squashed the whole thing with his fork.

His father and Billy Buck came in. Jody knew from the sound on the floor that both of them were wearing flat-heeled shoes, but he peered under the table to make sure. His father turned off the oil lamp, for the day had arrived, and he looked stern and disciplinary, but Billy Buck didn't look at Jody at all. He avoided the shy questioning eyes of the boy and soaked a whole piece of toast in his coffee.

Carl Tiflin said crossly, "You come with us after breakfast!"

Jody had trouble with his food then, for he felt a kind of doom in the air. After Billy had tilted his saucer and drained the coffee which had slopped into it, and had wiped his hands on his jeans, the two men stood up from the table and went out into the morning light together, and Jody respectfully followed a little behind them. He tried to keep his mind from running ahead, tried to keep it absolutely motionless.

His mother called, "Carl! Don't you let it keep him from school."

They marched past the cypress, where a singletree hung from a limb to butcher the pigs on, and past the black iron kettle, so it was not a pig killing. The sun shone over the hill and threw long, dark shadows of the trees and buildings. They crossed a stubble-field to shortcut to the barn. Jody's father unhooked the door and they went in. They had been walking toward the sun on the way down. The barn was black as night in contrast and warm from the hay and from the beasts. Jody's father moved over toward the one box stall. "Come here!" he ordered. Jody could begin to see things now. He looked into the box stall and then stepped back quickly.

A red pony colt was looking at him out of the stall. Its tense ears were forward and a light of disobedience was in its eyes. Its coat was rough and thick as an airedale's fur and its mane was long and tangled. Jody's throat collapsed in on itself and cut his breath short.

"He needs a good currying," his father said, "and if I ever hear of you not feeding him or leaving his stall dirty, I'll sell him off in a minute."

Jody couldn't bear to look at the pony's eyes any more. He gazed down at his hands for a moment, and he asked very shyly, "Mine?" No one answered him. He put his hand out toward the pony. Its grey nose came close, sniffing loudly, and then the lips drew back and the strong teeth closed on Jody's fingers. The pony shook its head up and down and seemed to laugh with amusement. Jody regarded his bruised fingers. "Well," he said with pride—"Well, I guess he can bite all right." The two men laughed, somewhat in relief. Carl Tiflin went out of the barn and walked up a sidehill to be by himself, for he was embarrassed, but Billy Buck stayed. It was easier to talk to Billy Buck. Jody asked again—"Mine?"

Billy became professional in tone. "Sure! That is, if you look out for him and break him right. I'll show you how. He's just a colt. You can't ride him for some time."

Jody put out his bruised hand again, and this time the red pony let his nose be rubbed. "I ought to have a carrot," Jody said. "Where'd we get him, Billy?"

"Bought him at a sheriff's auction," Billy explained. "A show went broke in Salinas and had debts. The sheriff was selling off their stuff."

The pony stretched out his nose and shook the forelock from his wild eyes. Jody stroked the nose a little. He said softly, "There isn't a—saddle?"

Billy Buck laughed. "I'd forgot. Come along."

In the harness room he lifted down a little saddle of red morocco leather. "It's just a show saddle," Billy Buck said disparagingly. "It isn't practical for the brush, but it was cheap at the sale."

Jody couldn't trust himself to look at the saddle either, and he couldn't speak at all. He brushed the shining red leather with his fingertips, and after a long time he said, "It'll look pretty on him though." He thought of the grandest and prettiest things he knew. "If he hasn't a name already, I think I'll call him Gabilan Mountains," he said.

Billy Buck knew how he felt. "It's a pretty long name. Why don't you just call him Gabilan? That means hawk. That would be a fine name for him." Billy felt glad. "If you will collect tail hair, I might be able to make a hair rope for you sometime. You could use it for a hackamore."

Jody wanted to go back to the box stall. "Could I lead him to school, do you think—to show the kids?"

But Billy shook his head. "He's not even halter-broke yet. We had a time getting him here. Had to almost drag him. You better be starting for school though."

"I'll bring the kids to see him here this afternoon," Jody said.

Six boys came over the hill half an hour early that afternoon, running hard, their heads down, their forearms working, their breath whistling. They swept by the house and cut across the stubble-field to the barn. And then they stood self-consciously before the pony, and then they looked at Jody with eyes in which there was a new admiration and a new respect. Before today Jody had been a boy, dressed in overalls and a blue shirt—quieter than most, even suspected of being a little cowardly. And now he was different. Out of a thousand centuries they drew the ancient admiration of the footman for the horseman. They knew instinctively that a man on a horse is spiritually as well as physically bigger than a man on foot. They knew that Jody had been miraculously lifted out of equality with them, and had been placed over them. Gabilan put his head out of the stall and sniffed them.

"Why'n't you ride him?" the boys cried. "Why'n't you braid his tail with ribbons like in the fair?" "When you going to ride him?"

Jody's courage was up. He too felt the superiority of the horseman. "He's not old enough. Nobody can ride him for a long time. I'm going to train him on the long halter. Billy Buck is going to show me how."

"Well, can't we even lead him around a little?"

"He isn't even halter-broke," Jody said. He wanted to be completely alone when he took the pony out the first time. "Come and see the saddle."

They were speechless at the red morocco saddle, completely shocked out of comment. "It isn't much use in the brush," Jody explained. "It'll look pretty on him though. Maybe I'll ride bareback when I go into the brush."

"How you going to rope a cow without a saddle horn?"

"Maybe I'll get another saddle for every day. My father might want me to help him with the stock." He let them feel the red saddle, and showed them the brass chain throat-latch on the bridle and the big brass buttons at each temple where the headstall and brow band crossed. The whole thing was too wonderful. They had to go away after a little while, and each boy, in his mind, searched among his possessions for a bribe worthy of offering in return for a ride on the red pony when the time should come.

Jody was glad when they had gone. He took brush and currycomb from the wall, took down the barrier of the box stall and stepped cautiously in. The pony's eyes glittered, and he edged around into kicking position. But Jody touched him on the shoulder and rubbed his high arched neck as he had always seen Billy Buck do, and he crooned "So-o-o Boy," in a deep voice. The pony gradually relaxed his tenseness. Jody curried and brushed until a pile of dead hair lay in the stall and until the pony's coat had taken on a deep red shine. Each time he finished he thought it might have been done better. He braided the mane into a dozen little pigtails, and he braided the forelock, and then he undid them and brushed the hair out straight again.

Jody did not hear his mother enter the barn. She was angry when she came, but when she looked in at the pony and at Jody working over him, she felt a curious pride rise up in her. "Have you forgot the wood-box?" she asked gently. "It's not far off from dark and there's not a stick of wood in the house, and the chickens aren't fed."

Jody quickly put up his tools. "I forgot, ma'am."

"Well, after this do your chores first. Then you won't forget. I expect you'll forget lots of things now if I don't keep an eye on you."

"Can I have carrots from the garden for him, ma'am?"

She had to think about that. "Oh—I guess so, if you only take the big tough ones."

"Carrots keep the coat good," he said, and again she felt the curious rush of pride.

Jody never waited for the triangle to get him out of bed after the coming of the pony. It became his habit to creep out of bed even before his mother was awake, to slip into his clothes and to go quietly down to the barn to see Gabilan. In the grey quiet mornings when the land and the brush and the houses and the trees were silver-grey and black like a photograph negative, he stole toward the barn, past the sleeping stones and the sleeping cypress tree. The turkeys, roosting in the tree out of coyotes' reach, clicked drowsily. The fields glowed with a grey frost-like light and in the dew the tracks of rabbits and of field mice stood out sharply. The good dogs came stiffly out of their little houses, hackles up and deep growls in their throats. Then they caught Jody's scent, and their stiff tails rose up and waved a greeting—Doubletree Mutt with the big thick tail, and Smasher, the incipient shepherd—then went lazily back to their warm beds.

It was a strange time and a mysterious journey, to Jody—an extension of a dream. When he first had the pony he liked to torture himself during the trip by thinking Gabilan would not be in his stall, and worse, would never have been there. And he had other delicious little self-induced pains. He thought how the rats had gnawed ragged holes in the red saddle, and how the mice had nibbled Gabilan's tail until it was stringy and thin. He usually ran the last little way to the barn. He unlatched the rusty hasp of the barn door and stepped in, and no matter how quietly he opened the door, Gabilan was always looking at him over the barrier of the box stall and Gabilan whinnied softly and stamped his front foot, and his eyes had big sparks of red fire in them like oak-wood embers.

Sometimes, if the work horses were to be used that day, Jody found Billy Buck in the barn harnessing and currying. Billy stood with him and looked long at Gabilan and he told Jody a great many things about horses. He explained that they were terribly afraid for their feet, so that one must make a practice of lifting the legs and patting the hooves and ankles to remove their terror. He told Jody how horses love conversation. He must talk to the pony all the time, and tell him the reasons for everything. Billy wasn't sure a horse could understand everything that was said to him, but it was impossible to say how much was understood. A horse never kicked up a fuss if some one he liked explained things to him. Billy could give examples, too. He had known, for instance, a horse nearly dead beat with fatigue to perk up when told it was only a little farther to his destination. And he had known a horse paralyzed with fright to come out of it when his rider told him what it was that was frightening him. While he talked in the mornings, Billy Buck cut twenty or thirty straws into neat three-inch lengths and stuck them into his hatband. Then during the whole day, if he wanted to pick his teeth or merely to chew on something, he had only to reach up for one of them.

Jody listened carefully, for he knew and the whole country knew that Billy Buck was a fine hand with horses. Billy's own horse was a stringy cayuse with a hammer head, but he nearly always won the first prizes at the stock trials. Billy could rope a steer, take a double half-hitch about the horn with his riata, and dismount, and his horse would play the steer as an angler plays a fish, keeping a tight rope until the steer was down or beaten.

Every morning, after Jody had curried and brushed the pony, he let down the barrier of the stall, and Gabilan thrust past him and raced down the barn and into the corral. Around and around he galloped, and sometimes he jumped forward and landed on stiff legs. He stood quivering, stiff ears forward, eyes rolling so that the whites showed, pretending to be frightened. At last he walked snorting to the water-trough and buried his nose in the water up to the nostrils. Jody was proud then, for he knew that was the way to judge a horse. Poor horses only touched their lips to the water, but a fine spirited beast put his whole nose and mouth under, and only left room to breathe.

Then Jody stood and watched the pony, and he saw things he had never noticed about any other horse, the sleek, sliding flank muscles and the cords of the buttocks, which flexed like a closing fist, and the shine the sun put on the red coat. Having seen horses all his life, Jody had never looked at them very closely before. But now he noticed the moving ears which gave expression and even inflection of expression to the face. The pony talked with his ears. You could tell exactly how he felt about everything by the way his ears pointed. Sometimes they were stiff and upright and sometimes lax and sagging. They went back when he was angry or fearful, and forward when he was anxious and curious and pleased; and their exact position indicated which emotion he had.

Billy Buck kept his word. In the early fall the training began. First there was the halter-breaking, and that was the hardest because it was the first thing. Jody held a carrot and coaxed and promised and pulled on the rope. The pony set his feet like a burro when he felt the strain. But before long he learned. Jody walked all over the ranch leading him. Gradually he took to dropping the rope until the pony followed him unled wherever he went.

And then came the training on the long halter. That was slower work. Jody stood in the middle of a circle, holding the long halter. He clucked with his tongue and the pony started to walk in a big circle, held in by the long rope. He clucked again to make the pony trot, and again to make him gallop. Around and around Gabilan went thundering and enjoying it immensely. Then he called, "Whoa," and the pony stopped. It was not long until Gabilan was perfect at it. But in many ways he was a bad pony. He bit Jody in the pants and stomped on Jody's feet. Now and then his ears went back and he aimed a tremendous kick at the boy. Everytime he did one of these bad things, Gabilan settled back and seemed to laugh to himself.

Billy Buck worked at the hair rope in the evenings before the fireplace. Jody collected tail hair in a bag, and he sat and watched Billy slowly constructing the rope, twisting a few hairs to make a string and rolling two strings together for a cord, and then braiding a number of cords to make the rope. Billy rolled the finished rope on the floor under his foot to make it round and hard.

The long halter work rapidly approached perfection. Jody's father, watching the pony stop and start and trot and gallop, was a little bothered by it.

"He's getting to be almost a trick pony," he complained. "I don't like trick horses. It takes all the—dignity out of a horse to make him do tricks. Why, a trick horse is kind of like an actor—no dignity, no character of his own." And his father said, "I guess you better be getting him used to the saddle pretty soon."

Jody rushed for the harness-room. For some time he had been riding the saddle on a sawhorse. He changed the stirrup length over and over, and could never get it just right. Sometimes, mounted on the sawhorse in the harness-room, with collars and hames and tugs hung all about him, Jody rode out beyond the room. He carried his rifle across the pommel. He saw the fields go flying by, and he heard the beat of the galloping hoofs.

It was a ticklish job, saddling the pony the first time. Gabilan hunched and reared and threw the saddle off before the cinch could be tightened. It had to be replaced again and again until at last the pony let it stay. And the cinching was difficult, too. Day by day Jody tightened the girth a little more until at last the pony didn't mind the saddle at all.

Then there was the bridle. Billy explained how to use a stick of licorice for a bit until Gabilan was used to having something in his mouth. Billy explained, "Of course we could force-break him to everything, but he wouldn't be as good a horse if we did. He'd always be a little bit afraid, and he wouldn't mind because he wanted to."

The first time the pony wore the bridle he whipped his head about and worked his tongue against the bit until the blood oozed from the corners of his mouth. He tried to rub the headstall off on the manger. His ears pivoted about and his eyes turned red with fear and with general rambunctiousness. Jody rejoiced, for he knew that only a mean-souled horse does not resent training.

And Jody trembled when he thought of the time when he would first sit in the saddle. The pony would probably throw him off. There was no disgrace in that. The disgrace would come if he did not get right up and mount again. Sometimes he dreamed that he lay in the dirt and cried and couldn't make himself mount again. The shame of the dream lasted until the middle of the day.

Gabilan was growing fast. Already he had lost the long-leggedness of the colt; his mane was getting longer and blacker. Under the constant currying and brushing his coat lay as smooth and gleaming as orange-red lacquer. Jody oiled the hoofs and kept carefully trimmed so they would not crack.

The hair rope was nearly finished. Jody's father gave him an old pair of spurs and bent in the side bars and cut down the strap and took up the chainlets until they fitted. And then one day Carl Tiflin said:

"The pony's growing faster than I thought. I guess you can ride him by Thanksgiving. Think you can stick on?"

"I don't know," Jody said shyly. Thanksgiving was only three weeks off. He hoped it wouldn't rain, for rain would spot the red saddle.

Gabilan knew and liked Jody by now. He nickered when Jody came across the stubble-field, and in the pasture he came running when his master whistled for him. There was always a carrot for him every time.

Billy Buck gave him riding instructions over and over. "Now when you get up there, just grab tight with your knees, and keep your hands away from the saddle, and if you get throwed, don't let that stop you. No matter how good a man is, there's always some horse can pitch him. You just climb up again before he gets to feeling smart about it. Pretty soon, he won't throw you no more, and pretty soon he can't throw you no more. That's the way to do it."

"I hope it don't rain before," Jody said.

"Why not? Don't want to get throwed in the mud?"

That was partly it, and also he was afraid that in the flurry of bucking Gabilan might slip and fall on him and break his leg or his hip. He had seen that happen to men before, had seen how they writhed on the ground like squashed bugs, and he was afraid of it.

He practiced on the sawhorse how he would hold the reins in his left hand and a hat in his right hand. If he kept his hands thus busy, he couldn't grab the horn if he felt himself going off. He didn't like to think of what would happen if he did grab the horn. Perhaps his father and Billy Buck would never speak to him again, they would be so ashamed. The news would get about and his mother would be ashamed too. And in the school yard—it was too awful to contemplate.

He began putting his weight in a stirrup when Gabilan was saddled, but he didn't throw his leg over the pony's back. That was forbidden until Thanksgiving.

Every afternoon he put the red saddle on the pony and cinched it tight. The pony was learning already to fill his stomach out unnaturally large while the cinching was going on, and then to let it down when the straps were fixed. Sometimes Jody led him up to the brush line and let him drink from the round green tub, and sometimes he led him up through the stubble-field to the hilltop from which it was possible to see the white town of Salinas and the geometric fields of the great valley, and the oak trees clipped by the sheep. Now and then they broke through the brush and came to little cleared circles so hedged in that the world was gone and only the sky and the circle of brush were left from the old life. Gabilan liked these trips and showed it by keeping his head very high and by quivering his nostrils with interest. When the two came back from an expedition they smelled of the sweet sage they had forced through.

Time dragged on toward Thanksgiving, but winter came fast. The clouds swept down and hung all day over the land and brushed the hilltops, and the winds blew shrilly at night. All day the dry oak leaves drifted down from the trees until they covered the ground, and yet the trees were unchanged.

Jody had wished it might not rain before Thanksgiving, but it did. The brown earth turned dark and the trees glistened. The cut ends of the stubble turned black with mildew; the haystacks greyed from exposure to the damp, and on the roofs the moss, which had been all summer as grey as lizards, turned a brilliant yellow-green. During the week of rain, Jody kept the pony in the box stall out of the dampness, except for a little time after school when he took him out for exercise and to drink at the water-trough in the upper corral. Not once did Gabilan get wet.

The wet weather continued until little new grass appeared. Jody walked to school dressed in a slicker and short rubber boots. At length one morning the sun came out brightly. Jody, at his work in the box stall, said to Billy Buck, "Maybe I'll leave Gabilan in the corral when I go to school today."

"Be good for him to be out in the sun," Billy assured him. "No animal likes to be cooped up too long. Your father and me are going back on the hill to clean the leaves out of the spring." Billy nodded and picked his teeth with one of his little straws.

"If the rain comes, though—" Jody suggested.

"Not likely to rain today. She's rained herself out." Billy pulled up his sleeves and snapped his arm bands. "If it comes on to rain— why a little rain don't hurt a horse."

"Well, if it does come on to rain, you put him in, will you, Billy? I'm scared he might get cold so I couldn't ride him when the time comes."

"Oh sure! I'll watch out for him if we get back in time. But it won't rain today."

And so Jody, when he went to school left Gabilan standing out in the corral.

Billy Buck wasn't wrong about many things. He couldn't be. But he was wrong about the weather that day, for a little after noon the clouds pushed over the hills and the rain began to pour down. Jody heard it start on the schoolhouse roof. He considered holding up one finger for permission to go to the outhouse and, once outside, running for home to put the pony in. Punishment would be prompt both at school and at home. He gave it up and took ease from Billy's assurance that rain couldn't hurt a horse. When school was finally out, he hurried home through the dark rain. The banks at the sides of the road spouted little jets of muddy water. The rain slanted and swirled under a cold and gusty wind. Jody dog-trotted home, slopping through the gravelly mud of the road.

From the top of the ridge he could see Gabilan standing miserably in the corral. The red coat was almost black, and streaked with water. He stood head down with his rump to the rain and wind. Jody arrived running and threw open the barn door and led the wet pony in by his forelock. Then he found a gunny sack and rubbed the soaked hair and rubbed the legs and ankles. Gabilan stood patiently, but he trembled in gusts like the wind.

When he had dried the pony as well as he could, Jody went up to the house and brought hot water down to the barn and soaked the grain in it. Gabilan was not very hungry. He nibbled at the hot mash, but he was not very much interested in it, and he still shivered now and then. A little steam rose from his damp back.

It was almost dark when Billy Buck and Carl Tiflin came home. "When the rain started we put up at Ben Herche's place, and the rain never let up all afternoon," Carl Tiflin explained. Jody looked reproachfully at Billy Buck and Billy felt guilty.

"You said it wouldn't rain," Jody accused him.

Billy looked away. "It's hard to tell, this time of year," he said, but his excuse was lame. He had no right to be fallible, and he knew it.

"The pony got wet, got soaked through."

"Did you dry him off?"

"I rubbed him with a sack and I gave him hot grain."

Billy nodded in agreement.

"Do you think he'll take cold, Billy?"

"A little rain never hurt anything," Billy assured him.

Jody's father joined the conversation then and lectured the boy a little. "A horse," he said, "isn't any lap-dog kind of thing." Carl Tiflin hated weakness and sickness, and he held a violent contempt for helplessness.

Jody's mother put a platter of steaks on the table and boiled potatoes and boiled squash, which clouded the room with their steam. They sat down to eat. Carl Tiflin still grumbled about weakness put into animals and men by too much coddling.

Billy Buck felt bad about his mistake. "Did you blanket him?" he asked.

"No. I couldn't find any blanket. I laid some sacks over his back."

"We'll go down and cover him up after we eat, then." Billy felt better about it then. When Jody's father had gone in to the fire and his mother was washing dishes, Billy found and lighted a lantern. He and Jody walked through the mud to the barn. The barn was dark and warm and sweet. The horses still munched their evening hay. "You hold the lantern!" Billy ordered. And he felt the pony's legs and tested the heat of the flanks. He put his cheek against the pony's grey muzzle and then he rolled up the eyelids to look at the eyeballs and he lifted the lips to see the gums, and he put his fingers inside the ears. "He don't seem so chipper," Billy said. "I'll give him a rubdown."

Then Billy found a sack and rubbed the pony's legs violently and he rubbed the chest and the withers. Gabilan was strangely spiritless. He submitted patiently to the rubbing. At last Billy brought an old cotton comforter from the saddle-room, and threw it over the pony's back and tied it at neck and chest with string.

"Now he'll be all right in the morning," Billy said.

Jody's mother looked up when he got back to the house. "You're late up from bed," she said. She held his chin in her hard hand and brushed the tangled hair out of his eyes and she said, "Don't worry about the pony. He'll be all right. Billy's as good as any horse doctor in the country."

Jody hadn't known she could see his worry. He pulled gently away from her and knelt down in front of the fireplace until it burned his stomach. He scorched himself through and then went in to bed, but it was a hard thing to go to sleep. He awakened after what seemed a long time. The room was dark but there was a greyness in the window like that which precedes the dawn. He got up and found his overalls and searched for the legs, and then the clock in the other room struck two. He laid his clothes down and got back into bed. It was broad daylight when he awakened again. For the first time he had slept through the ringing of the triangle. He leaped up, flung on his clothes and went out of the door still buttoning his shirt. His mother looked after him for a moment and then went quietly back to her work. Her eyes were brooding and kind. Now and then her mouth smiled a little but without changing her eyes at all.

Jody ran on toward the barn. Halfway there he heard the sound he dreaded, the hollow rasping cough of a horse. He broke into a sprint then. In the barn he found Billy Buck with the pony. Billy was rubbing its legs with his strong thick hands. He looked up and smiled gaily. "He just took a little cold," Billy said. "We'll have him out of it in a couple of days."

Jody looked at the pony's face. The eyes were half closed and the lids thick and dry. In the eye corners a crust of hard mucus stuck. Gabilan's ears hung loosely sideways and his head was low. Jody put out his hand, but the pony did not move close to it. He coughed again and his whole body constricted with the effort. A little stream of thin fluid ran from his nostrils.

Jody looked back at Billy Buck. "He's awful sick, Billy."

"Just a little cold, like I said," Billy insisted. "You go get some breakfast and then go back to school. I'll take care of him."

"But you might have to do something else. You might leave him."

"No, I won't. I won't leave him at all. Tomorrow's Saturday. Then you can stay with him all day." Billy had failed again, and he felt badly about it. He had to cure the pony now.

Jody walked up to the house and took his place listlessly at the table. The eggs and bacon were cold and greasy, but he didn't notice it. He ate his usual amount. He didn't even ask to stay home from school. His mother pushed his hair back when she took his plate. "Billy'll take care of the pony," she assured him.

He moped through the whole day at school. He couldn't answer any questions nor read any words. He couldn't even tell anyone the pony was sick, for that might make him sicker. And when school was finally out he started home in dread. He walked slowly and let the other boys leave him. He wished he might continue walking and never arrive at the ranch.

Billy was in the barn, as he had promised, and the pony was worse. His eyes were almost closed now, and his breath whistled shrilly past an obstruction in his nose. A film covered that part of the eyes that was visible at all. It was doubtful whether the pony could see any more. Now and then he snorted, to clear his nose, and by the action seemed to plug it tighter. Jody looked dispiritedly at the pony's coat. The hair lay rough and unkempt and seemed to have lost all of its old luster. Bill stood quietly beside the stall. Jody hated to ask, but he had to know.

"Billy, is he—is he going to get well?"

Billy put his fingers between the bars under the pony's jaw and felt about. "Feel here," he said and he guided Jody's fingers to a large lump under the jaw. "When that gets bigger, I'll open it up and then he'll get better."

Jody looked quickly away, for he had heard about that lump. "What is it the matter with him?"

Billy didn't want to answer, but he had to. He couldn't be wrong three times. "Strangles," he said shortly, "but don't you worry about that. I'll pull him out of it. I've seen them get well when they were worse than Gabilan is. I'm going to steam him now. You can help."

"Yes," Jody said miserably. He followed Billy into the grain room and watched him make the steaming bag ready. It was a long canvas nose bag with straps to go over a horse's ears. Billy filled it one-third full of bran and then he added a couple of handfuls of dried hops. On top of the dry substance he poured a little carbolic acid and a little turpentine. "I'll be mixing it all up while you run to the house for a kettle of boiling water," Billy said.

When Jody came back with the steaming kettle, Billy buckled the straps over Gabilan's head and fitted the bag tightly around his nose. Then through a little hole in the side of the bag he poured the boiling water on the mixture. The pony started away as a cloud of strong steam rose up, but then the soothing fumes crept through his nose and into his lungs, and the sharp steam began to clear out the nasal passages. He breathed loudly. His legs trembled in an ague, and his eyes closed against the biting cloud. Billy poured in more water and kept the steam rising for fifteen minutes. At last he set down the kettle and took the bag from Gabilan's nose. The pony looked better. He breathed freely, and his eyes were open wider than they had been.

"See how good it makes him feel," Billy said. "Now we'll wrap him up in the blanket again. Maybe he'll be nearly well by morning."

"I'll stay with him tonight," Jody suggested.

"No. Don't you do it. I'll bring my blankets down here and put them in the hay. You can stay tomorrow and steam him if he needs it."

The evening was falling when they went to the house for their supper. Jody didn't even realize that some one else had fed the chickens and filled the wood-box. He walked up past the house to the dark brush line and took a drink of water from the tub. The spring water was so cold that it stung his mouth and drove a shiver through him. The sky above the hills was still light. He saw a hawk flying so high that it caught the sun on its breast and shone like a spark. Two blackbirds were driving him down the sky, glittering as they attacked their enemy. In the west, the clouds were moving in to rain again.

Jody's father didn't speak at all while the family ate supper, but after Billy Buck had taken his blankets and gone to sleep in the barn, Carl Tiflin built a high fire in the fireplace and told stories. He told about the wild man who ran naked through the country and had a tail and ears like a horse, and he told about the rabbit-cats of Moro Cojo that hopped into the trees for birds. He revived the famous Maxwell brothers who found a vein of gold and hid the traces of it so carefully that they could never find it again.

Jody sat with his chin in his hands; his mouth worked nervously, and his father gradually became aware that he wasn't listening very carefully. "Isn't that funny?" he asked.

Jody laughed politely and said, "Yes, sir." His father was angry and hurt, then. He didn't tell any more stories. After a while, Jody took a lantern and went down to the barn. Billy Buck was asleep in the hay, and, except that his breath rasped a little in his lungs, the pony seemed to be much better. Jody stayed a little while, running his fingers over the red rough coat, and then he took up the lantern and went back to the house. When he was in bed, his mother came into the room.

"Have you enough covers on? It's getting winter."

"Yes, ma'am."

"Well, get some rest tonight." She hesitated to go out, stood uncertainly. "The pony will be all right," she said.

Jody was tired. He went to sleep quickly and didn't awaken until dawn. The triangle sounded, and Billy Buck came up from the barn before Jody could get out of the house.

"How is he?" Jody demanded.

Billy always wolfed his breakfast. "Pretty good. I'm going to open that lump this morning. Then he'll be better maybe."

After breakfast, Billy got out his best knife, one with a needle point. He whetted the shining blade a long time on a little carborundum stone. He tried the point and the blade again and again on his calloused thumb-ball, and at last he tried it on his upper lip.

On the way to the barn, Jody noticed how the young grass was up and how the stubble was melting day by day into the new green crop of volunteer. It was a cold sunny morning.

As soon as he saw the pony, Jody knew he was worse. His eyes

were closed and sealed shut with dried mucus. His head hung so low
that his nose almost touched the straw of his bed. There was a little
groan in each breath, a deep-seated, patient groan.

Billy lifted the weak head and made a quick slash with the knife,
Jody saw the yellow pus run out. He held up the head while Billy
swabbed out the wound with weak carbolic acid salve.

"Now he'll feel better," Billy assured him. "That yellow poison
is what makes him sick."

Jody looked unbelieving at Billy Buck. "He's awful sick."

Billy thought a long time what to say. He nearly tossed off a careless assurance, but he saved himself in time. "Yes, he's pretty sick,"
he said at last. "I've seen worse ones get well. If he doesn't get pneu-
monia, we'll pull him through. You stay with him. If he gets worse,
you can come and get me."

For a long time after Billy went away, Jody stood beside the pony,
stroking him behind the ears. The pony didn't flip his head the way
he had done when he was well. The groaning in his breathing was
becoming more hollow.

Doubletree Mutt looked into the barn, his big tail waving provocatively, and Jody was so incensed at his health that he found a
hard black clod on the floor and deliberately threw it. Doubletree
Mutt went yelping away to nurse a bruised paw.

In the middle of the morning, Billy Buck came back and made
another steam bag. Jody watched to see whether the pony improved
this time as he had before. His breathing eased a little, but he did
not raise his head.

The Saturday dragged on. Late in the afternoon Jody went to
the house and brought his bedding down and made up a place to
sleep in the hay. He didn't ask permission. He knew from the way
his mother looked at him that she would let him do almost anything.
That night he left a lantern burning on a wire over the box stall.
Billy had told him to rub the pony's legs every little while.

At nine o'clock the wind sprang up and howled around the barn.
And in spite of his worry, Jody grew sleepy. He got into his
blankets and went to sleep, but the breathy groans of the pony
sounded in his dreams. And in his sleep he heard a crashing noise
which went on and on until it awakened him. The wind was rush-

ing through the barn. He sprang up and looked down the lane of stalls. The barn door had blown open, and the pony was gone.

He caught the lantern and ran outside into the gale, and he saw Gabilan weakly shambling away into the darkness, head down, legs working slowly and mechanically. When Jody ran up and caught him by the forelock, he allowed himself to be led back and put into his stall. His groans were louder, and a fierce whistling came from his nose. Jody didn't sleep any more then. The hissing of the pony's breath grew louder and sharper.

He was glad when Billy Buck came in at dawn. Billy looked for a time at the pony as though he had never seen him before. He felt the ears and flanks. "Jody," he said, "I've got to do something you won't want to see. You run up to the house for a while."

Jody grabbed him fiercely by the forearm. "You're not going to shoot him?"

Billy patted his hand. "No. I'm going to open a little hole in his windpipe so he can breathe. His nose is filled up. When he gets well, we'll put a little brass button in the hole for him to breathe through."

Jody couldn't have gone away if he had wanted to. It was awful to see the red hide cut, but infinitely more terrible to know it was being cut and not to see it. "I'll stay right here," he said bitterly. "You sure you got to?"

"Yes. I'm sure. If you stay, you can hold his head. If it doesn't make you sick, that is."

The fine knife came out again and was whetted again just as carefully as it had been the first time. Jody held the pony's head up and the throat taut, while Billy felt up and down for the right place. Jody sobbed once as the bright knife point disappeared into the throat. The pony plunged weakly away and then stood still, trembling violently. The blood ran thickly out and up the knife and across Billy's hand and into his shirtsleeve. The sure square hand sawed out a round hole in the flesh, and the breath came bursting out of the hole, throwing a fine spray of blood. With the rush of oxygen, the pony took a sudden strength. He lashed out with his hind feet and tried to rear, but Jody held his head down while Billy mopped the new wound with carbolic salve. It was a good job.

The blood stopped flowing and the air puffed out the hole and sucked it in regularly with a little bubbling noise.

The rain brought in by the night wind began to fall on the barn roof. Then the triangle rang for breakfast. "You go up and eat while I wait," Billy said. "We've got to keep this hole from plugging up."

Jody walked slowly out of the barn. He was too dispirited to tell Billy how the barn door had blown open and let the pony out. He emerged into the wet grey morning and sloshed up to the house, taking a perverse pleasure in splashing through all the puddles. His mother fed him and put dry clothes on. She didn't question him. She seemed to know he couldn't answer questions. But when he was ready to go back to the barn she brought him a pan of steaming meal. "Give him this," she said.

But Jody did not take the pan. He said, "He won't eat anything," and ran out of the house. At the barn, Billy showed him how to fix a ball of cotton on a stick, with which to swab out the breathing hole when it became clogged with mucus.

Jody's father walked into the barn and stood with them in front of the stall. At length he turned to the boy. "Hadn't you better come with me? I'm going to drive over the hill." Jody shook his head. "You better come on, out of this," his father insisted.

Billy turned on him angrily. "Let him alone. It's his pony, isn't it?"

Carl Tiflin walked away without saying another word. His feelings were badly hurt.

All morning Jody kept the wound open and the air passing in and out freely. At noon the pony lay wearily down on his side and stretched his nose out.

Billy came back. "If you're going to stay with him tonight, you better take a little nap," he said. Jody went absently out of the barn. The sky had cleared to a hard thin blue. Everywhere the birds were busy with worms that had come to the damp surface of the ground.

Jody walked to the brush line and sat on the edge of the mossy tub. He looked down at the house and at the old bunkhouse and at the dark cypress tree. The place was familiar, but curiously changed. It wasn't itself any more, but a frame for things that were happening. A cold wind blew out of the east now, signifying that the rain was over for a little while. At his feet Jody could see the little arms of new weeds spreading out over the ground. In the mud about the spring were thousands of quail tracks.

Doubletree Mutt came sideways and embarrassed up through the vegetable patch, and Jody, remembering how he had thrown the clod, put his arm about the dog's neck and kissed him on his wide black nose. Doubletree Mutt sat still, as though he knew some solemn thing was happening. His big tail slapped the ground gravely. Jody pulled a swollen tick out of Mutt's neck and popped it dead between his thumb-nails. It was a nasty thing. He washed his hands in the cold spring water.

Except for the steady swish of the wind, the farm was very quiet. Jody knew his mother wouldn't mind if he didn't go in to eat his lunch. After a little while he went slowly back to the barn. Mutt crept into his own little house and whined softly to himself for a long time.

Billy Buck stood up from the box and surrendered the cotton swab. The pony still lay on his side and the wound in his throat bellowsed in and out. When Jody saw how dry and dead the hair looked, he knew at last that there was no hope for the pony. He had seen the dead hair before on dogs and on cows, and it was a sure sign. He sat heavily on the box and let down the barrier of the box stall. For a long time he kept his eyes on the moving wound, and at last he dozed, and the afternoon passed quickly. Just before dark his mother brought in a deep dish of stew and left it for him and went away. Jody ate a little of it, and, when it was dark, he set the lantern on the floor by the pony's head so he could watch the wound and keep it open. And he dozed again until the night chill awakened him. The wind was blowing fiercely, bringing the north cold with it. Jody brought a blanket from his bed in the hay and wrapped himself in it. Gabilan's breathing was quiet at last; the hole in his throat moved gently. The owls flew through the hayloft, shrieking and looking for mice. Jody put his hands down on his head and slept. In his sleep he was aware that the wind had increased. He heard it slamming about the barn.

It was daylight when he awakened. The barn door had swung

open. The pony was gone. He sprang up and ran out into the morning light.

The pony's tracks were plain enough, dragging through the frost-like dew on the young grass, tired tracks with little lines between them where the hoofs had dragged. They headed for the brush line halfway up the ridge. Jody broke into a run and followed them. The sun shone on the sharp white quartz that stuck through the ground here and there. As he followed the plain trail, a shadow cut across in front of him. He looked up and saw a high circle of black buzzards, and the slowly revolving circle dropped lower and lower. The solemn birds soon disappeared over the ridge. Jody ran faster then, forced on by panic and rage. The trail entered the brush at last and followed a winding route among the tall sage bushes.

At the top of the ridge Jody was winded. He paused, puffing noisily. The blood pounded in his ears. Then he saw what he was looking for. Below, in one of the little clearings in the brush, lay the red pony. In the distance, Jody could see the legs moving slowly and convulsively. And in a circle around him stood the buzzards, waiting for the moment of death they know so well.

Jody leaped forward and plunged down the hill. The wet ground muffled his steps and the brush hid him. When he arrived, it was all over. The first buzzard sat on the pony's head and its beak had just risen dripping with dark eye fluid. Jody plunged into the circle like a cat. The black brotherhood arose in a cloud, but the big one on the pony's head was too late. As it hopped along to take off, Jody caught its wing tip and pulled it down. It was nearly as big as he was. The free wing crashed into his face with the force of a club, but he hung on. The claws fastened on his leg and the wing elbows battered his head on either side. Jody groped blindly with his free hand. His fingers found the neck of the struggling bird. The red eyes looked into his face, calm and fearless and fierce; the naked head turned from side to side. Then the beak opened and vomited a stream of putrefied fluid. Jody brought up his knee and fell on the great bird. He held the neck to the ground with one hand while his other found a piece of sharp white quartz. The first blow broke the beak sideways and black blood spurted from the twisted, leathery mouth corners. He struck again and missed. The red fearless eyes still looked at him, impersonal and unafraid and detached.

He struck again and again, until the buzzard lay dead, until its head was a red pulp. He was still beating the dead bird when Billy Buck pulled him off and held him tightly to calm his shaking.

Carl Tiflin wiped the blood from the boy's face with a red bandana. Jody was limp and quiet now. His father moved the buzzard with his toe. "Jody," he explained, "the buzzard didn't kill the pony. Don't you know that?"

"I know it," Jody said wearily.

It was Billy Buck who was angry. He had lifted Jody in his arms, and had turned to carry him home. But he turned back on Carl Tiflin. " 'Course he knows it," Billy said furiously. "Jesus Christ! man, can't you see how he'd feel about it?"

The Conversion of St. Wilfrid

by RUDYARD KIPLING

Rudyard Kipling's animal stories are well known and loved and many of them will be remembered when his gospel of the "white man's burden" is ancient history, as peculiar and incredible as the dinosaur. "The Conversion of St. Wilfrid" is one of a series of stories which Puck of Pook's Hill brings to life for two children who first saw him on Midsummer Day. It is as much and as little for children as Shakespeare's "Midsummer Night's Dream," where Puck also uses ancient magic to bring wisdom to mortals.

THEY had bought peppermints up at the village, and were coming home past little St. Barnabas's church, when they saw Jimmy Kidbrooke, the carpenter's baby, kicking at the churchyard gate, with a shaving in his mouth and the tears running down his cheeks.

Una pulled out the shaving and put in a peppermint. Jimmy said he was looking for his grand-daddy—he never seemed to take much notice of his father—so they went up between the old graves, under the leaf-dropping limes, to the porch, where Jim trotted in, looked about the empty church, and screamed like a gate-hinge.

Young Sam Kidbrooke's voice came from the bell-tower, and made them jump.

"Why, Jimmy," he called, "what are you doin' here? Fetch him, Father!"

Old Mr. Kidbrooke stumped downstairs, jerked Jimmy on to his shoulder, stared at the children beneath his brass spectacles, and stumped back again. They laughed: it was so exactly like Mr. Kidbrooke.

"It's all right," Una called up the stairs. "We found him, Sam. Does his mother know?"

"He's come off by himself. She'll be just about crazy," Sam answered.

"Then I'll run down street and tell her." Una darted off.

"Thank you, Miss Una. Would you like to see how we're mendin' the bell-beams, Mus' Dan?"

Dan hopped up, and saw young Sam lying on his stomach in a most delightful place among beams and ropes, close to the five great bells. Old Mr. Kidbrooke on the floor beneath was planing a piece of wood, and Jimmy was eating the shavings as fast as they came away. He never looked at Jimmy; Jimmy never stopped eating; and the broad gilt-bobbed pendulum of the church clock never stopped swinging across the white-washed wall of the tower.

Dan winked through the sawdust that fell on his up-turned face. "Ring a bell," he called.

"I mustn't do that, but I'll buzz one of 'em a bit for you," said Sam. He pounded on the sound-bow of the biggest bell, and waked a hollow groaning boom that ran up and down the tower like creepy feelings down your back. Just when it almost began to hurt, it died away in a hurry of beautiful sorrowful cries, like a wine-glass rubbed with a wet finger. The pendulum clanked—one loud clank to each silent swing.

Dan heard Una return from Mrs. Kidbrooke's, and ran down to fetch her. She was standing by the font staring at some one who kneeled at the altar rail.

"Is that the lady who practises the organ?" she whispered.

"No. She's gone into the organ-place. Besides, she wears black," Dan replied.

The figure rose and came down the nave. It was a white-haired man in a long white gown with a sort of scarf looped low on the neck, one end hanging over his shoulder. His loose long sleeves were embroidered with gold, and a deep strip of gold embroidery waved and sparkled round the hem of his gown.

"Go and meet him," said Puck's voice behind the font. "It's only Wilfrid."

"Wilfrid who?" said Dan. "You come along too."

"Wilfrid—Saint of Sussex, and Archbishop of York. *I* shall wait till he asks me." He waved them forward. Their feet squeaked on the old grave slabs in the centre aisle. The Archbishop raised one hand with a pink ring on it, and said something in Latin. He was very handsome, and his thin face looked almost as silvery as his thin circle of hair.

"Are you alone?" he asked.

"Puck's here, of course," said Una. "Do you know him?"

"I know him better now than I used to." He beckoned over Dan's shoulder, and spoke again in Latin. Puck pattered forward, holding himself as straight as an arrow. The Archbishop smiled.

"Be welcome," said he. "Be very welcome."

"Welcome to you also, O Prince of the Church," Puck replied. The Archbishop bowed his head and passed on, till he glimmered like a white moth in the shadow by the font.

"He does look awfully princely," said Una. "Isn't he coming back?"

"Oh yes. He's only looking over the church. He's very fond of churches," said Puck. "What's that?"

The Lady who practises the organ was speaking to the blower-boy behind the organ-screen. "We can't very well talk here," Puck whispered. "Let's go to Panama Corner."

He led them to the end of the south aisle, where there is a slab of iron which says in queer, long-tailed letters *Orate p. annema Jhone Coline*. The children always called it Panama Corner.

The Archbishop moved slowly about the little church, peering at the old memorial tablets, and the new glass windows. The Lady who practises the organ began to pull out stops and rustle hymn-books behind the screen.

"I hope she'll do all the soft lacey tunes—like treacle on porridge," said Una.

"I like the trumpety ones best," said Dan. "Oh, look at Wilfrid! He's trying to shut the altar gates!"

"Tell him he mustn't," said Puck, quite seriously.

"He can't, anyhow," Dan muttered, and tiptoed out of Panama Corner while the Archbishop patted and patted at the carved gates that always sprang open again beneath his hand.

"That's no use, sir," Dan whispered. "Old Mr. Kidbrooke says altar-gates are just *the* one pair of gates which no man can shut. He made 'em so himself."

The Archbishop's blue eyes twinkled. Dan saw that he knew all about it.

"I beg your pardon," Dan stammered—very angry with Puck.

"Yes, I know! He made them so Himself." The Archbishop smiled, and crossed to Panama Corner, where Una dragged up a certain padded arm-chair for him to sit on.

The organ played softly. "What does that music say?" he asked.

Una dropped into the chant without thinking: " 'Oh, all ye works of the Lord, bless ye the Lord; praise him and magnify him for ever.' We call it the Noah's Ark, because it's all lists of things—beasts and birds and whales, you know."

"Whales?" said the Archbishop quickly.

"Yes— 'O ye whales, and all that move in the waters,' " Una hummed—" 'Bless ye the Lord'—it sounds like a wave turning over, doesn't it?"

"Holy Father," said Puck with a demure face, "is a little seal also 'one who moves in the water'?"

"Eh? Oh yes—yess!" he laughed. "A seal moves wonderfully in the waters. Do the seal come to my island still?"

Puck shook his head. "All those little islands have been swept away."

"Very possible. The tides ran fiercely down there. Do you know the land of the Sea-calf, maiden!"

"No—but we've seen seals—at Brighton."

"The Archbishop is thinking of a little farther down the coast. He means Seal's Eye—Selsea—down Chichester way—where he converted the South Saxons," Puck explained.

"Yes—yess; if the South Saxons did not convert me," said the Archbishop, smiling. "The first time I was wrecked was on that coast. As our ship took ground and we tried to push her off, an old fat fellow, I remember, reared breast high out of the water, and scratched his head with his flipper as if he were saying 'What *does* that respectable person with the pole think he is doing?' I was very wet and miserable, but I could not help laughing, till the natives came down and attacked us."

"What did you do?" Dan asked.

"One couldn't very well go back to France, so one tried to make them go back to the shore. All the South Saxons are born wreckers, like my own Northumbrian folk. I was bringing over a few things for my old church at York, and some of the natives laid hands on them, and—and I'm afraid I lost my temper."

"It is said," Puck's voice was wickedly meek, "that there was a great fight."

"Eh, but I must ha' been a silly lad." Wilfrid spoke with a sudden thick burr in his voice. He coughed, and took up his silvery tones again. "There was no fight really. My men thumped a few of them, but the tide rose half an hour before its time, with a strong wind, and we backed off. What I wanted to say, though, was that the seas about us were full of sleek seals watching the scuffle. My good Eddi—my chaplain—insisted that they were demons. Yes—yess! That was my first acquaintance with the South Saxons and their seals."

"But not the only time you were wrecked, was it?" said Dan.

"Alas, no! On sea and land my life seems to have been one long shipwreck." He looked at the Jhone Coline slab as old Hobden sometimes looks into the fire. "Ah, well!"

"But did you ever have any more adventures among the seals?" said Una, after a pause.

"Oh, the seals! I beg your pardon. They are the important things. Yes—yess! I went back to the South Saxons after twelve—fifteen years. No, I did not come by water, but overland from my own Northumbria, to see what I could do. It's little one *can* do with that class of native except make them stop killing each other and themselves—"

"Why did they kill themselves?" Una asked, her chin in her hand.

"Because they were heathen. When they grew tired of life (as if they were the only people!) they would jump into the sea. They called it going to Wotan. It wasn't want of food always—by any means. A man would tell you that he felt grey in the heart, or a woman would say that she saw nothing but long days in front of her; and they'd saunter away to the mud-flats and—that would be the end of them, poor souls, unless one headed them off! One had to run quick, but one can't allow people to lay hands on themselves because they happen to feel grey. Yes—yess! Extraordinary people, the South Saxons. Disheartening, sometimes. . . . What does that say now?" The organ had changed tune again.

"Only a hymn for next Sunday," said Una. " 'The Church's One Foundation.' Go on, please, about running over the mud. I should like to have seen you."

"I dare say you would, and I really *could* run in those days. Ethelwalch the king gave me some five or six muddy parishes by the sea, and the first time my good Eddi and I rode there we saw a man slouching along the slob, among the seals at Manhood End. My good Eddi disliked seals—but he swallowed his objections and ran like a hare."

"Why?" said Dan.

"For the same reason that I did. We thought it was one of our people going to drown himself. As a matter of fact, Eddi and I were nearly drowned in the pools before we overtook him. To cut a long story short, we found ourselves very muddy, very breathless, being quietly made fun of in good Latin by a very well-spoken person. No—he'd no idea of going to Wotan. He was fishing on his own beaches, and he showed us the beacons and turf-heaps that divided his lands from the Church property. He took us to his own house, gave us a good dinner, some more than good wine, sent a guide with us into Chichester, and became one of my best and most refreshing friends. He was a Meon by descent, from the west edge of the kingdom; a scholar educated, curiously enough, at Lyons, my old school; had travelled the world over, even to Rome, and was a brilliant talker. We found we had scores of acquaintances in common. It seemed he was a small chief under King Ethelwalch, and I fancy the King was somewhat afraid of him. The South Saxons mistrust a man who talks too well. Ah! *Now*, I've left out the very point of my story! He kept a great grey-muzzled old dog-seal that he had brought up from a pup. He called it Padda—after one of my clergy. It *was* rather like fat, honest old Padda. The creature followed him everywhere, and nearly knocked down my good Eddi when we first met him. Eddi loathed it. It used to sniff at his thin legs and cough at him. I can't say I ever took much notice of it (I was not fond of animals), till one day Eddi came to me with a circumstantial account of some witchcraft that Meon worked. He would tell the seal to go down to the beach the last thing at night, and bring him word of the weather. When it came back, Meon might say to his slaves, 'Padda thinks we shall have wind to-morrow. Haul up the boats!' I spoke to Meon casually about the story, and he laughed.

"He told me he could judge by the look of the creature's coat and the way it sniffed what weather was brewing. Quite possible. One need not put down everything one does not understand to the work of bad spirits—or good ones, for that matter." He nodded towards Puck, who nodded gaily in return.

"I say so," he went on, "because to a certain extent I have been made a victim of that habit of mind. Some while after I was settled at Selsea, King Ethelwalch and Queen Ebba ordered their people to be baptized. I fear I'm too old to believe that a whole nation can change its heart at the King's command, and I had a shrewd suspicion that their real motive was to get a good harvest. No rain had fallen for two or three years, but as soon as we had finished baptizing, it fell heavily, and they all said it was a miracle."

"And was it?" Dan asked.

"Everything in life is a miracle, but"—the Archbishop twisted the heavy ring on his finger—"I should be slow—ve-ry slow should I be—to assume that a certain sort of miracle happens whenever lazy and improvident people say they are going to turn over a new leaf if they are paid for it. My friend Meon had sent his slaves to the font, but he had not come himself, so the next time I rode over—to return a manuscript—I took the liberty of asking why. He was perfectly open about it. He looked on the King's action as a heathen attempt to curry favour with the Christians' God through me the Archbishop, and he would have none of it. 'My dear man,' I said, 'admitting that that is the case, surely you, as an educated person, don't believe in Wotan and all the other hobgoblins any more than Padda here.' The old seal was hunched up on his ox-hide behind his master's chair.

" 'Even if I don't,' he said, 'why should I insult the memory of my father's Gods? I have sent you a hundred and three of my rascals to christen. Isn't that enough?'

" 'By no means,' I answered. 'I want *you*.'

" 'He wants us! What do you think of that, Padda?' He pulled the seal's whiskers till it threw back its head and roared, and he pretended to interpret. 'No! Padda says he won't be baptized yet awhile. He says you'll stay to dinner and come fishing with me to-morrow, because you're overworked and need a rest.'

" 'I wish you'd keep yon brute in its proper place,' I said, and Eddi, my chaplain, agreed.

" 'I do,' said Meon. 'I keep him just next my heart. He can't tell a lie, and he doesn't know how to love any one except me. It 'ud be the same if I were dying on a mud-bank, wouldn't it, Padda?'

" 'Augh! Augh!' said Padda, and put up his head to be scratched.

"Then Meon began to tease Eddi: 'Padda says, if Eddi saw his Archbishop dying on a mud-bank Eddi would tuck up his gown and run. Padda knows Eddi can run too! Padda came into Wittering Church last Sunday—all wet—to hear the music, and Eddi ran out.'

"My good Eddi rubbed his hands and his shins together, and flushed. 'Padda is a child of the Devil, who is the father of lies!' he cried, and begged my pardon for having spoken. I forgave him.

" 'Yes. You are just about stupid enough for a musician,' said Meon. 'But here he is. Sing a hymn to him, and see if he can stand it. You'll find my small harp beside the fireplace.'

"Eddi, who is really an excellent musician, played and sang for quite half an hour. Padda shuffled off his ox-hide, hunched himself on his flippers before him, and listened with his head thrown back. Yes—yess! A rather funny sight! Meon tried not to laugh, and asked Eddi if he were satisfied.

"It takes some time to get an idea out of my good Eddi's head. He looked at me.

" 'Do you want to sprinkle him with holy water, and see if he flies up the chimney? Why not baptize him?' said Meon.

"Eddi was really shocked. I thought it was bad taste myself.

" 'That's not fair,' said Meon. 'You call him a demon and a familiar spirit because he loves his master and likes music, and when I offer you a chance to prove it, you won't take it. Look here! I'll make a bargain. I'll be baptized if you'll baptize Padda too. He's more of a man than most of my slaves.'

" 'One doesn't bargain—or joke—about these matters," I said. He was going altogether too far.

" 'Quite right,' said Meon, 'I shouldn't like any one to joke about

Padda. Padda, go down to the beach and bring us to-morrow's weather!'

"My good Eddi must have been a little overtired with his day's work. 'I am a servant of the Church,' he cried. 'My business is to save souls, not to enter into fellowships and understandings with accursed beasts.'"

" 'Have it your own narrow way," said Meon. 'Padda, you needn't go.' The old fellow flounced back to his ox-hide at once.

" 'Man could learn obedience at least from that creature,' said Eddi, a little ashamed of himself. Christians should not curse.

" 'Don't begin to apologise just when I am beginning to like you,' said Meon. 'We'll leave Padda behind to-morrow—out of respect to your feelings. Now let's go to dinner. We must be up early to-morrow for the whiting.'

"The next was a beautiful crisp autumn morning—a weather breeder, if I had taken the trouble to think; but it's refreshing to escape from kings and converts for half a day. We three went by ourselves in Meon's smallest boat, and we got on the whiting near an old wreck, a mile or so off shore. Meon knew the marks to a yard, and the fish were keen. Yes—yess! A perfect morning's fishing! If a bishop can't be a fisherman, who can?" He twiddled his ring again. "We stayed there a little too long, and while we were getting up our stone, down came the fog. After some discussion, we decided to row for the land. The ebb was just beginning to make round the point, and sent us all ways at once like a coracle."

"Selsea Bill," said Puck under his breath. "The tides run something furious there."

"I believe you," said the Archbishop. "Meon and I have spent a good many evenings arguing as to where exactly we drifted. All I know is we found ourselves in a little rocky cove that had sprung up round us out of the fog, and a swell lifted the boat on to a ledge, and she broke up beneath our feet. We had just time to shuffle through the weed before the next wave. The sea was rising.

" 'It's rather a pity we didn't let Padda go down to the beach last night,' said Meon. 'He might have warned us this was coming.'

" 'Better fall into the hands of God than the hands of demons,' said Eddi, and his teeth chattered as he prayed. A nor'-west breeze had just got up—distinctly cool.

" 'Save what you can of the boat,' said Meon, 'we may need it,' and we had to drench ourselves again, fishing out stray planks."

"What for?" said Dan.

"For firewood. We did not know when we should get off. Eddi had flint and steel, and we found dry fuel in the old gulls' nests and lit a fire. It smoked abominably, and we guarded it with boat-planks up-ended between the rocks. One gets used to that sort of thing if one travels. Unluckily I'm not so strong as I was. I fear I must have been a trouble to my friends. It was blowing a full gale before midnight. Eddi wrung out his cloak, and tried to wrap me in it, but I ordered him on his obedience to keep it. However, he held me in his arms all the first night, and Meon begged his pardon for what he'd said the night before—about Eddi running away if he found me on a sandbank, you remember.

" 'You are right in half your prophecy,' said Eddi. 'I've tucked up my gown, at any rate.' (The wind had blown it over his head.) 'Now let us thank God for His mercies.'

" 'Hum!' said Meon. 'If this gale lasts, we stand a very fair chance of dying of starvation.'

" 'If it be God's will that we live, God will provide,' said Eddi. 'At least help me to sing to Him.' The wind almost whipped the words out of his mouth but he braced himself against a rock and sang psalms.

"I'm glad I never concealed my opinion—from myself—that Eddi was a better man than I. Yet I have worked hard in my time —very hard! Yes—yess! So the morning and evening were our second day on that islet. There was rainwater in the rock pools, and, as a Churchman, I knew how to fast, but I admit we were hungry. Meon fed our fire chip by chip to eke it out, and they made me sit over it, the dear fellows, when I was too weak to object. Meon held me in his arms the second night, just like a child. My good Eddi was a little out of his senses, and imagined himself teaching a York choir to sing. Even so he was beautifully patient with them.

"I heard Meon whisper, 'If this keeps up we shall go to our Gods. I wonder what Wotan will say to me. He must know I don't believe in him. On the other hand, I can't do what Ethelwalch finds so easy —curry favour with your God at the last minute, in the hope of being saved—as you call it. How do you advise, Bishop?'

" 'My dear man,' I said, 'if that is your honest belief, I take it upon myself to say you had far better not curry favour with any God. But if it's only your Jutish pride that holds you back, lift me up, and I'll baptize you even now.'

" 'Lie still,' said Meon. 'I could judge better if I were in my own hall. But to desert one's fathers' Gods even—if one doesn't believe in them—in the middle of a gale, isn't quite— What would you do yourself?'

"I was lying in his arms, kept alive by the warmth of his big, steady heart. It did not seem to me the time or the place for subtle arguments, so I answered, 'No, I certainly should not desert my God.' I don't see, even now, what else I could have said.

" 'Thank you. I'll remember that, if I live,' said Meon, and I must have drifted back to my dreams about Northumbria and beautiful France, for it was broad daylight when I heard him calling on Wotan in that high, shaking, heathen yell that I detest so.

" 'Lie quiet. I'm giving Wotan his chance,' he said. Our dear Eddi ambled up, still beating time to his imaginary choir.

" 'Yes. Call on your Gods,' he cried, 'and see what gifts they will send you. They are gone on a journey, or they are hunting.'

"I assure you the words were not out of his mouth when old Padda shot from the top of a cold wrinkled swell, drove himself over the weedy ledge, and landed fair in our laps with a rock-cod between his teeth. I could not help smiling at Eddi's face. 'A miracle! A miracle!' he cried, and kneeled down to clean the cod.

" 'You've been a long time winding us, my son,' said Meon. 'Now fish—fish for all our lives. We're starving, Padda.'

"The old fellow flung himself quivering like a salmon backward into the boil of the currents round the rocks, and then Meon said, 'We're safe. I'll send him to fetch help when this wind drops. Eat and be thankful.'

"I never tasted anything so good as those rock codlings we took from Padda's mouth and half roasted over the fire. Between his plunges Padda would hunch up and purr over Meon with the tears running down his face. I never knew before that seals could weep for joy—as I have wept.

" 'Surely,' said Eddi, with his mouth full, 'God has made the seal the loveliest of His creatures in the water. Look how Padda breasts the current! He stands up against it like a rock. Now watch the chain of bubbles where he dives; and now—there is his wise head under that rock-ledge! Oh, a blessing be on thee, my little brother Padda!'

" 'You *said* he was a child of the Devil!' Meon laughed.

" 'There I sinned,' poor Eddi answered. 'Call him here, and I will ask his pardon. God sent him out of the storm to humble me, a fool.'

" 'I won't ask you to enter into fellowships and understandings with any accursed brute,' said Meon rather unkindly. 'Shall we say he was sent to our Bishop as the ravens were sent to your prophet Elijah?'

" 'Doubtless that is so,' said Eddi. 'I will write it so if I live to get home.'

" 'No—no!' I said. 'Let us three poor men kneel and thank God for His mercies.'

"We kneeled, and old Padda shuffled up and thrust his head under Meon's elbows. I laid my hand upon it and blessed him. So did Eddi.

" 'And now, my son,' I said to Meon, 'shall I baptize thee?'

" 'Not yet,' said he. 'Wait till we are well ashore and at home. No God in any Heaven shall say that I came to him or left him because I was wet and cold. I will send Padda to my people for a boat. Is that witchcraft, Eddi?'

" 'Why, no. Surely Padda will go and pull them to the beach by the skirts of their gowns as he pulled me in Wittering Church to ask me to sing. Only then I was afraid, and did not understand,' said Eddi.

" 'You are understanding now,' said Meon, and at a wave of his arm off went Padda to the mainland, making a wake like a war-boat till we lost him in the rain. Meon's people could not bring a boat across for some hours; even so it was ticklish work among the rocks in that tideway. But they hoisted me aboard, too stiff to move, and Padda swam behind us, barking and turning somersaults all the way to Manhood End!"

"Good old Padda!" murmured Dan.

"When we were quite rested and re-clothed, and his people had been summoned—not an hour before—Meon offered himself to be baptized."

"Was Padda baptized too?" Una asked.

"No, that was only Meon's joke. But he sat blinking on his ox-hide in the middle of the hall. When Eddi (who thought I wasn't looking) made a little cross in holy water on his wet muzzle, he kissed Eddi's hand. A week before Eddi wouldn't have touched him. *That* was a miracle, if you like! But seriously, I was more glad than I can tell you to get Meon. A rare and splendid soul that never looked back—never looked back!" The Archbishop half closed his eyes.

"But, sir," said Puck, most respectfully, "haven't you left out what Meon said afterwards?" Before the Bishop could speak he turned to the children and went on: "Meon called all his fishers and ploughmen and herdsmen into the hall and he said: 'Listen, men! Two days ago I asked our Bishop whether it was fair for a man to desert his fathers' Gods in a time of danger. Our Bishop said it was not fair. You needn't shout like that, because you are all Christians now. My red war-boat's crew will remember how near we all were to death when Padda fetched them over to the Bishop's islet. You can tell your mates that even in that place, at that time, hanging on the wet weedy edge of death, our Bishop, a Christian, counselled me, a heathen, to stand by my fathers' Gods. I tell you now that a faith which takes care that every man shall keep faith, even though he may save his soul by breaking faith, is the faith for a man to believe in. So I believe in the Christian God, and in Wilfrid His Archbishop, and in the Church that Wilfrid rules. You have been baptized once by the King's orders. I shall not have you baptized again; but if I find any more old women being sent to Wotan, or any girls dancing on the sly before Balder, or any men talking about Thun or Lok or the rest, I will teach you with my own hands how to keep faith with the Christian God. Go out quietly; you'll find a couple of beefs on the beach.' Then of course they shouted 'Hurrah!' which meant 'Thor help us!' and—I think you laughed, sir?"

"I think you remember it all too well," said the Archbishop, smiling. "It was a joyful day for me. I had learned a great deal on that rock where Padda found us.—Yes—yess! One should deal kindly with all the creatures of God, and gently with their masters. But one learns late."

He rose, and his gold-embroidered sleeves rustled thickly.

The organ clacked and took deep breaths.

"Wait a minute," Dan whispered. "She's going to do the trumpety one. It takes all the wind you can pump. It's in Latin, sir."

"There is no other tongue," the Archbishop answered.

"It's not a real hymn," Una explained. "She does it as a treat after her exercises. She isn't a real organist, you know. She just comes down here sometimes, from the Albert Hall."

"Oh, what a miracle of a voice!" said the Archbishop.

It rang out suddenly from a dark arch of lonely noises—every word spoken to the very end.

> "Dies Iræ dies illâ
> Solvet sæclum in favilla.
> Teste David cum Sibylla."

The Archbishop caught his breath and moved forward.
The music carried on by itself a while.

"Now it's calling all the light out of the windows," Una whispered to Dan.

"I think it's more like a horse neighing in battle," he whispered back. The voice cried

> "Tuba mirum spargens sonum
> Per sepulchra regionum."

Deeper and deeper the organ dived down, but far below its deepest note they heard Puck's voice joining in the last line,

> "Coget omnes ante thronum."

As they looked in wonder, for it sounded like the dull jar of one of the very pillars shifting, the little fellow turned and went out through the south door.

"Now's the sorrowful part, but it's very beautiful." Una found herself speaking to the empty chair in front of her.

"What are you doing that for?" Dan said behind her. "You spoke so politely, too."

"I don't know . . . I thought . . ." said Una. "Funny!"

" 'Tisn't. It's the part you like best," Dan grunted.

The music had turned soft—full of little sounds that chased each other on wings across the broad gentle flood of the main tune. But the voice was ten times lovelier than the music.

"Recordare Jesu pie,
Quod sum causa Tuae viae,
Ne me perdas illâ die!"

There was no more. They moved out into the centre-aisle.

" 'That you?" the Lady called as she shut the lid. "I thought I heard you, and I played it on purpose."

"Thank you awfully," said Dan. "We hoped you would, so we waited. Come on, Una, it's pretty nearly dinner-time."

Chanticleer and Pertelote

(as told by the Nun's Chaplain)

by CHAUCER

We must accept Chaucer's own word that this is not the story of a cock and a hen. But Chaucer's acute perception of the characteristics of animals (as well as the characteristics of human beings) makes this mediaeval allegory from "The Canterbury Tales" a joy to all lovers of animals as well as to all lovers of literature.

A poor widow, somewhat steep in age,
On a time, dwelt in a narrow cottage
Beside a grove, standing in a dale.
This widow, of whom I tell my tale,
Since that day when she was last a wife
In patience led a quiet, simple life,
For little was her wealth and her intaking.
And of this little, she must needs be making
The best, to keep herself and her two lasses.
Three large sows she had, but neither horse nor asses,
Three cows, and one good sheep that was called Mall.
The walls were sooty in her room and hall
In which she ate her usual frugal meal.
Of pungent spices she needed never a deal,
No dainty morsel passed her lips and throat,
Her diet was according to her coat.
Repletion never yet had made her sick,
A temperate diet was her only physic,
And exercise, and heart's sufficiency.
The gout had never stopped her dance, and she

Feared not apoplexy's ruin on her head.
She drank no wine, neither white nor red;
Her table was most served with white and black:
White milk, black bread of which she found no lack,
Broiled bacon, and sometimes an egg, boiled hard,
For she had, as her pride, a poultry yard.
   A yard she had, enclosed with fence and ditch,
In which she kept a cock called Chanticleer.
In all the land, this rooster had no peer
For crowing. His voice was merrier than the merry note
That on feast days within the church each throat
Intones, and surer from his roost his crowing time
Than is a clock, or brave cathedral chime.
By nature knew he the sun's course and rising,
Both winter, and when days are equalising,
For when the day had reached fifteen degrees,
He crew, and on the moment, if you please.
His comb was redder than fine coral
And crenelated like a castle wall;
His bill was black, and as fine jet it shone,
Like azure were the feet he stood upon;
His nails were whiter than the lily flower,
And like burnt gold his coat in his proud hour.
This gentle cock did reign, as lord and king
O'er seven hens—a very pleasant thing:
They were his sisters and his paramours
And very like to him, in point of colours:
Of whom one, with fairest colours on her throat
Was called the lovely damsel Pertelote.
Courteous she was, discreet and debonnair,
Companionable, and bore herself so fair
Since that day that she was seven nights old
That truly she had the heart in hold
Of Chanticleer, locked up in every limb;
He loved her so, it was great joy to him.
But such delight it was to hear them sing,
When upward the bright sun began to spring,
In sweet accord, "My love has left the land."

For in that time, as you may understand,
Both birds and beasts could speak and also sing.
    And so befell, that one day at dawning
As Chanticleer, among his sisters all
Sat on the perch that was within the hall
And next him sat this same fair Pertelote,
That Chanticleer, asleep, groaned in his throat,
As one who, in his dreams, is troubled sore,
And when Dame Pertelote thus heard him roar
She was aghast, and said, "O, dear my heart,
What aileth you, that you should groan and start?
You are a wondrous sleeper—fie, for shame!"
And he answered and said, "My lovely dame,
I pray you that you take it not amiss,
I never dreamt of mischief such as this
Before, and still my heart is sore with fright.
Now God," quoth he, "my dream interpret right.
And keep my body out of chains, by Grace.
I dreamt that as I roamed around this place,
Within our yard, right there I saw a beast
Was like a hound, and would have made arrest
Upon my body, and would have had me dead.
His color was between a yellow and red,
And tippèd was his tail and both his ears
With black, unlike his other hairs.
His snoot was small, and glowing was his eye:
Still of his glance, for fear, I almost die!
This caused my groaning, doubtless."
    "Fie," quoth she, "out on you, heartless!
Alas," quoth she, "for by that God above,
Now have you lost my heart and all my love.
I cannot love a coward, by my faith.
For truly, what so any woman saith,
We all desire, if such a thing can be,
To have our husbands hardy, wise and free,
And trusty, and no miser, and no fool,
Nor one that stands aghast at every tool
Of war, and yet no boaster, God above!

How dare you say, for shame, unto your love
That there was anything on earth you feared.
Have you no man's heart, you who have a beard?
Alas, and can you be afraid of dreams?
Nothing, God knows, but vanity's in dreams.
Dreams are engendered of repletions
And often of gas, and of complications
When humours are too abundant in a wight.
Surely this dream, which you have met tonight
Cometh of a superfluous supply
Of the red choler you are vexèd by.
Which causeth folk to fear, in their dreams,
Sharp arrows, and bright fire with red gleams,
Just as the humour of melancholy
Causeth many a man in sleep to cry
For fear of black bears, or a great black bull,
Or else black devils, that would sinners pull
To hell. Of other humours could I tell you also
That cause many a man in sleep great woe,
But I would speak as little as I can.
    "Lo, Cato, who was so wise a man,
Said he not 'Put no trust in dreams.'
Now for God's love, but take some laxative;
On peril of my soul, that it may live,
I counsel you most well—I do not lie,
That both of choler and of melancholy
You purge yourself, and that you may not tarry,
Though in this town is no apothecary,
I shall myself in herbal lore instruct you,
That shall to health and your best good conduct you;
And in our very yard those herbs mature
Which have that potent property, by nature,
To purge your stomach and your colon too.
Forget not this, by God's own love for you.
You are choleric in your chief complexion,
Therefore avoid the sun in his ascension,
Nor eat the food made up of humours hot,
For if you do, I'll wager you a groat

That you will have an ague or tertian fever
Will take you off—and I am no deceiver.
A day or two I'll give you digestives
Of worms, before you take your laxatives
Of laurel, centaury and fumitory,
Or else of hellebore, raised for God's glory,
Or caper spurge, or of the buckthorn's berry,
Or ground ivy, a plant that makes you merry.
Pluck them just as they grow and eat them up.
Be merry, husband, for if well you sup,
You dread no dream. Now I can say no more."
    "Madame," he said, "I thank you for your lore,
Nevertheless, as touching Master Cato,
Who is for wisdom less renowned than Plato,
Though he bade men of dreams to have no fear,
By God, it doth in ancient books appear
That many a man of great authority,
Wiser than Cato was—I tell it ye—
Says quite the opposite of what he said,
And has determined, by experience dread,
That dreams be both a sign and signatory
Of joys like heaven, or grief like purgatory,
Which folk have taste of in their present life.
Let's make of this no argument nor strife.
The theory never proves so much as fact.
    "One of the greatest authors, that attract
All wise men, says that once two fellows went
On pilgrimage, having full good intent;
And happened so, they came into a town
Wherein was such a running up and down
Of people, and such scanty lodging space
They did not find so much as one poor place
In which they both might be lodged together,
Wherefore they must, since it was cold, wet weather,
Part company, and go where each was able
To get a roof. Now one lodged in a stable,
Far from a house, with oxen and farm stuff.
The other man was lodgèd well enough,

As was his chance or fortune; you can see
Chance rules all men, of high or low degree.
  "It so befell that long ere it was day
This man dreamt in his bed, as there he lay,
How his companion dear began to call
And said, 'Alas, for in an ox's stall,
This night I shall be murdered where I lie,
Now help me, my good brother, ere I die;
In all haste come and save me, friend,' he said.
The man starts up from sleep as from the dead;
But when he had awakened, then indeed,
Went back to bed, and gave his dream no heed.
He thought the vision but a vanity,
Though twice in sleep he dreamt. How can this be?
A third time then his friend stood by his bed,
Or so he thought, and said, 'Now I am dead;
Behold my bloody wounds, both deep and wide!
Arise up early in the morning tide,
And at the west gate of the town,' quoth he
'A cart laden with dung there shalt thou see,
In which my corpse is hid full secretly.
Cause this cart to be stopped at once, and boldly.
My gold has caused my murder, sooth to say.'
And told then of his dying, in what way
The men had fallen on him. Pale of hue
His countenance. Trust well the dream was true,
For on the morrow, soon as it was day,
To his friend's inn this fellow took his way
And when he came up to the ox's stall,
Upon his comrade he began to call.
  "The black browed hostler answered him anon
And said, 'Good sir, your traveling mate is gone,
As soon as it was day, he left the town.'
This man began to feel suspicion,
Remembering his dream—he would not wait,
But found, departing from the town's west gate
A dung cart, gotten up in the same way
As he had heard his murdered comrade say;

And with a strong heart he began to cry
Vengeance and justice on this felony:—
'My good friend here was murdered overnight
And in this cart he lieth stark—a sight
I here demand the officers should see,
Those men who should enforce the law,' said he.
'Harrow, alas—here lies my comrade slain.'
What should I add unto this tale of pain?
The people started up, and cast to ground
The cart and dung, and in the midst they found
The dead man, newly murdered. Oh, just God!
How Thou dost always murderous deed betray.
Murder will out—we see that day by day.
Murder is so loathsome and abominable
To God, who is so just and reasonable,
That He will not allow it hid to be,
Though it abide a year, or two or three,
Murder will out, and you can write it down.
And so forthwith, the sheriff of that town
Seized on the carter—punching him so sore,
So wracked the landlord—punching him the more,
That soon their deed of wickedness came out
And they were hanged—and went to hell, no doubt.
 "Here men may see they should hold dreams in dread,
And certainly in that same book I read,
Right in the very chapter following this,
(I speak not idly, by all joy and bliss,)
Two men that would have journeyed over sea,
For certain cause, into a far countree,
If the fierce wind had not contrary blown,
And made them tarry in a city, known
Throughout the world for its fine haven-side,
But on a day, and just at eventide,
The wind began to change, as they desired.
Joyful and glad the two men then retired
And planned to sail right early. Then to one
There came a marvel. Before night was done
He dreamt a man stood up by his bedside

Commanding him that he should there abide—
Bespoke him thus, 'If thou tomorrow wend,
Thou shalt be drowned. My tale is at an end.'
He woke and told his fellow what he dreamed,
And prayed him stay, because to him it seemed
Wiser; that day he prayed him to abide.
His companion, that lay by his bed's side,
Began to laugh. His ridicule came fast.
'No dream,' quoth he, 'can so my heart aghast
That I should hesitate to have my way.
I set no store on dreams, by night or day.
For dreams, they be but vanities and japes.
Men dream day after day of owls or apes,
And many a bewilderment withal;
Men dream of things that have not been, nor shall.
But since I see that thou wilt here abide,
And thus waste wilfully thy time and tide,
God knows it paineth me, and so good day.'
And so he took his leave and went his way.
But ere half of his course was safely sailed,
I know not why, nor what mischance prevailed,
Calamitously the ship's bottom rent,
And ship and man under the water went,
In sight of other shipping by its side
That sailed with them, and at the selfsame tide.
And therefore, lovely Pertelote so dear,
By such examples mayest thou learn and fear
Lest any man should be so wildly reckless
To ignore dreams, for I say to thee, doubtless,
That many a dream is mighty cause for dread.

    .   .   .   .

  "And furthermore, I would have you look well
In the old testament, of Daniel,
If he held dreams as only vanity.
Read too of Joseph, and there shall ye see
How dreams are sometimes (I do not say all)
Warnings of things that shall sometime befall.
Look on the King of Egypt, my lord Pharaoh,

His baker and his cup bearer also,
How well they knew the consequence of dreams.
Whoso will search the acts of men, meseems
May read of dreaming many a wondrous thing.
    "Lo, mighty Croesus, who was Lydia's king,
Dreamt he not that he sat upon a tree,
Which signified that he should hanged be?
Lo here, Andromache, bold Hector's wife,
Upon that day that Hector lost his life,
She dreamt the night before,—she could not waken—
How that the life of Hector would be taken
If on that day he armed and went to fight.
She warned him, but he did not heed it right,
He went to battle, and in mortal strife
The great Achilles took from him his life.
But this history is all too long to tell,
Also, it is near day—I may not dwell
Longer on it—in short, to make an end,
I say I know this dream can but portend
Adversity, and I say furthermore
That I do set by laxatives no store,
For they are poisonous, I know it well.
I won't take them; the devil can, in hell.
    "Now let us speak of mirth, and end all this,
For Madame Pertelote, as I know bliss,
Of one thing God has sent me greatest grace;
For when I see the beauty of your face,
You are so scarlet-red about your eye,
It causeth all my mortal fear to die;
For also, surely, as *In principio*
Mulier est hominis confusio;
Madame, the meaning of this Latin is—
Woman is all man's joy and all his bliss.
For when I feel at night your soft, smooth side,
Albeit that I may not on you ride
Because our perch is made so small, alas,
I am so full of joy and of solace
That I defy both prophecy and dream."

And with that word he flew down from the beam,
For it was day, and all his hens flew down,
And with a chuck, he called them all around,
For he had found a kernel in the yard.
Royal he was, he was no more afraid,
He feathered Pertelote a score of times,
And trod as oft, ere that the bell told primes.
He looked as though he were a lion brown,
And on his toes he pranced up and down,
He would not deign to set his feet to ground.
He cockaroo'd when he a kernel found,
And to him ran his ladies, one and all.
Thus royal, as a prince is in his hall
I leave this Chanticleer in his good pasture,
And later I will tell you his adventure.

    When that the month in which the world began,
That is called March, when Our Lord first made man,
When March was passed, and thirty day beside,
It happed that Chanticleer in all his pride,
His seven spouses walking by his side,
Cast up his eyes unto the great, bright sun
That in the sign of Taurus had already run
Twenty degrees and one—and somewhat more,
And knew by instinct—by no other lore—
That it was prime, and crew with blissful cry.
"The sun," he said, "has climbed the eastern sky
Forty degrees and one, and more, y-wis.
Dame Pertelote, who are my worldly bliss,
Hearken these blissful birds; hark how they sing.
And see the fresh, gay flowers, how they spring.
Full is my heart of joy and revelling."
But suddenly there came a woeful thing,
For ever the latter end of joy is woe.
God knows that worldly joy doth swiftly go;
And if a rhetorician could fair write,
He in a chronicle might safe indite
This fact, for sovereign notability.

    Now every wise man, let him hark to me,

This story is as true, I undertake,
As is the tale of Launcelot of the Lake,
That women hold in such great reverence.
—Now will I turn again to my last sentence.
   A pied fox, full of sly iniquity
That in the grove had lived out summers three,
Let high imagination provoke
His soul, that night, and through the hedges broke
Into the yard, where Chanticleer the fair
Was wont, and eke his damsels to repair;
And in a bed of wortweed still he lay,
Till there had passed a few hours of the day,
Biding his time on Chanticleer to fall,
As gladly do these homicides—yes, all
That patience have to wait and murder men.
Oh false murderer, lurking in thy den,
Oh new Iscariot, new Ganilon!
Oh false dissembling one, oh Greek Simon
Who brought tall Troy so utterly to sorrow!
Oh Chanticleer, accursed be that morrow
When thou into the yard flew from thy beams.
For thou wast warned, and fully, in thy dreams,
That such a day was perilous to thee.
 But that thing God forsees must surely be,
According to the doctrine of some scholars.
Be witness also, any accomplished scholar,
That in the schools is great altercation
In this matter, unusual disputation,
Which hath involved a hundred thousand men.
But I cannot set forth the case again
As can the holy doctor Augustine,
Or Boethius, or Bishop Bradwardine,
Whether our God's most holy foreknowing
Forceth me by fate to do a thing,
(By fate I mean just plain necessity)
Or else, if free will may be granted me
To do that same thing, or to do it not,
Though God foreknows it, ere it shall be wrought;

Or if His knowing constrains not at all
But by necessity conditional.
I will not try to make these matters clear,
My tale is of a cock, as ye may hear,
That took his council of his wife, oh sorrow,
To walk forth in the yard, upon that morrow
That he had dreamed the dream which you have heard.
I'd take no dame's cold council, by my word.
Women's advice brought mankind first to woe!
And made our father Adam, exiled, go
From Paradise, where he was full at ease.
But since I know not whom I may displease
If I th'advice of women folk should blame,
Pass over it, I speak but as a game,
  .   .   .   .   .   .

These are the rooster's words, and never mine
I can no harm in women folk divine.
    Fair in the sun, to bathe her merrily
Lieth Pertelote, and all her sisters she
Has by her side. And Chanticleer so free
Sang merrier than a mermaid in the sea,
For *Physiologus* sayeth truthfully
How that mermaids sing well and merrily.
And it befell that as he cast his eye
Among the wortweeds, at a butterfly,
He was aware of this fox crouching low.
No thing caused our cock then to wish to crow,
But he cried out, "Cok, cok," and up he started
As one that is afraid and panic hearted.
Instinctively a beast desires to flee
His natural enemy, if he should see
The beast, though never before he'd seen it with his eye.
    This Chanticleer, when he did him espy,
He would have fled, but that the fox anon
Said, "Gentle sir, alas, where have you gone?
Be ye afraid of me, that am your friend?
Now certes, I am worse than were a fiend
If I to you wished harm and villany.

I am not come upon your home to spy,
But truthfully, the reason I came here
Was but to hear you sing, brave Chanticleer.
For by my faith, you sing more merrily
Than any angel in God's choristery;
Therewith, you have in music more feeling
Than had Boethius, or any that can sing.
My lord your father (God his good soul bless!)
And your fair mother, of her gentleness,
Honoured my house with visits, to my ease,
And surely, sir, full fain would I you please,
For as men speak of singing, without disguise
I'd say, so might I have the use of my two eyes,
Save you, I never heard a singer sing
As did your father, at the break of morning.
Truly, 'twas from his heart, all of his song,
And for to make his singing the more strong
He would so take pains, that with both his eyes
He had to wink, so loud he raised his cries,
And stood upon his toes—melodious din,
And stretchèd forth his neck so long and thin.
And also, he was of such discretion
There was no one in any region
Your sire in song or wisdom might surpass.
Indeed, I've read in Sir Burnel the Ass,
Among his verses, that there was a cock,
Because a priest's son gave him once a knock
Upon his leg, when he was young and weak,
He made him lose his benefice, and seek
Another. There is no comparison
Between the wisdom and discretion
Of your own father, and his subtlety.
Now sing out, sir, for fair Saint Charity,
Let's see: can you your father imitate?"
    Chanticleer beat his wings, he did not wait.
No thought of Reynard's treasonous will had he,
He was so ravished by his flattery.
    This Chanticleer stood high upon his toes,

Stretching his neck, and held his two eyes closed,
And started crowing loudly, the poor dunce,
And Lord Reynard, the fox, arose at once
And caught brave Chanticleer by his bright throat
And bore him to the woods, oh sorry note!
For there was yet no man that him pursued.
Oh destiny that may not be eschewed!
Alas, that Chanticleer flew from the beams!
Alas, his wife, who reckoned not of dreams!
And on a Friday all this mischief fell.
Oh Venus, who art pleasure's queen, as well
As beauty's, since thy slave was Chanticleer,
And in thy service did more than his peer,
More for delight than world to multiply,
Why wouldst thou suffer him this day to die?
Oh Gaufred, dear master, in thy pain,
When that thy worthy king, Richard, was slain
With bolt, complained his death so sore,
Why have I not thine eloquence and lore,
That Friday for to chide, as well did ye?
(For on a Friday truly slain was he.)
Then would I show you how I could complain
For Chanticleer, his terror and his pain.

   Surely, no such cry or lamentation
Was ever heard from ladies, when great Ilium
Was won, and Pyrrhus with his bare sword,
When he had caught King Priam by the beard
And slain him (as tells us the Aeneid)
As shrieked out all the chickens in that yard,
When they had seen poor Chanticleer, his beak
Upon the fox's back. Fair Pertelote, her shriek
Was louder and more sovereign than the wife
Of Hasdrubal, when that lord lost his life
And Roman arms laid mighty Carthage low.
She was so full of anger and of woe
That willfully she leapt into the fire
And, steadfast heart, died at her city's pyre.
Oh, woeful hens, even so cried ye
As when foul Nero burnt up the city

Of Rome, lamented all the senator's wives
Because their noble lords had lost their lives;
Guiltless as lambs, this Nero had them slain.
Now will I turn me to my tale again.

    This good widow and her daughters, too,
Heard the hens cry out "Alas," and knew
Something amiss, and out of doors they darted
And saw the fox, who toward the grove had started,
Upon his back bearing the cock away;
They cried, "Out! harrow!" then, and "wellaway!"
"Ha, ha the fox!" and after him they ran,
And eke with staves ran many another man.
Colly our dog ran, Talbot and Gerland
And Malkin with a distaff in her hand;
The cow and calf ran, even the very hogs,
Crazed as they were by barking of the dogs
And shouting of the men, and women's cry;
They ran so hard they thought that they would die.
They yelled as fiends yell in the midst of hell;
The ducks cried as though men were out to kill them;
The geese for fear flew out over the trees;
Out of the hive up buzzed a swarm of bees;
So hideous was the noise, a! ben'cite!
Surely Jack Straw and all of his army
Made no such noise, nor any half so shrill,
When they were chasing Flanders men to kill,
As on that day was made, chasing the fox.
They brought out horns of brass and horns of box,
Of horn, of bone, in which they blew and pooped,
And therewithal they shriekèd and they whooped.
It seemed as though the very heavens would fall.
Now good my friends, I pray you hearken all.

    Lo, how fortune turneth suddenly
The hope and pride of even an enemy!
This cock, that lay upon the fox's back,
In all his fear, unto the fox he spake
And said, "Sir, if I were as ye
Then should I say, (as God gives aid to me)
Turn ye again, turn, ye proud peasants all.

A very pestilence upon ye fall.
Now am I come unto this deep wood's side,
Will ye or not, the cock shall here abide;
I will eat him, by my tail, and that anon."
The fox replied, "In faith, it shall be done."
And as he spake the word, no sooner said,
The cock flew from his mouth, deliverèd,
And high upon a tree he flew anon.
And when Sir Reynard saw that he was gone,
"Alas, Oh Chanticleer, alas!" quoth he,
"I fear that I have done you injury!
I frightened you by seizing you so hard
And rushing with you hither from your yard;
But, sir, I did it with no ill intent.
Come down, and I will tell you what I meant.
I will tell you the truth, upon mine oath."
    "Nay then," quoth cock, "I call shame on us both,
And first I scorn myself, both blood and bones,
If thou beguile me oftener than once.
Thou shalt not flatter me—I have grown wise.
I will not sing, and singing shut my eyes.
For he that winketh when he needs to see,
All wilfully, God free him ne'er from thee."
    "Nay," quoth the fox, "but God give him mischance
That is so indiscrete of governance
That jangleth when he should be like the grave."
    Lo, such it is to be reckless—not brave,
And negligent and trust in flattery.
But ye who hold this tale to be but folly,
As of a fox, or of a cock and hen,
Take to yourselves the moral, my good men.
For St. Paul saith that all that written is,
For our improvement it is writ, y-wis.
Take ye the fruit, and let the chaff blow past.
And now, good God, if such thou wilt at last,
As saith our Lord, so make us all good men;
And bring us to His highest bliss.   Amen.
                           Modern English version by E. L. M.

Hey Diddle, Diddle, the Cat

by EDEN PHILLPOTTS

*How a warm-hearted old man learned to love a cat,
and how he outwitted the man who tried to outwit
him forms as amusing and heart-warming a tale as any
I know.*

WHEN you be done larning, you might so well stop living,
and for my part, though I'm sixty-five, I thank God as I
can still gather useful knowledge when it comes my way.

For example, but four years ago, I had my eyes opened about a
matter on which I'd thought wrong for more than half a century.
I never could understand man or woman who loved a beast; and
when I see an old maid dote on her cat, or an old bachelor share
the best off his own plate with his dog, I scorned 'em. And when the
creatures came to a bad end, as pets so often will, and their owners
weren't above shedding a tear for 'em, I said, in my ignorance, they
did ought to be ashamed, and called 'em weak-minded zanies to let
a dumb animal reign over 'em in such a fashion. But I don't put on
no airs and graces now when I see anybody fretting for a sick or
dead creature; because I be in the same boat myself.

As a widow man and pretty well-to-do, I be one of them that
count at Ponsworthy, and have always tried to keep up the dignity
of the village and be a good neighbor and help on the welfare of us
all in my small way. And being addicted to childer, though never
blessed or cursed with none, I made friends with the young things
and stood well in their opinion.

So it came about that, as I minded their birthdays pretty often, a
sharp little maid axed me when mine might be; and I told her, doubting not that she'd forget again. Daisy Bird she was called, the young-

est daughter of my particular friend, Martin Bird, of the all-sorts shop.

Well, Daisy remembered, and on my birthday she brought me a kitten just old enough to leave his mother. 'Twas a cat of a well-known mother, but the father was wrapped in mystery, as fathers too often are. The kitling weren't nothing to praise, nor yet to blame—just a very every day young cat, with a piebald face and a bit of yellow and black dabbed about over a white ground. His eyes were doubtful and Daisy promised me as they'd turn a nice green when he'd growed a bit, same as his mother's; and if you'd look my gift-cat in the mouth, you'd have seen 'twas pink as a rose, with just the beginning of small, pearly teeth coming. No tail to name; but there again Daisy came to the rescue and solemnly vowed that he had the promise of a very fine tail, if I'd only be patient about it.

'Twas to be called "Sunny Jim," and she much hoped I'd take to it and be a kind friend to it; and if I did not, it had got to be drowned.

I paused at that, for I had meant to beg Daisy to carry it home and let me take the kind will for the deed. But when I see the little thing so trustful and so wishful to please, and so well satisfied with me from the first; and when I understood it was a choice between life along with me and death in the river, I hesitated. Daisy picked him up and put him in my hand; and if he'd shown any sauce, or turned against me, it would have been "good-by." But he knew 'twas touch and go; and whenever does a cat do a thing that makes against its own prosperity? He looked up in my face and purred, with the little gruff purr as young cats have, and rubbed his small carcass against my waistcoat, as if he'd found the very person he was wanting. So there it stood; I kept him, and let him have his run and his fill, and watched him grow into a very ugly cat in other eyes, but not ugly to me—never to me.

I always says that it's a beautiful thing to see the contentment of animals. No doubt it only happens because they've got no wits and no power to compare their lot with any other; but whatever it be —horse or donkey, dog or cat, only let him know he's welcome and have got a man or woman friend, and he'll cleave to the lowliest lot and be just so cheerful and good-natured and faithful along with a tinker as a king. They'll fit in, make themselves part of the home, feel 'tis the one place in the world that matters, however poor and humble, and go about the troublesome business of being alive, with such pluck and patience and good appetite that they be often a lesson to us grumbling, grizzling humans.

No dog or cat will ever look on the dark side of things. Nature have made 'em hopeful. They be quick to scent pleasure, and though there's a good and bad among 'em and some more easily cast down than others, they be prone to welcome life and give of their best in exchange for small mercies.

My Sunny Jim was a very well-named cat. He had what you might call a reasonable mind, and if he'd lacked the many virtues that came out in him, still I'd have been bound in common justice to rate him as a very worthy chap—along of his amazing affection for me. He seemed to know from the first as I had no use for domestic animals, and he said to himself: "Then I'll break you in and make you properly mad about me and conquer your hard heart."

He went about it very cunning, too. He knew I was a terrible clean old man and liked my house to be so spick and span as myself; and so he began by showing me what cleanliness really was; and a more fussy cat from his youth up I have never met. His father must have been a gentleman for sartain. You felt the cat had good blood in him, he was so nice. Never a hair out of place you might say, and he'd lick himself and wash his chops sometimes after a sup and bite till I'd shout at him to let be. Mud was his abomination, and if he come in with a speck on his pads, he'd bite and fidget, as if he was pulling off a pair of gloves; and he never thanked me more grateful nor purred louder than when I gave him his brush and comb. But to tell truth, I humored him in that matter, and finding what a godsend it was to him to have a rub from time to time, I met him there and kept an old brush a' purpose.

At six months I knew he'd got me, and I was a lot too fond of the cat; and on his birthday, which Daisy Bird remembered, us gave Sunny Jim a party, and Daisy and half a score of childer agreed to come. 'Twas a great success. Us provided him with three sardines and a drop of cream, and long after the party was over and the childer gone, he sat polishing up. Then, when he felt perfection inside and out, he just give a sigh of satisfaction and tucked in his paws and sat quite silent thinking over the day's fine doing.

As for mice, he was a very fine performer, but my house never had no mice in it as he soon found, so he went down three doors to Mrs. Wilkinson's, where there were scores of dozens, and he never drawed a blank there. Not that he'd often eat a mouse; but he was a mighty hunter of 'em—a proper mouse-tiger, you might say —though not much a one for birds. He seldom went afield and never laid a paw to fur or feathers, like many a hard-bitten poacher of a cat, as makes a shameful end soon or late on gamekeeper's gallows.

He slept along with me, at my bed-foot, and I'd trained him to come in for his supper an hour or so after dark. But he liked the evening hour and the moth time. Then he'd sit on the party wall and take the air, or join a cat chorus perhaps, but all like a gentleman; and he never went too far, or done anything to be ashamed of. A wife or two he may have had, but all well within honor; and he wouldn't fight nor nothing like that, for the good reason that he weighed about five pounds heavier than any cat at Ponsworthy, and no other tom in his right senses would have took him on for a moment.

He supped with me, and by ten o'clock we was both to bed. Then when he was stretched at my feet and the candle out, I'd bid him say his prayers, and he'd purr gentle and steady; and for a good few years the last sound I have heard, as I closed my eyes, was Sunny Jim saying his prayers.

Mrs. Wilkinson warned me, strangely enough, just a week afore the crash came.

"You be putting that tortoiseshell tom afore your God, Peter Blount," she said to me, "and 'tis terrible dangerous, for the Almighty's jealous as the grave, and you may get a nasty awakener."

A proper prophet the woman was, for seven nights later, just afore the hour when the cat was due—a moony night in autumn, bright and peaceful, with the owls calling each other in Western Wood—I heard a harsh, sharp sound which I knowed for a heavy air-gun; and not liking it none too well at that late hour, I went in my garden instanter to call Sunny Jim.

The back side of my house gave on waste land that ran up to furze brakes, and I was going to give a look over the wall and see who it might be prowling round, when my cat crawled up to me on three legs. I picked him up and took him in to the lamp; and then I found as he'd got his shoulder all smashed by a bullet.

I kept my head and ministered to the poor soul, and he fixed his eyes upon me and seemed to ask if it was to be a fatal matter. For a time I thought he was sinking, for he lay cruel still with his eyes shut, breathing hard; but then, seeing he weren't in no immediate danger of death, I offered him water, which he lapped, and after that I picked him up so tender as I might, put him in a big vegetable basket, with a bit of blanket in the bottom, and carried him over to see Billy Blades.

Bill weren't a man I liked, being a doubtful customer in many ways, and said to have shortened his wife's life by unkindness; but he was a very clever vet and properly renowned for his knowledge of four-footed creatures. He was a great dog-fancier without a doubt, and though 'twas whispered he fancied other people's dogs a thought too often, yet the skill was there; so I took Sunny Jim to see the man, and he was home by good luck and gave me all his attention. The cat knew perfectly well what his doctor was up to and behaved like a Christian under the search.

"His shoulder blade be smashed to pieces," said Billy, "and if the ball had took him an inch lower, it would have gone through the creature and slain him. The man who done this made a bad shot, I reckon, and when he found he'd only winged the cat, he ran for it, knowing the creature would have strength to get home and give the show away."

"But why should any mortal man want for to kill my cat?" I asked.

"For his skin," explained Billy Blades. "Cat and coney be worth money nowadays. A skin like this here will dye black and be worth fifteen shillings, or a pound, to any man; and that's why a good few cats have failed to come home lately. But I bain't going to say he won't live. I think he may. He's in good health and in his prime by the look of him, and he's got a patient sort of nature. You see how he bears up. If all goes well and there's no fatal poison in the wound, he'll very likely make a good recovery. Us can't tell yet; but if, as may happen, the wound gets ugly in a few days, then I'll give him a whiff of chloroform and see into the evil and find if the bullet's there."

"I can take hope then?" I asked.

"You can," he said, "but not too much. He's hard hit."

So all was dreadful suspense, and nought could be done for a time till the extent of the danger showed.

I took Sunny Jim home, and, to my great thanksgiving he ate a bit of raw mutton, as I cut off a leg and minced for him. Not much, but enough to keep up his strength; and he got a little sleep also off and on, though I did not; and in the morning, I carried him down, and he just lay, patient and resigned, on his little mat by the kitchen fire, while I swallowed my breakfast.

But my rage knew no bounds, and if I could have catched the anointed devil as done it, I'd have choked his breath out of him between my hands. I never did feel so properly hard to any fellow-creature before; and to this day when I see the vision of thicky cat crawling home on three legs, with the moonlight on his poor, terrified eyes, I feel a thrill of hate and passion.

Next morning it was round the village like a flame of fire that Sunny Jim had been shot and might die of it, and a proper rally of neighbors—women, children, and men—streamed along to see him and say how cruel vexed they was on my account, and to hope that Sunny Jim might be spared. 'Twas the general opinion that no neighbor could have sunk to such a crime, for none was known to bear me a grudge, nor yet him.

Billy Blades came morning and evening to view the patient. And then he gave me a ray of hope, for, in a week, he believed the wound was clean and wouldn't get no worse. In fact, it began to heal very nice outside, and now the danger was whether Sunny Jim's sinews would join up too, or whether they would not. And much depended upon that. He couldn't put his paw down yet, of course, but Job never beat him for patience. He didn't like me out of his sight, however, and wouldn't let down his victuals for anybody but me.

And then in my wrath I issued an advertisement, for I was death on bringing the sinner to justice and felt if a man had done the crime he must be had up and disgraced afore the magistrates; while if it was only a wicked, hard-hearted boy, then the least they could do to him, for his own salvation and my satisfaction, would be a damned good hiding.

And I wrote with my own hand six advertisements offering £5 reward for the name of the man, or boy, as had shot my famous cat. One I stuck on my front gate, one on the guide post at the cross roads outside the Ponsworthy, one in Martin Bird's shop window, one in the post office, one by the uppingstock, outside "The Green Man" public house, and the other in the bar of the same.

People marveled at the sight of such big money, and they said, behind my back, as I must be a millionaire, or else going weak in my head; but it was a fortnight afore any response reached me, and then I had the surprise of my life on hearing the sinner's name.

I learnt it of a Friday, when Billy Blades dropped in for a look at Sunny Jim, and he said he was very pleased indeed with the cat's progress, and now felt it was safe to assure me he'd made a recovery and was out of danger.

"The ligaments be joined up beautiful," said Billy, "and the bone have growed together. You see how he can use his leg and trust it again; and he could trust it more than he do, only he's nervous yet. But, though he may go a thought lame for life, it will be nothing to interfere with his pleasure. And in time even the lameness may wear off altogether, when the muscles and sinews get used to the change."

Then I thanked Blades with all my heart and shook his hand and told him I thought he was a very clever man and must send in his account.

"And now 'tis all over," he said, "I'll tell you another thing about this here cat, and that's the name of the party as tried to shoot him and failed."

"You know!" I cried out. "Then I thank Providence, Billy; and never shall I part from a five-pound note with better will."

"No, you won't," he answered. "You'll hate to part, Peter; but life's life and cats are cats, and a fiver is a fiver, so just you keep your nerve and take it as it comes. I shot your cat. I was poking about in the furzes with a new air-gun, and seeing the beggar airing himself, I thought a quid for his skin was worth while, me being harder up than usual. So I fired to drop him, but he moved and so was saved

alive. Then he was gone like a streak; and so was I, because I knowed
you'd fetch him along to me so soon as you could, if he weren't done
for. But I'm right down glad to have saved him and be nearly so fond
of the chap now as you are yourself."

"You God-forgotten villain!" I cried to the wretch, trembling
white with rage.

"I know," he answered. "That's all right, and you can lay it on
so thick as you please and cuss till you're winded. But you understand the situation, don't you? You summons me, and I get a dressing down and a caution and a fine. And the fine will be ten shillings
and sixpence; and time don't stand still and the matter will soon be
forgot; and I get your five pounds."

"Hookem snivey beast!" I said to him. "That ban't all, I promise
you! My five pound you may have; but I'll ruin your business and
set every honest man and woman against you, and hound you out of
Ponsworthy. By God's light I will!"

He laughed his hateful, coarse laugh, and his sharp nose grew
sharper than ever.

"You do your worstest and welcome, Peter Blount," he said. "I
ban't much afraid. There ain't no other vet within ten miles that I
know about, and the farmers don't care how wicked a man may be,
so long as he knows how to cure their things. So you give me my
fiver, and then have me up for trying to shoot your cat. And always
remember that I'm terrible glad I missed his vitals—though how I
failed I can't guess, for 'twas bright moonlight and I was as sober as
I am now."

I blazed up at that and ordered him out of my house, and he went;
and I bided awake three parts of the night thinking on the awful
ways of human nature and the hateful surprises that may be hid in
your next-door neighbor and familiar friend. In fact I cussed Billy to
hell and raged against him something furious; and first thing next
morning I went up to Martin Bird and catched him taking down his
shutters, and told him the monstrous tale.

It interested him a lot, and he seemed to think it funny in a way,
though for my part I didn't see nothing funny to it.

"To give the traitor as shot Sunny Jim four pound, ten shilling
for his trouble, be a bit of a joke sure enough," said Martin Bird.
"Of course, you'll have the satisfaction of getting him up afore the

justices and turning public opinion against him; but after all, as he
very truly said, a cat's only a cat—masterpiece though your cat is
known to be—and the law must hold an even balance between man
and man; and when you think of the dark crimes that human nature
will do at a pinch, the law have to keep a bit up its sleeve for the
murderers and such like. And so, no doubt, ten and six for a cat be
about the justice of it."

"I don't want no vengeance like that," I told Martin. "We all know
vengeance be the Lord's; and to speak plain, I'm a lot more set now
on keeping my five-pound note than on having that beastly toad
afore the beaks. It ain't the money, but the shame; for he'll have the
laugh against me to my dying day if he gets the cash."

"He will," admitted Martin. "Billy Blades is an artful item best
of times, and it would hit him much harder to withhold your money
than have him up."

"But how can it be done in honesty?" I asked. "There it is in plain
black and white. I offer five pounds to know who shot my cat; and
he told me."

Martin Bird said it was a very pretty problem, but he didn't give
up all hope of solving it. He was a clever man, as them with a barrow-
load of children must be, if they want to keep their young and themselves out of the workhouse, and he promised me he'd look in during
the evening if any light struck upon the subject.

"Anyway, 'tis Saturday, and you can well leave his claim unsettled
till you decide whether to summon him," said Bird to me.

So I went home to Sunny Jim, and couldn't help feeling that anything less than the law against Billy would be treachery to my cat.
And yet again, there was no doubt that Billy had been wondrous
clever with the animal, and so healed his shoulder that he was to have
the blessing of his leg. For what be the fulness of life to a cat on three
legs? Bill had, in fact, made good his own evil work in a manner of
speaking, and I was abound to admit that, once the cat was in his
hands, he might have finished the murder, and I shouldn't have been
none the wiser.

I couldn't see my duty all day, and the more I thought on Billy
Blades the more I detested him, for he'd played a devilish part, and
not been ashamed to confess it for blood money. So, when Martin

strolled in, after he'd shut up his shop, and asked for a spot of whisky, I weren't no forwarder than in the morn. But, if anything I hated worse than ever the thought of handing my five pounds to the assassin.

Martin stroked Sunny Jim for a bit and watched him walk, and said that by the look of it he was making a very brave recovery.

"The bone be joined up and the sinews going on fine," I told Bird, "and I shall leave him to nature now, for I won't have that cat-murderer in my house no more."

"Well," answered Martin, "I believe I see the way out for you. It come to me, like the Light to Paul while I was cutting off a pound of bacon. If you want to diddle Billy Blades, it can be done, and you've only got to say the word."

"I do," I said. "I never felt to want nothing so much."

"Right," he answered. "Say no more, Peter, but just go about your business and leave the rest to me."

'Twas a very puzzling direction, and I asked Martin to speak a thought plainer; but he refused.

"See what happens o' Monday morning," was all he would answer. And so, full of wonder and quite in the dark, I had to leave it at that.

Then Bird went his way after a lot of whisky, but he explained that I needn't grudge it, because he was going to take a tidy bit of trouble on my account. And when he was gone, me and Sunny Jim toddled off to bed. He couldn't quite get upstairs yet, so I had to carry him; and I reckoned that the poor hero had lost about three of his nine lives by this fearful adventure.

Nought happened Sunday, though, as I found afterward, Martin had been so busy as a bee on my account; and when Monday came, afore I'd done my breakfast, and while the cat was washing his face after his, the mystery began to unfold. But when I say "washing his face" I must tell you that Sunny Jim could only polish up one side as yet, for his right front paw couldn't work to perfection so far; and 'twas among his greatest griefs, while he was recovering, that the right side of his head and his right whisker and right ear had to go untended. I done what I could, but nought to satisfy him.

Then who should come in but Andy White, the waterkeeper, a very knowledgeable man with the rare gift to see in the dark.

"Well, White," I axed, "and what might you want?"

"Five pounds," he said. "I know who 'twas tried to slay your cat."

I leapt out of my chair as if I was sitting on fire.

"Guy Fawkes and angels!" I cried. "D'you tell me you done it, Andy?"

"Me done it!" he said. "No, Peter Blount, I ban't a cat shooter as ever I heard tell about. And I'm sorry you think I'd so demean myself. 'Twas Neddy Tutt, that young rip from Falcon Farm. He's got an air-gun and the deed was his."

Well, for the life of me I couldn't see even yet what was afoot, and after Andy had said he'd be round with proofs for his money a bit later and had gone to work, I sat marveling at his news.

And then, just as Mrs. Bassett come in to tidy up for me and see after one thing and another, which she performed regular for half a crown a week, who should knock at the door but Willie Stockman, the shoesmith.

"Hullo, Willie, and what can I do for you?" I asked the young man. He was rather a favorite of mine, for he had a kind heart and kept his widowed mother.

"Ban't what you can do for me, master, but what I can do for you," he answered. "Come in the garden and I'll tell you something you be wishful to know."

So I stepped out, and Sunny Jim, he stepped out with me. You'd have thought the blessed cat was in the know, for he sat and looked at Willie without winking while he spoke.

" 'Tis no less a job than the business of this poor creature," said Stockman. "I happened to be going home in the moonlight with my young woman, and just as us came through the furze brakes up over, I marked a chap with a gun. He lifted it and let fly, and then he was sloking off, and he came full upon us, Peter, and gave us 'Good night.' And 'twas that poaching rascal, Timothy Bamsey, from Lower Town. So now you know what you want to know. And I may say your five pounds be going to push on our wedding. There's no hurry, however, till you've got the proofs of the crime."

Of course, I thanked him very grateful; and when he was gone I beginned slow and sure to see the terrible cunning of Martin Bird. In fact, I'd never have given the man credit for such amazing stratagems; and even that weren't all, for an hour later, as I was digging a

few potatoes in the sun, and the cat was practising his game leg
gentle, and seeing if he could clean his claws on the stem of my lilac
bush according to his daily use, if Timothy Bamsey himself didn't
heave up the road! A hugeous young man—six foot three inches of
wickedness, by all accounts. I knew him by sight, no more, and I
also knew he'd only escaped clink by the skin of his teeth after a
row over the pheasants down to Squire Mannering's preserve. But
there he was, and he stopped at the gate and asked in a big voice if I
could tell him where I lived.

"Do 'e know the man round about here what had his cat shot
long ago?" says Timothy Bamsey to me, and I left my fork sticking
in the ground and went down to him.

"I'm the man," I said, "and what about it?" For I felt sure he was
come to own the felony and claim the fiver, same as Billy Blades
had done. I felt fierce, I admit, for I was getting in a miz-maze along
of all this plotting. I'd almost forgot Billy, and for the moment I
felt as if I stood face to face with the real, living villain at last.

But he soon undeceived me.

"Well, I know who shot your cat, Master. By chance I was going
home along behind these here houses on the right, and just as I
came down, I see a man in the moonlight lift a gun and fire—an air-
gun it was, for there weren't no explosion, but just a whiss and a
jolt, like what air-guns make. Then he runned forward to take up
his prey; but he found nought. He cussed something terrible, and
was just making off, when he very near ran into me and tried to hide
his face. But I see him so plain as I see you this minute."

"And who was the man, Timothy Bamsey?" I asked, so stern as
I could.

"Willie Stockman, the shoesmith," he answered. "There ain't
no manner of doubt about it, I assure you. And I'll have my fiver, if
it's all one, Mr. Blount."

Well, my head was spinning now till I thought it would roll off
in the road.

"Us'll talk about this another time," I said to the man. "There's
a mystery here, and I must seek my friends afore I do ought in such
a dark matter. I'm very much obliged to you, and you'll hear of me

again presently; but I don't part with no five-pound notes for the
minute, for it begins to look as if I should have to summon half the
parish afore I get to the bitter truth."

"I've told 'e the truth," he says, "and you owe me five pounds."

"I may, or I may not; but be sure justice shall be done," I said.
And with that he went off, leaving me in a proper confusion of
brain till the evening come. Then Martin Bird dropped in to hear
the result of his work. And when he did hear it he was terrible
pleased.

"Now," he said, "you stand in a firm position, for here be a cloud
of witnesses, Peter, and one man's word is as good as another's, and
better for that matter. Because everybody knows Billy Blades is a
liar, and nobody would take his word against t'others. So all you
need to say is that you don't know who the deuce to believe among
'em, which is true. And then you keep your money in your pocket!"

"A masterpiece of politics, Martin!" I said. "And gratefully I
thank you for it, but while Sunny Jim's living, it's always in the
power of a wicked man to have the last word and lay him out.
Don't you forget that."

"I haven't," answered Bird, who fairly staggered me with his
wondrous brain power. "I haven't overlooked the future, and what
I advise you to do be this, Peter: Ax the whole crew of 'em in to
supper one night, and give 'em a tidy feed and a bit of baccy to
each, and a bottle of whisky also. Do 'em a treat; then they'll all
be your friends for life."

"And Blades also?" I asked.

"Certainly Blades. He's the one that matters most. 'Cause we know
he done it in reality. Then, when they be got together and their
bellies filled and their pipes drawing suent and their glasses topped
up, you can tell 'em, amiable like, that they be a pack of bare-faced
liars, and you find such a lot of men shot your cat that you ain't
going to make no distinctions, but trust to the goodwill and gentlemanly feeling of 'em all never to do it no more. It will run you in a
pound or so, but you're a snug man and won't be none the worse."

"You've took the lead in this matter," I said, "and I'll go through
with it according as you direct. All I ask is that you come to the
feed with the rest."

Which Martin Bird did do; and, God's my Judge, I never want

to spend a pleasanter evening. They all obeyed my invite; and they all laughed fit to die when I told 'em they was a set of low-down, lying blackguards; and Billy Blades had to be seen home after, for he was blind afore the finish, singing shameful songs, as be long gone out of print, thank the watching Lord.

Sunny Jim, he much enjoyed his evening, also, and got nothing but kind words. And rabbit pie being very near his favorite food, he done himself so well as any of us. But the merriment tired him, and you can't blame the dear chap for not seeing the joke quite so clear as Billy and Timothy and Martin and Andy and Neddy and Willie saw it.

'Twas a good night, however, and me and Sunny Jim felt very glad to get to bed when the boys had gone.

And this I can say: no hand was ever lifted to my cat again. He walked on his way rejoicing, and though I ban't going to pretend he was ever quite the same light-hearted high-spirited party as of old, yet his higher qualities still shine out of him; and he's all the world to me.

Billy Blades was round only a night ago, and he thought as Sunny Jim ought to live a good five year yet. So I be contented in my mind about him; and while there's a purr left in him, I shall be his very willing servant and faithful friend.

But never again! Life be a cloudy and difficult business enough at best without mixing yourself up with the dumb things and letting a creature without a soul into your heart. I won't love nought on four feet no more. They get too terrible a grip upon your vitals —specially if you're a lonely old blid, without much else to set store by, same as me.

The Black Cat

by EDGAR ALLAN POE

Poe's classic tale of cruelty and horror cannot be omitted from any anthology of animal stories.

FOR the most wild, yet most homely narrative which I am about to pen, I neither expect nor solicit belief. Mad indeed would I be to expect it in a case where my very senses reject their own evidence. Yet mad am I not—and very surely do I not dream. But to-morrow I die, and to-day I would unburthen my soul. My immediate purpose is to place before the world plainly, succinctly, and without comment, a series of mere household events. In their consequences these events have terrified—have tortured—have destroyed me. Yet I will not attempt to expound them. To me they presented little but horror—to many they will seem less terrible than *baroques*. Hereafter, perhaps, some intellect may be found which will reduce my phantasm to the commonplace—some intellect more calm, more logical, and far less excitable than my own, which will perceive, in the circumstances I detail with awe, nothing more than an ordinary succession of very natural causes and effects.

From my infancy I was noted for the docility and humanity of my disposition. My tenderness of heart was even so conspicuous as to make me the jest of my companions. I was especially fond of animals, and was indulged by my parents with a great variety of pets. With these I spent most of my time, and never was so happy as when feeding and caressing them. This peculiarity of character grew with my growth, and in my manhood I derived from it one of my principal sources of pleasure. To those who have cherished an affection for a faithful and sagacious dog, I need hardly be at the trouble of explaining the nature or the intensity of the gratification thus derivable. There is something in the unselfish and self-sacrificing love of a brute which goes directly to the heart of him who has had frequent occasion to test the paltry friendship and gossamer fidelity of mere *Man*.

I married early, and was happy to find in my wife a disposition not uncongenial with my own. Observing my partiality for domestic pets, she lost no opportunity of procuring those of the most agreeable kind. We had birds, gold-fish, a fine dog, rabbits, a small monkey, and *a cat*.

This latter was a remarkably large and beautiful animal, entirely black, and sagacious to an astonishing degree. In speaking of his intelligence, my wife, who at heart was not a little tinctured with superstition, made frequent allusion to the ancient popular notion which regarded all black cats as witches in disguise. Not that she was ever *serious* upon this point, and I mention the matter at all for no better reason than that it happens just now to be remembered.

Pluto—this was the cat's name—was my favorite pet and playmate. I alone fed him, and he attended me wherever I went about the house. It was even with difficulty that I could prevent him from following me through the streets.

Our friendship lasted in this manner for several years, during which my general temperament and character—through the instrumentality of the Fiend Intemperance—had (I blush to confess it) experienced a radical alteration for the worse. I grew, day by day, more moody, more irritable, more regardless of the feelings of others. I suffered myself to use intemperate language to my wife. At length, I even offered her personal violence. My pets of course were made to feel the change in my disposition. I not only neglected but ill-used them. For Pluto, however, I still retained sufficient regard to restrain me from maltreating him, as I made no scruple of maltreating the rabbits, the monkey, or even the dog, when by accident, or through affection, they came in my way. But my disease grew upon me—for what disease is like Alcohol!—and at length even Pluto, who was now becoming old, and consequently somewhat peevish—even Pluto began to experience the effects of my ill-temper.

One night, returning home much intoxicated from one of my haunts about town, I fancied that the cat avoided my presence. I seized him, when, in his fright at my violence, he inflicted a slight wound upon my hand with his teeth. The fury of a demon instantly possessed me. I knew myself no longer. My original soul seemed at once to take its flight from my body, and a more than fiendish malevolence, gin-nurtured, thrilled every fiber of my frame. I took from my waistcoat-pocket a pen-knife, opened it, grasped the poor beast by the throat, and deliberately cut one of its eyes from the socket! I blush, I burn, I shudder, while I pen the damnable atrocity.

When reason returned with the morning—when I had slept off the fumes of the night's debauch—I experienced a sentiment half of horror, half of remorse, for the crime of which I had been guilty, but it was at best a feeble and equivocal feeling, and the soul remained untouched. I again plunged into excess, and soon drowned in wine all memory of the deed.

In the meantime the cat slowly recovered. The socket of the lost eye presented, it is true, a frightful appearance, but he no longer appeared to suffer any pain. He went about the house as usual, but, as might be expected, fled in extreme terror at my approach. I had so much of my old heart left as to be at first grieved by this evident dislike on the part of a creature which had once so loved me. But this feeling soon gave place to irritation. And then came, as if to my final and irrevocable overthrow, the spirit of PERVERSENESS. Of this spirit philosophy takes no account. Yet I am not more sure that my soul lives than I am that perverseness is one of the primitive impulses of the human heart—one of the indivisible primary faculties or sentiments which give direction to the character of Man. Who has not, a hundred times, found himself committing a vile or a silly action for no other reason than because he knows he should *not?* Have we not a perpetual inclination, in the teeth of our best judgment, to violate that which is *Law,* merely because we understand it to be such? This spirit of perverseness, I say, came to my final overthrow. It was this unfathomable longing of the soul *to vex itself* —to offer violence to its own nature—to do wrong for the wrong's sake only—that urged me to continue and finally to consummate the injury I had inflicted upon the unoffending brute. One morning, in cool blood, I slipped a noose about its neck and hung it to the limb of a tree; hung it with the tears streaming from my eyes, and with the bitterest remorse at my heart; hung it *because* I knew that it had loved me, and *because* I felt it had given me no reason of offense; hung it *because* I knew that in so doing I was committing a sin—a deadly sin that would so jeopardize my immortal soul as to place it, if such a thing were possible, even beyond the reach of the infinite mercy of the Most-Merciful and Most Terrible God.

On the night of the day on which this cruel deed was done, I was aroused from sleep by the cry of fire. The curtains of my bed were in flames. The whole house was blazing. It was with great difficulty that my wife, a servant, and myself, made our escape from the conflagration. The destruction was complete. My entire worldly wealth was swallowed up, and I resigned myself thenceforward to despair.

I am above the weakness of seeking to establish a sequence of cause and effect between the disaster and the atrocity. But I am detailing a chain of facts, and wish not to leave even a possible link imperfect. On the day succeeding the fire, I visited the ruins. The walls with one exception had fallen in. This exception was found in a compartment wall, not very thick, which stood about the middle of the house, and against which had rested the head of my bed. The plastering had here in great measure resisted the action of the fire, a fact which I attributed to its having been recently spread. About this wall a dense crowd were collected, and many persons seemed to be examining a particular portion of it with very minute and eager attention. The words "Strange!" "Singular!" and other similar expressions, excited my curiosity. I approached and saw, as if graven in *bas relief* upon the white surface the figure of a gigantic *cat*. The impression was given with an accuracy truly marvelous. There was a rope about the animal's neck.

When I first beheld this apparition—for I could scarcely regard it as less—my wonder and my terror were extreme. But at length reflection came to my aid. The cat, I remembered, had been hung in a garden adjacent to the house. Upon the alarm of fire this garden had been immediately filled by the crowd, by some one of whom the animal must have been cut from the tree and thrown through an open window into my chamber. This had probably been done with the view of arousing me from sleep. The falling of other walls had compressed the victim of my cruelty into the substance of the freshly-spread plaster; the lime of which, with the flames and the *ammonia* from the carcass, had then accomplished the portraiture as I saw it.

Although I thus readily accounted to my reason, if not altogether to my conscience, for the startling fact just detailed, it did not the less fail to make a deep impression upon my fancy. For months I could not rid myself of the phantasm of the cat, and during this period there came back into my spirit a half-sentiment that seemed, but was not, remorse. I went so far as to regret the loss of the animal, and to look about me among the vile haunts which I now habitually frequented for another pet of the same species, and of somewhat similar appearance, with which to supply its place.

One night, as I sat half-stupefied in a den of more than infamy, my attention was suddenly drawn to some black object, reposing upon the head of one of the immense hogsheads of gin or of rum, which constituted the chief furniture of the apartment. I had been looking steadily at the top of this hogshead for some minutes, and what now caused me surprise was the fact that I had not sooner perceived the object thereupon. I approached it, and touched it with my hand. It was a black cat—a very large one—fully as large as Pluto, and closely resembling him in every respect but one. Pluto had not a white hair upon any portion of his body; but this cat had a large, although indefinite splotch of white, covering nearly the whole region of the breast.

Upon my touching him he immediately arose, purred loudly, rubbed against my hand, and appeared delighted with my notice. This, then, was the very creature of which I was in search. I at once offered to purchase it of the landlord; but this person made no claim to it—knew nothing of it—had never seen it before.

I continued my caresses, and when I prepared to go home the animal evinced a disposition to accompany me. I permitted it to do so, occasionally stooping and patting it as I proceeded. When it reached the house it domesticated itself at once, and became immediately a great favorite with my wife.

For my own part, I soon found a dislike to it arising within me. This was just the reverse of what I had anticipated, but—I know not how or why it was—its evident fondness for myself rather disgusted and annoyed. By slow degrees these feelings of disgust and annoyance rose into the bitterness of hatred. I avoided the creature; a certain sense of shame, and the remembrance of my former deed of cruelty, preventing me from physically abusing it. I did not, for some weeks, strike or otherwise violently ill-use it, but gradually —very gradually—I came to look upon it with unutterable loathing, and to flee silently from its odious presence as from the breath of a pestilence.

What added, no doubt, to my hatred of the beast was the discovery, on the morning after I brought it home, that, like Pluto, it also had been deprived of one of its eyes. This circumstance, however, only endeared it to my wife, who, as I have already said, possessed in a high degree that humanity of feeling which had once been my distinguishing trait, and the source of many of my simplest and purest pleasures.

With my aversion to this cat, however, its partiality for myself seemed to increase. It followed my footsteps with a pertinacity which it would be difficult to make the reader comprehend. Whenever I sat, it would crouch beneath my chair or spring upon my knees, covering me with its loathsome caresses. If I arose to walk it would get between my feet and thus nearly throw me down, or, fastening its long and sharp claws in my dress, clamber in this manner to my breast. At such times, although I longed to destroy it with a blow, I was yet withheld from so doing, partly by a memory of my former crime, but chiefly—let me confess it at once—by absolute *dread* of the beast.

This dread was not exactly a dread of physical evil—and yet I should be at a loss how otherwise to define it. I am almost ashamed to own—yes, even in this felon's cell, I am almost ashamed to own —that the terror and horror with which the animal inspired me had been heightened by one of the merest chimeras it would be possible to conceive. My wife had called my attention more than once to the character of the mark of white hair, of which I have spoken, and which constituted the sole visible difference between the strange beast and the one I had destroyed. The reader will remember that this mark, although large, had been originally very indefinite, but by slow degrees—degrees nearly imperceptible, and which for a long time my reason struggled to reject as fanciful—it had at length assumed a rigorous distinctness of outline. It was now the representation of an object that I shudder to name—and for this above all I loathed and dreaded, and would have rid myself of the monster *had I dared*—it was now, I say, the image of a hideous—of a ghastly thing—of the GALLOWS!—O, mournful and terrible engine of horror and of crime—of agony and of death!

And now was I indeed wretched beyond the wretchedness of mere humanity. And *a brute beast*—whose fellow I had contemptuously destroyed—*a brute beast* to work out for *me*—for me a man, fashioned in the image of the High God—so much of insufferable woe! Alas! neither by day nor by night knew I the blessing of rest any more! During the former the creature left me no moment alone; and in the latter I started hourly from dreams of unutterable fear, to find the hot breath of *the thing* upon my face, and its vast weight —an incarnate nightmare that I had no power to shake off—incumbent eternally upon my *heart!*

Beneath the pressure of torments such as these, the feeble remnant of the good within me succumbed. Evil thoughts became my sole intimates—the darkest and most evil of thoughts. The moodiness of my usual temper increased to hatred of all things and of all mankind; while from the sudden frequent and ungovernable outbursts of a fury to which I now blindly abandoned myself, my uncomplaining wife, alas! was the most usual and the most patient of sufferers.

One day she accompanied me upon some household errand into the cellar of the old building which our poverty compelled us to inhabit. The cat followed me down the steep stairs, and nearly throwing me headlong, exasperated me to madness. Uplifting an ax, and forgetting in my wrath the childish dread which had hitherto stayed my hand, I aimed a blow at the animal, which of course would have proved instantly fatal had it descended as I wished. But this blow was arrested by the hand of my wife. Goaded by the interference into a rage more than demoniacal, I withdrew my arm from her grasp and buried the ax in her brain. She fell dead upon the spot without a groan.

This hideous murder accomplished, I set myself forthwith and with entire deliberation to the task of concealing the body. I knew that I could not remove it from the house, either by day or by night, without the risk of being observed by the neighbors. Many projects entered my mind. At one period I thought of cutting the corpse into minute fragments and destroying them by fire. At another I resolved to dig a grave for it in the floor of the cellar. Again, I deliberated about casting it in the well in the yard—about packing it in a box, as if merchandise, with the usual arrangements, and so getting a porter to take it from the house. Finally I hit upon what I considered a far better expedient than either of these. I determined to wall it up in the cellar—as the monks of the middle ages are recorded to have walled up their victims.

For a purpose such as this the cellar was well adapted. Its walls were loosely constructed and had lately been plastered throughout with a rough plaster, which the dampness of the atmosphere had prevented from hardening. Moreover, in one of the walls was a projection caused by a false chimney or fireplace, that had been filled up and made to resemble the rest of the cellar. I made no doubt that I could readily displace the bricks at this point, insert the corpse, and wall the whole up as before, so that no eye could detect anything suspicious.

And in this calculation I was not deceived. By means of a crowbar I easily dislodged the bricks, and having carefully deposited the body against the inner wall, I propped it in that position, while with little trouble I relaid the whole structure as it originally stood. Having procured mortar, sand, and hair with every possible precaution, I prepared a plaster which could not be distinguished from the old, and with this I very carefully went over the new brick-work. When I had finished I felt satisfied that all was right. The wall did not present the slightest appearance of having been disturbed. The rubbish on the floor was picked up with the minutest care. I looked around triumphantly, and said to myself—"Here at last, then, my labor has not been in vain."

My next step was to look for the beast which had been the cause of so much wretchedness, for I had at length firmly resolved to put it to death. Had I been able to meet with it at the moment there could have been no doubt of its fate, but it appeared that the crafty animal had been alarmed at the violence of my previous anger, and forbore to present itself in my present mood. It is impossible to describe or to imagine the deep, the blissful sense of relief which the absence of the detested creature occasioned in my bosom. It did not make its appearance during the night—and thus for one night at least since its introduction into the house I soundly and tranquilly slept, aye, *slept* even with the burden of murder upon my soul!

The second and the third day passed, and still my tormentor came not. Once again I breathed as a freeman. The monster, in terror, had fled the premises forever! I should behold it no more! My happiness was supreme! The guilt of my dark deed disturbed me but little. Some few inquiries had been made, but these had been readily answered. Even a search had been instituted—but of course nothing was to be discovered. I looked upon my future felicity as secured.

Upon the fourth day of the assassination, a party of the police came very unexpectedly into the house, and proceeded again to make rigorous investigation of the premises. Secure, however, in the inscrutability of my place of concealment, I felt no embarrassment whatever. The officers bade me accompany them in their search. They left no nook or corner unexplored. At length, for the third or fourth time, they descended into the cellar. I quivered nòt in a muscle. My heart beat calmly as that of one who slumbers in innocence. I walked the cellar from end to end. I folded my arms upon my bosom, and roamed easily to and fro. The police were thoroughly satisfied, and prepared to depart. The glee at my heart was too strong to be restrained. I burned to say if but one word by way of triumph, and to render doubly sure their assurance of my guiltlessness.

"Gentlemen," I said at last, as the party ascended the steps, "I delight to have allayed your suspicions. I wish you all health, and a little more courtesy. By the by, gentlemen, this—this is a very well-constructed house." [In the rabid desire to say something easily, I scarcely knew what I uttered at all.] "I may say an *excellently* well-constructed house. These walls—are you going, gentlemen?—these walls are solidly put together;" and here, through the mere frenzy of bravado, I rapped heavily with a cane which I held in my hand upon that very portion of the brick-work behind which stood the corpse of the wife of my bosom.

But may God shield and deliver me from the fangs of the archfiend! No sooner had the reverberation of my blows sunk into silence than I was answered by a voice from within the tomb!—by a cry, at first muffled and broken, like the sobbing of a child, and then quickly swelling into one long, loud, and continuous scream, utterly anomalous and inhuman—a howl—a wailing shriek, half of horror and half of triumph, such as might have arisen only out of hell, conjointly from the throats of the damned in their agony and of the demons that exult in the damnation.

Of my own thoughts it is folly to speak. Swooning, I staggered to the opposite wall. For one instant the party upon the stairs remained motionless, through extremity of terror and of awe. In the next a dozen stout arms were toiling at the wall. It fell bodily. The corpse, already greatly decayed and clotted with gore, stood erect before the eyes of the spectators. Upon its head, with red extended mouth and solitary eye of fire, sat the hideous beast whose craft had seduced me into murder, and whose informing voice had consigned me to the hangman. I had walled the monster up within the tomb!

How They Brought the Good News from Ghent to Aix

by ROBERT BROWNING

I think this poem is about the horse Roland. Certainly we never learn what the good news was, so how can we be concerned with it, or with anything but the gallant horse?

I

I sprang to the stirrup, and Joris, and he;
I galloped, Dirck galloped, we galloped all three;
"Good speed!" cried the watch, as the gate-bolts undrew;
"Speed!" echoed the wall to us galloping through;
Behind shut the postern, the lights sank to rest,
And into the midnight we galloped abreast.

II

Not a word to each other; we kept the great pace
Neck by neck, stride by stride, never changing our place;
I turned in my saddle and made its girth tight,
Then shortened each stirrup, and set the pique right,
Rebuckled the cheek-strap, chained slacker the bit,
Nor galloped less steadily Roland a whit.

III

'Twas moonset at starting; but while we drew near
Lokeren, the cocks crew and twilight dawned clear;
At Boom, a great yellow star came out to see;
At Düffeld, 'twas morning as plain as could be;
And from Mecheln church-steeple we heard the half chime,
So Joris broke silence with, "Yet there is time!"

IV

At Aerschot, up leaped of a sudden the sun,
And against him the cattle stood black every one,
To stare thro' the mist at us galloping past,
And I saw my stout galloper Roland at last,
With resolute shoulders, each butting away
The haze, as some bluff river headland its spray.

V

And his low head and crest, just one sharp ear bent back
For my voice, and the other pricked out on his track;
And one eye's black intelligence,—ever that glance
O'er its white edge at me, his own master, askance!
And the thick heavy spume flakes which aye and anon
His fierce lips shook upwards in galloping on.

VI

By Hasselt, Dirck groaned; and cried Joris, "Stay spur!
Your Roos galloped bravely, the fault's not in her,
We'll remember at Aix"—for one heard the quick wheeze
Of her chest, saw the stretched neck and staggering knees,
And sunk tail, and horrible heave of the flank,
As down on her haunches she shuddered and sank.

VII

So we were left galloping, Joris and I,
Past Looz and past Tongres, no cloud in the sky;
The broad sun above laughed a pitiless laugh,
'Neath our feet broke the brittle bright stubble like chaff;
Till over by Dalhem a dome-spire sprang white,
And "Gallop," gasped Joris, "for Aix is in sight!"

VIII

"How they'll greet us!"—and all in a moment his roan
Rolled neck and croup over, lay dead as a stone;
And there was my Roland to bear the whole weight

Of the news which alone could save Aix from her fate,
With his nostrils like pits full of blood to the brim,
And with circles of red for his eye-sockets' rim.

IX

Then I cast loose my buffcoat, each holster let fall,
Shook off both my jack-boots, let go belt and all,
Stood up in the stirrup, leaned, patted his ear,
Called my Roland his pet-name, my horse without peer;
Clapped my hands, laughed and sang, any noise, bad or good,
Till at length into Aix Roland galloped and stood.

X

And all I remember is, friends flocking round
As I sat with his head 'twixt my knees on the ground;
And no voice but was praising this Roland of mine,
As I poured down his throat our last measure of wine,
Which (the burgesses voted by common consent)
Was no more than his due who brought good news from Ghent.

The Song of the Falcon

by MAXIM GORKI

This allegory by Maxim Gorki, one of the great writers of Russia, one of the great revolutionary leaders of Russia, is about a falcon . . . is about freedom . . . is about those who cannot understand the willingness to fight for freedom until we die. But Maxim Gorki understood the worth of the battle. . . .

SIGHING lazily at the shore, the slumbering sea lies calm and motionless in the distance, diffused with the columbine sheen of the moon. Velvety and black it blends there with the blue southern sky and sleeps soundly, reflecting the transparent woof of the immobile and fleecy clouds through which gleam the golden arabesques of the stars. It appears as if the heavens stoop lower and lower over the sea, anxious to grasp what the weltering waves are murmuring as they creep drowsily on to the shore.

The mountains, overgrown with countless trees, bend fantastically to the northeast, hoist their summits into the blue void above them, while their dry and rugged outlines bathe in the warm caressing haze of the southern night.

Gravely thoughtful stand the mountains, casting dark and gloomy shadows upon the stately green crests of waves, enshrouding them, as if wishing to thwart their sole element and muffle the incessant splashes and sighs of the foam—sounds that infringe upon the mysterious tranquillity which holds sway over all things jointly with the turquoise silvery light of the moon, still hidden beyond the mountain ridges.

"A-lah-ah ak-bar! . . ." murmurs softly Nadír-Rahím-Ogli, a tall, gray, old and sage Crimean herdsman of sombre aspect, burned dark by the sun of the south.

We are lying on the sand at the foot of a colossal boulder which long since broke off from its native mountain, and now, overgrown with surly and dismal moss, scowls in dark shadows. The side facing seaward is covered with silt and sea-weeds, washed upon it by the waves; from the distance it appears indistinguishable from the narrow land streak which separates the mountains from the sea. The flame of the wood-pile casts a glaring light upon the side facing the mountains; it flickers, and shadows run across the ancient rock designed with a network of deep rents. It seems possessed of thought and feeling.

Rahím and I are boiling fish-soup from freshly-caught sculpins, and both of us are in that peculiar frame of mind when all appears visionary and spiritualistic; when one is apt to fathom his own mind; the heart so pure, so buoyant and, at last, free from all other desires save one—to contemplate.

Meanwhile, the sea fondles the shore and the waves wail with tender sadness, as if they are asking heat from our fire. From time to time one detects a note more daring and crafty. This is one of the many waves which has fearlessly crept well-nigh over to us. Rahím has already compared the waves to women, suspecting them of the desire to embrace and kiss us. He is lying with chest upon the sand, leaning on his elbows, and gazing thoughtfully into the hazy distance. His head, resting on the palm of his hand, is turned seaward. His shaggy sheepskin hat has shifted down the nape of his neck, while a refreshing breeze, wafted from the sea, caresses his furrowed forehead. He is philosophizing, unmindful of my presence, just as if he were addressing himself to the sea:

"A man faithful to God goes to heaven. But he who does not serve God and the Prophet? Perhaps he is in that foam? . . . And those silvery patches on the surface of the water may even be he. Who can tell? . . ."

The dark and mighty sea now throbs in lambent light as if carelessly scattered by the moon which has already emerged from under the jagged mountain tops. It is now pensively emitting its light upon the sea which sighs softly as she meets it and upon the shore and rock beside which both of us are lying.

"Rahím! . . . Tell me a story!" I beg of the old man.

"What for?" interrogates Rahím, without even turning to look at me.

"Just so! I love your stories."

"I have already told them all to you. . . . I have no others. . . ."

By this he intimates that I should entreat him, which I do accordingly.

"Would you like to hear an old song?" assents Rahím.

I declare my eagerness for it. Whereupon in a dismal recitative tone, endeavouring to preserve the original melody of the steppe-song and dreadfully jumbling together the Russian words, he recites:

I

"High into the mountains crawled a Snake, and there, in a damp gorge, he lay all shrivelled up into a knot, gazing upon the sea.

"Deep in the sky shone the sun, and the mountains breathed forth sultry heat into heaven. Below, the billows rushed themselves against the rocks.

"And along the gorge, through darkness and splashing, a torrent bounding over the rocks, rushed to meet the sea.

"Seething in white foam, hoary and vigourous, it cut through the rocks, falling into the sea, roaring angrily.

"Suddenly, into the gorge wherein the Snake lay shrivelled up, a Falcon fell from heaven, his bosom broken and feathers stained with blood.

"With a sharp cry he dropped upon the earth and in impotent wrath beat his head against the hard rock.

"Alarmed, the Snake at first hastily retreated, but soon grasped that the bird had but a few more minutes to live; he crawled over nearer to him and hissed directly into his eyes:

" 'Art thou dying?'

" 'Yes, I am dying,' replied the Falcon, heaving a deep sigh. 'I have lived gloriously! . . . I have known happiness! . . . I have fought heroically! . . . I have beheld heaven! . . . Thou wilt not see it so near thee! . . . O, thou unfortunate!'

" 'Pooh, what's heaven?—an empty place. . . . How am I to creep up there? Besides, this place suits me very much . . . 'tis damp and warm!'

"Thus rejoined the Snake to the free bird, smiling inwardly at such nonsense.

"And he reasoned thus: 'Fly or creep, the end is known: all will die—all into dust will turn. . . .'

"But all at once the daring Falcon shook his wings, raised himself slightly above the ground and viewed the stifled gorge. Through the gray rock water gushed, and a putrid smell pervaded the dark cleft.

"His strength all mustered up, his heart replete with grief and anguish, he shouted:

" 'O, if for the last time I could rise to heaven! . . . There, to the wounds of my bosom I would clutch my enemy . . . and, strangled, he would die in my blood! O joy of battle!'

"The Snake then reasoned again:

" 'Heaven, must indeed, be a splendid place to live in, that he so doth sigh!'

"And to the bird of Freedom he held forth thus:

" 'Draw nearer to the brink of the gorge and throw thyself down. Perchance thy wings once more will bear thee up, and thou wilt live a while longer in thine native element!'

"And the Falcon shuddered, and, uttering a faint cry, drew nearer to the steep, sliding with his claws on the slime of the stone. And spreading his wings, he flashed fire from his eyes, sighing heavily as he rolled downward.

"And like a stone tumbling down the rocks, he fell swiftly, breaking his pinions and losing his feathers.

"His blood washed off, and, caught by the waves of the torrent, he was carried into the sea, bedecked with foam.

"And the billows of the sea, roaring dismally, dashed themselves against the rocks. . . . And the corpse of the bird was lost in the waste of the sea. . . ."

II

"Lying in the gorge, the Snake brooded long over the death of the bird and its passionate craving for heaven.

"And into that distance, which forever flatters one to dream of happiness, he directed his eyes.

" 'What is it that he, the dead Falcon, could have seen in that bottomless and never-ending desert? Wherefore do such as he, no longer alive, stir one's soul with their love of flight to heaven? What is clear to them up there? I, of course, could easily make knowledge of all, were I to ascend there but for a fleeting moment.'

"Said and done. Into a circle all curled up, the Snake soared into the air, flashing in the sun like a narrow ribbon.

" 'What is born to crawl—will never fly!' Unmindful of this truth he fell back on the rock, hurt but not killed, and laughed:

" 'So that's what makes the flight into heaven so delightful! It's —the fall! . . . Ridiculous birds! Having little knowledge of the earth, they feel out of place on it; aspire to high heavens and seek life in a sultry desert. Light there is in abundance and emptiness unbound, 'tis true. But where's one to get food and support for a living body! Wherefore, then, have pride? Wherefore all reproaches? Is it not a mask to disguise the madness of one's desires and the unfitness for life's affairs? Ridiculous birds! Their words will no longer enchant me! . . . I know better now! I beheld the sky. . . . I ascended it, explored it and even experienced the sensation of falling, but have escaped destruction; on the contrary, it has only strengthened the confidence in myself. Let those who shun earthly life live by deceit. . . . As for myself, I know the truth now, and in their invocations I have lost my faith. An earthly creature—on earth I shall remain!'

"And curled up into a ball, he lay on the rock flattered by pride.

"The whole surface of the sea was now bathed in bright splendour and the billows menacingly dashed themselves against the rocks.

"In their lion-like roar resounded the song of the proud bird; the rocks quaked from their blows, the sky shuddered from the menacing song:

" '*To the madness of the brave we sing praise!*'

"Madness of the brave—that's the wisdom of life. O, brave Falcon! In battle with thy enemies thou hast bled! . . . But there will come a time when the drops of the seething blood will scintillate like sparks in the darkness of life, enkindling many a brave heart with a maddening thirst for freedom and light!

"Be it that thou art dead! . . . But in the song of the brave and strong in spirit thou always will be a living precedent, a proud invocation to freedom and light!

"We chant the song of praise to the madness of the brave!"

Tranquil is the opal-tinged surface of the sea and wailing gloomily the waves sweep along the shore. I utter not a word as I gaze at Rahím who has just concluded reciting his song of the brave Falcon to the sea. Silvery patches reflected from the moonbeams begin to cover the whole surface of the sea. . . . Our fish soup is beginning to boil.

Splashing defiantly, one of the waves sweeps playfully along the shore, reaching Rahím's head.

"Whither bound? . . . Away!" threatens Rahím with his hand, and the wave submissively rolls back into the sea.

In Rahím's sally, personifying the waves, I find nothing to laugh at. All about us is strangely alive, soft and caressing. The sea is inspiringly calm and one feels that in its fresh breath, still uncooled from the day's heat, is hidden much mighty, suppressed strength. Over the dark blue firmament, in golden patterns of stars, is inscribed something solemn, fascinating the soul, confounding the mind with a sweet expectancy of some revelation.

Everything slumbers, but with a tensified semi-wakefulness, and it seems as if in the next second all things will suddenly awaken and resound in tuneful harmony of inexplicably sweet strains. These sounds will tell of the mysteries of the universe, unfold them to the mind which they will then extinguish like a will-o'-the-wisp, drawing the soul far, far away into the dark blue void, whence the trembling figures of the stars meeting it will also resound with the divine harmony of revelation.

The Crocodile

AN EXTRAORDINARY INCIDENT

by FIODOR DOSTOIEVSKI

*Another Russian story, a satire on Russian society,
some will say, and not an animal story at all. Yet how
could Dostoievski have satirized the society of petty
officialdom in Czarist Russia exactly as he does had the
crocodile not been put on exhibition?*

I

ON THE thirteenth of January of this present year, 1865, at
half-past twelve in the day, Elena Ivanovna, the wife of my
cultured friend Ivan Matveitch, who is a colleague in the same department, and may be said to be a distant relation of mine, too, expressed the desire to see the crocodile now on view at a fixed charge
in the Arcade. As Ivan Matveitch had already in his pocket his ticket
for a tour abroad (not so much for the sake of his health as for the
improvement of his mind), and was consequently free from his
official duties and had nothing whatever to do that morning, he
offered no objection to his wife's irresistible fancy, but was positively aflame with curiosity himself.

"A capital idea!" he said, with the utmost satisfaction. "We'll
have a look at the crocodile! On the eve of visiting Europe it is as
well to acquaint ourselves on the spot with its indigenous inhabitants." And with these words, taking his wife's arm, he set off with
her at once for the Arcade. I joined them, as I usually do, being
an intimate friend of the family. I have never seen Ivan Matveitch in
a more agreeable frame of mind than he was on that memorable
morning—how true it is that we know not beforehand the fate that

awaits us! On entering the Arcade he was at once full of admiration for the splendours of the building, and when we reached the shop in which the monster lately arrived in Petersburg was being exhibited, he volunteered to pay the quarter-rouble for me to the crocodile owner—a thing which had never happened before. Walking into a little room, we observed that besides the crocodile there were in it parrots of the species known as cockatoo, and also a group of monkeys in a special case in a recess. Near the entrance, along the left wall stood a big tin tank that looked like a bath covered with a thin iron grating, filled with water to the depth of two inches. In this shallow pool was kept a huge crocodile, which lay like a log absolutely motionless and apparently deprived of all its faculties by our damp climate, so inhospitable to foreign visitors. This monster at first aroused no special interest in any one of us.

"So this is the crocodile!" said Elena Ivanovna, with a pathetic cadence of regret. "Why, I thought it was . . . something different."

Most probably she thought it was made of diamonds. The owner of the crocodile, a German, came out and looked at us with an air of extraordinary pride.

"He has a right to be," Ivan Matveitch whispered to me, "he knows he is the only man in Russia exhibiting a crocodile."

This quite nonsensical observation I ascribe also to the extremely good-humoured mood which had overtaken Ivan Matveitch, who was on other occasions of rather envious disposition.

"I fancy your crocodile is not alive," said Elena Ivanovna, piqued by the irresponsive stolidity of the proprietor, and addressing him with a charming smile in order to soften his churlishness—a manœuvre so typically feminine.

"Oh, no, madam," the latter replied in broken Russian; and instantly moving the grating half off the tank, he poked the monster's head with a stick.

Then the treacherous monster, to show that it was alive, faintly stirred its paws and tail, raised its snout and emitted something like a prolonged snuffle.

"Come, don't be cross, Karlchen," said the German caressingly, gratified in his vanity.

"How horrid that crocodile is! I am really frightened," Elena

Ivanovna twittered, still more coquettishly. "I know I shall dream of him now."

"But he won't bite you if you do dream of him," the German retorted gallantly, and was the first to laugh at his own jest, but none of us responded.

"Come, Semyon Semyonitch," said Elena Ivanovna, addressing me exclusively, "let us go and look at the monkeys. I am awfully fond of monkeys; they are such darlings . . . and the crocodile is horrid."

"Oh, don't be afraid, my dear!" Ivan Matveitch called after us, gallantly displaying his manly courage to his wife. "This drowsy denison of the realms of the Pharaohs will do us no harm." And he remained by the tank. What is more, he took his glove and began tickling the crocodile's nose with it, wishing, as he said afterwards, to induce him to snort. The proprietor showed his politeness to a lady by following Elena Ivanovna to the case of monkeys.

So everything was going well, and nothing could have been foreseen. Elena Ivanovna was quite skittish in her raptures over the monkeys, and seemed completely taken up with them. With shrieks of delight she was continually turning to me, as though determined not to notice the proprietor, and kept gushing with laughter at the resemblance she detected between these monkeys and her intimate friends and acquaintances. I, too, was amused, for the resemblance was unmistakable. The German did not know whether to laugh or not, and so at last was reduced to frowning. And it was at that moment that a terrible, I may say unnatural, scream set the room vibrating. Not knowing what to think, for the first moment I stood still, numb with horror, but noticing that Elena Ivanovna was screaming too, I quickly turned round—and what did I behold! I saw—oh, heavens!—I saw the luckless Ivan Matveitch in the terrible jaws of the crocodile, held by them round the waist, lifted horizontally in the air and desperately kicking. Then—one moment, and no trace remained of him. But I must describe it in detail, for I stood all the while motionless, and had time to watch the whole process taking place before me with an attention and interest such as I never remember to have felt before. "What," I thought at that critical moment, "what if all that had happened to me instead of to Ivan Matveitch—how unpleasant it would have been for me!"

But to return to my story. The crocodile began by turning the unhappy Ivan Matveitch in his terrible jaws so that he could swallow his legs first; then bringing up Ivan Matveitch, who kept trying to jump out and clutching at the sides of the tank, sucked him down again as far as his waist. Then bringing him up again, gulped him down, and so again and again. In this way Ivan Matveitch was visibly disappearing before our eyes. At last, with a final gulp, the crocodile swallowed my cultured friend entirely, this time leaving no trace of him. From the outside of the crocodile we could see the protuberances of Ivan Matveitch's figure as he passed down the inside of the monster. I was on the point of screaming again when destiny played another treacherous trick upon us. The crocodile made a tremendous effort, probably oppressed by the magnitude of the object he had swallowed, once more opened his terrible jaws, and with a final hiccup he suddenly let the head of Ivan Matveitch pop out for a second, with an expression of despair on his face. In that brief instant the spectacles dropped off his nose to the bottom of the tank. It seemed as though that despairing countenance had only popped out to cast one last look on the objects around it, to take its last farewell of all earthly pleasures. But it had not time to carry out its intention; the crocodile made another effort, gave a gulp and instantly it vanished again—this time for ever. This appearance and disappearance of a still living human head was so horrible, but at the same—either from its rapidity and unexpectedness or from the dropping of the spectacles—there was something so comic about it that I suddenly quite unexpectedly exploded with laughter. But pulling myself together and realising that to laugh at such a moment was not the thing for an old family friend, I turned at once to Elena Ivanovna and said with a sympathetic air:

"Now it's all over with our friend Ivan Matveitch!"

I cannot even attempt to describe how violent was the agitation of Elena Ivanovna during the whole process. After the first scream she seemed rooted to the spot, and stared at the catastrophe with apparent indifference, though her eyes looked as though they were starting out of her head; then she suddenly went off into a heart-rending wail, but I seized her hands. At this instant the proprietor, too, who had at first been also petrified by horror, suddenly clasped his hands and cried, gazing upwards:

"Oh my crocodile! *Oh mein allerliebster Karlchen! Mutter, Mutter, Mutter!*"

A door at the rear of the room opened at this cry, and the *Mutter*, a rosy-cheeked, elderly but dishevelled woman in a cap made her appearance, and rushed with a shriek to her German.

A perfect Bedlam followed. Elena Ivanovna kept shrieking out the same phrase, as though in a frenzy, "Flay him! flay him!" apparently entreating them—probably in a moment of oblivion—to flay somebody for something. The proprietor and *Mutter* took no notice whatever of either of us; they were both bellowing like calves over the crocodile.

"He did for himself! He will burst himself at once, for he did swallow a *ganz* official!" cried the proprietor.

"*Unser Karlchen, unser allerliebster Karlchen wird sterben,*" howled his wife.

"We are bereaved and without bread!" chimed in the proprietor.

"Flay him! flay him! flay him!" clamoured Elena Ivanovna, clutching at the German's coat.

"He did tease the crocodile. For what did your man tease the crocodile?" cried the German, pulling away from her. "You will if *Karlchen wird* burst, therefore pay, *das war mein Sohn, das war mein einziger Sohn.*"

I must own I was intensely indignant at the sight of such egoism in the German and the cold-heartedness of his dishevelled *Mutter*; at the same time Elena Ivanovna's reiterated shriek of "Flay him! flay him!" troubled me even more and absorbed at last my whole attention, positively alarming me. I may as well say straight off that I entirely misunderstood this strange exclamation: it seemed to me that Elena Ivanovna had for the moment taken leave of her senses, but nevertheless wishing to avenge the loss of her beloved Ivan Matveitch, was demanding by way of compensation that the crocodile should be severely thrashed, while she was meaning something quite different. Looking round at the door, not without embarrassment, I began to entreat Elena Ivanovna to calm herself, and above all not to use the shocking word "flay." For such a reactionary desire here, in the midst of the Arcade and of the most cultured society, not two paces from the hall where at this very minute Mr. Lavrov was perhaps delivering a public lecture, was not only impossible but unthinkable, and might at any moment bring upon us the hisses of culture and the caricatures of Mr. Stepanov. To my horror I was immediately proved to be correct in my alarmed suspicions: the curtain that divided the crocodile room from the little entry where the quarter-roubles were taken suddenly parted, and in the opening there appeared a figure with moustaches and beard, carrying a cap, with the upper part of its body bent a long way forward, though the feet were scrupulously held beyond the threshold of the crocodile room in order to avoid the necessity of paying the entrance money.

"Such a reactionary desire, madam," said the stranger, trying to avoid falling over in our direction and to remain standing outside the room, "does no credit to your development, and is conditioned by lack of phosphorus in your brain. You will be promptly held up to shame in the *Chronicle of Progress* and in our satirical prints . . ."

But he could not complete his remarks; the proprietor coming to himself, and seeing with horror that a man was talking in the crocodile room without having paid entrance money, rushed furiously at the progressive stranger and turned him out with a punch from each fist. For a moment both vanished from our sight behind a curtain, and only then I grasped that the whole uproar was about nothing. Elena Ivanovna turned out quite innocent; she had, as I have mentioned already, no idea whatever of subjecting the crocodile to a degrading corporal punishment, and had simply expressed the desire that he should be opened and her husband released from his interior.

"What! You wish that my crocodile be perished!" the proprietor yelled, running in again. "No! let your husband be perished first, before my crocodile! . . . *Mein Vater* showed crocodile, *mein Grossvater* showed crocodile, *mein Sohn* will show crocodile, and I will show crocodile! All will show crocodile! I am known to *ganz Europa*, and you are not known to *ganz Europa*, and you must pay me a *strafe!*"

"*Ja, ja,*" put in the vindictive German woman, "we shall not let you go. *Strafe*, since Karlchen is burst!"

"And, indeed, it's useless to flay the creature," I added calmly, anxious to get Elena Ivanovna away home as quickly as possible, "as our dear Ivan Matveitch is by now probably soaring somewhere in the empyrean."

"My dear"—we suddenly heard, to our intense amazement, the voice of Ivan Matveitch—"my dear, my advice is to apply direct to the superintendent's office, as without the assistance of the police the German will never be made to see reason."

These words, uttered with firmness and aplomb, and expressing an exceptional presence of mind, for the first minute so astounded us that we could not believe our ears. But, of course, we ran at once to the crocodile's tank, and with equal reverence and incredulity listened to the unhappy captive. His voice was muffled, thin and even squeaky, as though it came from a considerable distance. It reminded one of a jocose person who, covering his mouth with a pillow, shouts from an adjoining room, trying to mimic the sound of two peasants calling to one another in a deserted plain or across a wide ravine— a performance to which I once had the pleasure of listening in a friend's house at Christmas.

"Ivan Matveitch, my dear, and so you are alive!" faltered Elena Ivanovna.

"Alive and well," answered Ivan Matveitch, "and, thanks to the Almighty, swallowed without any damage whatever. I am only uneasy as to the view my superiors may take of the incident; for after getting a permit to go abroad I've got into a crocodile, which seems anything but clever."

"But, my dear, don't trouble your head about being clever; first of all we must somehow excavate you from where you are," Elena Ivanovna interrupted.

"Excavate!" cried the proprietor. "I will not let my crocodile be excavated. Now the *publicum* will come many more, and I will *fünfzig* kopecks ask and Karlchen will cease to burst."

"*Gott sei dank!*" put in his wife.

"They are right," Ivan Matveitch observed tranquilly; "the principles of economics before everything."

"My dear! I will fly at once to the authorities and lodge a complaint, for I feel that we cannot settle this mess by ourselves."

"I think so too," observed Ivan Matveitch; "but in our age of industrial crisis it is not easy to rip open the belly of a crocodile without economic compensation, and meanwhile the inevitable question presents itself: What will the German take for his crocodile? And with it another: How will it be paid? For, as you know, I have no means . . ."

"Perhaps out of your salary . . ." I observed timidly, but the proprietor interrupted me at once.

"I will not the crocodile sell; I will for three thousand the crocodile sell! I will for four thousand the crocodile sell! Now the *publicum* will come very many. I will for five thousand the crocodile sell!"

In fact he gave himself insufferable airs. Covetousness and a revolting greed gleamed joyfully in his eyes.

"I am going!" I cried indignantly.

"And I! I too! I shall go to Andrey Osipitch himself. I will soften him with my tears," whined Elena Ivanovna.

"Don't do that, my dear," Ivan Matveitch hastened to interpose. He had long been jealous of Andrey Osipitch on his wife's account, and he knew she would enjoy going to weep before a gentleman of refinement, for tears suited her. "And I don't advise you to do so either, my friend," he added, addressing me. "It's no good plunging headlong in that slap-dash way; there't no knowing what it may lead to. You had much better go to-day to Timofey Semyonitch, as though to pay an ordinary visit; he is an old-fashioned and by no means brilliant man, but he is trustworthy, and what matters most of all, he is straightforward. Give him my greetings and describe the circumstances of the case. And since I owe him seven roubles over our last game of cards, take the opportunity to pay him the money; that will soften the stern old man. In any case his advice may serve as a guide for us. And meanwhile take Elena Ivanovna home. . . . Calm yourself, my dear," he continued, addressing her. "I am weary of these outcries and feminine squabblings, and should like a nap. It's soft and warm in here, though I have hardly had time to look round in this unexpected haven."

"Look round! Why, is it light in there?" cried Elena Ivanovna in a tone of relief.

"I am surrounded by impenetrable night," answered the poor captive; "but I can feel and, so to speak, have a look round with my hands. . . . Good-bye; set your mind at rest and don't deny your-

self recreation and diversion. Till tomorrow! And you, Semyon
Semyonitch, come to me in the evening, and as you are absent-
minded and may forget it, tie a knot in your handkerchief."

I confess I was glad to get away, for I was overtired and somewhat
bored. Hastening to offer my arm to the disconsolate Elena Ivanovna,
whose charms were only enhanced by her agitation, I hurriedly led
her out of the crocodile room.

"The charge will be another quarter-rouble in the evening," the
proprietor called after us.

"Oh, dear, how greedy they are!" said Elena Ivanovna, looking
at herself in every mirror on the walls of the Arcade, and evidently
aware that she was looking prettier than usual.

"The principles of economics," I answered with some emotion,
proud that passers-by should see the lady on my arm.

"The principles of economics," she drawled in a touching little
voice. "I did not in the least understand what Ivan Matveitch said
about those horrid economics just now."

"I will explain to you," I answered, and began at once telling her
of the beneficial effects of the introduction of foreign capital into our
country, upon which I had read an article in the *Petersburg News*
and the *Voice* that morning.

"How strange it is," she interrupted, after listening for some time.
"But do leave off, you horrid man. What nonsense you are talking.
. . . Tell me, do I look purple?"

"You look perfect, and not purple!" I observed, seizing the opportunity to pay her a compliment.

"Naughty man!" she said complacently. "Poor Ivan Matveitch,"
she added a minute later, putting her little head on one side coquettishly. "I am really sorry for him. Oh, dear!" she cried suddenly,
"how is he going to have his dinner . . . and . . . and . . . what
will he do . . . if he wants anything?"

"An unforeseen question," I answered, perplexed in my turn. To
tell the truth, it had not entered my head, so much more practical are
women than we men in the solution of the problems of daily life!

"Poor dear! how could he have got into such a mess . . . nothing
to amuse him, and in the dark. . . . How vexing it is that I have
no photograph of him. . . . And so now I am a sort of widow,"

she added, with a seductive smile, evidently interested in her new position. "Hm! . . . I am sorry for him, though."

It was, in short, the expression of the very natural and intelligible grief of a young and interesting wife for the loss of her husband. I took her home at last, soothed her, and after dining with her and drinking a cup of aromatic coffee, set off at six o'clock to Timofey Semyonitch, calculating that at that hour all married people of settled habits would be sitting or lying down at home.

Having written this first chapter in a style appropriate to the incident recorded, I intend to proceed in a language more natural though less elevated, and I beg to forewarn the reader of the fact.

II

The venerable Timofey Semyonitch met me rather nervously, as though somewhat embarrassed. He led me to his tiny study and shut the door carefully, "that the children may not hinder us," he added with evident uneasiness. There he made me sit down on a chair by the writing-table, sat down himself in an easy chair, wrapped round him the skirts of his old wadded dressing-gown, and assumed an official and even severe air, in readiness for anything, though he was not my chief nor Ivan Matveitch's, and had hitherto been reckoned as a colleague and even a friend.

"First of all," he said, "take note that I am not a person in authority, but just such a subordinate official as you and Ivan Matveitch. . . . I have nothing to do with it, and do not intend to mix myself up in the affair."

I was surprised to find that he apparently knew all about it already. In spite of that I told him the whole story over in detail. I spoke with positive excitement, for I was at that moment fulfilling the obligations of a true friend. He listened without special surprise, but with evident signs of suspicion.

"Only fancy," he said, "I always believed that this would be sure to happen to him."

"Why, Timofey Semyonitch? It is a very unusual incident in itself . . ."

"I admit it. But Ivan Matveitch's whole career in the service was leading up to this end. He was flighty—conceited indeed. It was always 'progress' and ideas of all sorts, and this is what progress brings people to!"

"But this is a most unusual incident and cannot possibly serve as a general rule for all progressives."

"Yes, indeed it can. You see, it's the effect of over-education, I assure you. For over-education leads people to poke their noses into all sorts of places, especially where they are not invited. Though perhaps you know best," he added, as though offended. "I am an old man and not of much education. I began as a soldier's son, and this year has been the jubilee of my service."

"Oh, no, Timofey Semyonitch, not at all. On the contrary, Ivan Matveitch is eager for your advice; he is eager for your guidance. He implores it, so to say, with tears."

"So to say, with tears! Hm! Those are crocodile's tears and one cannot quite believe in them. Tell me, what possessed him to want to go abroad? And how could he afford to go? Why, he has no private means!"

"He had saved the money from his last bonus," I answered plaintively. "He only wanted to go for three months—to Switzerland . . . to the land of William Tell."

"William Tell? Hm!"

"He wanted to meet the spring at Naples, to see the museums, the customs, the animals . . ."

"Hm! The animals! I think it was simply from pride. What animals? Animals, indeed! Haven't we animals enough? We have museums, menageries, camels. There are bears quite close to Petersburg! And here he's got inside a crocodile himself . . ."

"Oh, come, Timofey Semyonitch! The man is in trouble, the man appeals to you as to a friend, as to an older relation, craves for advice—and you reproach him. Have pity at least on the unfortunate Elena Ivanovna!"

"You are speaking of his wife? A charming little lady," said Timofey Semyonitch, visibly softening and taking a pinch of snuff with relish. "Particularly prepossessing. And so plump, and always putting her pretty little head on one side. . . . Very agreeable. Andrey Osipitch was speaking of her only the other day."

"Speaking of her?"

"Yes, and in very flattering terms. Such a bust, he said, such eyes, such hair. . . . A sugar-plum, he said, not a lady—and then he laughed. He is still a young man, of course." Timofey Semyonitch blew his nose with a loud noise. "And yet, young though he is, what a career he is making for himself."

"That's quite a different thing, Timofey Semyonitch."

"Of course, of course."

"Well, what do you say then, Timofey Semyonitch?"

"Why, what can I do?"

"Give advice, guidance, as a man of experience, a relative! What are we to do? What steps are we to take? Go to the authorities and . . ."

"To the authorities? Certainly not," Timofey Semyonitch replied hurriedly. "If you ask my advice, you had better, above all, hush the matter up and act, so to speak, as a private person. It is a suspicious incident, quite unheard of. Unheard of, above all; there is no precedent for it, and it is far from creditable. . . . And so, discretion above all. . . . Let him lie there a bit. We must wait and see . . ."

"But how can we wait and see, Timofey Semyonitch? What if he is stifled there?"

"Why should he be? I think you told me that he made himself fairly comfortable there?"

I told him the whole story over again. Timofey Semyonitch pondered.

"Hm!" he said, twisting his snuff-box in his hands. "To my mind it's really a good thing he should lie there a bit, instead of going abroad. Let him reflect at his leisure. Of course he mustn't be stifled, and so he must take measures to preserve his health, avoiding a cough, for instance, and so on. . . . And as for the German, it's my personal opinion he is within his rights, and even more so than the other side, because it was the other party who got into *his* crocodile without asking permission, and not *he* who got into Ivan Matveitch's crocodile without asking permission, though, so far as I recollect, the latter has no crocodile. And a crocodile is private property, and so it is impossible to slit him open without compensation."

"For the saving of human life, Timofey Semyonitch."

"Oh, well, that's a matter for the police. You must go to them."

"But Ivan Matveitch may be needed in the department. He may be asked for."

"Ivan Matveitch needed? Ha-ha! Besides, he is on leave, so that we may ignore him—let him inspect the countries of Europe! It will be a different matter if he doesn't turn up when his leave is over. Then we shall ask for him and make inquiries."

"Three months! Timofey Semyonitch, for pity's sake!"

"It's his own fault. Nobody thrust him there. At this rate we should have to get a nurse to look after him at government expense, and that is not allowed for in the regulations. But the chief point is that the crocodile is private property, so that the principles of economics apply in this question. And the principles of economics are paramount. Only the other evening, at Luka Andreitch's, Ignaty Prokofyitch was saying so. Do you know Ignaty Prokofyitch? A capitalist, in a big way of business, and he speaks so fluently. 'We need industrial development,' he said; 'there is very little development among us. We must create it. We must create capital, so we must create a middle-class, the so-called bourgeoisie. And as we haven't capital we must attract it from abroad. We must, in the first place, give facilities to foreign companies to buy up lands in Russia as is done now abroad. The communal holding of land is poison, is ruin.' And, you know, he spoke with such heat; well, that's all right for him—a wealthy man, and not in the service. 'With the communal system,' he said, 'there will be no improvement in industrial development or agriculture. Foreign companies,' he said, 'must as far as possible buy up the whole of our land in big lots, and then split it up, split it up, split it up, in the smallest parts possible'—and do you know he pronounced the words 'split it up' with such determination—'and then sell it as private property. Or rather, not sell it, but simply let it. When,' he said, 'all the land is in the hands of foreign companies they can fix any rent they like. And so the peasant will work three times as much for his daily bread and he can be turned out at pleasure. So that he will feel it, will be submissive and industrious, and will work three times as much for the same wages. But as it is, with the commune, what does he care? He knows he won't die of hunger, so he is lazy and drunken. And meanwhile money will be attracted into Russia, capital will be created and the bourgeoisie will spring up. The English political and literary paper, *The Times*, in an article the other day on our finances stated that the reason our financial position was so unsatisfactory was that we had no middle-class, no big fortunes, no accommodating proletariat.' Ignaty Prokofyitch speaks well. He is an orator. He wants to lay a report on the subject before the authorities, and then to get it published in the *News*. That's something very different from verses like Ivan Matveitch's . . ."

"But how about Ivan Matveitch?" I put in, after letting the old man babble on.

Timofey Semyonitch was sometimes fond of talking and showing that he was not behind the times, but knew all about things.

"How about Ivan Matveitch? Why, I am coming to that. Here we are, anxious to bring foreign capital into the country—and only consider: as soon as the capital of a foreigner, who has been attracted to Petersburg, has been doubled through Ivan Matveitch, instead of protecting the foreign capitalist, we are proposing to rip open the belly of his original capital—the crocodile. Is it consistent? To my mind, Ivan Matveitch, as the true son of his fatherland, ought to rejoice and to be proud that through him the value of a foreign crocodile has been doubled and possibly even trebled. That's just what is wanted to attract capital. If one man succeeds, mind you, another will come with a crocodile, and a third will bring two or three of them at once, and capital will grow up about them—there you have a bourgeoisie. It must be encouraged."

"Upon my word, Timofey Semyonitch!" I cried, "you are demanding almost supernatural self-sacrifice from poor Ivan Matveitch."

"I demand nothing, and I beg you, before everything—as I have said already—to remember that I am not a person in authority and so cannot demand anything of any one. I am speaking as a son of the fatherland, that is, not as the *Son of the Fatherland*, but as a son of the fatherland. Again, what possessed him to get into the crocodile? A respectable man, a man of good grade in the service, lawfully married—and then to behave like that! Is it consistent?"

"But it was an accident."

"Who knows? And where is the money to compensate the owner to come from?"

"Perhaps out of his salary, Timofey Semyonitch?"

"Would that be enough?"

"No, it wouldn't, Timofey Semyonitch," I answered sadly. "The proprietor was at first alarmed that the crocodile would burst, but as soon as he was sure that it was all right, he began to bluster and was delighted to think that he could double the charge for entry."

"Treble and quadruple perhaps! The public will simply stampede the place now, and crocodile owners are smart people. Besides, it's not Lent yet, and people are keen on diversions, and so I say again, the great thing is that Ivan Matveitch should preserve his incognito, don't let him be in a hurry. Let everybody know, perhaps, that he is in the crocodile, but don't let them be officially informed of it. Ivan Matveitch is in particularly favourable circumstances for that, for he is reckoned to be abroad. It will be said he is in the crocodile, and we will refuse to believe it. That is how it can be managed. The great thing is that he should wait; and why should he be in a hurry?"

"Well, but if . . ."

"Don't worry, he has a good constitution . . ."

"Well, and afterwards, when he has waited?"

"Well, I won't conceal from you that the case is exceptional in the highest degree. One doesn't know what to think of it, and the worst of it is there is no precedent. If we had a precedent we might have something to go by. But as it is, what is one to say? It will certainly take time to settle it."

A happy thought flashed upon my mind.

"Cannot we arrange," I said, "that if he is destined to remain in the entrails of the monster and it is the will of Providence that he should remain alive, that he should send in a petition to be reckoned as still serving?"

"Hm! . . . Possibly as on leave and without salary . . ."

"But couldn't it be with salary?"

"On what grounds?"

"As sent on a special commission."

"What commission and where?"

"Why, into the entrails, the entrails of the crocodile. . . . So to speak, for exploration, for investigation of the facts on the spot. It would, of course, be a novelty, but that is progressive and would at the same time show zeal for enlightenment."

Timofey Semyonitch thought a little.

"To send a special official," he said at last, "to the inside of a crocodile to conduct a special inquiry is, in my personal opinion, an absurdity. It is not in the regulations. And what sort of special inquiry could there be there?"

"The scientific study of nature on the spot, in the living subject. The natural sciences are all the fashion nowadays, botany. . . . He could live there and report his observations. . . . For instance, concerning digestion or simply habits. For the sake of accumulating facts."

"You mean as statistics. Well, I am no great authority on that subject, indeed I am no philosopher at all. You say 'facts'—we are overwhelmed with facts as it is, and don't know what to do with them. Besides, statistics are a danger."

"In what way?"

"They are a danger. Moreover, you will admit he will report facts, so to speak, lying like a log. And, can one do one's official duties lying like a log? That would be another novelty and a dangerous one; and again, there is no precedent for it. If we had any sort of precedent for it, then, to my thinking, he might have been given the job."

"But no live crocodiles have been brought over hitherto, Timofey Semyonitch."

"Hm . . . yes," he reflected again. "Your objection is a just one, if you like, and might indeed serve as a ground for carrying the matter further; but consider again, that if with the arrival of living crocodiles government clerks begin to disappear, and then on the ground that they are warm and comfortable there, expect to receive the official sanction for their position, and then take their ease there . . . you must admit it would be a bad example. We should have every one trying to go the same way to get a salary for nothing."

"Do your best for him, Timofey Semyonitch. By the way, Ivan Matveitch asked me to give you seven roubles he had lost to you at cards."

"Ah, he lost that the other day at Nikifor Nikiforitch's. I remember. And how gay and amusing he was—and now!"

The old man was genuinely touched.

"Intercede for him, Timofey Semyonitch!"

"I will do my best. I will speak in my own name, as a private person, as though I were asking for information. And meanwhile, you find out indirectly, unofficially, how much would the proprietor consent to take for his crocodile?"

Timofey Semyonitch was visibly more friendly.

"Certainly," I answered. "And I will come back to you at once to report."

"And his wife . . . is she alone now? Is she depressed?"

"You should call on her, Timofey Semyonitch."

"I will. I thought of doing so before; it's a good opportunity. . . . And what on earth possessed him to go and look at the crocodile. Though, indeed, I should like to see it myself."

"Go and see the poor fellow, Timofey Semyonitch."

"I will. Of course, I don't want to raise his hopes by doing so. I shall go as a private person. . . . Well, good-bye, I am going to Nikifor Nikiforitch's again; shall you be there?"

"No, I am going to see the poor prisoner."

"Yes, now he is a prisoner! . . . Ah, that's what comes of thoughtlessness!"

I said good-bye to the old man. Ideas of all kinds were straying through my mind. A good-natured and most honest man, Timofey Semyonitch, yet, as I left him, I felt pleased at the thought that he had celebrated his fiftieth year of service, and that Timofey Semyonitches are now a rarity among us. I flew at once, of course, to the Arcade to tell poor Ivan Matveitch all the news. And, indeed, I was moved by curiosity to know how he was getting on in the crocodile and how it was possible to live in a crocodile. And, indeed, was it possible to live in a crocodile at all? At times it really seemed to me as though it were all an outlandish, monstrous dream, especially as an outlandish monster was the chief figure in it.

III

And yet it was not a dream, but actual, indubitable fact. Should I be telling the story if it were not? But to continue.

It was late, about nine o'clock, before I reached the Arcade, and I had to go into the crocodile room by the back entrance, for the German had closed the shop earlier than usual that evening. Now in the seclusion of domesticity he was walking about in a greasy old frock-coat, but he seemed three times as pleased as he had been in the morning. It was evident that he had no apprehensions now, and that the public had been coming "many more." The *Mutter* came out later, evidently to keep an eye on me. The German and the *Mutter* frequently whispered together. Although the shop was closed he charged me a quarter-rouble. What unnecessary exactitude!

"You will every time pay; the public will one rouble, and you one quarter pay; for you are the good friend of your good friend; and I a friend respect . . ."

"Are you alive, are you alive, my cultured friend?" I cried, as I approached the crocodile, expecting my words to reach Ivan Matveitch from a distance and to flatter his vanity.

"Alive and well," he answered, as though from a long way off or from under the bed, though I was standing close beside him. "Alive and well; but of that later. . . . How are things going?"

As though purposely not hearing the question, I was just beginning with sympathetic haste to question him how he was, what it was like in the crocodile, and what, in fact, there was inside a crocodile. Both friendship and common civility demanded this. But with capricious annoyance he interrupted me.

"How are things going?" he shouted, in a shrill and on this occasion particularly revolting voice, addressing me peremptorily as usual.

I described to him my whole conversation with Timofey Semyonitch down to the smallest detail. As I told my story I tried to show my resentment in my voice.

"The old man is right," Ivan Matveitch pronounced as abruptly as usual in his conversation with me. "I like practical people, and can't endure sentimental milk-sops. I am ready to admit, however, that your idea about a special commission is not altogether absurd. I certainly have a great deal to report, both from a scientific and from an ethical point of view. But now all this has taken a new and unexpected aspect, and it is not worth while to trouble about mere salary. Listen attentively. Are you sitting down?"

"No, I am standing up."

"Sit down on the floor if there is nothing else, and listen attentively."

Resentfully I took a chair and put it down on the floor with a bang, in my anger.

"Listen," he began dictatorially. "The public came to-day in masses. There was no room left in the evening, and the police came in to keep order. At eight o'clock, that is, earlier than usual, the proprietor thought it necessary to close the shop and end the exhibition to count the money he had taken and prepare for to-morrow more conveniently. So I know there will be a regular fair to-morrow. So we may assume that all the most cultivated people in the capital, the ladies of the best society, the foreign ambassadors, the leading lawyers and so on, will all be present. What's more, people will be flowing here from the remotest provinces of our vast and interesting empire. The upshot of it is that I am the cynosure of all eyes, and though hidden to sight, I am eminent. I shall teach the idle crowd. Taught by experience, I shall be an example of greatness and resignation to fate! I shall be, so to say, a pulpit from which to instruct mankind. The mere biological details I can furnish about the monster I am inhabiting are of priceless value. And so, far from repining at what has happened, I confidently hope for the most brilliant of careers."

"You won't find it wearisome?" I asked sarcastically.

What irritated me more than anything was the extreme pomposity of his language. Nevertheless, it all rather disconcerted me. "What on earth, what, can this frivolous blockhead find to be so cocky about?" I muttered to myself. "He ought to be crying instead of being cocky."

"No!" he answered my observation sharply, "for I am full of great ideas, only now can I at leisure ponder over the amelioration of the lot of humanity. Truth and light will come forth now from the crocodile. I shall certainly develop a new economic theory of my own and I shall be proud of it—which I have hitherto been prevented from doing by my official duties and by trivial distractions. I shall refute everything and be a new Fourier. By the way, did you give Timofey Semyonitch the seven roubles?"

"Yes, out of my own pocket," I answered, trying to emphasise that fact in my voice.

"We will settle it," he answered·superciliously. "I confidently expect my salary to be raised, for who should get a rise if not I? I am of the utmost service now. But to business. My wife?"

"You are, I suppose, inquiring after Elena Ivanovna?"

"My wife?" he shouted, this time in a positive squeal.

There was no help for it! Meekly, though gnashing my teeth, I told him how I had left Elena Ivanovna. He did not even hear me out.

"I have special plans in regard to her," he began impatiently. "If I am celebrated *here*, I wish her to be celebrated *there*. Savants, poets, philosophers, foreign mineralogists, statesmen, after conversing in the morning with me, will visit her *salon* in the evening. From next week onwards she must have an 'At Home' every evening. With my salary doubled, we shall have the means for entertaining, and as the entertainment must not go beyond tea and hired footmen —that's settled. Both here and there they will talk of me. I have long thirsted for an opportunity for being talked about, but could not attain it, fettered by my humble position and low grade in the service. And now all this has been attained by a simple gulp on the part of the crocodile. Every word of mine will be listened to, every utterance will be thought over, repeated, printed. And I'll teach them what I am worth! They shall understand at last what abilities they have allowed to vanish in the entrails of a monster. 'This man might have been Foreign Minister or might have ruled a kingdom,' some will say. 'And that man did not rule a kingdom,' others will say. In what way am I inferior to a Garnier-Pagesishky or whatever they are called? My wife must be a worthy second—I have brains, she has beauty and charm. 'She is beautiful, and that is why she is his wife,' some will say. 'She is beautiful *because* she is his wife,' others will amend. To be ready for anything let Elena Ivanovna buy to-morrow the Encyclopædia edited by Andrey Kraevsky, that she may be able to converse on any topic. Above all, let her be sure to read the political leader in the *Petersburg News*, comparing it every day with the *Voice*. I imagine that the proprietor will consent to take me sometimes with the crocodile to my wife's brilliant *salon*. I will be in a tank in the middle of the magnificent drawing-room, and I will scintillate with witticisms which I will prepare in the morning. To the statesmen I will impart my projects; to the poet I will speak in rhyme; with the ladies I can be amusing and charming without impropriety, since I shall be no danger to their husbands' peace of mind. To all the rest I shall serve as a pattern of resignation to fate and the will of Providence. I shall make my wife a brilliant literary lady; I shall bring her forward and explain her to the public; as my wife she must be full of the most striking virtues; and if they are right in calling Andrey Alexandrovitch our Russian Alfred de Musset, they will be still more right in calling her our Russian Yevgenia Tour."

I must confess that although this wild nonsense was rather in Ivan Matveitch's habitual style, it did occur to me that he was in a fever and delirious. It was the same, everyday Ivan Matveitch, but magnified twenty times.

"My friend," I asked him, "are you hoping for a long life? Tell me, in fact, are you well? How do you eat, how do you sleep, how do you breathe? I am your friend, and you must admit that the incident is most unnatural, and consequently my curiosity is most natural."

"Idle curiosity and nothing else," he pronounced sententiously, "but you shall be satisfied. You ask how I am managing in the entrails of the monster? To begin with, the crocodile, to my amusement, turns out to be perfectly empty. His inside consists of a sort of huge empty sack made of gutta-percha, like the elastic goods sold in the Gorohovy Street, in the Morskaya, and, if I am not mistaken, in the Voznesensky Prospect. Otherwise, if you think of it, how could I find room?"

"Is it possible?" I cried, in a surprise that may well be understood. "Can the crocodile be perfectly empty?"

"Perfectly," Ivan Matveitch maintained sternly and impressively. "And in all probability, it is so constructed by the laws of Nature. The crocodile possesses nothing but jaws furnished with sharp teeth, and besides the jaws, a tail of considerable length—that is all, properly speaking. The middle part between these two extremities is an empty space enclosed by something of the nature of gutta-percha, probably really gutta-percha."

"But the ribs, the stomach, the intestines, the liver, the heart?" I interrupted quite angrily.

"There is nothing, absolutely nothing of all that, and probably there never has been. All that is the idle fancy of frivolous travellers. As one inflates an air-cushion, I am now with my person inflating the crocodile. He is incredibly elastic. Indeed, you might, as the friend of the family, get in with me if you were generous and self-sacrificing enough—and even with you here there would be room to spare. I even think that in the last resort I might send for Elena Ivanovna. However, this void, hollow formation of the crocodile is quite in keeping with the teachings of natural science. If, for instance, one had to construct a new crocodile, the question would naturally present itself. What is the fundamental characteristic of the crocodile? The answer is clear: to swallow human beings. How is one, in constructing the crocodile, to secure that he should swallow people? The answer is clearer still: construct him hollow. It was settled by physics long ago that Nature abhors a vacuum. Hence the inside of the crocodile must be hollow so that it may abhor the vacuum, and consequently swallow and so fill itself with anything it can come across. And that is the sole rational cause why every crocodile swallows men. It is not the same in the constitution of man: the emptier a man's head is, for instance, the less he feels the thirst to fill it, and that is the one exception to the general rule. It is all as clear as day to me now. I have deduced it by my own observation and experience, being, so to say, in the very bowels of Nature, in its retort, listening to the throbbing of its pulse. Even etymology supports me, for the very word crocodile means voracity. Crocodile—*crocodillo*—is evidently an Italian word, dating perhaps from the Egyptian Pharaohs, and evidently derived from the French verb *croquer*, which means to eat, to devour, in general to absorb nourishment. All these remarks I intend to deliver as my first lecture in Elena Ivanovna's *salon* when they take me there in the tank."

"My friend, oughtn't you at least to take some purgative?" I cried involuntarily.

"He is in a fever, a fever, he is feverish!" I repeated to myself in alarm.

"Nonsense!" he answered contemptuously. "Besides, in my present position it would be most inconvenient. I knew, though, you would be sure to talk of taking medicine."

"But, my friend, how . . . how do you take food now? Have you dined to-day?"

"No, but I am not hungry, and most likely I shall never take food again. And that, too, is quite natural; filling the whole interior of the crocodile I make him feel always full. Now he need not be fed for some years. On the other hand, nourished by me, he will naturally impart to me all the vital juices of his body; it is the same as with some accomplished coquettes who embed themselves and their whole persons for the night in raw steak, and then, after their morning bath, are fresh, supple, buxom and fascinating. In that way nourishing the crocodile, I myself obtain nourishment from him, consequently we mutually nourish one another. But as it is difficult even for a crocodile to digest a man like me, he must, no doubt, be conscious of a certain weight in his stomach—an organ which he does not, however, possess—and that is why, to avoid causing the creature suffering, I do not often turn over, and although I could turn over I do not do so from humanitarian motives. This is the one drawback of my present position, and in an allegorical sense Timofey Semyonitch was right in saying I was lying like a log. But I will prove that even lying like a log—nay, that only lying like a log—one can revolutionise the lot of mankind. All the great ideas and movements of our newspapers and magazines have evidently been the work of men who were lying like logs; that is why they call them divorced from the realities of life—but what does it matter, their saying that! I am constructing now a complete system of my own, and you wouldn't believe how easy it is! You have only to creep into a secluded corner or into a crocodile, to shut your eyes, and you immediately devise a perfect millennium for mankind. When you went away this afternoon I set to work at once and have already invented three systems, now I am preparing the fourth. It is true that at first one must refute everything that has gone before, but from the crocodile it is so easy to refute it; besides, it all becomes clearer, seen from the inside of the crocodile. . . . There are some drawbacks, though small ones, in my position, however; it is somewhat damp here and covered with a sort of slime; moreover, there is a smell of india-rubber like the smell of my old goloshes. That is all, there are no other drawbacks."

"Ivan Matveitch," I interrupted, "all this is a miracle in which I can scarcely believe. And can you, can you intend never to dine again?"

"What trivial nonsense you are troubling about, you thoughtless, frivolous creature! I talk to you about great ideas, and you . . . Understand that I am sufficiently nourished by the great ideas which light up the darkness in which I am enveloped. The good-natured proprietor has, however, after consulting the kindly *Mutter*, decided with her that they will every morning insert into the monster's jaws a bent metal tube, something like a whistle pipe, by means of which I can absorb coffee or broth with bread soaked in it. The pipe has already been bespoken in the neighbourhood, but I think this is superfluous luxury. I hope to live at least a thousand years, if it is true that crocodiles live so long, which, by the way —good thing I thought of it—you had better look up in some natural history to-morrow and tell me, for I may have been mistaken and have mixed it up with some excavated monster. There is only one reflection rather troubles me: as I am dressed in cloth and have boots on, the crocodile can obviously not digest me. Besides, I am alive, and so am opposing the process of digestion with my whole will power; for you can understand that I do not wish to be turned into what all nourishment turns into, for that would be too humiliating for me. But there is one thing I am afraid of: in a thousand years the cloth of my coat, unfortunately of Russian make, may decay, and then, left without clothing, I might perhaps, in spite of my indignation, begin to be digested; and though by day nothing would induce me to allow it, at night, in my sleep, when a man's will deserts him, I may be overtaken by the humiliating destiny of a potato, a pancake, or veal. Such an idea reduces me to fury. This alone is an argument for the revision of the tariff and the encouragement of the importation of English cloth, which is stronger and so will withstand Nature longer when one is swallowed by a crocodile. At the first opportunity I will impart this idea to some statesman and at the same time to the political writers on our Petersburg dailies. Let them publish it abroad. I trust this will not be the only idea they will borrow from me. I foresee that every morning a regular crowd of them, provided with quarter-roubles from the editorial office, will be flocking around me to seize my ideas on the telegrams of the previous day. In brief, the future presents itself to me in the rosiest light."

"Fever, fever!" I whispered to myself.

"My friend, and freedom?" I asked, wishing to learn his views thoroughly. "You are, so to speak, in prison, while every man has a right to the enjoyment of freedom."

"You are a fool," he answered. "Savages love independence, wise men love order; and if there is no order . . ."

"Ivan Matveich, spare me, please!"

"Hold your tongue and listen!" he squealed, vexed at my interrupting him. "Never has my spirit soared as now. In my narrow refuge there is only one thing that I dread—the literary criticisms of the monthlies and the hiss of our satirical papers. I am afraid that thoughtless visitors, stupid and envious people and nihilists in general, may turn me into ridicule. But I will take measures. I am impatiently awaiting the response of the public to-morrow, and especially the opinion of the newspapers. You must tell me about the papers to-morrow."

"Very good; to-morrow I will bring a perfect pile of papers with me."

"To-morrow it is too soon to expect reports in the newspapers, for it will take four days for it to be advertised. But from to-day come to me every evening by the back way through the yard. I am intending to employ you as my secretary. You shall read the newspapers and magazines to me, and I will dictate to you my ideas and give you commissions. Be particularly careful not to forget the foreign telegrams. Let all the European telegrams be here every day. But enough; most likely you are sleepy by now. Go home, and do not think of what I said just now about criticisms: I am not afraid of it, for the critics themselves are in a critical position. One has only to be wise and virtuous and one will certainly get on to a pedestal. If not Socrates, then Diogenes, or perhaps both of them together—that is my future rôle among mankind."

So frivolously and boastfully did Ivan Matveitch hasten to express himself before me, like feverish weak-willed women who, as we are told by the proverb, cannot keep a secret. All that he told me about the crocodile struck me as most suspicious. How was it possible that the crocodile was absolutely hollow? I don't mind betting that he was bragging from vanity and partly to humiliate me. It is true that he was an invalid and one must make allowances for invalids; but I must frankly confess, I never could endure Ivan Matveitch. I have been trying all my life, from a child up, to escape from his tutelage and have not been able to! A thousand times over I have been tempted to break with him altogether, and every time I have been drawn to him again, as though I were still hoping to prove something to him or to revenge myself on him. A strange thing, this friendship! I can positively assert that nine-tenths of my friendship for him was made up of malice. On this occasion, however, we parted with genuine feeling.

"Your friend a very clever man!" the German said to me in an undertone as he moved to see me out; he had been listening all the time attentively to our conversation.

"*A propos*," I said, "while I think of it: how much would you ask for your crocodile in case any one wanted to buy it?"

Ivan Matveitch, who heard the question, was waiting with curiosity for the answer; it was evident that he did not want the German to ask too little; anyway, he cleared his throat in a peculiar way on hearing my question.

At first the German would not listen—was positively angry.

"No one will dare my own crocodile to buy!" he cried furiously, and turned as red as a boiled lobster. "Me not want to sell the crocodile! I would not for the crocodile a million thalers take. I took a hundred and thirty thalers from the public to-day, and I shall to-morrow ten thousand take, and then a hundred thousand every day I shall take. I will not him sell."

Ivan Matveitch positively chuckled with satisfaction. Controlling myself—for I felt it was a duty to my friend—I hinted coolly and reasonably to the crazy German that his calculations were not quite correct, that if he makes a hundred thousand every day, all Petersburg will have visited him in four days, and then there will be no one left to bring him roubles, that life and death are in God's hands, that the crocodile may burst or Ivan Matveitch may fall ill and die, and so on and so on.

The German grew pensive.

"I will him drops from the chemist's get," he said, after pondering, "and will save your friend that he die not."

"Drops are all very well," I answered, "but consider, too, that the thing may get into the law courts. Ivan Matveitch's wife may demand the restitution of her lawful spouse. You are intending to get rich, but do you intend to give Elena Ivanovna a pension?"

"No, me not intend," said the German in stern decision.

"No, we not intend," said the *Mutter*, with positive malignancy.

"And so would it not be better for you to accept something now, at once, a secure and solid though moderate sum, than to leave things to chance? I ought to tell you that I am inquiring simply from curiosity."

The German drew the *Mutter* aside to consult with her in a corner where there stood a case with the largest and ugliest monkey of his collection.

"Well, you will see!" said Ivan Matveitch.

As for me, I was at that moment burning with the desire, first, to give the German a thrashing, next, to give the *Mutter* an even sounder one, and, thirdly, to give Ivan Matveitch the soundest thrashing of all for his boundless vanity. But all this paled beside the answer of the rapacious German.

After consultation with the *Mutter* he demanded for his crocodile fifty thousand roubles in bonds of the last Russian loan with lottery voucher attached, a brick house in Gorohovy Street with a chemist's shop attached, and in addition the rank of Russian colonel.

"You see!" Ivan Matveitch cried triumphantly. "I told you so! Apart from this last senseless desire for the rank of a colonel, he is perfectly right, for he fully understands the present value of the monster he is exhibiting. The economic principle before everything!"

"Upon my word!" I cried furiously to the German. "But what should you be made a colonel for? What exploit have you performed? What service have you done? In what way have you gained military glory? You are really crazy!"

"Crazy!" cried the German, offended. "No, a person very sensible, but you very stupid! I have a colonel deserved for that I have a crocodile shown and in him a live *hofrath* sitting! And a Russian can crocodile not show and a live *hofrath* in him sitting! Me extremely clever man and much wish colonel to be!"

"Well, good-bye, then, Ivan Matveitch!" I cried, shaking with fury, and I went out of the crocodile room almost at a run.

I felt that in another minute I could not have answered for myself. The unnatural expectations of these two blockheads were insupportable. The cold air refreshed me and somewhat moderated my indignation. At last, after spitting vigorously fifteen times on each side, I took a cab, got home, undressed and flung myself into bed. What vexed me more than anything was my having become his secretary. Now I was to die of boredom there every evening, doing the duty of a true friend! I was ready to beat myself for it, and I did, in fact, after putting out the candle and pulling up the bedclothes, punch myself several times on the head and various parts of my body. That somewhat relieved me, and at last I fell asleep fairly soundly, in fact, for I was very tired. All night long I could dream of nothing but monkeys, but towards morning I dreamt of Elena Ivanovna.

IV

The monkeys I dreamed about, I surmise, because they were shut up in the case at the German's; but Elena Ivanovna was a different story.

I may as well say at once, I loved the lady, but I make haste—post-haste—to make a qualification. I loved her as a father, neither more nor less. I judge that because I often felt an irresistible desire to kiss her little head or her rosy cheek. And though I never carried out this inclination, I would not have refused even to kiss her lips. And not merely her lips, but her teeth, which always gleamed so charmingly like two rows of pretty, well-matched pearls when she laughed. She laughed extraordinarily often. Ivan Matveitch in demonstrative moments used to call her his "darling absurdity"—a name extremely happy and appropriate. She was a perfect sugar-plum, and that was all one could say of her. Therefore I am utterly at a loss to understand what possessed Ivan Matveitch to imagine his wife as a Russian Yevgenia Tour? Anyway, my dream, with the exception of the monkeys, left a most pleasant impression upon me, and going over all the incidents of the previous day as I drank my morning cup of tea, I resolved to go and see Elena Ivanovna at once on my way to the office—which, indeed, I was bound to do as the friend of the family.

In a tiny little room out of the bedroom—the so-called little drawing-room, though their big drawing-room was little too—Elena Ivanovna was sitting, in some half-transparent morning wrapper, on a smart little sofa before a little tea-table, drinking coffee out of a little cup in which she was dipping a minute biscuit. She was ravishingly pretty, but struck me as being at the same time rather pensive.

"Ah, that's you, naughty man!" she said, greeting me with an absent-minded smile. "Sit down, feather-head, have some coffee. Well, what were you doing yesterday? Were you at the masquerade?"

"Why, were you? I don't go, you know. Besides, yesterday I was visiting our captive. . . ." I sighed and assumed a pious expression as I took the coffee.

"Whom? . . . What captive? . . . Oh, yes! Poor fellow! Well, how is he—bored? Do you know . . . I wanted to ask you . . . I suppose I can ask for a divorce now?"

"A divorce!" I cried in indignation and almost spilled the coffee. "It's that swarthy fellow," I thought to myself bitterly.

There was a certain swarthy gentleman with little moustaches who was something in the architectural line, and who came far too often to see them, and was extremely skilful in amusing Elena Ivanovna. I must confess I hated him and there was no doubt that he had succeeded in seeing Elena Ivanovna yesterday either at the masquerade or even here, and putting all sorts of nonsense into her head.

"Why," Elena Ivanovna rattled off hurriedly, as though it were a lesson she had learnt, "if he is going to stay on in the crocodile, perhaps not come back all his life, while I sit waiting for him here! A husband ought to live at home, and not in a crocodile. . . ."

"But this was an unforeseen occurrence," I was beginning, in very comprehensible agitation.

"Oh, no, don't talk to me, I won't listen, I won't listen," she cried, suddenly getting quite cross. "You are always against me, you wretch! There's no doing anything with you, you will never give me any advice! Other people tell me that I can get a divorce because Ivan Matveitch will not get his salary now."

"Elena Ivanovna! is it you I hear!" I exclaimed pathetically. "What villain could have put such an idea into your head? And divorce on such a trivial ground as a salary is quite impossible. And poor Ivan Matveitch, poor Ivan Matveitch is, so to speak, burning with love for you even in the bowels of the monster. What's more, he is melting away with love like a lump of sugar. Yesterday while you were enjoying yourself at the masquerade, he was saying that he might in the last resort send for you as his lawful spouse to join him in the entrails of the monster, especially as it appears the crocodile is exceedingly roomy, not only able to accommodate two but even three persons. . . ."

And then I told her all that interesting part of my conversation the night before with Ivan Matveitch.

"What, what!" she cried, in surprise. "You want me to get into the monster too, to be with Ivan Matveitch? What an idea! And how am I to get in there, in my hat and crinoline? Heavens, what foolishness! And what should I look like while I was getting into it, and very likely there would be some one there to see me! It's absurd! And what should I have to eat there? And . . . and . . . and what should I do there when . . . Oh, my goodness, what will they think of next? . . . And what should I have to amuse me there? . . . You say there's a smell of gutta-percha? And what should I do if we quarrelled—should we have to go on staying there side by side? Foo, how horrid!"

"I agree, I agree with all those arguments, my sweet Elena Ivanovna," I interrupted, striving to express myself with that natural enthusiasm which always overtakes a man when he feels the truth is on his side. "But one thing you have not appreciated in all this, you have not realised that he cannot live without you if he is inviting you there; that is a proof of love, passionate, faithful, ardent love. . . . You have thought too little of his love, dear Elena Ivanovna!"

"I won't, I won't, I won't hear anything about it!" waving me off with her pretty little hand with glistening pink nails that had just been washed and polished. "Horrid man! You will reduce me to tears! Get into it yourself, if you like the prospect. You are his friend, get in and keep him company, and spend your life discussing some tedious science. . . ."

"You are wrong to laugh at this suggestion"—I checked the frivolous woman with dignity—"Ivan Matveitch has invited me as it is. You, of course, are summoned there by duty; for me, it would be an act of generosity. But when Ivan Matveitch described to me last night the elasticity of the crocodile, he hinted very plainly that there would be room not only for you two, but for me also as a friend of the family, especially if I wished to join you, and therefore . . ."

"How so, the three of us?" cried Elena Ivanovna, looking at me in surprise. "Why, how should we . . . are we going to be all three there together? Ha-ha-ha! How silly you both are! Ha-ha-ha! I shall certainly pinch you all the time, you wretch! Ha-ha-ha! Ha-ha-ha!"

And falling back on the sofa, she laughed till she cried. All this— the tears and the laughter—were so fascinating that I could not resist rushing eagerly to kiss her hand, which she did not oppose, though she did pinch my ears lightly as a sign of reconciliation.

Then we both grew very cheerful, and I described to her in detail all Ivan Matveitch's plans. The thought of her evening receptions and her *salon* pleased her very much.

"Only I should need a great many new dresses," she observed, "and so Ivan Matveitch must send me as much of his salary as possible and as soon as possible. Only . . . only I don't know about that," she added thoughtfully. "How can he be brought here in the tank? That's very absurd. I don't want my husband to be carried about in a tank. I should feel quite ashamed for my visitors to see it. . . . I don't want that, no, I don't."

"By the way, while I think of it, was Timofey Semyonitch here yesterday?"

"Oh, yes, he was; he came to comfort me, and do you know, we played cards all the time. He played for sweetmeats, and if I lost he was to kiss my hands. What a wretch he is! And only fancy, he almost came to the masquerade with me, really!"

"He was carried away by his feelings!" I observed. "And who would not be with you, you charmer?"

"Oh, get along with your compliments! Stay, I'll give you a pinch as a parting present. I've learnt to pinch awfully well lately. Well, what do you say to that? By the way, you say Ivan Matveitch spoke several times of me yesterday?"

"N-no, not exactly. . . . I must say he is thinking more now of the fate of humanity, and wants . . ."

"Oh, let him! You needn't go on! I am sure it's fearfully boring. I'll go and see him some time. I shall certainly go to-morrow. Only not to-day; I've got a headache, and besides, there will be such a lot of people there to-day. . . . They'll say, 'That's his wife,' and I shall feel ashamed. . . . Good-bye. You will be . . . there this evening, won't you?"

"To see him, yes. He asked me to go and take him the papers."

"That's capital. Go and read to him. But don't come and see me to-day. I am not well, and perhaps I may go and see some one. Good-bye, you naughty man."

"It's that swarthy fellow is going to see her this evening," I thought.

At the office, of course, I gave no sign of being consumed by these cares and anxieties. But soon I noticed some of the most progressive papers seemed to be passing particularly rapidly from hand to hand among my colleagues, and were being read with an extremely serious expression of face. The first one that reached me was the *News-sheet*, a paper of no particular party but humanitarian in general, for which it was regarded with contempt among us, though it was read. Not without surprise I read in it the following paragraph:

"Yesterday strange rumours were circulating among the spacious ways and sumptuous buildings of our vast metropolis. A certain well-known *bon-vivant* of the highest society, probably weary of the *cuisine* at Borel's and at the X. Club, went into the Arcade, into the place where an immense crocodile recently brought to the metropolis is being exhibited, and insisted on its being prepared for his dinner. After bargaining with the proprietor he at once set to work to devour him (that is, not the proprietor, a very meek and punctilious German, but his crocodile), cutting juicy morsels with his penknife from the living animal, and swallowing them with extraordinary rapidity. By degrees the whole crocodile disappeared into the vast recesses of his stomach, so that he was even on the point of attacking an ichneumon, a constant companion of the crocodile, probably imagining that the latter would be as savoury. We are by no means opposed to that new article of diet with which foreign *gourmands* have long been familiar. We have, indeed, predicted that it would come. English lords and travellers make up regular parties for catching crocodiles in Egypt, and consume the back of the monster cooked like beefsteak, with mustard, onions and potatoes. The French who followed in the train of Lesseps prefer the paws baked in hot ashes, which they do, however, in opposition to the English, who laugh at them. Probably both ways would be appreciated among us. For our part, we are delighted at a new branch of industry, of which our great and varied fatherland stands preeminently in need. Probably before a year is out crocodiles will be brought in hundreds to replace this first one, lost in the stomach of a Petersburg *gourmand*. And why should not the crocodile be acclimatised among us in Russia? If the water of the Neva is too cold for these interesting strangers, there are ponds in the capital and rivers and lakes outside it. Why not breed crocodiles at Pargolovo, for instance, or at Pavlovsk, in the Presnensky Ponds and in Samoteka in Moscow? While providing agreeable, wholesome nourishment for our fastidious *gourmands*, they might at the same time entertain the ladies who walk about these ponds and instruct the children in natural history. The crocodile skin might be used for making jewel-cases, boxes, cigar-cases, pocket-books, and possibly more than one thousand saved up in the greasy notes that are peculiarly beloved of merchants might be laid by in crocodile skin. We hope to return more than once to this interesting topic."

Though I had foreseen something of the sort, yet the reckless inaccuracy of the paragraph overwhelmed me. Finding no one with whom to share my impression, I turned to Prohor Savvitch who was sitting opposite to me, and noticed that the latter had been watching me for some time, while in his hand he held the *Voice* as though he were on the point of passing it to me. Without a word he took the *News-sheet* from me, and as he handed me the *Voice* he drew a line with his nail against an article to which he probably wished to call my attention. This Prohor Savvitch was a very queer man: a taciturn old bachelor, he was not on intimate terms with any of us, scarcely spoke to any one in the office, always had an opinion of his own about everything, but could not bear to impart it to any one.

He lived alone. Hardly any one among us had ever been in his lodging.

This was what I read in the *Voice*.

"Every one knows that we are progressive and humanitarian and want to be on a level with Europe in this respect. But in spite of all our exertions and the efforts of our paper we are still far from maturity, as may be judged from the shocking incident which took place yesterday in the Arcade and which we predicted long ago. A foreigner arrives in the capital bringing with him a crocodile which he begins exhibiting in the Arcade. We immediately hasten to welcome a new branch of useful industry such as our powerful and varied fatherland stands in great need of. Suddenly yesterday at four o'clock in the afternoon a gentleman of exceptional stoutness enters the foreigner's shop in an intoxicated condition, pays his entrance money, and immediately without any warning leaps into the jaws of the crocodile, who was forced, of course, to swallow him, if only from an instinct of self-preservation, to avoid being crushed. Tumbling into the inside of the crocodile, the stranger at once dropped asleep. Neither the shouts of the foreign proprietor, nor the lamentations of his terrified family, nor threats to send for the police made the slightest impression. Within the crocodile was heard nothing but laughter and a promise to flay him (*sic*), though the poor mammal, compelled to swallow such a mass, was vainly shedding tears. An uninvited guest is worse than a Tartar. But in spite of the proverb the insolent visitor would not leave. We do not know how to explain such barbarous incidents which prove our lack of culture and disgrace us in the eyes of foreigners. The recklessness of the Russian temperament has found a fresh outlet. It may be asked what was the object of the uninvited visitor? A warm and comfortable abode? But there are many excellent houses in the capital with very cheap and comfortable lodgings, with the Neva water laid on, and a staircase lighted by gas, frequently with a hall-porter maintained by the proprietor. We would call our readers' attention to the barbarous treatment of domestic animals: it is difficult, of course, for the crocodile to digest such a mass all at once, and now he lies swollen out to the size of a mountain, awaiting death in insufferable agonies. In Europe persons guilty of inhumanity towards domestic animals have long been punished by law. But in spite of our European enlightenment, in spite of our European pavements, in spite of the European architecture of our houses, we are still far from shaking off our time-honoured traditions.

"Though the houses are new, the conventions are old."

"And, indeed, the houses are not new, at least the staircases in them are not. We have more than once in our paper alluded to the fact that in the Petersburg Side in the house of the merchant Lukyanov the steps of the wooden staircase have decayed, fallen away, and have long been a danger for Afimya Skapidarov, a soldier's wife who works in the house, and is often obliged to go up the stairs with water or armfuls of wood. At last our predictions have come true: yesterday evening at half-past eight Afimya Skapidarov fell down with a basin of soup and broke her leg. We do not know whether Lukyanov will mend his staircase now, Russians are often wise after the event, but the victim of Russian carelessness has by now been taken to the hospital. In the same way we shall never cease to maintain that the house-porters who clear away the mud from the wooden pavement in the Viborgsky Side ought not to spatter the legs of passers-by, but should throw the mud up into heaps as is done in Europe," and so on, and so on.

"What's this?" I asked in some perplexity, looking at Prohor Savvitch. "What's the meaning of it?"

"How do you mean?"

"Why, upon my word! Instead of pitying Ivan Matveitch, they pity the crocodile!"

"What of it? They have pity even for a beast, a *mammal*. We must be up to Europe, mustn't we? They have a very warm feeling for crocodiles there too. He-he-he!"

Saying this, queer old Prohor Savvitch dived into his papers and would not utter another word.

I stuffed the *Voice* and the *News-sheet* into my pocket and collected as many old copies of the newspapers as I could find for Ivan Matveitch's diversion in the evening, and though the evening was far off, yet on this occasion I slipped away from the office early to go to the Arcade and look, if only from a distance, at what was going on there, and to listen to the various remarks and currents of opinion. I foresaw that there would be a regular crush there, and turned up the collar of my coat to meet it. I somehow felt rather shy—so unaccustomed are we to publicity. But I feel that I have no right to report my own prosaic feelings when faced with this remarkable and original incident.

Makel-Adel

by IVAN TURGENEFF

A man whom we cannot respect, and yet cannot help respecting, for he was generous beyond the tradition of his society, though his generosity was stained by those traditions. And a horse of which one would have said there was none like him. And yet . . .

I

AFTER the death of his friend, Nedopuskin, Tchertapkanoff again began to drink. As his money had all been spent, and his serfs had run away, hunting was out of the question. In spite of his situation, his self-importance was not lessened. On the contrary, the worse his affairs, the greater his pride.

One day as he was riding through a near-by village, a sound of screaming and brawling reached his ears. It came from the front of the inn.

"What is going on here?" he demanded imperiously of an old woman who was standing at the door of her cottage.

"God knows, sir! Our people are flogging a Jew."

"Why are they flogging him?"

"I don't know, sir. Why shouldn't they? Didn't he crucify our Saviour?"

Driving his horse into the throng, Tchertapkanoff struck out right and left. The people scattered, revealing the creature they had been ill-treating. He lay without moving, a small, haggard, darkish man in a caftan of hemp that was torn and dishevelled.

"Why, you have killed this Jew," cried Pantalei Tchertapkanoff, whirling his whip.

The angry voice seemed to arouse the prostrate man. He sprang to his feet, slipped behind Pantalei, and clung to his saddle-girth. At that the crowd burst into a laugh.

"Why did they strike you?" asked Pantalei.

"I cannot tell. Their cattle began to die and they appeared to think that I—"

"Ah, well for the moment keep close to my saddle and come with me." He turned to the people. "You know me, I live at my own place, Bessonovo. Lay a complaint against me if you like!"

Blowing out his breath importantly he rode slowly away.

Some days later, Perfishka, the only servant who had remained with him, announced there was a horseman at the door. Pantalei went out onto the stairs and saw in the yard the Jew he had rescued. The man was sitting proudly on a very fine Cossack horse. He had his cap under his arm, his feet in the straps above the stirrups, and the torn skirts of his caftan hanging on each side of the saddle. Pantalei stared without returning the man's obsequious greeting.

"Hallo, there!" he cried. "Get down if you don't want me to fetch you down."

The Jew at once obeyed, and approached, smiling and bowing, the reins in his hand.

"What do you want?" asked Pantalei.

"Does it please your grace to take a look at the horse?"

"Why, yes, and it is a fine horse. Where did you get it? Did you steal it?"

"Not at all, your grace. I am an honest Jew. I got it for your grace. A finer horse is not to be found in the whole district, nor one so good."

"The horse is not bad," Tchertapkanoff was too great a lover of horseflesh not to appreciate the animal's points, but he spoke indifferently.

"Put your hand on him, your grace; pat him on the neck." The other did so. "There! Do you see?"

Pantalei with a diffident air laid his hand on the horse's neck, stroked it twice, ran his fingers through the mane, then down along the spine to a certain spot above the loin, and pressed tightly on this spot. The horse immediately bent his back and with a sidelong glance at Pantalei, threw his forelegs forward. The Jew laughed, clapping his hands gently. "He knows his master!"

But Pantalei was instantly annoyed. "Now, don't lie," he cried. "I have no money to buy him and I don't take presents from a Jew."

"I should not dare offer you a present," cried the Jew. He added slyly, "I will wait for the money."

Tchertapkanoff reflected. "How much do you want?"

"What I paid myself. Two hundred roubles."

The horse was worth twice—perhaps three times—that amount. "And the money; when do you want it?"

"Whenever your grace pleases."

"That is no answer. Speak plainly, thou son of Herod. Am I to give you my note?"

"Well, then, we will say in six months. Is that your pleasure?"

Pantalei grunted. "I have no need of the saddle. Take it off."

"Well—why not, why not? I will take it off at once."

"The money shall be yours in six months. And mark you, not two hundred, but two hundred and fifty. Silence! I owe you two hundred and fifty."

He could not look the other in the face. "It is evidently a present," he thought. "The Jew is grateful."

"Your grace," began the other, somewhat emboldened, "according to Russian custom, we ought to shake hands—"

"Have you lost your senses?" cried the landowner and shouted for his sole remaining servant. "Perfishka! Here, take this horse to the stable. His name is Makel-Adel."

Turning away importantly, he was about to go up the stairs. Moved incomprehensibly, however, he ran back to the Jew and pressed his hand. "Tell no one," he cried and rushed away.

From the day Makel-Adel came into Pantalei's possession he was the interest and joy of his life. The horse was worthy of the care bestowed on him. Fire, flaming fire! and the dignity of a boyar. Indefatigable, steadfast, patient, and to feed he cost very little. If he paced, then it was as if you were being carried on hands; if he cantered you were rocked in a cradle and he went so swiftly that a rifle-bullet would hardly have overtaken him. His wind was marvellous and his feet were like steel; he never stumbled. To clear a ditch or a hedge was a trifle to him—and, his intelligence! If called, he came running with his head raised; if you told him to stand and left him, he would not stir. When you returned he would neigh softly, as if to say, "Here I am." Fear he had never known; in the densest darkness, in a driving snowstorm, he could find his way. If a stranger had approached him, he would have torn him with his teeth, and it would not have been well for any dog to come near. A blow on the head from one of his forefeet and there would have been a dog the less. Makel-Adel, also, was sensitive of his honour. The whip might be used, but only as an ornament.

How fondly Tchertapkanoff petted and cared for this horse. His coat shone like new silver. To a hand gliding over it it felt like clean velvet. Pantalei himself braided his mane, washed it and the tail with beer, and rubbed the hoofs with black ointment.

When he mounted Makel-Adel to take a ride—not to call on his neighbours, for with them he had no intercourse—but to ride over their fields or past their houses, he said to himself, "Fools, you can admire at a distance."

If a hunt was to take place in the neighbourhood, he would hasten to the meet, gambol with his horse before them, but never suffer anybody to approach him.

On one occasion a man had dashed after him, shouting: "Hallo, there! Ask whatever you like for your horse! A thousand roubles! More—anything you like. I would give my wife—and my children!"

Tchertapkanoff stopped Makel-Adel.

"If you were a king," said he, unconsciously paraphrasing Shakespeare, "and would give your whole kingdom for my horse, I would not take it."

He caused Makel-Adel to rear, swung him in the air on his hindlegs, and rushed off across the stubble. The man who had made the offer, and who was reputed to be a prince, dashed his cap on the ground, and threw himself ragingly with his face on the cap.

II

The time for payment drew on. Tchertapkanoff had not been able to put by fifty roubles towards the two hundred and fifty.

"If the Jew will not have any mercy, I will give him my house, my home, and ride away—die of hunger; but I cannot part from Makel-Adel."

Fate took pity on him. A distant female relative died, leaving him two thousand roubles, and he obtained the money one day before the payment fell due. He thought of nothing, not even of brandy —from the day Makel-Adel came he had not tasted a drop. He ran to the stable, kissed his friend above the nostrils, where a horse's skin is soft and tender. Returning to the house, he counted out two hundred and fifty roubles, tied them up and sealed the package. Then he threw himself on his back, and lay smoking and thinking how he would spend the rest of the money. He would buy some dogs, they should be of the genuine Kostroma breed. He would give Perfishka a new coat with yellow galloon in the seams. Eventually, still in a blissful frame of mind, he fell asleep.

But he had a bad dream. He was out hunting—not on Makel-Adel, but on a camel-like animal. A white fox came running toward him, he was about to whirl his whip and set the dogs on, when, instead of the whip he found he had only a whisk of linden bast in his hand; and the fox, running before him mockingly showed his tongue. He sprang from the camel, stumbled and—fell into the hands of a police-officer. He woke up; the room was dark, the cock had crowed a second time. Far away, he heard the neighing of a horse.

A cold shudder ran through him; he leaped out of bed, groped for his clothes, pulled them on, snatched the stable-key from under his pillow, and rushed out. The stable was in the far corner of the yard, its back to the open field. Tchertapkanoff's hands trembled so much that he could not at once find the keyhole. When he had found it, he could not at first turn the key.

"Malishka!" he cried softly, and heard no replying sound. He struggled with the key but it would not turn. He pushed and the door swung open—then it could not have been locked! Stepping over the threshold, he once more called the horse, this time by name. A mouse skittered through the straw but there was no other sound. Tchertapkanoff rushed to the one of the three stalls which had been occupied by Makel-Adel; it was empty. He reeled from the first stall into the second, then into the third—which was full of hay— and at last ran back to the yard.

"Perfishka! Perfishka!" he shouted. "Makel-Adel is stolen!"

The little Cossack came running in his shirt from the loft where he slept. Master and servant collided in the middle of the yard.

"A lanthorn—quick."

In the kitchen the fire was long since out. Flint and tinder were not at once to be found, and when found would not work. Pantalei tore the steel from the hands of the terror-stricken servant. At the end of several minutes a tallow dip was made to burn in the broken lanthorn, and Pantalei and the Cossack ran out with it to the stable.

The fence had long been in a dilapidated state; near the stable some feet of it lay flat. Perfishka cried: "Master, look here! It was not so yesterday."

Pantalei rushed to the spot. "Hoof-tracks!" Swinging himself over, he ran across the field, shouting: "Makel-Adel."

The dawn was appearing when at last, his clothes plastered with mud, he returned. He was sinking with weariness, but he drove Perfishka away. He did not go to bed, but sat on the chair nearest to the door, his head in his hands.

Throughout the whole disturbance none of the dogs had barked. To be sure, there were only two and they were still young. Moreover, the cold had forced them to dig themselves down under the ground. Still they might have barked.

"What shall I do now?" thought Pantalei. "Buy another horse? I have money enough, but where could I find another like him?"

"Pantalei Jeremeitsch!" cried Perfishka at the door. "That Jew— he is here."

Tchertapkanoff tore the door open. Terrified by the sight of his wild, dishevelled figure, the Jew, who had been standing behind Perfishka, took to his heels. In two leaps Pantalei overtook him and seized him by the throat.

"Have mercy, your grace!" groaned the Jew.

"Where is my horse? To whom have you sold him?"

His grip on the man's throat prevented him from answering.

"I will pay you the money, but I will murder you—"

"You have murdered him, master," cried Perfishka; but on Tchertapkanoff relaxing his grip, placing the Jew on a bench and pouring brandy down his throat, he revived sufficiently to answer questions. It then became clear he had no knowledge of the theft.

"Where did you buy the horse?"

"In the Koursk district, at the Fair of Sosna. I bought him of a Cossack."

"Old or young?"

"Of middle age."

"Had he owned the horse long?"

"He said so."

"Then it is he who has stolen him. What is your name?"

"Moshel Leiba."

"Leiba," said Pantalei, "come with me and let us look for Makel-Adel. We will go to the horse-fairs, to cities, villages, we will go everywhere. An inheritance has come to me and I will spend my last farthing in the search for my friend. Leiba, your soul is better than many a Christian soul. Have pity on me and come, for alone I cannot carry out my undertaking."

The Jew made answer—his business!—but Pantalei would not listen and eventually he induced him to go. The following day in a peasant waggon, they started. The house was intrusted to Perfishka and a deaf old woman who acted as cook.

A year passed. The old cook died; Perfishka was preparing to abandon the house when the deacon of the parish received a letter from Pantalei which told of his impending return.

A few days later he rode into the yard on Makel-Adel, and jumping off cast a triumphant glance around and cried loudly: "I have found him. Yes, in spite of ill-fate and my enemies."

With long strides he went toward the stable. Perfishka stared at him fixedly, for he had grown haggard and wore a gloomy look. Leading the horse into his former stall, Pantalei said: "There you are, home again at last."

The same day he hired a trustworthy watchman.

Pantalei resumed his previous way of life—but not quite as before. The day after his return, he called Perfishka in and related, in his deep voice, how he had found Makel-Adel. He sat with his face turned to the window, smoking his long-stemmed pipe; and Perfishka stood on the threshold with his hands behind him. Reverently the Cossack listened to the tale of futile journeys, and of how at length Pantalei had come to the annual fair at Romma. Nothing there, he had, at first, thought; but on the fifth day as he was making up his mind to depart, he had caught sight of Makel-Adel, hitched with three other horses to a telega. Makel-Adel had recognized him, neighed and tried to tear himself loose.

"It was not a Cossack who had him," continued Pantalei, "but a gipsy. I claimed the horse as mine; but the gipsy screamed as if I had been murdering him, swore he had bought it and offered to bring witnesses. I spat at him but paid his price—may the devil take him! In Karatchej district, once, deceived by Leiba, I attacked a Cossack —smashed his face; he turned out to be the son of a priest and I had to pay one hundred and fifty roubles. However, what is of importance is that I have Makel-Adel again. If you ever see a Cossack in the vicinity run at once and fetch me my gun."

Thus spoke Pantalei to his servant Perfishka; but he was not in reality as calm as he appeared, for, alas, in the depths of his soul he was not absolutely convinced that the horse he had brought back was Makel-Adel.

III

At times his doubts appeared to him senseless and he was happy; but at others they would, in spite of him, come creeping back, to gnaw at his heart till he was desperate. During the journey home, he had been too glad to have found Makel-Adel, to harbour suspicions; but after his return to Bessonovo, they came upon him in crowds. Nevertheless he would have torn to pieces any man who had dared to suggest that the horse was not the genuine Makel-Adel. Although he did not invite congratulations, he accepted them. However, as his suspicions took stronger hold, he tried to avoid people.

The physical difference between the two horses was not what disturbed him. The original Makel-Adel's tail and mane had been perhaps a trifle thinner, his ears more pointed, his legs shorter, his eyes brighter. It was rather a certain moral difference which made him suspicious. Whenever his master entered the stable, the former Makel-Adel would look up and neigh; whereas the new horse would continue to chew his hay. Neither animal stirred when his rider dismounted; but while the former responded to every call, the latter remained standing like a piece of wood. The first leaped higher and farther, the latter went more evenly in pace, but jumped more

in trotting and occasionally struck his fore and hind shoes together
—a thing that had never happened with the other. The new horse
was always shaking his ears; the other, if once he laid his back, kept
them so, on the watch for the slightest signal. If the old Makel-Adel
perceived any want of cleanliness about him, he would kick against
the walls of his stall; the present horse did not seem to care if he
stood knee-deep in dirt. If you placed the former with his head
against the wind, he would draw a breath from the depths of his
lungs and shake himself; while the latter would only snort. To the
former, damp and rain were disagreeable; the latter hardly noticed
them. He was undoubtedly of coarser grain; moreover, he was hard-
bitted and not as pleasant-tempered.

Thus reflected Tchertapkanoff. At times, however, when the
horse was flying over a newly-ploughed field or leaping to the bottom of a washed-out ravine, his rapture would check the beating
of his heart and he would cease to make comparisons, he would believe he had under him the real Makel-Adel.

The long-continued quest had cost more money than he could
afford and there could be no question of dogs of the Kostroma breed.
One morning Pantalei met, about five versts from Bessonova, the
same princely hunting party before whose eyes he had, eighteen
months ago, so proudly shown off the paces of his horse. As before,
a hare came bounding down the hillside, the dogs on its trail. Pantalei joined in the pursuit—not beside the hunt, but some two hundred yards away. A chasm hollowed out by water ran down the
declivity. Gradually narrowing, it came between Pantalei and the
pursuit. At the point where he would have to clear it, and where a
year and a half earlier he had actually cleared it, the gorge was
sixteen feet wide and a couple of fathoms deep. In anticipation of
his triumph, which he expected to renew, Pantalei shouted and
whirled his whip. The hunt galloped up, their eyes fixed on the daring horseman. . . .

Suddenly Makel-Adel reared, whirled to the left and, in spite of
Pantalei's efforts to make him leap the chasm, tore off along the
ravine. Burning with shame and wrath, almost weeping, he drove
the horse straight up the slope, away from the hunt. White with
foam and his flanks bloody, Makel-Adel came dashing home. Pantalei immediately shut himself up in his room, exclaiming, "No, it

is not he! He would have broken his neck rather than fail me."

Further enlightenment followed. Riding on Makel-Adel, he was one day picking his way through the back yard of the parsonage near the church of Bessonovo. Although he rode with his cap over his eyes, he was recognized. The deacon called to him.

"What a magnificent horse you have," said he. "You lost your first horse, but relying on Divine Providence you buy another not a whit inferior."

"What are you talking about?" interrupted Pantalei. "It is the same horse."

"Eh?" said the deacon, pulling his beard in surprise. "How can that be? Your horse was stolen two weeks before the feast of the Intercession last year; and we are now at the end of November."

"Well, what then?"

"Your horse is of the same silver grey as then. It seems to me he is even darker. But as you know, grey horses always grow lighter as they get older."

Pantalei trembled. How was it that this piece of common knowledge had not occurred to him? Furious with the deacon he roared at him, "You cursed pig-tail, get away from me," and galloped off.

Once he was again at home he sought, but in vain, to persuade himself that his horse, if not Makel-Adel, was at least a very good beast. He knew, however, that he would never mount him again.

"Perfishka!" he cried suddenly, "run to the public-house and bring me half a pitcher of brandy."

Night came; a tallow candle burned dimly on the table. Pantalei sat with flushed face and dull eyes. "Now is the time," he said in a weary but business-like tone. "I have had enough of this."

He drank his last glass of brandy, took his pistol from over the bed, loaded it, put a couple of percussion caps in his pocket and started for the stable. As he put the key in the door, the watchman, supposing him to be a thief, came running up.

"Have you no eyes?" cried Pantalei. "Get away quick."

The man stepped aside and Pantalei entered the stable where the false Makel-Adel was lying in his stall.

"Get up, you rascal," he cried, giving the horse a kick.

He untied the halter, pulled off the blanket, turned the beast about and led it into the yard and from thence into the field—to the dumb surprise of the watchman, who stood staring after him until at a bend in the road he disappeared.

The night was tolerably clear. On an ordinary occasion the cold air would have had an effect on Pantalei after his having drunk so much brandy, but he was suffering from another, stronger intoxication. He believed himself justified in what he was about to do, and his innocent victim followed him at a patient trot.

Near the edge of the forest was a small ravine half-filled with underbrush. Into this Pantalei descended, and the horse, slipping, came near to falling on him.

"Would you crush me, you cursed beast?" he cried, pulling out his pistol as if to defend himself. His voice, echoing along the narrow ravine, alarmed him. A bird flapped noisily through the tree-tops—it was as if in this desert, where he had not expected to meet a living soul, he had aroused a witness to his deed.

"Go to the devil, then!" he said, dropping the reins and striking the horse on the shoulder with the handle of the pistol. It turned and galloped away and he soon lost even the clatter of its hoofs.

Climbing slowly out Pantalei took the road homeward. He was dissatisfied with himself and it was a long time since he had had any food.

As he walked along, depressed and at the same time angry, something nudged him gently between the shoulders. He turned to see Makel-Adel standing in the middle of the road.

"Ah!" cried Tchertapkanoff, "so you have come to receive your death. You shall have it."

He levelled his pistol against the horse's forehead and fired. The poor beast tumbled sideways, struggled up, ran a few steps and fell. Pantalei, holding his hands to his ears, ran from it. His drunken folly, his rage, his self-satisfaction—all had vanished. Only a bitter sense of shame and the consciousness that this was also his own end, remained.

IV

Six weeks later, Perfishka stopped the police inspector as he was passing the house.

"I think—I am afraid Pantalei Jeremeitsch is dying. At first he drank heavily day after day, but now he has taken to his bed and is very ill. He cannot speak."

The police inspector dismounted from his telega.

"Have you called a priest? Has your master confessed? Has he received the sacrament?"

"I asked him both yesterday and today whether I should fetch the priest. 'Silence, you fool,' said he, 'don't meddle in affairs that don't concern you.' When I asked him today, he was only able to twitch his moustache."

"Does he drink much brandy?"

"An astonishing quantity. Have the goodness, sir, to come and see him."

In a damp and dark back chamber, covered with a horse-blanket and with a ragged cloak under his head instead of a pillow, lay Tchertapkanoff. He was no longer merely pale, but yellowish-green like a corpse. His eyes were sunken. He wore on his breast the inevitable arkalouk with the cartridge-box. The Persian cap with the red tassel covered his forehead down to the eyebrows. Upon the table by the bed stood an empty pitcher and above the bed-head a couple of water-colour drawings had been pinned to the wall by darning-needles. One of these pictures represented a stout man with a guitar in his hand, probably his dead friend, Nedopuskin; the other a horseman at full speed. The horse resembled those fabulous creatures which children draw on walls and fences; but the dappled skin, carefully shaded, the cartridge-box on the rider's breast, and the enormous moustache, suggested that the drawing was meant to represent Tchertapkanoff on Makel-Adel.

The inspector did not know what to do. "The man is practically dead," he thought. Nevertheless, he made an attempt to reach the passing soul. "Pantalei Jeremeitsch!" said he.

Tchertapkanoff slowly opened his eyes. They wandered from right to left, then fixed themselves on his visitor. The bluish lips moved.

"The nobleman of the old race, Pantalei Tchertapkanoff, is dying. He owes nobody, he asks nothing. Go!"

His lips fell together, his eyes closed, he lay rigid.

"Let me know when he dies," whispered the inspector as he left the room. "The proprieties must be observed. He must receive the last ointment."

Perfishka sent the same day for the priest, and next morning gave notice to the inspector. Pantalei Jeremeitsch had died during the night. Two persons followed his coffin: Perfishka and Moshel Leiba.

The Oldest Dog Story in Literature

It is almost impossible to find a literature which knows the dog and does not celebrate the dog's loyalty to his master, or man's loyalty to his dog. This story is from the Hindu "Mahabharata," one of the early sacred books of India.

KRISHNA, the God, was old and weary of this world; he desired to die and return to his Heavenly Father. He had left the bliss of Paradise only because he saw that the Pandava brothers, descendants of Bharata, and defenders of the good, were steadily being overcome by the Kaurava brothers, who stood for all that is evil. Only for this had he come down to earth and suffered the humiliation of clothing the soul of a god in the flesh of a man— only that the world might be rescued from the power of wickedness.

And now, after long years of tremendous strife, the War of the Bharatas was over; the Pandavas, the champions of righteousness, were once more the rulers of India. Then it was that Krishna, sick of mortality, prayed his Father in Heaven to let him return to the home of the Celestials, and the prayer was heard.

But with Krishna gone, the King of the Pandava, the good monarch Yudishthira, felt that there remained nothing worth while in this earthly existence; he yearned to join his beloved Krishna in the Realm Beyond. Bravely he and his four brothers and the wife, Draupadi, and their old hound set forth for Mount Meru, there to ascend unto Heaven.

But the way was long and toilsome. One after another of the brothers fell in death by the wayside; the long-enduring and beloved Draupadi at length dropped down on that steep road, never to rise again; and Yudishthira and his old, faithful dog tottered on alone toward the shining gates of Paradise.

Those gates were reached. Utterly forespent with weariness from his long journey, desolate over the loss of his wife and his brothers, he stood before the portals of God's City and humbly sought entrance. But bitter disappointment was to be his. The celestial doors were opened for *him*, but his weary, long-suffering, and steadfast old hound might not enter! Yudishthira saw within the walls the glories of Heaven; he saw, too, the faithful, gaunt dog cowering at his feet and gazing pleadingly up into its master's eyes; the king's heart was torn with longing and gratitude.

"O Wisest One, Mighty God Indra!" he cried, "this hound hath eaten with me, starved with me, suffered with me, loved me! Must I desert him now?"

"Yea," declared the God of Gods, Indra, "all the joys of Paradise are yours forever, but leave here your hound."

Then exclaimed Yudishthira in anguish.

"Can it be that a god can be so destitute of pity? Can it be that to gain this glory I must leave behind all that I love? Then let me lose such glory forever!"

And Yudishthira turned sadly toward his forlorn dog. But the mighty Indra called to him again.

"Do you not understand? The creature is unclean; it would defile the altar fires of Paradise! Know this indeed: into Heaven, such cannot enter."

Bravely then did Yudishthira answer—with the bravery of an animal turning upon its pursuers.

"It is declared in the Vedas that to spurn a creature in supplication is a sin equal to that of slaying a Brahman. Therefore, Lord Indra, not for all the joys of Heaven desert I this poor, humble, faithful hound! Behold him. So friendless except for me! So confiding in me! So beseeching me to be faithful! So sure to perish without my help! Could I do this—I who was called among men the Just, the Merciful?"

The brow of Indra darkened.

"It is decreed," he replied sternly. "As you know, the very merit of prayer itself is lost if a dog touches him who is praying. He who enters Paradise must enter pure. Beside the stony highway you left the wife Draupadi and your brothers. Surely for this common creature you will not give up the joys of the blessed!"

Gently Yudishthira laid his hand upon the hound's head and turned to depart.

"All powerful Indra," he answered quietly, but firmly, "the dead are dead; I could not succor them. There are four deadly sins: to reject a suppliant, to slay a nursing mother, to destroy a Brahman's possessions, and to injure an old friend. But to these I add a fifth, as sinful: *to desert the lowliest friend when you pass out of sorrow into good fortune!* Farewell, then, Lord Indra. I go—and my hound with me."

And lo! the hound suddenly vanished and in its stead stood the God of Justice, the great Lord Dharma! Like honey fell the words from his lips.

"Behold, son, you have suffered much! But now, since you would not enter Heaven lest your poor dog should be cast away, lo! there is none in Paradise shall sit above you! Enter. Justice and Love welcome you."

And his faithful hound, now transformed into the Lord Dharma, mighty God of the Just, walked beside him through the glittering streets of the Celestial City.

Æpyornis Island

by H. G. WELLS

H. G. Wells' satire "Æpyornis Island" is funny and shocking and thought provoking. It also introduces us to the strangest tame animal in all literature.

THE man with the scarred face leant over the table and looked at my bundle.

"Orchids?" he asked.

"A few," I said.

"Cypripediums?" he said.

"Chiefly," said I.

"Anything new?—I thought not. *I* did these islands twenty-five —twenty-seven years ago. If you find anything new here—well, it's brand new. I didn't leave much."

"I'm not a collector," said I.

"I was young then," he went on. "Lord! how I used to fly around." He seemed to take my measure. "I was in the East Indies two years, and in Brazil seven. Then I went to Madagascar."

"I know a few explorers by name," I said anticipating a yarn. "Who did you collect for?"

"Dawsons. I wonder if you've heard the name of Butcher ever?"

"Butcher—Butcher?" The name seemed vaguely present in my memory; then I recalled *Butcher* v. *Dawson.* "Why!" said I, "you are the man who sued them for four years' salary—got cast away on a desert island—"

"Your servant," said the man with the scar, bowing. "Funny case, wasn't it? Here was me, making a little fortune on that island, doing nothing for it neither, and them quite unable to give me notice. It often used to amuse me thinking over it while I was there. I did

218

calculations of it—big—all over the blessed atoll in ornamental figuring."

"How did it happen?" said I. "I don't rightly remember the case."

"Well—you've heard of the Æpyornis?"

"Rather. Andrews was telling me of a new species he was working on only a month or so ago. Just before I sailed. They've got a thigh bone, it seems, nearly a yard long. Monster the thing must have been!"

"I believe you," said the man with the scar. "It *was* a monster. Sinbad's roc was just a legend of 'em. But when did they find these bones?"

"Three or four years ago—'91 I fancy. Why?"

"Why?—Because *I* found 'em—Lord! it's nearly twenty years ago. If Dawsons hadn't been silly about that salary they might have made a perfect ring in 'em.—I couldn't help the infernal boat going adrift."

He paused. "I suppose it's the same place. A kind of swamp about ninety miles north of Antananarivo. Do you happen to know? You have to go to it along the coast by boats. You don't happen to remember, perhaps?"

"I don't. I fancy Andrews said something about a swamp."

"It must be the same. It's on the east coast. And somehow there's something in the water that keeps things from decaying. Like creosote it smells. It reminded me of Trinidad. Did they get any more eggs? Some of the eggs I found were a foot and a half long. The swamp goes circling round, you know, and cuts off this bit. It's mostly salt, too. Well— What a time I had of it! I found the things quite by accident. We went for eggs, me and two native chaps, in one of those rum canoes all tied together, and found the bones at the same time. We had a tent and provisions for four days, and we pitched on one of the firmer places. To think of it brings that odd tarry smell back even now. It's funny work. You go probing into the mud with iron rods, you know. Usually the egg gets smashed. I wonder how long it is since these Æpyornises really lived. The missionaries say the natives have legends about when they were alive, but I never heard any such stories myself. But certainly those eggs we got were as fresh as if they had been new-laid. Fresh! Carrying them down to the boat one of my nigger chaps dropped one on a rock and it smashed. How I lammed into the beggar! But sweet it was as if it was new-laid, not even smelly, and its mother dead these four hundred years perhaps. Said a centipede had bit him. However, I'm getting off the straight with the story. It had taken us all day to dig into the slush and get these eggs out unbroken, and we were all covered with beastly black mud, and naturally I was cross. So far as I knew they were the only eggs that had ever been got out not even cracked. I went afterward to see the ones they have at the Natural History Museum in London: all of them were cracked and just stuck together like a mosaic, and bits missing. Mine were perfect, and I meant to blow them when I got back. Naturally I was annoyed at the silly devil dropping three hours' work just on account of a centipede. I hit him about rather."

The man with the scar took out a clay pipe. I placed my pouch before him. He filled up absent-mindedly.

"How about the others? Did you get those home? I don't remember—"

"That's the queer part of the story. I had three others. Perfectly fresh eggs. Well, we put 'em in the boat, and then I went up to the tent to make some coffee, leaving my two heathens down by the beach—the one fooling about with his sting and the other helping him. It never occurred to me that the beggars would take advantage of the peculiar position I was in to pick a quarrel. But I suppose the centipede poison and the kicking I'd given him had upset the one—he was always a cantankerous sort—and he persuaded the other.

"I remember I was sitting and smoking and boiling up the water over a spirit-lamp business I used to take on these expeditions. Incidentally I was admiring the swamp under the sunset. All black and blood red it was, in streaks—a beautiful sight. And up beyond, the land rose grey and hazy to the hills, and the sky behind them red, like a furnace mouth. And fifty yards behind the back of me was these blessed heathen—quite regardless of the tranquil air of things —plotting to cut off with the boat and leave me all alone with three day's provisions and a canvas tent, and nothing to drink whatsoever, beyond a little keg of water. I heard a kind of yelp behind me, and there they were in this canoe affair—it wasn't properly a boat—and perhaps twenty yards from land. I realized what was up in a moment. My gun was in the tent, and besides I had no bullets—only duck shot. They knew that. But I had a little revolver in my pocket and I pulled that out as I ran down to the beach.

" 'Come back!' says I, flourishing it.

"They jabbered something at me, and the man that broke the egg jeered. I aimed at the other—because he was unwounded and had the paddle, and I missed. They laughed. However, I wasn't beat. I knew I had to keep cool, and I tried him again and made him jump with the whang of it. The third time I got his head, and over he went, and the paddle with him. It was a precious lucky shot for a revolver. I reckon it was fifty yards. He went right under. I don't know if he was shot, or simply stunned and drowned. Then I began to shout to the other chap to come back, but he huddled up in the canoe and refused to answer. So I fired out my revolver at him and never got near him.

"I felt a precious fool, I can tell you. There I was on this rotten, black beach, flat swamp all behind me, and the flat sea, cold after the sunset, and just this black canoe drifting steadily out to sea. I tell you I damned Dawsons and Jamrachs and Museums and all the rest of it just to rights. I bawled to this nigger to come back, until my voice went up into a scream.

"There was nothing for it but to swim after him and take my luck with the sharks. So I opened my claspknife and put it in my mouth and took off my clothes and waded in. As soon as I was in the water I lost sight of the canoe, but I aimed, as I judged, to head it off. I hoped the man in it was too bad to navigate it, and that it would keep on drifting in the same direction. Presently it came up over the horizon again to the south-westward. The afterglow of sunset was well over now and the dim of night creeping up. The stars were coming through the blue. I swam like a champion, though my legs and arms were soon aching.

"However, I came up to him by the time the stars were fairly out. As it got darker I began to see all manner of glowing things in the water—phosphorescence, you know. At times it made me giddy. I hardly knew which was stars and which was phosphorescence, and whether I was swimming on my head or my heels. The canoe was as black as sin, and the ripple under the bows like liquid fire. I was naturally chary of clambering up into it. I was anxious to see what he was up to first. He seemed to be lying cuddled up in a lump in the bow, and the stern was all out of water. The thing kept turning round slowly as it drifted—kind of waltzing, don't you know. I went to the stern and pulled it down, expecting him to wake up. Then I began to clamber in with my knife in my hand, and ready for a rush. But he never stirred. So there I sat in the stern of the little canoe, drifting away over the calm phosphorescent sea, and with all the host of the stars above me, waiting for something to happen.

"After a long time I called him by name, but he never answered. I was too tired to take any risks by going along to him. So we sat there. I fancy I dozed once or twice. When the dawn came I saw he was as dead as a doornail and all puffed up and purple. My three eggs and the bones were lying in the middle of the canoe, and the keg of water and some coffee and biscuits wrapped in a Cape 'Argus' by his feet, and a tin of methylated spirit underneath him. There was no paddle, nor in fact anything except the spirit tin that one could use as one, so I settled to drift until I was picked up. I held an inquest on him, brought in a verdict against some snake, scorpion, or centipede unknown, and sent him overboard.

"After that I had a drink of water and a few biscuits, and took a look round. I suppose a man low down as I was don't see very far; leastways, Madagascar was clean out of sight, and any trace of land at all. I saw a sail going south-westward—looked like a schooner, but her hull never came up. Presently the sun got high in the sky and began to beat down upon me. Lord!—it pretty near made my brains boil. I tried dipping my head in the sea, but after a while my eye fell on the Cape 'Argus,' and I lay down flat in the canoe and spread this over me. Wonderful things these newspapers. I never read one through thoroughly before, but it's odd what you get up to when you're alone, as I was. I suppose I read that blessed old Cape 'Argus' twenty times. The pitch in the canoe simply reeked with the heat and rose up into big blisters.

"I drifted ten days," said the man with the scar. "It's a little thing in the telling, isn't it? Every day was like the last. Except in the morning and the evening I never kept a lookout even—the blaze was so infernal. I didn't see a sail after the first three days, and those I saw took no notice of me. About the sixth night a ship went by scarcely half a mile away from me, with all its lights ablaze and its ports open, looking like a big firefly. There was music aboard. I stood up and shouted and screamed at it. The second day I broached one of the Æpyornis eggs, scraped the shell away at the end bit by bit, and tried it, and I was glad to find it was good enough to eat. A bit flavory—not bad, I mean, but with something of the taste of a duck's egg. There was a kind of circular patch about six inches across on one side of the yolk, and with streaks of blood and a white mark like a ladder in it that I thought queer, but I didn't understand what this meant at the time, and I wasn't inclined to be particular. The eggs lasted me three days, with biscuits and a drink of water. I chewed coffee berries too—invigorating stuff. The second egg I opened about the eighth day. And it scared me."

The man with the scar paused. "Yes," he said—"developing.

"I daresay you find it hard to believe. *I* did, with the thing before me. There the egg had been, sunk in that cold black mud, perhaps three hundred years. But there was no mistaking it. There was the —what is it?—embryo, with its big head and curved back and its heart beating under its throat, and the yolk shriveled up and great membranes spreading inside of the shell and all over the yolk. Here was I hatching out the eggs of the biggest of all extinct birds, in a little canoe in the midst of the Indian Ocean. If old Dawson had known that! It was worth four years' salary. What do *you* think?

"However, I had to eat that precious thing up, every bit of it, before I sighted the reef, and some of the mouthfuls were beastly unpleasant. I left the third one alone. I held it up to the light, but the shell was too thick for me to get any notion of what might be happening inside; and though I fancied I heard blood pulsing, it might have been the rustle of my own ears, like what you listen to in a seashell.

"Then came the atoll. Came out of the sunrise, as it were, suddenly, close up to me. I drifted straight toward it until I was about half a mile from shore—not more, and then the current took a turn, and I had to paddle as hard as I could with my hands and bits of the Æpyornis shell to make the place. However, I got there. It was just a common atoll about four miles round, with a few trees growing and a spring in one place and the lagoon full of parrot fish. I took the egg ashore and put it in a good place well above the tide lines and in the sun, to give it all the chance I could, and pulled the canoe up safe, and loafed about prospecting. It's rum how dull an atoll is. When I was a kid I thought nothing could be finer or·more adventurous than the Robinson Crusoe business, but that place was as monotonous as a book of sermons. I went round finding eatable things and generally thinking; but I tell you I was bored to·death before the first day was out. It shows my luck—the very day I landed the weather changed. A thunderstorm went by to the north and flicked its wing over the island, and in the night there came a drencher and a howling wind slap over us. It wouldn't have taken much, you know, to upset that canoe.

"I was sleeping under the canoe, and the egg was luckily among the sand higher up the beach, and the first thing I remember was a sound like a hundred pebbles hitting the boat at once and a rush of water over my body. I'd been dreaming of Antananarivo, and I sat up and holloaed to Intoshi to ask her what the devil was up, and clawed out at the chair where the matches used to be. Then I remembered where I was. There were phosphorescent waves rolling up as if they meant to eat me, and all the rest of the night as black as pitch. The air was simply yelling. The clouds seemed down on your head almost, and the rain fell as if heaven was sinking and they were baling out the waters above the firmament. One great roller came writhing at me, like a fiery serpent, and I bolted. Then I thought of the canoe, and ran down to it as the water went hissing back again, but the thing had gone. I wondered about the egg then, and felt my way to it. It was all right and well out of reach of the maddest waves, so I sat down beside it and cuddled it for company. Lord! what a night that was!

"The storm was over before morning. There wasn't a rag of cloud left in the sky when the dawn came, and all along the beach there were bits of plank scattered—which was the disarticulated skeleton, so to speak, of my canoe. However, that gave me something to do, for, taking advantage of two of the trees being together, I rigged up a kind of storm shelter with these vestiges. And that day the egg hatched.

"Hatched, sir, when my head was pillowed on it and I was asleep. I heard a whack and felt a jar and sat up, and there was the end of the egg pecked out and a rum little brown head looking out at me.

'Lord!' I said, 'you're welcome,' and with a little difficulty he came out.

"He was a nice friendly little chap, at first about the size of a small hen—very much like most other young birds, only bigger. His plumage was a dirty brown to begin with, with a sort of gray scab that fell off it very soon, and scarcely feathers—a kind of downy hair. I can hardly express how pleased I was to see him. I tell you, Robinson Crusoe don't make near enough of his loneliness. But here was interesting company. He looked at me and winked his eye from the front backward like a hen, and gave a chirp and began to peck about at once, as though being hatched three hundred years too late was just nothing. 'Glad to see you, Man Friday!' says I, for I had naturally settled he was to be called Man Friday if ever he was hatched, as soon as ever I found the egg in the canoe had developed. I was a bit anxious about his feed, so I gave him a lump of raw parrot fish at once. He took it and opened his beak for more. I was glad of that, for, under the circumstances, if he'd been fanciful, I should have had to eat him after all.

"You'd be surprised what an interesting bird that Æpyornis chick was. He followed me about from the very beginning. He used to stand by me and watch while I fished in the lagoon and go shares in anything I caught. And he was sensible, too. There were nasty green warty things, like pickled gherkins, used to lie about on the beach, and he tried one of these and it upset him. He never even looked at any of them again.

"And he grew. You could almost see him grow. And as I was never much of a society man, his quiet, friendly ways suited me to a T. For nearly two years we were as happy as we could be on that island. I had no business worries, for I knew my salary was mounting up at Dawsons'. We would see a sail now and then, but nothing ever came near us. I amused myself too by decorating the island with designs worked in sea-urchins and fancy shells of various kinds. I put ÆPYORNIS ISLAND all round the place very nearly, in big letters, like what you see done with colored stones at railway stations in the old country. And I used to lie watching the blessed bird stalking round and growing, growing, and think how I could make a living out of him by showing him about if ever I got taken off. After his first moult he began to get handsome, with a crest and a blue wattle, and a lot of green feathers at the behind of him. And then I used to puzzle whether Dawsons had any right to claim him or not. Stormy weather and in the rainy season we lay snug under the shelter I had made out of the old canoe, and I used to tell him lies about my friends at home. It was a kind of idyll, you might say. If only I had had some tobacco it would have been simply just like Heaven.

"It was about the end of the second year our little Paradise went wrong. Friday was then about fourteen feet high to the bill of him, with a big broad head like the end of a pickaxe, and two huge brown eyes with yellow rims set together like a man's—not out of sight of each other like a hen's. His plumage was fine—none of the half mourning style of your ostrich—more like a cassowary as far as color and texture go. And then it was he began to cock his comb at me and give himself airs and show signs of a nasty temper.

"At last came a time when my fishing had been rather unlucky and he began to hang about me in a queer, meditative way. I thought he might have been eating sea-cucumbers or something, but it was really just discontent on his part. I was hungry too, and when at last I landed a fish I wanted it for myself. Tempers were short that morning on both sides. He pecked at it and grabbed it, and I gave him a whack on the head to make him leave go. And at that he went for me. Lord!

"He gave me this in the face." The man indicated his scar. "Then he kicked me. It was like a cart horse. I got up, and seeing he hadn't finished I started off full tilt with my arms doubled up over my face. But he ran on those gawky legs of his faster than a race horse, and kept landing out at me with sledge-hammer kicks, and bringing his pickaxe down on the back of my head. I made for the lagoon, and went in up to my neck. He stopped at the water, for he hated getting his feet wet, and began to make a shindy, something like a peacock's, only hoarser. He started strutting up and down the beach. I'll admit I felt small to see this blessed fossil lording it there. And my head and face were all bleeding, and—well, my body just one jelly of bruises.

"I decided to swim across the lagoon and leave him alone for a bit, until the affair blew over. I shinned up the tallest palm-tree and sat there thinking of it all. I don't suppose I ever felt so hurt by anything before or since. It was the brutal ingratitude of the creature. I'd been more than a brother to him. I'd hatched him. Educated him. A great, gawky, out-of-date bird! And me a human being—heir of the ages and all that.

"I thought after a time he'd begin to see things in that light himself, and feel a little sorry for his behavior. I thought if I was to catch some nice little bits of fish, perhaps, and go to him presently in a casual kind of way, and offer them to him, he might do the sensible thing. It took me some time to learn how unforgiving and cantankerous an extinct bird can be. Malice!

"I won't tell you all the little devices I tried to get that bird round again. I simply can't. It makes my cheek burn with shame even now to think of the snubs and buffets I had from this infernal curiosity. I tried violence. I chucked lumps of coral at him from a safe distance, but he only swallowed them. I shied my open knife at him and almost lost it, though it was too big for him to swallow. I tried starving him out and struck fishing, but he took to picking along the beach at low water after worms, and rubbed along on that. Half my time I spent up to my neck in the lagoon, and the rest up the palm-trees. One of them was scarcely high enough, and when he caught me up it he had a regular Bank Holiday with the calves of my legs. It got unbearable. I don't know if you have ever tried sleeping up a palm-tree. It gave me the most horrible nightmares. Think of the shame of it too! Here was this extinct animal mooning about my island like a sulky duke, and me not allowed to rest the sole of my foot on the place. I used to cry with weariness and vexation. I told him straight that I didn't mean to be chased about a desert island by any damned anachronisms. I told him to go and peck a navigator of his own age. But he only snapped his beak at me. Great ugly bird—all legs and neck!

"I shouldn't like to say how long that went on altogether. I'd have killed him sooner if I'd known how. However, I hit on a way of settling him at last. It's a South American dodge. I joined all my fishing lines together with stems of seaweed and things, and made a stoutish string, perhaps twelve yards in length or more, and I fastened two lumps of coral rock to the ends of this. It took me some time to do, because every now and then I had to go into the lagoon or up a tree as the fancy took me. This I whirled rapidly round my head and then let it go at him. The first time I missed, but the next time the string caught his legs beautifully and wrapped round them again and again. Over he went. I threw it standing waist-deep in the lagoon, and as soon as he went down I was out of the water and sawing at his neck with my knife—

"I don't like to think of that even now. I felt like a murderer while I did it, though my anger was hot against him. When I stood over him and saw him bleeding on the white sand and his beautiful great legs and neck writhing in his last agony—Pah!

"With that tragedy, Loneliness came upon me like a curse. Good Lord! you can't imagine how I missed that bird. I sat by his corpse and sorrowed over him, and shivered as I looked round the desolate, silent reef. I thought of what a jolly little bird he had been when he was hatched, and of a thousand pleasant tricks he had played before he went wrong. I thought if I'd only wounded him I might have nursed him round into a better understanding. If I'd had any means of digging into the coral rock I'd have buried him. I felt exactly as if he was human. As it was I couldn't think of eating him, so I put him in the lagoon and the little fishes picked him clean. Then one day a chap cruising about in a yacht had a fancy to see if my atoll still existed.

"He didn't come a moment too soon, for I was about sick enough of the desolation of it, and only hesitating whether I should walk out into the sea and finish up the business that way, or fall back on the green things.

"I sold the bones to a man named Winslow—a dealer near the British Museum, and he says he sold them to old Havers. It seems Havers didn't understand they were extra large, and it was only after his death they attracted attention. They called 'em Æpyornis —what was it?"

"*Æpyornis vastus*," said I. "It's funny, the very thing was mentioned to me by a friend of mine. When they found an Æpyornis with a thigh a yard long they thought they had reached the top of the scale and called him *Æpyornis maximus*. Then some one turned up another thigh bone four feet six or more, and that they called *Æpyornis Titan*. Then your *vastus* was found after old Havers died, in his collection, and then a *vastissimus* turned up."

"Winslow was telling me as much," said the man with the scar. "If they get any more Æpyornises, he reckons some scientific swell will go and burst a blood-vessel. But it was a queer thing to happen to a man! wasn't it—altogether?"

Whippetsnapper

by FLORENCE HEALY

*Florence Healy was an undergraduate when she wrote
this story. I don't think she has written much since, but
it is as outrageous a piece of tomfoolery as any I know.*

LORD A. MONTAGUE WHIPPETSNAPPER was one of
the proudest men in merry England. And why not? He
owned what was acknowledged to be the finest kennel of racing
whippets in the Empire. His whippets had outdistanced whippets
from Australia, whippets from Germany, whippets from Cape
Town, whippets from Japan, and whippets from Russia. Lord A.
Montague Whippetsnapper was prouder of that race he had almost
lost to those young upstarts of Russian whippets than he was of
any other race his kennels had ever run. This was because that Russian race had brought Genevieve to the fore. Some pup named
Nedyovitch, and carrying the colors of the Commanding Cossacks,
had been tearing along snoot and snoot with Daniel of the Whippetsnapper Kennels. This wasn't a thing to worry about particularly,
if it wasn't that Daniel was inclined to lose his head at such times.
The crowd, knowing it, was going wild in a frenzy of excitement.
So Genevieve stepped in. She too knew about Daniel. (She was his
wife.) She realized that nothing could save the race if it depended
on Daniel. In a flash she was trotting ahead into first place herself.
Not that she wanted to. Genevieve sought no glory for herself. She
ran for God, King George, and the Whippetsnapper Kennels. And
how she ran! Even Nedyovitch was impressed to such a degree that
he forgot to say the race was unfair.

But it brought no joy to Genevieve. She had wanted Daniel to
win. She knew he would forgive her for taking the race for him.

That wasn't the point. She wanted *him* to win. So unhappy was she that she found it difficult to look pleasant and wag an obliging wag when A. Montague presented her with the key to the kennels.

"Genevieve," he had said, his voice quavering with emotion, "words fail me to express myself. I can only thank you."

"Montague," she had wagged half-heartedly, "you're welcome."

Then Genevieve had spent weeks brooding. She no longer lived with Daniel. Indeed she could not, for her philosophy of marriage had been disturbed. How could harmony exist where the wife had proved to be the stronger vessel? She lost her appetite—but she ate her food. There was no reason for breaking training. Especially now that she had no choice but a career. So it was that A. Montague, and Tobias, the trainer, and the assistant trainer, Henry (pronounced 'Hennery') had no suspicion that all was not well.

Genevieve weighed the question and pondered the problem right up to the morning of the Fishgate Handicap. Then, as she lay feverishly tossing on the straw of her box, the answer came. She would run this last race for the honor of the house; win it, undoubtedly; then, right at the peak of her popularity, would desert the racket to devote herself wholly and entirely to Daniel! It seemed very simple now that she knew how to look at it. Her appetite returned.

Tobias brought her breakfast early that morning, for which she was grateful. The pangs of hunger were unpleasant. He patted her on the head and made his usual morning remarks.

"Wuzzy wuzzy wuzzums?" said he seriously.

She woofed her greeting, "Woof, woof!"

"Diddums want ums breakfast?"

She snapped her agreement, "Snap, snap!"

"Then ums must shake hands," he decreed, offering his left.

She eyed it suspiciously but made no motion until he remembered that a gentleman offers his right and acted accordingly. Then she gave him her paw graciously, while her thoughts she gave to the subject of food.

This usually completed the greeting ceremony. Not so this morning. Tobias was in an especially good mood, it being the day of the handicap and all. He had another bright idea.

"Before ums can have ums breakwis ums must beg for it."

Beg for it! Beg for it indeed! Genevieve Whippetsnapper beg! The man must be ill.

She turned her back as a sign of indignation.

Tobias waited tapping his foot. "Well, willums beg?"

No answer.

"Then ums can eat without begging because ums is one fine bow-bow. So ums is."

And he put down the shredded wheat. The dish was clean in a flash.

Now Tobias thought she was finished when, as a matter of fact, she had only begun. Three weeks of eating with no heart in it, is equivalent to three weeks of no eating, she discovered, when the biscuits were gone. She stepped back and wagged, cajoling, for more.

Of course, Tobias didn't understand. He scratched his head. "Now what's the matter, Jen?"

She cocked her head and grinned.

"How many guesses can I have?"

She pushed the dish with her paw.

"What? More food?"

She jumped and clicked her heels with enthusiasm.

His voice saddened considerably. "Don't you know you shouldn't ask that, Genevieve?"

She did; but denied it by dropping her tail.

"Training rule number six," he said as though it were the judgment, "distinctly says 'two shredded wheat biscuits, in one cup of hot milk shall be the early rations for whippets in training.'"

Genevieve growled menacingly. She didn't think he had to use that tone.

Tobias was troubled. He hastened to explain, "It's not that I have anything against you personally, Genevieve. But you have to run that race to-day. And rules are rules."

She tried new tactics and wagged teasingly.

"I'm sorry, Genevieve. My orders, you know."

She sidled over and put her head and front paws in his lap.

"Nope," he said briskly because he felt he would weaken before long, "you can't have any, so run away and play." Then he pushed her from his knees before 'before long' came.

He hadn't meant to be rough. But emotion had gotten the best of him.

Genevieve looked hurt. He would have apologized but he felt he would cry, so he turned abruptly and left the kennel.

Genevieve tossed her head to restore her pride. She, Genevieve Whippetsnapper, had lowered herself to beg. Run for the pride of the Whippetsnapper family when they had broken hers? Hah!

And she thought a thought.

.   .   .   .

The Fishgate Handicap drew out such a crowd as *would* attend the Fishgate Handicap and it filled the grandstand to the uppermost tier. Gay colored hats mingled with gayer colored dresses and off-colored shoes. A. Montague Whippetsnapper wondered, in one fleeting wonder, just why dresses and shoes were never any closer than cousins, then dropped the subject. A. Montague Whippetsnapper was in his element, although it was only an element of tracks, trainers, dogs, and puppy-biscuits. He fitted his glasses to his eyes and trained them on the track. The whippets were being led out.

Now, a whippet race usually works this way. The dogs are held in leash at one end of the racing lane and the trainers at the other. Then the race begins. The assistant trainers release the dogs, while the trainers call them, enticing them on with threats or promises as the case may be. The dogs tear madly down the lane in their eagerness to reach the 'Boss.' The dog getting there first wins. And there you are.

That, as we mentioned above is the way the thing usually works. But that wasn't the way it worked this time. And nobody realized it more keenly than A. Montague Whippetsnapper.

They were a beautiful group of animals, those dogs that were led out by the assistant trainers. Just by looking at their sleek, well-groomed bodies, their rippling muscles, their wagging tails, and bright red tongues, one could tell exactly how that race should have come off.

The assistant trainers lined the animals up at the head of their respective lanes. Genevieve was in lane four with Hennery. The picture would have been a pretty one if the red of Genevieve's blanket had not clashed with Hennery's carrot-top. A. Montague

Whippetsnapper noticed the lack of harmony and turned to his secretary,

"Bodkins, do something about that color combination in the next race."

"Yes, your lordship," said the faithful Bodkins, writing as he spoke, "I shall have Hennery dye his hair."

By now the trainers were in place and all was in readiness. There was an awful moment of suspense before the gun. The Whippets eyed the crowd; some, former champions and present ones, arrogantly; some, newcomers, timidly; some, the fair sex, coyly; and Genevieve, not at all. Genevieve saw no crowded grandstand, nor waiting whippets, nor eager trainers, nor even God's sunshine. She had a picture in her mind to see, a picture of one lone, tempting shredded wheat biscuit.

One gun shot. Twenty loosened leashes. Twenty trainers calling "Here, Ludovic!"—"Here, Rags!"—"Here, Eleanor!"—"Come, Majesty." Twenty owners nervously biting their nails. Nineteen whippets tearing down the lane. One whippet at the head of the lane. A crowd roaring itself hoarse.

Tobias, at the foot of the lane, was struck. He called in a louder voice.

"Here, Genevieve!"

No attempt to run by Genevieve.

"Here Genevieve, Genevieve, Genevieve! Here Genevieve!"

Genevieve settled back on her haunches with ominous determination.

"Come on, now, and be est the sweetes, eetest, itty, bow-bow" . . . "Genevieve?" . . . "Genevieve, come here at once!"

A. Montague was beside himself. With a leap that was really remarkable for one of his years, he bounded to Tobias' side. His object was to try his own persuasive powers.

"Genevieve," said he, a bit more firmly, "come to papa Montague?"

She would not.

"Genevieve," said he, a bit more firmly, but none the less sweetly, "will you come to papa Montague?"

She would not.

"Genevieve," he said less sweetly, more firmly, and shook his fore-finger, "for the third and last time are you coming to papa Montague?"

She was not.

"Very well," he snapped, "I shall come to you, and when I do, mark my words, you snivelling mutt, I'll . . . ."

A gentle hand stayed his arm, the hand of A. Isabelle Whippetsnapper. "Don't do anything rash in public, father," said the daughter of the house of Whippetsnapper. "Let me have a try."

She leaned forward irresistibly. "Won't you come to *me*, Genevieve?" And was hurt to find that Genevieve would not.

"Father, let me try," said A. Junior Whippetsnapper, and as he spoke struck a "jolly-good-fellow" attitude. "Come on, old girl," he boomed, "be a sport."

Genevieve was no sport.

Mrs. A. Montague Whippetsnapper joined the family, weeping, "Genevieve," she snivelled, "you're breaking my heart!"

Genevieve had no objections to being a "heart-breaker!" She laid down in the dust and rolled in delight.

And the sorrowing family knelt side by side in the same dust. A. Montague Whippetsnapper, there was, and Mrs. A. Montague Whippetsnapper, with the children, A. Junior and A. Isabel. "Genevieve," it wailed, "please come to us." And Tobias a bit in the rear sobbed, "Genevieve."

The crowd was going wild with excitement and hilarity. Half of it joined the Whippetsnappers calling "Genevieve!" The younger bloods rooted for her in no uncertain manner. "Good girl, Jenny!" —"Don't let them bully you, Jen!"—"Atta girl!"—and similar terms of approbation.

A. Montague was mortified but gave the cue for his complete embarrassment himself. "Genevieve," he gulped, falling forward on his face. "My Genevieve!"

That was the end of sanity in the stands. The crowd seized the cue with delight, and sang at the top of its lungs, "Genevieve, My Genevieve," swaying in rhythm and the voices rang loud and clear.

> "Genevieve, my early love,
> The days may come,
> The days may go.
> But still the heart of memory clings

To whippet races, sports and things.
The spell is done.
The die is cast.
This very race will be your last.
Oh, Genevieve, my Genevieve!"

And later, as the seething Tobias led her back to the kennels, she hummed to herself.

"Woof, woof, woof, woof, woof, woof, woof,
Woof, woof, woof, woof,
Woof, woof, woof, woof,
Woof, woof, woof, woof, woof, woof, woof, woof.
Woof, woof, woof, woof, woof, woof, woof, woof.
Woof, woof, woof, woof,
Woof, woof, woof, woof,
Woof, woof, woof, woof, woof, woof, woof, woof.
Woof, woof, woof, woof, woof, woof, woof, woof!"

and thought of Daniel.

.   .   .   .

A. Montague Whippetsnapper paced his study in a towering rage. His heavily clad feet stamped the length of the room. His plus fours and vest alternately bagged and sagged with indignation. His watch swung like a pendulum at the end of its chain. His teeth champed a long cigarette holder. His head was rammed forward and motionless. A. Montague Whippetsnapper was in a "state." First, he had lost a race. Second, he had been publicly humiliated. Third, it was time for his weekly "state." The fact that he had lost thousands of pounds along with the race had nothing to do with the case. No Whippetsnapper had ever been mercenary. The Whippetsnappers were sportsmen for the joy of the sport and the publicity thereof.

Poor Bodkins had survived "states" for eleven years, 572 weeks, 572 "states" in all, yet he had never been able to conquer the fear he experienced on these occasions. So it was he cowered in the corner behind the humidor and tried to control his rapidly vibrating body.

A. Montague wheeled on him. "Bodkins," he roared, as Bodkins' legs gave way. "Send that fool of a trainer here!"

"Tobias, your lordship?" he aspired as he reeled toward the door.

"Tobias, my lordship," bellowed A. Montague. "Tobias."

"Yes, your lordship," he agreed. "Tobias."

Tobias was almost on the spot almost at once. Now Tobias had never before been present at one of A. Montague's "states" but he had imagination. So he vibrated on exactly the same wave-length as Bodkins. A. Montague noticed it.

"Stop that twitching!" he thundered.

Bodkins' vibrations were replaced by a castanet-like death-rattle. Tobias' vibrations doubled their frequency as he inquired,

"What twitching, your lordship?"

"Sit down," screamed A. Montague.

Tobias obliged.

"No, stand up," he snapped, having changed his mind.

Tobias obliged.

"Why," said A. Montague menacingly, "did that dog refuse to run?"

"I-I-I-I-I—"

"Why did that dog refuse to run?"

"I ddd-d-d-on't know, your lordship."

"Oh, you don't, don't you?" sneered the head of the house of Whippetsnapper. "Well, we'll soon make you know." And he banged the table with vehemence.

"Yes, your lordship."

"And if you're to blame, you useless piece of diseased meat, I'll I'll—" Exhausted by rage he fainted in the chair. Bodkins revived him with a practiced hand.

"Give a detailed account of yourself."

"Yes, your lordship. I was born in London, sir."

"Never mind all that. Start with this morning."

"Yes, your lordship. I arose with the lark."

"With what?"

"I mean the dawn, your lordship."

"Yes, you arose with the dawn. Then what?"

"I turned on the radio for my setting up exercises."

"Yes?"

"But I didn't take them."

"No?" He seized the clue gleefully. "Why not?"

"The radio wasn't working, your lordship!"

A. Montague Whippetsnapper was exasperated. He made several turns about the room full steam ahead then came to an abrupt stop.

"When did you first see Genevieve?"

"About seven-thirty, your lordship."

"What was she doing?"

"Sleeping, your lordship."

"What did you do!"

"I watched her, your lordship."

"What did she do then?"

"Went on sleeping, your lordship."

"But she woke up eventually?"

"Yes, your lordship."

"How did she wake?"

"Beautifully, your lordship. She always did have a sweet disposition."

"I mean did she wake herself, or did you wake her?"

"She woke herself, your lordship."

"Yes, I see. You're sure of that?"

"Yes, your lordship."

"Think now, there was no possible noise that could have awakened her?"

"Nothing, your lordship."

"No pins dropping or things?"

"Unless her own snoring, your Lordship."

"Hm."

He took another turn about the room and made a note on his pad. "I guess we may safely conclude that she woke herself."

A. Montague Whippetsnapper was puzzled now that he had exhausted that idea. He thought for a while, then did the logical thing in the end.

"What did you do then?"

"I gave her her breakfast."

"Which was?"

"Number six, your lordship, two shredded wheat biscuits in one cup of hot milk."

"Then what?"

"She ate it your lordship."

"How?"

"Oh, as though famished, your lordship, but, I may safely say she wasn't famished."

"What then?"

"Well, your lordship, I suppose you must know. Genevieve wasn't satisfied."

A. Montague looked as though he had been struck by a bolt from the blue. He trembled with rage.

"Not satisfied?" he roared.

"No, your lordship, she wanted more."

His lordship came forward on tip-toes, and looked him menacingly in the eye.

"Did you give it to her?"

"No, your lordship."

"No?" he screamed, "Why not?"

"Rule number six, your lordship?" Tobias was trembling again.

A. Montague was tip-toeing about the room, seething with rage.

"Do you mean to tell me," he hissed, "that you refused to give Genevieve another shredded wheat biscuit?"

"Yes, your lordship," he piped, "I was obeying rule number six."

"Damn rule number six. Damn all the rules. Bodkins, abolish all the rules! Damn all the rules."

"But your lordship . . ."

"Don't but me! Can't you use more common sense than to irritate a dog on the day of a race!"

"I didn't want to irritate you, your lordship."

"Irritate me! Irritate me, indeed! I don't get irritated. Bodkins, have you ever seen me irritated?"

Bodkins gulped an uncertain negative. A. Montague went on.

"To let one measly shredded wheat biscuit stand before the glory of the Whippetsnapper kennels! . . . Pah! You disgust me! . . . Pah! A shredded wheat biscuit!"

"But . . ."

"You're discharged! Take your pay in lieu of notice! A biscuit! One shredded wheat biscuit! Denying Genevieve! Get out of here! Get out!"

As the door closed behind him, the last thing Tobias heard was A. Montague Whippetsnapper sobbing, "This . . . this . . . and for . . . a . . . shredded . . . wheat. . . ."

.   .   .   .

Daniel sat with his back turned to Genevieve and shrugged his shoulders in a genuine devil-may-care gesture. Genevieve sidled up to him uncertainly, yet certainly.

"Woof?" she breathed in his ear tearfully.

"Woof!" he snapped moving away quickly.

"Woof?" she begged in her most pleading manner, and smiled at him coyly.

Finally he gave in. "Oh, well, woof!" he said feeling very foolish indeed.

She flung herself on him joyfully and the trouble was over. She kissed him, a pretty little peck, and he countered with a bear-hug. They both bear-hugged, then she tapped him on the shoulder.

"Last tag!" she cried.

"Last tag yourself!" he laughed and began chasing her.

She ran right. He ran right following her. She continued right. He cut across left and she ran into him head-on. They fell together on the floor.

"Whoopee!" whooped Daniel.

"Darling!" she cooed. And they began running again.

A shadow fell across the door-way. The shadow of A. Montague Whippetsnapper.

Genevieve whispered to Daniel. "Get square with him, Danny. He didn't do right by Tobias."

"No?" gasped Daniel.

"No," emphasized Genevieve.

A. Montague Whippetsnapper beckoned Genevieve to one side and engaged her in a long monologue. She was infinitely bored but listened with polite interest. At last he reached the home stretch and arose from his knees where he had gotten in a moment of excitement.

"Now," said he, "is us all friends again?"

"Woof! Woof!" woofed Genevieve, meaning "us is."

A. Montague was more than a little relieved as he realized that his personality had not been wasted. He patted her on the head with his right hand while the left mopped his brow.

"And ums will play with ums papa Montague?"

"Yipe! Yipe!" she yiped, meaning "sure thing."

"Genevieve," he sentimentalized, "you're a trump. You deserve a medal."

As there was no medal, she decided to take a leg. She picked the left of the Lordling's pair and began intensive work on the ankle.

"Wurra! Wurra!" he screamed. "Naughty, naught! OUCH! No must do."

But Genevieve was "doing" with a vengeance.

"Please, Genevieve," he gasped as he hopped, "be decent!"

But Genevieve was not "decent." She made some sort of a high-sign to Daniel who attacked the right.

"Help!" roared A. Montague Whippetsnapper alternating it with "Murder!"

"Snap! Snap!" snapped Daniel. And "Pull, pull," pulled Genevieve.

The sounds attracted Tobias to the door, where he stood dismally, his bag at his feet.

"Tobias," pleaded A. M. W. "Do something!"

"If I were your lordship," said Tobias gravely, "which I thank my God I am not, I shouldn't deny Genevieve."

"Help," screamed A. Montague.

"No!" screamed Tobias.

"I'll take you back on!" screamed A. Montague.

"I wouldn't come!" screamed Tobias.

And A. Montague was left to face the happy couple alone, with not a leg to stand on.

The King of the Cats

by STEPHEN VINCENT BENÉT

Stephen Vincent Benét's story of the social lion of the season is also about cats—who certainly have a king, as well as having been, each one of them, gods in Egypt —and they've never forgotten it. This is not only a charming fantasy, but also incorporates a part of the lore of cats which I would have had to print separately, had I not found it here.

"BUT, my *dear*," said Mrs. Culverin, with a tiny gasp, "you can't actually mean—a *tail!*"

Mrs. Dingle nodded impressively. "Exactly. I've actually seen him. Twice. Paris, of course, and then, a command appearance at Rome—we were in the Royal box. He conducted—my dear, you've never heard such effects from an orchestra—and, my dear," she hesitated slightly, "he conducted *with it*."

"How perfectly, fascinatingly too horrid for words!" said Mrs. Culverin in a dazed but greedy voice. "We *must* have him to dinner as soon as he comes over—he is coming over, isn't he?"

"The twelfth," said Mrs. Dingle with a gleam in her eyes. "The New Symphony people have asked him to be guest conductor for three special concerts—I do hope you can dine with *us* some night while he's here—he'll be very busy, of course—but he's promised to give us what time he can spare."

"Oh, thank you, dear," said Mrs. Culverin abstractedly, her last raid upon Mrs. Dingle's pet British novelist still fresh in her mind. "You're always so delightfully hospitable—but you mustn't wear yourself out—the rest of us must do *our* part—I know Harry and myself would be only too glad to—"

"That's very sweet of you, darling," Mrs. Dingle also remembered the larceny of the British novelist. "But we're just going to give Monsieur Tibault—sweet name, isn't it! They say he's descended from the Tybalt in *Romeo and Juliet* and that's why he doesn't like Shakespeare—we're just going to give Monsieur Tibault the simplest sort of time—a little reception after his first concert, perhaps. He hates," she looked around the table, "large, mixed parties. And then, of course, his—er—little idiosyncrasy." She coughed delicately. "It makes him feel a trifle shy with strangers."

"But I don't understand yet, Aunt Emily," said Tommy Brooks, Mrs. Dingle's nephew. "Do you really mean this Tibault bozo has a tail? Like a monkey and everything?"

"Tommy dear," said Mrs. Culverin crushingly, "in the first place Monsieur Tibault is not a bozo—he is a very distinguished musician—the finest conductor in Europe. And in the second place—"

"He has." Mrs. Dingle was firm. "He has a tail. He conducts with it."

"Oh, but honestly!" said Tommy, his ears pinkening. "I mean—of course, if you say so, Aunt Emily, I'm sure he has—but still, it sounds pretty steep, if you know what I mean! How about it, Professor Tatto?"

Professor Tatto cleared his throat. "Tck," he said, putting his finger tips together cautiously. "I shall be very anxious to see this Monsieur Tibault. For myself, I have never observed a genuine specimen of *homo caudatus*, so I should be inclined to doubt, and yet . . . In the Middle Ages, for instance, the belief in men—er—tailed or with caudal appendages of some sort, was both widespread and, as far as we can gather, well founded. As late as the eighteenth century, a Dutch sea captain with some character for veracity recounts the discovery of a pair of such creatures in the island of Formosa. They were in a low state of civilization, I believe, but the appendages in question were quite distinct. And in 1860 Dr. Grimbrook, the English surgeon, claims to have treated no less than three African natives with short but evident tails—though his testimony rests upon his unsupported word. After all, the thing is not impossible—though doubtless unusual. Web feet—rudimentary gills—these occur with some frequency. The appendix we have with us always. The chain of our descent from the apelike form is by no means complete. For that matter," he beamed around the table, "what can we call the last few vertebræ of the normal spine but the beginnings of a rudimentary tail? Oh, yes—yes—it's possible—quite —that in an extraordinary case—a reversion to type—a survival—"

"I told you so," said Mrs. Dingle triumphantly. "*Isn't* it fascinating? Isn't it, Princess?"

The Princess Vivrakanarda's eyes, blue as a field of larkspur, fathomless as the center of heaven, rested lightly for a moment on Mrs. Dingle's excited countenance.

"Ve-ry fascinating," she said, in a voice like stroked, golden velvet. "I should like ve-ry much to meet this Monsieur Tibault."

"Well, *I* hope he breaks his neck!" said Tommy Brooks under his breath—but nobody ever paid much attention to Tommy.

Nevertheless, as the time for Monsieur Tibault's arrival in these States drew nearer and nearer, people in general began to wonder whether the Princess had spoken quite truthfully—for there was no doubt of the fact that, up till then, she had been the unique sensation of the season—and you know what social lions and lionesses are.

It was a Siamese season, and genuine Siamese were at quite as much of a premium as Russian accents had been in the quaint old days when the Chauve-Souris was a novelty. The Siamese Art Theater, imported at terrific expense, was playing to packed houses at the Century Theater. *Gushuptzgu,* an epic novel of Siamese farm life, in nineteen closely printed volumes, had just been awarded the Nobel Prize. Prominent pet-and-newt dealers reported no cessation in the appalling demand for Siamese cats. And upon the crest of this wave of interest in things Siamese the Princess Vivrakanarda poised with the elegant nonchalance of a Hawaiian water baby upon his surf-board. She was indispensable. She was incomparable. She was everywhere.

Youthful, enormously wealthy, allied on one hand to the Royal Family of Siam and on the other to the Cabots (and yet with the first eighteen of her twenty-one years shrouded from speculation in a golden zone of mystery), the mingling of races in her had produced an exotic beauty as distinguished as it was strange. She moved with a feline, effortless grace, and her skin was as if it had been gently powdered with tiny grains of the purest gold—yet the blueness of her eyes, set just a trifle slantingly, was as pure and startling as the sea on the rocks of Maine. Her brown hair fell to her knees —she had been offered extraordinary sums by the Master Barbers' Protective Association to have it shingled. Straight as a waterfall tumbling over brown rocks, it had a vague perfume of sandalwood and suave spices and held tints of rust and the sun. She did not talk very much—but then she did not have to—her voice had an odd, small, melodious huskiness that haunted the mind. She lived alone and was reputed to be very lazy—at least it was known that she slept during most of the day—but at night she bloomed like a moonflower, and a depth came into her eyes.

It was no wonder that Tommy Brooks fell in love with her. The wonder was that she let him. There was nothing exotic or distinguished about Tommy—he was just one of those pleasant, normal young men who seem created to carry on the bond business by reading the newspapers in the University Club during most of the day, and can always be relied upon at night to fill an unexpected hole in a dinner party. It is true that the Princess could hardly be said to do more than tolerate any of her suitors—no one had ever seen those aloof and arrogant eyes enliven at the entrance of any male. But she seemed to be able to tolerate Tommy a little more than the rest—and that young man's infatuated daydreams were beginning to be beset by smart solitaires and imaginary apartments on Park Avenue when the famous Monsieur Tibault conducted his first concert at Carnegie Hall.

Tommy Brooks sat beside the Princess. The eyes he turned upon her were eyes of longing and love, but her face was as impassive as a Benda mask, and the only remark she made during the preliminary bustlings was that there seemed to be a number of people in the audience. But Tommy was relieved, if anything, to find her even a little more aloof than usual, for, ever since Mrs. Culverin's dinner party, a vague disquiet as to the possible impression which this Tibault creature might make upon her had been growing in his mind. It shows his devotion that he was present at all. To a man whose simple Princetonian nature found in "Just a Little Love, a

Little Kiss," the quintessence of musical art, the average symphony was a positive torture, and he looked forward to the evening's program itself with a grim, brave smile.

"Ssh!" said Mrs. Dingle breathlessly. "He's coming!" It seemed to the startled Tommy as if he were suddenly back in the trenches under a heavy barrage, as Monsieur Tibault made his entrance to a perfect bombardment of applause.

Then the enthusiastic noise was sliced off in the middle, and a gasp took its place—a vast, windy sigh, as if every person in that multitude had suddenly said "Ah!" For the papers had not lied about him. The tail was there.

They called him theatric—but how well he understood the uses of theatricalism! Dressed in unrelieved black from head to foot (the black dress shirt had been a special token of Mussolini's esteem), he did not walk on, he strolled, leisurely, easily, aloofly, the famous tail curled nonchalantly about one wrist—a suave, black panther lounging through a summer garden with that little mysterious weave of the head that panthers have when they pad behind bars—the glittering darkness of his eyes unmoved by any surprise or elation. He nodded, twice in regal acknowledgment, as the clapping reached an apogee of frenzy. To Tommy there was something dreadfully reminiscent of the Princess in the way he nodded. Then he turned to his orchestra.

A second and louder gasp went up from the audience at this point, for, as he turned, the tip of that incredible tail twined with dainty carelessness into some hidden pocket and produced a black baton. But Tommy did not even notice. He was looking at the Princess instead.

She had not even bothered to clap, at first, but now . . . Poor Tommy had never seen her moved like this, never. She was not applauding, her hands were clenched in her lap, but her whole body was rigid, rigid as a steel bar, and the blue flowers of her eyes were bent upon the figure of Monsieur Tibault in a terrible concentration. The pose of her entire figure was so still and intense that for an instant Tommy had the lunatic idea that any moment she might leap from her seat beside him as lightly as a moth, and land, with no sound, at Monsieur Tibault's side to—yes—to rub her proud head against his coat in worship. Even Mrs. Dingle would notice in a moment.

"Princess—" he said, in a horrified whisper, "Princess—"

Slowly the tenseness of her body relaxed, her eyes veiled again, she grew calm.

"Yes, Tommy?" she said, in her usual voice, but there was still something about her . . .

"Nothing, only—oh, hang—he's starting!" said Tommy, as Monsieur Tibault, his hands loosely clasped before him, turned and *faced* the audience. His eyes dropped, his tail switched once impressively, then gave three little preliminary taps with his baton on the floor.

Seldom has Gluck's overture *Iphigenie in Aulis* received such an ovation. But it was not until the Eighth Symphony that the hysteria of the audience reached its climax. Never before had the New Symphony been played so superbly—and certainly never before had it been led with such genius. Three prominent conductors in the audience were sobbing with the despairing admiration of envious children toward the close, and one at least was heard to offer wildly ten thousand dollars to a well-known facial surgeon there present for a shred of evidence that tails of some variety could by any stretch of science be grafted upon a normally decaudate form. There was no doubt about it—no mortal hand and arm, be they ever so dexterous, could combine the delicate *élan* and powerful grace displayed in every gesture of Monsieur Tibault's tail.

A sable staff, it dominated the brasses like a flicker of black lightning; an ebon, elusive whip, it drew the last exquisite breath of melody from the wood winds and ruled the stormy strings like a magician's rod. Monsieur Tibault bowed and bowed again—roar after roar of frenzied admiration shook the hall to its foundations —and when he finally staggered, exhausted, from the platform, the president of the Wednesday Sonata Club was only restrained by force from flinging her ninety-thousand-dollar string of pearls after him in an excess of esthetic appreciation. New York had come and seen—and New York was conquered. Mrs. Dingle was immediately besieged by reporters, and Tommy Brooks looked forward to the "little party" at which he was to meet the new hero of the hour

with feelings only a little less lugubrious than those that would have
come to him just before taking his seat in the electric chair.

The meeting between his princess and Monsieur Tibault was
worse and better than he expected. Better because, after all,
they did not say much to each other—and worse because it seemed
to him, somehow, that some curious kinship of mind between
them made words unnecessary. They were certainly the most
distinguished-looking couple in the room, as he bent over her hand.
"So darlingly foreign, both of them, and yet so different," babbled
Mrs. Dingle—but Tommy couldn't agree.

They were very different—yes—the dark, lithe stranger with
that bizarre appendage tucked carelessly in his pocket, and the blue-
eyed, brown-haired girl. But that difference only accentuated what
they had in common—something in the way they moved, in the
suavity of their gestures, in the set of their eyes. Something deeper,
even, than race. He tried to puzzle it out—then, looking around at
the others, he had a flash of revelation. It was as if that couple were
foreign, indeed—not only to New York but to all common humanity. As if they were polite guests from a different star.

Tommy did not have a happy evening, on the whole. But his
mind worked slowly, and it was not until much later that the
mad suspicion came upon him in full force.

Perhaps he is not to be blamed for his lack of immediate com-
prehension. The next few weeks were weeks of bewildered misery
for him. It was not that the Princess' attitude toward him had
changed—she was just as tolerant of him as before, but Monsieur
Tibault was always there. He had a faculty of appearing as out of
thin air—he walked, for all his height, as lightly as a butterfly—
and Tommy grew to hate that faintest shuffle on the carpet that
announced his presence as he had never hated the pound of the guns.

And then, hang it all, the man was so smooth, so infernally, un-
ruffably smooth! He was never out of temper, never embarrassed.
He treated Tommy with the extreme of urbanity, and yet his eyes
mocked, deep down, and Tommy could do nothing. And gradually,
the Princess became more and more drawn to this stranger, in a
soundless communion that found little need for speech—and that,
too, Tommy saw and hated, and that, too, he could not mend.

He began to be haunted not only by Monsieur Tibault in the flesh but by Monsieur Tibault in the spirit. He slept badly, and when he slept he dreamed—of Monsieur Tibault, a man no longer, but a shadow, a specter, the limber ghost of an animal whose words came purringly between sharp little pointed teeth. There was certainly something odd about the whole shape of the fellow—his fluid ease, the mold of his head, even the cut of his finger nails—but just what it was escaped Tommy's intensest cogitation. And when he did put his finger on it at length, at first he refused to believe.

A pair of petty incidents decided him, finally, against all reason. He had gone to Mrs. Dingle's, one winter afternoon, hoping to find the Princess. She was out with his aunt, but was expected back for tea, and he wandered idly into the library to wait. He was just about to switch on the lights, for the library was always dark even in summer, when he heard a sound of light breathing that seemed to come from the leather couch in the corner. He approached it cautiously and dimly made out the form of Monsieur Tibault, curled up on the couch, peacefully asleep.

The sight annoyed Tommy so that he swore under his breath and was back near the door on his way out, when the feeling we all know and hate, the feeling that eyes we cannot see are watching us, arrested him. He turned back—Monsieur Tibault had not moved a muscle of his body to all appearance—but his eyes were open now. And those eyes were black and human no longer. They were green —Tommy could have sworn it—and he could have sworn that they had no bottom and gleamed like little emeralds in the dark. It lasted only a moment, for Tommy pressed the light-button automatically—and there was Monsieur Tibault, his normal self, yawning a little but urbanely apologetic, but it gave Tommy time to think. Nor did what happened a trifle later increase his peace of mind.

They had lit a fire and were talking in front of it—by now, Tommy hated Monsieur Tibault so thoroughly that he felt that odd yearning for his company that often occurs in such cases. Monsieur Tibault was telling some anecdote, and Tommy was hating him worse than ever for basking with such obvious enjoyment in the heat of the flames and the ripple of his own voice.

Then they heard the street door open, and Monsieur Tibault jumped up—and, jumping, caught one sock on a sharp corner of the brass fire rail and tore it open in a jagged flap. Tommy looked down mechanically at the tear—a second's glance, but enough—for Monsieur Tibault, for the first time in Tommy's experience, lost his temper completely. He swore violently in some spitting, foreign tongue—his face distorted suddenly—he clapped his hand over his sock. Then, glaring furiously at Tommy, he fairly sprang from the room, and Tommy could hear him scaling the stairs in long, agile bounds. Tommy sank into a chair, careless for once of the fact that he heard the Princess' light laugh in the hall. He didn't want to see the Princess. He didn't want to see anybody. There had been something revealed when Monsieur Tibault had torn that hole in his sock—and it was not the skin of a man. Tommy had caught a glimpse of—black plush. Black velvet. And then had come Monsieur Tibault's sudden explosion of fury. Good *Lord*—did the man wear black velvet stockings under his ordinary socks? Or could he —could he—but here Tommy held his fevered head in his hands.

He went to Professor Tatto that evening with hypothetical questions, but as he did not dare confide his real suspicions to the Professor, the hypothetical answers he received served only to confuse him the more. Then he thought of Billy Strang. Billy was a good sort, and his mind had a turn for the bizarre. Billy might be able to help.

He couldn't get hold of Billy for three days, and lived through the interval in a fever of impatience. But finally they had dinner together at Billy's apartment, where his queer books were, and Tommy was able to blurt out the whole disordered jumble of his suspicions.

Billy listened without interrupting until Tommy was quite through. Then he pulled at his pipe. "But, my dear man—" he said protestingly.

"Oh, I know—I know," said Tommy, and waved his hands, "I know I'm crazy—you needn't tell me that—but I tell you, the man's a cat all the same—no, I don't see how he could be, but he is—why, hang it, in the first place, everybody knows he's got a *tail!*"

"Even so," said Billy Strang, puffing. "Oh, my dear Tommy, I don't doubt you saw, or think you saw, everything you say. But, even so . . ." He shook his head.

"But what about those other birds, werwolves and things?" said Tommy.

Billy looked dubious. "We-ll," he admitted, "you've got me there, of course. At least—a tailed man *is* possible. And the yarns about werwolves go back far enough so that—well, *I* wouldn't say there aren't or haven't been werwolves—but then I'm willing to believe more things than most people. But a wer-cat—or a man that's a cat and a cat that's a man—honestly, Tommy—"

"If I don't get some real advice I'll go clean off my hinge. For heaven's sake, tell me something to *do!*"

"Lemme think," said Billy. "First, you're pizen-sure this man is—"

"A cat. Yeah," and Tommy nodded violently.

"Check. And second—if it doesn't hurt your feelings, Tommy—you're afraid this girl you're in love with has—er—at least a streak of—felinity—in her—and so she's drawn to him?"

"Oh, Lord, Billy, if I only knew!"

"Well—er—suppose she really is, too, you know—would you still be keen on her?"

"I'd marry her if she turned into a dragon every Wednesday!" said Tommy fervently.

Billy smiled. "H'm," he said, "then the obvious thing to do is to get rid of this Monsieur Tibault. Lemme think."

He thought about two pipes full, while Tommy sat on pins and needles. Then, finally, he burst out laughing.

"What's so darn funny?" said Tommy aggrievedly.

"Nothing, Tommy, only I've just thought of a stunt—something so blooming crazy—but if he is—h'm—what you think he is—it *might* work—" And, going to the bookcase, he took down a book.

"If you think you're going to quiet my nerves by reading me a bedtime story—"

"Shut up, Tommy, and listen to this—if you really want to get rid of your feline friend."

"What is it?" asked Tommy gloomily.

"Book of Agnes Repplier's. About cats. Listen.

" 'There is also a Scandinavian version of the ever famous story

which Sir Walter Scott told to Washington Irving, which Monk
Lewis told to Shelley, and which, in one form or another, we find
embodied in the folklore of every land'—now, Tommy, pay attention—'the story of the traveler who saw within a ruined abbey, a
procession of cats, lowering into a grave a little coffin with a crown
upon it. Filled with horror, he hastened from the spot; but when he
had reached his destination he could not forbear relating to a friend
the wonder he had seen. Scarcely had the tale been told when his
friend's cat, who lay curled up tranquilly by the fire, sprang to its
feet, cried out, "Then I am the King of the Cats!" and disappeared
in a flash up the chimney.'

"Well?" said Billy, shutting the book.

"By gum!" said Tommy, staring. "By gum! Do you really think
there's a chance?"

"*I* think we're both in the boobyhatch. But if you want to try it—"

"Try it! I'll spring it on him the next time I see him. But—listen
—I can't make it a ruined abbey—"

"Oh, use your imagination! Make it Central Park. Tell it as if
it happened to you—seeing the funeral procession and all that. You
can lead into it somewhere—let's see—some general line—oh, yes—
'Strange, isn't it, how fact so often copies fiction? Why, only yesterday—' See?"

"Strange, isn't it, how fact so often copies fiction," repeated
Tommy dutifully. "Why, only yesterday—"

"I happened to be strolling through Central Park when I saw
something very odd."

"I happened to be strolling through—here, gimme that book!"
said Tommy, "I want to learn the rest of it by heart!"

Mrs. Dingle's farewell dinner to the famous Monsieur Tibault,
on the occasion of his departure for his Western tour, was looked
forward to with the greatest expectations. Not only could everybody be there, including the Princess Vivrakananda, but Mrs. Dingle,
a hinter if there ever was one, had let it be known that at this
dinner an announcement of very unusual interest to Society might
be made. So everyone, for once, was almost on time, except for
Tommy. He was at least fifteen minutes early, for he wanted to
have speech with his aunt alone. Unfortunately, however, he had

hardly taken off his overcoat when she was whispering some news in his ear so rapidly that he found it difficult to understand a word of it.

"And you mustn't breathe it to a soul!" she ended, beaming. "That is, not before the announcement—I think we'll have *that* with the salad—people never pay very much attention to salad—"

"Breathe what, Aunt Emily?" said Tommy, confused.

"The Princess, darling—the dear Princess and Monsieur Tibault —they just got engaged this afternoon, dear things! Isn't it *fascinating?*"

"Yeah," said Tommy, and started to walk blindly through the nearest door. His aunt restrained him.

"Not there, dear—not in the library. You can congratulate them later. They're just having a sweet little moment alone there now." And she turned away to harry the butler, leaving Tommy stunned.

But his chin came up after a moment. He wasn't beaten yet.

"Strange, isn't it, how often fact copies fiction?" he repeated to himself in dull mnemonics, and, as he did so, he shook his fist at the closed library door.

Mrs. Dingle was wrong, as usual. The Princess and Monsieur Tibault were not the library—they were in the conservatory, as Tommy discovered when he wandered aimlessly past the glass doors.

He didn't mean to look, and after a second he turned away. But that second was enough.

Tibault sat in a chair and she was crouched on a stool at his side, while his hand, softly, smoothly, stroked her brown hair. Black cat and Siamese kitten. Her face was hidden from Tommy, but he could see Tibault's face. And he could hear.

They were not talking, but there was a sound between them. A warm and contented sound like the murmur of giant bees in a hollow tree—a golden, musical rumble, deep-throated, that came from Tibault's lips and was answered by hers—a golden purr.

Somehow Tommy found himself back in the drawing room, shaking hands with Mrs. Culverin, who said frankly that she had seldom seen him look so pale.

The first two courses of the dinner passed Tommy like dreams, but Mrs. Dingle's cellar was notable, and by the middle of the meat course he began to come to himself. He had only one resolve now.

For the next few moments he tried desperately to break into the conversation, but Mrs. Dingle was talking, and even Gabriel will have a time interrupting Mrs. Dingle. At last, though, she paused for breath, and Tommy saw his chance.

"Speaking of that," said Tommy piercingly, without knowing in the least what he was referring to, "speaking of that—"

"As I was saying," said Professor Tatto. But Tommy would not yield. The plates were being taken away. It was time for salad.

"Speaking of that," he said again, so loudly and strangely that Mrs. Culverin jumped, and an awkward hush fell over the table. "Strange, isn't it, how often fact copies fiction?" There, he was started. His voice rose even higher. "Why, only today I was strolling through—" and, word for word, he repeated his lesson. He could see Tibault's eyes glowing at him as he described the funeral. He could see the Princess, tense.

He could not have said what he had expected might happen when he came to the end. But it was not bored silence everywhere, to be followed by Mrs. Dingle's acrid, "Well, Tommy, is that *quite* all?"

He slumped back in his chair, sick at heart. He was a fool, and his last resource had failed. Dimly he heard his aunt's voice saying, "Well, then—" and realized that she was about to make the fatal announcement.

But just then Monsieur Tibault spoke.

"One moment, Mrs. Dingle," he said, with extreme politeness, and she was silent. He turned to Tommy.

"You are—positive, I suppose, of what you saw this afternoon, Brooks?" he said in tones of light mockery.

"Absolutely," said Tommy sullenly. "Do you think I'd—"

"Oh, no, no, no," Monsieur Tibault waved the implication aside, "but—such an interesting story—one likes to be sure of the details—and, of course, you *are* sure—*quite* sure—that the kind of crown you describe was on the coffin?"

"Of course," said Tommy, wondering, "but—"

"Then I'm the King of the Cats!" cried Monsieur Tibault in a voice of thunder, and, even, as he cried it, the house lights blinked —there was the soft thud of an explosion that seemed muffled in cotton wool from the minstrel galley—and the scene was lit for a second by an obliterating and painful burst of light that vanished in an instant and was succeeded by heavy, blinding clouds of white, pungent smoke.

"Oh, those *horrid* photographers," came Mrs. Dingle's voice in a melodious wail. "I *told* them not to take the flashlight picture till dinner was over, and now they've taken it *just* as I was nibbling lettuce!"

Someone tittered a little nervously. Someone coughed. Then, gradually, the veils of smoke dislimned and the green and black spots in front of Tommy's eyes died away.

They were blinking at each other like people who have just come out of a cave into brilliant sun. Even yet their eyes stung with the fierceness of that abrupt illumination, and Tommy found it hard to make out the faces across the table from him.

Mrs. Dingle took command of the half-blinded company with her accustomed poise. She rose, glass in hand. "And now, dear friends," she said in a clear voice, "I'm sure all of us are very happy to—" Then she stopped, open-mouthed, an expression of incredulous horror on her features. The lifted glass began to spill its contents on the tablecloth in a little stream of amber. As she spoke she had turned directly to Monsieur Tibault's place at the table—and Monsieur Tibault was no longer there.

Some say there was a bursting flash of fire that disappeared up the chimney—some say it was a giant cat that leaped through the window at a bound, without breaking the glass. Professor Tatto puts it down to a mysterious chemical disturbance operating only over Monsieur Tibault's chair. Be that as it may, one thing is certain—in the instant of fictive darkness which followed the glare of the flashlight, Monsieur Tibault, the great conductor, disappeared forever from mortal sight, tail and all.

Mrs. Culverin swears he was an international burglar and that she was just about to unmask him, but no one who sat at that historic table believes her. No, there are no sound explanations, but Tommy thinks he knows, and he will never be able to pass a cat again without wondering.

Mrs. Tommy is quite of her husband's mind regarding cats—she was Gretchen Woolwine, of Chicago (*you* know the Woolwines!) —for Tommy told her his whole story.

Doubtless it would have been more romantic to relate how Tommy's daring won him his princess—but, unfortunately, it would not be veracious. For the Princess Vivrakanarda, also, is with us no longer. Her nerves, shattered by the spectacular dénouement of Mrs. Dingle's dinner, required a sea voyage, and from that voyage she has never returned to America.

Of course, there are the usual stories—one hears of her, a nun in a Siamese convent, or a masked dancer at *Le Jardin de ma Sœur*— one hears that she has been murdered in Patagonia or married in Trebizond—but, as far as can be ascertained, not one of these gaudy fables has the slightest basis in fact. I believe that Tommy, in his heart of hearts, is quite convinced that the sea voyage was only a pretext, and that by some unheard-of means she has managed to rejoin the formidable Monsieur Tibault, in fact, that in some ruined city or subterranean palace they reign together now, King and Queen of all the mysterious Kingdom of Cats. But that, of course, is quite impossible.

Sredni Vashtar

by SAKI

Saki's (H. H. Munro's) humor has been described as tory by no less an authority than Christopher Morley. Yet no radical has treated the vapid antics of the upper and middle-class Englishman with more biting wit than he. His best known animal story, and indeed, his best known story, Tobermory, has been re-printed so often that I dare not include it here. Instead, in Sredni Vashtar, we find two very strange pets . . . and Saki's savage hatred of the cruelty of adults to children, which is perhaps as great and terrible as any cruelty that exists in the world.

CONRADIN was ten years old, and the doctor had pronounced his professional opinion that the boy would not live another five years. The doctor was silky and effete, and counted for little, but his opinion was endorsed by Mrs. De Ropp, who counted for nearly everything. Mrs. De Ropp was Conradin's cousin and guardian, and in his eyes she represented those three-fifths of the world that are necessary and disagreeable and real; the other two-fifths, in perpetual antagonism to the foregoing, were summed up in himself and his imagination. One of these days Conradin supposed he would succumb to the mastering pressure of wearisome necessary things—such as illnesses and coddling restrictions and drawn-out dulness. Without his imagination, which was rampant under the spur of loneliness, he would have succumbed long ago.

Mrs. De Ropp would never, in her honestest moments, have confessed to herself that she disliked Conradin, though she might have been dimly aware that thwarting him "for his good" was a duty which she did not find particularly irksome. Conradin hated her with a desperate sincerity which he was perfectly able to mask. Such few pleasures as he could contrive for himself gained an added relish from the likelihood that they would be displeasing to his guardian, and from the realm of his imagination she was locked out —an unclean thing, which should find no entrance.

In the dull, cheerless garden, overlooked by so many windows that were ready to open with a message not to do this or that, or a reminder that medicines were due, he found little attraction. The few fruit-trees that it contained were set jealously apart from his plucking, as though they were rare specimens of their kind blooming in an arid waste; it would probably have been difficult to find a market-gardener who would have offered ten shillings for their entire yearly produce. In a forgotten corner, however, almost hidden behind a dismal shrubbery, was a disused tool-shed of respectable proportions, and within its walls Conradin found a haven, something that took on the varying aspects of a playroom and a cathedral. He had peopled it with a legion of familiar phantoms, evoked partly from fragments of history and partly from his own brain, but it also boasted two inmates of flesh and blood. In one corner lived a ragged-plumaged Houdan hen, on which the boy lavished an affection that had scarcely another outlet. Further back in the gloom stood a large hutch, divided into two compartments, one of which was fronted with close iron bars. This was the abode of a large polecat-ferret, which a friendly butcher-boy had once smuggled, cage and all, into its present quarters, in exchange for a long-secreted hoard of small silver. Conradin was dreadfully afraid of the lithe, sharp-fanged beast, but it was his most treasured possession. Its very presence in the tool-shed was a secret and fearful joy, to be kept scrupulously from the knowledge of the Woman, as he privately dubbed his cousin. And one day, out of Heaven knows what material, he spun the beast a wonderful name, and from that moment it grew into a god and a religion. The Woman indulged in religion once a week at a church near by, and took Conradin with her, but to him the church service was an alien rite in the House of Rimmon. Every Thursday in the dim and musty silence of the tool-shed, he worshipped with mystic and elaborate ceremonial before the wooden hutch where dwelt Sredni Vashtar, the great ferret. Red flowers in their season and scarlet berries in the winter-time were offered at his shrine, for he was a god who laid some special stress on the fierce impatient side of things, as opposed to the Woman's religion, which, as far as Conradin could observe, went to great lengths in the contrary direction. And on great festivals, powdered nutmeg was strewn in front of his hutch, an important feature of the offering being that the nutmeg had to be stolen. These festivals were of irregular occurrence, and were chiefly appointed to celebrate some passing event. On one occasion, when Mrs. De Ropp suffered from acute toothache for three days, Conradin kept up the festival during the entire three days, and almost succeeded in persuading himself that Sredni Vashtar was personally responsible for the toothache. If the malady had lasted for another day the supply of nutmeg would have given out.

The Houdan hen was never drawn into the cult of Sredni Vashtar. Conradin had long ago settled that she was an Anabaptist. He did not pretend to have the remotest knowledge as to what an Anabaptist was, but he privately hoped that it was dashing and not very respectable. Mrs. De Ropp was the ground plan on which he based and detested all respectability.

After a while Conradin's absorption in the tool-shed began to attract the notice of his guardian. "It is not good for him to be pottering down there in all weathers," she promptly decided, and at breakfast one morning she announced that the Houdan hen had been sold and taken away overnight. With her short-sighted eyes she peered at Conradin, waiting for an outbreak of rage and sorrow, which she was ready to rebuke with a flow of excellent precepts and reasoning. But Conradin said nothing: there was nothing to be said. Something perhaps in his white set face gave her a momentary qualm, for at tea that afternoon there was toast on the table, a delicacy which she usually banned on the ground that it was bad for him; also because the making of it "gave trouble," a deadly offence in the middle-class feminine eye.

"I thought you liked toast," she exclaimed, with an injured air, observing that he did not touch it.

"Sometimes," said Conradin.

In the shed that evening there was an innovation in the worship of the hutch-god. Conradin had been wont to chant his praises, tonight he asked a boon.

"Do one thing for me, Sredni Vashtar."

The thing was not specified. As Sredni Vashtar was a god he must be supposed to know. And choking back a sob as he looked at that other empty corner, Conradin went back to the world he so hated.

And every night, in the welcome darkness of his bedroom, and every evening in the dusk of the tool-shed, Conradin's bitter litany went up: "Do one thing for me, Sredni Vashtar."

Mrs. De Ropp noticed that the visits to the shed did not cease, and one day she made a further journey of inspection.

"What are you keeping in that locked hutch?" she asked. "I believe it's guinea-pigs. I'll have them all cleared away."

Conradin shut his lips tight, but the Woman ransacked his bedroom till she found the carefully hidden key, and forthwith marched down to the shed to complete her discovery. It was a cold afternoon, and Conradin had been bidden to keep to the house. From the furthest window of the dining-room the door of the shed could just be seen beyond the corner of the shrubbery, and there Conradin stationed himself. He saw the Woman enter, and then he imagined her opening the door of the sacred hutch and peering down with her short-sighted eyes into the thick straw bed where his god lay hidden. Perhaps she would prod at the straw in her clumsy impatience. And Conradin fervently breathed his prayer for the last time. But he knew as he prayed that he did not believe. He knew that the Woman would come out presently with that pursed smile he loathed so well on her face, and that in an hour or two the gardener would carry away his wonderful god, a god no longer, but a simple brown ferret in a hutch. And he knew that the Woman would triumph always as she triumphed now, and that he would grow ever more sickly under her pestering and domineering and superior wisdom, till one day nothing would matter much more with him, and the doctor would be proved right. And in the sting and misery of his defeat, he began to chant loudly and defiantly the hymn of his threatened idol:

Sredni Vashtar went forth,
His thoughts were red thoughts, and his teeth were white.
His enemies called for peace, but he brought them death.
Sredni Vashtar the Beautiful.

And then of a sudden he stopped his chanting and drew closer to the window-pane. The door of the shed still stood ajar as it had been left, and the minutes were slipping by. They were long minutes, but they slipped by nevertheless. He watched the starlings running and flying in little parties across the lawn; he counted them over and over again, with one eye always on that swinging door. A sour-faced maid came in to lay the table for tea, and still Conradin stood and waited and watched. Hope had crept by inches into his heart, and now a look of triumph began to blaze in his eyes that had only known the wistful patience of defeat. Under his breath, with a furtive exultation, he began once again the pæan of victory and devastation. And presently his eyes were rewarded: out through the doorway came a long, low, yellow-and-brown beast, with eyes a-blink at the waning daylight, and dark wet stains around the fur of jaws and throat. Conradin dropped on his knees. The great pole-cat-ferret made its way down to a small brook at the foot of the garden, drank for a moment, then crossed a little plank bridge and was lost to sight in the bushes. Such was the passing of Sredni Vashtar.

"Tea is ready," said the sour-faced maid; "where is the mistress?"

"She went down to the shed some time ago," said Conradin.

And while the maid went to summon her mistress to tea, Conradin fished a toasting-fork out of the sideboard drawer and proceeded to toast himself a piece of bread. And during the toasting of it and the buttering of it with much butter and the slow enjoyment of eating it, Conradin listened to the noises and silences which fell in quick spasms beyond the dining-room door. The loud foolish screaming of the maid, the answering chorus of wondering ejaculations from the kitchen region, the scuttering footsteps and hurried embassies for outside help, and then, after a lull, the scared sobbings and the shuffling tread of those who bore a heavy burden into the house.

"Whoever will break it to the poor child? I couldn't for the life of me!" exclaimed a shrill voice. And while they debated the matter among themselves, Conradin made himself another piece of toast.

Argos

by HOMER

No anthology of animal stories would be complete without the home-coming of far-wandering Odysseus, and the love of a dog, which penetrates even the disguise which the goddess Athene had given her favorite, in order that he might return safely home from the ten year siege of Troy and his ten years' wandering on the wine dark sea.

THERE lay the dog Argos, full of vermin. Yet now when he was aware of Odysseus standing by, he wagged his tail and wagged both his ears, but he had not now the strength to draw nearer to his master. But Odysseus looked aside and wiped away a tear that he easily hid from Eumaeus, and said,

"Eumaeus, verily this is a great marvel, this hound lying here in the dung. Truly he is goodly of growth, but I know not certainly if he have speed with his beauty, or if he be only comely, as are men's trencher dogs that their lords keep for the pleasure of the eye."

Then swineherd Eumaeus answered, "In very truth this is the dog of a man that has died in a far land. If he were what he once was in limb and in the feats of the chase, when Odysseus left him to go to Troy, soon wouldst thou marvel at the sight of his swiftness and his strength. There was no beast that could flee from him in the deep places of the wood; he was ever the keenest hound on a track. But now he is held in an evil case, and his lord has perished far from his own country, and the careless women take no charge of him" . . .

Therewith he passed within the fair-lying house, and went straight to the hall, to the company of the proud wooers.

But upon Argos came the fate of black death, even in the hour that he beheld Odysseus again, in the twentieth year.

Battling a Sea Monster

by VICTOR HUGO

The horror of the formless is perhaps the greatest horror man knows. And the octopus, that inchoate monster of the deep is, if not the most terrifying of all creatures, at least the most horrible of those with which literature has made us familiar. Victor Hugo in "Toilers of the Deep" gives us this blood curdling episode.

DRAWN in another direction by the pangs of hunger, Gilliatt pursued his search for food without much reflection. He wandered, not in the gorge, but outside among the smaller rocks where the *Durande*, ten weeks before, had first struck upon the sunken reef.

For the search that Gilliatt was prosecuting, this part was more favorable than the interior. At low water the crabs are accustomed to crawl out into the air. They seem to like to warm themselves in the sun, where they swarm, sometimes to the disgust of loiterers, who see in these creatures, with their awkward sidelong gait, climbing clumsily from crack to crack upon the rocks, a species of sea vermin.

For two months Gilliatt had lived almost entirely upon these creatures.

This time, however, the crayfish and crabs were both wanting. The tempest had driven them into their solitary retreats, and they had not yet mustered up courage to venture abroad.

Gilliatt held his open knife in his hand, and from time to time scraped a cockle from under the bunches of seaweed, and ate it as he walked on.

As Gilliatt was trying to make up his mind to be content with the sea-urchins and the *châtaignes de mer*, a little clattering noise at his feet aroused his attention. A large crab, startled by his approach, had just dropped into a pool. The water was shallow, and he did not lose sight of it.

He chased the crab along the base of the rock; but the crab moved fast, and suddenly disappeared.

It had buried itself in some crevice under the rock.

Gilliatt clutched the projections of the rock, and leaned over to look where it shelved away under the water.

As he suspected, there was an opening in which the creature had evidently taken refuge. It was more than a crevice; it was a kind of porch.

The water beneath it was not deep, and the bottom, covered with large pebbles, was plainly visible. The stones were green and clothed with *confervæ*, indicating that they were never dry. They looked like the tops of a number of infants' heads, covered with a kind of green hair.

Holding his knife between his teeth, Gilliatt descended, by the aid of his feet and hands, from the upper part of the escarpment, and leaped into the water. It reached almost to his shoulders.

He made his way through the porch, and found himself in a blind passage, with a roof shaped like a rude arch over his head. The walls were polished and slippery. The crab was nowhere visible.

As Gilliatt advanced the light grew fainter, so that he began to lose the power to distinguish objects.

When he had gone about fifteen yards the vaulted roof overhead ended. He had penetrated beyond the low passage. There was more space here, and consequently more daylight. The pupils of his eyes, moreover, had dilated, and he could see pretty clearly. . . . His vision became clearer and clearer. He was astonished. He found himself in an extraordinary palace of shadows; saw before his eyes a vaulted roof, fantastic columns, purple, blood-like stains, the vegetation rich with gems, and at the farther end, a crypt or sanctuary, and a huge stone which resembled an altar. . . .

Nearer the molded arch, he noticed low, dark grottoes, caves within caves. The entrance to the nearest was out of the water, and easily approached.

Nearer still than this recess he noticed, above the level of the water, and within reach of his hand, a horizontal fissure.

It seemed to him probable that the crab had taken refuge there, and he plunged his hand in as far as he was able, and groped in that dusky aperture.

Suddenly he felt himself seized by the arm. A strange, indescribable horror thrilled him.

Some living thing, thin, rough, flat, cold, and slimy had twisted itself round his naked arm, in the dark depth below. It crept towards his chest. Its pressure was like a tightening cord, its steady persistence like that of a screw. In another instant the same mysterious spiral form had wound around his wrist and elbow, and had reached his shoulder. A sharp point penetrated beneath the armpit.

Gilliatt recoiled, but he had scarcely power to move! He was, as it were, nailed to the place. With his left hand, which was disengaged, he seized his knife, which he still held between his teeth, and with that hand gripping the knife, he supported himself against the rocks, while he made a desperate effort to withdraw his arm; but he only succeeded in disturbing his persecutor, which wound itself tighter. It was supple as leather, strong as steel, cold as night.

A second form, sharp, elongated, and narrow issued from the crevice like a tongue out of monstrous jaws.

It seemed to lick his naked body; then suddenly stretching out, it became longer and thinner, as it crept over his skin, and wound itself around him. At the same time a terrible sensation of pain, utterly unlike any he had ever known, made all his muscles contract. It seemed as if innumerable suckers had fastened themselves in his flesh and were about to drink his blood.

A third long undulating shape issued from the hole in the rock, seemed to feel its way around his body to lash itself around his ribs like a cord, and fix itself there.

Intense agony is dumb. Gilliatt uttered no cry. There was sufficient light for him to see the repulsive forms which had wound themselves about him.

A fourth ligature—but this one swift as an arrow—darted towards his stomach, and wound around him.

It was impossible to sever or tear away the slimy bands which were twisted tightly around his body, and which were adhering to it at a number of points. Each of these points was the focus of frightful and singular pangs. It seemed as if innumerable small mouths were devouring him at the same time.

A fifth long, slimy, ribbon-shaped strip issued from the hole. It passed over the others, and wound itself tightly around his chest. The compression increased his sufferings. He could scarcely breathe.

These living thongs were pointed at their extremities, but broadened like the blade of a sword towards its hilt. All five evidently belonged to the same center. They crept and glided about him; he felt the strange points of pressure, which seemed to him like so many mouths, change their position from time to time.

Suddenly a large, round, flattened, glutinous mass issued from beneath the crevice. It was the center; the five thongs were attached to it like spokes to the hub of a wheel. On the opposite side of this disgusting monster appeared the beginning of three other similar tentacles, the ends of which remained under the rock. In the middle of this slimy mass were two eyes.

These eyes were fixed on Gilliatt.

He recognized the devil-fish.

It is difficult for those who have not seen it to believe in the existence of the devil-fish. Compared with this creature, the ancient hydras are insignificant. . . .

The devil-fish has no muscular organization, no menacing cry, no breast-plate, no horn, no dart, no claw, no tail with which to hold or bruise; no cutting fins, or wings with nails, no prickles, no sword, no electric discharge, no poison, no claws, no beak, no jaws. Yet he is of all creatures the most formidably armed.

What, then, is the devil-fish? It is a huge cupping-glass.

The swimmer who, attracted by the beauty of the spot, ventures among reefs far out to sea, where still waters hide rocks, or in unknown caverns abounding in marine plants, testacea, and crustacea, under the deep portals of the ocean, runs the risk of meeting it. If that fate should be yours, be not curious, but fly. The intruder enters there dazzled, but quits the spot in terror.

This frightful monster which is so often encountered amid the rocks in the open sea, is of a grayish color, about five feet long, and about the thickness of a man's arm. It is ragged in outline, and in shape strongly resembles a closed umbrella, without a handle. This irregular mass advances slowly towards you. Suddenly it opens, and eight radii issue abruptly from around a face with two eyes. These radii are alive; their undulation is like lambent flames; they resemble, when opened, the spokes of a wheel measuring four or five feet in diameter.

This monster winds itself around its victim, covering and entangling him in its long folds. Underneath it is yellow; above, it is of a dull grayish hue. It is spider-like in form, but its tints are those of the chameleon. When irritated it becomes violent. Its most horrible characteristic is its softness.

Its folds strangle; its contact paralyzes.

It has the aspect of gangrened or scabrous flesh. It is a monstrous embodiment of disease.

It clings to its prey, and cannot be torn away—a fact which is due to its power of exhausting air. The eight antennæ, large at their roots, diminish gradually, and end in needle-like points. Underneath each of these feelers are two rows of suckers, decreasing in size, the largest ones near the head, the smallest at the extremities. Each row contains twenty-five of these. There are, therefore, fifty suckers to each feeler, and the creature possesses four hundred in all. These suckers act like cupping-glasses.

They are cartilaginous substances, cylindrical, horny, and livid. Upon the large species they diminish gradually from the diameter of a five-franc piece to the size of a split pea. These small tubes can be thrust out and withdrawn by the animal at will. They are capable of piercing to a depth of more than an inch. . . .

While swimming, the devil-fish remains, so to speak, in its sheath. It swims with all its parts drawn close together. It might be likened to a sleeve sewed up with a closed fist within. This protuberance, which is the head, pushes the water aside and advances with an undulatory movement. The two eyes, though large, are indistinct, being the color of water.

When it is lying in ambush, or seeking its prey, it retires into itself as it were, becomes smaller and condenses itself. It is then scarcely distinguishable in the dim, submarine light. It looks like a mere ripple in the water. It resembles anything except a living creature.

The devil-fish is crafty. When one is least expecting it, it suddenly opens.

A glutinous mass, endowed with a malevolent will, what could be more horrible.

It is in the most beautiful azure depths of limpid water that this hideous, voracious, sea-monster delights.

It always conceals itself—a fact which increases its terrible associations. When they are seen, it is almost invariably after they have captured their victim.

At night, however, and particularly in the breeding season, it becomes phosphorescent. These horrible creatures have their passions, their submarine nuptials. Then it adores itself, glows, and illumines; and from some rock it can sometimes be discerned in the deep obscurity of the waves below, expanding with a pale irradiation—a spectral sun.

The devil-fish not only swims, but crawls. It is part fish, part reptile. It crawls upon the bed of the sea. At such times, it makes use of its eight feelers, and creeps along after the fashion of a swiftly moving caterpillar.

It has no blood, no bones, no flesh. It is soft and flabby; a skin with nothing inside. Its eight tentacles may be turned inside out like the fingers of a glove.

It has a single orifice in the center of its radii, which appears at first to be neither the vent nor the mouth. It is in fact both. It performs a double function.

The entire creature is cold.

The jelly-fish of the Mediterranean is repulsive. Contact with that animated gelatinous substance, in which the hands sink, and at which the nails tear ineffectually; which can be rent in twain without killing it, and which can be plucked off without entirely removing it, that soft and yet tenacious creature which slips through the fingers —is disgusting; but no horror can equal the sudden apparition of the devil-fish, that Medusa with its eight serpents.

No grasp is like the sudden strain of the cephalopod.

It is with the sucking apparatus that it attacks. The victim is oppressed by a vacuum drawing at numberless points; it is not a claw-ing or a biting, but an indescribable scarification. A tearing of the flesh is terrible, but less terrible than a sucking of the blood. Claws are harmless in comparison with the terrible action of these natural cupping-glasses. The claws of the wild beast enter your flesh; but with the cephalopod, it is you who enter the creature that attacks you.

The muscles swell, the fibers of the body are contorted, the skin cracks under the loathsome oppression, the blood spurts out and mingles horribly with the lymph of the monster, which clings to its victim by innumerable hideous mouths. The hydra incorporates it-self with the man; the man becomes one with the hydra. The specter lies upon you; the tiger can only devour you; the horrible devil-fish sucks your life-blood away. He draws you to and into himself; while bound down, glued fast, powerless, you feel yourself gradually emptied into this pouch, which is the monster itself. To be eaten alive is terrible; to be absorbed alive is horrible beyond expres-sion. . . .

Such was the creature in whose power Gilliatt had fallen.

The monster was the mysterious inmate of the grotto; the terrible genius of the place; a kind of marine demon.

The splendors of the cavern existed for it alone. . . .

Gilliatt had thrust his arm deep into the opening; the monster had snapped at it.

It held him fast, as the spider holds the fly.

He was in the water up to his belt; his naked feet clutching the slippery roundness of the huge stones at the bottom; his right arm bound and rendered powerless by the flat coils of the long tentacles of the creature, and his body almost hidden under the folds and crossfolds of this horrible bandage.

Of the eight arms of the devil-fish, three adhered to the rock, while five encircled Gilliatt. In this way, clinging to the granite on one side, and to its human prey on the other, it chained him to the rock. Two hundred and fifty suckers were upon him, torment-ing him with agony and loathing. He was grasped by gigantic hands, each finger of which was nearly a yard long, and furnished inside with living blisters eating into the flesh.

As we have said, it is impossible to tear one's self from the clutches of the devil-fish. The attempt only results in a firmer grasp. The monster clings with more determined force. Its efforts increase with those of his victim; every struggle produces a tightening of its ligatures.

Gilliatt had but one resource—his knife.

His left hand only was free. . . .

His open knife was in his hand.

The antennae of the devil-fish cannot be cut; it is a leathery substance upon which a knife makes no impression; it slips under the blade; to sever it would be to wound severely the victim's own flesh.

The creature is formidable, but there is a way of resisting it. The fishermen of Sark know it, and so does anyone who has seen them execute certain abrupt movements in the sea. Porpoises know it, too; they have a way of biting the cuttle-fish which decapitates it. Hence the frequent sight on the sea of headless pen-fish, polypuses, and cuttle-fish.

In fact, its only vulnerable part is its head.

Gilliatt was not ignorant of this fact.

He had never seen a devil-fish of this size. His first encounter was with one of the largest species. Any other man would have been overwhelmed with terror.

With the devil-fish, as with a furious bull, there is a certain instant in the conflict which must be seized. It is the instant when the bull lowers his neck; it is the instant when the devil-fish advances its head. The movement is rapid. One who loses that moment is irrevocably doomed.

The events we have described occupied only a few seconds, Gilliatt, however, felt the increasing power of the monster's innumerable suckers.

The monster is cunning; it tries first to stupefy its prey. It seizes and then pauses awhile.

Gilliatt grasped his knife; the sucking increased.

He looked at the monster, which seemed to return the look.

Suddenly it loosened from the rock its sixth antenna, and darting it at him, seized him by the arm.

At the same moment, it advanced its head with a quick movement. In one second more its mouth would have fastened on his breast. Bleeding in the sides, and with his two arms entangled, he would have been a dead man. But Gilliatt was watchful.

He avoided the antenna, and at the very instant the monster darted forward to fasten on his breast, he stuck it with the knife clinched in his left hand.

There were two convulsive movements in opposite directions—that of the devil-fish, and that of its prey.

The movements were as rapid as lightning.

Gilliatt had plunged the blade of his knife into the flat, slimy substance, and with a rapid movement, like the flourish of a whip-lash in the air, had described a circle round the two eyes, and wrenched off the head as a man would draw a tooth.

The struggle was ended. The slimy bands relaxed. The air-pump being broken, the vacuum was destroyed. The four hundred suckers, deprived of their sustaining power, dropped at once from the man and the rock. The mass sank to the bottom of the water.

Breathless with the struggle, Gilliatt could dimly discern on the stones at his feet two shapeless, slimy heaps, the head on one side, the rest of the monster on the other.

Nevertheless, fearing a convulsive return of the death agony, he recoiled to be out of reach of the dread tentacles.

But the monster was quite dead.

Gilliatt closed his knife.

Northwind

by HERBERT RAVENEL SASS

An Indian hunter, and a battle between two horses, and a theory which may be true concerning the origin of the wild horses on the barrier islands of Carolina.

IT WAS in the days when Moytoy of Tellequo was High Chief of the Cherokee nation that the wild chestnut stallion known afterward as Northwind left the savannahs of the Choctaw country and travelled to the Overhills of the Cherokees. He made this long journey because the Choctaw horse-hunters had been pressing him hard. A rumor had run through the tribe, started perhaps by some learned conjurer or medicine man, that the tall, long-maned chestnut stallion who was king of the wild horse herds was descended from the famous steed which the Prince Soto rode when, many years before, he led his Spaniards through the Choctaw lands far into the Mississippi wilderness and perished there.

This rumor sharpened the eagerness of the younger braves, for it was well known that Soto's horse had magic in him. That spring they hunted the wild stallion more persistently than ever; and at last, taking two sorrel mares with him, he struck northeastward, seeking safer pastures.

He did not find them in the Overhills, as the Cherokees called the high Smokies and the Blue Ridge where they lived and hunted. At dawn one May morning, as he lay on a bed of fresh sweet-scented grass near the middle of a natural pasture known as Long Meadow, a warning came to him. He raised his head high and sniffed the air, then jumped nimbly to his feet. For a half minute, however, he did not rouse the two mares lying on either side of him: and they, if they were aware of his movement, were content to await his signal.

He gave the signal presently, and the mares rose, their ears pricked, their nostrils quivering. A light breeze blew across the meadow from the north. The stallion faced south, for his sensitive nose told him that no foeman was approaching from the opposite direction. He knew that his ears had not deceived him and that the sound which he had heard was near at hand. But he did not know the exact quarter from which the sound had come; and though his large eyes were well adapted to the dim light, nowhere could he discern that sinister weaving movement of the tall, close-growing grass which would reveal the stealthy approach of bear or puma. So, for some minutes, he waited motionless, his head held high, every faculty keyed to the utmost.

Twenty yards away down the wind Corane the Raven, young warrior of the Cherokees, crouching low in the grass, watched the wild stallion eagerly. Himself invisible, he could see his quarry more and more plainly as the light grew stronger; and he knew already that the wits of this slim, long-maned chestnut horse, which had come over the mountains from the west, were worthy of his beauty and strength. With all his art—and the Raven prided himself on his skill as a still-hunter—and with all the conditions in his favor, he had been baffled. Having located the beds of the wild horses, he had left his own horse, Monito-Kinibic, at the edge of the woods and had crept through the grass as furtively as a lynx. But his approach had been detected when he was yet five lance-lengths distant, and since then the stallion had made no false move, had committed no error of judgment.

Corane the Raven knew the wild horses well. Most of them were small and wiry, already approaching the mustang type of later years; but in those early days, before inbreeding had proceeded very far, an occasional stallion still revealed unmistakably the fine qualities of blooded forebears. From his hiding place in the grass the young warrior, naked except for a light loincloth of deer-hide, studied the great chestnut carefully, thoughtfully, marvelling at the lithe symmetry of his powerful but beautifully moulded form, admiring his coolness and steadiness in the face of danger. The stallion showed no sign of fear. He did not fidget or caper nervously. Only his head moved slowly back and forth, while with all his powers of sight, scent and hearing he strove to locate the precise spot where his enemy was lurking.

The Raven smiled in approval; and presently he applied a test of another kind.

With his long spear he pushed the grass stems in front of him, causing the tops of the tall blades to quiver and wave. The movement was slight; yet even in the pale morning light the wild horse saw it. He watched the spot intently for some moments. Then he moved slowly and cautiously forward, the mares following in his tracks. He moved neither toward the danger nor away from it. Instead, he circled it, and the Raven realized at once what the stallion's purpose was. He intended to get down wind from the suspected spot, so that his nose could tell him whether an enemy hid there, and, if so, what kind of enemy it was.

The young warrior waited, curious to see the outcome. Suddenly the stallion's head jerked upward. He was well down the wind now and a puff of air had filled his nostrils with the manscent. A moment he stood at gaze; and in that moment one of the mares caught the tell-tale scent, snorted with terror and bolted at full speed. Close behind her raced the other mare; while the stallion, wheeling gracefully, followed at a slower pace, his eyes searching the grassy plain ahead.

The Raven had risen to his feet and stood in plain view, but the chestnut stallion scarcely glanced at him again. He was no longer a menace. Of greater importance now were other dangers unknown, invisible, yet possibly imminent.

The natural meadows of lush grass and maiden cane were perilous places for the unwary. In them the puma set his ambush; there the black bear often lurked; hidden in that dense cover, the Indian horse-hunter sometimes waited with their snares. The mares, in a frenzy of panic, were beyond their protector's control. Their nostrils full of the man-smell, they had forgotten all other perils. But the stallion had not forgotten. Before the mares had run fifty yards the thing that he feared happened.

Out of the grass a black bulk heaved upward, reared high with huge hairy arms outspread, fell forward with a deep grunting roar on the haunch of the foremost mare. Screaming like a mad thing, the mare reeled, staggered and went down. In a fraction of a second she was on her feet again, but the big mountain black bear, hurling himself on her hindquarters, crushed them to the ground.

Corane the Raven, racing forward at the sound of the mare's frenzied scream, was near enough to see part of what happened. He saw the wild stallion rear to his utmost height and come down with battering forefeet on the bear's back. He heard the stallion's loud squeal of fury, the bear's hoarse grunt of rage and pain. Next moment the mare was up again and running for her life, the stallion cantering easily behind her.

When the Raven reached the spot the bear had vanished; and the young Indian, marvelling at what he had seen, ran toward the woods-edge where his swift roan, Manito-Kinibic, awaited him.

In this way began the chase of the chestnut stallion—Northwind, as he was afterward known—that long hunt which Corane the Raven made long ago, even before the time of Atta-Kulla-Kulla the Wise. It was Dunmore the trader who first brought down from the Overhills the story of that hunt and told it one night in Nick Rounder's tavern in Charles Town. Dunmore had it from the Raven himself; and the Raven was known among the white traders and hunters as a truthful man. But he was known also as a man of few words, while Dunmore, great hunter and famous Indian fighter though he was, had a tongue more fluent than a play-actor's.

So it was probably Dunmore who put color into the story, and undoubtedly his quick brain, well warmed with rum that night in the tavern, filled in many details. The tale appealed to him, for he was a lover of horses; and this story of the feud between Northwind, the wild stallion, and Manito-Kinibic, the Raven's roan, concerned two horses which were paladins of their kind.

For the hunt which began that morning in Long Meadow became in large measure a contest between these two. It happened that the Raven had returned not long before from a peace mission to the Choctaws, and while in their country he had heard of the wonderful wild horse which was said to have in him the blood of the Prince Soto's steed and which had vanished from the savannahs after defying all attempts to capture him. In the Overhills wild horses were rare. When the Raven found the tracks of three of

them near Long Meadow about sunset one May day, he thought it
worth while to sleep that night near the meadow's edge and have a
look at the horses in the morning.

So at dawn he had tried to stalk them in their beds; and the moment he saw the wild stallion rise from his sleeping place in the
grass he knew that the great chestnut horse of which the Choctaws
had spoken stood before him. That morning in Long Meadow he
knew also that he could not rest until he had taken this matchless
wild horse for his own.

It would be a long hunt, for the stallion would not linger in the
Overhills. Small bands of wild horses occasionally crossed the mountains from the west, and always these migrating bands travelled
fast, pausing only to feed. Yet, though the hunt might carry him
far, Corane the Raven, as he ran swiftly across Long Meadow
toward the woods-edge where he had left Manito-Kinibic, had
little doubt as to its issue. This wild stallion was a great horse, beautiful, swift and strong—by far the finest wild horse that the Raven
had ever seen. But there was one other that was his equal in all things
except beauty; and that other was Manito-Kinibic, the Raven's
roan.

There was no chief of the Cherokees, the Creeks or the Choctaws
who had a horse that could match Manito-Kinibic. His like had
never been known in the Overhills. Dunmore the trader had seen
him and had wondered whence he came; for though the Raven
had taken him from the Chickasaws, whose country lay west of
the mountains, it was plain that this big-boned burly roan was not
of the Western or Southern wild breed, while his name, which in
the white man's tongue meant Rattlesnake, had to Dunmore's ear
a Northern sound.

Thick-bodied, wide-headed, short-maned, heavy-eared, Manito-
Kinibic was almost grotesquely ugly; yet in his very ugliness there
was a sinister, almost reptilian fascination, heightened by the metallic
sheen of his red-speckled coat, the odd flatness of his head and the
fixed stony glare of his small, deep-set eyes. No warrior of the
Cherokees except the Raven could ride him. Few could even approach him, for his temper was as arrogant as that of the royal
serpent for which he was named.

There lurked in him, too, a craftiness recalling the subtle cunning which the red men attributed to the rattlesnake and because of which they venerated the king of serpents almost as a god; and with this craftiness he harbored a savage hatred of the wild creatures which the Indians hunted, so that on the hunt he was even more eager, even more relentless than his rider. It was the Raven's boast that Manito-Kinibic could follow a trail which would baffle many a red hunter; that he could scent game at a greater distance than the wolf; that his ears were as keen as those of the deer; that he was as crafty as the fox and as ruthless as the weasel; and that he feared no wild beast of the forest, not even the puma himself.

Such was the horse that Corane the Raven rode on his long hunt. From the beginning of that hunt until its end Manito-Kinibic seemed to live for one thing only—the capture of the wild stallion whose scent he snuffed for the first time that morning in Long Meadow after the wild horse's encounter with the bear.

A few minutes after that encounter, the Raven had reached the woods-edge where he had left the big roan, had vaulted upon his back and, riding as swiftly as was prudent through the tall grass and beds of maiden cane, had struck the trail of the three wild horses near the spot where they had passed from the meadow at its lower end into the woods.

The trail was plain to the eye. The scent was strong where the wild horses had brushed through the rank grass. From that moment Manito-Kinibic knew what game it was that his rider hunted; and in that moment all the strange smouldering hatred of his nature was focused upon the wild stallion which, as his nose told him, had passed that way with one or two mares.

Manito-Kinibic leaped forward with long bounds, his nostrils dilated, his ears flattened against his head. Corane the Raven, smiling grimly, let him go. It might be true, as the Choctaws believed, that the wild stallion was sprung from the mighty horse of the Prince Soto himself. But surely this huge implacable horse that now followed on the wild one's trail must have in his veins the blood of the great black steed which the Evil Spirit bestrode when he stood, wrapped in cloud, on the bare summit of Younaguska peak and hurled those awful arrows of his that flashed like lightning.

Northwind, the chestnut stallion, had passed within sight of Younaguska, highest of the Balsams, which men in these days call

Caney Fork Bald; but that sombre mountain lay far behind him now, for he had crossed both the main ranges of the mountain bulwark and had begun to descend the eastern slope of the second and lesser range. From Long Meadow he led his mares southeastward at a steady gait, following in general the trend of the valleys and the downward-sloping ridges. The injured mare, though her haunch was raw and bloody where the bear's claws had raked it, kept pace with her companions; and the three traveled fast, pausing only once or twice to drink at some cold, clear, hemlock-shaded stream.

For the most part their course carried them through a virgin forest of oak, chestnut, hickory and other broad-leaved trees, clothing the ridges, the slopes and most of the valleys. Occasionally the stallion chose his own way, though as a rule he followed the narrow trails made by the deer; but when in the early forenoon he found a broader path through the woods, well-marked and evidently often used, he turned into it unhesitatingly and followed it without swerving. The wild horse of the southwestern savannahs recognized this path at once. It was one of the highways of the buffalo herds, a road trodden deep and hard through many centuries by thousands of hoofs.

The buffalo were far less abundant now on the eastern side of the mountains. Although the white men's settlements were still confined to a strip along the coast, white hunters sometimes penetrated the foothills and white traders encouraged the taking of pelts. The deer still abounded in almost incredible numbers, but the eastern buffalo herds were withdrawing gradually across the Appalachians. Small droves, however, still ranged the eastern foothills and kept open the deep-worn paths; and the main buffalo roads across the mountain barrier, wider than the narrow buffalo ruts of the Western plains, were still highways for wild creatures of many kinds. It was one of these main roads that the chestnut stallion and his mares were following; a road which would lead them with many windings down from the mountains into the hills and through the hills to the broad belt of rolling lands beyond which lay the swamps and savannahs of the Atlantic plain.

All that forenoon the Raven trailed his quarry. Both to the roan stallion and to his rider the trail was a plain one; and when the tracks of the wild horses turned into the buffalo path, the Raven knew that he had only to follow that highway through the woods. With a guttural word he restrained Manito-Kinibic's savage eagerness. So long as the wild horses kept to the buffalo road the task of following them would be simple. The Raven preferred that for the present the chestnut stallion should not know that he was pursued.

Half a bowshot ahead of the young warrior a troop of white-tails crossed the path, following a deer trail leading down the slope to a laurel-bordered stream. Once, at a greater distance, he saw a puma come out of the woods into the path, sit for a moment on its haunches, then vanish at a bound into the forest on the other side. Again and again wild turkeys ran into the woods on either hand, seldom taking wing; and with monotonous regularity ruffed grouse rose a few paces in front of him and whirred swiftly away.

About noon he killed a cock grouse in the path, pinning the bird to the ground with a light cane arrow tipped with bone; and he had scarcely remounted when around a curve of the path appeared the shaggy bulk of a huge buffalo bull. A moment the great beast stood motionless, blinking in astonishment, his massive head hanging low. Then, with surprising nimbleness, he turned and darted around the bend of the trail.

The Raven heard the stamping and trampling of many hoofs and gave Manito-Kinibic his head. The roan bounded forward and almost in an instant reached the bend of the path. At a word from his rider he halted; and the Raven, quivering with excitement, gazed with shining eyes upon a spectacle which sent the blood leaping through his veins—a herd of twenty buffalo pouring out of the path, crowding and jostling one another as they streamed down the mountainside through the woods, following a deer trail which crossed the buffalo road almost at right angles. Twice the young warrior bent his bow and drew the shaft to the head; and twice he lowered his weapon, unwilling to kill game which he must leave to the wolves.

Afternoon came and still the Raven rode on through the teeming mountain forest, following the deep-worn highway which the migrating herds through unknown centuries had carved across the Overhills. More keenly than ever now his eyes searched the path ahead. The wild stallion and his mares had probably grazed abundantly in Long Meadow before their early morning rest and had been interrupted; but by this time they should be hungry again, for since leaving Long Meadow they had not stopped to feed. Wherever the Raven saw the forest open a little ahead of him so that grass grew under the far-spaced trees, he halted and listened carefully. Before long in one of these grassy places he should find the three wild horses grazing. And he wished to avoid frightening them.

The path, which heretofore had wound around the mountain shoulders, dipped suddenly into a deep gorge-like valley at the bottom of which a torrent roared. The forest here was close and dark. The wild horses would not halt in this valley, for there was no grass to be had; and for a time the Raven relaxed his vigilance, letting his eyes stray from the path ahead.

From a tall hemlock on the mountainside a wild gobbler took wing, sailing obliquely across the valley, and the Raven saw an eagle, which had been perching on a dead tulip poplar, launch himself forward in swift pursuit. The young brave turned on his horse's back, gazing upward over his shoulder, eagerly watching the chase.

Without warning, Manito-Kinibic reared, swerved to the right and plunged forward. His rider, taken utterly by surprise, lurched perilously, yet somehow kept his seat. For an instant, as Manito-Kinibic reared again, the Raven saw a sinewy naked arm raised above a hideous grinning face daubed with vermilion and black. Steel-fingered hands clutched the Raven's leg; on the other side another hand clawed at his thigh. Out from the thicket into the path ahead leaped three more warriors, feathered and plumed with eagle-tails and hawk-wings, striped and mottled with the red and black paint of war. More dreadful than the hunting cry of the puma, the shrill war-whoop of the Muskogee split the air.

But for Manito-Kinibic the Rattlesnake, the chase of the chestnut stallion would have ended then. But the Muskogee war-party which waylaid Corane the Raven in the pass, hoping to take him alive for slavery or the torture, failed to reckon with the temper and strength of the mighty roan.

In an instant Manito-Kinibic had become a rearing, snorting fury, a raging devil of battering hoofs and gleaming teeth. The Raven saw one Muskogee go down before the plunging roan stallion. He saw another whose shoulder was red with something that was not war paint. He saw the three warriors in the path ahead leap for their lives into the thicket as Manito-Kinibic charged down upon them. Bending low on his horse's neck, he heard an arrow speed over him and, a half-second later, another arrow. Then, remembering that he was the son of a war captain, he rose erect, looked back, and flourishing the hand which still held his bow and spear, hurled at his enemies the Cherokee whoop of triumph.

Thenceforward for a time the Raven watched the path behind rather than the path ahead. The war parties of the Muskogee were often mounted, and the young Cherokee thought it likely that this party had horses concealed in the thickets near the path. They would probably pursue him, but with Manito-Kinibic under him he was safe. Yet for a while he gave the sure-footed roan his head, racing onward as swiftly as the uneven surface of the trail allowed. So it happened that he was driven by necessity into doing the thing which he had intended to avoid.

A mile beyond the scene of the ambush the valley widened. Here, encircled by forested heights, lay a level, sun-bathed meadow, sweet with clover and wild pea vine. Northwind and his mares had travelled far and fast. Urged on by his restless eagerness to get out of the dark forbidding mountains, perhaps impelled, too, by some mysterious premonition of danger, the great chestnut horse had permitted no halt for food. In this beautiful vivid green oasis in the wilderness of woods he halted at last.

The meadow was dotted with grazing deer. Clearly no enemy lurked there. With a joyful whinny Northwind turned aside from the path and led his consorts to the feast.

A half-hour later, an instant before the wariest of the white-tails had caught the warning sound, the wild stallion raised his head suddenly, listened intently for a moment, then, with a peremptory summons to the mares, trotted slowly with high head and tail toward the lower end of the meadow. Because wild creatures do not ordinarily rush headlong through the forest, he miscalculated the speed of the intruder whose hoof-beats he had heard. He was still near the middle of the meadow, while the mares, loath to leave the clover beds, were far behind him, when he saw the Raven on Manito-Kinibic dash out of the woods.

The young brave heard the wild stallion's snort of surprise, saw him leap forward and race for the buffalo path, while the mares

wheeled and galloped off to the left. In long beautiful bounds the
stallion skimmed over the grass to the meadow's lower end where
the path reëntered the forest. There he disappeared amid the
trees.

The damage having been done, the Raven let Manito-Kinibic do
his best for two or three miles. But the wild horse ran like the north
wind which blows across the summit of Unaka Kanoos. It was then
that the Raven named him, in honor of that north wind which is
the swiftest and keenest of all the winds of the mountains. Until
his rider checked him, Manito-Kinibic ran a good race. But they
saw the wild stallion no more that day.

Even among the Cherokees, great hunters and marvelously skilful trackers, it was considered a noteworthy thing that Corane the
Raven and Manito-Kinibic the Rattlesnake were able to follow the
trail of the chestnut stallion all the way from the eastern slope of
the Overhills to the Low Country of the Atlantic coast, more than
two hundred miles as the white man reckons distance. Certain circumstances aided the pursuers. Nearly always Northwind kept to
the game paths. Until he was well out of the mountains he followed
the buffalo road. For many miles through the upper foothills he
used the narrow paths trodden out by the deer. Always he chose
those paths which led him south or southeast, following the slope
of the land.

When he passed from the foothills into the rolling country where
the forest was more open and where many prairie-meadows lay em-
bosomed in the woods, the Raven's problem was somewhat harder;
and in the Low Country of the coastal plain, so utterly unlike his
mountain home, there were moments when the young warrior
saw defeat staring him in the face. Yet it was evident that the wild
stallion himself was not at home in this land of dense cypress swamps
and towering pinewoods, of vast canebrakes and wide wastes of
rushes, of dark sluggish rivers winding silently through moss-draped
mysterious forests.

If this was the land which some deep-seated instinct had impelled
him to seek, it was evidently not what he had expected it to be—
not a land like that which he had known westward of the mountains. It was rich beyond measure, affording pasturage of numer-

ous kinds. But in many respects it was strange to him, and his first night within its borders taught him that it bristled with dangers.

He rested that night near the end of a long woods-prairie or open savannah close to a tall canebrake bordering a great swamp. In the late afternoon he had grazed in the savannah amid herds of deer and flocks of tall gray cranes. The air was melodious with the songs of numberless birds. Over him, as he cropped the grass, passed many wild turkeys coming in from the woods to their roosts in the giant pines of the swamp. Around the margins of a marshy pond scores of graceful milk-white égrets walked to and fro amid hundreds of smaller herons of darker plumage. To the stallion it seemed that he had come to a land of plenty and of peace where no enemies lurked.

The night revealed his mistake. The swamp rang with the cries and roars of hunting beasts and with the long-drawn resonant bellowings of great alligators—a fearful chorus of the wilderness such as he had never heard before. Twice he saw round fiery eyes glaring at him out of the darkness. Once his nose told him that near at hand in the canebrake a puma was passing along one of the winding pathways through the canes. Sleep was impossible; yet, the night being very black, he judged it unsafe to move, fearing to run upon an invisible enemy. He spent the long hours standing, tense and rigid, his senses strained to the utmost, expecting each moment to feel the fangs or claws of some unknown foe.

How long the chestnut stallion remained in the wild swamp region of the Low Country cannot be told. Probably not long, for while food was abundant, the perils were too many. Nor can it be related how he avoided those perils and found his way at last to the edge of the wide salt marshes between the Low Country mainland and the barrier islands along the sea. Day after day Corane the Raven and Manito-Kinibic the Rattlesnake followed him in his wanderings; and day after day the Raven, patient with the long patience of his race, held fast to the resolution which he had formed at the beginning—the resolution not to attempt the capture of the wild stallion until the time should be fully ripe.

He had to wait long for that time, but in one respect fortune favored the young warrior. Except for the Muskogee ambush in the mountain pass, he suffered no interference at the hands of man and, indeed, saw scarcely a human face between the Overhills and the coast. Even when he had reached the white men's country—where, however, the settlements were still small and sparse—the wild horse's fear of human enemies kept both himself and his pursuers out of man's way. The spot where the long chase had its ending was as lonely as the remotest wilderness.

To Northwind, after his long journey, that spot seemed a paradise. To Corane the Raven, viewing it cautiously from the cover of the woods about noon of a warm cloudless June day, it seemed to combine all the conditions essential for his success. A dry level meadow carpeted with short thick grass and shaped like a broad spearhead lay between a converging river and creek which came together at the meadow's lower end. There, and for some distance along the shore, the land sloped sharply to the river, forming a little bluff about ten feet in height; while beyond the river lay vast marshes stretching for miles toward the hazy line of woods on the barrier isles.

The Raven took in these things at a glance; noted, too, with satisfaction that here and there in the meadow stood clumps of some dense, stiff-branched bush of a kind unknown in the mountains. Then, well pleased, his plan complete to the smallest detail, he let his eyes rest again upon that feature of the scene which was the most important and most gratifying of all.

Almost in the center of the meadow stood Northwind, the wild stallion, alert, arrogant, confident, a picture of lithe, clean-cut beauty and perfectly proportioned strength. But he no longer stood alone. Just beyond him grazed five mares, all of them bays and all of them of one size and build. The Raven knew at once that they were not wild horses and he surmised that they were strays from the white men's stock. But it mattered little whence they had come. The essential fact was that Northwind had taken them as his own, had become their master and protector.

Two hours before midnight, when the moon, almost at the full, swung high above the marshes beyond the river and the grassy expanse of the meadow was bathed in ghostly light, the Raven led Manito-Kinibic from his hiding place in the woods to the edge of the open. There the young brave halted. The big roan, his nostrils tingling with a scent which set his blood on fire, needed no word of instruction. He knew his part and would play it perfectly. Quivering with eagerness, yet too well trained to give way to the fury that possessed him, Manito-Kinibic moved out into the meadow at a slow walk, his hoofs making no sound.

The Raven waited until the roan had become a dim uncertain shape in the moonlight. Then, crouching low, the Indian stole to the nearest bush-clump, thence to another isolated thicket, and thence by a roundabout course to a third. He was halfway down the meadow when he heard the wild stallion's challenge and knew that Manito-Kinibic's keen nose had led the roan straight to his goal. Bending close to the ground, sometimes creeping on all fours, sometimes crawling like a snake, the Raven moved from bush-clump to bush-clump toward the sound.

A fresh breeze blew from the sea across the marshes. The wild stallion, resting with his mares near the meadow's lower end where the creek and river joined, could neither smell nor hear an enemy approaching from the direction of the woods. Manito-Kinibic was scarcely fifty paces distant when Northwind saw him.

A moment the wild horse stood at gaze, his muscles tense for the long leap which would launch him forward in swift flight. Then fear passed out of him and fury took its place. A glance had shown him what the intruder was—a lone stallion, riderless, unaccompanied by man, roaming at will and evidently seeking the bay mares. Loud and shrill rang Northwind's challenge. Instantly he charged his foe.

Manito-Kinibic the Rattlesnake was a veteran of many battles. The fiercest battle of his career was the one which he fought that night in the moonlit meadow where the long chase of the chestnut stallion had its end. Northwind, too, had conquered many rivals to make good his mastery of the wild horse herds; but never before had he faced an antagonist as formidable as the burly roan. With Manito-Kinibic lay the advantage of size and weight; with the wild horse the advantage of quickness and agility. In courage neither surpassed the other. In cunning each was the other's match.

Almost at once they took each other's measure and, despite their fury, fought with instinctive skill, each striving to utilize to the utmost those powers in which he excelled. After his first whirlwind charge, Northwind did not charge again. He knew after that first onset that he must not hurl himself recklessly against the roan's weight and bulk. This was an enemy too big to be overwhelmed; he must be cut to pieces with slashing hoofs and torn to ribbons with ripping, raking teeth. Hence the wild stallion whirled and circled, feinted and reared, dashed in and leaped clear again, like a skilful rapier-man whose opponent wields a broadsword—and wields it well.

For Manito-Kinibic was no blundering bruiser whose sole reliance was his strength. He, too, fought with cunning and skill, manœuvring with a lightness which belied his bulk, parrying and thrusting with an adroitness not much inferior to that of his opponent. But, apparently realizing the advantage which his weight gave him, he strove from the first for close quarters. Furiously, incessantly he forced the fighting, seeking to grip and hold his elusive enemy, rearing high to crush the wild horse with his battering hoofs, plunging forward with all his weight to drive his mighty shoulder against his foe and hurl him to the ground.

It was a fight too furious to last long. A stallion's hoofs and teeth are fearful weapons. A few minutes more must have brought a bloody end to the battle, though no man can say what that end would have been. Suddenly from a bush-clump a shadow darted, sped lightly across the grass, and vanished in a tuft of tall weeds. Northwind did not see it because it was behind him. If Manito-Kinibic saw it he gave no sign.

The battling stallions wheeled and reared, biting and plunging, striking with their forefeet, thrusting, parrying, feinting. Once more the roan hurled himself forward, his small eyes gleaming red, his teeth bared, his heavy hoofs stabbing the air; and once more his slim, long-maned opponent, light as a dancer, lithe as a panther, whirled aside, escaping destruction by an inch.

Again, as they fenced for an opening, rearing high, snorting and squealing, the wild horse's back was turned to the clump of weeds; and again the shadow darted forward, swiftly, noiselessly, gliding over the turf.

The next moment Corane the Raven crouched close behind the chestnut stallion. A half-second more, and he had swung his rawhide thong with the skill for which he was famous. Then, with a shout, he leaped for Manito-Kinibic's head.

Northwind was down. He lay on his side, motionless as a dead thing. The rawhide thong, weighted at its ends, was wrapped around his hind legs, binding them tightly together. The greatest miracle was not the skill with which the Raven had thrown his snare. More wonderful still was the quelling of Manito-Kinibic's battle-fury, the swiftness with which his master brought the raging roan under control. Yet this was merely the result of teaching, of long painstaking instruction. Corane the Raven, the most successful horse-hunter among the Cherokees, owed his success partly to the peculiar methods which he employed and partly to the perfect training of his famous roan.

Manito-Kinibic, his neck and shoulders bloody, his flanks heaving, stood quietly, gazing down at his fallen foe with eyes in which the fire of hatred still glowed; but Northwind, his silky sides streaked with red, lay inert, inanimate, seeming scarcely to breathe. He offered no resistance as the Raven with deft fingers slipped a strong hobble around the slim forelegs and made it fast above each fetlock. There was no terror, no fierceness in the wild horse's large eyes. Instead they seemed singularly calm and soft, as though the brain behind them was lulled with a vision of places far away and days long ago.

Yet, if the chestnut stallion, a prisoner at last, dreamed of some green, daisy-sprinkled forest-prairie beyond the mountains, the dream passed quickly. Presently the Raven removed the thong which had held Northwind's hind legs helpless; and instantly the wild horse came to life, panic-stricken, furious, frantic for his freedom.

For a moment he thought himself free. His hind legs were no longer bound. The hobble around his forelegs bound them only loosely. With a snort he heaved upward and leaped away in mad flight—only to pitch headlong to the ground with a force which almost drove the breath from his body. Up he scrambled once more and down again he plunged as his fettered forelegs crumpled under him. Five times he rose and five times he fell before he seemed to realize his helplessness.

For several minutes, then, he lay utterly still. The Raven had remounted Manito-Kinibic. The wild horse could not escape; yet it was well to be prepared for whatever might happen. The ordeal might be over in an hour, or, on the other hand, many hours might pass before Northwind's spirit was broken.

At last he struggled to his feet. The Raven circled him on the roan, watching him keenly. The captive's frenzy seemed to have passed. He was cooler now, steadier on his legs. Sudden anxiety which was almost panic gripped the young Indian. He recalled that once he had seen a hobbled wild horse travel a distance of half a bow-shot in short labored bounds before falling; and in a flash he had become aware of a danger hitherto unrealized.

Quickly he slipped from Manito-Kinibic's back and approached Northwind from behind, uncoiling the weighted rawhide thong which he had removed from the wild stallion's hind legs. He would snare those hind legs again and thus make certain of his captive.

By a margin of moments he was too late. Northwind wheeled, bounded forward, and this time he did not fall. He had learned what not one hobbled wild horse in a thousand ever discovered—that while a leap of normal length would throw him every time, he could travel at least a little distance at fair speed if his leaps were very short.

Another bound he made, another and another—stiff-legged, la-bored, heart-breaking—keeping his balance by a miracle. He was more than halfway to the river's edge when the hobble threw him, and though he fell heavily, almost in an instant he was on his feet again, bounding onward as before.

On the very verge of the low bluff the Raven, who had remounted as quickly as possible, drove Manito-Kinibic against the chestnut's flank in a last attempt to turn or throw him. Reeling from the blow, Northwind staggered on the brink. Then, rallying his strength for a supreme effort, he plunged sideways down the steep slope, and the water closed over him.

Some say he was drowned. The Raven never saw him again, though the moon shone brightly on the river. But the water is very deep beside that bluff and there the ebb tide is very strong and swift. It might have borne him quickly beyond the Indian's vision; and since the hobble allowed his forelegs some freedom of action, he might have made shift to swim.

At any rate, when Dunmore the trader told the story of the chestnut stallion that night in Nick Rounder's tavern, an old seafaring man, who was present, pricked up his ears and asked the trader certain questions. Then, with a great show of wonder and a string of sailor's oaths, he spun a queer yarn.

One midnight, he said, while his ship lay at anchor in a river-mouth between two barrier islands, the lookout sighted a big chestnut horse coming down the river with the tide. They manned a boat, got a rope over the horse's head and towed him to the sandy island shore. He seemed almost exhausted, his neck and shoulders were cut and bruised, and how he had come into the river was a mystery since his forelegs were hobbled. They could not take the horse aboard their vessel; so, after cutting the hobble, they left him lying on the beach, apparently more dead than alive. They expected to see his body there in the morning, but when they weighed anchor at sunrise he was gone.

Dunmore believed the old man's story; but others held that he had invented the tale on the spur of the moment, in the hope that the trader would stand him a noggin of rum. However that may be, an odd legend exists today on the barrier islands of the Carolina coast.

The story runs that the slim wiry ponies of those islands, rovers of the beaches and marsh flats, have in their veins the blood of De Soto's Andalusian horses abandoned nearly four centuries ago in the Mississippi wilderness six hundred miles away, beyond the mountains.

It seems a fantastic legend; yet the river in which Northwind made his last desperate bid for freedom passes quickly to the sea between two of those barrier isles.

The Witch Hare

by WALTER DE LA MARE

This legend is part of the old, old story of man who is not so far distant from animals but that he can become an animal at his pleasure. There are also stories of witch cats . . . and of course the werewolf. . . .

I WAS out thracking hares meself, and I seen a fine puss of a thing hopping, hopping in the moonlight, and whacking her ears about, now up, now down, and winking her great eyes, and —"Here goes," says I, and the thing was so close to me that she turned round and looked at me, and then bounced back, as well as to say, do your worst! So I had the least grain in life of *blessed powder* left, and I put it in the gun—and bang at her! My jewel, the scritch she gave would frighten a ridgment, and a mist, like, came betwixt me and her, and I seen her no more; but when the mist wint off I saw blood on the spot where she had been, and I followed its track, and at last it led me—whist, whisper—right up to Katey MacShane's door; and when I was at the thrashold, I heerd a murnin' within, a great murnin', and a groanin', and I opened the door, and there she was herself, sittin' quite content in the shape of a woman, and the black cat that was sittin' by her rose up its back and spit at me; but I went on never heedin', and asked the ould— how she was and what ailed her.

"Nothing," sis she.

"What's that on the floor?" sis I.

"Oh," she says, "I was cuttin' a billet of wood," she says, "wid the reaping hook," she says, "an I've wounded meself in the leg," she says, "and that's drops of my precious blood," she says.

The Knight and the Greyhound

by WALTER DE LA MARE

This is also a story which has been told many times in many different manners. We will perhaps recall other variations. I chose this because it was beautifully and simply written.

THERE was a certain valiant knight which had only one son, the which he loved so much, that he ordained for his keepers three nourishers or nurses. The first should give him suck, and feed him; the second should wash him, and keep him clean; and the third should bring him to his sleep and rest. The knight had also a greyhound and a falcon, which he also loved right well. The greyhound was so good that he never ran at any game, but he took it and held it till his master came. And if his master disposed him to go into any battel, if he should not speed therein, anone as he should mount upon his horse, the greyhound would take the horse-tail in his mouth, and draw backward, and would also howl and cry marvellouslie loud. By these signs, and the due observation thereof, the knight did always understand that his journey should have very ill success. The falcon was so gentle and hardy, that he was never cast off to his prey but he took it. The same knight had much pleasure in justing and tourney, so that upon a time under his castle he proclaimed a tournament, to the which came many great lords and knights. The knight entered into the tourney, and his ladie went with her maidens to see it: and as they went out, after went the nourishers, and left the child lying alone there in the cradle in the hall, where the greyhound lay near the wall, and the hawk or falcon standing upon a perch. In this hall there was a serpent lurking, or hid in a hole, to all of them in the castle unknown, the which when he perceived that they were all absent, he put his

291

head out of the hole, and when he saw none but the child lying in the cradle, he went out of his hole towards the cradle, for to have slain the child. The noble falcon perceiving that, made such a noise and rustling with her wings presently, that the greyhound awoke and rose up: and when he saw the serpent nigh the child, anone against him he leapt, and they both fought so long together, until that the serpent had grievously hurt and wounded the greyhound, that he bled so sore, that the earth about the cradle was all bloody. The greyhound, when that he felt himself grievously hurt and wounded, starts fiercely upon the serpent, and fought so sore together, and so eagerly, that between them the cradle was overcast with the child, the bottome upward. And because that the cradle had four pomels like feet falling towards the earth, they saved the child's life and his visage from any hurt. What can be more exprest to make good the wonder in the preservation of the child? Incontinently thereafter, with great pain the greyhound overcame and slew the serpent, and laid him down again in his place and licked his wounds. And anon after the just and tourney was done, the nourishers came first into the castle, and as they saw the cradle turned upside down upon the earth, compassed round about with blood, and that the greyhound was also bloody, they thought and said among themselves that the greyhound had slain the child, and were not so wise as to turn up the cradle again with the child, for to have seen what was thereof befallen; but they said, Let us run away, lest our master should put or lay any blame upon us, and so slay us. As they were thus running away, they met the knight's wife, and she said unto them, Wherefore make ye this sorrow, and whither will ye run? Then said they, O lady, wo and sorrow be to us, and to you. Why, said she, what is there happened? show me. The greyhound, they said, that our lord and master loved so well, hath devoured and slain your son, and lyeth by the wall all full of blood. As the lady heard this she presently fell to the earth, and began to weep and cry piteouslie, and said, Alace, O my dear son, are ye slain and dead? What shall I now do, that I have mine only son thus lost? Wherewithal came in the knight from the tourney, and beholding this lady thus crying and making sorrow, he demanded of her wherefore she made so great sorrow and lamentation. She answered him, O my lord, that greyhound that you have loved so much hath slain your only son, and lyeth by the wall, satiated with the blood of the child. The knight, very exceeding angry, went into the hall, and the greyhound went to meet him, and did fawn upon him, as he was wont to do, and the knight drew out his sword, and with one stroke smote off the greyhound's head, and then went to the cradle where the child lay and found his son all whole, and by the cradle the serpent slain; and then by diverse signs he perceived that the greyhound had killed the serpent for the defence of the child. Then with great sorrow and weeping he tare his hair, and said, Wo be to me, that for the words of my wife I have slain my good and best greyhound, the which hath saved my child's life, and hath slain the serpent, therefore I will put myself to penance. And so he brake his sword in three pieces, and went towards the Holy Land, and abode all the days of his life.

A Sailor's Yarn

by JOHN MASEFIELD

This is really an extended joke; but what a good joke it is. . . .

"ONCE upon a time there was a clipper ship called the *Mary,* and she was lying in Panama waiting for a freight. It was hot, and it was calm, and it was hazy, and the men aboard her were dead sick of the sight of her. They had been lying there all the summer, having nothing to do but to wash her down, and scrape the royal masts with glass, and make the chain cables bright. And aboard of her was a big A.B. from Liverpool, with a tattooed chest on him and an arm like a spar. And this man's name was Bill.

"Now, one day, while the captain of this clipper was sunning in the club, there came a merchant to him offering him a fine freight home and 'despatch' in loading. So the old man went aboard that evening in a merry temper, and bade the mates rastle the hands aft. He told them that they could go ashore the next morning for a 'liberty-day' of four-and-twenty hours, with twenty dollars pay to blue, and no questions asked if they came aboard drunk. So forward goes all hands merrily, to rout out their go-ashore things, their red handkerchiefs, and 'sombre-airers,' for to astonish the Dons. And ashore they goes the next morning, after breakfast, with their silver dollars in their fists, and the jolly-boat to take them. And ashore they steps, and 'So long' they says to the young fellows in the boat, and so up the Mole to the beautiful town of Panama.

"Now the next morning that fellow Bill I told you of was tacking down the city to the boat, singing some song or another. And when he got near to the jetty he went fumbling in his pocket for his pipe, and what should he find but a silver dollar that had slipped away and

294

been saved. So he thinks, 'If I go aboard with this dollar, why the hands'll laugh at me; besides, it's a wasting of it not to spend it.' So he casts about for some place where he could blue it in.

"Now close by where he stood there was a sort of a great store, kept by a Johnny Dago. And if I were to tell you of the things they had in it, I would need nine tongues and an oiled hinge to each of them. But Billy walked into this store, into the space inside, into like the 'tween decks, for to have a look about him before buying. And there were great bunches of bananas a-ripening against the wall. And sacks of dried raisins, and bags of dried figs, and melon seeds, and pomegranates enough to sink you. Then there were cotton bales, and calico, and silk of Persia. And rum in puncheons, and bottled ale. And all manner of sweets, and a power of a lot of chemicals. And anchors gone rusty, fished up from the bay after the ships were gone. And spare cables, all ranged for letting go. And ropes, and sails, and balls of marline stuff. Then there was blocks of all kinds, wood and iron. Dunnage there was, and scantling, likewise sea-chests with pictures on them. And casks of beef and pork, and paint, and peas, and peterolium. But for not one of these things did Billy care a handful of bilge.

"Then there were medical comforts, such as ginger and cala-vances. And plug tobacco, and coil tobacco, and tobacco leaf, and tobacco clippings. And such a power of a lot of bulls' hides as you never saw. Likewise there was tinned things like cocoa, and boxed things like China tea. And any quantity of blankets, and rugs, and donkeys' breakfasts. And oilskins there was, and rubber seaboots, shore-shoes, and Crimee shirts. Also dungarees, and soap, and matches, so many as you never heard tell. But no, not for one of these things was Bill going for to bargain.

"Then there were lamps and candles, and knives and nutmeg-graters, and things made of bright tin and saucers of red clay; and rolls of coloured cloth, made in the hills by the Indians. Bowls there were, painted with twisty-twirls by the folk of old time. And flutes from the tombs (of the Incas), and whistles that looked like flower-pots. Also fiddles and beautiful melodeons. Then there were paper roses for ornament, and false white flowers for graves; also paint-brushes and coir-brooms. There were cages full of parrots, both green and grey; and white cockatoos on perches a-nodding their' red crests; and Java love-birds a-billing, and parrakeets a-screaming, and little kittens for the ships with rats. And at the last of all there was a little monkey, chained to a sack of jib-hanks, who sat upon his tail a-grinning.

"Now Bill he sees this monkey, and he thinks he never see a cuter little beast, not never. And then he thinks of something, and he pipes up to the old Johnny Dago, and he says, pointing to the monkey:

" 'Hey-a Johnny! How much-a-take-a little munk?'

"So the old Johnny Dago looks at Bill a spell, and then says:

" 'I take-a five-a doll' that-a little munk.'

"So Billy planks down his silver dollar, and says:

" 'I give-a one doll', you cross-eyed Dago.'

"Then the old man unchained the monkey, and handed him to Bill without another word. And away the pair of them went, down the Mole to where the boats lay, where a lanchero took them off to the *Mary*.

"Now when they got aboard all hands came around Bill, saying: 'Why, Bill, whatever are you going to do with that there little monkey?' And Bill he said: 'You shut your heads about that there little monkey. I'm going to teach that little monkey how to speak. And when he can speak I'm going to sell him to a museum. And then I'll buy a farm. I won't come to sea any more.' So they just laugh at Bill, and by and by the *Mary* loaded, and got her hatches on, and sailed south-away, on the road home to Liverpool.

"Well, every evening, in the dog-watch, after supper, while the decks were drying from the washing-down, Bill used to take the monkey on the fo'c's'le head, and set him on the capstan. 'Well, ye little divvle,' he used to say, 'will ye speak? Are ye going to speak, hey?' and the monkey would just grin and chatter back at Billy, but never no Christian speech came in front of them teeth of his. And this game went on until they were up with the Horn, in bitter cold weather, running east like a stag, with a great sea piling up astern. And then one night, at eight bells, Billy came on deck for the first watch, bringing the monkey with him. It was blowing like sin, stiff and cold, and the *Mary* was butting through, and dipping her fo'c's'le under. So Bill takes the monkey, and lashes him down good and snug on the drum of the capstan, on the fo'c's'le head. 'Now, ye little divvle,' he said, 'will ye speak? Will ye speak, eh?' But the monkey just grinned at him.

"At the end of the first hour he came again. 'Are ye going to speak, ye little beggar?' he says, and the monkey sits and shivers, but never a word does the little beggar say. And it was the same at four bells, when the lookout man was relieved. But at six bells Billy came again, and the monkey looked mighty cold, and it was a wet perch where he was roosting, and his teeth chattered; yet he didn't speak, not so much as a cat. So just before eight bells, when the watch was nearly out, Billy went forward for the last time. 'If he don't speak now,' says Billy, 'overboard he goes for a dumb animal.'

"Well, the cold green seas had pretty nearly drowned that little monkey, and the spray had frozen him over like a jacket of ice, and right blue his lips were, and an icicle was a-dangling from his chin, and he was shivering like he had an ague. 'Well, ye little divvle,' says Billy, 'for the last time, will ye speak? Are ye going to speak, hey?' And the monkey spoke. '*Speak* is it? *Speak* is it?' he says. 'It's so cold it's enough to make a little fellow *swear*.'

"It's the solemn gospel truth that story is."

The Squaw

by BRAM STOKER

*This horrible story by the author of "Dracula" is com-
pletely incredible within its own terms, but I challenge
you to finish it without a shiver of real horror . . . and
that is why I have included it.*

NURNBERG at the time was not so much exploited as it has
been since then. Irving had not been playing *Faust,* and the
very name of the old town was hardly known to the great bulk of
the travelling public. My wife and I being in the second week of
our honeymoon, naturally wanted someone else to join our party,
so that when the cheery stranger, Elias P. Hutcheson, hailing from
Isthmian City, Bleeding Gulch, Maple Tree County, Neb., turned
up at the station at Frankfort, and casually remarked that he was
going on to see the most all-fired old Methuselah of a town in Yurrup,
and that he guessed that so much travelling alone was enough to
send an intelligent, active citizen into the melancholy ward of a daft
house, we took the pretty broad hint and suggested that we should
join forces. We found, on comparing notes afterwards, that we had
each intended to speak with some diffidence or hesitation so as not
to appear too eager, such not being a good compliment to the success
of our married life; but the effect was entirely marred by our both
beginning to speak at the same instant—stopping simultaneously and
then going on together again. Anyhow, no matter how, it was
done; and Elias P. Hutcheson became one of our party. Straightway Amelia and I found the pleasant benefit; instead of quarrelling,
as we had been doing, we found that the restraining influence of a
third party was such that we now took every opportunity of spoon-
ing in odd corners. Amelia declares that ever since she has, as the
result of that experience, advised all her friends to take a friend on
the honeymoon. Well, we "did" Nurnberg together, and much

298

enjoyed the racy remarks of our Transatlantic friend, who, from his quaint speech and his wonderful stock of adventures, might have stepped out of a novel. We kept for the last object of interest in the city to be visited the Burg, and on the day appointed for the visit strolled round the outer wall of the city by the eastern side.

The Burg is seated on a rock dominating the town, and an immensely deep fosse guards it on the northern side. Nurnberg has been happy in that it was never sacked; had it been it would certainly not be so spick and span perfect as it is at present. The ditch has not been used for centuries, and now its base is spread with teagardens and orchards, of which some of the trees are of quite respectable growth. As we wandered round the wall, dawdling in the hot July sunshine, we often paused to admire the views spread before us, and in especial the great plain covered with towns and villages and bounded with a blue line of hills, like a landscape of Claude Lorraine. From this we always turned with new delight on the city itself, with its myriad of quaint old gables and acre-wide red roofs dotted with dormer windows, tier upon tier. A little to our right rose the towers of the Burg, and nearer still, standing grim, the Torture Tower, which was, and is, perhaps, the most interesting place in the city. For centuries the tradition of the Iron Virgin of Nurnberg has been handed down as an instance of the horrors of cruelty of which man is capable; we had long looked forward to seeing it; and here at last was its home.

In one of our pauses we leaned over the wall of the moat and looked down. The garden seemed quite fifty or sixty feet below us, and the sun pouring into it with an intense, moveless heat like that of an oven. Beyond rose the grey, grim wall seemingly of endless height, and losing itself right and left in the angles of bastion and counterscarp. Trees and bushes crowned the wall, and above again towered the lofty houses on whose massive beauty Time has only set the hand of approval. The sun was hot and we were lazy; time was our own, and we lingered, leaning on the wall. Just below us was a pretty sight—a great black cat lying stretched in the sun, whilst round her gambolled prettily a tiny black kitten. The mother would wave her tail for the kitten to play with, or would raise her feet and push away the little one as an encouragement to further play. They were just at the foot of the wall, and Elias P. Hutcheson, in order to help the play, stopped and took from the walk a moderate sized pebble.

"See!" he said, "I will drop it near the kitten, and they will both wonder where it came from."

"Oh, be careful," said my wife; "you might hit the dear little thing!"

"Not me, ma'am," said Elias P. "Why, I'm as tender as a Maine cherry-tree. Lor, bless ye, I wouldn't hurt the poor pooty little critter more'n I'd scalp a baby. An' you may bet your variegated socks on that! See, I'll drop it fur away on the outside so's not to go near her!" Thus saying, he leaned over and held his arm out at full length and dropped the stone. It may be that there is some attractive force which draws lesser matters to greater; or more probably that the wall was not plumb but sloped to its base—we not noticing the inclination from above; but the stone fell with a sickening thud that came up to us through the hot air, right on the kitten's head, and shattered out its little brains then and there. The black cat cast a swift upward glance, and we saw her eyes like green fire fixed an instant on Elias P. Hutcheson; and then her attention was given to the kitten, which lay still with just a quiver of her tiny limbs, whilst a thin red stream trickled from a gaping wound. With a muffled cry, such as a human being might give, she bent over the kitten, licking its wound and moaning. Suddenly she seemed to realise that it was dead, and again threw her eyes up at us. I shall never forget the sight, for she looked the perfect incarnation of hate. Her green eyes blazed with lurid fire, and the white, sharp teeth seemed to almost shine through the blood which dabbled her mouth and whiskers. She gnashed her teeth, and her claws stood out stark and at full length on every paw. Then she made a wild rush up the wall as if to reach us, but when the momentum ended fell back, and further added to her horrible appearance for she fell on the kitten, and rose with her back fur smeared with its brains and blood. Amelia turned quite faint, and I had to lift her back from the wall. There was a seat close by in the shade of a spreading plane-tree, and here I placed her whilst she composed herself. Then I went back to Hutcheson, who stood without moving, looking down on the angry cat below.

As I joined him, he said:

"Wall, I guess that air the savagest beast I ever see—'cept once when an Apache squaw had an edge on a half-breed what they nick-named 'Splinters' 'cos of the way he fixed up her papoose which he stole on a raid just to show that he appreciated the way they had given his mother the fire torture. She got that kinder look so set on her face that it just seemed to grow there. She followed Splinters more'n three year till at last the braves got him and handed him over to her. They did say that no man, white or Injun, had ever been so long a-dying under the tortures of the Apaches. The only time I ever see her smile was when I wiped her out. I kem on the camp just in time to see Splinters pass in his checks, and he wasn't sorry to go either. He was a hard citizen, and though I never could shake with him after that papoose business—for it was bitter bad, and he should have been a white man, for he looked like one—I see he had got paid out in full. Durn me, but I took a piece of his hide from one of his skinnin posts an' had it made into a pocket-book. It's here now!" and he slapped the breast pocket of his coat.

Whilst he was speaking the cat was continuing her frantic efforts to get up the wall. She would take a run back and then charge up, sometimes reaching an incredible height. She did not seem to mind the heavy fall which she got each time but started with renewed vigour; and at every tumble her appearance became more horrible. Hutcheson was a kind-hearted man—my wife and I had both noticed little acts of kindness to animals as well as to persons—and he seemed concerned at the state of fury to which the cat had wrought herself.

"Wall now!" he said, "I du declare that that poor critter seems quite desperate. There! there! poor thing, it was all an accident—though that won't bring back your little one to you. Say! I wouldn't have had such a thing happen for a thousand! Just shows what a clumsy fool of a man can do when he tries to play! Seems I'm too darned slipperhanded to even play with a cat. Say Colonel!"—it was a pleasant way he had to bestow titles freely—"I hope your wife don't hold no grudge against me on account of this unpleasantness? Why, I wouldn't have had it occur on no account."

He came over to Amelia and apologised profusely, and she with her usual kindness of heart hastened to assure him that she quite understood that it was an accident. Then we all went again to the wall and looked over.

The cat missing Hutcheson's face had drawn back across the moat, and was sitting on her haunches as though ready to spring. Indeed, the very instant she saw him she did spring, and with a blind unreasoning fury, which would have been grotesque, only that it was so frightfully real. She did not try to run up the wall, but simply launched herself at him as though hate and fury could lend her wings to pass straight through the great distance between them. Amelia, woman-like, got quite concerned, and said to Elias P. in a warning voice:

"Oh! you must be very careful. That animal would try to kill you if she were here; her eyes look like positive murder."

He laughed out jovially. "Excuse me, ma'am," he said, "but I can't help laughin'. Fancy a man that has fought grizzlies an' Injuns bein' careful of bein' murdered by a cat!"

When the cat heard him laugh, her whole demeanour seemed to change. She no longer tried to jump or run up the wall, but went quietly over, and sitting again beside the dead kitten began to lick and fondle it as though it were alive.

"See!" said I, "the effect of a really strong man. Even that animal in the midst of her fury recognises the voice of a master, and bows to him!"

"Like a squaw!" was the only comment of Elias P. Hutcheson, as we moved on our way round the city fosse. Every now and then we looked over the wall and each time saw the cat following us. At first she had kept going back to the dead kitten, and then as the distance grew greater took it in her mouth and so followed. After a while, however, she abandoned this, for we saw her following all alone; she had evidently hidden the body somewhere. Amelia's alarm grew at the cat's persistence, and more than once she repeated her warning; but the American always laughed with amusement, till finally, seeing that she was beginning to be worried, he said:

"I say, ma'am, you needn't be skeered over that cat. I go heeled, I du!" Here he slapped his pistol pocket at the back of his lumbar region. "Why sooner'n have you worried, I'll shoot the critter, right here, an' risk the police interferin' with a citizen of the United States for carryin' arms contrairy to reg'lations!" As he spoke he looked over the wall, but the cat, on seeing him, retreated, with a growl, into a bed of tall flowers, and was hidden. He went on: "Blest if that ar critter ain't got more sense of what's good for her than most Christians. I guess we've seen the last of her! You bet, she'll go back now to that busted kitten and have a private funeral of it, all to herself!"

Amelia did not like to say more, lest he might, in mistaken kindness to her, fulfil his threat of shooting the cat: and so we went on and crossed the little wooden bridge leading to the gateway whence ran the steep paved roadway between the Burg and the pentagonal Torture Tower. As we crossed the bridge we saw the cat again down below us. When she saw us her fury seemed to return, and she made frantic efforts to get up the steep wall. Hutcheson laughed as he looked down at her, and said:

"Good-bye, old girl. Sorry I in-jured your feelin's, but you'll get over it in time! So long!" And then we passed through the long, dim archway and came to the gate of the Burg.

When we came out again after our survey of this most beautiful old place which not even the well-intended efforts of the Gothic restorers of forty years ago have been able to spoil—though their restoration was then glaring white—we seemed to have quite forgotten the unpleasant episode of the morning. The old lime tree with its great trunk gnarled with the passing of nearly nine centuries, the deep well cut through the heart of the rock by those captives of old, and the lovely view from the city wall whence we heard, spread over almost a full quarter of an hour, the multitudinous chimes of the city, had all helped to wipe out from our minds the incident of the slain kitten.

We were the only visitors who had entered the Torture Tower that morning—so at least said the old custodian—and as we had the place all to ourselves were able to make a minute and more satisfactory survey than would have otherwise been possible. The custodian, looking to us as the sole source of his gains for the day, was willing to meet our wishes in any way. The Torture Tower is truly a grim place, even now when many thousands of visitors have sent a stream of life, and the joy that follows life, into the place; but at the time I mention it wore its grimmest and most gruesome aspect. The dust of ages seemed to have settled on it, and the darkness and the horror of its memories seem to have become sentient in a way that would have satisfied the Pantheistic souls of Philo or Spinoza. The lower chamber where we entered was seemingly, in its normal state, filled with incarnate darkness; even the hot sunlight streaming in through the door seemed to be lost in the vast thickness of the walls, and only showed the masonry rough as when the builder's scaffolding had come down, but coated with dust and marked here and there with patches of dark stain which, if walls could speak, could have given their own dread memories of fear and pain. We were glad to pass up the dusty wooden staircase, the custodian leaving the outer door open to light us somewhat on our way; for to our eyes the one long-wick'd, evil-smelling candle stuck in a sconce on the wall gave an inadequate light. When we came up through the open trap in the corner of the chamber overhead, Amelia held on to me so tightly that I could actually feel her heart beat. I must say for my own part that I was not surprised at her fear, for this room was even more gruesome than that below. Here there was certainly more light, but only just sufficient to realise the horrible surroundings of the place. The builders of the tower had evidently intended that only they who should gain the top should have any of the joys of light and prospect. There, as we had noticed from below, were ranges of windows, albeit of mediæval smallness, but elsewhere in the tower were only a very few narrow slits such as were habitual in places of mediæval defence. A few of these only lit the chamber, and these so high up in the wall that from no part could the sky be seen through the thickness of the walls. In racks, and leaning in disorder against the walls, were a number of headsmen's swords, great double-handed weapons with broad blade and keen edge. Hard by were several blocks whereon the necks of the victims had lain, with here and there deep notches where the steel had bitten through the guard of flesh and shored into the wood. Round the chamber, placed in all sorts of irregular ways, were many implements of torture which made one's heart ache to see—chairs full of spikes which gave instant and excruciating pain; chairs and couches with dull knobs whose torture was seemingly less, but which, though slower, were equally efficacious; racks, belts, boots, gloves, collars, all made for compressing at will; steel baskets in which the head could be slowly crushed into a pulp if necessary; watchmen's hooks with long handle and knife that cut at resistance—this a specialty of the old Nurnberg police system; and many, many other devices for man's injury to man. Amelia grew quite pale with the horror of the things, but fortunately did not faint, for being a little overcome she sat down on a torture chair, but jumped up again with a shriek, all tendency to faint gone. We both pretended that it was the injury done to her dress by the dust of the chair, and the rusty spikes which had upset her, and Mr. Hutcheson acquiesced in accepting the explanation with a kind-hearted laugh.

But the central object in the whole of this chamber of horrors was the engine known as the Iron Virgin, which stood near the centre of the room. It was a rudely-shaped figure of a woman, something of the bell order, or, to make a closer comparison, of the figure of Mrs. Noah in the children's Ark, but without that slimness of waist and perfect *rondeur* of hip which marks the æsthetic type of the Noah family. One would hardly have recognised it as intended for a human figure at all had not the founder shaped on the forehead a rude semblance of a woman's face. This machine was coated with rust without, and covered with dust; a rope was fastened to a ring in the front of the figure, about where the waist should have been, and was drawn through a pulley, fastened on the wooden pillar which sustained the flooring above. The custodian pulling this rope showed that a section of the front was hinged like a door at one side; we then saw that the engine was of considerable thickness, leaving just room enough inside for a man to be placed. The door was of equal thickness and of great weight, for it took the custodian all his strength, aided though he was by the contrivance of the pulley, to open it. This weight was partly due to the fact that the door was of manifest purpose hung so as to throw its weight downwards, so that it might shut of its own accord when the strain was released. The inside was honeycombed with rust—nay more, the rust alone that comes through time would hardly have eaten so deep into the iron walls; the rust of the cruel stains was deep indeed! It was only, however, when we came to look at the inside of the door that the diabolical intention was manifest to the full. Here were several long spikes, square and massive, broad at the base and sharp at the points, placed in such a position that when the door should close the upper ones would pierce the eyes of the victim, and the lower ones his heart and vitals. The sight was too much for poor Amelia, and this time she fainted dead off, and I had to carry her down the stairs, and place her on a bench outside till she recovered. That she felt it to the quick was afterwards shown by the fact that my eldest son bears to this day a rude birthmark on his breast, which has, by family consent, been accepted as representing the Nurnberg Virgin.

When we got back to the chamber we found Hutcheson still opposite the Iron Virgin; he had been evidently philosophising, and now gave us the benefit of his thought in the shape of a sort of exordium.

"Well, I guess I've been learnin' somethin' here while madam has been gettin' over her faint. 'Pears to me that we're a long way behind the times on our side of the big drink. We uster think out on the plains that the Injun could give us points in tryin' to make a man oncomfortable; but I guess your old mediæval law-and-order party could raise him every time. Splinters was pretty good in his bluff on the squaw, but this here young miss held a straight flush all high on him. The points of them spikes air sharp enough still, though even the edges air eaten out by what uster be on them. It'd be a good thing for our Indian section to get some specimens of this here play-toy to send round to the Reservations jest to knock the stuffin' out of the bucks, and the squaws too, by showing them as how old civilisation lays over them at their best. Guess but I'll get in that box a minute jest to see how it feels!"

"Oh, no! no!" said Amelia. "It is too terrible!"

"Guess, ma'am, nothin's too terrible to the explorin' mind. I've been in some queer places in my time. Spent a night inside a dead horse while a prairie fire swept over me in Montana Territory—an' another time slept inside a dead buffler when the Comanches was on the war path an' I didn't keer to leave my kyard on them. I've been two days in a caved-in tunnel in the Billy Broncho gold mine in New Mexico, an' was one of the four shut up for three parts of a day in the caisson what slid over on her side when we was settin' the foundations of the Buffalo Bridge. I've not funked an odd experience yet, an' I don't propose to begin now!"

We saw that he was set on the experiment, so I said: "Well, hurry up, old man, and get through it quick!"

"All right, General," said he, "but I calculate we ain't quite ready yet. The gentlemen, my predecessors, what stood in that thar canister, didn't volunteer for the office—not much! And I guess there was some ornamental tyin' up before the big stroke was made. I want to go into this thing fair and square, so I must get fixed up proper first. I dare say this old galoot can rise some string and tie me up accordin' to sample?"

This was said interrogatively to the old custodian, but the latter, who understood the drift of his speech, though perhaps not appreciating to the full the niceties of dialect and imagery, shook his head. His protest was, however, only formal and made to be overcome. The American thrust a gold piece into his hand, saying, "Take it, pard! it's your pot; and don't be skeer'd. This ain't no necktie party that you're asked to assist in!" He produced some thin frayed rope and proceeded to bind our companion, with sufficient strictness for the purpose. When the upper part of his body was bound, Hutcheson said:

"Hold on a moment, Judge. Guess I'm too heavy for you to tote into the canister. You jest let me walk in, and then you can wash up regardin' my legs!"

Whilst speaking he had backed himself into the opening which was just enough to hold him. It was a close fit and no mistake. Amelia looked on with fear in her eyes, but she evidently did not like to say anything. Then the custodian completed his task by tying the American's feet together so that he was now absolutely helpless and fixed in his voluntary prison. He seemed to really enjoy it, and the incipient smile which was habitual to his face blossomed into actuality as he said:

"Guess this here Eve was made out of the rib of a dwarf! There ain't much room for a full-grown citizen of the United States to hustle. We uster make our coffins more roomier in Idaho territory. Now, Judge, you just begin to let this door down, slow, on to me. I want to feel the same pleasure as the other jays had when those spikes began to move toward their eyes!"

"Oh no! no! no!" broke in Amelia hysterically. "It is too terrible! I can't bear to see it—I can't! I can't!"

But the American was obdurate. "Say, Colonel," said he, "why not take madam for a little promenade? I wouldn't hurt her feelin's for the world; but now that I am here, havin' kem eight thousand miles, wouldn't it be too hard to give up the very experience I've been pinin' and pantin' fur? A man can't get to feel like canned goods every time! Me and the Judge here'll fix up this thing in no time, an' then you'll come back, an' we'll all laugh together!"

Once more the resolution that is born of curiosity triumphed, and Amelia stayed holding tight to my arm and shivering whilst the custodian began to slacken slowly inch by inch the rope that held back the iron door. Hutcheson's face was positively radiant as his eyes followed the first movement of the spikes.

"Well!" he said. "I guess I've not had enjoyment like this since I left Noo York. Bar a scrap with a French sailor at Wapping—an' that warn't much of a picnic neither—I've not had a show fur real pleasure in this dod-rotted Continent, where there ain't no b'ars nor no Injuns, an' where nary man goes heeled. Slow there, Judge! Don't you rush this business! I want a show for my money this game—I du!"

The Custodian must have had in him some of the blood of his predecessors in that ghastly tower, for he worked the engine with a deliberate and excruciating slowness which after five minutes, in which the outer edge of the door had not moved half as many inches, began to overcome Amelia. I saw her lips whiten, and felt her hold upon my arm relax. I looked around an instant for a place whereon to lay her, and when I looked at her again found that her eye had become fixed on the side of the Virgin. Following its direction I saw the black cat crouching out of sight. Her green eyes shone like danger lamps in the gloom of the place, and their colour was heightened by the blood which still smeared her coat and reddened her mouth. I cried out:

"The cat! look out for the cat!" for even then she sprang out before the engine. At this moment she looked like a triumphant demon. Her eyes blazed with ferocity, her hair bristled out till she seemed twice her normal size, and her tail lashed about as does a tiger's when the quarry is before it. Elias P. Hutcheson when he saw her was amused, and his eyes positively sparkled with fun as he said:

"Darned if the squaw hain't got on all her war paint! Jest give her a shove off if she comes any of her tricks on me, for I'm so fixed everlastingly by the boss, that durn my skin if I can keep my eyes

from her if she wants them! Easy there, Judge! Don't you slack that
ar rope or I'm euchered!"

At this moment Amelia completed her faint, and I had to clutch
hold of her round the waist or she would have fallen to the floor.
Whilst attending to her I saw the black cat crouching for a spring,
and jumped up to turn the creature out.

But at that instant, with a sort of hellish scream, she hurled herself, not as we expected at Hutcheson, but straight at the face of the
custodian. Her claws seemed to be tearing wildly as one sees in the
Chinese drawings of the dragon rampant, and as I looked I saw one
of them light on the poor man's eye, and actually tear through it
and down his cheek, leaving a wide band of red where the blood
seemed to spurt from every vein.

With a yell of sheer terror which came quicker than even his
sense of pain, the man leaped back, dropping as he did so the rope
which held back the iron door. I jumped for it, but was too late,
for the cord ran like lightning through the pulley-block, and the
heavy mass fell forward from its own weight.

As the door closed I caught a glimpse of our poor companion's
face. He seemed frozen with terror. His eyes stared with a horrible
anguish as if dazed, and no sound came from his lips.

And then the spikes did their work. Happily the end was quick,
for when I wrenched open the door they had pierced so deep that
they had locked in the bones of the skull through which they had
crushed, and actually tore him—it—out of his iron prison till, bound
as he was, he fell at full length with a sickly thud upon the floor,
the face turning upward as he fell.

I rushed to my wife, lifted her up and carried her out, for I feared
for her very reason if she should wake from her faint to such a
scene. I laid her on the bench outside and ran back. Leaning against
the wooden column was the custodian moaning in pain whilst he
held his reddening handkerchief to his eyes. And sitting on the head
of the poor American was the cat, purring loudly as she licked the
blood which trickled through the gashed sockets of his eyes.

I think no one will call me cruel because I seized one of the old
executioner's swords and shore her in two as she sat.

Riquet

by ANATOLE FRANCE

The wise urbanity of Anatole France is extended to the dog Riquet, who becomes a distinct personality— and yet very definitely remains a dog, in a dog's world.

QUARTER-DAY had come. With his sister and daughter, Monsieur Bergeret was leaving the dilapidated old house in the Rue de Seine to take up his abode in a modern flat in the Rue de Vaugirard. Such was the decision of Zoé and the Fates.

During the long hours of the morning, Riquet wandered sadly through the devastated rooms. His most cherished habits were upset. Strange men, badly dressed, rude and foul-mouthed, disturbed his repose. They penetrated even to the kitchen, where they stepped into his dish of biscuit and his bowl of fresh water. The chairs were carried off as fast as he curled himself up on them; the carpets were pulled roughly from under his weary limbs. There was no abiding-place for him, not even in his own home.

To his credit, be it said, that at first he attempted resistance. When the cistern was carried off he barked furiously at the enemy. But no one responded to his appeal; no one encouraged him, there was no doubt about it his efforts were regarded with disapproval. Mademoiselle Zoé said to him sharply: "Be quiet!" And Mademoiselle Pauline added: "Riquet, you are silly!"

Henceforth he would abstain from useless warnings. He would cease to strive alone for the public weal. In silence he deplored the devastation of the household. From room to room he sought in vain for a little quiet. When the furniture removers penetrated into a room where he had taken refuge, he prudently hid beneath an as yet unmolested table or chest of drawers. But this precaution proved worse than useless; for soon the pieces of furniture tottered over him, rose, then fell with a crash, threatening to crush him. Terrified, with his hair all turned up the wrong way, he fled to another refuge no safer than the first.

But these inconveniences and even dangers were as nothing to the agony he was suffering at heart. His sentiments were the most deeply affected.

The household furniture he regarded not as things inert, but as living benevolent creatures, beneficent spirits, whose departure foreshadowed cruel misfortunes. Dishes, sugar-basins, pots and pans, all the kitchen divinities; armchairs, carpets, cushions, all the fetishes of the hearth, its lares and its domestic gods had vanished. He could not believe that so great a disaster would ever be repaired. And sorrow filled his little heart to overflowing. Fortunately, Riquet's heart resembled human hearts in being easily distracted and quick to forget its misfortunes.

During the long absence of the thirsty workmen, when old Angélique's broom raised ancient dust from the floor, Riquet breathed an odour of mice and watched the flight of a spider; thus was his versatile mind diverted. But he soon relapsed into sadness.

On the day of departure, when he beheld things growing hourly worse and worse, he grew desperate. It seemed to him above all things disastrous when he saw the linen being piled in dark cases. Pauline with eager haste was putting her frock into a trunk. He turned away from her, as if she were doing something wrong. He shrank up against the wall and thought to himself: "Now the worst has come; this is the end of everything." Then, whether it were that he believed things ceased to exist when he did not see them, or whether he was simply avoiding a painful sight, he took care not to look in Pauline's direction. It chanced that as she was passing to and fro she noticed Riquet's attitude. It was sad: but to her it seemed funny, and she began to laugh. Then, still laughing, she called out: "Come here! Riquet, come to me!" But he did not stir from his corner, and would not even turn his head. He was not then in the mood to caress his young mistress, and, through some secret instinct, through a kind of presentiment, he was afraid of approaching the gaping trunk. Pauline called him several times. Then, as he did not respond, she went and took him up in her arms. "How un-

happy we are!" she said to him; "What is wrong then?" Her tone
was ironical. Riquet did not understand irony. He lay in Pauline's
arms, sad and inert, affecting to see nothing and to hear nothing.
"Riquet, look at me!" she said it three times and three times in vain.
Then, pretending to be in a rage: "Silly creature," she cried, "in
with you"; and she threw him into the trunk and shut the lid on
him. At that moment her aunt having called her, she went out of
the room, leaving Riquet in the trunk.

He was seized with wild alarm; for he was very far from supposing that he had been playfully thrown into the trunk for a mere
joke. Esteeming his situation about as bad as it could be, he was
desirous not to make it worse by any imprudence. So he remained
motionless for a few moments, holding his breath. Then he deemed
it expedient to explore his dark prison. With his paws he felt the
skirts and the linen on to which he had been so cruelly precipitated,
endeavouring to find some way out of this terrible place. He had
been thus engaged for two or three minutes, when he was called
by Monsieur Bergeret, who had been getting ready to go out.

"Riquet! Riquet! Come for a walk on the quays, that is the land
of glory. True, they have disfigured it by erecting a railway station
of hideous proportions and striking ugliness. Architecture is a lost
art. They have pulled down a nice-looking house at the corner of
the Rue du Bac. They will doubtless put some unsightly building in
its place. I trust that at least our architects may abstain from intro-
ducing onto the Quai d'Orsay that barbarous style of which they have
given such a horrid example at the corner of the Rue Washington
and the Champs Elysées! . . . Riquet! Riquet! Come for a walk
on the quays. That is a glorious land. But architecture has deterior-
ated sadly since the days of Gabriel and of Louis. . . . Where is
the dog? . . . Riquet! Riquet?"

The sound of Monsieur Bergeret's voice was a great consolation
to Riquet. He replied by making a noise with his paws, scratching
frantically against the wicker sides of the trunk.

"Where is the dog?" her father asked Pauline as she was returning with a pile of linen in her arms.

"He is in the trunk, Papa."

"What, in the trunk! Why is he there?" asked Monsieur Bergeret.

"Because he was silly," replied Pauline.

Monsieur Bergeret liberated his friend. Riquet followed him into the hall, wagging his tail. Then a sudden thought occurred to him. He went back into the room, ran up to Pauline and rubbed against her skirt. And not until he had wildly caressed her as evidence of his loyalty did he rejoin his master on the staircase. He would have felt himself deficient in wisdom and religious feeling had he failed to display these signs of affection to one who had been so powerful as to plunge him into a deep trunk.

In the street, Monsieur Bergeret and his dog beheld the sad sight of their household furniture scattered over the pavement. The removers had gone off to the public-house round the corner, leaving the plate-glass mirror of Mademoiselle Zoé's wardrobe to reflect the passing procession of girls, workmen, shopkeepers, and Beaux Arts students, of drays, carts and cabs, and the chemist's shop with its bottles and its serpents of Æsculapius. Leaning against a post was Monsieur Bergeret senior, smiling in his frame, mild, pale and delicate looking, with his hair ruffled. With affectionate respect the son contemplated his parent whom he moved away from the post. He likewise lifted out of harm's way Zoé's little table, which looked ashamed at finding itself in the street.

Meanwhile Riquet was patting his master's legs with his paws, looking up at him with sorrowing beautiful eyes, which seemed to say:

"Thou, who wert once so rich and so powerful, canst thou have become poor? Canst thou have lost thy power, O my master? Thou permittest men clothed in vile rags to invade thy sitting-room, thy bedroom, thy dining-room, to throw themselves upon thy furniture and pull it out of doors, to drag down the staircase thy deep armchair, thy chair and mine, for in it we repose side by side in the evening and sometimes in the morning too. I heard it groan in the arms of those tatterdemalions; that chair which is a fetish and a benignant spirit. Thou didst offer no resistance to the invaders. But if thou dost no longer possess any of those genii who once filled thy dwelling, if thou hast lost all, even those little divinities, which thou didst put on in the morning when getting out of bed, those slippers which I used to bite in my play, if thou art indigent and poor, O my Master, then what will become of me?"

THE MEDITATIONS OF RIQUET

I

Men, beasts and stones grow great as they come near and loom enormous when they are upon me. It is not so with me. I remain equally great wheresoever I am.

II

When my master places for me beneath the table the food which he was about to put into his own mouth, it is in order that he may tempt me and that he may punish me if I yield to temptation. For I cannot believe that he would deny himself for my sake.

III

The smell of dogs is sweet in the nostrils.

IV

My master keeps me warm when I lie behind him in his chair. It is because he is a god. In front of the fire-place is a hot stone. That stone is divine.

V

I speak when I please. From my master's mouth proceed likewise sounds which make sense. But his meaning is not so clear as that expressed by the sounds of my voice. Every sound that I utter has a meaning. From my master's lips come forth many idle noises. It is difficult but necessary to divine the thoughts of the master.

VI

To eat is good. To have eaten is better. For the enemy who lieth in wait to take your food is quick and crafty.

VII

All is flux and reflux. I alone remain.

VIII

I am in the center of all things; men, beasts and things, friendly and adverse, are ranged about me.

IX

In sleep one beholdeth men, dogs, horses, trees, forms pleasant and unpleasant. When one awaketh these forms have vanished.

X

Reflection. I love my master, Bergeret, because he is powerful and terrible.

XI

An action for which one has been beaten is a bad action. An action for which one has received caresses or food is a good action.

XII

At nightfall evil powers prowl round the house. I bark in order that my master may be warned and drive them away.

XIII

Prayer. O my master, Bergeret, god of courage, I adore thee. When thou art terrible, be thou praised. When thou art kind, be thou praised. I crouch at thy feet: I lick thy hands. When, seated before thy table spread, thou devourest meats in abundance, thou art very great and very beautiful. Very great art thou and very beautiful when, striking fire out of a thin splint of wood, thou changest night into day. Keep me in thine house and keep out every other dog. And thou, Angélique, the cook, divinity good and great, I fear thee and I venerate thee in order that thou mayest give me much to eat.

XIV

A dog who lacketh piety towards men and who scorneth the fetishes assembled in his master's house liveth a miserable and a wandering life.

XV

One day, from a broken pitcher, filled with water which was being carried across the parlour, water ran on to the polished floor. A thrashing must have been the punishment of that dirty pitcher.

XVI

Men possess the divine power of opening all doors. I by myself am only able to open a few. Doors are great fetishes which do not readily obey dogs.

XVII

The life of a dog is full of danger. If he would escape suffering he must be ever on the watch, during meals and even during sleep.

XVIII

It is impossible to know whether one has acted well towards men. One must worship them without seeking to understand them. Their wisdom is mysterious.

XIX

Invocation. O Fear, Fear august and maternal, Fear sacred and salutary, possess me, in danger fill me, in order that I may void that which is harmful, lest, casting myself upon the enemy, I suffer for my imprudence.

XX

Vehicles there are which horses pull through the street. They are terrible. Other vehicles there are which move themselves breathing loudly. These are also fearful. Men in rags are detestable, likewise such as carry baskets on their heads or roll casks. I do not love children who utter loud cries and flee from and pursue each other swiftly in the streets. The world is full of hostile and dreadful things.

For My Lady

by ALBERT R. WETJEN

The sperm whale, the greatest living mammal, fights, and hunts his terrible prey, and dies in this story that ranges over half the oceans of the world.

THERE were three of them fighting, and two of them hoped to eat the third. The thresher shark, one fork of his tail enormously elongated, leaped clear of the sea and brought that tail down with a crack that could be heard three miles away. There was a tremendous flurry in the water and into the thick of it the swordfish charged with all the fury and velocity of a shell shot from a gun, a white and bubbling wake streaming out behind him. His aim was true but the trouble was his target did not keep still. Instead of the pointed lance plunging home in a vital spot it met the blank wall of a mighty head that could have been solid India rubber for all the impression that was made. The sword glanced off. There was another flurry and then a pair of massive jaws sheared together and the swordfish was gone. He had been well over fifteen feet in length but that did not matter. He was little more than an appetizer.

The thresher shark turned to flee as disaster overtook his companion, but behind him there came in wrath and thunder some one hundred tons of vindictive sperm whale, seventy feet of energy, power and hunger. The chase spread over six miles of ocean. It went down to a depth of two hundred fathoms, came up again, twisted and turned and cork-screwed. And then at last, with a final desperate effort, the thresher, slender as a torpedo, flung himself clear of the sea, his steel-gray body glistening in the morning sun.

There was a roar as of a cataract behind him as the sperm breached too. The terrible jaws sheared together in mid-air and the thresher

317

fell in two halves. With a crash that shook the world the sperm struck the sea again, swallowed twice and then wallowed comfortably in the foam of his own commotion while he caught his breath, a feather of spray lifting at regular intervals from the S-shaped hole in the top of his head.

He was a remarkable creature in many ways, this whale. An eon or so ago his ancestors had run through the primeval forests and they had been very small. Now he was the biggest living thing in the world, black on top and shading imperceptibly to brown beneath; with a head that occupied fully one third of his body; with a long narrow under-jaw set with fifty conical ivory teeth; and with a cavernous mouth capable of swallowing two men whole. Inside that mouth myriads of tiny molluscs and other sea life made their home, just as innumerable of their relations made their home in the wrinkles and sea growths of the giant's skin.

That skin, too, was something to talk about. In places it was two feet thick and beneath it there was an incredible layer of solid and important fat, important and famous for many reasons. It not only wrapped the giant sperm with a blanket of protection that kept him warm and safe, but on that fat cities had been built and even nations. In the search for that fat far islands had been discovered, new coasts, new seas, new rivers, new harbors. Untold thousands of men and countless generations had been nourished upon it. The cachalot, the sperm whale (*Physeter macrocephalus* to be exact), was a creature of consequence.

Just now he was hungry in spite of the ton or so of fresh fish he had just consumed. He had a lot of bulk to keep up and he was usually hungry. It is a peculiar curse of nature that the more food any given creature must eat to keep itself alive the more energy it must expend to catch that food. And the more energy it expends the more food it must catch. It is rather involved but true, a very vicious circle. And so, after his little business with the swordfish and the thresher shark, our sperm was still hungry.

He decide to do something about it after a while and with a flick of his tail started off at a steady ten knots toward a feeding ground he was well acquainted with, and which he would never have left had it not been for a certain lady whale. In fact our sperm had been resting upon the surface of the sea after a hard fight with another bull when he had been attacked, during which process the lady had departed with the defeated rival, which was strictly against all the rules. He now dismissed that matter from his mind, however, and settled down to a steady passage that would take him across five degrees of latitude—a trifle for the cachalot, which ranges the world.

He did not pause to rest. When a whale is making a passage he holds a course as steady as if his brain possessed a compass and weariness appears to be a stranger to him. So our sperm drove on, hour after hour, his flukes boiling the sea and his mighty tail lashing his wake to foam. Toward evening a low but persistent pulsing caught his acute hearing and then the water ahead of him began to riffle and churn as if a great fire had been lighted under it. He checked his passage then, stopped and solemnly sat on his tail, lifting his massive head some twenty feet in the air and while in this position slowly revolving so that his little weak eyes, when he had completed the circle, had embraced the whole horizon.

He located the source of the noise and the direction of the disturbed water and, satisfied, he resumed his normal horizontal position, dug in with his flukes again and proceeded on his course. As he progressed a vast shadowy mass loomed closer and when he was near enough he could see it was a school of mullet, millions and millions of them, and millions and millions more, showing the careless prodigality of nature and the inexhaustible fertility of the sea.

From the vanguard of the school to the very rear was a matter of a full mile. In width the school ran perhaps half that distance but from the surface down to a depth of a hundred fathoms the mullet were packed so closely it seemed incredible they could swim. The air above was dark with vast flocks of screaming, diving birds, while the sea astern was dotted with countless other birds sitting on the water, too gorged to rise again. Upon the flanks of the moving mass swarmed hundreds of blue pointer sharks, several gray nurse sharks, a few killer whales and one gigantic tiger shark strayed far from his normal haunts. They were all eating with the tireless voracity of their kind, and how many they had consumed may not be known, but they had certainly made no appreciable inroads upon the mullet school. The mullet themselves were quite indifferent,

swimming steadily forward to some definite rendezvous, oblivious
to the ravenous swarms that beset them from above and below and
from all sides.

The sperm did not like fish generally. He would not have gone
out of his way by a hair's-breadth to search for them unless he had
been literally starving. But since here they were, right in his
path, he did not see why opportunity should be lost. So he opened
his cavern of a mouth and plowed through the heart of the school,
swallowing mullet by the hundred-weight in an absent-minded
manner, much like a man who has set himself the task of eating his
way through a not particularly tasty watermelon. He did not check
his speed nor did he deviate from the line of his passage, though
he had to redouble the thrust of his flukes to force himself ahead
against the solid wall of fish.

He broke clear at last and the school flowed on behind him as
if he had never passed through it. A gray nurse shark, a little excited
with so much going on, so far forgot himself as to try to tear a
chunk of blubber from the sperm's flank as he passed, and he died
rather appallingly under one flip of the mighty tail to toss, bottom-up,
a bloody pulp in the cachalot's wake.

The night fell and the sperm swam on. The moon, hanging a
golden ball in the star-filled sky, glinted on the somber marble of
his back and flung warm lights along his sides. A string of porpoise
swerved to give him passage, although they were warm-blooded
mammals and the sperm never ate his own kind. A ton-size batfish,
bad-tempered and vicious at being awakened, flicked his whip-like
tail that could cut another fish well-nigh in half. It rasped harm-
lessly against the sperm's great flat-fronted head and the next instant a fluke took the batfish across the back and sent him broken
and dying toward the ocean floor.

With the dawn the whale birds came winging in the sperm's
wake. There was always food where the whale was, fragments from
his own feasts or good pickings upon his vast back when he finally
condescended to lie motionless on the water. The birds could descend then and peck around the sea growths that clustered the skin
or dig out the tiny crustacea from the thick wrinkles, for a whale
supports more life on his hide than a dog does fleas.

It was afternoon when the sperm checked his steady gait. A spout appeared ahead of him, then another and another. The sea was covered with whales, old scarred bulls, young bulls, ancient cows, young mothers, here and there calves gamboling and diving and spouting. On the far horizon loomed the purple line of a coast. Above, the sky was clear blue. The sea was satin-smooth and green. The wind was too light to lift the ripples. And below, far below, there were the feeding grounds. The sperm drifted into the whale city and stopped. He was enormously hungry but he was also a little tired now. In an hour or two he would eat.

Down, far down, nearly five hundred fathoms down, there was another world. The darkness was a solid thing. Not a ray of green seeped down from above, not the ghost of a ray. Everything was black and icy cold and in this blackness and this coldness nightmares lived and moved, such nightmares as the mind may not even conceive. There was utter, unconscious and impartial cruelty. There were appetites so incredible that all the food in the world could not suffice them. Five hundred fathoms down nature had gone completely mad.

There were small fishes with immense eyes and no appreciable mouths. There were big fishes with no eyes and mouths that literally split the body. There were some shaped like balloons, some like sausages, some like cones and some as flat as a sheet of paper. There were fishes with lights along their sides, like the portholes of a vessel, spots of glowing phosphorescence. There were other fishes with clear lamps hung from the top of tall stems that grew from out of the head, a lure and a trap for prey. There were fishes that could swallow things larger than themselves and others that fastened upon their prey and leisurely ate it, a piece at a time, while it lived and went about its business. There were great gray snakes with manes like those of horses; and pallid white snakes that writhed in the ooze of the sea floor. But all of these lived beneath a terror greater than they were themselves; beneath the shadow, had there been shadows in that inky darkness, of an enormous nightmare with a soft yielding body, with a great rending beak like the beak of a parrot, with awful glassy goggle eyes and immense arms.

He drifted like a vast cloud through that cold and darkness, his strange body colored beautifully green and purple and glossy black, with splotches of sick gray between. He could, when he wished, move with lightning rapidity, spurting out a jet of water from an opening under his head, and he could move either backward or forward as he chose, but mostly he preferred to drift. Two of his arms were over fifty feet long, always moving about in the darkness, always probing and searching. And as soon as they touched anything eight other arms, forty feet long, leaped to aid them, to wrap around and draw the frantic prey toward the gaping parrot beak. Such arms they were!—fitted with suction cups fringed each with claws so that once they took hold they never let go. At the bases, where they joined the bloated egg-shaped body, they were as thick as a man and there was incredible power hidden within them.

They were seldom at rest, those terrible arms. Always and ever they itched for the feel of food and never was their owner even remotely satiated. He possessed the most powerful digestive juices in the world and from the time food passed through his beak until the time it was completely digested was a matter of minutes alone. He was nothing but a huge stomach, incredible and foul—a living horror. His name was *Architeuthis* but all men called him the deep-sea squid, the lord of the lower depths. And he *was* such a lord as long as he remained there, and until the whale came.

The sperm had sounded after his rest on the surface of the water, had gone down with one immense flip of his tail and plunged straight through the light green depths that changed to dark green, to a somber slatey hue and then grew dark and black. He did not go clear to the ocean floor. The pressure was too great for him there, and he straightened out after a while and swam slowly ahead, listening for a pulse in the water or for any other sound that would warn him that life was about. Below him, he knew, far below there were those luscious, soft and jelly-like squids upon which he doted, but they were too far down for him to venture. He had to search and wait. Sometime, sooner or later, one of those monstrous shapes would come spurting upward to the higher depths in search of food, for the sea floor never afforded enough to satisfy the stomach of a squid.

For an hour the sperm ranged up and down. Occasional shoals

of smaller fish brushed by him; once a massive white shark cut in front of him, forty feet of viciousness looking for a squid himself; once a tremendous swarm of black eels wriggled by on their way to their spawning grounds, and behind them undulated a great gray sea snake steadily swallowing up the rear guard. The sperm took no notice of all this. He was intent on squid, the principal and favorite food of the cachalot. But at the end of an hour, having located nothing, he began to ascend, rising up like a balloon with hardly a movement of his flukes. He had to breathe. Once every hour or so when he was under the sea he had to breathe again. He broke the surface with a washing of water that sounded like the combers breaking on a reef and his spout blew white and high. He rested for some minutes, filled his lungs with air and then went down again.

He was more fortunate this time. *Architeuthis* the squid had caught the rhythm of a shoal of great red schnapper passing above and, forgetting everything except his insatiable hunger, came upward from the depths, the water jet spurting from the hole beneath his head and his arms all trailing along after him.

He shot into the schnapper shoal like a monstrous cloud and his arms sprayed out, gathering the big fish toward him. They could not escape. From fifty feet away his arms fastened on them and brought them in; and the parrot beak opened and closed and opened and closed unwearied.

The squid was really so busy and the schnapper were disturbing the water so much he did not sense danger. The sperm had caught the rhythm of the passing shoal and the following disturbance and came shooting along to investigate. He did not need to come very close to tell what was happening. There was a vague muskiness in the water, the steady blur-blur of a water jet as the squid propelled himself, and so the sperm drove in.

The first thing the squid knew one of his arms slipped against a massive bulk that was certainly not a schnapper and then that arm was sheared off and was gone. Thereafter madness broke loose. The squid dived frantically and as he dived there shot from him a vast cloud of sepia to blacken the already black water in an effort to confuse the sperm. But the sperm was hunting by sound and not by sight. He caught the squid by the side of the head and furiously

backed. The squid just as furiously went ahead and there was a
tug of war for a while. The sperm knew and the squid knew that
if they reached another fifty fathoms down the pressure would
be too great and the sperm would have to abandon the fight. And
so they were locked.

Shaking his captive as a terrier shakes a rat, the sperm suddenly
plunged ahead as if to go down with the squid, but instead of doing
that he came up in a long arc and against the full forward thrust of
his flukes and his tail the squid battled in vain. Up and up they
fought, the mighty arms threshing about to get a hold upon the
sperm and the sperm shaking savagely. And at the last they shot
to the very surface of the sea where the bright sun looked down
upon the nightmare from the depths. The sperm closed his jaws
tight, wrenched a huge chunk of the jelly-like flesh from the squid's
side, bolted it and plunged into the fight again before the squid could
go down.

The squid had twisted to face his foe, to bring his arms into play.
They closed about the sperm like a living net and the parrot beak
scraped and rasped against the thick India rubber head, scoring
grooves in it but doing no other damage. The sperm's mighty jaws
sheared together and two arms were cropped clear, to lie writhing
and twisting like living serpents on the swells. He paid no attention
to them but, taking a fresh grip on the pulsing, jelly-like body, just
beneath the great goggling black eyes, the sperm calmly commenced
to eat his way through it in the same absent-minded manner he had
exhibited when he had eaten his way through the mullet school
the day before.

The whale birds gathered overhead in flocks. A young sperm calf
with its mother came cautiously closer and bolted the two cropped
arms. With a crash of his mighty tail the sperm warned them off
and went on with his meal. In an hour it was over and there showed
on the surface only a big greasy patch, a few fragments of squid the
birds were occupied with and the sperm, full fed at last, lazily
settling himself to sleep.

He spent many days thus with like companions. Sometimes he
would be successful in finding one of the great squids, sometimes
he would not. The feeding grounds were getting exhausted or the

squids were growing more cautious. Fewer and fewer ventured into the upper levels where food was more plentiful and, since no living sperm could go deep enough to force them up to the surface, the whale city slowly broke up, small pods of bulls and calves and cows leaving every day to seek fresh grounds.

Our sperm would have gone with them eventually but he was taken sick as all sperms are periodically.

Of all the squids he had eaten he was unable to digest the terrible pointed claws that fringed their arm suckers, and the terrible parrot beaks that guarded their mouths. These sat in his stomach and irritated it, passed into his intestines and irritated them. And so he was sick and in pain while mysterious processes inside him created layer after layer of fatty phlegm about these masses of beaks and claws, wrapping them in a covering that would protect the sperm's organs from their points and hardness. It was, in a measure, exactly like the oyster creating coat upon coat of nacre about some torturing substance that had found its way into its tender body, forming at last a pearl.

On the fourth day of the whale's sickness there came a strange thing across the sea. It had a long, gray-painted body and three tall masts clothed with white sails. The sperm lay upon the swells, feebly moving his flukes, while the long, gray-painted body moved close to him. Then something terrible happened. A long spear of fire struck him in the side and then expanded to blow open his whole body. He reared up, the sting of the bomb-harpoon waking him to action, and then with a tremendous flurry he went down, fathom after fathom of line snaking out behind him.

Down and down he went. He had never gone so deep before and the water seemed to close about him as tight as an iron band. He had to come up then, his lungs full of blood, and he shot from the sea twisting in agony, to fall back in the bloody welter which he threshed to bloodier foam. Twice more he attempted to sound but could not, and then he drifted with the swell, the foam subsiding about him, his flukes still making little feeble twitches until he died. Boats came out to secure him and dark-skinned Kanakas walked on his back.

On the poop deck of the whaling ship *Gunross* her two owners leaned on the rail and watched. One man was tall and lean, with a lantern jaw and fierce dark eyes. The other man was of medium height, broader, with a pock-marked face and a mouth that twisted up at one side.

"He must have been pretty sick to lay there and wait for us," said the tall man reflectively. His companion grunted:

"Hope he was sick enough."

The other man seemed to comprehend that strange statement.

"Hope so," he agreed.

They watched then until the last of the bloody foam had subsided and the boats were towing the sperm alongside, and then the tall man uttered a sharp exclamation and pointed.

"There's some!" he said, his voice tight.

The shorter man straightened with a sharp oath and then both of them moved simultaneously amidships where they launched the dinghy and, ignoring the questioning looks of their native crew, pulled rapidly to that spot where the sperm had died. They pulled steadily, with an air of tense excitement, and when they checked the boat they stared overside, awed by the several lumps of what looked like dirty tallow bobbing on the surface.

"Five pieces," said the tall man after a while.

"I've never seen so much together," agreed his companion. Their voices were hoarse and shaken. They reached over and lifted the stuff into the dinghy, grunting with the weight of it. And when they had done they stared down at the stuff as it lay oozing on the bottom boards.

"More'n two hundred pounds," said the tall man. He stared bleakly at his companion. The shorter man bent down and dug his fingers into one greasy mass. He brought them out again holding between them several squid claws and part of a parrot beak. He put them to his nostrils and closed his eyes at the sweet, earthy odor.

"It's ambergris all right," he said. "That whale was pretty sick."

The tall man still glared at him with bleak eyes.

"Worth fifteen dollars an ounce," he said thinly. "Maybe more. We're in luck this voyage."

The other nodded but said nothing. He seemed to be thinking. They got out their oars and pulled back for the ship. The native

crew was already cutting into the whale and the try-works amid-
ship were already blazing, while over the ship began to drift the
sickening, acrid reek of whale oil. When they came to cut open
the sperm's stomach in search for more ambergris they found another
thirty pounds. For them the dream of all whalers had come true.
They had made their fortune with one catch.

For two days the try-works flickered and blazed and the great
drums in the holds were filled with oil. Then the decks were cleaned
up; the native crew was sent below to rest. It was early night and
the tall man and the shorter man walked up and down the poop,
smoking their cigars and thinking. At the wheel a native peered intently at the glow of the compass bowl.

"We'll sell that stuff in 'Frisco," said the shorter man. "We'll be
rich."

"Yes, we'll be rich," agreed the tall man. They paced up and
down and then the short man went to the rail and looked over at
the water. The tall man came and stood behind him.

"I guess I'll quit the sea and get married," said the shorter man
reflectively. The tall man looked this way and that way along
the dark deck.

"I guess I'll quit the sea too," he said, and he struck hard with a
belaying pin he took from the rail. There was a faint splash then,
lost in the booming of the wind in the sail, in the slatting of lines and
the rattlings of blocks, in the wash of the water along the hull. The
tall man walked aft toward the helmsman, his cigar glowing contentedly between his lips.

"Seen anything of my partner?" asked the tall man idly. The
native stared up at him and shook his head, the whites of his eyes
bright in his face. He had been very busy steering. He had thought
the white men had been together. No, he had seen nothing.

"That's what I thought," said the tall man cryptically, and he
went below for a drink with a thin smile upon his lips.

The leading perfumer of San Francisco was extremely glad to
obtain the large supply of ambergris the whaling ship *Gunross*
brought in. The stuff was rare enough and the clever chemical sub-
stitutes science had produced were still not worthy of the best scents.
So, in the course of time, the squid's beaks and the sucker claws were
weaned from the mass; and many strange and mysterious trans-

fusions took place. Until at last a lovely woman stopped before a window and desired a little green bottle that was worth more than its weight in gold.

This lovely woman wore furs about her shoulders and pearls about her throat; soft and sensuous warmth, translucent beauty born out of sickness and of pain. She did not think of this, nor did her companion when he bought her the little green bottle. Why should they connect a little green bottle with a beautifully colored nightmare five hundred fathoms deep, with one hundred tons of sick whale resting upon a purple sea, with sweat and blood and death? And why should they care?

The Honk-honk Breed

by STEWART EDWARD WHITE

America's cattle country produced a breed of men whose humor expressed itself most typically in the "tall story." It also produced a breed of fowl. . . . But let Stewart Edward White tell his own story.

IT WAS Sunday at the ranch. For a wonder the weather had been favourable; the windmills were all working, the bogs had dried up, the beef had lasted over, the remuda had not strayed—in short, there was nothing to do. Sang had given us a baked bread-pudding with raisins in it. We filled it in—a wash basin full of it —on top of a few incidental pounds of *chile con,* baked beans, soda biscuits, "air tights," and other delicacies. Then we adjourned with our pipes to the shady side of the blacksmith's shop where we could watch the ravens on top the adobe wall of the corral. Somebody told a story about ravens. This led to road-runners. This suggested rattlesnakes. They started Windy Bill.

"Speakin' of snakes," said Windy, "I mind when they catched the great-granddaddy of all the bull-snakes up at Lead in the Black Hills. I was only a kid then. This wasn't no such tur'ble long a snake, but he was more'n a foot thick. Looked just like a sahuaro stalk. Man name of Terwilliger Smith catched it. He named this yere bull-snake Clarence, and got it so plumb gentle it followed him everywhere. One day old P. T. Barnum come along and wanted to buy this Clarence snake—offered Terwilliger a thousand cold—but Smith wouldn't part with the snake nohow. So finally they fixed up a deal so Smith could go along with the show. They shoved Clarence in a box in the baggage car, but after a while Mr. Snake gets so lonesome he gnaws out and starts to crawl back to find his

329

master. Just as he is half-way between the baggage car and the smoker, the couplin' give way—right on that heavy grade between Custer and Rocky Point. Well, sir, Clarence wound his head 'round one brake wheel and his tail around the other, and held that train together to the bottom of the grade. But it stretched him twenty-eight feet and they had to advertise him as a boa-constrictor."

Windy Bill's history of the faithful bullsnake aroused to reminiscence the grizzled stranger, who thereupon held forth as follows:

Wal, I've seen things and I've heerd things, some of them ornery, and some you'd love to believe, they was that gorgeous and improbable. Nat'ral history was always my hobby and sportin' events my special pleasure—and this yarn of Windy's reminds me of the only chanst I ever had to ring in business and pleasure and hobby all in one grand merry-go-round of joy. It come about like this:

One day, a few year back, I was sittin' on the beach at Santa Barbara watchin' the sky stay up, and wonderin' what to do with my year's wages, when a little squinch-eye round-face with big bow spectacles came and plumped down beside me.

"Did you ever stop to think," says he, shovin' back his hat, "that if the horsepower delivered by them waves on this beach in one single hour could be concentrated behind washin' machines, it would be enough to wash all the shirts for a city of four hundred and fifty-one thousand one hundred and thirty-six people?"

"Can't say I ever did," says I, squintin' at him sideways.

"Fact," says he; "and did it ever occur to you that if all the food a man eats in the course of a natural life could be gathered together at one time, it would fill a wagon-train twelve miles long?"

"You make me hungry," says I.

"And ain't it interestin' to reflect," he goes on, "that if all the finger nail parin's of the human race for one year was to be collected and subjected to hydraulic pressure it would equal in size the pyramid of Cheops?"

"Look yere," says I, sittin' up, "did *you* ever pause to excogitate that if all the hot air you is dispensin' was to be collected together it would fill a balloon big enough to waft you and me over that Bullyvard of Palms to yonder gin mill on the corner?"

He didn't say nothin' to that—just yanked me to my feet, faced me towards the gin mill above mentioned, and exerted considerable pressure on my arm in urgin' of me forward.

"You ain't so much of a dreamer, after all," thinks I. "In important matters you are plumb decisive."

We sat down at little tables, and my friend ordered a beer and a chicken sandwich.

"Chickens," says he, gazin' at the sandwich, "is a dollar apiece in this country, and plumb scarce. Did you ever pause to ponder over the returns chickens would give on small investment? Say you start with ten hens. Each hatches out thirteen aigs, of which allow a loss of say six for childish accidents. At the end of the year you has eighty chickens. At the end of two years that flock has increased to six hundred and twenty. At the end of the third year—"

He had the medicine tongue! Ten days later him and me was occupyin' of an old ranch fifty mile from anywhere. When they run stage-coaches this joint used to be a road-house. The outlook was on about a thousand little brown foothills. A road two miles four rods two foot eleven inches in sight run by in front of us. It come over one foothill and disappeared over another. I know just how long it was, for later in the game I measured it.

Out back was about a hundred little wire chicken corrals filled with chickens. We had two kinds. That was the doin's of Tuscarora. My pardner called himself Tuscarora Maxillary. I asked him once if that was his real name.

"It's the realest little old name you ever heerd tell of," says he. "I know, for I made it myself—liked the sound of her. Parents ain't got no rights to name their children. Parents don't have to be called them names."

Well, these chickens, as I said, was of two kinds. The first was these low-set, heavy-weight propositions with feathers on their laigs, and not much laigs at that, called Cochin Chinys. The other was a tall ridiculous outfit made up entire of bulgin' breast and gangle laigs. They stood about two foot and a half tall, and when they went to peck the ground their tail feathers stuck straight up to the sky. Tusky called 'em Japanese Games.

"Which the chief advantage of them chickens is," says he, "that in weight about 90 per cent. of 'em is breast meat. Now my idee is, that if we can cross 'em with these Cochin Chiny fowls we'll have a low-hung, heavy-weight chicken runnin' strong on breast meat. These Jap Games is too small, but if we can bring 'em up in size and shorten their laigs, we'll shore have a winner."

That looked good to me, so we started in on that idee. The theery was bully, but she didn't work out. The first broods we hatched growed up with big husky Cochin Chiny bodies and little short necks, perched up on laigs three foot long. Them chickens couldn't reach ground nohow. We had to build a table for 'em to eat off, and when they went out rustlin' for themselves they had to confine themselves to sidehills or flyin' insects. Their breasts was all right, though—"And think of them drumsticks for the boardin'-house trade!" says Tusky.

So far things wasn't so bad. We had a good grubstake. Tusky and me used to feed them chickens twicet a day, and then used to set around watchin' the playful critters chase grasshoppers up an' down the wire corrals, while Tusky figgered out what'd happen if somebody was dumfool enough to gather up somethin' and fix it in baskets or wagons or such. That was where we showed our ignorance of chickens.

One day in the spring I hitched up, rustled a dozen of the youngsters into coops, and druv over to the railroad to make our first sale. I couldn't fold them chickens up into them coops at first, but then I stuck the coops up on aidge and they worked all right, though I will admit they was a comical sight. At the railroad one of them towerist trains had just slowed down to a halt as I come up, and the towerists was paradin' up and down allowin' they was particular enjoyin' of the warm Californy sunshine. One old terrapin, with gray chin whiskers, projected over, with his wife, and took a peek through the slats of my coop. He straightened up like someone had touched him off with a red-hot poker.

"Stranger," said he, in a scared kind of whisper, "What's them?"

"Them's chickens," says I.

He took another long look.

"Marthy," says he to the old woman, "this will be about all! We come out from Ioway to see the Wonders of Californy, but I can't go nothin' stronger than this. If these is chickens, I don't want to see no Big Trees."

Well, I sold them chickens all right for a dollar and two bits, which was better than I expected, and got an order for more. About ten days later I got a letter from the commission house.

"We are returnin' a sample of your Arts and Crafts chickens with the lovin' marks of the teeth still onto him," says they. "Don't send any more till they stops pursuin' of the nimble grasshopper. Dentist bill will foller."

With the letter came the remains of one of the chickens. Tusky and I, very indignant, cooked her for supper. She was tough, all right. We thought she might do better biled, so we put her in the pot over night. Nary bit. Well, then we got interested. Tusky kep' the fire goin' and I rustled greasewood. We cooked her three days and three nights. At the end of that time she was sort of pale and frazzled, but still givin' points to three-year-old jerky on cohesion and other uncompromisin' forces of Nature. We buried her then, and went out back to recuperate.

There we could gaze on the smilin' landscape, dotted by about four hundred long-laigged chickens swoopin' here and there after grasshoppers.

"We got to stop that," says I.

"We can't," murmured Tusky, inspired. "We can't. It's born in 'em; it's a primal instinct, like the love of a mother for her young, and it can't be eradicated! Them chickens is constructed by a divine providence for the express purpose of chasin' grasshoppers, jest as the beaver is made for buildin' dams, and the cow-punchers is made for whisky and faro-games. We can't keep 'em from it. If we was to shut 'em in a dark cellar, they'd flop after imaginary grasshoppers in their dreams, and die emaciated in the midst of plenty. Jimmy, we're up agin the Cosmos, the oversoul—" Oh, he had the medicine tongue, Tusky had, and risin' on the wings of eloquence that way, he had me faded in ten minutes. In fifteen I was wedded solid to the notion that the bottom had dropped out of the chicken business. I think now that if we'd shut them hens up, we might have—still, I don't know; they was a good deal in what Tusky said.

"Tuscarora Maxillary," says I, "did you ever stop to entertain that beautiful thought that if all the dumfoolishness possessed now by the human race could be gathered together, and lined up along-side of us, the first feller to come along would say to it 'Why, hello Solomon!'"

We quit the notion of chickens for profit right then and there, but we couldn't quit the place. We hadn't much money, for one thing, and then we kind of liked loafin' around and raisin' a little garden truck, and—oh, well, I might as well say so, we had a notion about placers in the dry wash back of the house—you know how it is. So we stayed on, and kept a-raisin' these long-laigs for the fun of it. I used to like to watch 'em projectin' around, and I fed 'em twicet a day about as usual.

So Tusky and I lived alone there together, happy as ducks in Arizona. About oncet in a month somebody'd pike along the road. She wasn't much of a road, generally more chuck-holes than bumps, though sometimes it was the other way around. Unless it happened to be a man on horseback or maybe a freighter without the fear of God in his soul, we didn't have no words with them; they were too busy cussin' the highways and generally too mad for social discourses.

One day early in the year, when the 'dobe mud made ruts to add to the bumps, one of these automobeels went past. It was the first Tusky and me had seen in them parts, so we run out to view her. Owin' to the high spots on the road, she looked like one of these movin' picters, as to blur and wobble; sounded like a cyclone mingled with cuss-words, and smelt like hell on housecleanin' day.

"Which them folks don't seem to be enjoyin' of the scenery," says I to Tusky. "Do you reckon that there blue trail is smoke from the machine or remarks from the inhabitants thereof?"

Tusky raised his head and sniffed long and inquirin'.

"It's langwidge," says he. "Did you ever stop to think that all the words in the dictionary hitched end to end would reach—"

But at that minute I catched sight of somethin' brass lyin 'in the road. It proved to be a curled-up sort of horn with a rubber bulb on the end. I squoze the bulb and jumped twenty foot over the remark she made.

"Jarred off the machine," says Tusky.

"Oh, did it?" says I, my nerves still wrong. "I thought maybe it had growed up from the soil like a toadstool."

About this time we abolished the wire chicken corrals, because we needed some of the wire. Them long-laigs thereupon scattered all over the flat searchin' out their prey. When feed time come I had to screech my lungs out gettin' of 'em in, and then sometimes they didn't all hear. It was plumb discouragin', and I mighty nigh made up my mind to quit 'em, but they had come to be sort of pets, and I hated to turn 'em down. It used to tickle Tusky almost to death to see me out there hollerin' away like an old bull-frog. He used to come out reg'lar, with his pipe lit, just to enjoy me. Finally I got mad and opened up on him.

"Oh," he explains, "it just plumb amuses me to see the dumfool at his childish work. Why don't you teach 'em to come to that brass horn, and save your voice?"

"Tusky," says I, with feelin', "sometimes you do seem to get a glimmer of real sense."

Well, first off them chickens used to throw back-sommersets over that horn. You have no idee how slow chickens is to learn things. I could tell you things about chickens—say, this yere bluff about roosters bein' gallant is all wrong. I've watched 'em. When one finds a nice feed he gobbles it so fast that the pieces foller down his throat like yearlin's through a hole in the fence. It's only when he scratches up a measly one-grain quick-lunch that he calls up the hens and stands noble and self-sacrificin' to one side. That ain't the point, which is, that after two months I had them long-laigs so they'd drop everythin' and come kitin' at the *honk-honk* of that horn. It was a purty sight to see 'em, sailin' in from all directions twenty foot at a stride. I was proud of 'em, and named 'em the Honk-honk Breed. We didn't have no others, for by now the coyotes and bob-cats had nailed the straight-breds. There wasn't no wild cat or coyote could catch one of my Honk-honks, no, sir!

We made a little on our placer—just enough to keep interested. Then the supervisors decided to fix our road, and what's more, *they done it!* That's the only part in this yarn that's hard to believe, but, boys, you'll have to take it on faith. They ploughed her, and crowned her, and scraped her, and rolled her, and when they moved on we had the fanciest highway in the State of Californy.

That noon—the day they called her a job Tusky and I sat smokin' our pipes as per usual, when way over the foothills we seen a cloud of dust and faint to our ears was bore a whizzin' sound. The chickens was gathered under the cottonwood for the heat of the day, but they didn't pay no attention. Then faint, but clear, we heard another of them brass horns:

"Honk! honk!" says it, and every one of them chickens woke up, and stood at attention.

"Honk! honk!" it hollered clearer and nearer. Then over the hill come an automobeel, blowin' vigorous at every jump.

"My God!" I yells to Tusky, kickin' over my chair, as I springs to my feet. "Stop 'em! Stop 'em!"

But it was too late. Out the gate sprinted them poor devoted chickens, and up the road they trailed in vain pursuit. The last we seen of 'em was a minglin' of dust and dim figgers goin' thirty mile an hour after a disappearin' automobeel.

That was all we seen for the moment. About three o'clock the first straggler came limpin' in, his wings hangin', his mouth open, his eyes glazed with the heat. By sundown fourteen had returned. All the rest had disappeared utter; we never seen 'em again. I reckon they just naturally run themselves into a sunstroke and died on the road.

It takes a long time to learn a chicken a thing, but a heap longer to unlearn him. After that two or three of these yere automobeels went by every day, all a-blowin' of their horns, all kickin' up a hell of a dust. And every time them fourteen Honk-honks of mine took along after 'em, just as I'd taught 'em to do, layin' to get to their corn when they caught up. No more of 'em died, but that fourteen did get into elegant trainin'. After a while they got plumb to enjoyin' it. When you come right down to it, a chicken don't have many amusements and relaxations in this life. Searchin' for worms, chasin' grasshoppers, and wallerin' in the dust is about the limits of joys for chickens.

It was sure a fine sight to see 'em after they got well into the game. About nine o'clock every mornin' they would saunter down to the rise of the road where they would wait patient until a machine came along. Then it would warm your heart to see the enthusiasm of them. With exultant cackles of joy they'd trail in, reachin' out like quarter-horses, their wings half spread out, their eyes beamin' with delight. At the lower turn they'd quit. Then, after talkin' it over excited-like for a few minutes, they'd calm down and wait for another.

After a few months of this sort of trainin' they got purty good at it. I had one two-year-old rooster that made fifty-four mile an hour behind one of those sixty-horse-power Panhandles. When cars didn't come along often enough, they'd all turn out and chase jackrabbits. They wasn't much fun at that. After a short, brief sprint the rabbit would crouch down plumb terrified, while the Honk-honks pulled off triumphal dances around his shrinkin' form.

Our ranch got to be purty well known them days among automobeelists. The strength of their cars was horse-power, of course, but the speed of them they got to ratin' by chicken-power. Some of them used to come way up from Los Angeles just to try out a new car along our road with the Honk-honks for pace-makers. We charged them a little somethin', and then, too, we opened up the road-house and the bar, so we did purty well. It wasn't necessary to work any longer at that bogus placer. Evenin's we sat around outside and swapped yarns, and I bragged on my chickens. The chickens would gather round close to listen. They liked to hear their praises sung, all right. You bet they *sabe!* The only reason a chicken, or any other critter, isn't intelligent is because he hasn't no chance to expand.

Why, we used to run races with 'em. Some of us would hold two or more chickens back of a chalk line, and the starter'd blow the horn from a hundred yards to a mile away, dependin' on whether it was a sprint or for distance. We had pools on the results, gave odds, made books, and kept records. After the thing got knowed we made money hand over fist.

The stranger broke off abruptly and began to roll a cigarette.

"What did you quit it for, then?" ventured Charley, out of the hushed silence.

"Pride," replied the stranger solemnly. "Haughtiness of spirit."

"How so?" urged Charley, after a pause.

"Them chickens," continued the stranger, after a moment, "stood around listenin' to me a-braggin' of what superior fowls they was until they got all puffed up. They wouldn't have nothin' whatever to do with the ordinary chickens we brought in for eatin' purposes, but stood around lookin' bored. Then there wasn't no sport doin'. They got to be just like that Four Hundred you read about in the papers. It was one continual round of grasshopper balls, race meets, and afternoon hen-parties. They got idle and haughty, just like folks. Then come race suicide. They got to feelin' so aristocratic the hens wouldn't have no eggs."

Nobody dared say a word.

"Windy Bill's snake—" began the narrator genially.

"Stranger," broke in Windy Bill, with great emphasis, "as to that snake, I want you to understand this: yereafter in my estimation that snake is nothin' but an ornery angle-worm!"

On Cats

by T. S. ELIOT

It is amazing to find that T. S. Eliot, the learned and frequently obscure poet of the despair of modern civilization, is the author of these charming and completely comprehensible and very funny verses about cats. There are more of them—a great many more of them, but I like these two best, probably because my own cat is a "Jellicle cat." If you want a cat with a different personality, and a different name, I refer you with complete confidence to "Old Possum's Book of Practical Cats" from which these two poems were taken. I am sure you will find your own favorite cat described.

THE NAMING OF CATS

The Naming of Cats is a difficult matter,
    It isn't just one of your holiday games;
You may think at first I'm as mad as a hatter
When I tell you, a cat must have THREE DIFFERENT NAMES.
First of all, there's the name that the family use daily,
    Such as Peter, Augustus, Alonzo or James,
Such as Victor or Jonathan, George or Bill Bailey—
    All of them sensible everyday names.
There are fancier names if you think they sound sweeter,
    Some for the gentlemen, some for the dames:
Such as Plato, Admetus, Electra, Demeter—
    But all of them sensible everyday names.
But I tell you, a cat needs a name that's particular,
    A name that's peculiar, and more dignified,
Else how can he keep up his tail perpendicular,
    Or spread out his whiskers, or cherish his pride?

Of names of this kind, I can give you a quorum,
Such as Munkustrap, Quaxo, or Coricopat,
Such as Bombalurina, or else Jellylorum—
    Names that never belong to more than one cat.
But above and beyond there's still one name left over,
    And that is the name that you never will guess;
The name that No human research can discover—
    But the CAT HIMSELF KNOWS, and will never confess.
When you notice a cat in profound meditation,
    The reason, I tell you, is always the same:
His mind is engaged in a rapt contemplation
    Of the thought, of the thought, of the thought of his name:
        His ineffable effable
        Effanineffable
Deep and inscrutable singular Name.

THE SONG OF THE JELLICLES

                    Jellicle Cats come out tonight,
                    Jellicle Cats come one come all:
                    The Jellicle moon is shining bright—
                    Jellicles come to the Jellicle Ball.

Jellicle Cats are black and white,
Jellicle Cats are rather small;
Jellicle Cats are merry and bright,
And pleasant to hear when they caterwaul.
Jellicle Cats have cheerful faces,
Jellicle cats have bright black eyes;
They like to practice their airs and graces
And wait for the Jellicle Moon to rise.

Jellicle Cats develop slowly,
Jellicle Cats are not too big;
Jellicle Cats are roly-poly,
They know how to dance a gavotte and a jig.
Until the Jellicle Moon appears
They make their toilette and take their repose:

Jellicles wash behind their ears,
Jellicles dry between their toes.

Jellicle Cats are white and black,
Jellicle Cats are of moderate size;
Jellicles jump like a jumping jack,
Jellicle Cats have moonlit eyes.
They're quiet enough in the morning hours,
They're quiet enough in the afternoon,
Reserving their terpsichorean powers
To dance by the light of the Jellicle Moon.

Jellicle Cats are black and white,
Jellicle Cats (as I said) are small;
If it happens to be a stormy night
They will practice a caper or two in the hall.
If it happens the sun is shining bright
You would say they had nothing to do at all:
They are resting and saving themselves to be right
For the Jellicle Moon and the Jellicle Ball.

The Backbreaker's Bride

by HENRY WILLIAMSON

This is a beautiful and slightly mannered story of a young falcon, in an England that existed before the war made such leisurely and absorbed preoccupation with the training of a game bird a little unreal to all of us. Henry Williamson is a writer of very perceptive stories about animals: this is perhaps his best work.

THE eyesses had slept and awakened over a hundred times during the night as the mail train took them eastwards towards London. Although they were starving, they would not tear the two plucked pigeons lying beside them. They had no hunger. At Paddington they were taken out of the guard's van, and many people waiting in the vast and gloomy station wondered what made the shrill chattering inside the basket. In the luggage room, where they remained for several hours, they fell asleep, to awake when the lid was lifted.

The man looking at them was a colonel of cavalry, with gray mustache and sunburnt skin. With the expert eye of an experienced falconer he examined the plumage, to see whether the eyesses, or young peregrine falcons, had been taken too early from the eyrie on Lundy. Every season from time immemorial fishermen had scaled the cliff for the peregrine's young, receiving five pounds every midsummer for a cast of three. There were two eyries on the island, and the right to take the young falcons had been leased by the owner for many years: the subject of a legal contract.

The wildness of the three young birds in the basket assured their new owner that they were fresh taken; and signing the receipt form, he carried them to a car outside and drove through London and down into Kent, and to his home at the foot of the downs overlooking the English Channel.

Up the straight wooden wall-ladder to the loft over the coach-house he took the basket, gently turning the trembling birds out on the straw and leaving them with a bowl of water.

When the next morning came they were still crouched there. He picked them up in his thick leather gauntlets, into which they stuck their talons, not with intent to wound, but because their tautly strung nervous systems were shocked into a world without coherence or meaning.

Upon the leg of each bird he fixed two small Lahore bells and a jess, or strip of soft greased hide of the white whale, a swivel attached to it. The agony of his touch did not last long, for the falconer had brought a hack-board, whereon was placed food for them—three heaps of beef chopped up and mixed with hard-boiled eggs. He put it on the floor and left them. They did not feed. At five o'clock in the afternoon he returned and, without showing head or body, stretched up an arm, removed the hack-board, cleaned it under a tap in the stable wall, made three fresh heaps of the same food, mixed with rabbits' fur and pigeons' feathers. Quietly he placed the evening meal before them, and when he had gone they fed ravenously.

Twice a day for the next fortnight the hack-board was put over the edge of the trap-door, sometimes with strips of raw beef and dead rabbits tied to it. The eyesses became used to their food arriving, as it were, by itself. The falconer did not show himself with the food because he did not want them to associate the ideas of food arrival with man arrival; he wanted to train them when they were older to fly at rooks and magpies, and possibly gulls, on the downs; and a hawk that would scream or cry out to him when unhooded would be useless.

It was warm sunny weather, with wild doves nesting in the larches around the house, and oak leaves green and rustling outside the open window. The eyesses taught themselves to fly from beam to beam of the loft. Nearly all the baby-fluff had gone when the largest, a female bird, called falcon, after three days of indecision on the ivy-grown sill, launched herself into the air and, flapping wildly, clung to a lichened branch. One of her brothers, a male hawk, called tiercel, followed her after half an hour of shrill chattering.

At the end of another week, nearly every branch of the tree had been perched upon. For the first two evenings they returned to roost in the loft, but when the oak tree was familiar they slept there. The hack-board was now placed outside the loft, on a strip of grass, for they would not return under a roof once they were free. As soon as they saw it they jumped upon the hack-board and tore off their breakfast. Afterwards they returned to the tree, preening flight feathers, and nibbling dry skin fragments off legs and toes.

The falcon, larger than her brothers, was the first to venture again from the oak. She flew across the rose garden of the house, over a tennis lawn, and perched on an elm that overlooked a walled-in kitchen garden. Swifts, with their black curved wings that made a sound like *fere* as they tore through the wind, screamed their puny screams as they saw her, and her full liquid-brown eyes watched them. She rested for nearly an hour, snapping at bluebottles buzzing about her, watching the flight of birds and insects. She began to chatter as she dipped, for she was not yet confident of her wing-power.

The falconer, watching her, saw her suddenly cock her eye at the sky. He uttered an exclamation for, wheeling overhead, was a wild peregrine. Its flight was like a swift's, but its wings were broader at the elbow, from whence to the tips they narrowed to sharp points.

He watched the young falcon glide off the branch, and begin to ring above the kitchen garden with a series of sharp flaps followed by glides on level pinions. At every glide she depressed her tail and rose higher, and at the curves she gained speed again. When she had climbed five hundred feet, the stranger, who had swung round and now hung head-to-wind, closed his pinions and stooped upon her. She saw him and cried out in fear, but he swerved from the line of stoop and passed her, to turn under her and make his point above her again. His breast was a creamy white, barred with thin black lines, and two black mustachial patches on his cheeks gave him a fierce and beautiful appearance. Like the falcon, he had yellow legs; but his back was not brown, like hers, but a gray-blue.

He flew beside her, and she chattered at him, still being afraid. He was a wild tiercel, in his first mature plumage, which he wore with dashing pride. Suddenly he fell and, watching his stoop with thrilling delight, the falconer saw him miss a swift, immediately to make his point in a perfect swoop upwards and rejoin her.

Unknown to the Colonel, the wild tiercel was The Backbreaker, escaped from a mews on Salisbury Plain, where among falconers he was famed for his skill in swiftly maneuvering a rook into position to receive the grand stoop.

The next day he joined the three eyesses in the elm. He bore a starling in his talons. He plucked, skinned, and ate it as he stood on a bough, while they watched every beak-stroke, every rip, every gulp with the most eager curiosity. Someone else was watching too, for in the falconer's mind were plans for its capture.

The previous autumn he had been in Holland, to examine the hawk traps on the great plain of Valkenswaard, where for centuries a family of Dutchmen had taken migrating, or passage, hawks. It was the Colonel's ambition to reclaim an adult wild peregrine and train it to be as good a bird as the most famous hawks of olden time. A tiercel taken mature would be more dashing than an eyess that had never killed its own prey before being "reclaimed."

The eyesses grew strong of wing, and after breakfast every morning at sunrise they set their feathers straight and cleaned their talons, and then—away into the sky! The Colonel, who was a lonely widower since his only daughter's recent marriage, had learned a little about the training of falcons during his service on Indian plains, where the larger sacer falcons were flown at kites and gamebirds by native officers.

The young peregrines enjoyed their play in the air, chasing and stooping at each other through the sunlit wind. The wild tiercel came every day, joining in their games, and playing with the falcon more than with her brothers. Often they dashed down the wind, seen as specks from below, to swing round and be thrown up by the impetus of the swerve.

The Colonel used to lie in a deck-chair in the sun and watch them through glasses until they were beyond sight, where for an hour and more they tumbled and swooped and rejoiced in the cold untrodden ways of the lofty summer sky. Although they were beyond human sight aided by lenses and prisms, yet the movements of the man below were visible to four pairs of haughty dark eyes whenever he crossed one leg over the other or put his arms behind his white panama hat.

One day as he was lounging there, listening to the sea's continuous *ah-ah's* on the distant shore, he heard a hissing noise above, and

looked up in time to see the wild tiercel stoop upon a carrion crow
which had been stealing squabs or nestling pigeons from the larch
wood. The carrion crow cawed harshly and fled back towards the
trees; but before it could reach cover and hide in the maze of
branches, the tiercel in a magnificent stoop had hit it so accurately
that it was instantly killed. Its mate appeared out of the wood a few
seconds later in answer to its cawing, and The Backbreaker, who
had shot up to a pitch three hundred feet above the striking place,
stooped upon her. She avoided his line of stoop by a violent shift,
and the falconer heard the swishing as the tiercel turned on his back,
making the figure 6 and ripped with his talons as he passed under
her. She fell mortally wounded, her crop torn open, in the rose
garden; and running to her, the Colonel killed her with the blow
of a stick.

Three squabs were in the crop, and to his surprise one of them,
about three days old, was alive. He carried it away and put it in a
dovecot beside a tippler squab whose mother nourished it thenceforward as her own offspring. It was uninjured, having been swallowed whole by the crow. Eventually it grew to be a fine bird.

The falconer, filled with admiration for the prowess and skill of
the wild tiercel, visited a cobbler in the village who trapped sky-
larks during the autumn migration across the downs. This man made
him a bow-net after the pattern of the Dutch nets. Together they
fixed it in the paddock adjoining the stables.

For several days The Backbreaker had been coming morning and
evening to the hack-board, and feeding with the eyesses, who never
failed to return at mealtimes, crying *Way-ee*, *Way-ee* and shivering their wings when they saw him—a happy sign that they had not
learned to kill for themselves. Although they wailed to him and
showed no fear of him, they would not allow him to approach within
a yard of them. He was astonished at the wild bird's tameness until
he saw a bell on its leg, and then he realized that it must have escaped.
He was the more determined to recapture it.

Very soon, he thought, he would have to begin to break them in.
Within a week they must be caught, hooded, and each leashed to
its wooden block driven into the lawn. After an hour or two of
quiet perching, one would be perched on his wrist and carried

about, stroked with a feather and fed through the hood. The hood would be removed inside the shuttered coach-house, by candlelight, quietly during a meal, and put on again, but before the meal's end —lest the idea of hooding and termination of a meal be associated in their minds. The next stage would be to feed them in daylight and to break them in quietly to the putting on of the hood; for when hooded they could rest and grow calm. Afterwards would begin the training proper, a very patient work, to make them return to the lure—wings of a duck tied to a pad and swung on a string for the recall.

For the haggard tiercel, however, the reclaiming would be more severe. For two days and nights, by sunlight and candlelight, it would be stroked with a feather, handled gently, and prevented from sleeping. Then it would be starved. At the end of forty-eight hours, if all went well, its fierce and haughty spirit would be subdued, its sense of lordship over all in the open sky be dulled, its resentment of captivity gone, and it would submit to a hood patiently, and take food from its captor's hand.

The falconer bided his time. The bow-net was made, and fixed in the paddock. The squab that had escaped death in the crow's crop, and whose life was owed to The Backbreaker, was fully fledged when the day planned for the taking of the four peregrines arrived. Recently the wild tiercel had been roosting on the tower of the Norman church in the village nearby, and frequently the three slept with him. He was their protector. Once seventeen magpies had found one of the young male eyesses resting on a downland thorn, perched insecurely on a top spray in the sea breeze, and had mobbed him. They had pecked at him, knowing he was little, and tried to pull out his tail and flight feathers. The Backbreaker had seen them as he swooped in play at his favorite falcon; he had swept up with the wind two thousand feet above; he had poised for the grand stoop; he had tipped up, beating wings to increase the sheer of his dive headfirst—faster, faster, the wind screaming against his barbed strength—seventeen magpies were scattered like pieces of half-burnt paper, except one whose head spun away from its flattened body and fell seventy feet distant from the thorn bush. (Sixteen magpies fought for the body two minutes afterwards, but ants had the head, leaving horn and bone clean a day later.)

Now the falconer was waiting to take the four friends.

The net was circular, a yard across, with a pliant hazel-rod bent like a bow and tied to half the net's circumference. To the bow-net was attached fifty yards of line. The unattached half of the net was pegged to the ground, and the loose folds tucked under the hazel bow. Beside the bow was placed the hack-board, with dead rats and rabbits tied to it. Fifty yards away the falconer squatted in the grass, the smoke of his pipe straying into the quiet evening air among the gnats which rose and fell in dance over his head.

Seven was the usual feeding time, and the stable cock had sounded the hour three minutes when a speck appeared over the downs, and grew rapidly into the barb-shape of a swooping eyess. He fell like an arrowhead to the hack-board, where he was joined by the other eyess tiercel two minutes later. The falconer waited for the falcon eyess and the wild tiercel, but when at a quarter past seven they were still absent, he jerked the line so that the bow rose over the eyesses and they were caught in the spread circle of the net. How they chattered and struggled! Gently the hand-in-gauntlet held wings against sides, they were drawn out one at a time, and rufter hoods slipped over their heads and fastened with straps round their backs. Good-by to freedom, little Lundy tiercels! The light caps of leather, which were open at the back and permitted them to feed, blindfolded them; they ceased to struggle; swivels and leashes were attached to the jesses on their legs; the leashes tied to the larchwood blocks a hundred yards away in the grass.

The other hawks did not return to the hack-board, and the falconer concluded that the wild tiercel had killed for the falcon eyess. At sunset the pair returned to the church tower, where they slept. Before dawn the next morning the falconer arose and prepared fresh food on the hack-board, which he then took to the dewy grass of the paddock. He waited for half an hour, while the stars paled in the steely glow above him and the line of the downs grew dark as light flowed up to the zenith. Larks were already singing when a thrush flew to the elm and its bold ringing notes awoke the drowsiest birds. Swallows flew round him, and a cohort of swifts seemed to descend from the stars as though poured out of an unseen pitcher. The last star was dimmed when the eyess falcon suddenly appeared, The Backbreaker behind her, and she was about to alight upon the hack-board when the tiercel cried *chak-chek-chak!* and she swerved away, to make her point above the net and complain in a baby wail to the falconer. *Way-ee way-ee,* she wailed, but the tiercel swooped at her and drove her away. Once netted, twice shy, thought the falconer.

The cries were heard by the eyesses hooded and leashed in a disused chicken-house, and they too cried *way-ee way-ee.* Every time the eyess swooped down to the hack-board the tiercel drove her up, and *way-ee, way-ee,* she complained to the falconer, flying round his head, her bell tinkling, and crying *way-ee, way-ee, way-ee!*

To the Colonel, a sensitive and thoughtful man, the eyess seemed like a young bride, reluctant to leave a loved home, yet eager for love and life. The Backbreaker chattered and called her, her brothers wailed to her, as she circled above the paddock and cried to the one who was regarded as parent and guardian. A feeling of sadness came over him, as he stood and watched, the cord loose in his hand, for in that moment he realized how near to men were animals and birds in their desires and aspirations. "We're all the same," he murmured to himself.

He dropped the cord. He would try no further to net them. He walked to the house, followed by the young eyess. He was moved by her cries to him, and remembered his only daughter on her wedding eve.

"Go your ways, little falcon," he said. "That handsome fellow has first claim on you."

Then he stood still in amazement; for immediately he had spoken, the falcon dashed upwards to The Backbreaker, and together they flew up into the sky.

The eyess tiercels were trained and accounted for many thieving crows and magpies during happy hours of wandering with him and a spaniel on the downs. Buccaneer and Belfry they were called and lived to be old birds; but they never saw The Backbreaker or his mate again.

Far away over the Devon seaboard the pair ranged, from their eyrie on Bone Ledge where The Backbreaker had been born—he the direct heir to more than a hundred thousand years of fearlessness.

A Cat in the Family

by WINIFRED WILLIAMS

*Charming and heart-breaking; this sketch of two chil-
dren and a cat repeats the theme which we find so often
in stories about pets; that adults do not know or have
forgotten how important small animals are to children.*

IN THE northern English village in which I was raised, nearly
everybody kept a cat. There were very few dogs—a couple of
Scotch terriers and three racing whippets. When I was six I wanted
a dog—a collie—but whenever I asked for one, Father would say,
"If ever I have a dog, it'll be an Airedale. There's naught to touch an
Airedale. Just remember that, my lass." It was several years before
I realized that he didn't mean to have a dog of any sort.

For quite a while we didn't have a cat, either. Mother was tolerant
toward human weaknesses, she believed that mankind was improv-
ing, she gave food to beggars, when we had barely enough for ourselves, but she detested dogs and cats, especially cats. I guess she
thought the battle for cleanliness was hard enough without having a
cat leave hairs on the sofa and slop milk on her kitchen floor.

We lived in a small cottage in a street of narrow stone houses,
and as everybody had a cat except us, the mice in the neighboring
fields took to staying with us whenever they wanted to be indoors.
We often saw their sharp eyes under the cupboard in the living
room and heard them scuttle across the bedroom floors. Father set
traps for weeks, but he only caught one mouse.

"We'll have to get a cat," Father said at last. "There's naught else
for it." A few days afterward, Uncle Tom arrived with a kitten.

Uncle Tom was the universal provider. A few months after the
end of the World War, he had come home from India with a model
of the Taj Mahal, four painted cushion covers, several large, dead

350

butterflies, and six brass pots, all of which he distributed to admiring relatives. He got a job immediately, he never seemed to be short of money, and he would lend whatever he had to anybody.

"This," he said, putting the kitten on our hearthrug, "is as fine as ever I saw. And mind you treat it right."

He looked sharply at my brother, who, whenever he got a toy, took it to pieces to see what was inside. If the toy was strong, my brother got a hammer to speed up the demolition. He was seven years old, and curious. I was eleven and past the toy age.

My brother and I took to the kitten the moment we saw her. We called her Topsy, because it is a custom in England to call black female kittens Topsy. We trailed lengths of string across the carpet for her, and we were constantly fetching the milk jug from the cellar because we thought the kitten might need nourishment. I found that reading a book with a cat on my lap made the book seem better. We never saw the kitten catch a mouse, but the mice left us. Mother admitted that the kitten must be responsible for this strategic retreat, but her gratitude was cold. A cat, she said, was a nuisance. Once, when it made a mess on her kitchen floor, she went white with anger and disgust. She soon cured the cat of that sort of uncleanliness. My brother said unhappily that he believed she had slapped it. The kitten was lively and kept getting under Mother's feet. Whenever she tripped over it, she would wish loudly that it was in Timbuktu. We had no idea where Timbuktu was, nor had she, but we all knew it was far enough away. Sometimes when we came home from school, my brother and I would find the kitten mewing outside our door, and one of us would pick it up and hug it, trying to make up for Mother's unkindness.

Father was tolerant and good-natured toward the kitten, but his attitude changed after she broke Jack Johnson. Father had once gone on a day's trip to a seaside town and had brought back as a souvenir a china tobacco jar, shaped and colored like a Negro's head. It had a smiling face and white, even teeth, and when you wanted tobacco, you lifted the scalp off. Father told us that Jack Johnson was the greatest boxer in the world and that this was a model of his head. One evening, Jack Johnson was left on the edge of a chair, and the kitten, leaping from the floor onto the leather seat, knocked him off. He broke into twenty pieces.

"That damned cat!" Father roared. He went absolutely purple and said he would have the cat drowned. My brother and I were alarmed, for though we liked Jack Johnson, we liked the cat better. My brother picked her up and took her out into the street for a while to let Father's anger cool. Half an hour later, Uncle Tom came in, and, as nothing could take Father's mind off Jack Johnson, Uncle tactfully started a discussion of boxing. Father relieved his feelings in oratory and said nothing more about having the cat drowned. But he never liked Topsy after that, and if she sprang onto his knee, he pushed her off.

Topsy was soon out of infancy. She got through adolescence in a flash and emerged into handsome maturity. As cats go, she was very affectionate, but she had no discrimination; she would sidle up to Mother or Father with the same warmth that she showed to my brother and me, and no amount of coldness on their part convinced her that her love was not returned.

My brother got the idea of taking her to bed with him and letting her lie on his feet to keep them warm. He managed this for a while with secrecy and success, but one night I overheard him talking to the cat and was jealous. Naturally, I shouted to Mother, and she rushed upstairs to find Topsy escaping and cat hairs on the white bedspread. Next morning I saw the bedspread floating in a tub of soapy water in the wash cellar; Mother had a horror of germs.

The next problem was kittens. Uncle Tom said if Mother put the cat out every night what else could she expect, but I believe her innocent mind had never envisaged kittens. We saw Topsy getting heavier and slower, and Mother frowned every time she looked at her.

"They'll have to be drowned," Mother said. "The whole lot of 'em."

Four kittens were born—unluckily, while my brother and I were in school. Mother was uncommonly kind to Topsy for a week and never once wished her in Timbuktu, but on the tenth day Uncle Tom turned up and she told him that he'd have to do the drowning.

"You've got to keep one, unless you want to break the cat's heart," Uncle Tom said.

"I don't care," Mother said.

"No, but I do," Uncle Tom said. "And you'll keep one for a month and then I'll find it a home."

The arrangement worked out well. Topsy's maternal impulse seemed to last about a month, and apparently she never missed the three that Uncle Tom drowned. We didn't see him do the drowning, but he told us that the kittens felt absolutely nothing.

Topsy lived with us for nearly two years and had several litters, which Uncle Tom disposed of, always in the same way, and everybody was satisfied. Then Mother got sick and the doctor said she must lie flat in bed for a couple of months. It was decided that we should all go to live with Grandmother and Uncle Tom for a while, so that we could be properly cared for, but Grandmother said that she wouldn't have a cat in the house and that we must get rid of Topsy. My brother and I visited several neighbors and asked if they would keep a cat for us, but they all had cats and nobody wanted another. Even Uncle Tom said there was no way out. My brother and I talked things over and decided to take Topsy across the field to Farley's farm. Farley had two cats in his barn and we thought he might like a third. We dared not ask him, as he was an unpleasant man with a sharp temper, but we thought that if we left the cat in the field near the barn, she would find herself a home. We knew she had intelligence and initiative.

The evening before we were to go to Grandmother's, we carried out our plan. We waited until no one else was downstairs. Then I picked Topsy up and told my brother to come on. Topsy, who was used to being pushed around, made no sound, and we went out into the summer twilight. We took turns carrying her.

To get to Farley's farm, we had to go along Back Lane and through Spring Wood. The field on the other side of the lane was some nine feet below the roadway. We had reckoned that nine feet of wall would discourage Topsy from trying to return with us.

When we got to the wall, my brother suggested that we might sit with the cat for a while before dropping her over the other side, but I was feeling miserable and wanted to get the affair finished. I looked over the wall at the field beneath. My brother, who was hugging the cat, knew what I was thinking. "We can't let her drop that far," he said. "It might kill her."

I told him to climb down with her, since he was good at wall climbing, but he pointed out that I was older than he. It was an awkward wall, and neither of us liked the look of it. Finally we decided to toss a halfpenny. He lost, and started to climb down. When he had got a third of the way, I leaned over and gave him the cat, and then, tucking her under his left arm, he managed to get to the bottom. I noticed that his right knee was bleeding, but he didn't seem to mind, so I said nothing.

I sat on the wall and watched him run toward Farley's barn with Topsy in his arms. The long grass had been mown and there was only stubble left; Farley couldn't say we had damaged his crop. I began to feel queer in my stomach, and remembered that I had eaten six green gooseberries in the school yard that afternoon. I wondered if I was going to be sick. I watched my brother put the cat down beside the door of the barn and saw him start to run back. The cat streaked after him and they arrived at the wall simultaneously.

"Climb up, quick," I said. "We'll have to leave her in the field."

He started to scramble up the wall and I leaned over as far as I dared to give him a hand. I had an awful time getting him up. As I was dragging him over the rough top stones, I happened to turn my head and saw Topsy sitting on the wall beside me. She seemed very interested in the way my brother was climbing up. I guess she thought he was making hard work of it.

"What do we do now?" my brother asked, looking miserable.

"Let's run," I said. "She won't follow us all the way. She'll get tired."

We started to run and Topsy ran after us. Occasionally she would get a few yards ahead, and then she would stop and wait for us. We ran through Spring Wood and into Back Lane, but we couldn't shake her off. Halfway along the lane we had to stop because we were short of breath.

"We've got to run faster this time," my brother said. His face was white and he was trying not to cry.

"But we can't lose her just anywhere," I said. "Who'll look after her?"

"If we take her home, she'll get drowned," he said.

We all three started to run. When we got to the main street,

Topsy streaked ahead, and when we reached home, she was waiting for us on the doorstep, looking cool and self-possessed.

We found Uncle Tom in the living room, packing my clothes into a suitcase and singing "Waiting for the Robert E. Lee." It was his favorite song, but when I asked him once who Robert E. Lee was he said he didn't know, and he couldn't explain what "waiting on the levee" meant, either. He said a levee was something they had in America.

"Where've you two been?" he asked. "You look as if you've been running your legs off."

I said nothing. My brother sat on the sofa and stared into the fire. I could hear my grandmother walking around upstairs. With every step she took, the bedroom floor creaked.

"You've been up to something," Uncle Tom said. "Out with it."

I told him how we had tried to lose the cat and failed. Topsy had stretched herself out on the hearthrug. She must be pretty tired, I thought. I knew I was.

"Listen," Uncle Tom said. "You've had her a long time and you can't keep her now. But I won't drown her. Tomorrow night, as soon as I've finished work, I'll take her to a vet in Hampton, and he'll see she dies peaceful."

We thought that over. We didn't like the idea much.

"He'll just give her a whiff of something that'll send her to sleep for good. That's all. It'll cost me five shillings, but if you'll stop worrying and go off to bed I promise I'll do it."

It seemed the only way, and Topsy liked sleeping. She spent half the day asleep in front of the fire.

"All right," I said.

"There's milk and currant bread for your supper. It's on the kitchen table. Fetch it in here," Uncle Tom said, "and I'll tell you about the time I was in the Himalayas."

My brother went into the kitchen and came back with a saucer of milk, which he put on the hearthrug.

"When your mother gets better, I'll find a kitten for you," Uncle Tom said.

"We don't want one," I said.

"You'll feel different in a week or two," Uncle Tom said. "I once felt the same way about somebody—about something—and I got over it. That's the way it always is," he said, and started pushing the lid of my suitcase down and whistling "Waiting for the Robert E. Lee."

Miss Holloway's Goat

by LUIGI PIRANDELLO

*Pirandello, whom we are accustomed to find con-
cerned with the mysteries of personality, here presents
us with a problem that is in some degree outside his
usual field, and yet is very much within his usual preoccupation. Is a goat, bearded and offensive, the same
animal. . . . But I shan't give away the plot of this story.*

THERE is no doubt of it, Mr. Charles Trockley is always in
the right. I am even disposed to admit that Mr. Charles
Trockley could not possibly be in the wrong, Mr. Trockley and
the right being the same thing. Every gesture of Mr. Charles Trockley's, every glance, every word are rigid and precise, well-weighed
and safe in the assurance that everyone must immediately recognize the fact it is impossible for Mr. Charles Trockley, under any
circumstances, in connection with any question that may arise or
any incident that may occur, to harbor the wrong opinion or assume the wrong attitude.

He and I, by way of example, were born in the same year, the
same month and almost on the same day; he in England, I in Sicily.
Today, the fifteenth of June, he is forty-eight; I shall be forty-eight
on the twenty-eighth of June. Very well: how old shall we be, he
on the fifteenth and I on the twenty-eighth of next June? Mr.
Charles Trockley is not baffled by that; he does not hesitate for a
moment, but maintains with assurance that, on the fifteenth and the
twenty-eighth, respectively, of next June, he and I will be just one
year older, that is, forty-nine.

Could one think of telling Mr. Charles Trockley that he is wrong?

The years do not go by the same for all. I, in one day, in one hour,
may acquire more damage than he in ten years of his rigorously dis-

357

ciplined and well-preserved existence. I, owing to the deplorable state of my mind, may live more than a lifetime in the course of a single year. My body, weaker and less well-cared-for than his, has, assuredly, aged more in the past forty-eight years than Mr. Trockley's will in seventy. This is evidenced by the fact that, while his hair is silvery-white all over, his lobster-like face displays not the slightest trace of a wrinkle, and he is still youthfully spry enough to do a little fencing every morning.

But what does it all matter? All these idealistic and matter-of-fact considerations are, for Mr. Charles Trockley, a waste of time and without any reasonable foundation. For reason informs Mr. Charles Trockley that, as a matter of simple fact, on the fifteenth and the twenty-eighth, respectively, of next June, we shall be just one year older than we now are, that is, forty-nine.

Having told you this, I should now like for you to hear what happened to Mr. Charles Trockley recently; and then, ask yourselves whether or not he was in the wrong.

Last April, in following an Italian itinerary that had been mapped out for her by Baedeker, Miss Ethel Holloway, the very young and sprightly daughter of Sir W. H. Holloway, a very rich and highly respected English peer, arrived at Girgenti in Sicily to have a look at the marvelous ruins of the ancient Doric city. Enchanted with the landscape—a sea of white almond-blossoms—at this time of year, white almond-blossoms swaying to the warm zephyrs from off the African sea, she had decided to prolong her one-day stop-over at the big *Hôtel des Temples*, which, ideally situated, stands outside the very steep and squalid city, in the open country.

For twenty-two years, Mr. Charles Trockley has been English vice-consul at Girgenti, and every day for twenty-two years, at sundown, he has taken a walk, striding along at his usual nimble, even pace, from the hillside city down to the ruins of the Acragantian temples, standing airy and majestic upon the sharp ridge at the bottom of a slope, the Acraean hill, where stood of old the haughty marble town, hymned by Pindar as the fairest among the cities of men. The ancients were in the habit of remarking that the Acragantinians ate every day as if they expected to die the day after, but that they built their houses as if they were never going to die. They eat precious little now; for there is much want in the city and over the countryside; and as for the historic town, after so many wars, after being seven times sacked and as often put to the torch, there no longer remains so much as a trace of its houses. In their place, there stands an almond and olive grove, for this reason known as the *Bosco della Città*, or Civic Wood. And the long-maned ashen-hued olives, theoretically, run all the way up to the majestic temple columns, and appear to be uttering a requiem on behalf of these abandoned slopes. Under the ridge there flows, when times are propitious, the Acragantas, celebrated by Pindar as being rich in flocks and herds. A few straggling goats now cross the river's stony bed and climb the rocky ridge, to lie down and browse upon the scant pasturage to be found there, in the very shadow of the ancient Temple of Concord, which is still standing.

The goat-herd, drowsy and stupid-looking as an Arab, likewise stretches out upon the crumbling steps of the pronaos, and contrives to extract a few lugubrious notes from his reed-flute.

For Mr. Charles Trockley, this invasion of the temple by goats has always seemed a horrible profanation; and times without number, he has lodged a formal complaint with the custodians of monuments, without ever obtaining any other response than an indulgent and philosophic smile or a shrug of the shoulders. Literally trembling with indignation at these smiles and these shoulder-shrugs, Mr. Charles Trockley upon numerous occasions has besought me to accompany him on his daily walk. Now, it often happens that, either in the Temple of Concord, or in the Temple of Hera Lacinia, further up, or in the other one, commonly known as the Temple of the Giants—it often happens that, in one of these places, Mr. Trockley falls in with parties of his countrymen who have come to visit the ruins. And he, thereupon, with that indignation which time cannot wither nor custom stale, calls upon those present to bear witness to the profanation that is being committed: those goats there, stretched out and browsing in the shadow of the temple columns. But not all the British visitors, it must be stated, are inclined to share Mr. Trockley's wrath. Many of them even feel that there is a certain poetic touch in those goats, reclining thus in these temples which have been left standing in an oblivion-wrapped solitude in the midst of the plain. And more than one of the visitors, to Mr. Trockley's

great disgust, has gone so far as to remark what an altogether charming sight it was.

Particularly charmed, last April, was the very young and very
sprightly Miss Ethel Holloway. And even while the indignant vice-
consul was engaged in giving her certain valuable archæologic information that was not as yet to be found either in Baedeker or in
any other guidebook, Miss Holloway was so thoughtless as to turn
her back suddenly on Mr. Trockley and run up to a pretty little
black kid, only a few days old, which, amid the sprawling goats,
was leaping about here and there, as if the dancing sunlight were
full of enticing gnats; and then, after these violent exertions, it
would stand there as if appalled at what it had done; it was as if every
slightest sound, every breath of air, every tiniest shadow in the, for
it, as yet uncertain spectacle of life were sufficient cause for fear and
trembling.

On that particular day, I was with Mr. Trockley, and I was
greatly pleased to see the delight which the little English miss
manifested; it was charming to see her fall in love at first sight like
that with a little black kid—she was determined to buy it at any
cost; but I was also pained to see how poor Mr. Trockley suffered.

"Buy that kid?"

"Yes, yes! buy it, at once, at once!"

The little miss was trembling all over, just like her little black
pet; she doubtless did not so much as suspect that she could not have
offered Mr. Trockley a greater insult; how was she to know how
long and how ferociously he had hated those beasts? It was in vain
that Mr. Trockley endeavored to dissuade her, to bring her to see
all the trouble that she would have as a result of her purchase. He
had to give in, finally, and, out of respect for her father, had to go
up to the half-savage goat-herd to dicker over the price of the animal.

Miss Ethel Holloway, having taken out the money from her
purse, then informed Mr. Trockley that she wanted the kid turned
over to the manager of the *Hôtel des Temples*, and that, as soon as
she was back in London, she would telegraph, so that the darling
little thing, all expenses paid, could be sent to her at once; and she
went back to the hotel in a carriage, with the kid squirming and
bleating under her arms.

Against the light of the setting sun—a sun that was going down amid a fantastic fretwork of clouds, flaming above a sea that lay spread out beneath like a boundless golden mirror—I had a glimpse, within that black carriage, of a young blond head, as the slender and ardent Miss Holloway disappeared in a nimbus of gleaming light. I beheld all this; and to me, it was like a dream. And then, I understood that, being so far from her own country and from the accustomed sights and surroundings of her daily life, for her thus to have conceived such a passion for a little black kid could mean but one thing: it must mean that she was without a particle of that solid sense which so gravely governed the acts, thoughts, words, and deeds of Mr. Charles Trockley.

And what, then, did Miss Ethel Holloway have in place of solid sense?

Nothing but gross stupidity, maintained Mr. Charles Trockley, with a rage which it was all he could do to control, a rage that becomes something like a downright affliction with a man like him, who is usually so well-contained.

The reasons for Mr. Trockley's wrath are to be found in the events that followed the purchase of that black kid.

Miss Ethel Holloway left Girgenti the next day. From Sicily, she was bound for Greece, from Greece for Egypt, from Egypt for India.

It is in the nature of a miracle that, having returned safe and sound to London along about the end of November, she should have remembered, after eight months of travel and all the experiences which she surely must have had in the course of so long a trip, the little black kid which she had bought one far-away day, amid the ruins of the Acragantian temples in Sicily. No sooner was she back than she wrote, as she had promised, to Mr. Charles Trockley.

The *Hôtel des Temples* is closed every year from the middle of June to the first of November. The manager, to whom Miss Holloway had entrusted the kid, when he came to leave in the middle of June, had turned it over to the caretaker of the inn, but without any directions as to what was to be done with it, for he had been fed up more than once with all the trouble that the beast had given him. The caretaker waited from day to day for the vice-consul, Mr. Charles Trockley, who, the manager had told him, was to come and get the kid and send it on to England; but when no one showed up, he decided, by way of getting rid of the animal, to turn it over to the same goat-herd who had sold it to Miss Holloway, promising him that he could have it as a gift in case its owner, as seemed likely, was not going to send for it; otherwise if the vice-consul called for it, the goat-herd was to be reimbursed for its care and keep.

When, after nearly eight months, Miss Holloway's letter arrived from London, the manager of the *Hôtel des Temples*, the caretaker and the goat-herd were all vastly embarrassed; the manager for having entrusted the kid to the caretaker, the caretaker for having turned it over to the goat-herd, and the goat-herd for having in turn given it to another goat-herd with the same promises that had been made to him. And now, nobody knew where this other goat-herd was. They hunted for him for more than a month. At last, one fine day, Mr. Charles Trockley, seated in the vice-consul's office at Girgenti, looked up and saw before him a big overgrown horned beast, very smelly and covered with a scraggly manure-coated, mud-laden fleece of faded reddish hue; the animal, with deep, raucous, quivering bleats, stood there with its head down threateningly, as if demanding what was wanted of it, now that, against its will, they had brought it so far from its accustomed haunts.

But Mr. Charles Trockley was not in the least put out by his un-expected caller; not in the least; not he. He did not waste a moment, but proceeded to calculate rapidly the time that had elapsed between the first of April and the last of December; and he concluded, reasonably enough, that the pretty little black kid could very well be the filthy animal that stood before him. And without the faintest hesitation, he at once sent word to Miss Holloway that he was shipping her the kid, from Porto Empedocle, with the next home-faring British merchantman. And he put around the neck of this horrible beast a tag with Miss Ethel Holloway's address, and ordered it taken down to the port. There, he himself, at great risk to his dignity, led the restive animal by a rope down the quay, followed by a crowd of urchins; he saw it safely aboard the departing steamer, and then returned to Girgenti, quite sure that he had scrupulously fulfilled his duty, not by catering to Miss Holloway's deplorable whim, but by showing the proper respect to her father.

Yesterday, Mr. Charles Trockley came to see me, in such a condition of mind and body that, very much alarmed, I ran up to help him to a chair and had them bring him a glass of water.

"For the love of God, Mr. Trockley, what's happened?"

Still speechless, Mr. Trockley drew from his pocket a letter and handed it to me. It was a letter from Sir W. H. Holloway, British peer, and contained a string of vigorous insults, occasioned by the affront which Mr. Trockley had offered to Sir W. H. Holloway's daughter, Miss Ethel, by sending her that filthy, awful beast.

And this was the thanks that poor Mr. Trockley had for all his trouble.

But what was he to have expected of that utterly stupid Miss Holloway? Did she by any chance think that, after nearly eleven months, she would see arriving at London the same little black kid which she had beheld so timidly leaping about in the sun amid the columns of the ancient Greek Temple in Sicily? Was it possible? It was too much for Mr. Charles Trockley.

Perceiving the state he was in, I did my best to comfort him, assuring him that he was quite right, that Miss Ethel Holloway must be not only an extremely capricious, but an extremely unreasonable creature as well.

"Stupid! Stupid! Stupid!"

"Let us rather say 'unreasonable,' my dear Mr. Trockley. And yet, look, my friend" (I took the liberty of adding) "she left here last April with the pretty picture of that little black kid in her mind's eye; and—let us be fair to her—she could not well have foreseen (however irrational it may appear) that you were suddenly going to confront her with the very image of reason in the form of that monstrous animal you sent her."

"Well, then," and Mr. Trockley bristled up, "what should you say I ought to have done?"

"I cannot say, Mr. Trockley," I replied hastily and in some embarrassment; "I should not like to appear as unreasonable as that little miss back there in your country; but in your case, Mr. Trockley, do you want to know what I should have done? Either I should have sent word to Miss Ethel Holloway that her pretty little black kid had died of a broken heart; or else, I should have bought another little black kid, exactly like the one she purchased last April; and I should have sent it to her, quite safe in the assurance that Miss Ethel Holloway would never once give a thought to the fact that her little pet could not possibly be the same after eleven months. All this naturally implies, as you see, a recognition of the fact that Miss Ethel Holloway is utterly unreasonable, and that you are absolutely in the right, as always, my dear Mr. Trockley."

A Vendetta

by GUY DE MAUPASSANT

*Hate and death and the intelligence of an animal and
the persistence of mother love.*

THE widow of Paolo Saverini lived alone with her son in a
poor little house on the outskirts of Bonifacio. The city
built on an outjutting part of the mountain, in places even overhanging the sea, looks across the foamy straits toward the southern-
most coast of Sardinia. Around on the other side of the city is a kind
of *fjord* which serves as a port, and which, after a winding journey,
brings—as far as the first houses—the little Italian and Sardinian
fishing-smacks and, every two weeks, the old, wheezy steamer
which makes the trip to Ajaccio.

On the white mountain, the clump of houses makes an even
whiter spot. They look like the nests of wild birds, clinging to this
peak, overlooking this terrible passage where vessels rarely venture.
The wind, which blows uninterruptedly, has swept bare the forbidding coast; it engulfs itself in the narrow straits and lays waste both
sides. The pale streaks of foam, clinging to the black rocks, whose
countless peaks rise up out of the water, look like bits of rag floating
and drifting on the surface of the sea.

The house of Widow Saverini, clinging to the very edge of the
precipice, looked out, through its three windows, over this wild
and desolate picture. She lived there alone, with her son Antoine
and their dog Semillante, a big thin beast, with a long rough coat,
one of the kind of animals that is used for guarding the herds. The
young man took her with him when out hunting.

One night, after some kind of a quarrel, Antoine Saverini was
treacherously stabbed by Nicolas Ravolati, who escaped the same
evening to Sardinia.

When the old mother received the body of her child, which the neighbors had brought back to her, she did not cry, but she stayed there for a long time motionless, watching him; then, stretching her wrinkled hand over the body, she promised him a vendetta. She did not wish anybody near her, and she shut herself up beside the body with the dog, which howled continuously, standing at the foot of the bed, her head stretched toward her master and her tail between her legs. She did not move any more than did the mother, who now leaning over the body with a blank stare, was weeping silently and watching it.

The young man, lying on his back, dressed in his jacket of coarse cloth torn at the chest, seemed to be asleep; but he had blood all over him; on his shirt, which had been torn off in order to administer the first aid; on his vest, on his trousers, on his face, on his hands. Clots of blood had hardened in his beard and in his hair.

His old mother began to talk to him. At the sound of this voice the dog quieted down.

"Never fear, my boy, my little baby, you shall be avenged. Sleep, sleep, you shall be avenged, do you hear? It's your mother's promise! And she always keeps her word, your mother does, you know she does."

Slowly she leaned over him, pressing her cold lips to his dead ones.

Then Semillante began to howl again, with a long, monotonous, penetrating, horrible howl.

The two of them, the woman and the dog, remained there until morning.

Antoine Saverini was buried the next day, and soon his name ceased to be mentioned in Bonifacio.

He had no brothers, no cousins—no man to carry on the vendetta. Alone his mother thought of it; and she was an old woman.

On the other side of the straits, she saw, from morning until night, a little white speck on the coast. It was the little Sardinian village, Longosardo, where Corsican criminals take refuge when they are too closely pursued. They compose almost the entire population of this hamlet, opposite their native island, awaiting the time to return. She knew that Nicolas Ravolati had sought refuge in this village.

All alone, all day long, seated at her window, she was looking over there and thinking of revenge. How could she do anything without help—she, an invalid, and so near death? But she had promised, she had sworn on the body. She could not forget, she could not wait. What could she do? She thought stubbornly. The dog, dozing at her feet, would sometimes lift her head and howl. Since her master's death, she often howled thus, as though she were calling him, as though her beast's soul, inconsolable, too, had also kept something in memory which nothing could wipe out.

One night, as Semillante began to howl, the mother suddenly got hold of an idea—a savage, vindictive, fierce idea. She thought it over until morning; then, having arisen at daybreak, she went to church. She prayed, prostrate on the floor, begging the Lord to help her, to support her, to give to her poor, broken-down body the strength which she needed in order to avenge her son.

She returned home. In her yard, she had an old barrel, which served as a cistern; she turned it over, emptied it, made it fast to the ground with sticks and stones; then she chained Semillante to this improvised kennel.

All day and all night the dog howled. In the morning, the old woman brought her some water in a bowl; but nothing more; no soup, no bread.

Another day went by. Semillante, weakened, was sleeping. The following day, her eyes were shining, her hair was on end and she was pulling wildly at her chain.

All this day the old woman gave her nothing to eat. The beast, furious, was barking hoarsely. Another passed.

Then, at daybreak, Mother Saverini asked a neighbor for some straw. She took the old rags which had formerly been worn by her husband and stuffed them so as to make them look like a human body.

Having planted a stick in the ground, in front of Semillante's kennel, she tied to it this dummy, which seemed to be standing up. Then she made a head out of some old rags.

The dog, surprised, was watching this straw man, and was quiet, although famished. Then the old woman went to the store and bought a piece of black sausage. When she got home, she started a fire in the yard, near the kennel, and cooked the sausage. Semillante, wild, was jumping around and frothing at the mouth, her eyes fixed on the food, whose smell went right to her stomach.

Then, with the smoking sausage, the mother made a necktie for the dummy. She tied it very tightly around the neck, and when she had finished she untied the dog.

With one leap, the beast jumped at the dummy's throat, and, with her paws on his shoulders she began to tear at it. She would fall back with a piece of food in her mouth, then she would jump again, sinking her fangs into the ropes, and snatching a few pieces of meat she would fall back again, and once more spring forward. She was tearing the face with her teeth, and the whole collar had disappeared.

The old woman, motionless and silent, was watching eagerly. Then she chained the beast up again, made her fast for two more days, and began this strange exercise again.

For three months she trained her to this battle. She no longer chained her up, but just pointed to the dummy.

She had taught her to tear him up and to devour him without even hiding any food about his neck. Then, as a reward, she would give her a piece of sausage.

As soon as she would see the man, Semillante would begin to tremble, then she would look up to her mistress, who, lifting her finger, would cry "Go!"

When she thought that the proper time had come, the widow went to confession, and one Sunday morning she partook of communion with an ecstatic fervor; then, having put on men's clothes, looking like an old tramp, she struck a bargain with a Sardinian fisherman who carried her and her dog to the other side of the straits.

In a bag, she had a large piece of sausage. Semillante had had nothing to eat for two days. The old woman kept letting her smell the food, and goading her.

They got to Longosardi. The Corsican woman walked with a limp. She went to a baker's shop and asked for Nicolas Ravolati. He had taken up his old trade, that of carpenter. He was working alone at the back of his store.

The old woman opened the door and called:

"Say! Nicolas!"

He turned around; then she, releasing her dog, cried:

"Go, go! Eat him up! Eat him up!"

The maddened animal sprang for his throat. The man stretched out his arms, seized the dog and lolled to the ground. For a few seconds, he squirmed, beating the ground with his feet; then he stopped moving, while Semillante dug her fangs into his throat and tore it to ribbons. Two neighbors, seated before their door, remembered perfectly having seen an old beggar come out with a thin, black dog which was eating something its master was giving her.

At nightfall the old woman was home again. She slept well that night.

mehitabel's extensive past

by DON MARQUIS

(as told by archy the cockroach, who was once a vers libre poet,
and who could not work the capital letters on the typewriter
because he used the impact of his whole body to move one key.)

*Anyone who does not know archy the cock-roach
and mehitabel the alley cat and their many friends is un-
acquainted with the most famous ménage of the 1920's,
and really has missed an important part of our literature.
I can only give a sampling here: go read the rest yourself.*

mehitabel the cat claims that
she has a human soul
also and has transmigrated
from body to body and it
may be so boss you
remember i told you she accused
herself of being cleopatra once i
asked her about antony

anthony who she asked me are
you thinking of that
song about rowley and gammon and
spinach heigho for anthony rowley

no i said mark antony the
great roman the friend of
caesar surely cleopatra you
remember j caesar

listen archy she said i
have been so many different
people in my time and met
so many prominent gentlemen i
wont lie to you or stall i
do get my dates mixed sometimes
think of how much I have had a
chance to forget and i have
always made a point of not
carrying grudges over
from one life to the next archy

i have been
used something fierce in my time but
i am no bum sport archy
i am a free spirit archy i
look on myself as being
quite a romantic character oh the
queens i have been and the
swell feeds i have ate
a cockroach which you are
and a poet which you used to be
archy couldn't understand
my feelings at having come
down to this i have
had bids to elegant feeds where poets
and cockroaches would
neither be mentioned without a
laugh archy i have had
adventures but i
have never been an adventuress
one life up and the next life
down archy but always a lady
through it all and a
good mixer too always the
life of the party archy but never
anything vulgar always free footed
archy never tied down to

a job or housework yes looking
back on it all i can say is
i had some romantic
lives and some elegant times i
have seen better days archy but
whats the use of kicking kid its
all in the game like a gentleman
friend of mine used to say
toujours gai kid toujours gai he
was an elegant cat he used
to be a poet himself and he made up
some elegant poetry about me and him

lets hear it i said and
mehitabel recited

persian pussy from over the sea
demure and lazy and smug and fat
none of your ribbons and bells for me
ours is the zest of the alley cat
over the roofs from flat to flat
we prance with capers corybantic
what though a boot should break a slat
mehitabel us for the life romantic

we would rather be rowdy and gaunt and free
and dine on a diet of roach and rat

roach i said what do you
mean roach interrupting mehitabel
yes roach she said thats the
way my boy friend made it up
i climbed in amongst the typewriter
keys for she had an excited
look in her eyes go on mehitabel i
said feeling safer and she
resumed her elocution

we would rather be rowdy and gaunt and free
and dine on a diet of roach and rat

than slaves to a tame society
ours is the zest of the alley cat
fish heads freedom a frozen sprat
dug from the gutter with digits frantic
is better than bores and a fireside mat
mehitabel us for the life romantic

when the pendant moon in the leafless tree
clings and sways like a golden bat
i sing its light and my love for thee
ours is the zest of the alley cat
missiles around us fall rat a tat tat
but our shadows leap in a ribald antic
as over the fences the world cries scat
mehitabel us for the life romantic

persian princess i dont care that
for your pedigree traced by scribes pedantic
ours is the zest of the alley cat
mehitabel us for the life romantic

aint that high brow stuff
archy i always remembered it
but he was an elegant gent
even if he was a highbrow and a
regular bohemian archy him and
me went aboard a canal boat
one day and he got his head into
a pitcher of cream and couldn t get
it out and fell overboard
he came up once before he
drowned toujours gai kid he
gurgled and then sank for ever that
was always his words archy toujours
gai kid toujours gai i
have known some swell gents
in my time dearie

                              archy

Madame Jolicœur's Cat

by THOMAS A. JANVIER

Such a horrible man . . . such a clever cat. . . . Charming and light, and so French—as we like to think of France, before the war, before the turn of the century.

BEING somewhat of an age, and a widow of dignity—the late Monsieur Jolicœur has held the responsible position under Government of Ingénieur des Ponts et Chaussées—yet being also of a provocatively fresh plumpness, and a Marseillaise, it was of necessity that Madame Veuve Jolicœur, on being left lonely in the world save for the companionship of her adored Shah de Perse, should entertain expectations of the future that were antipodal and antagonistic: on the one hand, of an austere life suitable to a widow of a reasonable maturity and of an assured position; on the other hand, of a life, not austere, suitable to a widow still of a provocatively fresh plumpness and by birth a Marseillaise.

Had Madame Jolicœur possessed a severe temperament and a resolute mind—possessions inherently improbable, in view of her birthplace—she would have made her choice between these equally possible futures with a promptness and with a finality that would have left nothing at loose ends. So endowed, she would have emphasized her not excessive age by a slightly excessive gravity of dress and of deportment; and would have adorned it, and her dignified widowhood, by becoming dévote: and thereafter, clinging with a modest ostentation only to her piety, would have radiated, as time made its marches, an always increasingly exemplary grace. But as Madame Jolicœur did not possess a temperament that even bordered on severity, and as her mind was a sort that made itself up in at least twenty different directions in a single moment—as she was, in short,

an entirely typical and therefore an entirely delightful Provençale
—the situation was so much too much for her that, by the process
of formulating a great variety of irreconcilable conclusions, she left
everything at loose ends by not making any choice at all.

In effect, she simply stood attendant upon what the future had
in store for her: and meanwhile avowedly clung only, in default
of piety, to her adored Shah de Perse—to whom was given, as she
declared in disconsolate negligence of her still provocatively fresh
plumpness, all of the bestowable affection that remained in the
devastated recesses of her withered heart.

To preclude any possibility of compromising misunderstanding,
it is but just to Madame Jolicœur to explain at once that the personage thus in receipt of the contingent remainder of her blighted
affections—far from being, as his name would suggest, an Oriental
potentate temporarily domiciled in Marseille to whom she had
taken something more than a passing fancy—was a Persian superb
black cat; and a cat of such rare excellencies of character and of
acquirements as fully to deserve all of the affection that any heart
of the right sort—withered, or otherwise—was disposed to bestow
upon him.

Cats of his perfect beauty, of his perfect grace, possibly might be
found, Madame Jolicœur grudgingly admitted, in the Persian royal
catteries; but nowhere else in the Orient, and nowhere at all in the
Occident, she declared with an energetic conviction, possibly could
there be found a cat who even approached him in intellectual development, in wealth of interesting accomplishments, and, above
all, in natural sweetness of disposition—a sweetness so marked that
even under extreme provocation he never had been known to thrust
out an angry paw. This is not to say that the Shah de Perse was a
characterless cat, a lymphatic nonentity. On occasion—usually in
connection with food that was distasteful to him—he could have
his resentments; but they were manifested always with a dignified
restraint. His nearest approach to ill-mannered abruptness was to
bat with a contemptuous paw the offending morsel from his plate;
which brusque act he followed by fixing upon the bestower of unworthy food a coldly, but always politely, contemptuous stare. Ordinarily, however, his displeasure—in the matter of unsuitable food,
or in other matters—was exhibited by no more overt action than his

retirement to a corner—he had his choices in corners, governed by
the intensity of his feelings—and there seating himself with his back
turned scornfully to an offending world. Even in his kindliest corner,
on such occasions, the expression of his scornful back was as a whole
volume of wingéd words!

But the rare little cat tantrums of the Shah de Perse—if to his so
gentle excesses may be applied so strong a term—were but as sun-
spots on the effulgence of his otherwise constant amiability. His reg-
nant desires, by which his worthy little life was governed, were to
love and to please. He was the most cuddlesome cat, Madame Jolicœur unhesitatingly asserted, that ever had lived; and he had a purr
—softly thunderous and winningly affectionate—that was in keeping with his cuddlesome ways. When, of his own volition, he would
jump into her abundant lap and go to burrowing with his little soft
round head beneath her soft round elbows, the while gurglingly
purring forth his love for her, Madame Jolicœur, quite justifiably,
at times was moved to tears. Equally was his sweet nature exhibited
in his always eager willingness to show off his little train of cat accomplishments. He would give his paw with a courteous grace to
any lady or gentleman—he drew the caste line rigidly—who asked
for it. For his mistress, he would spring to a considerable height and
clutch with his two soft paws—never by any mistake scratching—
her outstretched wrist, and so would remain suspended while he
delicately nibbled from between her fingers her edible offering.
For her, he would make an almost painfully real pretence of being
a dead cat: extending himself upon the rug with an exaggeratedly
death-like rigidity—and so remaining until her command to be alive
again brought him briskly to rub himself, rising on his hind legs and
purring mellowly, against her comfortable knees.

All of these interesting tricks, with various others that may be
passed over, he would perform with a lively zest whenever set at
them by a mere word of prompting; but his most notable trick was
a game in which he engaged with his mistress not at word of command, but—such was his intelligence—simply upon her setting the
signal for it. The signal was a close-fitting white cap—to be quite
frank, a night-cap—that she tied upon her head when it was desired that the game should be played.

It was of the game that Madame Jolicœur should assume her cap with an air of detachment and aloofness: as though no such entity as the Shah de Perse existed, and with an insisted-upon disregard of the fact that he was watching her alertly with his great golden eyes. Equally was it of the game that the Shah de Perse should affect— save for his alert watching—a like disregard of the doings of Madame Jolicœur: usually by an ostentatious pretence of washing his up-raised hind leg, or by a like pretence of scrubbing his ears. These conventions duly having been observed, Madame Jolicœur would seat herself in her especial easy-chair, above the relatively high back of which her night-capped head a little rose. Being so seated, always with the air of aloofness and detachment, she would take a book from the table and make a show of becoming absorbed in its contents. Matters being thus advanced, the Shah de Perse would make a show of becoming absorbed in searchings for an imaginary mouse —but so would conduct his fictitious quest for that supposititious animal as eventually to achieve for himself a strategic position close behind Madame Jolicœur's chair. Then, dramatically, the pleasing end of the game would come: as the Shah de Perse—leaping with the distinguishing grace and lightness of his Persian race—would flash upward and "surprise" Madame Jolicœur by crowning her white-capped head with his small black person, all a-shake with triumphant purrs! It was a charming little comedy—and so well understood by the Shah de Perse that he never ventured to essay it under other, and more intimate, conditions of night-cap use; even as he never failed to engage in it with spirit when his white lure properly was set for him above the back of Madame Jolicœur's chair. It was as though to the Shah de Perse the white night-cap of Madame Jolicœur, displayed in accordance with the rules of the game, were an oriflamme: akin to, but in minor points differing from, the helmet of Navarre.

Being such a cat, it will be perceived that Madame Jolicœur had reason in her avowed intention to bestow upon him all of the bestowable affection remnant in her withered heart's devastated recesses; and, equally, that she would not be wholly desolate, having such a cat to comfort her, while standing impartially attendant upon the decrees of fate.

To assert that any woman not conspicuously old and quite conspicuously of a fresh plumpness could be left in any city isolate, save for a cat's company, while the fates were spinning new threads for her, would be to put a severe strain upon credulity. To make that assertion specifically of Madame Jolicœur, and specifically—of all cities in the world!—of Marseille, would be to strain credulity fairly to the breaking point. On the other hand, to assert that Madame Jolicœur, in defence of her isolation, was disposed to plant machine-guns in the doorway of her dwelling—a house of modest elegance on the Pavé d'Amour, at the crossing of the Rue Bausset—would be to go too far. Nor indeed—aside from the fact that the presence of such engines of destruction would not have been tolerated by the other residents of the quietly respectable Pavé d'Amour—was Madame Jolicœur herself, as has been intimated, temperamentally inclined to go to such lengths as machine-guns in maintenance of her somewhat waveringly desired privacy in a merely cat-enlivened solitude.

Between these widely separated extremes of conjectural possibility lay the mediate truth of the matter: which truth—thus resembling precious gold in its valueless rock matrix—lay embedded in, and was to be extracted from, the irresponsible utterances of the double row of loosely hung tongues, always at hot wagging, ranged along the two sides of the Rue Bausset.

Madame Jouval, a milliner of repute—delivering herself with the generosity due to a good customer from whom an order for a trousseau was a not unremote possibility, yet with the acumen perfected by her professional experiences—summed her views of the situation, in talk with Madame Vic, proprietor of the Vic bakery, in these words: "It is of the convenances, and equally is it of her own melancholy necessities, that this poor Madame retires for a season to sorrow in a suitable seclusion in the company of her sympathetic cat. Only in such retreat can she give vent fitly to her desolating grief. But after storm comes sunshine: and I am happily assured by her less despairing appearance, and by the new mourning that I have been making for her, that even now, from the bottomless depth of her affliction, she looks beyond the storm."

"I well believe it!" snapped Madame Vic. "That the appearance of Madame Jolicœur at any time has been despairing is a matter that has escaped my notice. As to the mourning that she now wears, it is a defiance of all propriety. Why, with no more than that of colour in her frock"—Madame Vic upheld her thumb and finger infinitesimally separated—"and with a mere pin-point of a flower in her bonnet, she would be fit for the opera!"

Madame Vic spoke with a caustic bitterness that had its roots. Her own venture in second marriage had been catastrophic—so catastrophic that her neglected bakery had gone very much to the bad. Still more closely to the point, Madame Jolicœur—incident to finding entomologic specimens misplaced in her breakfast-rolls—had taken the leading part in an interchange of incivilities with the bakery's proprietor, and had withdrawn from it her custom.

"And even were her mournings not a flouting of her short year of widowhood," continued Madame Vic, with an acrimony that abbreviated the term of widowhood most unfairly—"the scores of eligible suitors who openly come streaming to her door, and are welcomed there, are as trumpets proclaiming her audacious intentions and her indecorous desires. Even Monsieur Brisson is in that outrageous procession! Is it not enough that she should entice a repulsively bald-headed notary and an old rake of a major to make their brazen advances, without suffering this anatomy of a pharmacien to come treading on their heels?—he with his hands imbrued in the life-blood of the unhappy old woman whom his mismade prescription sent in agony to the tomb! Pah! I have no patience with her! She and her grief and her seclusion and her sympathetic cat, indeed! It all is a tragedy of indiscretion—that shapes itself as a revolting farce!"

It will be observed that Madame Vic, in framing her bill of particulars, practically reduced her alleged scores of Madame Jolicœur's suitors to precisely two—since the bad third was handicapped so heavily by that notorious matter of the mismade prescription as to be a negligible quantity, quite out of the race. Indeed, it was only the preposterous temerity of Monsieur Brisson—despairingly clutching at any chance to retrieve his broken fortunes—that put him in the running at all. With the others, in such slighting terms referred to by Madame Vic—Monsieur Peloux, a notary of standing, and the Major Gontard, of the Twenty-ninth of the Line—the case was different. It had its sides.

"That this worthy lady reasonably may desire again to wed," declared Monsieur Fromagin, actual proprietor of the Épicerie Russe—an establishment liberally patronized by Madame Jolicœur —"is as true as that when she goes to make her choosings between these estimable gentlemen she cannot make a choice that is wrong."

Madame Gauthier, a clear-starcher of position, to whom Monsieur Fromagin thus addressed himself, was less broadly positive. "That is a matter of opinion," she answered; and added: "To go no further than the very beginning, Monsieur should perceive that her choice has exactly fifty chances in the hundred of going wrong: lying, as it does, between a meagre, sallow-faced creature of a death-white baldness, and a fine big pattern of a man, strong and ruddy, with a close-clipped but abundant thatch on his head, and a moustache that admittedly is superb!"

"Ah, there speaks the woman!" said Monsieur Fromagin, with a patronizing smile distinctly irritating. "Madame will recognize— if she will but bring herself to look a little beyond the mere outside —that what I have advanced is not a matter of opinion but of fact. Observe: Here is Monsieur Peloux to whose trifling leanness and aristocratic baldness the thoughtful give no attention—easily a notary in the very first rank. As we all know, his services are sought in cases of the most exigent importance—"

"For example," interrupted Madame Gauthier, "the case of the insurance solicitor, in whose countless defraudings my own brother was a sufferer: a creature of a vileness, whose deserts were unnumbered ages of dungeons—and who, thanks to the chicaneries of Monsieur Peloux, at this moment walks free as air!"

"It is of the professional duty of advocates," replied Monsieur Fromagin, sententiously, "to defend their clients; on the successful discharge of that duty—irrespective of minor details—depends their fame. Madame neglects the fact that Monsieur Peloux, by his masterly conduct of the case that she specifies, won for himself from his legal colleagues an immense applause."

"The more shame to his legal colleagues!" commented Madame Gauthier curtly.

"But leaving that affair quite aside," continued Monsieur Fromagin airily, but with insistence, "here is this notable advocate who reposes his important homages at Madame Jolicœur's feet: he a man of an age that is suitable, without being excessive; who has in the community an assured position; whose more than moderate wealth is known. I insist, therefore, that should she accept his homages she would do well."

"And I insist," declared Madame Gauthier stoutly, "that should she turn her back upon the Major Gontard she would do most ill!"

"Madame a little disregards my premises," Monsieur Fromagin spoke in a tone of forbearance, "and therefore a little argues—it is the privilege of her sex—against the air. Distinctly, I do not exclude from Madame Jolicœur's choice that gallant Major: whose rank—now approaching him to the command of a regiment, and fairly equalling the position at the bar achieved by Monsieur Peloux—has been won, grade by grade, by deeds of valour in his African campaignings which have made him conspicuous even in the army that stands first in such matters of all the armies of the world. Moreover —although, admittedly, in that way Monsieur Peloux makes a better showing—he is of an easy affluence. On the Camargue he has his excellent estate in vines, from which comes a revenue more than sufficing to satisfy more than modest wants. At Les Martigues he has his charming coquette villa, smothered in the flowers of his own planting, to which at present he makes his agreeable escapes from his military duties; and in which, when his retreat is taken, he will pass softly his sunset years. With these substantial points in his favour, the standing of the Major Gontard in this matter practically is of a parity with the standing of Monsieur Peloux. Equally, both are worthy of Madame Jolicœur's consideration: both being able to continue her in the life of elegant comfort to which she is accustomed; and both being on a social plane—it is of her level accurately —to which the widow of an ingénieur des ponts et chaussées neither steps up nor steps down. Having now made clear, I trust, my reasonings, I repeat the proposition with which Madame took issue: When Madame Jolicœur goes to make her choosings between these estimable gentlemen she cannot make a choice that is wrong."

"And I repeat, Monsieur," said Madame Gauthier, lifting her basket from the counter, "that in making her choosings Madame Jolicœur either goes to raise herself to the heights of a matured happiness, or to plunge herself into bald-headed abysses of despair. Yes, Monsieur, that far apart are her choosings!" And Madame Gauthier added, in communion with herself as she passed to the street with her basket: "As for me, it would be that adorable Major by a thousand times!"

As was of reason, since hers was the first place in the matter, Madame Jolicœur herself carried on debatings—in the portion of her heart that had escaped complete devastation—identical in essence with the debatings of her case which went up and down the Rue Bausset.

Not having become dévote—in the year and more of opportunity open to her for a turn in that direction—one horn of her original dilemma had been eliminated, so to say, by atrophy. Being neglected, it had withered: with the practical result that out of her very indecisions had come a decisive choice. But to her new dilemma, of which the horns were the Major and the Notary—in the privacy of her secret thoughts she made no bones of admitting that this dilemma confronted her—the atrophying process was not applicable; at least, not until it could be applied with a sharp finality. Too long dallied with, it very well might lead to the atrophy of both of them in dudgeon; and thence onward, conceivably, to her being left to cling only to the Shah de Perse for all the remainder of her days.

Therefore, to the avoidance of that too radical conclusion, Madame Jolicœur engaged in her debatings briskly: offering to herself, in effect, the balanced arguments advanced by Monsieur Fromagin in favour equally of Monsieur Peloux and of the Major Gontard; taking as her own, with moderating exceptions and emendations, the views of Madame Gauthier as to the meagreness and pallid baldness of the one and the sturdiness and gallant bearing of the other; considering, from the standpoint of her own personal knowledge in the premises, the Notary's disposition toward a secretive reticence that bordered upon severity, in contrast with the cordially frank and debonair temperament of the Major; and, at the back of all, keeping well in mind the fundamental truths that opportunity ever is evanescent and that time ever is on the wing.

As the result of her debatings, and not less as the result of experience gained in her earlier campaigning, Madame Jolicœur took up a strategic position nicely calculated to inflame the desire for, by assuming the uselessness of, an assault. In set terms, confirming par-

ticularly her earliér and more general avowal, she declared equally
to the Major and to the Notary that absolutely the whole of her
bestowable affection—of the remnant in her withered heart avail-
able for distribution—was bestowed upon the Shah de Perse: and
so, with an alluring nonchalance, left them to draw the logical conclusion that their strivings to win that desirable quantity were idle
—since a definite disposition of it already had been made.

The reply of the Major Gontard to this declaration was in keeping with his known amiability, but also was in keeping with his
military habit of command. "Assuredly," he said, "Madame shall
continue to bestow, within reason, her affections upon Monsieur le
Shah; and with them that brave animal—he is a cat of ten thousand
—shall have my affections as well. Already, knowing my feeling
for him, we are friends—as Madame shall see to her own convincing." Addressing himself in tones of kindly persuasion to the Shah
de Perse, he added: "Viens, Monsieur!"—whereupon the Shah de
Perse instantly jumped himself to the Major's knee and broke forth,
in response to a savant rubbing of his soft little jowls, into his
gurgling purr. "Voilà, Madame!" continued the Major. "It is to be
perceived that we have our good understandings, the Shah de Perse
and I. That we all shall live happily together tells itself without
words. But observe"—of a sudden the voice of the Major thrilled
with a deep earnestness, and his style of address changed to a familiarity that only the intensity of his feeling condoned—"I am resolved
that to me, above all, shall be given thy dear affections. Thou shalt
give me the perfect flower of them—of that fact rest thou assured.
In thy heart I am to be the very first—even as in my heart thou thyself art the very first of all the world. In Africa I have had my suc-
cesses in my conquests and holdings of fortresses. Believe me, I
shall have an equal success in conquering and in holding the sweet-
est fortress in France!"

Certainly, the Major Gontard had a bold way with him. But that
it had its attractions, not to say its compellings, Madame Jolicœur
could not honestly deny.

On the part of the Notary—whose disposition, fostered by his
profession, was toward subtlety rather than toward boldness—
Madame Jolicœur's declaration of cat rights was received with no
such belligerent blare of trumpets and beat of drums. He met it with

a light show of banter—beneath which, to come to the surface later, lay hidden dark thoughts.

"Madame makes an excellent pleasantry," he said with a smile of the blandest. "Without doubt, not a very flattering pleasantry— but I know that her denial of me in favour of her cat is but a jesting at which we both may laugh. And we may laugh together the better because, in the roots of her jesting, we have our sympathies. I also have an intensity of affection for cats"—to be just to Monsieur Peloux, who loathed cats, it must be said that he gulped as he made this flagrantly untruthful statement—"and with this admirable cat, so dear to Madame, it goes to make itself that we speedily become enduring friends."

Curiously enough—a mere coincidence, of course—as the Notary uttered these words so sharply at points with veracity, in the very moment of them, the Shah de Perse stiffly retired into his sulkiest corner and turned what had every appearance of being a scornful back upon the world.

Judiciously ignoring this inopportunely equivocal incident, Monsieur Peloux reverted to the matter in chief and concluded his deliverance in these words: "I well understand, I repeat, that Madame for the moment makes a comedy of herself and of her cat for my amusing. But I persuade myself that her droll fancyings will not be lasting, and that she will be serious with me in the end. Until then —and then most of all—I am at her feet humbly: an unworthy, but a very earnest, suppliant for her good-will. Should she have the cruelty to refuse my supplication, it will remain with me to die in an unmerited despair!"

Certainly, this was an appeal—of a sort. But even without perceiving the mitigating subtlety of its comminative final clause—so skilfully worded as to leave Monsieur Peloux free to bring off his threatened unmeritedly despairing death quite at his own convenience—Madame Jolicœur did not find it satisfying. In contrast with the Major Gontard's ringingly audacious declarations of his habits in dealing with fortresses, she felt that it lacked force. And, also—this, of course, was a sheer weakness—she permitted herself to be influenced appreciably by the indicated preferences of the Shah de Perse: who had jumped to the knee of the Major with an

affectionate alacrity; and who undeniably had turned on the Notary
—either by chance or by intention—a back of scorn.

As the general outcome of these several developments, Madame
Jolicœur's debatings came to have in them—if I so may state the
trend of her mental activities—fewer bald heads and more moustaches; and her never severely set purpose to abide in a loneliness relieved only by the Shah de Perse was abandoned root and branch.

While Madame Jolicœur continued her debatings—which, in their
modified form, manifestly were approaching her to conclusions—
water was running under bridges elsewhere.

In effect, her hesitancies produced a period of suspense that gave
opportunity for, and by the exasperating delay of it stimulated, the
resolution of the Notary's dark thoughts into darker deeds. With
reason, he did not accept at its face value Madame Jolicœur's declaration touching the permanent bestowal of her remnant affections;
but he did believe that there was enough in it to make the Shah de
Perse a delaying obstacle to his own acquisition of them. When ob-
stacles got in this gentleman's way it was his habit to kick them out
of it—a habit that had not been unduly stunted by half a lifetime
of successful practice at the criminal bar.

Because of his professional relations with them, Monsieur Peloux
had an extensive acquaintance among criminals of varying shades of
intensity—at times, in his dubious doings, they could be useful to him
—hidden away in the shadowy nooks and corners of the city; and he
also had his emissaries through whom they could be reached. All the
conditions thus standing attendant upon his convenience, it was a
facile matter for him to make an appointment with one of these
disreputables at a cabaret of bad record in the Quartier de la Tour-
ette: a region—bordering upon the north side of the Vieux Port—
that is at once the oldest and the foulest quarter of Marseille.

In going to keep this appointment—as was his habit on such occasions, in avoidance of possible spying upon his movements—he
went deviously: taking a cab to the Bassin de Carènage, as though
some maritime matter engaged him, and thence making the transit
of the Vieux Port in a bateau mouche. It was while crossing in the
ferryboat that a sudden shuddering beset him: as he perceived with

horror—but without repentance—the pit into which he descended. In his previous, always professional, meetings with criminals his position had been that of unassailable dominance. In his pending meeting—since he himself would be not only a criminal but an inciter to crime—he would be, in the essence of the matter, the under dog. Beneath his seemly black hat his bald head went whiter than even its normal deathly whiteness, and perspiration started from its every pore. Almost with a groan, he removed his hat and dried with his handkerchief what were in a way his tears of shame.

Over the interview between Monsieur Peloux and his hireling —cheerfully moistened, on the side of the hireling, with absinthe of a vileness in keeping with its place of purchase—decency demands the partial drawing of a veil. In brief, Monsieur Peloux—his guilty eyes averted, the shame-tears streaming afresh from his bald head —presented his criminal demand and stated the sum that he would pay for its gratification. This sum—being in keeping with his own estimate of what it paid for—was so much in excess of the hireling's views concerning the value of a mere cat-killing that he fairly jumped at it.

"Be not disturbed, Monsieur!" he replied, with the fervour of one really grateful, and with the expansive extravagance of a Marseillais keyed up with exceptionally bad absinthe. "Be not disturbed in the smallest! In this very coming moment this camel of a cat shall die a thousand deaths; and in but another moment immeasurable quantities of salt and ashes shall obliterate his justly despicable grave! To an instant accomplishment of Monsieur's wishes I pledge wholeheartedly the word of an honest man."

Actually—barring the number of deaths to be inflicted on the Shah de Perse, and the needlessly defiling concealment of his burial-place—this radical treatment of the matter was precisely what Monsieur Peloux desired; and what, in terms of innuendo and euphuism, he had asked for. But the brutal frankness of the hireling, and his evident delight in sinning for good wages, came as an arousing shock to the enfeebled remnant of the Notary's better nature—with a resulting vacillation of purpose to which he would have risen superior had he been longer habituated to the ways of crime.

"No! No!" he said weakly. "I did not mean that—by no means all of that. At least—that is to say—you will understand me, my good man, that enough will be done if you remove the cat from Marseille. Yes, that is what I mean—take it somewhere. Take it to Cassis, to Arles, to Avignon—where you will—and leave it there. The railway ticket is my charge—and, also, you have an extra napoléon for your refreshment by the way. Yes, that suffices. In a bag, you know—and soon!"

Returning across the Vieux Port in the bateau mouche, Monsieur Peloux no longer shuddered in dread of crime to be committed—his shuddering was for accomplished crime. On his bald head, unheeded, the gushing tears of shame accumulated in pools.

When leaves of absence permitted him to make retirements to his coquette little estate at Les Martigues, the Major Gontard was as another Cincinnatus: with the minor differences that the lickerish cookings of the brave Marthe—his old femme de ménage: a veritable protagonist among cooks, even in Provence—checked him on the side of severe simplicity; that he would have welcomed with effusion lictors, or others, come to announce his advance to a regiment; and that he made no use whatever of a plow.

In the matter of the plow, he had his excuses. His two or three acres of land lay on a hillside banked in tiny terraces—quite unsuited to the use of that implement—and the whole of his agricultural energies were given to the cultivation of flowers. Among his flowers, intelligently assisted by old Michel, he worked with a zeal bred of his affection for them; and after his workings, when the cool of evening was come, smoked his pipe refreshingly while seated on the vine-bowered estrade before his trim villa on the crest of the slope: the while sniffing with a just interest at the fumes of old Marthe's cookings, and placidly delighting in the ever-new beauties of the sunsets above the distant mountains and their near-by reflected beauties in the waters of the Étang de Berre.

Save in his professional relations with recalcitrant inhabitants of Northern Africa, he was of a gentle nature, this amiable warrior: ever kindly, when kindliness was deserved, in all his dealings with mankind. Equally, his benevolence was extended to the lower orders of animals—that it was understood, and reciprocated, the willing jumping of the Shah de Perse to his friendly knee made manifest—and was exhibited in practical ways. Naturally, he was a liberal contributor to the funds of the Société protectrice des animaux; and, what was more to the purpose, it was his well-rooted habit to do such protecting as was necessary, on his own account, when he chanced upon any suffering creature in trouble or in pain.

Possessing these commendable characteristics, it follows that the doings of the Major Gontard in the railway station at Pas de Lanciers—on the day sequent to the day on which Monsieur Peloux was the promoter of a criminal conspiracy—could not have been other than they were. Equally does it follow that his doings produced the doings of the man with the bag.

Pas de Lanciers is the little station at which one changes trains in going from Marseille to Les Martigues. Descending from a first-class carriage, the Major Gontard awaited the Martigues train—his leave was for two days, and his thoughts were engaged pleasantly with the breakfast that old Marthe would have ready for him and with plans for his flowers. From a third-class carriage descended the man with the bag, who also awaited the Martigues train. Presently —the two happening to come together in their saunterings up and down the platform—the Major's interest was aroused by observing that within the bag went on a persistent wriggling; and his interest was quickened into characteristic action when he heard from its interior, faintly but quite distinctly, a very pitiful half-strangled little mew!

"In another moment," said the Major, addressing the man sharply, "that cat will be suffocated. Open the bag instantly and give it air!"

"Pardon, Monsieur," replied the man, starting guiltily. "This excellent cat is not suffocating. In the bag it breathes freely with all its lungs. It is a pet cat, having the habitude to travel in this manner; and, because it is of a friendly disposition, it is accustomed thus to make its cheerful little remarks." By way of comment upon this explanation, there came from the bag another half-strangled mew that was not at all suggestive of cheerfulness. It was a faint miserable mew —that told of cat despair!

At that juncture a down train came in on the other side of the platform, a train on its way to Marseille.

"Thou art a brute!" said the Major, tersely. "I shall not suffer thy cruelties to continue!" As he spoke, he snatched away the bag from its uneasy possessor and applied himself to untying its confining cord. Oppressed by the fear that goes with evil-doing, the man hesitated for a moment before attempting to retrieve what constructively was his properly.

In that fateful moment the bag opened and a woebegone little black cat-head appeared; and then the whole of a delighted little black cat-body emerged—and cuddled with joy-purrs of recognition in its deliverer's arms! Within the sequent instant the recognition was mutual. "Thunder of guns!" cried the Major. "It is the Shah de Perse!"

Being thus caught red-handed, the hireling of Monsieur Peloux cowered. "Brigand!" continued the Major. "Thou hast ravished away this charming cat by the foulest of robberies. Thou art worse than the scum of Arab camp-followings. And if I had thee to myself, over there in the desert," he added grimly, "thou shouldst go the same way!"

All overawed by the Major's African attitude, the hireling took to whining. "Monsieur will believe me when I tell him that I am but an unhappy tool—I, an honest man whom a rich tempter, taking advantage of my unmerited poverty, has betrayed into crime. Monsieur himself shall judge me when I have told him all!" And then —with creditably imaginative variations on the theme of a hypothetical dying wife in combination with six supposititious starving children—the man came close enough to telling all to make clear that his backer in cat-stealing was Monsieur Peloux!

With a gasp of astonishment, the Major again took the word. "What matters it, animal, by whom thy crime was prompted? Thou art the perpetrator of it—and to thee comes punishment! Shackles and prisons are in store for thee! I shall—"

But what the Major Gontard had in mind to do toward assisting the march of retributive justice is immaterial—since he did not do it. Even as he spoke—in these terms of doom that qualifying conditions rendered doomless—the man suddenly dodged past him, bolted across the platform, jumped to the foot-board of a carriage of the just-starting train, cleverly bundled himself through an open window, and so was gone: leaving the Major standing lonely, with impotent rage filling his heart, and with the Shah de Perse all a purring cuddle in his arms!

Acting on a just impulse, the Major Gontard sped to the telegraph office. Two hours must pass before he could follow the miscreant; but the departed train ran express to Marseille, and telegraphic heading-off was possible. To his flowers, and to the romance of a breakfast that old Marthe by then was in the very act of preparing for him, his thoughts went in bitter relinquishment: but his purpose was stern! Plumping the Shah de Perse down anyway on the telegraph table, and seizing a pen fiercely, he began his writings. And then, of a sudden, an inspiration came to him that made him stop in his writings—and that changed his flames of anger into flames of joy.

His first act under the influence of this new and better emotion was to tear his half-finished dispatch into fragments. His second act was to assuage the needs, physical and psychical, of the Shah de Perse—near to collapse for lack of food and drink, and his little cat feelings hurt by his brusque deposition on the telegraph table—by carrying him tenderly to the buffet; and there—to the impolitely over-obvious amusement of the buffetière—purchasing cream without stint for the allaying of his famishings. To his feasting the Shah de Perse went with the avid energy begotten of his bag-compelled long fast. Dipping his little red tongue deep into the saucer, he lapped with a vigour that all cream-splattered his little black nose. Yet his admirable little cat manners were not forgotten: even in the very thick of his eager lappings—pathetically eager, in view of the cause of them—he purred forth gratefully, with a gurgling chokiness, his earnest little cat thanks.

As the Major Gontard watched this pleasing spectacle his heart was all aglow within him and his face was of a radiance comparable only with that of an Easter-morning sun. To himself he was saying: "It is a dream that has come to me! With the disgraced enemy in retreat, and with the Shah de Perse for my banner, it is that I hold victoriously the whole universe in the hollow of my hand!"

While stopping appreciably short of claiming for himself a clutch upon the universe, Monsieur Peloux also had his satisfactions on the evening of the day that had witnessed the enlèvement of the Shah de Perse. By his own eyes he knew certainly that that iniquitous kidnapping of a virtuous cat had been effected. In the morning the hireling had brought to him in his private office the unfortunate Shah de Perse—all unhappily bagged, and even then giving vent to his pathetic complainings—and had exhibited him, as a pièce justificatif, when making his demand for railway fare and the promised extra napoléon. In the mid-afternoon the hireling had returned, with the satisfying announcement that all was accomplished: that he had carried the cat to Pas de Lanciers, of an adequate remoteness, and there had left him with a person in need of a cat who received him willingly. Being literally true, this statement had in it so convincing a ring of sincerity that Monsieur Peloux paid down in full the blood-money and dismissed his bravo with commendation. Thereafter, being alone, he rubbed his hands—gladly thinking of what was in the way to happen in sequence to the permanent removal of this cat stumbling-block from his path. Although professionally accustomed to consider the possibilities of permutation, the known fact that petards at times are retroactive did not present itself to his mind.

And yet—being only an essayist in crime, still unhardened—certain compunctions beset him as he approached himself, on the to-be eventful evening of that eventful day, to the door of Madame Jolicœur's modestly elegant dwelling on the Pavé d'Amour. In the back of his head were justly self-condemnatory thoughts, to the general effect that he was a blackguard and deserved to be kicked. In the dominant front of his head, however, were thoughts of a more agreeable sort: of how he would find Madame Jolicœur all torn and rent by the bitter sorrow of her bereavement; of how he would pour into her harried heart a flood of sympathy by which that injured organ would be soothed and mollified; of how she would be lured along gently to requite his tender condolence with a softening gratitude—that presently would merge easily into the yet softer phrase of love! It was a well-made program, and it had its kernel of reason in his recognized ability to win bad causes—as that of the insurance solicitor—by emotional pleadings which in the same breath lured to lenience and made the intrinsic demerits of the cause obscure.

"Madame dines," was the announcement that met Monsieur Peloux when, in response to his ring, Madame Jolicœur's door was opened for him by a trim maid-servant. "But Madame already has continued so long her dining," added the maid-servant, with a glint in her eyes that escaped his preoccupied attention, "that in but an-

other instant must come the end. If M'sieu' will have the amiability
to await her in the salon, it will be for but a point of time!"

Between this maid-servant and Monsieur Peloux no love was lost.
Instinctively he was aware of, and resented, her views—practically
identical with those expressed by Madame Gauthier to Monsieur
Fromagin—touching his deserts as compared with the deserts of the
Major Gontard. Moreover, she had personal incentives to take her
revenges. From Monsieur Peloux, her only vail had been a miserable two-franc Christmas box. From the Major, as from a perpetually
verdant Christmas-tree, boxes of bonbons and five-franc pieces at
all times descended upon her in showers.

Without perceiving the curious smile that accompanied this young
person's curiously cordial invitation to enter, he accepted the invitation and was shown into the salon: where he seated himself—a left-
handedness of which he would have been incapable had he been less
perturbed—in Madame Jolicœur's own special chair. An anatomical
vagary of the Notary's meagre person was the undue shortness of
his body and the undue length of his legs. Because of this eccentricity
of proportion, his bald head rose above the back of the chair to a
height approximately identical with that of its normal occupant.

His waiting time—extending from its promised point to what
seemed to him to be a whole geographical meridian—went slowly.
To relieve it, he took a book from the table, and in a desultory manner turned the leaves. While thus perfunctorily engaged, he heard
the clicking of an opening door, and then the sound of voices: of
Madame Jolicœur's voice, and of a man's voice—which latter, coming nearer, he recognized beyond all doubting as the voice of the
Major Gontard. Of other voices there was not a sound: whence the
compromising fact was obvious that the two had gone through that
long dinner together, and alone! Knowing, as he did, Madame Jolicœur's habitual disposition toward the convenances—willingly to
be boiled in oil rather than in the smallest particular to abrade them
—he perceived that only two explanations of the situation were possible: either she had lapsed of a sudden into madness; or—the
thought was petrifying—the Major Gontard had won out in his
French campaigning on his known conquering African lines. The
cheerfully sane tone of the lady's voice forbade him to clutch at

the poor solace to be found in the first alternative—and so forced him to accept the second. Yielding for a moment to his emotions, the death-whiteness of his bald head taking on a still deathlier pallor, Monsieur Peloux buried his face in his hands and groaned.

In that moment of his obscured perception a little black personage trotted into the salon on soundless paws. Quite possibly, in his then overwrought condition, had Monsieur Peloux seen this personage enter he would have shrieked—in the confident belief that before him was a cat ghost! Pointedly, it was not a ghost. It was the happy little Shah de Perse himself—all a-frisk with the joy of his blessed home-coming and very much alive! Knowing, as I do, many of the mysterious ways of little cat souls, I even venture to believe that his overbubbling gladness largely was due to his sympathetic perception of the gladness that his home-coming had brought to two human hearts.

Certainly, all through that long dinner the owners of those hearts had done their best, by their pettings and their pamperings of him, to make him a participant in their deep happiness; and he, gratefully respondent, had made his affectionate thankings by going through all of his repertory of tricks—with one exception—again and again. Naturally, his great trick, while unexhibited, repeatedly had been referred to. Blushing delightfully, Madame Jolicœur had told about the night-cap that was a necessary part of it; and had promised— blushing still more delightfully—that at some time, in the very remote future, the Major should see it performed. For my own part, because of my knowledge of little cat souls, I am persuaded that the Shah de Perse, while missing the details of this love-laughing talk, did get into his head the general trend of it; and therefore did trot on in advance into the salon with his little cat mind full of the notion that Madame Jolicœur immediately would follow him—to seat herself, duly night-capped, book in hand, in signal for their game of surprises to begin.

Unconscious of the presence of the Shah de Perse, tortured by the gay tones of the approaching voices, clutching his book vengefully as though it were a throat, his bald head beaded with the sweat of agony and the pallor of it intensified by his poignant emotion, Monsieur Peloux sat rigid in Madame Jolicœur's chair!

"It is declared," said Monsieur Brisson, addressing himself to Madame Jouval, for whom he was in the act of preparing what was spoken of between them as "the tonic," a courteous euphuism, "that that villain Notary, aided by a bandit hired to his assistance, was engaged in administering poison to the cat; and that the brave animal, freeing itself from the bandit's holdings, tore to destruction the whole of his bald head—and then triumphantly escaped to its home!"

"A sight to see is that head of his!" replied Madame Jouval. "So swathed is it in bandages, that the turban of the Grand Turk is less!" Madame Jouval spoke in tones of satisfaction that were of reason —already she had held conferences with Madame Jolicœur in regard to the trousseau.

"And all," continued Monsieur Brisson, with rancour, "because of his jealousies of the cat's place in Madame Jolicœur's affections— the affections which he so hopelessly hoped, forgetful of his own repulsiveness, to win for himself!"

"Ah, she has done well, that dear lady," said Madame Jouval warmly. "As between the Notary—repulsive, as Monsieur justly terms him—and the charming Major, her instincts rightly have directed her. To her worthy cat, who aided in her choosing, she has reason to be grateful. Now her cruelly wounded heart will find solace. That she should wed again, and happily, was Heaven's will."

"It was the will of the baggage herself!" declared Monsieur Brisson with bitterness. "Hardly had she put on her travesty of a mourning than she began her oglings of whole armies of men!"

Aside from having confected with her own hands the mourning to which Monsieur Brisson referred so disparagingly, Madame Jouval was not one to hear calmly the ascription of the term baggage—the word has not lost in its native French, as it has lost in its naturalized English, its original epithetical intensity—to a patroness from whom she was in the very article of receiving an order for an exceptionally rich trousseau. Naturally, she bristled. "Monsieur must admit at least," she said sharply, "that her oglings did not come in his direction;" and with an irritatingly smooth sweetness added: "As to the dealings of Monsieur Peloux with the cat, Monsieur doubtless speaks with an assured knowledge. Remembering, as we all do, the affair of the unhappy old woman, it is easy to perceive that to Monsieur, above all others, any one in need of poisonings would come!"

The thrust was so keen that for the moment Monsieur Brisson met it only with a savage glare. Then the bottle that he handed to Madame Jouval inspired him with an answer. "Madame is in error," he said with politeness. "For poisons it is possible to go variously elsewhere—as, for example, to Madame's tongue." Had he stopped with that retort courteous, but also searching, he would have done well. He did ill by adding to it the retort brutal: "But that old women of necessity come to me for their hair-dyes is another matter. That much I grant to Madame with all good will."

Admirably restraining herself, Madame Jouval replied in tones of sympathy: "Monsieur receives my commiserations in his misfortunes." Losing a large part of her restraint, she continued, her eyes glittering: "Yet Monsieur's temperament clearly is over-sanguine. It is not less than a miracle of absurdity that he imagined: that he, weighted down with his infamous murderings of scores of innocent old women, had even a chance the most meagre of realizing his ridiculous aspirations of Madame Jolicœur's hand!" Snatching up her bottle and making for the door, without any restraint whatever she added: "Monsieur and his aspirations are a tragedy of stupidity —and equally are abounding in all the materials for a farce at the Palais de Cristal!"

Monsieur Brisson was cut off from opportunity to reply to this outburst by Madame Jouval's abrupt departure. His loss of opportunity had its advantages. An adequate reply to her discharge of such a volley of home truths would have been difficult to frame.

In the Vic bakery, between Madame Vic and Monsieur Fromagin, a discussion was in hand akin to that carried on between Monsieur Brisson and Madame Jouval—but marked with a somewhat nearer approach to accuracy in detail. Being sequent to the settlement of Monsieur Fromagin's monthly bill—always a matter of nettling dispute—it naturally tended to develop its own asperities.

"They say," observed Monsieur Fromagin, "that the cat—it was among his many tricks—had the habitude to jump on Madame Jolicœur's head when, for that purpose, she covered it with a nightcap. The use of the cat's claws on such a covering, and, also, her hair being very abundant—"

"*Very* abundant!" interjected Madame Vic; and added: "She, she is of a richness to buy wigs by the scores!"

"It was his custom, I say," continued Monsieur Fromagin with insistence, "to steady himself after his leap by using lightly his claws. His illusion in regard to the bald head of the Notary, it would seem, led to the catastrophe. Using his claws at first lightly, according to his habit, he went on to use them with a truly savage energy—when he found himself as on ice on that slippery eminence and verging to a fall."

"They say that his scalp was peeled away in strips and strings!" said Madame Vic. "And all the while that woman and that reprobate of a Major standing by in shrieks and roars of laughter—never raising a hand to save him from the beast's ferocities! The poor man has my sympathies. He, at least, in all his doings—I do not for a moment believe the story that he caused the cat to be stolen—observed rigidly the convenances: so recklessly shattered by Madame Jolicœur in her most compromising dinner with the Major alone!"

"But Madame forgets that their dinner was in celebration of their betrothal—following Madame Jolicœur's glad yielding, in just gratitude, when the Major heroically had rescued her deserving cat from the midst of its enemies and triumphantly had restored it to her arms."

"It is the man's part," responded Madame Vic, "to make the best of such matters. In the eyes of all right-minded women her conduct has been of a shamelessness from first to last: tossing and balancing the two of them for months upon months; luring them, and countless others with them, to her feet; declaring always that for her disgusting cat's sake she will have none of them; and ending by pretending brazenly that for her cat's sake she bestows herself—second-hand remnant that she is—on the handsomest man for his age, concerning his character it is well to be silent; that she could find for herself in all Marseille! On such actions, on such a woman, Monsieur, the saints in heaven look down with an agonized scorn!"

"Only those of the saints, Madame," said Monsieur Fromagin, warmly taking up the cudgels for his best customer, "as in the matter of second marriages, prior to their arrival in heaven, have had regrettable experiences. Equally, I venture to assert, a like qualification applies to a like attitude on earth. That Madame has her prejudices, incident to her misfortunes, is known."

"That Monsieur has his brutalities, incident to his regrettable bad breeding, also is known. His present offensiveness, however, passes all limits. I request him to remove himself from my sight." Madame Vic spoke with dignity.

Speaking with less dignity, but with conviction—as Monsieur Fromagin left the bakery—she added: "Monsieur, effectively, is a camel! I bestow upon him my disdain!"

Alice in Wonderland

by LEWIS CARROLL

Was the baby a pig? was the pig an animal? And what about the Cheshire cat? It doesn't really matter. No anthology of animal stories would be complete without some of the beasts that Alice found in Wonderland.

THE door led right into a large kitchen, which was full of smoke from one end to the other: the Duchess was sitting on a three-legged stool in the middle, nursing a baby: the cook was leaning over the fire, stirring a large cauldron which seemed to be full of soup.

"There's certainly too much pepper in that soup!" Alice said to herself, as well as she could for sneezing.

There was certainly too much of it in the *air*. Even the Duchess sneezed occasionally; and as for the baby, it was sneezing and howling alternately without a moment's pause. The only two creatures in the kitchen, that did *not* sneeze, were the cook, and a large cat, which was lying on the hearth and grinning from ear to ear.

"Please would you tell me," said Alice, a little timidly, for she was not quite sure whether it was good manners for her to speak first, "why your cat grins like that?"

"It's a Cheshire-Cat," said the Duchess, "and that's why. Pig!"

She said the last word with such sudden violence that Alice quite jumped; but she saw in another moment that it was addressed to the baby, and not to her, so she took courage, and went on again:—

"I didn't know that Cheshire-Cats always grinned; in fact, I didn't know that cats *could* grin."

"They all can," said the Duchess; "and most of 'em do."

"I don't know of any that do," Alice said very politely, feeling quite pleased to have got into a conversation.

"You don't know much," said the Duchess; "and that's a fact."

Alice did not at all like the tone of this remark, and thought it would be as well to introduce some other subject of conversation. While she was trying to fix on one, the cook took the cauldron of soup off the fire, and at once set to work throwing everything within her reach at the Duchess and the baby—the fire-irons came first; then followed a shower of sauce-pans, plates, and dishes. The Duchess took no notice of them even when they hit her; and the baby was howling so much already, that it was quite impossible to say whether the blows hurt it or not.

"Oh, *please* mind what you're doing!" cried Alice, jumping up and down in an agony of terror. "Oh, there goes his *precious* nose!" as an unusually large sauce-pan flew close by it, and very nearly carried it off.

"If everybody minded their own business," the Duchess said, in a hoarse growl, "the world would go round a deal faster than it does."

"Which would *not* be an advantage," said Alice, who felt very glad to get an opportunity of showing off a little of her knowledge. "Just think what work it would make with the day and night! You see the earth takes twenty-four hours to turn round on its axis—"

"Talking of axes," said the Duchess, "chop off her head!"

Alice glanced rather anxiously at the cook, to see if she meant to take the hint; but the cook was busily stirring the soup, and seemed not to be listening, so she went on again: "Twenty-four hours, I *think;* or is it twelve? I—"

"Oh, don't bother *me!*" said the Duchess. "I never could abide figures!" And with that she began nursing her child again, singing a sort of lullaby to it as she did so, and giving it a violent shake at the end of every line:—

> "Speak roughly to your little boy,
>   And beat him when he sneezes:
> He only does it to annoy,
>   Because he knows it teases."

> ### CHORUS
>
> (in which the cook and the baby joined):—
>
> "Wow! wow! wow!"

While the Duchess sang the second verse of the song, she kept tossing the baby violently up and down, and the poor little thing howled so, that Alice could hardly hear the words:—

"I speak severely to my boy,
    I beat him when he sneezes;
For he can thoroughly enjoy
    The pepper when he pleases!"

CHORUS

"Wow! wow! wow!"

"Here! You may nurse it a bit, if you like!" the Duchess said to Alice, flinging the baby at her as she spoke. "I must go and get ready to play croquet with the Queen," and she hurried out of the room. The cook threw a frying-pan after her as she went, but it just missed her.

Alice caught the baby with some difficulty, as it was a queer-shaped little creature, and held out its arms and legs in all directions, "just like a star-fish," thought Alice. The poor little thing was snorting like a steam-engine when she caught it, and kept doubling itself up and straightening itself out again, so that altogether, for the first minute or two, it was as much as she could do to hold it.

As soon as she had made out the proper way of nursing it (which was to twist it up into a sort of knot, and then keep tight hold of its right ear and left foot, so as to prevent its undoing itself), she carried it out into the open air. "If I don't take this child away with me," thought Alice, "they're sure to kill it in a day or two. Wouldn't it be murder to leave it behind?" She said the last words out loud, and the little thing grunted in reply (it had left off sneezing by this time). "Don't grunt," said Alice; "that's not at all a proper way of expressing yourself."

The baby grunted again, and Alice looked very anxiously into its face to see what was the matter with it. There could be no doubt that it had a *very* turn-up nose, much more like a snout than a real nose: also its eyes were getting extremely small for a baby: altogether Alice did not like the look of the thing at all. "But perhaps it was only sobbing," she thought, and looked into its eyes again, to see if there were any tears.

No, there were no tears. "If you're going to turn into a pig, my dear," said Alice, seriously, "I'll have nothing more to do with you. Mind now!" The poor little thing sobbed again (or grunted, it was impossible to say which), and they went on for some while in silence.

Alice was just beginning to think to herself, "Now, what am I to do with this creature, when I get it home?" when it grunted again, so violently, that she looked down into its face in some alarm. This time there could be *no* mistake about it: it was neither more nor less than a pig, and she felt that it would be quite absurd for her to carry it any further.

So she set the little creature down, and felt quite relieved to see it trot away quietly into the wood. "If it had grown up," she said to herself, "it would have made a dreadfully ugly child: but it makes rather a handsome pig, I think." And she began thinking over other children she knew, who might do very well as pigs, and was just saying to herself "if one only knew the right way to change them—" when she was a little startled by seeing the Cheshire-Cat sitting on a bough of a tree a few yards off.

The Cat only grinned when it saw Alice. It looked good-natured, she thought: still it had *very* long claws and a great many teeth, so she felt that it ought to be treated with respect.

"Cheshire-Puss," she began, rather timidly, as she did not at all know whether it would like the name: however, it only grinned a little wider. "Come, it's pleased so far," thought Alice, and she went on. "Would you tell me, please, which way I ought to go from here?"

"That depends a good deal on where you want to get to," said the Cat.

"I don't much care where—" said Alice.

"Then it doesn't matter which way you go," said the Cat.

"—so long as I get *somewhere*," Alice added as an explanation.

"Oh, you're sure to do that," said the Cat, "if you only walk long enough."

Alice felt that this could not be denied, so she tried another question. "What sort of people live about here?"

"In *that* direction," the Cat said, waving its right paw round, "lives a Hatter: and in *that* direction," waving the other paw, "lives a March Hare. Visit either you like: they're both mad."

"But I don't want to go among mad people," Alice remarked.

"Oh, you can't help that," said the Cat: "we're all mad here. I'm mad. You're mad."

"How do you know I'm mad?" said Alice.

"You must be," said the Cat, "or you wouldn't have come here."

Alice didn't think that proved it at all: however, she went on: "And how do you know that you're mad?"

"To begin with," said the Cat, "a dog's not mad. You grant that?"

"I suppose so," said Alice.

"Well, then," the Cat went on, "you see a dog growls when it's angry, and wags its tail when it's pleased. Now *I* growl when I'm pleased, and wag my tail when I'm angry. Therefore I'm mad."

"*I* call it purring, not growling," said Alice.

"Call it what you like," said the Cat. "Do you play croquet with the Queen to-day?"

"I should like it very much," said Alice, "but I haven't been invited yet."

"You'll see me there," said the Cat, and vanished.

Alice was not much surprised at this, she was getting so well used to queer things happening. While she was still looking at the place where it had been, it suddenly appeared again.

"By-the-bye, what became of the baby?" said the Cat. "I'd nearly forgotten to ask."

"It turned into a pig," Alice answered very quietly, just as if the Cat had come back in a natural way.

"I thought it would," said the Cat, and vanished again.

Alice waited a little, half expecting to see it again, but it did not appear, and after a minute or two she walked on in the direction in which the March Hare was said to live. "I've seen hatters before," she said to herself: "the March Hare will be much the most interesting, and perhaps, as this is May, it won't be raving mad—at least not so mad as it was in March." As she said this, she looked up, and there was the Cat again, sitting on a branch of a tree.

"Did you say 'pig,' or 'fig'?" said the Cat.

"I said 'pig,'" replied Alice; "and I wish you wouldn't keep appearing and vanishing so suddenly: you make one quite giddy!"

"All right," said the Cat; and this time it vanished quite slowly, beginning with the end of the tail, and ending with the grin, which remained some time after the rest of it had gone.

"Well! I've often seen a cat without a grin," thought Alice; "but a grin without a cat! It's the most curious thing I ever saw in all my life!"

The Urban Rat and the Suburban Rat

by GUY WETMORE CARRYL

The works of Guy Wetmore Carryl are out of print, and they should not be. His "Fables for the Frivolous" are all as amusing and as cleverly rhymed and as full of unexpected twists as this one. They are not all about animals, however.

A metropolitan rat invited
    His country cousin in town to dine;
The country cousin replied, "Delighted."
    And signed himself, "Sincerely thine."
The town rat treated the country cousin
            To half a dozen
            Kinds of wine.

He served him terrapin, kidneys devilled,
    And roasted partridge, and candied fruit;
In Little Neck Clams at first they revelled,
    And then in Pommery, *sec* and *brut;*
The country cousin exclaimed: "Such feeding
            Proclaims your breeding
            Beyond dispute!"

But just as, another bottle broaching,
    They came to chicken *en casserole*
A ravenous cat was heard approaching,
    And, passing his guest a finger-bowl,
The town rat murmured, "The feast is ended."
            And then descended
            The nearest hole.

His cousin followed him, helter-skelter,
  And, pausing beneath the pantry floor,
He glanced around at their dusty shelter
  And muttered, "This is a beastly bore.
My place as an epicure resigning,
        I'll try this dining
          In town no more.

"You must dine some night at my rustic cottage;
  I'll warn you now that it's simple fare:
A radish or two, a bowl of pottage,
  And the wine that's known as *ordinaire*,
But for holes I haven't to make a bee-line,
        No prowling feline
          Molests me there.

"You smile at the lot of a mere commuter,
  You think that my life is hard, mayhap,
But I'm sure than you I am far acuter:
  I ain't afraid of no cat nor trap."
The city rat could but meekly stammer,
        "Don't use such grammar,
          My worthy chap."

He dined next night with his poor relation,
  And caught dyspepsia, and lost his train,
He waited an hour in the lonely station,
  And said some things that were quite profane.
"I'll never," he cried, in tones complaining,
        "Try entertaining
          That rat again."

It's easy to make a memorandum
  About THE MORAL these verses teach:
De gustibus non est disputandum;
  The meaning of which Etruscan speech
Is wheresoever you're hunger quelling
        Pray keep your dwelling
          In easy reach.

Blue-Jays

by MARK TWAIN

Mark Twain needs no introduction to an American audience. He is one of our classics.

ANIMALS talk to each other, of course. There can be no question about that; but I suppose there are very few people who can understand them. I never knew but one man who could. I knew he could, however, because he told me so himself. He was a middle-aged, simple-hearted miner, who had lived in a lonely corner of California, among the woods and mountains, a good many years, and had studied the ways of his only neighbours, the beasts and the birds, until he believed he could accurately translate any remark which they made. This was Jim Baker. According to Jim Baker, some animals have only a limited education and use only very simple words, and scarcely ever a comparison or a flowery figure; whereas, certain other animals have a large vocabulary, a fine command of language and a ready and fluent delivery; consequently this latter talk a great deal; they like it; they are conscious of their talent, and they enjoy "showing off." Baker said that, after long and careful observation, he had come to the conclusion that the blue-jays were the best talkers he had found among birds and beasts. Said he:

"There's more *to* a blue-jay than any other creature. He has got more moods and more different kinds of feelings than other creatures; and, mind you, whatever a blue-jay feels, he can put into language. And no mere commonplace language, either, but rattling, out-and-out book-talk—and bristling with metaphor, too—just bristling! And as for command of language—why, *you* never see a blue-jay get stuck for a word. No man ever did. They just boil out of him! And another thing: I've noticed a good deal and there's no bird, or cow, or anything that uses as good grammar as a blue-jay. You may say a cat uses good grammar. Well, a cat does—but you let a cat get excited, once; you let a cat get to pulling fur with another cat on a shed, nights, and you'll hear grammar that will give you the lockjaw. Ignorant people think it's the *noise* which fighting cats make that is so aggravating, but it ain't so; it's the sickening grammar they use. Now I've never heard a jay use bad grammar but very seldom; and when they do, they are as ashamed as a human; they shut right down and leave.

"You may call a jay a bird. Well, so he is, in a measure—because he's got feathers on him, and don't belong to no church, perhaps; but otherwise he is just as much a human as you be. And I'll tell you for why. A jay's gifts, and instincts, and feelings, and interests cover the whole ground. A jay hasn't got any more principle than a Congressman. A jay will lie, a jay will steal, a jay will deceive, a jay will betray; and, four times out of five, a jay will go back on his solemnest promise. The sacredness of an obligation is a thing which you can't cram into no blue-jay's head. Now, on top of all this, there's another thing: a jay can out-swear any gentleman in the mines. You think a cat can swear. Well, a cat can; but you give a blue-jay a subject that calls for his reserve powers, and where is your cat? Don't talk to *me*—I know too much about this thing. And there's yet another thing: in the one little particular of scolding— just good, clean, out-and-out scolding—a blue-jay can lay over anything, human or divine. Yes, sir, a jay is everything that a man is. A jay can cry, a jay can laugh, a jay can feel shame, a jay can reason and plan and discuss, a jay likes gossip and scandal, a jay has got a sense of humour, a jay knows when he is an ass just as well as you do —maybe better. If a jay ain't human, he better take in his sign, that's all. Now I am going to tell you a perfectly true fact about some blue-jays.

"When I first begun to understand jay language correctly, there was a little incident happened here. Seven years ago, the last man in this region but me moved away. There stands his house—been empty ever since; a log house, with a plank roof—just one big room, and no more; no ceiling—nothing between the rafters and the floor. Well, one Sunday morning I was sitting out here in front of my cabin with my cat, taking the sun, and looking at the blue hills, and

listening to the leaves rustling so lonely in the trees, and thinking of
the home away yonder in the States, that I hadn't heard from in
thirteen years, when a blue-jay lit on that house, with an acorn in
his mouth, and says, 'Hello, I reckon I've struck something!' When
he spoke, the acorn fell out of his mouth and rolled down the
roof, of course, but he didn't care; his mind was all on the thing
he had struck. It was a knot-hole in the roof. He cocked his head to
one side, shut one eye and put the other one to the hole, like a 'possum looking down a jug; then he glanced up with his bright eyes,
gave a wink or two with his wings—which signifies gratification,
you understand—and says, 'It looks like a hole, it's located like a
hole—blamed if I don't believe it *is* a hole!'

"Then he cocked his head down and took another look; he glances
up perfectly joyful this time; winks his wings and his tail both, and
says, 'Oh, no, this ain't no fat thing, I reckon! If I ain't in luck!—
why, it's a perfectly elegant hole!' So he flew down and got that
acorn, and fetched it up and dropped it in, and was just tilting his
head back with the heavenliest smile on his face, when all of a sudden he was paralyzed into a listening attitude, and that smile faded
gradually out of his countenance like breath off'n a razor, and the
queerest look of surprise took its place. Then he says, 'Why, I didn't
hear it fall!' He cocked his eye at the hole again and took a long
look; raised up and shook his head; stepped around to the other side
of the hole, and took another look from that side; shook his head
again. He studied a while, then he just went into the *de*tails—walked
round and round the hole, and spied into it from every point of the
compass. No use. Now he took a thinking attitude on the comb
of the roof, and scratched the back of his head with his right foot
a minute, and finally says, 'Well, it's too many for *me*, that's certain;
must be a mighty long hole; however, I ain't got no time to fool
around here; I got to 'tend to business; I reckon it's all right—chance
it, anyway!'

"So he flew off and fetched another acorn and dropped it in, and
tried to flirt his eyes to the hole quick enough to see what become of
it, but he was too late. He held his eyes there as much as a minute;
then he raised up and sighed, and says, 'Confound it, I don't seem
to understand this thing, no way; however, I'll tackle her again.'
He fetched another acorn, and done his level best to see what

become of it, but he couldn't. He says, 'Well, *I* never struck no such hole as this before; I'm of the opinion it's a totally new kind of a hole.' Then he begun to get mad. He held in for a spell, walking up and down the comb of the roof, and shaking his head and muttering to himself; but his feelings got the upper hand of him presently, and he broke loose and cussed himself black in the face. I never see a bird take on so about a little thing. When he got through, he walks to the hole and looks in again for a half a minute; then he says, 'Well, you're a long hole, and a deep hole, and a mighty singular hole altogether—but I've started in to fill you, and I'm d——d if I *don't* fill you, if it takes a hundred years!'

"And with that, away he went. You never see a bird work so since you was born. He laid into his work like a nigger, and the way he hove acorns into that hole for about two hours and a half was one of the most exciting and astonishing spectacles I ever struck. He never stopped to take a look any more—he just hove 'em in, and went for more. Well, at last he could hardly flop his wings, he was so tuckered out. He comes a-dropping down, once more, sweating like an ice-pitcher, drops his acorn in and says, '*Now* I guess I've got the bulge on you by this time!' So he bent down for a look. If you'll believe me, when his head come up again he was just pale with rage. He says, 'I've shoveled acorns enough in there to keep the family thirty years, and if I can see a sign of one of 'em, I wish I may land in a museum with a belly full of sawdust in two minutes!'

"He just had strength enough to crawl up on to the comb and lean his back agin the chimbly, and then he collected his impressions and begun to free his mind. I see in a second that what I had mistook for profanity in the mines was only just the rudiments, as you may say.

"Another jay was going by, and heard him doing his devotions, and stops to inquire what was up. The sufferer told him the whole circumstance, and says, 'Now, yonder's the hole, and if you don't believe me, go and look for yourself.' So this fellow went and looked, and comes back and says, 'How many did you say you put in there?' 'Not any less than two tons,' says the sufferer. The other jay went and looked again. He couldn't seem to make it out, so he raised a yell, and three more jays come. They all examined the hole, they all made the sufferer tell it over again, then they all discussed it, and got off as many leather-headed opinions about it as an average crowd of humans could have done.

"They called in more jays; then more and more, till pretty soon this whole region 'peared to have a blue flush about it. There must have been five thousand of them; and such another jawing and disputing and ripping and cussing, you never heard. Every jay in the whole lot put his eye to the hole, and delivered a more chuckle-headed opinion about the mystery than the jay that went there before him. They examined the house all over, too. The door was standing half-open, and at last one old jay happened to go and light on it and look in. Of course, that knocked the mystery galley-west in a second. There lay the acorns, scattered all over the floor. He flopped his wings and raised a whoop. 'Come here!' he says, 'Come here, everybody; hang'd if this fool hasn't been trying to fill up a house with acorns!' They all came a-swooping down like a blue cloud, and as each fellow lit on the door and took a glance, the whole absurdity of the contract that that first jay had tackled hit him home, and he fell over backwards suffocating with laughter, and the next jay took his place and done the same.

"Well, sir, they roosted around here on the house-top and the trees for an hour, and guffawed over that thing like human beings. It ain't no use to tell me a blue-jay hasn't got a sense of humour, because I know better. And memory, too. They brought jays here from all over the United States to look down that hole, every summer for three years. Other birds, too. And they could all see the point, except an owl that come from Nova Scotia to visit the Yo Semite, and he took this thing in on his way back. He said he couldn't see anything funny in it. But then, he was a good deal disappointed about Yo Semite, too."

The Pope's Mule

by ALPHONSE DAUDET

They say the elephant remembers. . . . But this is the story of a mule, whose memory was equally remarkable, and whose revenge was prodigious.

O F ALL the pretty sayings, proverbs, adages, with which our Provençal peasantry decorate their discourse, I know of none more picturesque or more peculiar than this:—for fifteen leagues around my mill, when they speak of a spiteful and vindictive man, they say: "That fellow! distrust him! he's like the Pope's mule who kept her kick for seven years."

I tried for a long time to find out whence that proverb came, what that Pope's mule was, and why she kept her kick for seven years. No one could give me any information on the subject, not even Francet Mamaï, my old fife-player, though he knows his Provençal legends to the tips of his fingers. Francet thought, as I did, that there must be some ancient chronicle of Avignon behind it, but he had never heard of it otherwise than as a proverb.

"You won't find it anywhere except in the Grasshoppers' Library," said the old man, laughing.

The idea struck me as a good one; and as the Grasshoppers' Library is close at my door, I shut myself up there for over a week.

It is a wonderful library, admirably stocked, open to poets night and day, and served by little librarians with cymbals who make music for you all the time. I spent some delightful days there, and after a week of researches (on my back) I ended by discovering what I wanted, namely: the story of the mule and that famous kick which she kept for seven years. The tale is pretty, though rather naïve, and I shall try to tell it to you just as I read it yesterday in a manuscript colored by the weather, smelling of good dried lavender and tied with the Virgin's threads—as they call gossamer in these parts.

411

Whoso did not see Avignon in the days of the Popes has seen
nothing. For gayety, life, animation, the excitement of festivals,
never was a town like it. From morning till night there was nothing but processions, pilgrimages, streets strewn with flowers, draped
with tapestries, cardinals arriving by the Rhone, banners in the
breeze, galleys dressed in flags, the Pope's soldiers chanting Latin
on the squares, and the tinkling rattle of the begging friars; while
from garret to cellar of houses that pressed, humming, round the
great papal palace like bees around their hive, came the tick-tack of
lace-looms, the to-and-fro of shuttles weaving the gold thread of
chasubles, the tap-tap of the goldsmith's chasing-tools tapping on
the chalices, the tuning of choir-instruments at the lute-makers, the
songs of the spinners at their work; and above all this rose the sound
of bells, and always the echo of certain tambourines coming from
away down there on the bridge of Avignon. Because, with us, when
the people are happy they must dance—they must dance; and as in
those days the streets were too narrow for the *farandole,* fifes and
tambourines posted themselves on the bridge of Avignon in the
fresh breeze of the Rhone, and day and night folks danced, they
danced. Ah! the happy times! the happy town! Halberds that did
not wound, prisons where the wine was put to cool; no hunger, no
war. That's how the Popes of the Comtat governed their people; and
that's why their people so deeply regretted them.

There was one Pope especially, a good old man called Boniface.
Ah! that one, many were the tears shed in Avignon when he was
dead. He was so amiable, so affable a prince! He laughed so merrily
on the back of his mule! And when you passed him, were you only
a poor little gatherer of madder-roots, or the grand provost of the
town, he gave you his benediction so politely! A real Pope of
Yvetot, but a Yvetot of Provence, with something delicate in his
laugh, a sprig of sweet marjoram in his cardinal's cap, and never a
Jeanneton,—the only Jeanneton he was ever known to have, that
good Father, was his vineyard, his own little vineyard which he
planted himself, three leagues from Avignon, among the myrtles
of Château-Neuf.

Every Sunday, after vespers, the good man paid court to his vineyard; and when he was up there, sitting in the blessed sun, his mule

near him, his cardinals stretched out beneath the grapevines, he would order a flask of the wine of his own growth to be opened, —that beautiful wine, the color of rubies, which is now called the *Château-Neuf des Papes,* and he sipped it with sips, gazing at his vineyard tenderly. Then, the flask empty, the day fading, he rode back joyously to town, the Chapter following; and when he crossed the bridge of Avignon through the tambourines and the *farandoles,* his mule, set going by the music, paced along in a skipping little amble, while he himself beat time to the dance with his cap, which greatly scandalized the cardinals but made the people say: "Ah! the good prince! Ah! the kind Pope!"

What the Pope loved best in the world, next to his vineyard of Château-Neuf, was his mule. The good man doted on that animal. Every evening before he went to bed he went to see if the stable was locked, if nothing was lacking in the manger; and never did he rise from table without seeing with his own eyes the preparation of a great bowl of wine in the French fashion with sugar and spice, which he took to his mule himself, in spite of the remarks of his cardinals. It must be said that the animal was worth the trouble. She was a handsome black mule, with reddish points, sure-footed, hide shining, back broad and full, carrying proudly her thin little head decked out with pompons and ribbons, silver bells and streamers; gentle as an angel withal, innocent eyes, and two long ears, always shaking, which gave her the look of a downright good fellow. All Avignon respected her, and when she passed through the streets there were no civilities that the people did not pay her; for every one knew there was no better way to stand well at court, and that the Pope's mule, for all her innocent look, had led more than one man to fortune,—witness Tistet Védène and his amazing adventure.

This Tistet Védène was, in point of fact, an impudent young rogue, whom his father, Guy Védène, the goldsmith, had been forced to turn out of his house, because he would not work and only debauched the apprentices. For six months Tistet dragged his jacket through all the gutters of Avignon, but principally those near the papal palace; for the rascal had a notion in his head about the Pope's mule, and you shall now see what mischief was in it.

One day when his Holiness was riding all alone beneath the ramparts, behold our Tistet approaching him and saying, with his hands clasped in admiration:

"Ah! *mon Dieu*, Holy Father, what a fine mule you are riding! Just let me look at her. Ah! Pope, what a beautiful mule she is! The Emperor of Germany hasn't her equal."

And he stroked her and spoke to her softly as if to a pretty young lady:

"Come here, my treasure, my jewel, my pearl—"

And the good Pope, quite touched, said to himself:

"What a nice young fellow; how kind he is to my mule!"

And the next day what do you think happened? Tistet Védène changed his yellow jacket for a handsome lace alb, a purple silk hood, shoes with buckles; and he entered the household of the Pope, where no one had ever yet been admitted but sons of nobles and nephews of cardinals. That's what intriguing means! But Tistet was not satisfied with that.

Once in the Pope's service, the rascal continued the game he had played so successfully. Insolent to every one, he showed attentions and kindness to none but the mule, and he was always to be met with in the courtyards of the palace with a handful of oats, or a bunch of clover, shaking its pink blooms at the window of the Holy Father as if to say: "Hein! who's that for, hey?" Time and again this happened, so that, at last, the good Pope, who felt himself getting old, left to Tistet the care of looking after the stable and of carrying to the mule his bowl of wine,—which did not cause the cardinals to laugh.

Nor the mule either. For now, at the hour her wine was due she beheld half a dozen little pages of the household slipping hastily into the hay with their hoods and their laces; and then, soon after, a good warm smell of caramel and spices pervaded the stable, and Tistet Védène appeared bearing carefully the bowl of hot wine. Then the poor animal's martyrdom began.

That fragrant wine she loved, which kept her warm and gave her wings, they had the cruelty to bring it into her stall and let her smell of it; then, when her nostrils were full of the perfume, away! and the beautiful rosy liquor went down the throats of those young scamps! And not only did they steal her wine, but they were like devils, those young fellows, after they had drunk it. One pulled her ears, another her tail. Quiquet jumped on her back, Béluguet put his hat on her head, and not one of the rascals ever thought that with one good kick of her hind-legs the worthy animal could send them all to the polar star, and farther still if she chose. But no! you are not the Pope's mule for nothing—that mule of benedictions and plenary indulgences. The lads might do what they liked, she was never angry with them; it was only Tistet Védène whom she hated. He, indeed! when she felt him behind her, her hoofs itched; and reason enough too. That good-for-nothing Tistet played her such villainous tricks. He had such cruel ideas and inventions after drinking.

One day he took it into his head to make her go with him into the belfry, high up, very high up, to the peak of the palace! What I am telling you is no tale; two hundred thousand Provençal men and women saw it. Imagine the terror of that unfortunate mule, when, after turning for an hour, blindly, round a corkscrew staircase and climbing I don't know how many steps, she found herself all of a sudden on a platform blazing with light, while a thousand feet below her she saw a diminutive Avignon, the booths in the market no bigger than nuts, the Pope's soldiers moving about their barrack like little red ants, and down there, bright as a silver thread, a microscopic little bridge on which they were dancing, dancing. Ah! poor beast! what a panic! At the cry she gave, all the windows of the palace shook.

"What's the matter? what are they doing to my mule?" cried the good Pope, rushing out upon his balcony.

Tistet Védène was already in the courtyard pretending to weep and tear his hair.

"Ah! great Holy Father, what's the matter, indeed! *Mon Dieu!* What will become of us? There's your mule gone up to the belfry."

"All alone?"

"Yes, great Holy Father, all alone. Look up there, high up. Don't you see the tips of her ears pointing out—like two swallows?"

"Mercy!" cried the poor Pope, raising his eyes. "Why, she must have gone mad! She'll kill herself! Come down, come down, you luckless thing!"

Pécaïre! she wanted nothing so much as to come down. But how?
which way? The stairs? not to be thought of; they can be mounted,
those things; but as for going down! why, they are enough to break
one's legs a hundred times. The poor mule was in despair, and while
circling round and round the platform with her big eyes full of
vertigo she thought of Tistet Védène.

"Ah! bandit, if I only escape—what a kick tomorrow morning!"

That idea of a kick put some courage into her heart; without it
she never could have held good. . . . At last, they managed to save
her; but 'twas quite a serious affair. They had to get her down with
a derrick, ropes, and a sling. You can fancy what humiliation it was
for a Pope's mule to see herself suspended at that height, her four
hoofs swimming in the void like a cockchafer hanging to a string.
And all Avignon looking at her!

The unfortunate beast could not sleep at night. She fancied she
was still turning round and round that cursed platform while the
town laughed below, and again she thought of the infamous Tistet
and the fine kick of her heels she would let fly at him next day. Ah!
friends, what a kick! the dust of it would be seen as far as Pampérigouste.

Now, while this notable reception was being made ready for him
in the Pope's stable what do you think Tistet Védène was about?
He was descending the Rhone on a papal galley, singing as he went
his way to the Court of Naples with a troop of young nobles whom
the town of Avignon sent every year to Queen Jeanne to practise
diplomacy and fine manners. Tistet Védène was not noble; but the
Pope was bent on rewarding him for the care he had given to his
mule, and especially for the activity he displayed in saving her
from her perilous situation.

The mule was the disappointed party on the morrow!

"Ah! the bandit! he suspected something," she thought, shaking
her silver bells. "No matter for that, scoundrel; you'll find it when
you get back, that kick; I'll keep it for you!"

And she kept it for him.

After Tistet's departure the Pope's mule returned to her tranquil
way of life and her usual proceedings. No more Quiquet, no more
Béluguet in the stable. The good old days of the spiced wine came
back, and with them good-humor, long siestas, and the little gavotte

step as she crossed the bridge of Avignon. Nevertheless, since her adventure a certain coldness was shown to her in the town. Whisperings were heard as she passed, old people shook their heads, children laughed and pointed to the belfry. The good Pope himself no longer had quite the same confidence in his friend, and when he let himself go into a nice little nap on her back of a Sunday, returning from his vineyard, he always had this thought latent in his mind: "What if I should wake up there on the platform!" The mule felt this, and she suffered, but said nothing; only, whenever the name of Tistet Védène was uttered in her hearing, her long ears quivered, and she struck the iron of her shoes hard upon the pavement with a little snort.

Seven years went by. Then, at the end of those seven years, Tistet Védène returned from the Court of Naples. His time was not yet finished over there, but he had heard that the Pope's head mustard-bearer had died suddenly at Avignon, and as the place seemed a good one, he hurried back in haste to solicit it.

When this intriguing Védène entered the palace the Holy Father did not recognize him, he had grown so tall and so stout. It must also be said that the good Pope himself had grown older, and could not see much without spectacles.

Tistet was not abashed.

"What, great Holy Father! you don't remember me? It is I, Tistet Védène."

"Védène?"

"Why, yes, you know the one that took the wine to your mule."

"Ah! yes, yes,—I remember. A good little fellow, that Tistet Védène! And now, what do you want of me?"

"Oh! very little, great Holy Father. I came to ask— By the bye, have you still got her, that mule of yours? Is she well? Ah! good! I came to ask you for the place of the chief mustard-bearer who lately died."

"Mustard-bearer, you! Why, you are too young. How old are you?"

"Twenty-two, illustrious pontiff; just five years older than your mule. Ah! palm of God, what a fine beast she is! If you only knew how I love her, that mule,—how I pined for her in Italy! Won't you let me see her?"

"Yes, my son, you shall see her," said the worthy Pope, quite touched. "And as you love her so much I must have you live near her. Therefore, from this day I attach you to my person as chief mustard-bearer. My cardinals will cry out, but no matter! I'm used to that. Come and see me to-morrow, after vespers, and you shall receive the insignia of your rank in presence of the whole Chapter, and then I will show you the mule and you shall go to the vineyard with us, hey! hey!"

I need not tell you if Tistet Védène was content when he left the palace, and with what impatience he awaited the ceremony of the morrow. And yet there was one more impatient and more content than he: it was the mule. After Védène's return, until vespers on the following day that terrible animal never ceased to stuff herself with oats, and practise her heels on the wall behind her. She, too, was preparing for the ceremony.

Well, on the morrow, when vespers were said, Tistet Védène made his entry into the papal courtyard. All the grand clergy were there; the cardinals in their red robes, the devil's advocate in black velvet, the convent Abbots in their small mitres, the wardens of Saint-Agrico, the violet hoods of the Pope's household, the lower clergy also, the Pope's guard in full uniform, the three penitential brotherhoods, the hermits of Mont-Ventoux, with their sullen faces, and the little clerk who walks behind them with a bell, the flagellating friars naked to the waist, the ruddy sextons in judge's gowns, all, all, down to the givers of holy water, and the man who lights and him who puts out the candles—not one was missing. Ah! 'twas a fine ordination! Bells, firecrackers, sunshine, music, and always those frantic tambourines leading the *farandole* over there, on the bridge.

When Védène appeared in the midst of this great assembly, his fine bearing and handsome face sent a murmur of admiration through the crowd. He was truly a magnificent Provençal; but of the blond type, with thick hair curling at the tips, and a dainty little beard, that looked like slivers of fine metal fallen from the chisel of his father, the goldsmith. The rumor ran that the fingers of Queen Jeanne had sometimes played in the curls of that golden beard; and, in truth, the Sieur de Védène had the self-glorifying air and the abstracted look of men that queens have loved. On this day, in order to do honor to his native town, he had substituted for his Neapolitan clothes a tunic edged with pink, *à la Provençale,* and in his hood there quivered a tall feather of the Camargue ibis.

As soon as he entered the new official bowed with a gallant air, and approached the high portico where the Pope was waiting to give him the insignias of his rank, namely, a wooden spoon and a saffron coat. The mule was at the foot of the steps, saddled and bridled, all ready to go to the vineyard; as he passed beside her, Tistet Védène smiled pleasantly, and stopped to give her a friendly pat or two on the back, glancing, as he did so, out of the corner of his eye to see if the Pope noticed it. The position was just right, —the mule let fly her heels.

"There, take it, villain! Seven years have I kept it for thee!"

And she gave him so terrible a kick,—so terrible that even at Pampérigouste the smoke was seen, a whirlwind of blond dust, in which flew the feather of an ibis, and that was all that remained of the unfortunate Tistet Védène!

Mule kicks are not usually so destructive; but this was a papal mule; and then, just think! she had kept it for him for seven years. There is no finer example of ecclesiastical rancor.

The Oracle of the Dog

by GILBERT K. CHESTERTON

G. K. Chesterton's Father Brown stories rank with Conan Doyle's, with Edgar Allan Poe's, with a few others, as detective stories which are also literature. And this is also an animal story—about a dog, and a priest who knew what dogs could and could not do.

"YES," said Father Brown, "I always like a dog so long as he isn't spelled backwards."

Those who are quick in talking are not always quick in listening. Sometimes even their brilliancy produces a sort of stupidity. Father Brown's friend and companion was a young man with a stream of ideas and stories, an enthusiastic young man named Fiennes, with eager blue eyes and blond hair that seemed to be brushed back not merely with a hair-brush but with the wind of the world as he rushed through it. But he stopped in the torrent of his talk in a momentary bewilderment, before he saw the priest's very simple meaning.

"You mean that people make too much of them?" he said. "Well, I don't know. They're marvelous creatures. Sometimes I think they know a lot more than we do."

Father Brown said nothing; but continued to stroke the head of the big retriever in a half abstracted but apparently soothing fashion.

"Why," said Fiennes, warming again to his monologue, "there was a dog in the case I've come to see you about; what they call the 'Invisible Murderer Case,' you know. It's a strange story, but from my point of view the dog is about the strangest thing in it. Of course, there's the mystery of the crime itself, and how old Druce can have been killed by somebody else when he was all alone in the summer-house—"

The hand stroking the dog stopped for a moment in its rhythmic movement; and Father Brown said calmly,

"Oh, it was a summer-house, was it?"

"I thought you'd read all about it in the papers," answered Fiennes. "Stop a minute; I believe I've got a cutting that will give you all the particulars." He produced a strip of newspaper from his pocket and handed it to the priest who began to read it.

"Many mystery stories, about men murdered behind locked doors and windows and murderers escaping without means of entrance and exit, have come true in the course of the extraordinary events at Cranston on the coast of Yorkshire, where Colonel Druce was found stabbed from behind by a dagger that has entirely disappeared from the scene, and apparently even from the neighborhood. The summer-house in which he died was indeed accessible at one entrance—the ordinary doorway which looked down the central walk of the garden toward the house. But by a combination of events almost to be called a coincidence, it appears that both the path and the entrance were watched during the crucial time, and there is a chain of witnesses who confirm each other. The summer-house stands at the extreme end of the garden where there is no exit or entrance of any kind.

"The central garden path is a lane between two ranks of tall delphiniums, planted so close that a stray step off the path would leave its traces; and both path and plants run right up to the very mouth of the summer-house, so that no straying from that straight path could fail to be observed, and no other mode of entrance can be imagined.

"Oscar Floyd, secretary to the murdered man, testified that he had been in a position to overlook the whole garden from the time when Colonel Druce last appeared alive in the doorway to the time when he was found dead; as he, Floyd, had been on the top of a stepladder clipping the garden hedge. Janet Druce, the dead man's daughter, confirmed this, saying that she had sat on the terrace of the house throughout that time and had seen Floyd at his work. Touching some part of the time, this is again supported by Donald Druce, her brother, who overlooked the garden standing at his bedroom window in his dressing-gown, for he had risen late.

"Lastly the account is consistent with that given by Dr. Valentine, a neighbor, who called for a time to talk with Miss Druce on the terrace, and by the Colonel's solicitor, Mr. Aubrey Traill, who was apparently the last to see the murdered man alive—presumably with the exception of the murderer. All are agreed that the course of events is as follows: about half-past three in the afternoon Miss Druce went down the path to ask her father when he would like tea; but he said he did not want any and was waiting to see Traill, his lawyer, who was to be sent to him in the summer-house.

"The girl then came away and met Traill coming down the path; she directed him to her father and he went in as directed. About half an hour afterwards he came out again, the Colonel coming with him to the door and showing himself to all appearance in health and even in high spirits. He had been somewhat annoyed earlier in the day by his son's irregular hours, but seemed to recover his temper in a perfectly normal fashion; and had been rather markedly genial in receiving other visitors, including two of his nephews who came over for the day. But as these were out walking during the whole period of the tragedy, they had no evidence to give.

"It is said indeed that the Colonel was not on very good terms with Dr. Valentine, but that gentleman only had a brief interview with the daughter of the house, to whom he is supposed to be paying serious attentions. Traill, the solicitor, says he left the Colonel entirely alone in the summer-house, and this is confirmed by Floyd's bird's-eye view of the garden which showed nobody else passing the only entrance.

"Ten minutes later Miss Druce again went down the garden and had not reached the end of the path when she saw her father, who was conspicuous by his white linen coat, lying in a heap on the floor. She uttered a scream which brought others to the spot; and on entering the place they found the Colonel lying dead beside his basket chair which was also upset. Dr. Valentine, who was still in the immediate neighborhood, testified that the wound was made by some sort of stiletto, entering under the shoulder blade and piercing the heart. The police have searched the neighborhood for such a weapon but no trace of it can be found."

"So Colonel Druce wore a white coat, did he?" said Father Brown as he put down the paper.

"Trick he learned in the tropics," replied Fiennes with some wonder. "He'd had some queer adventures there, by his own account; and I fancy this dislike of Valentine was connected with the doctor coming from the tropics, too. But it's all an infernal puzzle.

"The account there is pretty accurate; I didn't see the tragedy, in the sense of the discovery; I was out walking with the young nephews and the dog—the dog I wanted to tell you about. But I saw the stage set for it as described; the straight lane between the blue flowers right up to the dark entrance, and the lawyer going down it in his blacks and his silk hat, and the red head of the secretary showing high above the green hedge as he worked on it with his shears. This red-haired secretary Floyd is quite a character, a breathless bounding sort of fellow, always doing everybody's work as he was doing the gardener's."

"What about the lawyer?" asked Father Brown.

There was a silence and then Fiennes spoke quite slowly for him. "Traill struck me as a singular man. In his fine black clothes he was almost foppish, yet you can hardly call him fashionable. For he wore a pair of long luxuriant black whiskers such as haven't been seen since Victorian times. He had rather a grave face and a fine grave manner, but every now and then he seemed to remember to smile. And when he showed his white teeth he seemed to lose a little of his dignity and there was something faintly fawning about him. It may have been only embarrassment, for he would also fidget with his cravat, and his tie pin, which were at once handsome and unusual, like himself.

"If I could think of anybody—but what's the good, when the whole thing's impossible? Nobody knows who did it. Nobody knows how it could be done. At least there's only one exception I'd make, and that's why I really mentioned the whole thing. The dog knows."

Father Brown sighed and then said absently, "You were there as a friend of young Donald, weren't you? He didn't go on your walk with you?"

"No," replied Fiennes smiling. "The young scoundrel had gone to bed that morning and got up that afternoon. I went with his cousins, two young officers from India; and our conversation was trivial enough. I remember the elder, whose name I think is Herbert Druce, and who is an authority on horse breeding, talked about nothing but a mare he had bought; while his brother Harry seemed to be brooding on his bad luck at Monte Carlo. I only mention it to show you, in the light of what happened on our walk, that there was nothing psychic about us. The dog was the only mystic in our company."

"What sort of a dog was he?" asked the priest.

"Same breed as that one," answered Fiennes. "He's a big black retriever named Nox, and a suggestive name too; for I think what he did more of a mystery than the murder.

"You know Druce's house and garden are by the sea; we walked about a mile from it along the sands and then turned back, going the other way. We passed a rather curious rock called the Rock of Fortune, famous in the neighborhood because it's one of those examples of one stone barely balanced on another, so that a touch would knock it over. It is not really very high, but the hanging outline of it makes it look a little wild and sinister. Just then the question arose of whether it was time to go back to tea, and even then I think I had a premonition that time counted for a good deal in the business.

"Neither Herbert Druce nor I had a watch; so we called out to his brother, who was some paces behind, having stopped to light his pipe under the hedge. Hence it happened that he shouted out the hour, which was twenty past four, in his big voice through the growing twilight; and somehow the loudness of it made it sound like the proclamation of something tremendous. According to Dr. Valentine's testimony, poor Druce had actually died just about half-past four.

"Well, they said we needn't go home for ten minutes and we walked a little farther along the sands doing nothing in particular; throwing stones for the dog and throwing sticks into the sea for him to swim after. And then the curious thing happened.

"Nox had just brought back Herbert's walking-stick out of the sea, and his brother had thrown his in also. The dog swam out again, but just about what must have been the stroke of the half hour, he stopped swimming. He came back again on to the shore and stood in front of us. Then he suddenly threw up his head and sent up a howl or wail of woe if ever I heard one in the world.

" 'What the devil's the matter with the dog?' asked Herbert, but none of us could answer. There was a long silence after the brute's wailing and whining died away on the desolate shore; and then the silence was broken. As I live, it was broken by a faint and far off shriek, like the shriek of a woman from beyond the hedges inland. We didn't know what it was then; but we knew afterwards. It was the cry the girl gave when she first saw the body of her father."

"You went back, I suppose," said Father Brown patiently. "What happened then?"

"I'll tell you what happened then," said Fiennes, with a grim emphasis. "When we got back into that garden the first thing we saw was Traill the lawyer; I can see him now with his black hat and black whiskers relieved against the perspective of the blue flowers stretching down to the summer-house with the sunset and the strange outline of the Rock of Fortune in the distance. His face and figure were in shadow against the sunset; but I swear the white teeth were showing in his head and he was smiling.

"The moment Nox saw the man, the dog dashed forward and stood in the middle of the path barking at him madly, murderously volleying out curses that were almost verbal in their dreadful distinctness of hatred. And the man doubled up and fled along the path between the flowers."

Father Brown sprang to his feet with a startling impatience.

"So the dog denounced him, did he?" he cried. "The oracle of the dog condemned him. Did you see what birds were flying, and are you sure whether they were on the right hand or the left? Did you consult the augurs about the sacrifices? Surely you didn't omit to cut open the dog, and examine his entrails. That is the sort of scientific test you heathen humanitarians seem to trust, when you are thinking of taking away the life and honor of a man."

Fiennes sat gaping for an instant before he found breath to say, "Why, what's the matter with you? What have I done now?"

A sort of anxiety came back into the priest's eyes.

"I'm most awfully sorry," he said, with sincere distress, "I beg your pardon for being so rude, pray forgive me."

Fiennes looked at him curiously. "I sometimes think you are more of a mystery than any of the mysteries," he said. "But as for the lawyer, I don't go only by the dog; there are other curious details too. He struck me as a smooth, smiling, equivocal sort of person and one of his tricks seemed like a sort of hint. You know the doctor and the police were on the spot very quickly, Valentine was brought back when walking away from the house, and he telephoned instantly. That, with the secluded house, small numbers and enclosed space made it pretty possible to search everybody who could have been near; and everybody was thoroughly searched—for a weapon. The whole house, garden and shore were combed for a weapon. The disappearance of the dagger is almost as crazy as the disappearance of the man."

"The disappearance of the dagger," said Father Brown nodding. He seemed to have become suddenly attentive.

"Well," continued Fiennes, "I told you that man Traill had a trick of fidgeting with his tie and tie pin—especially his tie pin. His pin, like himself, was at once showy and old-fashioned. It had been one of those stones with concentric colored rings that look like an eye; and his own concentration on it got on my nerves, as if he had been a cyclops with one eye in the middle of his body. But the pin was not only large but long; and it occurred to me that his anxiety about its adjustment was because it was even longer than it looked, as long as a stiletto in fact."

Father Brown nodded thoughtfully. "Was any other instrument ever suggested?" he asked.

"There was another suggestion," answered Fiennes, "from one of the young Druces; the cousins I mean. Neither Herbert nor Harry Druce would have struck one at first as likely to be of assistance in scientific detection; but Harry had been in the Indian Police and knew something about such things. Indeed in his own way he was quite clever; and I rather fancy he had been too clever; I mean he had left the police through breaking some red-tape regulations and taking some sort of risk and responsibility of his own.

"Anyhow he was in some sense a detective out of work, and threw himself into this business with more than the ardor of an amateur and it was with him that I had an argument about the weapon, an argument that led to something new. It began by his countering my description of the dog barking at Traill; and he said that a dog at his worst didn't bark but growled."

"He was quite right there," observed the priest.

"This young fellow went on to say, that, if it came to that, he'd heard Nox growling at other people before then; and among others at Floyd the secretary. I retorted that his own argument answered itself; for the crime couldn't be brought home to two or three people, and least of all to Floyd who was as innocent as a harum scarum schoolboy, and had been seen by everybody all the time perched above the garden hedge.

" 'I know there's difficulties anyhow,' said my colleague, 'but I wish you'd come with me down the garden a minute. I want to show you something I don't think any one else has seen.' This was on the very day of the discovery, and the garden was just as it had been; the stepladder was still standing by the hedge; and just under the hedge my guide stooped and disentangled something from the deep grass. It was the shears used for clipping the hedge; and on the point of one of them was a smear of blood."

There was a short silence and then Father Brown said suddenly: "What was the lawyer there for?"

"He told us the Colonel sent for him to alter his will," answered Fiennes. "The Colonel was a very wealthy man and his will was important. Traill wouldn't tell us the alterations at that stage; but I have since heard, only this morning in fact, that most of the money was transferred from the son to the daughter. I told you that Druce was wild with my friend Donald over his dissipated hours."

"The question of motive has been rather shadowed by the question of method," observed Father Brown thoughtfully. "At that moment, apparently, Miss Druce was the immediate gainer by the death."

"Good God! What a cold-blooded way of talking," cried Fiennes, staring at him. "You don't really mean to hint that she—"

"Is going to marry that Dr. Valentine?" asked the other. "What sort of a man is he?"

"He—Valentine—man with a beard; very pale, very handsome; rather foreign looking. The name doesn't seem quite English somehow. But he is liked and respected in the place and is a skilled and devoted surgeon."

"So devoted a surgeon," said Father Brown, "that he had surgical instruments with him when he went to call on the young lady at tea time. For he must have used a lancet or something, and he never seems to have gone home."

Fiennes sprang to his feet and looked at him in a heat of inquiry. "You suggest he might have used the very same lancet—"

Father Brown shook his head. "All these suggestions are fancies just now," he said. "The problem is not who did it or what did it, but how it was done. We might find many men and even many tools; pins and shears and lancets. But how did a man get into the room? *How did even a pin get into it?*"

He was staring reflectively at the ceiling as he spoke.

"Well, what would you do about it?" asked the young man. "You have a lot of experience, what would you advise now?"

"I'm afraid I'm not much use," said Father Brown with a sigh. "I can't suggest very much without having ever been near the place or the people. For the moment you can only go on with local inquiries. I gather that your friend from the Indian Police is more or less in charge of your inquiry down there. I should run down and see how he is getting on. There may be news already."

As his guests, the biped and the quadruped, disappeared, Father Brown took up his pen and went back to his interrupted occupation of planning a course of lectures on the Encyclical De Rerum Novarum. The subject was a large one and he had to recast it more than once, so that he was somewhat similarly employed some two days later when the big black dog again came bounding into the room and sprawling all over him with enthusiasm and excitement. The master who followed the dog shared the excitement if not the enthusiasm. His blue eyes seemed to start from his head and his eager face was even a little pale.

"You told me," he said abruptly and without preface, "to find out what Harry Druce was doing. Do you know what he's done? He's killed himself."

Father Brown's lips moved only faintly and there was nothing practical about what he was saying; nothing that has anything to do with this story or this world.

"You give me the creeps sometimes," said Fiennes. "Did you—did you expect this?"

"I thought it possible," said Father Brown, "that was why I asked you to go and see what he was doing. I hoped you might not be too late."

"It was I who found him," said Fiennes rather huskily. "It was the ugliest and most uncanny thing I ever knew. I went down that old garden again and I knew there was something new and unnatural about it besides the murder. The flowers still tossed about in blue masses on each side of the black entrance into the old gray summer-house; but to me the blue flowers looked like blue devils dancing before some dark cavern of the underworld. The queer notion grew on me that there was something wrong with the very shape of the sky.

"And then I saw what it was. The Rock of Fortune always rose in the background beyond the garden hedge and against the sea. And the Rock of Fortune was gone."

Father Brown had lifted his head and was listening intently.

"It was as if a mountain had walked away out of a landscape or a moon fallen from the sky; though I knew, of course, that a touch at any time would have tipped the thing over. Something possessed me and I rushed down that garden path like the wind and went crashing through the hedge as if it were a spider's web. On the shore I found the loose rock fallen from its pedestal and poor Harry Druce lay like a wreck underneath it. One arm was thrown round it in a sort of embrace as if he had pulled it down on himself; and in the other hand was clenched a scrap of paper on which he had scrawled the words, 'The Rock of Fortune falls on the fool.' "

"It was the Colonel's will that did that," observed Father Brown. "The young man had staked everything on profiting himself by Donald's disgrace, especially when his uncle sent for him on the same day as the lawyer, and welcomed him with so much warmth. Otherwise he was dumb; he'd lost his police job; he was beggared at Monte Carlo. And he killed himself when he found he'd killed his kinsman for nothing. That's the whole story."

Fiennes stared. "But look here," he cried, "how do you come to know the whole story, or to be sure it's the true story? You've been sitting here a hundred miles away writing a sermon; do you mean to tell me you really know what happened already? If you've really come to the end, where in the world do you begin? What started you off with your own story?"

Father Brown jumped up.

"The dog!" he cried, "the dog, of course! You had the whole story in your hands in the business of the dog on the beach, if you'd only noticed the dog properly."

Fiennes stared still more. "But you told me just now that my feelings about the dog were all nonsense, and the dog had nothing to do with it!"

"The dog had everything to do with it," said Father Brown, "as you'd have found out if you'd only treated the dog as a dog, not as God Almighty, judging the souls of men."

He paused in an embarrassed way for a moment, and then said, with a rather pathetic air of apology:

"The truth is that I happen to be awfully fond of dogs. And it seemed to me that in all this lurid halo of dog superstitions nobody was really thinking about the poor dog at all. To begin with a small point, about his barking at the lawyer or growling at the secretary. You asked how I could guess things a hundred miles away; but honestly it's mostly to your credit, for you described people so well that I know the types.

"A man like Traill who frowns usually and smiles suddenly, a man who fiddles with things, especially at his throat, is a nervous, easily embarrassed man. I shouldn't wonder if Floyd the efficient secretary is nervy and jumpy too; otherwise he wouldn't have cut his fingers on the shears and dropped them when he heard Janet Druce scream.

"Now dogs hate nervous people. I don't know whether they make the dog nervous too; or whether, being after all a brute, he is a bit of a bully. But anyhow there was nothing in poor Nox protesting against those people, except that he disliked them for being afraid of him.

"But when we come to that business by the seashore, things are much more interesting. I didn't understand that tale of the dog going in and out of the water; it didn't seem to me a doggy thing to do. If Nox had been very much upset about something else, he might possibly have refused to go after the stick at all. But when once a dog is actually chasing a thing, a stone or a stick or a rabbit, my experience is that he won't stop for anything but the most peremptory command, and not always for that. That he should turn round because his mood changed seems to me unthinkable."

"But he did turn around," insisted Fiennes, "and came back without the stick."

"He came back without the stick for the best reason in the world," replied the priest. "He came back because he couldn't find it. He whined because he couldn't find it. That's the sort of thing a dog really does whine about. He came back to complain seriously of the conduct of the stick. Never had such a thing happened before. Never had an eminent and distinguished dog been so treated by a rotten old walking stick."

"Why, what had the walking stick done?" inquired the young man.

"It had sunk," said Father Brown.

Fiennes said nothing but continued to stare, and it was the priest who continued, "It had sunk because it was not really a stock but a rod of steel with a very thin shell of cane and a sharp point. In other words, it was a sword stick. I suppose a murderer never got rid of a bloody weapon so oddly and yet so naturally as by throwing it into the sea for a retriever."

"I begin to see what you mean," admitted Fiennes, "but even if a sword stick was used I have no guess of how it was used."

"I had a sort of guess," said Father Brown, "right at the beginning when you said the word summer-house. And another when you said that Druce wore a white coat."

He was leaning back, looking at the ceiling, and began like one going back to his own first thoughts and fundamentals.

"All that discussion about detective stories like the Yellow Room, about a man found dead in sealed chambers which no one could enter, does not apply to the present case; because it is a summer-house. When we talk of a Yellow Room, or any room, we imply walls that are really homogeneous and impenetrable. But a summer-house is not make like that; it is often made, as it was in this case, of closely interlaced but still separate boughs and strips of wood, in which there are chinks here and there. There was one of them just behind Druce's back as he sat in his chair up against the wall. But just as the room was a summer-house, so the chair was a basket chair. That also was a lattice of loop-holes.

"Lastly, the summer-house was close up under the hedge; and you have just told me that it was really a thin hedge. A man standing outside it could easily see, amid a network of twigs and branches and canes, one white spot of the Colonel's coat as plain as the white of a target.

"Now you left the geography a little vague; but it was possible to put two and two together. You said the Rock of Fortune was not really high; but you also said it could be seen dominating the garden like a mountain peak. In other words, it was very near the end of the garden, though your walk had taken you a long way round to it. Also, it isn't likely the young lady really howled so as to be heard half a mile. She gave an ordinary involuntary cry, and yet you heard it on the shore. And among other interesting things that you told me, may I remind you that you said Harry Druce had fallen behind to light his pipe under a hedge?"

Fiennes shuddered slightly. "You mean he drew his blade there and sent it through the hedge at the white spot? But surely it was a very odd chance and a very sudden choice. Besides, he couldn't be certain the old man's money had passed to him, and as a fact it hadn't."

Father Brown's face became animated.

"You misunderstand the man's character," he said, as if he himself had known the man all his life. "A curious but not unknown type of character. If he had really *known* the money would come to him, I seriously believe he wouldn't have done it."

"Isn't that rather paradoxical?" asked the other.

"This man was a gambler," said the priest, "and a man in disgrace for having taken risks and anticipated orders. Now the temptation of that type of man is to do a mad thing precisely because the risk will be wonderful in retrospect. He wants to say, 'Nobody but I could have seized that chance or seen that it was then or never. Anybody would say I was mad to risk it; but that is how fortunes are made, by the man mad enough to have a little foresight.'

"In short, it is the vanity of guessing. It is the megalomania of the gambler. The more incongruous the coincidence, the more instantaneous the decision, the more likely he is to snatch the chance. The accident, the very triviality of the white speck and the hole in the hedge intoxicated him like a vision of the world's desire. Nobody clever enough to see such a combination of accidents could be cowardly enough not to use them! That is how the devil talks to the gambler."

Fiennes was musing.

"It's queer," he said, "that the dog really was in the story after all."

"The dog could almost have told you the story, if he could talk," said the priest. "All I complain of is that because he couldn't talk you made up his story for him and made him talk with the tongues of men and angels. It's part of something I've noticed more and more in the modern world, appearing in all sorts of newspaper rumors and conversational catchwords. People readily swallow the untested claims of this, that, or the other. It's drowning all your old rationalism and skepticism, it's coming in like a sea; and the name of it is superstition."

He stood up abruptly, his face heavy with a sort of frown, and went on talking almost as if he were alone. "It's the first effect of not believing in God that you lose your common sense, and can't see things as they are. A dog is an omen and a cat is a mystery and a pig is a mascot and a beetle is a scarab, calling up all the menagerie of polytheism from Egypt and old India; Dog Anubis and great green-eyed Pasht and all the holy howling Bulls of Bashan reeling back to the bestial gods of the beginning, escaping into elephants and snakes and crocodiles; and all because you are frightened of three words: Homo Factus Est."

The young man got up with a little embarrassment, almost as if he had overheard a soliloquy. He called to the dog and left the room with vague but breezy farewells.

But he had to call the dog twice; for the dog had remained behind quite motionless for a moment, looking up steadily at Father Brown as the wolf looked at St. Francis.

The Wild Goat's Kid

by LIAM O'FLAHERTY

Exquisite prose and exquisite sensitivity make this one of the stories I am most proud to include in this anthology.

HER nimble hoofs made music on the crags all winter, as she roamed along the cliff-tops over the sea.

During the previous autumn, when goats were mating, she had wandered away, one of a small herd that trotted gaily after a handsome fellow, with a splendid gray-black hide and winding horns. It was her first mating. Then, with the end of autumn, peasant boys came looking for their goats. The herd was broken up. The gallant buck was captured and slain by two hungry dogs from the village of Drumranny. The white goat alone remained. She had wandered too far away from her master's village. He couldn't find her. She was given up as lost.

So that she became a wild one of the cliffs, where the sea-gulls and the cormorants were lords, and the great eagle of Moher soared high over the thundering sea. Her big, soft, yellow eyes became wild from looking down often at the sea, with her long chin whiskers swaying gracefully in the wind. She was a long, slender thing, with short, straight horns and ringlets of matted hair trailing far down on either haunch.

With her tail in the air, snorting, tossing her horns, she fled when anybody approached. Her hoofs would patter over the crags until she was far away. Then she would stand on some eminence and turn about to survey the person who had disturbed her, calmly, confident in the power of her slender legs to carry her beyond pursuit.

She roamed at will. No stone fence however high could resist her long leap, as she sprang on muscular thighs that bent like silk.

She was so supple that she could trot on the top of a thin fence, carelessly, without a sound except the gentle tapping of her delicate hoofs. She hardly ever left the cliff-tops. There was plenty of food there, for the winter was mild, and the leaves and grasses that grew between the crevices of the crags were flavoured by the strong, salt taste of the brine carried up on the wind. She grew sleek and comely.

Toward the end of winter a subtle change came over her. Her hearing became more acute. She took fright at the least sound. She began to shun the sea except on very calm days, when it did not roar. She ate less. She grew very particular about what she ate. She hunted around a long time before she chose a morsel. She often went on her knees, reaching down to the bottom of a crevice to nibble at a briar that was inferior to the more accessible ones. She became corpulent. Her udder increased.

Winter passed. Green leaves began to sprout. Larks sang in the morning. There was sweetness in the air and a great urge of life. The white goat, one morning a little after dawn, gave birth to a grey-black kid.

The kid was born in a tiny, green glen under an overhanging ledge of low rock that sheltered it from the wind. It was a male kid, an exquisite, fragile thing, tinted delicately with many colours. His slender belly was milky white. The insides of his thighs were of the same colour. He had deep rings of gray, like bracelets, above his hoofs. He had black knee-caps on his forelegs, like pads, to protect him when he knelt to take his mother's teats into his silky, black mouth. His back and sides were gray-black. His ears were black, long, and drooping with the weakness of infancy.

The white goat bleated over him, with soft eyes and shivering flanks, gloating over the exquisite thing that had been created within her by the miraculous power of life. And she had this delicate creature all to herself, in the wild solitude of the beautiful little glen, within earshot of the murmuring sea, with little birds whistling their spring songs around about her, and the winds coming with their slow whispers over the crags. The first tender hours of her first motherhood were undisturbed by any restraint, not even by the restraint of a mate's presence. In absolute freedom and quiet, she watched with her young.

How she manœuvered to make him stand! She breathed on him
to warm him. She raised him gently with her forehead, uttering
strange, soft sounds to encourage him. Then he stood up, trembling, staggering, swaying on his curiously long legs. She became
very excited, rushing around him, bleating nervously, afraid that
he should fall again. He fell. She was in agony. Bitter wails came
from her distended jaws and she crunched her teeth. But she renewed her efforts, urging the kid to rise, to rise and live . . . to
live, live, live.

He rose again. Now he was steadier. He shook his head. He
wagged his long ears as his mother breathed into them. He took a
few staggering steps, came to his padded knees, and rose again immediately. Slowly, gently, gradually, she pushed him toward her
udder with her horns. At last he took the teat within his mouth, he
pushed joyously, sank to his knees and began to drink.

She stayed with him all day in the tiny glen, just nibbling a few
mouthfuls of the short grass that grew around. Most of the time she
spent exercising her kid. With a great show of anxiety and importance, she brought him on little expeditions across the glen to
the opposite rock, three yards away and back again. At first he
staggered clumsily against her side, and his tiny hoofs often lost
their balance on tufts of grass, such was his weakness. But he gained
strength with amazing speed, and the goat's joy and pride increased.
She suckled and caressed him after each tiny journey.

When the sun had set he was able to walk steadily, to take little
short runs, to toss his head. They lay all night beneath the shelter
of the ledge, with the kid between his mother's legs, against her
warm udder.

Next morning she hid him securely in a crevice of the neighbouring crag, in a small groove between two flags that were covered
with a withered growth of wild grass and ferns. The kid crawled
instinctively into the warm hole without any resistance to the
gentle push of his mother's horns. He lay down with his head
toward his doubled hind legs, and closed his eyes. Then the goat
scraped the grass and fern-stalks over the entrance hole with her
fore feet, and she hurried away to graze, as carelessly as if she had no
kid hidden.

All the morning, as she grazed hurriedly and fiercely around the crag, she took great pains to pretend that she was not aware of her kid's nearness. Even when she grazed almost beside the hiding-place, she never noticed him, by look or by cry. But still, she pricked her little ears at every distant sound.

At noon she took him out and gave him suck. She played with him on a grassy knoll and watched him prance about. She taught him how to rear on his hind legs and fight the air with his forehead. Then she put him back into his hiding-place and returned to graze. She continued to graze until nightfall.

Just when she was about to fetch him from his hole and take him to the overhanging ledge to rest for the night, a startling sound reached her ears. It came from afar, from the south, from beyond a low fence that ran across the crag on the skyline. It was indistinct, barely audible, a deep, purring sound. But to the ears of the mother-goat, it was loud and ominous as a thunderclap. It was the heavy breathing of a dog sniffing the wind.

She listened stock-still, with her head in the air and her short tail lying stiff along her back, twitching one ear. The sound came again. It was nearer. Then there was a patter of feet. Then a clumsy, black figure hurtled over the fence and dropped on to the crag, with awkward secrecy. The goat saw a black dog, a large, curly fellow, standing by the fence in the dim twilight, with his fore paw raised and his long, red tongue hanging. Then he shut his mouth suddenly, and raising his snout upward sniffed several times, contracting his nostrils as he did so, as if in pain. Then he whined savagely, and trotted toward the goat sideways.

She snorted. It was a sharp, dull thud, like a blow from a rubber sledge. Then she rapped the crag three times with her left fore foot, loudly and sharply. The dog stood still and raised his fore paw again. He bent down his head and looked at her with narrowed eyes. Then he licked his breast and began to run swiftly to the left. He was running toward the kid's hiding-place, with his tail stretched out straight and his snout to the wind.

With another fierce snort the goat charged him at full speed, in order to cut him off from his advance on the kid's hiding-place. He stopped immediately when she charged. The goat halted too, five yards from the hiding-place, between the dog and the hiding-place, facing the dog.

The dog stood still. His eyes wandered around in all directions, with the bashfulness of a sly brute, caught suddenly in an awkward position. Then slowly he raised his bloodshot eyes to the goat. He bared his fangs. His mane rose like a fan. His tail shot out. Picking his steps like a lazy cat, he approached her without a sound. The goat shivered along her left flank, and she snorted twice in rapid succession.

When he was within six yards of her he uttered a ferocious roar —a deep, rumbling sound in his throat. He raced toward her, and leaped clean into the air, as if she were a fence that he was trying to vault. She parried him subtly with her horns, like a swordthrust, without moving her fore feet. Her sharp horns just grazed his belly as he whizzed past her head. But the slight blow deflected his course. Instead of falling on his feet, as he had intended cunningly to do, between the goat and the kid, he was thrown to the left and fell on his side, with a thud. The goat whirled about and charged him.

But he had arisen immediately and jerked himself away, with his haunches low down, making a devilish scraping and yelping and growling noise. He wanted to terrify the kid out of his hiding-place. Then it would be easy to overpower the goat, hampered by the task of hiding the kid between her legs.

The kid uttered a faint, querulous cry, but the goat immediately replied with a sharp, low cry. The kid mumbled something indistinct, and then remained silent. There was a brushing sound among the ferns that covered him. He was settling himself down farther. The goat trotted rigidly to the opposite side of the hiding-place to face the dog again.

The dog had run away some distance, and lay on his belly, licking his paws. Now he meant to settle himself down properly to the prolonged attack, after the failure of his first onslaught. He yawned lazily and made peculiar, mournful noises, thrusting his head into the air and twitching his snout. The goat watched every single movement and sound, with her ears thrust forward past her horns. Her great, soft eyes were very wild and timorous in spite of the valiant posture of her body, and the terrific force of the blows she delivered occasionally on the hard crag with her little hoofs.

The dog remained lying for half an hour or so, continuing his weird pantomime. The night fell completely. Everything became unreal and ghostly under the light of the distant myriads of stars. An infant moon had arisen. The sharp rushing wind and the thunder of the sea only made the silent loneliness of the night more menacing to the white goat, as she stood bravely on the limestone crag defending her newborn young. On all sides the horizon was a tumultuous line of barren crag, dented with shallow glens and seamed with low, stone fences that hung like tattered curtains against the rim of the sky.

Then the dog attacked again. Rising suddenly, he set off at a long, swinging gallop, with his head turned sideways toward the goat, whining as he ran. He ran around the goat in a wide circle, gradually increasing his speed. A white spot on his breast flashed and vanished as he rose and fell in the undulating stretches of his flight. The goat watched him, fiercely rigid from tail to snout. She pawed the crag methodically, turning around on her own ground slowly to face him.

When he passed his starting-point, he was flying at full speed, a black ball shooting along the gloomy surface of the crag, with a sharp rattle of claws. The rattle of his claws, his whining and the sharp tapping of the goat's fore feet as she turned about, were the only sounds that rose into the night from this sinister engagement.

He sped round and round the goat, approaching her imperceptibly each round, until he was so close that she could see his glittering eyes and the white lather of rage on his half-open jaws. She became slightly dizzy and confused, turning about so methodically in a confined space, confused and amazed by the subtle strategy of the horrid beast. His whining grew louder and more savage. The rattle of his claws was like the clamour of hailstones driven by a wind. He was upon her.

He came in a whirl on her flank. He came with a savage roar that deafened her. She shivered and then stiffened in rigid silence to receive him. The kid uttered a shrill cry. Then the black bulk hurtled through the air, close up, with hot breathing, snarling, with reddened fangs and . . . smash.

He had dived for her left flank. But as he went past her head she turned like lightning and met him again with her horns. This time she grazed his side, to the rear of the shoulder. He yelped and tumbled sideways, rolling over twice. With a savage snort she was upon him. He was on his haunches, rising, when her horns thudded into his head. He went down again with another yelp. He rolled over and then suddenly, with amazing speed, swept to his feet, whirled about on swinging tail and dived for her flank once more. The goat uttered a shriek of terror. He had passed her horns. His fangs had embedded themselves in the matted ringlet that trailed along her right flank. The dog's flying weight, swinging on to the ringlet as he fell, brought her to her haunches.

But she was ferocious now. As she wriggled to her feet beside the rolling dog that gripped her flank, she wrenched herself around and gored him savagely in the belly. He yelled and loosed his hold. She rose on her hind legs in a flash, and with a snort she gored him again. Her sharp, pointed horns penetrated his side between the ribs. He gasped and shook his four feet in the air. Then she pounded on him with her fore feet, beating his prostrate body furiously. Her little hoofs pattered with tremendous speed for almost a minute. She beat him blindly, without looking at him.

Then she suddenly stopped. She snorted. The dog was still. He was dead. Her terror was passed. She lifted her right fore foot and shook it with a curious movement. Then she uttered a wild, joyous cry and ran toward her kid's hiding-place.

Night passed with a glorious dawn that came over a rippling sea from the west. A wild, sweet dawn, scented with dew and the many perfumes of the germinating earth. The sleepy sun rose brooding from the sea, golden and soft, searching far horizons with its concave shafts of light. The dawn was still. Still and soft and pure.

The white goat and her kid were traveling eastward along the cliff-tops over the sea. They had traveled all night, flying from the horrid carcass of the beast that lay stretched on the crag beside the little glen. Now they were far away, on the summit of the giant white Precipice of Cahir. The white goat rested to give suck to her kid, and to look out over the cliff-top at the rising sun.

Then she continued her flight eastward, pushing her tired kid before her gently with her horns.

Then the Witch Came

by E. LOUISE MALLY

JOYCE came hopping down the stairs. She hadn't had breakfast yet, but she wasn't going to go to breakfast till she was ready to. She was going out to the room under the back porch and see the new kittens. Mother had said, last night, "It's your bedtime, Joyce. You can play with the kittens all you want, tomorrow. They won't run away."

The Stork had brought the kittens to Crazy. It must have been sometime around supper time. Anyway, after Joyce had finished supper, Helen had called her into the kitchen, and had said, "Guess what—" and then had taken her out to the room under the porch, and there, on the dirt floor, was a box, and Crazy was in it, and four new, blind squirmy kittens. Then Mother had said, "It's your bedtime. . . ."

Mother didn't like cats. She didn't like Helen either. Helen was the maid. Mother had said to Father, when Joyce was supposed to be asleep, "Helen is so young. I hate to let her go. And Joyce seems to love her. But I really think . . ." Helen was nice. Helen played with Joyce. Now she had the kittens to play with.

Under the porch, it was still cool, though it was late May, and yesterday had been a warm day. There was a faint smell of cat, and the clean smell of the dirt floor, and of all the out of doors, since there was no door on the room. Joyce came in, and touched Crazy tentatively. Helen had said that the cat would not like to have her babies touched, and perhaps would not like to be touched herself, now that she had the new kittens. But Crazy made the kind of screechy mewing sound she always made when Joyce petted her, and then turned over to feed her babies. Joyce watched, fascinated.

441

Joyce had told Mother, a long time ago, that she wanted a baby
sister, and Mother had said she must write to the Stork. So Helen
had written the letter to the Stork for her, and posted it, but there
hadn't been an answer. Not long after, the Stork had brought a
brother to Mary, who lived up the street and already had two other
brothers. Mother had said Joyce hadn't been on the porch, for the
Stork to see her, and the Stork must have made a mistake. But Joyce
had carefully said she wanted a sister—she wasn't at all sure that
she would like to have a brother, younger or older. Boys teased
all the time. Now the Stork had come again, and had brought the
kittens to Crazy. They might be almost as good as a sister, for a
while. Of course, when they got to be full grown cats, they wouldn't
play all the time, and you couldn't play with them yet.

Joyce stood and looked at the kittens, and made up a story about
them. The biggest kitten was not an ordinary cat at all. He was a
cat out of a fairy tale. And he would grow up to be an enormous
cat—and he would come to Joyce and say, "We are going off to
the kingdom of the cats. I was born to be a king in the kingdom of
the cats. And we want you to come with us. Because you love us.
Beside, you are really a fairy person, and you are to be queen in
Catland." And then they would form a procession, and she would
walk beside the prince. And when they came to the kingdom of the
cats she would have a crown, and . . .

Helen came out and said, "Well, have you named the kittens yet?"

"He's Prince Charming." Joyce pointed to the largest kitten.

Helen giggled. "That's no kind of a name for a cat. Beside, I
think it's a little girl cat."

Before they went in to breakfast, Helen had named three of the
cats—Blacky, Whitey and Tiny. But Joyce named the biggest kitten Boots—that could be either a girl or a boy, and besides, it was
a sort of fairy-tale name—though it wasn't as good as Prince Charming.

Father had just finished breakfast when Joyce came in. Joyce
said, "Can we take the kittens with us when we go to Paris-France
to buy for your store?"

Father laughed. "The kittens will be grown cats before we go to
Europe. We can't take five cats to Europe with us."

"We can take Crazy, can't we?"

Mother said, "We'll see." When Mother said, "We'll see," it always meant no. Joyce knew they weren't going to Europe soon. Father had been planning to go, this summer, but late last summer someone in Europe had been killed, and there was a strip in the funny paper about Austria got hungry and used some grease, and that was the names of countries that were fighting. Joyce hadn't understood about the war at first. Uncle John had come, visiting, and Joyce had climbed up in his lap and said, "We're going to Paris-France next year."

"You can't go to Paris-France, because you don't speak French," Uncle John had said, imitating her.

"I do too speak French," Joyce said. "I can say bonjour. I can say artichoke."

"But what will you say when you want some milk for your cat?" Uncle John had asked. "Crazy won't eat artichokes."

"I will say 'meow,'" Joyce said, and laughed delightedly. "I will say, 'Milch, bitte.' Mother says I speak German very nicely."

"But you can't speak German in France," Uncle John said in mock horror. "The French will put you in prison."

Joyce said, "Why?"

But she knew about the war now. She was a big girl—she was almost six. And Mother was knitting sweaters for the Belgium babies. But Mother said, "Please don't tell me about it," when people wanted to talk about the war. Mother did not like excitement. When Joyce had been a little girl, she had been like Mother. Mother had taken her to see *Hansel and Gretel,* and she had cried through the whole play. She had cried when the children had been lost in the forest, and when the witch wanted to eat the children, and finally when the children killed the witch. Mother said, "Don't you want to go home?" But Joyce had not wanted to go—if she weren't there to see how it came out, she'd never be sure the witch didn't eat the children. So Mother gave her chocolates out of a box on the back of the theater seat.

But that had been when she was four years old. Now she liked excitement. She liked the stories about the war that Helen told her and she liked the fairy stories—especially fairy stories where the prince rescued the enchanted princess. She would take Boots to Europe, and he would kill the Kaiser. Then the war would be over. And Boots would be the Prince.

The kittens grew very quickly. They were almost as much fun as Joyce had thought they would be. But you couldn't play with them all day long—Mother said there wasn't anything you would want to do *all* the time—it would be very monotonous. But Joyce thought there must be something. If she had a baby sister . . .

She went up the street to play with Mary, and with Alice and Margaret. They played hide-and-go-seek. Joyce would have liked that, but she could never run as fast as Mary or Margaret. Once in a while she caught Alice, but she was It most of the time. When she said, "Let's play something else," Mary said,

"No fair. You just want to stop playing 'cause you're It. My mama says you have to play when you're It."

But later they played house. Joyce went home and got her dolls and her dress-up clothes. She and Alice were the grown-up lady sisters, and Mary and Margaret were the father and the mother. When the sisters went to balls, Mary and Margaret said, "Don't you look nice, my dears." At the balls, everybody wanted to dance with Joyce and Alice.

But when they came home from the ball, Margaret said, "There were burglars. They stole the children."

Joyce knew the dolls were really hidden back of the couch— she could see the biggest doll's leg sticking out. She did not want to cry in front of her friends—it was silly to cry when she knew it was just pretend. She turned, facing the street, and saw her mother and Mrs. Lawrence, her mother's best friend, coming out of her house. Mother had her hat on—she must be going somewhere—downtown or calling. Joyce ran down the street to say good-bye to her mother.

Joyce's mother said, "I thought you were busy playing. What is it? Do you want me to bring you something?"

Joyce had tears in her eyes. She shook her head and didn't say anything, but threw her arms around her mother's neck, pulling her face down, so that she could kiss her. Mother was wearing some kind of perfume that smelt of flowers, and her dress was flowered, and there were flowers in her hat.

Joyce was crying when she came back to Mary and Margaret and Alice. "I don't want Mother to go to town," she said. She knew she was crying because the burglars had stolen the children. She wasn't going to tell anyone that. When they stopped playing, after a while, she took her dolls home with her.

Helen wasn't working for Joyce's mother any more. The new maid was a very dependable woman, Mother said. She didn't like cats either.

After Joyce had gone to bed that night, she heard the doorbell ring, and then a man's voice—she didn't know who it was. It might be burglars—and they would carry away Father and Mother. Only Joyce would be left—and she would go to the fairies, and they would rescue Father and Mother from the burglars. But when she woke the next morning there hadn't been any burglars. Only a friend of Father's.

"No one you know, Joyce," Mother said.

She ate breakfast—oatmeal, and she didn't like oatmeal, but she ate it all. She looked at a picture book—she didn't go to school yet, and Mother didn't have time to read to her this morning. Mother said, "Go on out of doors and play." So she went to look for the kittens. And the kittens weren't there.

The kittens weren't there, and Crazy wasn't there. She called frantically, but they didn't come. Often before, when she had called, the kittens hadn't come. She went to look for them, in the yard, and then up and down the street. Then she went in and told Mother that the kittens were lost, and Mother came out and called. Mother said they must be somewhere, and of course they would come home at mealtime. But noon came, and evening, and they didn't come home.

Mother said cats often ran away. Mother said, "We will get you a dog, later. Dogs are faithful."

"I don't want a dog," Joyce said. "I want my cats." She was crying.

Two mornings later, when Joyce was dressing, Mother said to hurry and go down stairs—that the kittens had come back. But when she got downstairs, there was no sign of them. Mother helped Joyce look for them again, but they couldn't find the kittens. Mother said they must have run away again. She couldn't understand it.

Early in the fall, Aunt Charlotte, Mother's sister, came on a visit. The second day after Aunt Charlotte had come, they went down town to Father's store. And Mother said to Joyce, "Go over and see what Aunt Charlotte is looking at."

It wasn't anything but a black broadcloth suit. When Joyce came back to tell Mother that, Mother was talking to the elevator man.

While Aunt Charlotte was visiting, Father went to New York to buy for his store. And Mother and Aunt Charlotte sat up late, talking. Aunt Charlotte was giggling a lot, and talking about someone called Alan. Joyce didn't listen all the time. She was making up a story about the first day in school—she was going to start school in three days. She would be very good, and never whisper in class, and the teacher would say she was the best little girl in the first grade. If Mother came in to see if she were asleep, now, Joyce would close her eyes hard, and pretend to be asleep. She had done that before—though Mother always seemed to know she wasn't asleep. Joyce couldn't understand that. Perhaps she lay too quietly— Mother said Joyce kicked in her sleep. . . . Mother wasn't coming into the room now. Mother was talking to Aunt Charlotte, still. Joyce heard her own name—they weren't talking about Alan anymore. Then she heard her mother say, "So I gave the cat and the kittens to the elevator man at the store. And I helped Joyce hunt for them."

Joyce screwed up her face. She was not going to cry. Because then Mother would see, if she came in, that she had not been asleep. But someday she would run off. She would run off to the kingdom of the cats, and *she* would be a cat. And then Mother would not like her either.

A Passion in the Desert

by HONORÉ DE BALZAC

*Strange and memorable is this story of the love be-
tween a man and a panther in this unusual story by the
author of "The Human Comedy."*

"THE sight was fearful!" she cried, as we quit M. Martin's menagerie.

She had seen that fearless wild-beast tamer going through his
marvelous performance in a cage of hyenas.

"How can it be possible," she went on, "to so tame those creatures as to be sure of them?"

"It is an enigma to you," I replied, "yet still it is naturally a fact."

"Ah!" she exclaimed, her lips quivering incredulously.

"You think, then, that beasts are without feeling?" I asked. "Be
assured by me that they are taught by us all of our vices and virtues
—those of civilization."

Amazement was expressed in her look.

"At the time I first saw M. Martin, I, like you, exclaimed my
amazement," I went on. "It happened that I was seated alongside an
old soldier, his right leg amputated, who had attracted my notice
by his appearance as I went into the show. His face showed the
dauntless look of the Napoleonic wars, disfigured as it was with battle's scars. This old hero, besides, had a frank, jolly style which,
wherever I come across it, is always attractive to me. Undoubtedly
he was one of those old campaigners who are surprised at nothing,
who can make a jest on the last grimaces of a dying comrade, or will
bury his friend or rifle his body with gayety; give a challenge to
every bullet with composure; make a short shriving for himself or
others; and usually, as the saying goes, fraternize with the Devil. He

closely watched the proprietor of the exhibition as he entered the cage, curling his lip, that peculiar sign of contemptuous satire which better informed men assume to signify how superior they are to the dupes. The veteran smiled when I exclaimed at the cool daring of M. Martin, he gave a toss of the head, and, with a knowing grimace, said: 'An old game!'

" 'Old game,' said I, 'what do you mean? You will greatly oblige me if you can explain the secret of the mysterious power of this man.'

"We came to be acquainted after a while, and went to dine at the first café we saw after quitting the menagerie. After a bottle of champagne with our dessert, which burnished up his memory and rendered it very vivid, he narrated a circumstance in his early history which showed very conclusively that he had ample reason to style M. Martin's performance 'an old game.' "

When we arrived at her house she so teased me, and was withal so charming, making me a number of such pretty promises, that I consented to write the yarn narrated by the veteran hero for her benefit. On the morrow I sent her this adventure, which might well be headed: "The French in Egypt."

During the expedition to Upper Egypt under General Desaix, a Provençal soldier, who had fallen into the clutches of the Maugrabins, was marched by these marauders, these tireless Arabs, into the deserts lying beyond the cataracts of the Nile.

So as to put a sufficient distance between themselves and the French army, to insure their greater safety, the Maugrabins made forced marches and rested only during the night. They then encamped around a well shaded by palm-trees, under which they had previously concealed a store of provisions. Never dreaming that their prisoner would think of escaping, they satisfied themselves by merely tying his hands, then lay down to sleep, after having regaled themselves on a few dates and given provender to their horses.

When the courageous Provençal noted that they slept soundly and could no longer watch his movements, he made use of his teeth to steal a scimitar, steadied the blade between his knees, cut through the thongs which bound his hands; in an instant he was free. He at once seized a carbine and a long dirk, then took the precaution of providing himself with a stock of dried dates, a small bag of oats, some powder and bullets, and a scimitar hung around his waist; he mounted one of the horses and spurred on in the direction in which he supposed the French army to be. So impatient was he to see a bivouac again that he pressed on the already tired courser at such a speed that its flanks were lacerated with the spurs: soon the poor animal, utterly exhausted, fell dead, leaving the Frenchman alone in the midst of the desert.

After walking for a long time in the sand, with all the courage and firmness of an escaped convict, the soldier was obliged to stop, as the day had already come to an end. Despite the beauty of an Oriental night, with its exquisite sky, he felt that he could not, though he fain would, continue on his weary way. Fortunately he had come to a small eminence, on the summit of which grew a few palm-trees whose verdure shot into the air and could be seen from afar; this had brought hope and consolation to his heart.

His fatigue was so great that he threw himself down on a block of granite capriciously fashioned by Nature into the semblance of a camp-bed, and, without taking any precaution for defense, was soon fast in sleep. He had made the sacrifice of his life. His last waking thought was one of regret. He repented having left the Maugrabins, whose nomad life seemed to smile on him now that he was far from them and from all hope of succour.

He was awakened by the sun, whose pitiless rays fell with their intensest heat on the granite, and produced a most intolerable sense of torridness—for he had most stupidly placed himself away from the shadow cast by the verdant and majestic fronds of the palm-trees. He looked at these solitary monarchs and shuddered—they reminded him of the graceful shafts crowned with waving foliage which characterize the Saracenic columns in the cathedral of Arles.

But when, after counting the palm-trees, he cast his eyes around him, the most horrible despair took possession of his soul. The dark, forbidding sands of the desert spread farther than sight could reach in every direction, and glittered with a dull luster like steel struck by light. It was a limitless ocean that he saw. It might have been a sea of ice or a chain of lakes that lay mirrored around him. A fiery vapour carried in streaks formed perpetual heat-waves over this heaving continent. The sky was glowing with an Oriental splendour of insupportable translucence, disappointing, inasmuch as it leaves naught for the imagination to exceed. Heaven, earth, both were on fire.

The silence was awful in its wild, tremendous majesty. Infinitude, immensity, closed in upon the soul from every side. Not a cloud in the sky, not a breath in the air, not a rift on the bosom of the sand, which was ever moving in ever-diminishing wavelets, scarcely disturbing the surface; the horizon fell into space, traced by a slim line of light, definite as the edge of a sabre—as in summer seas a beam of light just divides the earth from the heaven which meets it.

The Provençal threw his arms around the trunk of one of the palm-trees, as though it were the body of a friend; and there, in the shelter of its slender, straight shadow cast by it upon the granite, he wept. Then sitting down he remained motionless, contemplating with awful dread the implacable scene which Nature stretched out before him. He cried aloud to measure the solitude. His voice, lost in the hollows of the hillocks, sounded in the distance with a faint resonance, but aroused no echo—the echo was in the soldier's heart. The Provençal was two-and-twenty; he loaded his carbine.

"Time enough yet," he muttered to himself, laying on the ground the weapon which alone could give him deliverance.

Looking by turns at the burnished black expanse and the blue immensity of the sky, the soldier dreamed of France—he smelt with delight, in his longing fancy, the gutters of Paris—he remembered the towns through which he had passed, the faces of his fellow-soldiers, the most trivial incidents of his life.

His Southern imagination saw the stones of his dearly loved Provence in the undulating play of the heat which spread in waves over the outspread sheet of the desert. Fearing the dangers of this cruel mirage, he went down the opposite side of the knoll from that up which he had come on the previous day. How great was his joy when he discerned a natural grotto, formed of immense blocks of granite, the foundation of the rising ground. The remains of a rug showed that this place had at one time been inhabited; a short distance therefrom were some date-palms laden with fruit. There arose in his heart that instinct which binds us to life. He now hoped to live long enough to see the approach of some wandering Arabs, who should pass that way; perhaps, who should say? he might hear the sound of cannon; for at that time Bonaparte was traversing Egypt.

These thoughts inspired him with new life. The palm-tree near him seemed to bend under its weight of ripe fruit. The Frenchman shook down some of the clusters, and, when he tasted the unhoped-for manna, he felt convinced that the palms had been cultivated by some former inhabitant—the rich and luscious flavour of the fresh meat of the dates was an attestation of the care of his unknown predecessor. Like all Provençals, he passed from the gloom of dark despair to an almost insane joy.

He went up again, running, to the top of the hillock, where he devoted the remainder of the day to cutting down one of the sterile palm-trees which, the previous night, had served him as a shelter. A vague memory made him think of the wild beasts of the desert. He foresaw that they would most likely come to drink at the spring which was visible, bubbling through the sand, at the base of the rock, but which lost itself in the desert farther down. He resolved to guard himself against their unwelcome visits to his hermitage by felling a tree which should fall across the entrance.

Despite his diligence and the strength which the dread of being devoured in his sleep lent him, he was unable to cut the palm-tree in pieces during the day, but he was successful in felling it. At eventide the monarch of the desert tumbled down; the noise of its falling resounded far and wide like a moan from Solitude's bosom; the soldier shuddered as though he heard a voice predicting evil.

But like an heir who mourns not his parent's decease, he stripped off from this beautiful tree the arching green fronds, its poetic adornment, and used them in forming a couch on which to rest.

Fatigued by his labours, he soon fell asleep under the red vault of his damp, cool cave.

In the middle of the night his sleep was disturbed by an extraordinary sound. He sat up; the profound silence that reigned around enabled him to distinguish the alternating rhythm of a respiration whose savage energy could not possibly be that of a human being.

A deadly terror, increased yet more by the silence, the darkness, his racing fancy, froze his heart within him. He felt his hair rise on end, as his eyes, dilated to their utmost, perceived through the gloom two faint amber lights. At first he attributed these lights to the delusion of his vision, but presently the vivid brilliance of the night aided him to gradually distinguish the objects around him in the cave, when he saw, within the space of two feet of him, a huge animal lying at rest. Was it a lion? Was it a tiger? Was it a crocodile?

The Provençal was not sufficiently well educated to know under what sub-species his enemy should be classed; his fear was but the greater because his ignorance led him to imagine every terror at once. He endured most cruel tortures as he noted every variation of the breathing which was so near him; he dared not make the slightest movement.

An odour, pungent like that of a fox, but more penetrating, as it were, more profound, filled the cavern. When the Provençal became sensible of this, his terror reached the climax, for now he could no longer doubt the proximity of a terrible companion, whose royal lair he utilized as a bivouac.

Presently the reflection of the moon, as it slowly descended to the horizon, lighted up the den, rendering gradually visible the gleaming, resplendent, and spotted skin of a panther.

This lion of Egypt lay asleep curled up like a great dog, the peaceful possessor of a kennel at the door of some sumptuous hôtel; its eyes opened for a moment, then closed again; its face was turned toward the Frenchman. A thousand confused thoughts passed through the mind of the tiger's prisoner. Should he, as he at first thought of doing, kill it with a shot from his carbine? But he saw plainly that there was not room enough in which to take proper aim; the muzzle would have extended beyond the animal—the bullet would miss the mark. And what if it were to wake!—this fear kept him motionless and rigid.

He heard the pulsing of his heart beating in the dreadful silence and he cursed the too violent pulsations which his surging blood brought on, lest they should awaken the mighty creature from sleep —that slumber which gave him time to think and plan over his escape.

Twice did he place his hand upon his scimitar, intending to cut off his enemy's head; but the difficulty of severing the close-haired skin caused him to renounce this daring attempt. To miss was *certain* death. He preferred the chances of a fair fight, and made up his mind to await the daylight. The dawn did not give him long to wait. It came.

He could now examine the panther at his ease; its muzzle was smeared with blood.

"It's had a good dinner," he said, without troubling himself to speculate whether the feast might have been of human flesh or not. "It won't be hungry when it wakes."

It was a female. The fur on her belly and thighs was glistening white. Many small spots like velvet formed beautiful bracelets round her paws; her sinuous tail was also white, ending in black rings. The back of her dress was yellow, like unburnished gold, very lissome and soft, and had the characteristic blotches in the shape of pretty rosettes, which distinguish the panther from every other species *felis*.

This formidable hostess lay tranquilly snoring in an attitude as graceful and easy as that of a cat on the cushions of an ottoman. Her bloody paws, nervous and well armed, were stretched out before her head, which rested on the back of them, while from her muzzle radiated her straight, slender whiskers, like threads of silver.

If he had seen her lying thus, imprisoned in a cage, the Provençal would doubtless have admired the grace of the creature and the .ivid contrasts of colour which gave her robe an imperial splendour; but just then his sight was jaundiced by sinister forebodings.

The presence of the panther, even asleep, had the same effect upon him as the magnetic eyes of a snake are said to have on the nightingale.

The soldier's courage oozed away in the presence of this silent danger, though he was a man who gathered courage at the mouths of cannon belching forth shot and shell. And yet a bold thought brought daylight to his soul and sealed up the source from whence issued the cold sweat which gathered on his brow. Like men driven to bay, who defy death and offer their bodies to the smiter, so he, seeing in this merely a tragic episode, resolved to play his part with honour to the last.

"The day before yesterday," said he, "the Arabs might have killed me."

So considering himself as already dead, he waited bravely, but with anxious curiosity, the awakening of his enemy.

When the sun appeared the panther suddenly opened her eyes; then she stretched out her paws with energy, as if to get rid of cramp.

Presently she yawned and showed the frightful armament of her teeth, and the pointed tongue rough as a rasp.

"She is like a dainty woman," thought the Frenchman, seeing her rolling and turning herself about so softly and coquettishly. She licked off the blood from her paws and muzzle, and scratched her head with reiterated grace of movement.

"Good, make your little toilet," said the Frenchman to himself; he recovered his gayety with his courage. "We are presently about to give each other good-morning," and he felt for the short poniard that he had abstracted from the Maugrabins. At this instant the panther turned her head toward him and gazed fixedly at him, without otherwise moving.

The rigidity of her metallic eyes and their insupportable luster made him shudder. The beast approached him; he looked at her caressingly, staring into those bright eyes in an effort to hypnotize her—to soothe her. He let her come quite close to him before stirring; then with a movement both gentle and amorous, as though he were caressing the most beautiful of women, he passed his hand over her whole body, from the head to the tail, scratching the flexible vertebræ which divided the yellow back of the panther. The animal slightly moved her tail in pleasure, and her eyes grew soft and gentle; and when for the third time the Frenchman had accomplished this interested flattery, she gave vent to purrings like those by which cats express their satisfaction; but they issued from a throat so deep, so powerful, that they resounded through the cave like the last chords of an organ rolling along the vaulted roof of a church. The Provençal, seeing the value of his caresses, redoubled them until they completely soothed and lulled this imperious female.

When he felt assured that he had extinguished the ferocity of his capricious companion, whose hunger had so luckily been appeased the day before, he got up to leave the grotto. The panther let him go out, but when he reached the summit of the little knoll she sprang up and bounded after him with the lightness of a sparrow hopping from twig to twig on a tree, and rubbed against his legs, arching her back after the manner of a domestic cat. Then regarding her guest with eyes whose glare had somewhat softened, she gave vent to that wild cry which naturalists compare to the grating of a saw.

"Madame is exacting," said the Frenchman, smiling.

He was bold enough to play with her ears; he stroked her belly and scratched her head good and hard with his nails. He was encouraged with his success, and tickled her skull with the point of his dagger, watching for an opportune moment to kill her, but the hardness of the bone made him tremble, dreading failure.

The sultana of the desert showed herself gracious to her slave; she lifted her head, stretched out her neck, and betrayed her delight by the tranquillity of her relaxed attitude. It suddenly occurred to the soldier that, to slay this savage princess with one blow, he must stab deep in the throat.

He raised the blade, when the panther, satisfied, no doubt, threw herself gracefully at his feet and glanced up at him with a look in which, despite her natural ferocity, a glimmer of good-will was apparent. The poor Provençal, thus frustrated for the nonce, ate his dates as he leaned against one of the palm-trees, casting an interrogating glance from time to time across the desert, in quest of some deliverer, and on his terrible companion, watching the chances of her uncertain clemency.

The panther looked at the place where the date-stones fell; and, each time he threw one, she examined the Frenchman with an eye of evident distrust. However, the examination seemed to be favourable to him, for, when he had eaten his frugal meal, she licked his boots with her powerful rough tongue, cleaning off in a marvelous manner the dust which was caked in the wrinkles.

"Ah! but how when she is really hungry?" thought the Provençal. In spite of the shudder caused by his thought, his attention was curiously drawn to the symmetrical proportions of the animal, which was certainly one of the most splendid specimens of its race. He began to measure them with his eye. She was three feet in height at the shoulders and four feet in length, not counting her tail; this powerful weapon was nearly three feet long, and rounded like a cudgel. The head, large as that of a lioness, was distinguished by an intelligent, crafty expression. The cold cruelty of the tiger dominated, and yet it bore a vague resemblance to the face of a wanton woman. Indeed, the countenance of this solitary queen had something of the gayety of a Nero in his cups; her thirst for blood was slaked, now she wished for amusement.

The soldier tried if he might walk up and down; the panther left him freedom, contenting herself with following him with her eyes, less like a faithful dog watching his master's movements with affectionate solicitude, than a huge Angora cat uneasy and suspicious of every movement.

When he looked around he saw, by the spring, the carcass of his horse; the panther had dragged the remains all that distance, and had eaten about two-thirds of it already. The sight reassured the Frenchman, it made it easy to explain the panther's absence and the forbearance she had shown him while he slept.

This first good luck emboldened the soldier to think of the future. He conceived the wild idea of continuing on good terms with his companion and to share her home, to try every means to tame her and endeavour to turn her good graces to his account.

With these thoughts he returned to her side, and had the unspeakable joy of seeing her wag her tail with an almost imperceptible motion as he approached. He sat down beside her, fearlessly, and they began to play together. He took her paws and muzzle, twisted her ears, rolled her over on her back, and stroked her warm delicate flanks. She allowed him to do whatever he liked, and, when he began to stroke the fur on her feet, she carefully drew in her murderously savage claws, which were sharp and curved like a Damascus sword.

The Frenchman kept one hand on his poniard, and thought to watch his chance to plunge it into the belly of the too confiding animal; but he was fearful lest he might be strangled in her last convulsive struggles; besides this, he felt in his heart a sort of remorse which bade him respect this hitherto inoffensive creature that had done him no hurt. He seemed to have found a friend in the boundless desert, and, half-unconsciously, his mind reverted to his old sweetheart whom he had, in derision, nicknamed "Mignonne" by way of contrast because she was so furiously jealous; during the whole period of their intercourse he lived in dread of the knife with which she ever threatened him.

This recollection of his youthful days suggested the idea of making the panther answer to this name, now that he began to admire with less fear her graceful swiftness, agility, and softness. Toward the close of the day he had so familiarized himself with his perilous position that he was half in love with his dangerous situation and its painfulness. At last his companion had grown so far tamed that she had caught the habit of looking up at him whenever he called in a falsetto voice "Mignonne."

At the setting of the sun Mignonne, several times in succession, gave a long, deep, melancholy cry.

"She has been well brought up," thought the light-hearted soldier; "she says her prayers." But this jesting thought only occurred to him when he noticed that his companion still retained her pacific attitude.

"Come, my little blonde, I'll let you go to bed first," he said to her, counting on the activity of his own legs to run away as soon as she was asleep; to reach as great distance as possible, and seek some other shelter for the night.

With the utmost impatience the soldier waited the hour of his flight. When it arrived he started off vigorously in the direction of the Nile; but hardly had he made a quarter of a league in the sand when he heard the panther bounding after him; at intervals giving out that saw-like cry which was more terrible than her leaping gait.

"Ah!" said he, "she's fallen in love with me; she has never met anyone before; it is really flattering to be her first love."

So thinking he fell into one of those treacherous quicksands, so menacing to travelers, and from which it is an impossibility to save one's self. Finding himself caught he gave a shriek of alarm. The panther seizing his collar with her teeth, and springing vigorously backward, drew him as by magic out of the sucking sand.

"Ah, Mignonne!" cried the soldier, enthusiastically kissing her; "we are bound to each other now—for life and death! But no tricks, mind!" and he retraced his steps.

From that time the desert was inhabited for him. It contained a being to whom he could talk and whose ferocity was now lulled into gentleness, although he could not explain to himself this strange friendship. Anxious as he was to keep awake and on guard, as it were, he gradually succumbed to his excessive fatigue of body and mind; he threw himself on the floor of the cave and slept soundly.

On awakening, Mignonne was absent; he climbed the hillock and afar off saw her returning in the long bounds characteristic of those animals, who cannot run owing to the extreme flexibility of the vertebral column.

Mignonne arrived with bloody jaws; she received the wonted caresses, the tribute her slave hastened to pay, and showed by her purring how transported she was. Her eyes, full of languor, rested more kindly on the Provençal than on the previous day, and he addressed her as he would have done a domestic animal.

"Ah! mademoiselle, you're a nice girl, aren't you? Just see now! we like to be petted, don't we? Are you not ashamed of yourself? So you've been eating some Arab or other, eh? well, that doesn't matter. They're animals, the same as you are; but don't take to crunching up a Frenchman, bear that in mind, or I shall not love you any longer."

She played like a dog with its master, allowing herself to be rolled over, knocked about, stroked, and the rest, alternately; at times she would coax him to play by putting her paw upon his knee and making a pretty gesture of solicitation.

Some days passed in this manner. This companionship allowed the Provençal to properly appreciate the sublime beauties of the desert. He had now discovered in the rising and setting of the sun sights utterly unknown to the world. He knew what it was to tremble when over his head he heard the hiss of a bird's wing, which occurred so rarely, or when he saw the clouds changing like many-coloured travelers melting into each other. In the night-time he studied the effects of the moon upon the ocean of sand, where the simoom made waves swift of movement and rapid in their changes. He lived the life of the East; he marveled at its wonderful pomp; then, after having reveled in the sight of a wind-storm over the plain where the madly whirling sands made red, dry mists, and death-bearing clouds, he would welcome the night with joy, for then fell the blissful freshness of the light of the stars, and he listened to imaginary music in the skies.

Thus solitude taught him to unroll the treasures of dreams. He passed long hours in remembering mere nothings—trifles, and comparing his past life with the present.

In the end he grew passionately fond of his panther; for some sort of affection was a necessity.

Whether it was that his own will powerfully projected had modified that of his companion, or whether, because she had found abundant food in her predatory excursions in the desert, she respected the man's life, he feared no longer for it, for she became exceedingly tame.

Most of his time he devoted to sleep, but he was compelled to watch like a spider in its web, that the moment of his deliverance might not escape him, in case any should come his way over that line marked by the horizon. His shirt he had sacrificed in the making of a flag, which he attached to the top of a palm-tree from which he had broken the foliage. Taught by necessity, he found the means of keeping it spread out, by fastening twigs and wedges to the corners; for the fitful breeze might not be blowing at the moment when the passing traveler was looking over the desert.

Nevertheless there were long hours of gloom, when he had abandoned hope; then he played with his panther. He had come to understand the different inflexions of her voice, the expression of her eyes; he had studied the capricious patterns of the rosettes that marked her golden robe. Mignonne was not even angry when he took hold of the tuft at the end of her tail to count the black and white rings, those graceful ornaments which glistened in the sun like precious gems. It afforded him pleasure to contemplate the supple, lithe, soft lines of her lissome form, the whiteness of her belly, the graceful poise of her head. But it was especially when she was playing that he took the greatest pleasure in looking at her. The agility and youthful lightness of her movements were a continual wonder to him. He was amazed at the supple way in which she bounded, crept, and glided, or clung to the trunk of palm-trees, or rolled over, crouching sometimes to the ground and gathering herself together for her mighty spring; how she washed herself and combed down her fur. He noted that however vigorous her spring might be, however slippery the block of granite upon which she landed, she would stop, motionless, at the one word "Mignonne."

One day, under a bright midday sun, a great bird hovered in the sky. The Provençal left his panther to gaze at this new guest; but after pausing for a moment the deserted sultana uttered a deep growl.

"God take me! I do believe that she is jealous," he cried, seeing the rigid look appearing again in the metallic eyes. "The soul of Virginie has passed into her body, that's sure!"

The eagle disappeared in the ether, and the soldier admired the panther again, recalled by her evident displeasure, her rounded flanks, and the perfect grace of her attitude. She was as pretty as a woman. There were youth and grace in her form. The blond fur of her robe shaded, with delicate gradations, to the dead-white tones of her furry thighs; the vivid sunshine brought out in its fullness the brilliancy of this living gold and its variegated brown spots with indescribable luster.

The Provençal and the panther looked at each other with a look pregnant with meaning. She trembled with delight (the coquettish creature) when she felt her friend scratch the strong bones of her skull with his nails. Her eyes glittered like lightning-flashes—then she closed them tightly.

"She has a soul!" cried he, looking at the stillness of this queen of the sands, golden like them, white as their waving light, solitary and burning as themselves.

"Well," said she, "I have read your defense of the beasts, but now tell me the end of this friendship between two beings who seemed to understand each other so thoroughly."

"Ah! there you are!" I replied. "It finished as all great passions end—by a misunderstanding. I believe that both sides imagine treachery; pride prevents an explanation, the rupture comes to pass through obstinacy."

"And sometimes on pleasant occasions," said she, "a glance, a word, an exclamation is all-sufficient. Well, tell me the end of the story."

"That is horribly difficult. But you will understand it the better if I give it you in the words of the old veteran, as he finished the bottle of champagne and exclaimed:

"'I don't know how I could have hurt her, but she suddenly turned on me in a frenzy, seizing my thigh with her sharp teeth, and yet (I thought of this afterward) not cruelly. I imagined that she intended devouring me, and I plunged my poniard in her throat. She rolled over with a cry that rent my soul; she looked at me in her death-struggle, but without anger. I would have given the whole world—my Cross, which I had not yet gained, all, everything—to restore her life to her. It was as if I had assassinated a real human being, a friend. When the soldiers who had seen my flag came to my rescue they found me in tears. Ah! well, monsieur,' he resumed, after a momentary pause, eloquent by its silence, 'I went through the wars in Germany, Spain, Russia, and France; I have marched my carcass well-nigh the world over, but I have seen nothing comparable to the desert. Ah! it is most beautiful! glorious!'

" 'What were your feelings there?' I asked.

" 'They can not be told, young man. Besides, I do not always regret my panther, my bouquet of palms. I must, indeed, be sad for that. In the desert, see you, there is all, and there is nothing.'

" 'But wait!—explain that!'

" 'Well, then,' he replied, with an impatient gesture, 'God is there, man is not.' "

A Tent in Agony

by STEPHEN CRANE

Stephen Crane is generally known for his grim realism: "The Red Badge of Courage"; "The Open Boat" . . . and to animal lovers for his terrible story, "A Dark Brown Dog." Here we have a different animal, and a very different mood.

FOUR men once came to a wet place in the roadless forest to fish. They pitched their tent fair upon the brow of a pine-clothed ridge of riven rocks whence a bowlder could be made to crash through the brush and whirl past the trees to the lake below. On fragrant hemlock boughs they slept the sleep of successful fishermen, for upon the lake alternately the sun made them lazy and the rain made them wet. Finally they ate the last bit of bacon, and smoked, and burned the last fearful and wonderful hoe-cake.

Immediately a little man volunteered to stay and hold the camp while the remaining three should go the Sullivan county miles to a farmhouse for supplies. They gazed at him dismally. "There's only one of you—the devil make a twin," they said in parting malediction, and disappeared down the hill in the known direction of a distant cabin. When it came night and the hemlocks began to sob, they had not returned. The little man sat close to his companion, the campfire, and encouraged it with logs. He puffed fiercely at a heavy built brier, and regarded a thousand shadows which were about to assault him. Suddenly he heard the approach of the unknown, crackling the twigs and rustling the dead leaves. The little man arose slowly to his feet, his clothes refused to fit his back, his pipe dropped from his mouth, his knees smote each other. "Hah!" he bellowed hoarsely in menace. A growl replied and a bear paced into the light of the fire. The little man supported himself upon a sapling and regarded his visitor.

The bear was evidently a veteran and a fighter, for the black of his coat had become tawny with age. There was confidence in his gait and arrogance in his small, twinkling eye. He rolled back his lips and disclosed his white teeth. The fire magnified the red of his mouth. The little man had never before confronted the terrible, and he could not wrest it from his breast. "Hah!" he roared. The bear interpreted this as the challenge of a gladiator. He approached warily. As he came near, the boots of fear were suddenly upon the little man's feet. He cried out and then darted around the campfire. "Ho!" said the bear to himself, "this thing won't fight—it runs. Well, suppose I catch it." So upon his features there fixed the animal look of going—somewhere. He started intensely around the campfire. The little man shrieked and ran furiously. Twice around they went.

The hand of heaven sometimes falls heavily upon the righteous. The bear gained.

In desperation the little man flew into the tent. The bear stopped and sniffed at the entrance. He scented the scent of many men. Finally he ventured in.

The little man crouched in a distant corner. The bear advanced, creeping, his blood burning, his hair erect, his jowls dripping. The little man yelled and rustled clumsily under the flap at the end of the tent. The bear snarled awfully and made a jump and a grab at his disappearing game. The little man, now without the tent, felt a tremendous paw grab his coat tails. He squirmed and wriggled out of his coat like a schoolboy in the hands of an avenger. The bear howled triumphantly and jerked the coat into the tent and took two bites, a punch and a hug before he discovered his man was not in it. Then he grew not very angry, for a bear on a spree is not a black-haired pirate. He is merely a hoodlum. He lay down on his back, took the coat on his four paws and began to play uproariously with it. The most appalling, bloodcurdling whoops and yells came to where the little man was crying in a tree-top, and froze his blood. He moaned a little speech meant for a prayer and clung convulsively to the bending branches. He gazed with tearful wistfulness at where his comrade, the campfire, was giving dying flickers and crackles. Finally, there was a roar from the tent which eclipsed all roars; a snarl which it seemed would shake the stolid silence of the mountain and cause it to shrug its granite shoulders. The little man quaked and shriveled to a grip and a pair of eyes. In the glow of the embers he saw the white tent quiver and fall with a crash. The bear's merry play had disturbed the centre pole and brought a chaos of canvas upon his head.

Now the little man became the witness of a mighty scene. The tent began to flounder. It took flopping strides in the direction of the lake. Marvelous sounds came from within—rips and tears and great groans and pants. The little man went into giggling hysterics.

The entangled monster failed to extricate himself before he had walloped the tent frenziedly to the edge of the mountain. So it came to pass that three men, clambering up the hill with bundles and baskets, saw their tent approaching.

It seemed to them like a white-robed phantom pursued by hornets. Its moans riffled the hemlock twigs.

The three men dropped their bundles and scurried to one side, their eyes gleaming with fear. The canvas avalanche swept past them. They leaned, faint and dumb, against trees and listened, their blood stagnant. Below them it struck the base of a great pine tree, where it writhed and struggled. The three watched its convolutions a moment and then started terrifically for the top of the hill. As they disappeared, the bear cut loose with a mighty effort. He cast one disheveled and agonized look at the white thing and then started wildly for the inner recesses of the forest.

The three fear-stricken individuals ran to the rebuilt fire. The little man reposed by it, calmly smoking. They sprang at him and overwhelmed him with interrogations. He contemplated darkness and took a long, pompous puff. "There's only one of me—and the devil made a twin," he said.

For the Love of a Man

by JACK LONDON

*This excerpt from the "Call of the Wild" has been
included in so many anthologies that I hesitated for a
long time before I decided that it was certainly the best
animal story Jack London had ever written, and that it
was one of the greatest animal stories in American literature.*

WHEN John Thornton froze his feet in the previous December, his partners had made him comfortable and left him
to get well, going on themselves up the river to get out a raft of saw-
logs for Dawson. He was still limping slightly at the time he rescued Buck, but with the continued warm weather even the slight
limp left him. And here, lying by the river bank through the long
spring days, watching the running water, listening lazily to the
songs of birds and the hum of nature, Buck slowly won back his
strength.

A rest comes very good after one has traveled three thousand
miles, and it must be confessed that Buck waxed lazy as his wounds
healed, his muscles swelled out, and the flesh came back to cover
his bones. For that matter, they were all loafing,—Buck, John Thornton, and Skeet and Nig,—waiting for the raft to come that was to
carry them down to Dawson. Skeet was a little Irish setter who
early made friends with Buck, who, in a dying condition, was unable to resent her first advances. She had the doctor trait which
some dogs possess; and as a mother cat washes her kittens, so she
washed and cleansed Buck's wounds. Regularly, each morning
after he had finished his breakfast, she performed her self-appointed
task, till he came to look for her ministrations as much as he did for
Thornton's. Nig, equally friendly, though less demonstrative, was a

465

huge black dog, half bloodhound and half deerhound, with eyes
that laughed and a boundless good nature. To Buck's surprise these
dogs manifested no jealousy toward him. They seemed to share
the kindliness and largeness of John Thornton. As Buck grew
stronger they enticed him into all sorts of ridiculous games, in which
Thornton himself could not forbear to join; and in this fashion
Buck romped through his convalescence and into a new existence.
Love, genuine passionate love, was his for the first time. This he had
never experienced at Judge Miller's down in the sun-kissed Santa
Clara Valley. With the Judge's sons, hunting and tramping, it had
been a working partnership; with the Judge's grandsons, a sort of
pompous guardianship; and with the Judge himself, a stately and
dignified friendship. But love that was feverish and burning, that
was adoration, that was madness, it had taken John Thornton to
arouse.

This man had saved his life, which was something; but, further,
he was the ideal master. Other men saw to the welfare of their
dogs from a sense of duty and business expediency; he saw to the
welfare of his as if they were his own children, because he could
not help it. And he saw further. He never forgot a kindly greeting
or a cheering word, and to sit down for a long talk with them
("gas" he called it) was as much his delight as theirs. He had a way
of taking Buck's head roughly between his hands, and resting his
own head upon Buck's, of shaking him back and forth, the while
calling him ill names that to Buck were love names. Buck knew no
greater joy than that rough embrace and the sound of murmured
oaths, and at each jerk back and forth it seemed that his heart would
be shaken out of his body, so great was its ecstasy. And when, released, he sprang to his feet, his mouth laughing, his eyes eloquent,
his throat vibrant with unuttered sound, and in that fashion remained without movement, John Thornton would reverently ex-
claim, "God! you can all but speak!"

Buck had a trick of love expression that was akin to hurt. He would
often seize Thornton's hand in his mouth and close so fiercely that
the flesh bore the impress of his teeth for some time afterward. And
as Buck understood the oaths to be love words, so the man understood this feigned bite for a caress.

For the most part, however, Buck's love was expressed in adoration. While he went wild with happiness when Thornton touched him or spoke to him, he did not seek these tokens. Unlike Skeet, who was wont to shove her nose under Thornton's hand and nudge and nudge till petted, or Nig, who would stalk up and rest his great head on Thornton's knee, Buck was content to adore at a distance. He would lie by the hour, eager, alert, at Thornton's feet, looking up into his face, dwelling upon it, studying it, following with keenest interest each fleeting expression, every movement or change of feature. Or, as chance might have it, he would lie farther away, to the side or rear, watching the outlines of the man and the occasional movements of his body. And often, such was the communion in which they lived, the strength of Buck's gaze would draw John Thornton's head around, and he would return the gaze, without speech, his heart shining out of his eyes as Buck's heart shone out.

For a long time after his rescue, Buck did not like Thornton to get out of his sight. From the moment he left the tent to when he entered it again, Buck would follow at his heels. His transient masters since he had come into the Northland had bred in him a fear that no master could be permanent. He was afraid that Thornton would pass out of his life as Perrault and François and the Scotch half-breed had passed out. Even in the night, in his dreams, he was haunted by this fear. At such times he would shake off sleep and creep through the chill to the flap of the tent, where he would stand and listen to the sound of his master's breathing.

But in spite of this great love he bore John Thornton, which seemed to bespeak the soft civilizing influence, the strain of the primitive, which the Northland had aroused in him, remained alive and active. Faithfulness and devotion, things born of fire and roof, were his; yet he retained his wildness and wiliness. He was a thing of the wild, come in from the wild to sit by John Thornton's fire, rather than a dog of the soft Southland stamped with the marks of generations of civilization. Because of his very great love, he could not steal from this man, but from any other man, in any other camp, he did not hesitate an instant; while the cunning with which he stole enabled him to escape detection.

His face and body were scored by the teeth of many dogs, and he fought as fiercely as ever and more shrewdly. Skeet and Nig were too good-natured for quarreling,—besides, they belonged to

John Thornton; but the strange dog, no matter what the breed or
valor, swiftly acknowledged Buck's supremacy or found himself
struggling for life with a terrible antagonist. And Buck was merci-
less. He had learned well the law of club and fang, and he never
forewent an advantage or drew back from a foe he had started on
the way to Death. He had lessoned from Spitz, and from the chief
fighting dogs of the police and mail, and knew there was no middle
course. He must master or be mastered; while to show mercy was
a weakness. Mercy did not exist in the primordial life. It was misunderstood for fear, and such misunderstandings made for death.
Kill or be killed, eat or be eaten, was the law; and this mandate,
down out of the depths of Time, he obeyed.

He was older than the days he had seen and the breaths he had
drawn. He linked the past with the present, and the eternity behind
him throbbed through him in a mighty rhythm to which he swayed
as the tides and seasons swayed. He sat by John Thornton's fire, a
broad-breasted dog, white-fanged and long-furred; but behind him
were the shades of all manner of dogs, half-wolves and wild wolves,
urgent and prompting, tasting the savor of the meat he ate, thirsting
for the water he drank, scenting the wind with him, listening with
him and telling him the sounds made by the wild life in the forest,
dictating his moods, directing his actions, lying down to sleep with
him when he lay down, and dreaming with him and beyond him
and becoming themselves the stuff of his dreams.

So peremptorily did these shades beckon him, that each day mankind and the claims of mankind slipped farther from him. Deep in
the forest a call was sounding, and as often as he heard this call,
mysteriously thrilling and luring, he felt compelled to turn his back
upon the fire and the beaten earth around it, and to plunge into the
forest, and on and on, he knew not where or why; nor did he wonder where or why, the call sounding imperiously, deep in the forest.
But as often as he gained the soft unbroken earth and the green
shade, the love for John Thornton drew him back to the fire again.

Thornton alone held him. The rest of mankind was as nothing.
Chance travelers might praise or pet him; but he was cold under it
all, and from a too demonstrative man he would get up and walk
away. When Thornton's partners, Hans and Pete, arrived on the
long-expected raft, Buck refused to notice them till he learned they

were close to Thornton; after that he tolerated them in a passive sort of way, accepting favors from them as though he favored them by accepting. They were of the same large type as Thornton, living close to the earth, thinking simply and seeing clearly; and ere they swung the raft into the big eddy by the sawmill at Dawson, they understood Buck and his ways, and did not insist upon an intimacy such as obtained with Skeet and Nig.

For Thornton, however, his love seemed to grow and grow. He, alone among men, could put a pack upon Buck's back in the summer traveling. Nothing was too great for Buck to do, when Thornton commanded. One day (they had grub-staked themselves from the proceeds of the raft and left Dawson for the head-waters of the Tanana) the men and dogs were sitting on the crest of a cliff which fell away, straight down, to naked bed-rock three hundred feet below. John Thornton was sitting near the edge, Buck at his shoulder. A thoughtless whim seized Thornton, and he drew the attention of Hans and Pete to the experiment he had in mind. "Jump, Buck!" he commanded, sweeping his arm out and over the chasm. The next instant he was grappling with Buck on the extreme edge, while Hans and Pete were dragging them back into safety.

"It's uncanny," Pete said, after it was over and they had caught their speech.

Thornton shook his head. "No, it is splendid, and it is terrible, too. Do you know, it sometimes makes me afraid."

"I'm not hankering to be the man that lays hands on you while he's around," Pete announced conclusively, nodding his head toward Buck.

"Py Jingo!" was Han's contribution, "not mineself either."

It was at Circle City, ere the year was out, that Pete's apprehensions were realized. "Black" Burton, a man evil-tempered and malicious, had been picking a quarrel with a tenderfoot at the bar, when Thornton stepped good-naturedly between. Buck, as was his custom, was lying in a corner, head on paws, watching his master's every action. Burton struck out, without warning, straight from the shoulder. Thornton was sent spinning, and saved himself from falling only by clutching the rail of the bar.

Those who were looking on heard what was neither bark nor

yelp, but a something which is best described as a roar, and they
saw Buck's body rise up in the air as he left the floor for Burton's
throat. The man saved his life by instinctively throwing out his arm,
but was hurled backward to the floor with Buck on top of him.
Buck loosed his teeth from the flesh of the arm and drove in again
for the throat. This time the man succeeded only in partly blocking,
and his throat was torn open. Then the crowd was upon Buck, and
he was driven off; but while a surgeon checked the bleeding, he
prowled up and down, growling furiously, attempting to rush in,
and being forced back by an array of hostile clubs. A "miners'
meeting," called on the spot, decided that the dog had sufficient
provocation, and Buck was discharged. But his reputation was made,
and from that day his name spread through every camp in Alaska.

Later on, in the fall of the year, he saved John Thornton's life
in quite another fashion. The three partners were lining a long and
narrow poling-boat down a bad stretch of rapids on the Forty-Mile
Creek. Hans and Pete moved along the bank, snubbing with a thin
Manila rope from tree to tree, while Thornton remained in the boat,
helping its descent by means of a pole, and shouting directions to
the shore. Buck, on the bank, worried and anxious, kept abreast of
the boat, his eyes never off his master.

At a particularly bad spot, where a ledge of barely submerged
rocks jutted out into the river, Hans cast off the rope, and, while
Thornton poled the boat out into the stream, ran down the bank
with the end in his hand to snub the boat when it had cleared the
ledge. This it did, and was flying down-stream in a current as swift
as a mill-race, when Hans checked it with the rope and checked too
suddenly. The boat flirted over and snubbed in to the bank bottom up, while Thornton, flung sheer out of it, was carried down-
stream toward the worst part of the rapids, a stretch of wild water
in which no swimmer could live.

Buck had sprung in on the instant; and at the end of three hundred yards, amid a mad swirl of water, he overhauled Thornton.
When he felt him grasp his tail, Buck headed for the bank, swimming with all his splendid strength. But the progress shoreward was
slow; the progress down-stream amazingly rapid. From below came
the fatal roaring where the wild current went wilder and was rent
in shreds and spray by the rocks which thrust through like the

teeth of an enormous comb. The suck of the water as it took the beginning of the last steep pitch was frightful, and Thornton knew that the shore was impossible. He scraped furiously over a rock, bruised across a second, and struck a third with crushing force. He clutched its slippery top with both hands, releasing Buck, and above the roar of the churning water shouted: "Go, Buck! Go!"

Buck could not hold his own, and swept on down-stream, struggling desperately, but unable to win back. When he heard Thornton's command repeated, he partly reared out of the water, throwing his head high, as though for a last look, then turned obediently toward the bank. He swam powerfully and was dragged ashore by Pete and Hans at the very point where swimming ceased to be possible and destruction began.

They knew that the time a man could cling to a slippery rock in the face of that driving current was a matter of minutes, and they ran as fast as they could up the bank to a point far above where Thornton was hanging on. They attached the line with which they had been snubbing the boat to Buck's neck and shoulders, being careful that it should neither strangle him nor impede his swimming, and launched him into the stream. He struck out boldly, but not straight enough into the stream. He discovered the mistake too late, when Thornton was abreast of him and a bare half-dozen strokes away while he was being carried helplessly past.

Hans promptly snubbed with the rope, as though Buck were a boat. The rope thus tightening on him in the sweep of the current, he was jerked under the surface, and under the surface he remained till his body struck against the bank and he was hauled out. He was half drowned, and Hans and Pete threw themselves upon him, pounding the breath into him and the water out of him. He staggered to his feet and fell down. The faint sound of Thornton's voice came to them, and though they could not make out the words of it, they knew that he was in his extremity. His master's voice acted on Buck like an electric shock. He sprang to his feet and ran up the bank ahead of the men to the point of his previous departure.

Again the rope was attached and he was launched, and again he struck out, but this time straight into the stream. He had miscalculated once, but he would not be guilty of it a second time. Hans paid out the rope, permitting no slack, while Pete kept it clear of coils. Buck held on till he was on a line straight above Thornton; then he turned, and with the speed of an express train headed down upon him. Thornton saw him coming, and, as Buck struck him like a battering ram, with the whole force of the current behind him, he reached up and closed with both arms around the shaggy neck. Hans snubbed the rope around the tree, and Buck and Thornton were jerked under the water. Strangling, suffocating, sometimes one uppermost and sometimes the other, dragging over the jagged bottom, smashing against rocks and snags, they veered in to the bank.

Thornton came to, belly downward and being violently propelled back and forth across a drift log by Hans and Pete. His first glance was for Buck, over whose limp and apparently lifeless body Nig was setting up a howl, while Skeet was licking the wet face and closed eyes. Thornton was himself bruised and battered, and he went carefully over Buck's body, when he had been brought around, finding three broken ribs.

"That settles it," he announced. "We camp right here." And camp they did, till Buck's ribs knitted and he was able to travel.

That winter, at Dawson, Buck performed another exploit, not so heroic, perhaps, but one that put his name many notches higher on the totem-pole of Alaskan fame. This exploit was particularly gratifying to the three men; for they stood in need of the outfit which it furnished, and were enabled to make a long-desired trip into the virgin East, where miners had not yet appeared. It was brought about by a conversation in the Eldorado Saloon, in which men waxed boastful of their favorite dogs. Buck, because of his record, was the target for these men, and Thornton was driven stoutly to defend him. At the end of half an hour one man stated that his dog could start a sled with five hundred pounds and walk off with it; a second bragged six hundred for his dog; and a third, seven hundred.

"Pooh! pooh!" said John Thornton; "Buck can start a thousand pounds."

"And break it out? and walk off with it for a hundred yards?" demanded Matthewson, a Bonanza King, he of the seven hundred vaunt.

"And break it out, and walk off with it for a hundred yards," John Thornton said coolly.

"Well," Matthewson said, slowly and deliberately, so that all could hear, "I've got a thousand dollars that says he can't. And there it is." So saying, he slammed a sack of gold dust of the size of a bologna sausage down upon the bar.

Nobody spoke. Thornton's bluff, if bluff it was, had been called. He could feel a flush of warm blood creeping up his face. His tongue had tricked him. He did not know whether Buck could start a thousand pounds. Half a ton! The enormousness of it appalled him. He had great faith in Buck's strength and had often thought him capable of starting such a load; but never, as now, had he faced the possibility of it, the eyes of a dozen men fixed upon him, silent and waiting. Further, he had no thousand dollars; nor had Hans or Pete.

"I've got a sled standing outside now, with twenty fifty-pound sacks of flour on it," Matthewson went on with brutal directness; "so don't let that hinder you."

Thornton did not reply. He did not know what to say. He glanced from face to face in the absent way of a man who has lost the power of thought and is seeking somewhere to find the thing that will start it going again. The face of Jim O'Brien, a Mastodon King and old-time comrade, caught his eyes. It was as a cue to him, seeming to rouse him to do what he would never have dreamed of doing.

"Can you lend me a thousand?" he asked, almost in a whisper.

"Sure," answered O'Brien, thumping down a plethoric sack by the side of Matthewson's. "Though it's little faith I'm having, John, that the beast can do the trick."

The Eldorado emptied its occupants into the street to see the test. The tables were deserted, and the dealers and gamekeepers came forth to see the outcome of the wager and to lay odds. Several hundred men, furred and mittened, banked around the sled within easy distance. Matthewson's sled, loaded with a thousand pounds of flour, had been standing for a couple of hours, and in the intense cold (it was sixty below zero) the runners had frozen fast to the hard-packed snow. Men offered odds of two to one that Buck could not budge the sled. A quibble arose concerning the phrase "break

out." O'Brien contended it was Thornton's privilege to knock the
runners loose, leaving Buck to "break it out" from a dead standstill.
Matthewson insisted that the phrase included breaking the runners
from the frozen grip of the snow. A majority of the men who had
witnessed the making of the bet decided in his favor, whereat the
odds went up to three to one against Buck.

There were no takers. Not a man believed him capable of the
feat. Thornton had been hurried into the wager, heavy with doubt;
and now that he looked at the sled itself, the concrete fact, with the
regular team of ten dogs curled up in the snow before it, the more
impossible the task appeared. Matthewson waxed jubilant.

"Three to one!" he proclaimed. "I'll lay you another thousand
at that figure, Thornton. What d'ye say?"

Thornton's doubt was strong in his face, but his fighting spirit
was aroused—the fighting spirit that soars above odds, fails to recognize the impossible, and is deaf to all save the clamor for battle. He
called Hans and Pete to him. Their sacks were slim, and with his
own the three partners could rake together only two hundred dollars. In the ebb of their fortunes, this sum was their total capital;
yet they laid it unhesitatingly against Matthewson's six hundred.

The team of ten dogs was unhitched, and Buck, with his own
harness, was put into the sled. He had caught the contagion of the
excitement, and he felt that in some way he must do a great thing
for John Thornton. Murmurs of admiration at his splendid appearance went up. He was in perfect condition, without an ounce of
superfluous flesh, and the one hundred and fifty pounds that he
weighed were so many pounds of grit and virility. His furry coat
shone with the sheen of silk. Down the neck and across the shoulders, his mane, in repose as it was, half bristled and seemed to lift
with every movement, as though excess of vigor made each particular hair alive and active. The great breast and heavy forelegs
were no more than in proportion with the rest of the body, where
the muscles showed in tight rolls underneath the skin. Men felt
these muscles and proclaimed them hard as iron, and the odds went
down to two to one.

"Gad, sir! Gad, sir!" spluttered a member of the latest dynasty,
a king of the Skookum Benches. "I offer you eight hundred for him,
sir, before the test, sir; eight hundred just as he stands."

Thornton shook his head and stepped to Buck's side.

"You must stand off from him," Matthewson protested. "Free play and plenty of room."

The crowd fell silent; only could be heard the voices of the gamblers vainly offering two to one. Everybody acknowledged Buck a magnificent animal, but twenty fifty-pound sacks of flour bulked too large in their eyes for them to loosen their pouch-strings.

Thornton knelt down by Buck's side. He took his head in his two hands and rested cheek on cheek. He did not playfully shake him, as was his wont, or murmur soft love curses; but he whispered in his ear. "As you love me, Buck. As you love me," was what he whispered. Buck whined with suppressed eagerness.

The crowd was watching curiously. The affair was growing mysterious. It seemed like a conjuration. As Thornton got to his feet, Buck seized his mittened hand between his jaws, pressing in with his teeth and releasing slowly, half-reluctantly. It was the answer, in terms, not of speech, but of love. Thornton stepped well back.

"Now, Buck," he said.

Buck tightened the traces, then slackened them for a matter of several inches. It was the way he had learned.

"Gee!" Thornton's voice rang out, sharp in the tense silence.

Buck swung to the right, ending the movement in a plunge that took up the slack and with a sudden jerk arrested his one hundred and fifty pounds. The load quivered, and from under the runners arose a crisp crackling.

"Haw!" Thornton commanded.

Buck duplicated the manœuvre, this time to the left. The crackling turned into a snapping, the sled pivoting and the runners slipping and grating several inches to the side. The sled was broken out. Men were holding their breaths, although they were intensely unconscious of the fact.

"Now, MUSH!"

Thornton's command cracked out like a pistol-shot. Buck threw himself forward, tightening the traces with a jarring lunge. His whole body was gathered compactly together in the tremendous effort, the muscles writhing and knotting like live things under the silky fur. His great chest was low to the ground, his head forward and down, while his feet were flying like mad, the claws scarring

the hard-packed snow in parallel grooves. The sled swayed and
trembled, half-started forward. One of his feet slipped, and one
man groaned aloud. Then the sled lurched ahead in what appeared
a rapid succession of jerks, though it never really came to a dead
stop again . . . half an inch . . . an inch . . . two inches. . . .
The jerks perceptibly diminished; as the sled gained momentum,
he caught them up, till it was moving steadily along.

Men gasped and began to breathe again, unaware that for a moment they had ceased to breathe. Thornton was running behind,
encouraging Buck with short, cheery words. The distance had been
measured off, and as he neared the pile of firewood which marked
the end of the hundred yards, a cheer began to grow and grow,
which burst into a roar as he passed the firewood and halted at command. Every man was tearing himself loose, even Matthewson.
Hats and mittens were flying in the air. Men were shaking hands,
it did not matter with whom, and bubbling over in a general in-
coherent babel.

But Thornton fell on his knees beside Buck. Head was against
head, and he was shaking him back and forth. Those who hurried
up heard him cursing Buck, and he cursed him long and fervently,
and softly and lovingly.

"Gad, sir! Gad, sir!" spluttered the Skookum Bench king. "I'll
give you a thousand for him, sir, a thousand, sir—twelve hundred,
sir."

Thornton rose to his feet. His eyes were wet. The tears were
streaming frankly down his cheeks. "Sir," he said to the Skookum
Bench king, "no, sir. You can go to hell, sir. It's the best I can do
for you, sir."

Buck seized Thornton's hand in his teeth. Thornton shook him
back and forth. As though animated by a common impulse, the
onlookers drew back to a respectful distance; nor were they again
indiscreet enough to interrupt.

Kashtanka

by ANTON CHEKHOV

*Chekhov's bitter irony does not desert him when he
enters the animal kingdom. One might say that this is a
faithful dog, but I do not think that was the author's
intent.*

I

MISBEHAVIOUR

A YOUNG dog, a reddish mongrel, between a dachshund and
a "yard-dog," very like a fox in face, was running up and
down the pavement looking uneasily from side to side. From time to
time she stopped and, whining and lifting first one chilled paw and
then another, tried to make up her mind how it could have happened
that she was lost.

She remembered very well how she had passed the day, and how,
in the end, she had found herself on this unfamiliar pavement.

The day had begun by her master Luka Alexandritch's putting
on his hat, taking something wooden under his arm wrapped up in
a red handkerchief, and calling: "Kashtanka, come along!"

Hearing her name the mongrel had come out from under the
work-table, where she slept on the shavings, stretched herself
voluptuously and run after her master. The people Luka Alexandritch worked for lived a very long way off, so that, before he
could get to any one of them, the carpenter had several times to
step into a tavern to fortify himself. Kashtanka remembered that
on the way she had behaved extremely improperly. In her delight
that she was being taken for a walk she jumped about, dashed barking after the trams, ran into yards, and chased other dogs. The car-

penter was continually losing sight of her, stopping, and angrily shouting at her. Once he had even, with an expression of fury in his face, taken her fox-like ear in his fist, smacked her, and said emphatically: "Pla-a-ague take you, you pest!"

After having left the work where it had been bespoken, Luka Alexandritch went into his sister's and there had something to eat and drink; from his sister's he had gone to see a bookbinder he knew; from the bookbinder's to a tavern, from the tavern to another crony's, and so on. In short, by the time Kashtanka found herself on the unfamiliar pavement, it was getting dusk, and the carpenter was as drunk as a cobbler. He was waving his arms and, breathing heavily, muttered:

"In sin my mother bore me! Ah, sins, sins! Here now we are walking along the street and looking at the street lamps, but when we die, we shall burn in a fiery Gehenna. . . ."

Or he fell into a good-natured tone, called Kashtanka to him, and said to her: "You, Kashtanka, are an insect of a creature, and nothing else. Beside a man, you are much the same as a joiner beside a cabinet-maker. . . ."

While he talked to her in that way, there was suddenly a burst of music. Kashtanka looked round and saw that a regiment of soldiers was coming straight towards her. Unable to endure the music, which unhinged her nerves, she turned round and round and wailed. To her great surprise, the carpenter, instead of being frightened, whining and barking, gave a broad grin, drew himself up to attention, and saluted with all his five fingers. Seeing that her master did not protest, Kashtanka whined louder than ever, and dashed across the road to the opposite pavement.

When she recovered herself, the band was not playing and the regiment was no longer there. She ran across the road to the spot where she had left her master, but alas, the carpenter was no longer there. She dashed forward, then back again and ran across the road once more, but the carpenter seemed to have vanished into the earth. Kashtanka began sniffing the pavement, hoping to find her master by the scent of his tracks, but some wretch had been that way just before in new rubber goloshes, and now all delicate scents were mixed with an acute stench of india-rubber, so that it was impossible to make out anything.

Kashtanka ran up and down and did not find her master, and meanwhile it had got dark. The street lamps were lighted on both sides of the road, and lights appeared in the windows. Big, fluffy snow-flakes were falling and painting white the pavement, the horses' backs and the cabmen's caps, and the darker the evening grew the whiter were all these objects. Unknown customers kept walking incessantly to and fro, obstructing her field of vision and shoving against her with their feet. (All mankind Kashtanka divided into two uneven parts: masters and customers; between them there was an essential difference: the first had the right to beat her, and the second she had the right to nip by the calves of their legs.) These customers were hurrying off somewhere and paid no attention to her.

When it got quite dark, Kashtanka was overcome by despair and horror. She huddled up in an entrance and began whining piteously. The long day's journeying with Luka Alexandritch had exhausted her, her ears and her paws were freezing, and, what was more, she was terribly hungry. Only twice in the whole day had she tasted a morsel: she had eaten a little paste at the bookbinder's, and in one of the taverns she had found a sausage skin on the floor, near the counter—that was all. If she had been a human being she would have certainly thought: "No, it is impossible to live like this! I must shoot myself!"

II

A MYSTERIOUS STRANGER

But she thought of nothing, she simply whined. When her head and back were entirely plastered over with the soft feathery snow, and she had sunk into a painful doze of exhaustion, all at once the door of the entrance clicked, creaked, and struck her on the side. She jumped up. A man belonging to the class of customers came out. As Kashtanka whined and got under his feet, he could not help noticing her. He bent down to her and asked:

"Doggy, where do you come from? Have I hurt you? O, poor thing, poor thing. . . . Come, don't be cross, don't be cross. . . . I am sorry."

Kashtanka looked at the stranger through the snow-flakes that hung on her eyelashes, and saw before her a short, fat little man, with a plump, shaven face wearing a top hat and a fur coat that swung open.

"What are you whining for?" he went on, knocking the snow off her back with his fingers. "Where is your master? I suppose you are lost? Ah, poor doggy! What are we going to do now?"

Catching in the stranger's voice a warm, cordial note, Kashtanka licked his hand, and whined still more pitifully.

"Oh, you nice funny thing!" said the stranger. "A regular fox! Well, there's nothing for it, you must come along with me! Perhaps you will be of use for something. . . . Well!"

He clicked with his lips, and made a sign to Kashtanka with his hand, which could only mean one thing: "Come along!" Kashtanka went.

Not more than half an hour later she was sitting on the floor in a big, light room, and, leaning her head against her side, was looking with tenderness and curiosity at the stranger who was sitting at the table, dining. He ate and threw pieces to her. . . . At first he gave her bread and the green rind of cheese, then a piece of meat, half a pie and chicken bones, while through hunger she ate so quickly that she had not time to distinguish the taste, and the more she ate the more acute was the feeling of hunger.

"Your masters don't feed you properly," said the stranger, seeing with what ferocious greediness she swallowed the morsels without munching them. "And how thin you are! Nothing but skin and bones. . . ."

Kashtanka ate a great deal and yet did not satisfy her hunger, but was simply stupefied with eating. After dinner she lay down in the middle of the room, stretched her legs and, conscious of an agreeable weariness all over her body, wagged her tail. While her new master, lounging in an easy-chair, smoked a cigar, she wagged her tail and considered the question, whether it was better at the stranger's or at the carpenter's. The stranger's surroundings were poor and ugly; besides the easy-chairs, the sofa, the lamps and the rugs, there was nothing, and the room seemed empty. At the carpenter's the whole place was stuffed full of things: he had a table, a bench, a heap of shavings, planes, chisels, saws, a cage with a goldfinch, a basin. . . . The stranger's room smelt of nothing, while there was always a thick fog in the carpenter's room, and a glorious smell of glue, varnish, and shavings. On the other hand, the stranger had one great superiority—he gave her a great deal to eat and, to do him full justice, when Kashtanka sat facing the table and looking wistfully at him, he did not once hit or kick her, and did not once shout: "Go away, damned brute!"

When he had finished his cigar her new master went out, and a minute later came back holding a little mattress in his hands.

"Hey, you dog, come here!" he said, laying the mattress in the corner near the dog. "Lie down here, go to sleep!"

Then he put out the lamp and went away. Kashtanka lay down on the mattress and shut her eyes; the sound of a bark rose from the street, and she would have liked to answer it, but all at once she was overcome with unexpected melancholy. She thought of Luka Alexandritch, of his son Fedyushka, and her snug little place under the bench. . . . She remembered on the long winter evenings, when the carpenter was planing or reading the paper aloud, Fedyushka usually played with her. . . . He used to pull her from under the bench by her hind legs, and play such tricks with her, that she saw green before her eyes, and ached in every joint. He would make her walk on her hind legs, use her as a bell, that is, shake her violently by the tail so that she squealed and barked, and give her tobacco to sniff. . . . The following trick was particularly agonising: Fedyushka would tie a piece of meat to a thread and give it to Kashtanka, and then, when she had swallowed it he would, with a loud laugh, pull it back again from her stomach, and the more lurid were her memories the more loudly and miserably Kashtanka whined.

But soon exhaustion and warmth prevailed over melancholy. She began to fall asleep. Dogs ran by in her imagination: among them a shaggy old poodle, whom she had seen that day in the street with a white patch on his eye and tufts of wool by his nose. Fedyushka ran after the poodle with a chisel in his hand, then all at once he too was covered with shaggy wool, and began merrily barking beside Kashtanka. Kashtanka and he good-naturedly sniffed each other's noses and merrily ran down the street. . . .

III

When Kashtanka woke up it was already light, and a sound rose from the street, such as only comes in the day-time. There was not a soul in the room. Kashtanka stretched, yawned and, cross and ill-humoured, walked about the room. She sniffed the corners and the furniture, looked into the passage and found nothing of interest there. Besides the door that led into the passage there was another door. After thinking a little Kashtanka scratched on it with both paws, opened it, and went into the adjoining room. Here on the bed, covered with a rug, a customer, in whom she recognised the stranger of yesterday, lay asleep.

"Rrrrr . . ." she growled, but recollecting yesterday's dinner, wagged her tail, and began sniffing.

She sniffed the stranger's clothes and boots and thought they smelt of horses. In the bedroom was another door, also closed. Kashtanka scratched at the door, leaned her chest against it, opened it, and was instantly aware of a strange and very suspicious smell. Foresee-ing an unpleasant encounter, growling and looking about her, Kash-tanka walked into a little room with a dirty wall-paper and drew back in alarm. She saw something surprising and terrible. A grey gander came straight towards her, hissing, with its neck bowed down to the floor and its wings outspread. Not far from him, on a little mattress, lay a white tom-cat; seeing Kashtanka, he jumped up, arched his back, wagged his tail with his hair standing on end and he, too, hissed at her. The dog was frightened in earnest, but not caring to betray her alarm, began barking loudly and dashed at the cat. . . . The cat arched his back more than ever, mewed and gave Kashtanka a smack on the head with his paw. Kashtanka jumped back, squatted on all four paws, and craning her nose towards the cat, went off into loud, shrill barks; meanwhile the gander came up behind and gave her a painful peck in the back. Kashtanka leapt up and dashed at the gander.

"What's this?" They heard a loud angry voice, and the stranger came into the room in his dressing-gown, with a cigar between his teeth. "What's the meaning of this? To your places!"

He went up to the cat, flicked him on his arched back, and said:

"Fyodor Timofeyitch, what's the meaning of this? Have you got up a fight? Ah, you old rascal! Lie down!"

And turning to the gander he shouted: "Ivan Ivanitch, go home!"

The cat obediently lay down on his mattress and closed his eyes. Judging from the expression of his face and whiskers, he was displeased with himself for having lost his temper and got into a fight. Kashtanka began whining resentfully, while the gander craned his neck and began saying something rapidly, excitedly, distinctly, but quite unintelligibly.

"All right, all right," said his master, yawning. "You must live in peace and friendship." He stroked Kashtanka and went on: "And you, red-hair, don't be frightened. . . . They are capital company, they won't annoy you. Stay, what are we to call you? You can't go on without a name, my dear."

The stranger thought a moment and said: "I tell you what . . . you shall be Auntie. . . . Do you understand? Auntie!"

And repeating the word "Auntie" several times he went out. Kashtanka sat down and began watching. The cat sat motionless on his little mattress, and pretended to be asleep. The gander, craning his neck and stamping, went on talking rapidly and excitedly about something. Apparently it was a very clever gander; after every long tirade, he always stepped back with an air of wonder and made a show of being highly delighted with his own speech. . . . Listening to him and answering "R-r-r-r," Kashtanka fell to sniffing the corners. In one of the corners she found a little trough in which she saw some soaked peas and a sop of rye crusts. She tried the peas; they were not nice; she tried the sopped bread and began eating it. The gander was not at all offended that the strange dog was eating his food, but, on the contrary, talked even more excitedly, and to show his confidence went to the trough and ate a few peas himself.

IV

MARVELS ON A HURDLE

A little while afterwards the stranger came in again, and brought a strange thing with him like a hurdle, or like the figure II. On the crosspiece on the top of this roughly made wooden frame hung a bell, and a pistol was also tied to it; there were strings from the tongue of the bell, and the trigger of the pistol. The stranger put the frame in the middle of the room, spent a long time tying and untying something, then looked at the gander and said: "Ivan Ivanitch, if you please!"

The gander went up to him and stood in an expectant attitude.

"Now then," said the stranger, "let us begin at the very beginning. First of all, bow and make a curtsey! Look sharp!"

Ivan Ivanitch craned his neck, nodded in all directions, and scraped with his foot.

"Right. Bravo. . . . Now die!"

The gander lay on his back and stuck his legs in the air. After performing a few more similar, unimportant tricks, the stranger suddenly clutched at his head, and assuming an expression of horror, shouted: "Help! Fire! We are burning!"

Ivan Ivanitch ran to the frame, took the string in his beak, and set the bell ringing.

The stranger was very much pleased. He stroked the gander's neck and said:

"Bravo, Ivan Ivanitch! Now pretend that you are a jeweller selling gold and diamonds. Imagine now that you go to your shop and find thieves there. What would you do in that case?"

The gander took the other string in his beak and pulled it, and at once a deafening report was heard. Kashtanka was highly delighted with the bell ringing, and the shot threw her into so much ecstasy that she ran round the frame barking.

"Auntie, lie down!" cried the stranger; "be quiet!"

Ivan Ivanitch's task was not ended with the shooting. For a whole hour afterwards the stranger drove the gander round him on a cord, cracking a whip, and the gander had to jump over barriers and through hoops; he had to rear, that is, sit on his tail and wave his legs in the air. Kashtanka could not take her eyes off Ivan Ivanitch, wriggled with delight, and several times fell to running after him with shrill barks, After exhausting the gander and himself, the stranger wiped the sweat from his brow and cried:

"Marya, fetch Havronya Ivanovna here!"

A minute later there was the sound of grunting. . . . Kashtanka growled, assumed a very valiant air, and to be on the safe side, went nearer to the stranger. The door opened, an old woman looked in, and, saying something, led in a black and very ugly sow. Paying no attention to Kashtanka's growls, the sow lifted up her little hoof and grunted good-humouredly. Apparently it was very agreeable to her to see her master, the cat, and Ivan Ivanitch. When she went up to the cat and gave him a light tap on the stomach with her hoof, and then made some remark to the gander, a great deal of good-nature was expressed in her movements, and the quivering of her tail. Kashtanka realised at once that to growl and bark at such a character was useless.

The master took away the frame and cried: "Fyodor Timofeyitch, if you please!"

The cat stretched lazily, and reluctantly, as though performing a duty, went up to the sow.

"Come, let us begin with the Egyptian pyramid," began the master.

He spent a long time explaining something, then gave the word of command, "One . . . two . . . three!" At the word "three" Ivan Ivanitch flapped his wings and jumped on to the sow's back. . . . When, balancing himself with his wings and his neck, he got a firm foothold on the bristly back, Fyodor Timofeyitch listlessly and lazily, with manifest disdain, and with an air of scorning his art and not caring a pin for it, climbed on to the sow's back, then reluctantly mounted on to the gander, and stood on his hind legs. The result was what the stranger called the Egyptian pyramid. Kashtanka yapped with delight, but at that moment the old cat yawned and, losing his balance, rolled off the gander. Ivan Ivanitch lurched and fell off too. The stranger shouted, waved his hands, and began explaining something again. After spending an hour over the pyramid their indefatigable master proceeded to teach Ivan Ivanitch to ride on the cat, then began to teach the cat to smoke, and so on.

The lesson ended in the stranger's wiping the sweat off his brow and going away. Fyodor Timofeyitch gave a disdainful sniff, lay down on his mattress, and closed his eyes; Ivan Ivanitch went to the trough, and the pig was taken away by the old woman. Thanks to the number of her new impressions, Kashtanka hardly noticed how

the day passed, and in the evening she was installed with her mattress in the room with the dirty wall-paper, and spent the night in
the society of Fyodor Timofeyitch and the gander.

V

TALENT! TALENT!

A month passed.

Kashtanka had grown used to having a nice dinner every evening,
and being called Auntie. She had grown used to the stranger too, and
to her new companions. Life was comfortable and easy.

Every day began in the same way. As a rule, Ivan Ivanitch was
the first to wake up, and at once went up to Auntie or to the cat,
twisting his neck, and beginning to talk excitedly and persuasively,
but, as before, unintelligibly. Sometimes he would crane up his head
in the air and utter a long monologue. At first Kashtanka thought
he talked so much because he was very clever, but after a little
time had passed, she lost all her respect for him; when he went up
to her with his long speeches she no longer wagged her tail, but
treated him as a tiresome chatterbox, who would not let anyone
sleep and, without the slightest ceremony, answered him with
"R-r-r-r!"

Fyodor Timofeyitch was a gentleman of a very different sort.
When he woke he did not utter a sound, did not stir, and did not
even open his eyes. He would have been glad not to wake, for, as
was evident, he was not greatly in love with life. Nothing interested
him, he showed an apathetic and nonchalant attitude to everything,
he disdained everything and, even while eating his delicious dinner,
sniffed contemptuously.

When she woke Kashtanka began walking about the room and
sniffing the corners. She and the cat were the only ones allowed
to go all over the flat; the gander had not the right to cross the
threshold of the room with the dirty wall-paper, and Havronya
Ivanovna lived somewhere in a little outhouse in the yard and made
her appearance only during the lessons. Their master got up late,
and immediately after drinking his tea began teaching them their
tricks. Every day the frame, the whip, and the hoop were brought in,
and every day almost the same performance took place. The lesson

lasted three or four hours, so that sometimes Fyodor Timofeyitch was so tired that he staggered about like a drunken man, and Ivan Ivanitch opened his beak and breathed heavily, while their master became red in the face and could not mop the sweat from his brow fast enough.

The lesson and the dinner made the day very interesting, but the evenings were tedious. As a rule, their master went off somewhere in the evening and took the cat and the gander with him. Left alone, Auntie lay down on her little mattress and began to feel sad. . . .

Melancholy crept on her imperceptibly and took possession of her by degrees, as darkness does of a room. It began with the dog's losing every inclination to bark, to eat, to run about the rooms, and even to look at things; then vague figures, half dogs, half human beings, with countenances attractive, pleasant, but incomprehensible, would appear in her imagination; when they came Auntie wagged her tail, and it seemed to her that she had somewhere, at some time, seen them and loved them. . . . And as she dropped asleep, she always felt that those figures smelt of glue, shavings, and varnish.

When she had grown quite used to her new life, and from a thin, long mongrel, had changed into a sleek, well-groomed dog, her master looked at her one day before the lesson and said:

"It's high time, Auntie, to get to business. You have kicked up your heels in idleness long enough. I want to make an artiste of you. . . . Do you want to be an artiste?"

And he began teaching her various accomplishments. At the first lesson he taught her to stand and walk on her hind legs, which she liked extremely. At the second lesson she had to jump on her hind legs and catch some sugar, which her teacher held high above her head. After that, in the following lessons she danced, ran tied to a cord, howled to music, rang the bell, and fired the pistol, and in a month could successfully replace Fyodor Timofeyitch in the "Egyptian Pyramid." She learned very eagerly and was pleased with her own success; running with her tongue out on the cord, leaping through the hoop, and riding on old Fyodor Timofeyitch, gave her the greatest enjoyment. She accompanied every successful trick with a shrill, delighted bark, while her teacher wondered, was also delighted, and rubbed his hands.

"It's talent! It's talent!" he said. "Unquestionable talent! You will certainly be successful!"

And Auntie grew so used to the word talent, that every time her master pronounced it, she jumped up as if it had been her name.

VI

AN UNEASY NIGHT

Auntie had a doggy dream that a porter ran after her with a broom, and she woke up in a fright.

It was quite dark and very stuffy in the room. The fleas were biting. Auntie had never been afraid of darkness before, but now, for some reason, she felt frightened and inclined to bark.

Her master heaved a loud sigh in the next room, then soon afterwards the sow grunted in her sty, and then all was still again. When one thinks about eating one's heart grows lighter, and Auntie began thinking how that day she had stolen the leg of a chicken from Fyodor Timofeyitch, and had hidden it in the drawing-room, between the cupboard and the wall, where there were a great many spiders' webs and a great deal of dust. Would it not be as well to go now and look whether the chicken leg were still there or not? It was very possible that her master had found it and eaten it. But she must not go out of the room before morning, that was the rule. Auntie shut her eyes to go to sleep as quickly as possible, for she knew by experience that the sooner you go to sleep the sooner the morning comes. But all at once there was a strange scream not far from her which made her start and jump up on all four legs. It was Ivan Ivanitch, and his cry was not babbling and persuasive as usual, but a wild, shrill, unnatural scream, like the squeak of a door opening. Unable to distinguish anything in the darkness, and not understanding what was wrong, Auntie felt still more frightened and growled: "R-r-r-r. . . ."

Some time passed, as long as it takes to eat a good bone; the scream was not repeated. Little by little Auntie's uneasiness passed off and she began to doze. She dreamed of two big black dogs with tufts of last year's coat left on their haunches and sides; they were eating out of a big basin some swill, from which there came a white steam and a most appetising smell; from time to time they looked round at Auntie, showed their teeth and growled: "We are not going to give you any!" But a peasant in a fur-coat ran out of the house and drove them away with a whip; then Auntie went up to the basin and began eating, but as soon as the peasant went out of the gate, the two black dogs rushed at her growling, and all at once there was again a shrill scream.

"K-gee! K-gee-gee!" cried Ivan Ivanitch.

Auntie woke, jumped up and, without leaving her mattress, went off into a yelping bark. It seemed to her that it was not Ivan Ivanitch that was screaming but someone else, and for some reason the sow again grunted in her sty.

Then there was the sound of shuffling slippers, and the master came into the room in his dressing-gown with a candle in his hand. The flickering light danced over the dirty wall-paper and the ceiling, and chased away the darkness. Auntie saw that there was no stranger in the room. Ivan Ivanitch was sitting on the floor and was not asleep. His wings were spread out and his beak was open, and altogether he looked as though he were very tired and thirsty. Old Fyodor Timofeyitch was not asleep either. He, too, must have been awakened by the scream.

"Ivan Ivanitch, what's the matter with you?" the master asked the gander. "Why are you screaming? Are you ill?"

The gander did not answer. The master touched him on the neck, stroked his back, and said: "You are a queer chap. You don't sleep yourself, and you don't let other people. . . ."

When the master went out, carrying the candle with him, there was darkness again. Auntie felt frightened. The gander did not scream, but again she fancied that there was some stranger in the room. What was most dreadful was that this stranger could not be bitten, as he was unseen and had no shape. And for some reason she thought that something very bad would certainly happen that night. Fyodor Timofeyitch was uneasy too. Auntie could hear him shifting on his mattress, yawning and shaking his head.

Somewhere in the street there was a knocking at a gate and the sow grunted in her sty. Auntie began to whine, stretched out her front-paws and laid her head down upon them. She fancied that in the knocking at the gate, in the grunting of the sow, who was for some reason awake, in the darkness and the stillness, there was something as miserable and dreadful as in Ivan Ivanitch's scream. Everything was in agitation and anxiety, but why? Who was the stranger who could not be seen? Then two dim flashes of green gleamed for a minute near Auntie. It was Fyodor Timofeyitch, for the first time of their whole acquaintance coming up to her. What did he want? Auntie licked his paw, and not asking why he had come, howled softly and on various notes.

"K-gee!" cried Ivan Ivanitch. "K-g-ee!"

The door opened again and the master came in with a candle.

The gander was sitting in the same attitude as before, with his beak open, and his wings spread out, his eyes were closed.

"Ivan Ivanitch!" his master called him.

The gander did not stir. His master sat down before him on the floor, looked at him in silence for a minute, and said:

"Ivan Ivanitch, what is it? Are you dying? Oh, I remember now, I remember!" he cried out, and clutched at his head. "I know why it is! It's because the horse stepped on you to-day! My God! My God!"

Auntie did not understand what her master was saying, but she saw from his face that he, too, was expecting something dreadful. She stretched out her head towards the dark window, where it seemed to her some stranger was looking in, and howled.

"He is dying, Auntie!" said her master, and wrung his hands. "Yes, yes, he is dying! Death has come into your room. What are we to do?"

Pale and agitated, the master went back into his room, sighing and shaking his head. Auntie was afraid to remain in the darkness, and followed her master into his bedroom. He sat down on the bed and repeated several times: "My God, what's to be done?"

Auntie walked about round his feet, and not understanding why she was wretched and why they were all so uneasy, and trying to understand, watched every movement he made. Fyodor Timofeyitch, who rarely left his little mattress, came into the master's bedroom too, and began rubbing himself against his feet. He shook his head as though he wanted to shake painful thoughts out of it, and kept peeping suspiciously under the bed.

The master took a saucer, poured some water from his wash-stand into it, and went to the gander again.

"Drink, Ivan Ivanitch!" he said tenderly, setting the saucer before him; "drink, darling."

But Ivan Ivanitch did not stir and did not open his eyes. His master bent his head down to the saucer and dipped his beak into the water, but the gander did not drink, he spread his wings wider than ever, and his head remained lying in the saucer.

"No, there's nothing to be done now," sighed his master. "It's all over. Ivan Ivanitch is gone!"

And shining drops, such as one sees on the window-pane when it rains, trickled down his cheeks. Not understanding what was the matter, Auntie and Fyodor Timofeyitch snuggled up to him and looked with horror at the gander.

"Poor Ivan Ivanitch!" said the master, sighing mournfully. "And I was dreaming I would take you in the spring into the country, and would walk with you on the green grass. Dear creature, my good comrade, you are no more! How shall I do without you now?"

It seemed to Auntie that the same thing would happen to her, that is, that she too, there was no knowing why, would close her eyes, stretch out her paws, open her mouth, and everyone would look at her with horror. Apparently the same reflections were passing through the brain of Fyodor Timofeyitch. Never before had the old cat been so morose and gloomy.

It began to get light, and the unseen stranger who had so frightened Auntie was no longer in the room. When it was quite daylight, the porter came in, took the gander, and carried him away. And soon afterwards the old woman came in and took away the trough.

Auntie went into the drawing-room and looked behind the cupboard; her master had not eaten the chicken bone, it was lying in its place among the dust and spiders' webs. But Auntie felt sad and dreary and wanted to cry. She did not even sniff at the bone, but went under the sofa, sat down there, and began softly whining in a thin voice.

VII

AN UNSUCCESSFUL DÉBUT

One fine evening the master came into the room with the dirty wall-paper, and, rubbing his hands, said:

"Well. . . ."

He meant to say something more, but went away without saying it. Auntie, who during her lessons had thoroughly studied his face and intonations, divined that he was agitated, anxious and, she fancied, angry. Soon afterwards he came back and said:

"To-day I shall take with me Auntie and Fyodor Timofeyitch. To-day, Auntie, you will take the place of poor Ivan Ivanitch in the 'Egyptian Pyramid.' Goodness knows how it will be! Nothing is ready, nothing has been thoroughly studied, there have been few rehearsals! We shall be disgraced, we shall come to grief!"

Then he went out again, and a minute later, came back in his fur-coat and top hat. Going up to the cat he took him by the fore-paws and put him inside the front of his coat, while Fyodor Timofeyitch appeared completely unconcerned, and did not even trouble to open his eyes. To him it was apparently a matter of absolute indifference whether he remained lying down, or were lifted up by his paws, whether he rested on his mattress or under his master's fur-coat. . . .

"Come along, Auntie," said her master.

Wagging her tail, and understanding nothing, Auntie followed him. A minute later she was sitting in a sledge by her master's feet and heard him, shrinking with cold and anxiety, mutter to himself:

"We shall be disgraced! We shall come to grief!"

The sledge stopped at a big strange-looking house, like a soup-ladle turned upside down. The long entrance to this house, with its three glass doors, was lighted up with a dozen brilliant lamps. The doors opened with a resounding noise and, like jaws, swallowed up the people who were moving to and fro at the entrance. There were a great many people, horses, too, often ran up to the entrance, but no dogs were to be seen.

The master took Auntie in his arms and thrust her in his coat, where Fyodor Timofeyitch already was. It was dark and stuffy there, but warm. For an instant two green sparks flashed at her; it was the cat, who opened his eyes on being disturbed by his neighbour's cold rough paws. Auntie licked his ear, and, trying to settle herself as comfortably as possible, moved uneasily, crushed him under her cold paws, and casually poked her head out from under the coat, but at once growled angrily, and tucked it in again. It seemed to her that she had seen a huge, badly lighted room, full of monsters; from behind screens and gratings, which stretched on both sides of the room, horrible faces looked out: faces of horses with horns, with long ears, and one fat, huge countenance with a tail instead of a nose, and two long gnawed bones sticking out of his mouth.

The cat mewed huskily under Auntie's paws, but at that moment the coat was flung open, the master said, "Hop!" and Fyodor Timofeyitch and Auntie jumped to the floor. They were now in a little room with grey plank walls; there was no other furniture in it but a little table with a looking-glass on it, a stool, and some rags hung about the corners, and instead of a lamp or candles, there was a bright fan-shaped light attached to a little pipe fixed in the wall. Fyodor Timofeyitch licked his coat which had been ruffled by Auntie, went under the stool, and lay down. Their master, still agitated and rubbing his hands, began undressing. . . . He undressed as he usually did at home when he was preparing to get under the rug, that is, took off everything but his underlinen, then he sat down on the stool, and, looking in the looking-glass, began playing the most surprising tricks with himself. . . . First of all he put on his head a wig, with a parting and with two tufts of hair standing up like horns, then he smeared his face thickly with something white, and over the white colour painted his eye-brows, his moustaches, and red on his cheeks. His antics did not end with that. After smearing his face and neck, he began putting himself into an extraordinary and incongruous costume, such as Auntie had never seen before, either in houses or in the street. Imagine very full trousers, made of chintz covered with big flowers, such as is used in working-class houses for curtains and covering furniture, trousers which buttoned up just under his armpits. One trouser leg was made of brown chintz, the other of bright yellow. Almost lost in these, he then put on a short chintz jacket, with a big scalloped collar, and a gold star on the back, stockings of different colours, and green slippers. . . .

Everything seemed going round before Auntie's eyes and in her soul. The white-faced, sack-like figure smelt like her master, its voice, too, was the familiar master's voice, but there were moments when Auntie was tortured by doubts, and then she was ready to run away from the parti-coloured figure and to bark. The new place, the fan-shaped light, the smell, the transformation that had taken place in her master—all this aroused in her a vague dread and a fore-boding that she would certainly meet with some horror such as the big face with the tail instead of a nose. And then, somewhere through the wall, some hateful band was playing, and from time to time she heard an incomprehensible roar. Only one thing reassured her—that was the imperturbability of Fyodor Timofeyitch. He dozed with the utmost tranquillity under the stool, and did not open his eyes even when it was moved.

A man in a dress coat and a white waistcoat peeped into the little room and said:

"Miss Arabella has just gone on. After her—you."

Their master made no answer. He drew a small box from under the table, sat down, and waited. From his lips and his hands it could be seen that he was agitated, and Auntie could hear how his breathing came in gasps.

"Monsieur George, come on!" someone shouted behind the door. Their master got up and crossed himself three times, then took the cat from under the stool and put him in the box.

"Come, Auntie," he said softly.

Auntie, who could make nothing out of it, went up to his hands, he kissed her on the head, and put her beside Fyodor Timofeyitch. Then followed darkness. . . . Auntie trampled on the cat, scratched at the walls of the box, and was so frightened that she could not utter a sound, while the box swayed and quivered, as though it were on the waves. . . .

"Here we are again!" her master shouted aloud: "here we are again!"

Auntie felt that after that shout the box struck against something hard and left off swaying. There was a loud deep roar, someone was being slapped, and that someone, probably the monster with the tail instead of a nose, roared and laughed so loud that the locks of the box trembled. In response to the roar, there came a shrill, squeaky laugh from her master, such as he never laughed at home.

"Ha!" he shouted, trying to shout above the roar. "Honoured friends! I have only just come from the station! My granny's kicked the bucket and left me a fortune! There is something very heavy in the box, it must be gold, ha! ha! I bet there's a million here! We'll open it and look. . . ."

The lock of the box clicked. The bright light dazzled Auntie's eyes, she jumped out of the box, and, deafened by the roar, ran quickly round her master, and broke into a shrill bark.

"Ha!" exclaimed her master. "Uncle Fyodor Timofeyitch! Beloved Aunt, dear relations! The devil take you!"

He fell on his stomach on the sand, seized the cat and Auntie, and fell to embracing them. While he held Auntie tight in his arms, she glanced round into the world into which fate had brought her and, impressed by its immensity, was for a minute dumbfounded with amazement and delight, then jumped out of her master's arms, and to express the intensity of her emotions, whirled round and round on one spot like a top. This new world was big and full of bright light; wherever she looked, on all sides, from floor to ceiling there were faces, faces, faces, and nothing else.

"Auntie, I beg you to sit down!" shouted her master. Remembering what that meant, Auntie jumped on to a chair, and sat down. She looked at her master. His eyes looked at her gravely and kindly as always, but his face, especially his mouth and teeth, were made grotesque by a broad immovable grin. He laughed, skipped about, twitched his shoulders, and made a show of being very merry in the presence of the thousands of faces. Auntie believed in his merriment, all at once felt all over her that those thousands of faces were looking at her, lifted up her fox-like head, and howled joyously.

"You sit there, Auntie," her master said to her, "while Uncle and I will dance the Kamarinsky."

Fyodor Timofeyitch stood looking about him indifferently, waiting to be made to do something silly. He danced listlessly, carelessly, sullenly, and one could see from his movements, his tail and his ears, that he had a profound contempt for the crowd, the bright light, his

master and himself. When he had performed his allotted task, he
gave a yawn and sat down.

"Now, Auntie!" said her master, "we'll have first a song, and
then a dance, shall we?"

He took a pipe out of his pocket, and began playing. Auntie, who
could not endure music, began moving uneasily in her chair and
howled. A roar of applause rose from all sides. Her master bowed,
and when all was still again, went on playing. . . . Just as he took
one very high note, someone high up among the audience uttered a
loud exclamation:

"Auntie!" cried a child's voice, "why it's Kashtanka!"

"Kashtanka it is!" declared a cracked drunken tenor. "Kashtanka!
Strike me dead, Fedyushka, it is Kashtanka. Kashtanka! here!"

Someone in the gallery gave a whistle, and two voices, one a boy's
and one a man's, called loudly: "Kashtanka! Kashtanka!"

Auntie started, and looked where the shouting came from. Two
faces, one hairy, drunken and grinning, the other chubby, rosy-
cheeked and frightened-looking, dazed her eyes as the bright light
had dazed them before. . . . She remembered, fell off the chair,
struggled on the sand, then jumped up, and with a delighted yap
dashed towards those faces. There was a deafening roar, interspersed
with whistles and a shrill childish shout: "Kashtanka! Kashtanka!"

Auntie leaped over the barrier, then across someone's shoulders.
She found herself in a box: to get into the next tier she had to leap
over a high wall. Auntie jumped, but did not jump high enough, and
slipped back down the wall. Then she was passed from hand to
hand, licked hands and faces, kept mounting higher and higher, and
at last got into the gallery. . . .

Half an hour afterwards, Kashtanka was in the street, following
the people who smelt of glue and varnish. Luka Alexandritch staggered and instinctively, taught by experience, tried to keep as far
from the gutter as possible.

"In sin my mother bore me," he muttered. "And you, Kashtanka,
are a thing of little understanding. Beside a man, you are like a joiner
beside a cabinet-maker."

Fedyushka walked beside him, wearing his father's cap. Kashtanka looked at their backs, and it seemed to her that she had been

following them for ages, and was glad that there had not been a break for a minute in her life.

She remembered the little room with dirty wall-paper, the gander, Fyodor Timofeyitch, the delicious dinners, the lessons, the circus, but all that seemed to her now like a long, tangled, oppressive dream.

A Friendly Rat

by W. H. HUDSON

We have heard of cats and dogs who became friends, against the dictates of instinct, but here is something much stranger. The author of "Green Mansions" and "The Purple Land" gives us a charming sketch.

MOST of our animals, also many creeping things, such as our "wilde wormes in woods," common toads, natterjacks, newts, and lizards, and stranger still, many insects, have been tamed and kept as pets.

Badgers, otters, foxes, hares, and voles are easily dealt with; but that any person should desire to fondle so prickly a creature as a hedgehog, or so diabolical a mammalian as the bloodthirsty flat-headed little weasel, seems very odd. Spiders, too, are uncomfortable pets; you can't caress them as you could a dormouse; the most you can do is to provide your spider with a clear glass bottle to live in, and teach him to come out in response to a musical sound, drawn from a banjo or fiddle, to take a fly from your fingers and go back again to its bottle.

An acquaintance of the writer is partial to adders as pets, and he handles them as freely as the schoolboy does his innocuous ring-snake; Mr. Benjamin Kidd once gave us a delightful account of his pet humble-bees, who used to fly about his room, and come at call to be fed, and who manifested an almost painful interest in his coat buttons, examining them every day as if anxious to find out their true significance. Then there was my old friend, Miss Hopely, the writer on reptiles, who died recently, aged 99 years, who tamed newts, but whose favourite pet was a slow-worm. She was never tired of expatiating on its lovable qualities. One finds Viscount

Grey's pet squirrels more engaging, for these are wild squirrels in a wood in Northumberland, who quickly find out when he is at home and make their way to the house, scale the walls, and invade the library; then, jumping upon his writing-table, are rewarded with nuts, which they take from his hand. Another Northumbrian friend of the writer keeps, or kept, a pet cormorant, and finds him no less greedy in the domestic than in the wild state. After catching and swallowing fish all the morning in a neighbouring river, he wings his way home at meal-times, screaming to be fed, and ready to devour all the meat and pudding he can get.

The list of strange creatures might be extended indefinitely, even fishes included; but who has ever heard of a tame pet rat? Not the small white, pink-eyed variety, artificially bred, which one may buy at any dealer's, but a common brown rat, *Mus decumanus*, one of the commonest wild animals in England and certainly the most disliked. Yet this wonder has been witnessed recently in the village of Lelant, in West Cornwall. Here is the strange story, which is rather sad and at the same time a little funny.

This was not a case of "wild nature won by kindness"; the rat simply thrust itself and its friendship on the woman of the cottage: and she, being childless and much alone in her kitchen and living-room, was not displeased at its visits: on the contrary, she fed it; in return the rat grew more and more friendly and familiar towards her, and the more familiar it grew, the more she liked the rat. The trouble was, she possessed a cat, a nice gentle animal not often at home, but it was dreadful to think of what might happen at any moment should pussy walk in when her visitor was with her. Then, one day, pussy did walk in when the rat was present, purring loudly, her tail held stiffly up, showing that she was in her usual sweet temper. On catching sight of the rat, she appeared to know intuitively that it was there as a privileged guest, while the rat on its part seemed to know, also by intuition, that it had nothing to fear. At all events these two quickly became friends and were evidently pleased to be together, as they now spent most of the time in the room, and would drink milk from the same saucer, and sleep bunched up together, and were extremely intimate.

By and by the rat began to busy herself making a nest in a corner of the kitchen under a cupboard, and it became evident that there would soon be an increase in the rat population. She now spent her time running about and gathering little straws, feathers, string, and anything of the kind she could pick up, also stealing or begging for strips of cotton, or bits of wool and thread from the work-basket. Now it happened that her friend was one of those cats with huge tufts of soft hair on the two sides of her face; a cat of that type, which is not uncommon, has a quaint resemblance to a Mid-Victorian gentleman with a pair of magnificent side-whiskers of a silky softness covering both cheeks and flowing down like a double beard. The rat suddenly discovered that this hair was just what she wanted to add a cushion-like lining to her nest, so that her naked pink little ratlings should be born into the softest of all possible worlds. At once she started plucking out the hairs, and the cat, taking it for a new kind of game, but a little too rough to please her, tried for a while to keep her head out of reach and to throw the rat off. But she wouldn't be thrown off, and as she persisted in flying back and jumping at the cat's face and plucking the hairs, the cat quite lost her temper and administered a blow with her claws unsheathed.

The rat fled to her refuge to lick her wounds, and was no doubt as much astonished at the sudden change in her friend's disposition as the cat had been at the rat's new way of showing her playfulness. The result was that when, after attending her scratches, she started upon her task of gathering soft materials, she left the cat severely alone. They were no longer friends; they simply ignored one another's presence in the room. The little ones, numbering about a dozen, presently came to light and were quietly removed by the woman's husband, who didn't mind his missis keeping a rat, but drew the line at one.

The rat quickly recovered from her loss and was the same nice affectionate little thing she had always been to her mistress; then a fresh wonder came to light—cat and rat were fast friends once more! This happy state of things lasted a few weeks; but, as we know, the rat was married, though her lord and master never appeared on the scene, indeed, he was not wanted; and very soon it became plain to see that more little rats were coming. The rat is an exceedingly prolific creature; she can give a month's start to a rabbit and beat her at the end by about 40 points.

Then came the building of the nest in the same old corner, and when it got to the last stage and the rat was busily running about in search of soft materials for the lining, she once more made the discovery that those beautiful tufts of hair on her friend's face were just what she wanted, and once more she set vigorously to work pulling the hairs out. Again, as on the former occasion, the cat tried to keep her friend off, hitting her right and left with her soft pads, and spitting a little, just to show that she didn't like it. But the rat was determined to have the hairs, and the more she was thrown off the more bent was she on getting them, until the breaking-point was reached and puss, in a sudden rage, let fly, dealing blow after blow with lightning rapidity and with all the claws out. The rat, shrieking with pain and terror, rushed out of the room and was never seen again, to the lasting grief of her mistress. But its memory will long remain like a fragrance in the cottage—perhaps the only cottage in all this land where kindly feelings for the rat are cherished.

The Stuff of Dreams

by HELEN DORE BOYLSTON

Who can help loving Shah, even though he is a little silly?

SHAH first met Sadie Thompson in the apple tree.
He was lying far out on a branch in the sun, his taffy-colored paws tucked under his chest, his golden ruff a halo around his flower-like little face. The red-gold plume of his tail flowed back along the limb. In all the spring morning there was no sound except the twittering of birds. The warm sweetness of the earth drifted up to him. His eyes closed.

Something scrambled under the fence at the back of the garden. Shah's eyes flew open. He stared, incredulous. She was coming across the yard, Shah's *own* yard, invading it, mincing and dainty, a half-grown black kitten with high white boots and small yellow eyes, as expressionless as marbles. She was larger than Shah and her fur was very short and sleek.

She made straight for the tree, climbed it with impressive, ripping bounds, and approached Shah on his branch, heedless of his frightened hissing. He backed away as far as the limb would permit, but she came on steadily. The orange of Shah's eyes was drowned in black. He arched with enormous tail.

Reserve was unknown to Sadie. She loomed over him. She breathed on him. She sniffed along his quivering and appalled whiskers, her blackness very smooth beside his golden fluffiness. Her tongue rasped on his coral nose, worked along his cheek, and up to his tufted ear.

Somewhere, at some other time, another tongue had licked him so. Another paw had lain across his back. And it had been pleasant.

502

His terror subsided and he relaxed, bowing his head to the onslaught.

When he had been washed until his bright fur stood up in long, damp spears all over his body, Sadie settled on the limb beside him and did her nails. Her tail hung down behind her, long, black, and elegant.

Shah looked at it. Sadie wasn't noticing. Her wrinkling nose was buried in the spread toes of a hind foot. Shah reached out a tentative claw and hooked the tail. Sadie nibbled on. Emboldened, Shah patted her face and shrank back when she put down her leg and rose. But she only moved along the limb, pausing to look over her shoulder at him.

"Prrrt!" she said.

Shah pattered after her, enchanted.

She dashed down the tree trunk, head first, and sprang to the ground. Shah was admiring but embarrassed. After a moment of indecision he peered down the vast wall of the trunk. It had a great many smooth places, and the ground was so far away! In sudden obstinacy Shah turned, lowered himself over the limb, and backed down ignominiously, clinging to the friendly bark, his furry stomach pressed close against it. The ground received him at last and he hurried after Sadie.

She ran along the garden path to a tangle of grass and bushes at the back—a dank, cool jungle. Shah's eyes were very big as he pushed through behind her. She squeezed under the fence, and Shah, following, entered a new world of space and sun and weeds.

While he hesitated, bewildered, Sadie made a black streak into the air after a bug, missed it, came down without a sound, and melted into nothing behind a clump of grass. Shah brightened and his whiskers moved forward. He crouched and sprang, his little body an orange flame in the sun. They met, head on, and, clutching each other, rolled among the weeds. Sadie's hind feet encountered Shah's chin and she kicked it with steady rhythm. Her fur filled his mouth.

Sadie tore herself free at last and fled. Shah bounded after her, tail high.

The grass blurred greenly past him and gave place to low, gray mounds. Shah halted with a little bounce. Gray dust settled on him and strange odors came to his nose. Sadie was prowling, long and sinuous, on the top of one of the mounds. Her tail twitched and her whiskers quivered.

Shah sniffed and was backing away in distaste when a thin, sweet smell, drifting on a breeze, drew him forward again. He set his paws down carefully, avoiding bits of broken glass, a doll's wig, and a heap of lemon rinds. Flashes of sunlight jumped from tin can to tin can, and something stirred under his paws. He spat sharply, but the smell drew him on, up the mound, to where a condensed-milk can lay on its side. A little trickle of milk came from it.

"Mrrrt!" Shah called.

Sadie came in a scrambling run. Her eyes glittered. Shah drew back graciously and waited until her round, black head was bent over the rich find. Then he joined her; red cheek against black, they lapped up the thick sweetness.

Shah withdrew first, leaving Sadie the last drop. He shook out his ruff, and, sitting down, was lifting a paw to his whiskers when his nose caught the first whiff of something which stirred him to the very tips of his toes. His paw dropped. He rose; moving with the stiffness of one hypnotized, he went straight up the mound of ashes and down the other side. His nose had not deceived him. There it lay, his for the taking, brown and shiny, dried by wind and sun, washed by rain, but still pungent—an exquisite fish head!

Shah gazed upon it in silent rapture. Never, in all his life, had such a gift been laid before him. Never before had his nose been blessed with such an odor—succulent, soul-stirring, beautiful. A high, tenor purr began in his little chest. Sadie was forgotten. His ears were deaf to the sound of a low, excited yowl. He realized nothing until Sadie shot under his chin and crouched, growling, over his treasure.

Shah's ears flattened against his head in shocked surprise. Then they lifted and he stepped forward, confidently, to share. It was over in an instant! Claws raked his nose and he fell back, blinded with pain, his mouth opening in a soundless shriek. He shook his head and wiped at his nose with a trembling paw, but the pain wouldn't come off. The sound of snarling continued.

When Shah could see, he moved a prudent distance away and sat down. His whiskers drooped miserably and his eyes were very big.

The change in Sadie was beyond belief. She was no longer the motherly little cat, nor the gay companion, but a stranger from whose body came a sickening, brassy odor of hatred. Her eyes blazed and her tail lashed the ashes into a semicircle of dust.

Even as Shah watched, her teeth sank deep into the fish head with a crackling sound. Shah's mouth watered. Outraged, he saw her lift his personal property from the ground, saw it sticking out on either side of her head, crisp and tempting. Its fragrance almost overcame him.

Still crouching, Sadie turned with a weaving motion of her head and was gone—back along the way they had come. Her tail was not jaunty now. It slithered behind her, close to the ground. Shah hurried after her, keeping at a safe distance. She darted under the fence into his own garden and Shah cried out at the added insult.

In the middle of the garden, on the new grass, Sadie laid Shah's fish head down with tenderness and gloating. Shah stood still. Sadie walked around the prize, glancing out of the corner of her eye at the anxious little figure beyond. Her whiskers twitched and the corners of her mouth curled upward. Then, elaborately unaware of him, she inserted a paw beneath the jewel, flipped it into the air, batted it a foot or two in Shah's direction; and when he stepped forward, all eagerness, she sprang upon it, growling.

The black pools of Shah's eyes blazed. His whiskers stood forward until they almost met before his stinging nose. The watered silk of his flanks, burning red and orange in the sun, trembled with the explosions of his breath.

Sadie danced before the fish head in curves and arabesques. She curled around it. She killed it with pomp, restored it to life with ceremony. She was a black feather, a drift of smoke, an exclamation point of delight. And all the while her eyes glittered at Shah's agony.

He was pacing back and forth now, unable to endure that sight, unable to tear his eyes from it. The brush of his tail drooped behind him. Another drop of blood was gathering on his nose.

At that moment George, Shah's own Scottie, came around a distant corner of the house. Shah's tail swept upward and the furrows of anxiety on his forehead were smooth stripes again. He opened his mouth in a long wail for help. George, always the gentleman, removed his nose from the trail of his own affairs and waved his tail in response, but he had not understood, and after a moment went on his way. Shah's tail dropped slowly down.

The game continued.

The noon sun shone in benign indifference. The little heat waves over the garden were saturated with the smell of fish, and insects, emerging from under stones, toiled through the wilderness of grass in search of it. Shah's tongue trembled over his lips as Sadie paused in her frolicking to bite into the dream of dreams. It crunched brownly, and Shah wailed aloud.

The door of Shah's kitchen opened and the cook's voice issued from it. Sadie, startled, turned to look, leaving the fish head unprotected for the briefest of moments. In that moment Shah was a silent golden streak across the grass. His teeth met between bones and he fled, straight for that open door, and through it into the warm kitchen. He crept into the steamy darkness under the stove and waited there, breathless.

Presently there was a commotion in the kitchen. Windows were thrown open and the cook's voice was shrill. Her lumps of feet shadowed back and forth in front of Shah's hiding place with increasing rapidity. They paused. There were grunts, a thump, and heavy breathing near the floor. Shah's heart pounded in his throat, but he remained motionless. Then his eyes and the cook's met over the fish head.

A hand, at the end of a fat arm, came under the stove, groped, caught Shah by the scruff of his neck, and dragged him out. His treasure was wrenched from his jaws—though not before he had left long red marks on the cook's arm. He hit the floor, hard. The kitchen door was jerked open, and the fish head sailed through it in a splendid arc. Shah raced through the door after it, but he was too late. The triumphant Sadie was already climbing into the apple tree, carrying the fish head.

He followed her grimly, but without hope.

She clambered on, far up into the topmost branches, wedged the fish head into a little crotch, and bunched herself on a limb just below.

Shah began his vigil slightly farther down. Neither looked at the other. Above them the fish head was a brown triangle against the tender green of new leaves.

Shah had eaten nothing since the few drops of condensed milk that morning and his inside was a large and drafty emptiness, but he made no move to descend. One taffy paw was tucked under his chest. The other extended along the limb, and upon this, after a while, he rested his chin. His golden whiskers lay back along his cheeks until their curving tips touched his ruff. His tail hung down, and his orange eyes were fixed, unblinking, on the brown triangle above.

Sadie was two solid black circles melting together against the sky —a large one, and a small one with ears. Her yellow eyes stared at nothing.

The kitchen door opened and a familiar and beloved voice called out words that Shah knew.

"Shah!" it said. "Come! *Dinner!*"

Shah's head lifted and the emptiness inside him began to ache, but he remained where he was. He gave one beseeching little cry when the door closed, but that was all.

The shadow of the tree trunk grew longer. A breeze stirred among the leaves and blew away a swarm of gnats which had been jigging around Shah's head. There was a sudden fluttering as a pair of robins invaded the tree, hopping from twig to twig, chattering. Shah and Sadie looked up hungrily, but continued glued to their branches. The leaves whispered above them. From far away a sound of hammering came to them on the wind. The air was sweet with the smell of grass and heavy with wood smoke. Shah's coral nose quivered. His emptiness was a sharp pain now, and he shifted uneasily on his branch. Sadie did not move.

The beloved voice called again, from an open window, and Shah called back desperately. The porch door opened at once, and She came out, hurrying across the garden to the apple tree. Shah's chest fur trembled with the hopeful beating of his heart. His little face, furrowed with hunger, peered down at Her.

"Shah—my foolish! What is it? Come down! Come, Shah, *dinner!*"

Shah didn't wail, this time. He squalled, pink mouth wide, ears back.

Sadie stared but said nothing.

"Come, Shah! Dinner!"

"Eee-yow!" Shah screamed, clinging to his branch. His emptiness roared in his ears.

After a time She went away.

The brown tree shadows slowly deepened to blue and a chill crept into the air. Shah wrapped his tail around him for warmth. The leaves hung motionless, and the robins, with a final twitter, swooped away. Sadie was a motionless black lump. In the west the wings of the sunset trailed scarlet across a lemon-yellow sky, and the breath of the fields was a white mist. Lights came on in Shah's house.

Something moved in the gloom below. She had returned—with a ladder. Shah mewed hysterically, peeking over his branch. The ladder scraped against the tree trunk and was still, but the tree shook a little, and Her voice came nearer, speaking to Shah. At the sound of it Sadie uncoiled and stretched upward, swift and black. Shah heard the lovely crunch as her teeth met in the fish head. Unseen leaves rustled violently, higher up. Shah followed instantly.

His heart sank as he climbed, for Her voice was suddenly angry. "*Bad!*" it said. But he went on up, little and orange and determined. Sadie had settled down again, beside the fish head. There was no comfortable place for Shah and he was forced to lie upward along a branch and hold with his claws.

After a moment he looked down. She was on the ground again, and taking away the ladder in an unpleasant silence. Then Her feet swished across the grass. The kitchen door was a sudden oblong of light—then darkness.

The first stars were flaring above him when Shah heard, far in the distance, the terrifying wail of a fire siren. It grew louder every second. All the doors of his house opened and there was running in the driveway. Out in the road passing cars drew hastily to one side with a squealing of brakes; there was more running, and a babel of voices.

Two long cones of light swept down the highway and the screaming wail came with them. They swung ponderously at the driveway entrance and crept in, drawing behind them something long, and high, and red. It clattered. The wailing died away to a whine and ceased. An engine throbbed—stopped. In the silence Her voice spoke, alone, apologetic.

There was laughter, and more clattering. The cones of light

moved, turned, and focused on the suddenly golden tree. Shah's claws almost lost their grip.

People tramped across the grass carrying another ladder, very long, very red. Other people made a semicircle of grinning faces on the edge of the light.

The ladder reared into the air and grew longer and longer. It squeaked, and Shah's ears pricked forward nervously. His eyes widened in terror as the uppermost prongs of it reached a level with his face and remained there, not resting against anything. A dark shape in a glaring red hat detached itself from the group below and began to mount the ladder, which swayed. The figure came steadily higher, nearer and nearer to the paralyzed Shah. It said something to the people below in a voice quite like George's—a definite bark—and the ladder squeaked again.

Just over Shah's head there was a stealthy, frightened movement. It was very slight, but Shah heard it and looked up. Sadie's branch was empty! She had gone only the night knew where—and she had left the fish head behind!

Everything else was forgotten. Shah was a whirlwind among the leaves.

When a large masculine hand closed on the scruff of his neck he scarcely knew it. Crisp brownness filled his mouth, pricked his throat until his eyes bulged, drowned his nostrils with its exquisite pungency. His teeth met in crackling succulence. His ecstatic purr was strained through scales and delicious, crumbling bones.

Shah came down the ladder dangling from the hand, not hearing the cheers which burst the darkness. Into the circle of light Her hands reached to take him—Her dear hands that understood. He nestled into them, exhausted but trusting.

One of Her fingers touched his treasure gingerly. Her eyes were close, peering. Her voice said:—

"Good heaven! A *fish head!*"

There was a pause during which Shah's round eyes looked up at Her happily, glistening with pride.

"So that was it!" She said at last. And She laughed—an odd, quavering little laugh. Shah was lifted suddenly and held close under Her chin, and together they went away, out of the blinding light, to the warm shelter of the kitchen.

The fish head was buried in the hollow of Her neck—safe at last.

Lady into Fox

by DAVID GARNETT

*The horror of the end of this fantasy is testimony to
the completeness with which it convinces us of its reality.*

WONDERFUL or supernatural events are not so uncommon,
rather they are irregular in their incidence. Thus there may
be not one marvel to speak of in a century, and then often enough
comes a plentiful crop of them; monsters of all sorts swarm suddenly
upon the earth, comets blaze in the sky, eclipses frighten nature,
meteors fall in rain, while mermaids and sirens beguile, and sea-
serpents engulf every passing ship, and terrible cataclysms beset humanity.

But the strange event which I shall here relate came alone, unsupported, without companions into a hostile world, and for that
very reason claimed little of the general attention of mankind. For
the sudden changing of Mrs. Tebrick into a vixen is an established
fact which we may attempt to account for as we will. Certainly it
is in the explanation of the fact, and the reconciling of it with our
general notions that we shall find most difficulty, and not in accepting for true a story which is so fully proved, and that not by one
witness but by a dozen, all respectable, and with no possibility of
collusion between them.

But here I will confine myself to an exact narrative of the event
and all that followed on it. Yet I would not dissuade any of my
readers from attempting an explanation of this seeming miracle because up till now none has been found which is entirely satisfactory.
What adds to the difficulty to my mind is that the metamorphosis
occurred when Mrs. Tebrick was a full-grown woman, and that it
happened suddenly in so short a space of time. The sprouting of a

tail, the gradual extension of hair all over the body, the slow change of the whole anatomy by a process of growth, though it would have been monstrous, would not have been so difficult to reconcile to our ordinary conceptions, particularly had it happened in a young child.

But here we have something very different. A grown lady is changed straightway into a fox. There is no explaining that away by any natural philosophy. The materialism of our age will not help us here. It is indeed *a miracle;* something from outside our world altogether; an event which we would willingly accept if we were to meet it invested with the authority of Divine Revelation in the Scriptures, but which we are not prepared to encounter almost in our time, happening in Oxfordshire amongst our neighbours.

The only things which go any way towards an explanation of it are but guesswork, and I give them more because I would not conceal anything, than because I think they are of any worth.

Mrs. Tebrick's maiden name was certainly Fox, and it is possible that such a miracle happening before, the family may have gained their name as a *soubriquet* on that account. They were an ancient family, and have had their seat at Tangley Hall time out of mind. It is also true that there was a half-tame fox once upon a time chained up at Tangley Hall in the inner yard, and I have heard many speculative wiseacres in the public-houses turn that to great account—though they could not but admit that "there was never one there in Miss Silvia's time." At first I was inclined to think that Silvia Fox, having once hunted when she was a child of ten and having been blooded, might furnish more of an explanation. It seems she took great fright or disgust at it, and vomited after it was done. But now I do not see that it has much bearing on the miracle itself, even though we know that after that she always spoke of the "poor foxes" when a hunt was stirring and never rode to hounds till after her marriage when her husband persuaded her to it.

She was married in the year 1879 to Mr. Richard Tebrick, after a short courtship, and went to live after their honeymoon at Rylands, near Stokoe, Oxon. One point indeed I have not been able to ascertain and that is how they first became acquainted. Tangley Hall is over thirty miles from Stokoe, and is extremely remote. Indeed to this day there is no proper road to it, which is all the more remarkable as it is the principal, and indeed the only, manor house for several miles around.

Whether it was from a chance meeting on the roads, or less romantic but more probable, by Mr. Tebrick becoming acquainted with her uncle, a minor canon at Oxford, and thence being invited by him to visit Tangley Hall, it is impossible to say. But however they became acquainted the marriage was a very happy one. The bride was in her twenty-third year. She was small, with remarkably small hands and feet. It is perhaps worth noting that there was nothing at all foxy or vixenish in her appearance. On the contrary, she was a more than ordinarily beautiful and agreeable woman. Her eyes were of a clear hazel but exceptionally brilliant, her hair dark, with a shade of red in it, her skin brownish, with a few dark freckles and little moles. In manner she was reserved almost to shyness, but perfectly self-possessed, and perfectly well-bred.

She had been strictly brought up by a woman of excellent principles and considerable attainments, who died a year or so before the marriage. And owing to the circumstance that her mother had been dead many years, and her father bed-ridden, and not altogether rational for a little while before his death, they had few visitors but her uncle. He often stopped with them a month or two at a stretch, particularly in winter, as he was fond of shooting snipe, which are plentiful in the valley there. That she did not grow up a country hoyden is to be explained by the strictness of her governess and the influence of her uncle. But perhaps living in so wild a place gave her some disposition to wildness, even in spite of her religious upbringing. Her old nurse said: "Miss Silvia was always a little wild at heart," though if this was true it was never seen by anyone else except her husband.

On one of the first days of the year 1880, in the early afternoon, husband and wife went for a walk in the copse on the little hill above Rylands. They were still at this time like lovers in their behaviour and were always together. While they were walking they heard the hounds and later the huntsman's horn in the distance. Mr. Tebrick had persuaded her to hunt on Boxing Day, but with great difficulty, and she had not enjoyed it (though of hacking she was fond enough).

Hearing the hunt, Mr. Tebrick quickened his pace so as to reach the edge of the copse, where they might get a good view of the hounds if they came that way. His wife hung back, and he, holding her hand, began almost to drag her. Before they gained the edge of the copse she suddenly snatched her hand away from his very violently and cried out, so that he instantly turned his head.

Where his wife had been the moment before was a small fox, of a very bright red. It looked at him very beseechingly, advanced towards him a pace or two, and he saw at once that his wife was looking at him from the animal's eyes. You may well think if he were aghast: and so maybe was his lady at finding herself in that shape, so they did nothing for nearly half-an-hour but stare at each other, he bewildered, she asking him with her eyes as if indeed she spoke to him: "What am I now become? Have pity on me, husband, have pity on me for I am your wife."

So that with his gazing on her and knowing her well, even in such a shape, yet asking himself at every moment: "Can it be she? Am I not dreaming?" and her beseeching and lastly fawning on him and seeming to tell him that it was she indeed, they came at last together and he took her in his arms. She lay very close to him, nestling under his coat and fell to licking his face, but never taking her eyes from his.

The husband all this while kept turning the thing in his head and gazing on her, but he could make no sense of what had happened, but only comforted himself with the hope that this was but a momentary change, and that presently she would turn back again into the wife that was one flesh with him.

One fancy that came to him, because he was so much more like a lover than a husband, was that it was his fault, and this because if anything dreadful happened he could never blame her but himself for it.

So they passed a good while, till at last the tears welled up in the poor fox's eyes and she began weeping (but quite in silence), and she trembled too as if she were in a fever. At this he could not contain his own tears, but sat down on the ground and sobbed for a great while, but between his sobs kissing her quite as if she had been a woman, and not caring in his grief that he was kissing a fox on the muzzle.

They sat thus till it was getting near dusk, when he recollected himself, and the next thing was that he must somehow hide her, and then bring her home.

He waited till it was quite dark that he might the better bring her into her own house without being seen, and buttoned her inside his topcoat, nay, even in his passion tearing open his waistcoat and his shirt that she might lie the closer to his heart. For when we are overcome with the greatest sorrow we act not like men or women but like children whose comfort in all their troubles is to press themselves against their mother's breast, or if she be not there to hold each other tight in one another's arms.

When it was dark he brought her in with infinite precautions, yet not without the dogs scenting her, after which nothing could moderate their clamour.

Having got her into the house, the next thing he thought of was to hide her from the servants. He carried her to the bedroom in his arms and then went downstairs again.

Mr. Tebrick had three servants living in the house, the cook, the parlourmaid, and an old woman who had been his wife's nurse. Besides these women there was a groom or a gardener (whichever you choose to call him), who was a single man and so lived out, lodging with a labouring family about half a mile away.

Mr. Tebrick going downstairs pitched upon the parlourmaid.

"Janet," says he, "Mrs. Tebrick and I have had some bad news, and Mrs. Tebrick was called away instantly to London and left this afternoon, and I am staying to-night to put our affairs in order. We are shutting up the house, and I must give you and Mrs. Brant a month's wages and ask you to leave to-morrow morning at seven o'clock. We shall probably go away to the Continent, and I do not know when we shall come back. Please tell the others, and now get me my tea and bring it into my study on a tray."

Janet said nothing for she was a shy girl, particularly before gentlemen, but when she entered the kitchen Mr. Tebrick heard a sudden burst of conversation with many exclamations from the cook.

When she came back with his tea, Mr. Tebrick said: "I shall not require you upstairs. Pack your own things and tell James to have the wagonette ready for you by seven o'clock to-morrow morning to take you to the station. I am busy now, but I will see you again before you go."

When she had gone Mr. Tebrick took the tray upstairs. For the first moment he thought the room was empty, and his vixen got away, for he could see no sign of her anywhere. But after a moment he saw something stirring in a corner of the room, and then behold! she came forth dragging her dressing-gown, into which she had somehow struggled.

This must surely have been a comical sight, but poor Mr. Tebrick was altogether too distressed then or at any time afterwards to divert himself at such ludicrous scenes. He only called to her softly:

"Silvia—Silvia. What do you do here?" And then in a moment saw for himself what she would be at, and began once more to blame himself heartily—because he had not guessed that his wife would not like to go naked, notwithstanding the shape she was in. Nothing would satisfy him then till he had clothed her suitably, bringing her dresses from the wardrobe for her to choose. But as might have been expected, they were too big for her now, but at last he picked out a little dressing-jacket that she was fond of wearing sometimes in the mornings. It was made of a flowered silk, trimmed with lace, and the sleeves short enough to sit very well on her now. While he tied the ribands his poor lady thanked him with gentle looks and not without some modesty and confusion. He propped her up in an arm-chair with some cushions, and they took tea together, she very delicately drinking from a saucer and taking bread and butter from his hands. All this showed him, or so he thought, that his wife was still herself; there was so little wildness in her demeanour and so much delicacy and decency, especially in her not wishing to run naked, that he was very much comforted, and began to fancy they could be happy enough if they could escape the world and live always alone.

From this too sanguine dream he was aroused by hearing the gardener speaking to the dogs, trying to quiet them, for ever since he had come in with his vixen they had been whining, barking and growling, and all as he knew because there was a fox within doors and they would kill it.

He started up now, calling to the gardener that he would come down to the dogs himself to quiet them, and bade the man go indoors again and leave it to him. All this he said in a dry, compelling kind of voice which made the fellow do as he was bid, though it was against his will, for he was curious. Mr. Tebrick went down-stairs, and taking his gun from the rack loaded it and went out into the yard. Now there were two dogs, one a handsome Irish setter that was his wife's dog (she had brought it with her from Tangley Hall on her marriage); the other was an old fox terrier called Nelly that he had had ten years or more.

When he came out into the yard both dogs saluted him by bark-ing and whining twice as much as they did before, the setter jump-ing up and down at the end of his chain in a frenzy, and Nelly shiver-ing, wagging her tail, and looking first at her master and then at the house door, where she could smell the fox right enough.

There was a bright moon, so that Mr. Tebrick could see the dogs as clearly as could be. First he shot his wife's setter dead, and then looked about him for Nelly to give her the other barrel, but he could see her nowhere. The bitch was clean gone, till, looking to see how she had broken her chain, he found her lying hid in the back of her kennel. But that trick did not save her, for Mr. Tebrick, after trying to pull her out by her chain and finding it useless—she would not come,—thrust the muzzle of his gun into the kennel, pressed it into her body and so shot her. Afterwards, striking a match, he looked in at her to make certain she was dead. Then, leaving the dogs as they were, chained up, Mr. Tebrick went in-doors again and found the gardener, who had not yet gone home, gave him a month's wages in lieu of notice and told him he had a job for him yet—to bury the two dogs and that he should do it that same night.

But by all this going on with so much strangeness and authority on his part, as it seemed to them, the servants were much troubled. Hearing the shots while he was out in the yard his wife's old nurse, or Nanny, ran up to the bedroom though she had no business there, and so opening the door saw the poor fox dressed in my lady's little jacket lying back in the cushions, and in such a reverie of woe that she heard nothing.

Old Nanny, though she was not expecting to find her mistress there, having been told that she was gone that afternoon to London, knew her instantly, and cried out:

"Oh, my poor precious! Oh, poor Miss Silvia! What dreadful

change is this?" Then, seeing her mistress start and look at her, she cried out:

"But never fear, my darling, it will all come right, your old Nanny knows you, it will all come right in the end."

But though she said this she did not care to look again, and kept her eyes turned away so as not to meet the foxy slit ones of her mistress, for that was too much for her. So she hurried out soon, fearing to be found there by Mr. Tebrick, and who knows, perhaps shot, like the dogs, for knowing the secret.

Mr. Tebrick had all this time gone about paying off his servants and shooting his dogs as if he were in a dream. Now he fortified himself with two or three glasses of strong whisky and went to bed, taking his vixen into his arms, where he slept soundly. Whether she did or not is more than I or anybody else can say.

In the morning when he woke up they had the place to themselves, for on his instructions the servants had all left first thing: Janet and the cook to Oxford, where they would try and find new places, and Nanny going back to the cottage near Tangley, where her son lived, who was the pigman there.

So with that morning there began what was now to be their ordinary life together. He would get up when it was broad day, and first thing light the fire downstairs and cook the breakfast, then brush his wife, sponge her with a damp sponge, then brush her again, in all this using scent very freely to hide somewhat her rank odour. When she was dressed he carried her downstairs and they had their breakfast together, she sitting up to table with him, drinking her saucer of tea, and taking her food from his fingers, or at any rate being fed by him. She was still fond of the same food that she had been used to before her transformation, a lightly boiled egg or slice of ham, a piece of buttered toast or two, with a little quince and apple jam. While I am on the subject of her food, I should say that reading in the encyclopedia he found that foxes on the Continent are inordinately fond of grapes, and that during the autumn season they abandon their ordinary diet for them, and then grow exceedingly fat and lose their offensive odour.

This appetite for grapes is so well confirmed by Æsop, and by passages in the Scriptures, that it is strange Mr. Tebrick should not have known it. After reading this account he wrote to London for a basket of grapes to be posted to him twice a week and was rejoiced to find that the account in the encyclopedia was true in the most important of these particulars. His vixen relished them exceedingly and seemed never to tire of them, so that he increased his order first from one pound to three pounds and afterwards to five. Her odour abated so much by this means that he came not to notice it at all except sometimes in the mornings before her toilet.

What helped him most to make living with her bearable for him was that she understood him perfectly—yes, every word he said, and though she was dumb she expressed herself very fluently by looks and signs though never by the voice.

Thus he frequently conversed with her, telling her all his thoughts and hiding nothing from her, and this the more readily because he was very quick to catch her meaning and her answers.

"Puss, Puss," he would say to her, for calling her that had been a habit with him always. "Sweet Puss, some men would pity me living alone here with you after what has happened, but I would not change places while you were living with any man for the whole world. Though you are a fox I would rather live with you than any woman. I swear I would, and that too if you were changed to anything." But then, catching her grave look, he would say: "Do you think I jest on these things, my dear? I do not. I swear to you, my darling, that all my life I will be true to you, will be faithful, will respect and reverence you who are my wife. And I will do that not because of any hope that God in His mercy will see fit to restore your shape, but solely because I love you. However you may be changed, my love is not."

Then anyone seeing them would have sworn that they were lovers, so passionately did each look on the other.

Often he would swear to her that the devil might have power to work some miracles, but that he would find it beyond him to change his love for her.

These passionate speeches, however they might have struck his wife in an ordinary way, now seemed to be her chief comfort. She would come to him, put her paw in his hand and look at him with sparkling eyes shining with joy and gratitude, would pant with eagerness, jump at him and lick his face.

Now he had many little things which busied him in the house—getting his meals, setting the room straight, making the bed and so forth. When he was doing his housework it was comical to watch his vixen. Often she was as it were beside herself with vexation and distress to see him in his clumsy way doing what she could have done so much better had she been able. Then, forgetful of the decency and the decorum which she had at first imposed upon herself never to run upon all fours, she followed him everywhere, and if he did one thing wrong she stopped him and showed him the way of it. When he had forgot the hour for his meal she would come and tug his sleeve and tell him as if she spoke: "Husband, are we to have no luncheon to-day?"

This womanliness in her never failed to delight him, for it showed she was still his wife, buried as it were in the carcase of a beast but with a woman's soul. This encouraged him so much that he debated with himself whether he should not read aloud to her, as he often had done formerly. At last, since he could find no reason against it, he went to the shelf and fetched down a volume of the "History of Clarissa Harlowe," which he had begun to read aloud to her a few weeks before. He opened the volume where he had left off, with Lovelace's letter after he had spent the night waiting fruitlessly in the copse.

"*Good God!*

What is now to become of me?

My feet benumbed by midnight wanderings through the heaviest dews that ever fell; my wig and my linen dripping with the hoar-frost dissolving on them!

Day but just breaking . . ." etc.

While he read he was conscious of holding her attention, then after a few pages the story claimed all his, so that he read on for about half-an-hour without looking at her. When he did so he saw that she was not listening to him, but was watching something with strange eagerness. Such a fixed intent look was on her face that he was alarmed and sought the cause of it. Presently he found that her gaze was fixed on the movements of her pet dove which was in its cage hanging in the window. He spoke to her, but she seemed displeased, so he laid "Clarissa Harlowe" aside. Nor did he ever repeat the experiment of reading to her.

Yet that same evening, as he happened to be looking through his writing table drawer with Puss beside him looking over his elbow, she spied a pack of cards, and then he was forced to pick them out to please her, then draw them from their case. At last, trying first one thing, then another, he found that what she was after was to play piquet with him. They had some difficulty at first in contriving for her to hold her cards and then to play them, but this was at last overcome by his stacking them for her on a sloping board, after which she could flip them out very neatly with her claws as she wanted to play them. When they had overcome this trouble they played three games, and most heartily she seemed to enjoy them. Moreover she won all three of them. After this they often played a quiet game of piquet together, and cribbage too. I should say that in marking the points at cribbage on the board he always moved her pegs for her as well as his own, for she could not handle them or set them in the holes.

The weather, which had been damp and misty, with frequent downpours of rain, improved very much in the following week, and, as often happens in January, there were several days with the sun shining, no wind and light frosts at night, these frosts becoming more intense as the day went on till bye and bye they began to think of snow.

With this spell of fine weather it was but natural that Mr. Tebrick should think of taking his vixen out of doors. This was something he had not yet done, both because of the damp rainy weather up till then and because the mere notion of taking her out filled him with alarm. Indeed he had so many apprehensions beforehand that at one time he resolved totally against it. For his mind was filled not only with the fear that she might escape from him and run away, which he knew was groundless, but with more rational visions, such as wandering curs, traps, gins, spring guns, besides a dread of being seen with her by the neighbourhood. At last however he resolved on it, and all the more as his vixen kept asking him in the gentlest way: "Might she not go into the garden?" Yet she always listened very submissively when he told her that he was afraid if they were seen together it would excite the curiosity of their neighbours; besides this, he often told her of his fears for her on account of dogs. But one day she answered this by leading him into the hall and pointing boldly to his gun. After this he resolved to take her, though with full precautions. That is he left the house door open so that in case of need she could beat a swift retreat, then he took his gun under his arm, and lastly he had her well wrapped up in a little fur jacket lest she should take cold.

He would have carried her too, but that she delicately disengaged herself from his arms and looked at him very expressively to say that she would go by herself. For already her first horror of being seen to go upon all fours was worn off; reasoning no doubt upon it, that either she must resign herself to go that way or else stay bed-ridden all the rest of her life.

Her joy at going into the garden was inexpressible. First she ran this way, then that, though keeping always close to him, looking very sharply with ears cocked forward first at one thing, then another and then up to catch his eye.

For some time indeed she was almost dancing with delight, running round him, then forward a yard or two, then back to him and gambolling beside him as they went round the garden. But in spite of her joy she was full of fear. At every noise, a cow lowing, a cock crowing, or a ploughman in the distance hulloaing to scare the rooks, she started, her ears pricked to catch the sound, her muzzle wrinkled up and her nose twitched, and she would then press herself against his legs. They walked round the garden and down to the pond where there were ornamental waterfowl, teal, widgeon and mandarin ducks, and seeing these again gave her great pleasure. They had always been her favourites, and now she was so overjoyed to see them that she behaved with very little of her usual self-restraint. First she stared at them, then bouncing up to her husband's knee sought to kindle an equal excitement in his mind. Whilst she rested her paws on his knee she turned her head again and again towards the ducks as though she could not take her eyes off them, and then ran down before him to the water's edge.

But her appearance threw the ducks into the utmost degree of consternation. Those on shore or near the bank swam or flew to the centre of the pond, and there huddled in a bunch; and then, swimming round and round, they began such a quacking that Mr. Tebrick was nearly deafened. As I have before said, nothing in the ludicrous way that arose out of the metamorphosis of his wife (and such incidents were plentiful) ever stood a chance of being smiled at by him. So in this case, too, for realising that the silly ducks thought his wife a fox indeed and were alarmed on that account he found painful that spectacle which to others might have been amusing.

Not so his vixen, who appeared if anything more pleased than ever when she saw in what a commotion she had set them, and began cutting a thousand pretty capers. Though at first he called to her to come back and walk another way, Mr. Tebrick was overborne by her pleasure and sat down, while she frisked around him happier far than he had seen her ever since the change. First she ran up to him in a laughing way, all smiles, and then ran down again to the water's edge and began frisking and frolicking, chasing her own brush, dancing on her hind legs even, and rolling on the ground, then fell to running in circles, but all this without paying any heed to the ducks.

But they, with their necks craned out all pointing one way, swam to and fro in the middle of the pond, never stopping their quack, quack, quack, and keeping time too, for they all quacked in chorus. Presently she came further away from the pond, and he, thinking they had had enough of this sort of entertainment, laid hold of her and said to her:

"Come, Silvia, my dear, it is growing cold, and it is time we went indoors. I am sure taking the air has done you a world of good, but we must not linger any more."

She appeared then to agree with him, though she threw half a glance over her shoulder at the ducks, and they both walked soberly enough towards the house.

When they had gone about halfway she suddenly slipped round and was off. He turned quickly and saw the ducks had been following them.

So she drove them before her back into the pond, the ducks running in terror from her with their wings spread, and she not pressing them, for he saw that had she been so minded she could have caught two or three of the nearest. Then, with her brush waving above her, she came gambolling back to him so playfully that he stroked her indulgently, though he was first vexed, and then rather puzzled that his wife should amuse herself with such pranks.

But when they got within doors he picked her up in his arms, kissed her and spoke to her.

"Silvia, what a light-hearted childish creature you are. Your courage under misfortune shall be a lesson to me, but I cannot, I cannot bear to see it."

Here the tears stood suddenly in his eyes, and he lay down upon the ottoman and wept, paying no heed to her until presently he was aroused by her licking his cheek and his ear.

After tea she led him to the drawing room and scratched at the door till he opened it, for this was part of the house which he had shut up, thinking three or four rooms enough for them now, and to save the dusting of it. Then it seemed she would have him play to her on the pianoforte: she led him to it, nay, what is more, she would herself pick out the music he was to play. First it was a fugue of Handel's, then one of Mendelssohn's Songs Without Words, and then "The Diver," and then music from Gilbert and Sullivan; but each piece of music she picked out was gayer than the last one. Thus they sat happily engrossed for perhaps an hour in the candle light until the extreme cold in that unwarmed room stopped his playing and drove them downstairs to the fire. Thus did she admirably comfort her husband when he was dispirited.

Yet next morning when he woke he was distressed when he found that she was not in the bed with him but was lying curled up at the foot of it. During breakfast she hardly listened when he spoke, and then impatiently, but sat staring at the dove.

Mr. Tebrick sat silently looking out of the window for some time, then he took out his pocketbook; in it there was a photograph of his wife taken soon after their wedding. Now he gazed and gazed upon those familiar features, and now he lifted his head and looked at the animal before him. He laughed then bitterly, the first and last time for that matter that Mr. Tebrick ever laughed at his wife's transformation, for he was not very humorous. But this laugh was sour and painful to him. Then he tore up the photograph into little pieces, and scattered them out of the window, saying to himself: "Memories will not help me here," and turning to the vixen he saw that she was still staring at the caged bird, and as he looked he saw her lick her chops.

He took the bird into the next room, then acting suddenly upon the impulse, he opened the cage door and set it free, saying as he did so:

"Go, poor bird! Fly from this wretched house while you still remember your mistress who fed you from her coral lips. You are not a fit plaything for her now. Farewell, poor bird! Farewell! Unless," he added with a melancholy smile, "you return with good tidings like Noah's dove."

But, poor gentleman, his troubles were not over yet, and indeed one may say that he ran to meet them by his constant supposing that his lady should still be the same to a tittle in her behaviour now that she was changed into a fox.

Without making any unwarrantable suppositions as to her soul or what had now become of it (though we could find a good deal to the purpose on that point in the system of Paracelsus), let us consider only how much the change in her body must needs affect her ordinary conduct. So that before we judge too harshly of this unfortunate lady, we must reflect upon the physical necessities and infirmities and appetites of her new condition, and we must magnify the fortitude of her mind which enabled her to behave with decorum, cleanliness and decency in spite of her new situation.

Thus she might have been expected to befoul her room, yet never could anyone, whether man or beast, have shown more nicety in such matters. But at luncheon Mr. Tebrick helped her to a wing of chicken, and leaving the room for a minute to fetch some water which he had forgot, found her at his return on the table crunching the very bones. He stood silent, dismayed and wounded to the heart at this sight. For we must observe that this unfortunate husband thought always of his vixen as that gentle and delicate woman she had lately been. So that whenever his vixen's conduct went beyond that which he expected in his wife he was, as it were, cut to the quick, and no kind of agony could be greater to him than to see her thus forget herself. On this account it may indeed be regretted that Mrs. Tebrick had been so exactly well-bred, and in particular that her table manners had always been scrupulous. Had she been in the habit, like a continental princess I have dined with, of taking her leg of chicken by the drumstick and gnawing the flesh, it had been far better for him now. But as her manners had been perfect, so the lapse of them was proportionately painful to him. Thus in this instance he stood as it were in silent agony till she had finished her hideous crunching of the chicken bones and had devoured every scrap. Then he spoke to her gently, taking her on to his knee, stroking her fur and fed her with a few grapes, saying to her:

"Silvia, Silvia, is it so hard for you? Try and remember the past, my darling, and by living with me we will quite forget that you are no longer a woman. Surely this affliction will pass soon, as suddenly as it came, and it will all seem to us like an evil dream."

Yet though she appeared perfectly sensible of his words and gave him sorrowful and penitent looks like her old self, that same afternoon, on taking her out, he had all the difficulty in the world to keep her from going near the ducks.

There came to him then a thought that was very disagreeable to him, namely, that he dare not trust his wife alone with any bird or she would kill it. And this was the more shocking to him to think of since it meant that he durst not trust her as much as a dog even. For we may trust dogs who are familiars, with all the household pets; nay more, we can put them upon trust with anything and know they will not touch it, not even if they be starving. But things were come to such a pass with his vixen that he dared not in his heart trust her at all. Yet she was still in many ways so much more woman than fox that he could talk to her on any subject and she would understand him, better far than the oriental women who are kept in subjection can ever understand their masters unless they converse on the most trifling household topics.

Thus she understood excellently well the importance and duties of religion. She would listen with approval in the evening when he said the Lord's Prayer, and was rigid in her observance of the Sabbath. Indeed, the next day being Sunday he, thinking no harm, proposed their usual game of piquet, but no, she would not play. Mr. Tebrick, not understanding at first what she meant, though he was usually very quick with her, he proposed it to her again, which she again refused, and this time, to show her meaning, made the sign of the cross with her paw. This exceedingly rejoiced and comforted him in his distress. He begged her pardon, and fervently thanked God for having so good a wife, who, in spite of all, knew more of her duty to God than he did. But here I must warn the reader from inferring that she was a papist because she then made the sign of the cross. She made that sign to my thinking only on compulsion because she could not express herself except in that way. For she had been brought up as a true Protestant, and that she still was one is confirmed by her objection to cards, which would have been less than nothing to her had she been a papist. Yet that evening, taking her into the drawing room so that he might play her some sacred music, he found her after some time cowering away from him in the farthest corner of the room, her ears flattened back and an expression of the greatest anguish in her eyes. When he spoke to her she licked his hand, but remained shivering for a long time at his feet and showed the clearest symptoms of terror if he so much as moved towards the piano.

On seeing this and recollecting how ill the ears of a dog can bear with our music, and how this dislike might be expected to be even greater in a fox, all of whose senses are more acute from being a wild creature, recollecting this he closed the piano and taking her in his arms, locked up the room and never went into it again. He could not help marvelling though, since it was but two days after she had herself led him there, and even picked out for him to play and sing those pieces which were her favourites.

That night she would not sleep with him, neither in the bed nor on it, so that he was forced to let her curl herself up on the floor. But neither would she sleep there, for several times she woke him by trotting around the room, and once when he had got sound asleep by springing on the bed and then off it, so that he woke with a violent start and cried out, but got no answer either, except hearing her trotting round and round the room. Presently he imagines to himself that she must want something, and so fetches her food and water, but she never so much as looks at it, but still goes on her rounds, every now and then scratching at the door.

Though he spoke to her, calling her by her name, she would pay no heed to him, or else only for the moment. At last he gave her up and said to her plainly: "The fit is on you now Silvia to be a fox, but I shall keep you close and in the morning you will recollect yourself and thank me for having kept you now."

So he lay down again, but not to sleep, only to listen to his wife running about the room and trying to get out of it. Thus he spent what was perhaps the most miserable night of his existence. In the morning she was still restless, and was reluctant to let him wash and brush her, and appeared to dislike being scented but as it were to bear with it for his sake. Ordinarily she had taken the greatest pleasure imaginable in her toilet, so that on this account, added to his sleepless night, Mr. Tebrick was utterly dejected, and it was then that he resolved to put a project into execution that would show him, so he thought, whether he had a wife or only a wild vixen in his house. But yet he was comforted that she bore at all with him, though so restlessly that he did not spare her, calling her a "bad wild fox." And then speaking to her in this manner: "Are you not ashamed, Silvia, to be such a madcap, such a wicked hoyden? You who were particular in dress. I see it was all vanity—now you have not your former advantages you think nothing of decency."

His words had some effect with her too, and with himself, so that by the time he had finished dressing her they were both in the lowest state of spirits imaginable and neither of them far from tears.

Breakfast she took soberly enough, and after that he went about getting his experiment ready, which was this. In the garden he gathered together a nosegay of snowdrops, those being all the flowers he could find, and then going into the village of Stokoe bought a Dutch rabbit (that is a black and white one) from a man there who kept them.

When he got back he took his flowers and at the same time set down the basket with the rabbit in it, with the lid open. Then he called to her: "Silvia, I have brought some flowers for you. Look, the first snowdrops."

At this she ran up very prettily, and never giving as much as one glance at the rabbit which had hopped out of its basket, she began to thank him for the flowers. Indeed she seemed indefatigable in shewing her gratitude, smelt them, stood a little way off looking at them, then thanked him again. Mr. Tebrick (and this was all part of his plan) then took a vase and went to find some water for them, but left the flowers beside her. He stopped away five minutes, timing it by his watch and listening very intently, but never heard the rabbit squeak. Yet when he went in what a horrid shambles was spread before his eyes. Blood on the carpet, blood on the armchairs and antimacassars, even a little blood spurtled on to the wall, and what was worse, Mrs. Tebrick tearing and growling over a piece of the skin and the legs, for she had eaten up all the rest of it. The poor gentleman was so heartbroken over this that he was like to have done himself an injury, and at one moment thought of getting his gun, to have shot himself and his vixen too. Indeed the extremity of his grief was such that it served him a very good turn, for he was so entirely unmanned by it that for some time he could do nothing but weep, and fell into a chair with his head in his hands, and so kept weeping and groaning.

After he had been some little while employed in this dismal way, his vixen, who had by this time bolted down the rabbit, skin, head, ears and all, came to him and putting her paws on his knees, thrust her long muzzle into his face and began licking him. But he, looking at her now with different eyes, and seeing her jaws still sprinkled with fresh blood and her claws full of the rabbit's fleck, would have none of it.

But though he beat her off four or five times even to giving her blows and kicks, she still came back to him, crawling on her belly and imploring his forgiveness with wide-open sorrowful eyes. Before he had made this rash experiment of the rabbit and the flowers, he had promised himself that if she failed in it he would have no more feeling or compassion for her than if she were in truth a wild vixen out of the woods. This resolution, though the reasons for it had seemed to him so very plain before, he now found more difficult to carry out than to decide on. At length after cursing her and beating her off for upwards of half-an-hour, he admitted to himself that he still did care for her, and even loved her dearly in spite of all, whatever pretence he affected towards her. When he had acknowledged this he looked up at her and met her eyes fixed upon him, and held out his arms to her and said:

"Oh, Silvia, Silvia, would you had never done this! Would I had never tempted you in a fatal hour! Does not this butchery and eating of raw meat and rabbit's fur disgust you? Are you a monster in your soul as well as in your body? Have you forgotten what it is to be a woman?"

Meanwhile, with every word of his, she crawled a step nearer on her belly and at last climbed sorrowfully into his arms. His words then seemed to take effect on her and her eyes filled with tears and she wept most penitently in his arms, and her body shook with her sobs as if her heart were breaking. This sorrow of hers gave him the strangest mixture of pain and joy that he had ever known, for his love for her returning with a rush, he could not bear to witness her pain and yet must take pleasure in it as it fed his hopes of her one day returning to be a woman. So the more anguish of shame his vixen underwent, the greater his hopes rose, till his love and pity for her increasing equally, he was almost wishing her to be nothing more than a mere fox than to suffer so much by being half-human.

At last he looked about him somewhat dazed with so much weeping, then set his vixen down on the ottoman, and began to clean up the room with a heavy heart. He fetched a pail of water and washed out all the stains of blood, gathered up the two antimacassars and fetched clean ones from the other rooms. While he went about this work his vixen sat and watched him very contritely with her nose between her two front paws, and when he had done he brought in some luncheon for himself, though it was already late, but none for her, she having lately so infamously feasted. But water he gave her and a bunch of grapes. Afterwards she led him to the small tortoise-shell cabinet and would have him open it. When he had done so she motioned to the portable stereoscope which lay inside. Mr. Tebrick instantly fell in with her wish and after a few trials adjusted it to her vision. Thus they spent the rest of the afternoon together very happily looking through the collection of views which he had purchased, of Italy, Spain and Scotland. This diversion gave her great apparent pleasure and afforded him considerable comfort. But that night he could not prevail upon her to sleep in bed with him, and finally allowed her to sleep on a mat beside the bed where he could stretch down and touch her. So they passed the night, with his hand upon her head.

The next morning he had more of a struggle than ever to wash and dress her. Indeed at one time nothing but holding her by the scruff prevented her from getting away from him, but at last he achieved his object and she was washed, brushed, scented and dressed, although to be sure this left him better pleased than her, for she regarded her silk jacket with disfavour.

Still at breakfast she was well mannered though a trifle hasty with her food. Then his difficulties with her began for she would go out, but as he had his housework to do, he could not allow it. He brought her picture books to divert her, but she would have none of them but stayed at the door scratching it with her claws industriously till she had worn away the paint.

At first he tried coaxing her and wheedling, gave her cards to play patience and so on, but finding nothing would distract her from going out, his temper began to rise, and he told her plainly that she must wait his pleasure and that he had as much natural obstinacy as she had. But to all that he said she paid no heed whatever but only scratched the harder.

Thus he let her continue until luncheon, when she would not sit up, or eat off a plate, but first was for getting on to the table, and when that was prevented, snatched her meat and ate it under the table. To all his rebukes she turned a deaf or sullen ear, and so they each finished their meal eating little, either of them, for till she would sit at table he would give her no more, and his vexation had taken away his own appetite. In the afternoon he took her out for her airing in the garden.

She made no pretence now of enjoying the first snowdrops or the view from the terrace. No—there was only one thing for her now —the ducks, and she was off to them before he could stop her. Luckily they were all swimming when she got there (for a stream running into the pond on the far side it was not frozen there).

When he had got down to the pond, she ran out on to the ice, which would not bear his weight, and though he called her and begged her to come back she would not heed him but stayed frisking about, getting as near the ducks as she dared, but being circumspect in venturing on to the thin ice.

Presently she turned on herself and began tearing off her clothes, and at last by biting got off her little jacket and taking it in her mouth stuffed it into a hole in the ice where he could not get it. Then she ran hither and thither a stark naked vixen, and without giving a glance to her poor husband who stood silently now upon the bank, with despair and terror settled in his mind. She let him stay there most of the afternoon till he was chilled through and through and worn out with watching her. At last he reflected how she had just stripped herself and how in the morning she struggled against being dressed, and he thought perhaps he was too strict with her and if he let her have her own way they could manage to be happy somehow together even if she did eat off the floor. So he called out to her then:

"Silvia, come now, be good, you shan't wear any more clothes if you don't want to, and you needn't sit at table neither, I promise. You shall do as you like in that, but you must give up one thing, and that is you must stay with me and not go out alone, for that is dangerous. If any dog came on you he would kill you."

Directly he had finished speaking she came to him joyously, began fawning on him and prancing round him so that in spite of his vexation with her, and being cold, he could not help stroking her.

"Oh, Silvia, are you not wilful and cunning? I see you glory in being so, but I shall not reproach you but shall stick to my side of the bargain, and you must stick to yours."

He built a big fire when he came back to the house and took a glass or two of spirits also, to warm himself up, for he was chilled to the very bone. Then, after they had dined, to cheer himself he took another glass, and then another, and so on till he was very merry, he thought. Then he would play with his vixen, she encouraging him with her pretty sportiveness. He got up to catch her then and finding himself unsteady on his legs, he went down on to all fours. The long and the short of it is that by drinking he drowned all his sorrow; and then would be a beast too like his wife, though she was one through no fault of her own, and could not help it. To what lengths he went then in that drunken humour I shall not offend my readers by relating, but shall only say that he was so drunk and sottish that he had a very imperfect recollection of what had passed when he woke the next morning. There is no exception to the rule that if a man drink heavily at night the next morning will show the other side to his nature. Thus with Mr. Tebrick, for as he had been beastly, merry and a very dare-devil the night before, so on his awakening was he ashamed, melancholic and a true penitent before his Creator. The first thing he did when he came to himself was to call out to God to forgive him for his sin, then he fell into earnest prayer and continued so for half-an-hour upon his knees. Then he got up and dressed but continued very melancholy for the whole of the morning. Being in this mood you may imagine it hurt him to see his wife running about naked, but he reflected it would be a

bad reformation that began with breaking faith. He had made a
bargain and he would stick to it, and so he let her be, though sorely
against his will.

For the same reason, that is because he would stick to his side of
the bargain, he did not require her to sit up at table, but gave her
her breakfast on a dish in the corner, where to tell the truth she on
her side ate it all up with great daintiness and propriety. Nor did she
make any attempt to go out of doors that morning, but lay curled
up in an armchair before the fire dozing. After lunch he took her
out, and she never so much as offered to go near the ducks, but
running before him led him on to take her a longer walk. This he consented to do very much to her joy and delight. He took her through
the fields by the most unfrequented ways, being much alarmed
lest they should be seen by anyone. But by good luck they walked
above four miles across country and saw nobody. All the way his
wife kept running on ahead of him, and then back to him to lick
his hand and so on, and appeared delighted at taking exercise. And
though they started two or three rabbits and a hare in the course of
their walk she never attempted to go after them, only giving them a
look and then looking back to him, laughing at him as it were for
his warning cry of "Puss! come in, no nonsense now!"

Just when they got home and were going into the porch they
came face to face with an old woman. Mr. Tebrick stopped short
in consternation and looked about for his vixen, but she had run
forward without any shyness to greet her. Then he recognized the
intruder, it was his wife's old nurse.

"What are you doing here, Mrs. Cork?" he asked her.

Mrs. Cork answered him in these words:

"Poor thing. Poor Miss Silvia! It is a shame to let her run about
like a dog. It is a shame, and your own wife too. But whatever she
looks like, you should trust her the same as ever. If you do she'll
do her best to be a good wife to you, if you don't I shouldn't wonder
if she did turn into a proper fox. I saw her, sir, before I left, and
I've had no peace of mind. I couldn't sleep thinking of her. So I've
come back to look after her, as I have done all her life, sir," and she
stooped down and took Mrs. Tebrick by the paw.

Mr. Tebrick unlocked the door and they went in. When Mrs.
Cork saw the house she exclaimed again and again: "The place was

a pigstye. They couldn't live like that, a gentleman must have some
body to look after him. She would do it. He could trust her with
the secret."

Had the old woman come the day before it is likely enough that
Mr. Tebrick would have sent her packing. But the voice of conscience being woken in him by his drunkenness of the night before
he was heartily ashamed of his own management of the business,
moreover the old woman's words that "it was a shame to let her
run about like a dog," moved him exceedingly. Being in this mood
the truth is he welcomed her.

But we may conclude that Mrs. Tebrick was as sorry to see her
old Nanny as her husband was glad. If we consider that she had
been brought up strictly by her when she was a child, and was now
again in her power, and that her old nurse could never be satisfied
with her now whatever she did, but would always think her wicked
to be a fox at all, there seems good reason for her dislike. And it is
possible, too, that there may have been another cause as well, and
that is jealousy. We know her husband was always trying to bring
her back to be a woman, or at any rate to get her to act like one,
may she not have been hoping to get him to be like a beast himself
or to act like one? May she not have thought it easier to change
him thus than ever to change herself back into being a woman? If
we think that she had had a success of this kind only the night before,
when he got drunk, can we not conclude that this was indeed the
case, and then we have another good reason why the poor lady
should hate to see her old nurse?

It is certain that whatever hopes Mr. Tebrick had of Mrs. Cork
affecting his wife for the better were disappointed. She grew steadily
wilder and after a few days so intractable with her that Mr. Tebrick
again took her under his complete control.

The first morning Mrs. Cork made her a new jacket, cutting
down the sleeves of a blue silk one of Mrs. Tebrick's and trimming
it with swan's down, and directly she had altered it, put it on her
mistress, and fetching a mirror would have her admire the fit of it.
All the time she waited on Mrs. Tebrick the old woman talked to
her as though she were a baby, and treated her as such, never thinking perhaps that she was either the one thing or the other, that is
either a lady to whom she owed respect and who had rational powers

exceeding her own, or else a wild creature on whom words were wasted. But though at first she submitted passively, Mrs. Tebrick only waited for her Nanny's back to be turned to tear up her pretty piece of handiwork into shreds, and then ran gaily about waving her brush with only a few ribands still hanging from her neck.

So it was time after time (for the old woman was used to having her own way) until Mrs. Cork would, I think, have tried punishing her if she had not been afraid of Mrs. Tebrick's row of white teeth, which she often showed her, then laughing afterwards, as if to say it was only play.

Not content with tearing off the dresses that were fitted on her, one day Silvia slipped upstairs to her wardrobe and tore down all her old dresses and made havoc with them, not sparing her wedding dress either, but tearing and ripping them all up so that there was hardly a shred or rag left big enough to dress a doll in. On this, Mr. Tebrick, who had let the old woman have most of her management to see what she could make of her, took her back under his own control.

He was sorry enough now that Mrs. Cork had disappointed him in the hopes he had had of her, to have the old woman, as it were, on his hands. True she could be useful enough in many ways to him, by doing the housework, the cooking and mending, but still he was anxious since his secret was in her keeping, and the more now that she had tried her hand with his wife and failed. For he saw that vanity had kept her mouth shut if she had won over her mistress to better ways, and her love for her would have grown by getting her own way with her. But now that she had failed she bore her mistress a grudge for not being won over, or at the best was become indifferent to the business, so that she might very readily blab.

For the moment all Mr. Tebrick could do was to keep her from going into Stokoe to the village, where she would meet all her old cronies and where there were certain to be any number of inquiries about what was going on at Rylands and so on. But as he saw that it was clearly beyond his power, however vigilant he might be, to watch over the old woman and his wife, and to prevent anyone from meeting with either of them, he began to consider what he could best do.

Since he had sent away his servants and the gardener, giving out a story of having received bad news and his wife going away to London where he would join her, their probably going out of England and so on, he knew well enough that there would be a great deal of talk in the neighbourhood.

And as he had now stayed on, contrary to what he had said, there would be further rumour. Indeed, had he known it, there was a story already going round the country that his wife had run away with Major Solmes, and that he was gone mad with grief, that he had shot his dogs and his horses and shut himself up alone in the house and would speak with no one. This story was made up by his neighbours not because they were fanciful or wanted to deceive, but like most tittle-tattle to fill a gap, as few like to confess ignorance, and if people are asked about such or such a man they must have something to say, or they suffer in everybody's opinion, are set down as dull or "out of the swim." In this way I met not long ago with someone who, after talking some little while and not knowing me or who I was, told me that David Garnett was dead, and died of being bitten by a cat after he had tormented it. He had long grown a nuisance to his frends as an exorbitant sponge upon them, and the world was well rid of him.

Hearing this story of myself diverted me at the time, but I fully believe it has served me in good stead since. For it set me on my guard as perhaps nothing else would have done, against accepting for true all floating rumour and village gossip, so that now I am by second nature a true sceptic and scarcely believe anything unless the evidence for it is conclusive. Indeed I could never have got to the bottom of this history if I had believed one tenth part of what I was told, there was so much of it that was either manifestly false or absurd, or else contradictory to the ascertained facts. It is therefore only the bare bones of the story which you will find written here, for I have rejected all the flowery embroideries which would be entertaining reading enough, I daresay, for some, but if there be any doubt of the truth of a thing it is poor sort of entertainment to read about in my opinion.

To get back to our story: Mr. Tebrick having considered how much the appetite of his neighbours would be whetted to find out the mystery by his remaining in that part of the country, determined that the best thing he could do was to remove.

After some time turning the thing over in his mind, he decided that no place would be so good for his purpose as old Nanny's cottage. It was thirty miles away from Stokoe, which in the country means as far as Timbuctoo does to us in London. Then it was near Tangley, and his lady having known it from her childhood would feel at home there, and also it was utterly remote, there being no village near it or manor house other than Tangley Hall, which was now untenanted for the greater part of the year. Nor did it mean imparting his secret to others, for there was only Mrs. Cork's son, a widower, who being out at work all day would be easily outwitted, the more so as he was stone deaf and of a slow and saturnine disposition. To be sure there was little Polly, Mrs. Cork's granddaughter, but either Mr. Tebrick forgot her altogether, or else reckoned her as a mere baby and not to be thought of as a danger.

He talked the thing over with Mrs. Cork, and they decided upon it out of hand. The truth is the old woman was beginning to regret that her love and her curiosity had ever brought her back to Rylands, since so far she had got much work and little credit by it.

When it was settled, Mr. Tebrick disposed of the remaining business he had at Rylands in the afternoon, and that was chiefly putting out his wife's riding horse into the keeping of a farmer near by, for he thought he would drive over with his own horse, and the other spare horse tandem in the dogcart.

The next morning they locked up the house and they departed, having first secured Mrs. Tebrick in a large wicker hamper where she would be tolerably comfortable. This was for safety, for in the agitation of driving she might jump out, and on the other hand, if a dog scented her and she were loose, she might be in danger of her life. Mr. Tebrick drove with the hamper beside him on the front seat, and spoke to her gently very often.

She was overcome by the excitement of the journey and kept poking her nose first through one crevice, then through another, turning and twisting the whole time and peeping out to see what they were passing. It was a bitterly cold day, and when they had gone about fifteen miles they drew up by the roadside to rest the horses and have their own luncheon, for he dared not stop at an inn. He knew that any living creature in a hamper, even if it be only an old fowl, always draws attention; there would be several loafers most likely who would notice that he had a fox with him, and even if he left the hamper in the cart the dogs at the inn would be sure to sniff out her scent. So not to take any chances he drew up at the side of the road and rested there, though it was freezing hard and a northeast wind blowing.

He took down his precious hamper, unharnessed his two horses, covered them with rugs and gave them their corn. Then he opened the basket and let his wife out. She was quite beside herself with joy, running hither and thither, bouncing up on him, looking about her and even rolling on the ground. Mr. Tebrick took this to mean that she was glad at making this journey and rejoiced equally with her. As for Mrs. Cork, she sat motionless on the back seat of the dogcart well wrapped up, eating her sandwiches, but would not speak a word. When they had stayed there half-an-hour Mr. Tebrick harnessed the horses again, though he was so cold he could scarcely buckle the straps, and put his vixen in her basket, but seeing that she wanted to look about her, he let her tear away the osiers with her teeth till she had made a hole big enough for her to put her head out of.

They drove on again and then the snow began to come down and that in earnest, so that he began to be afraid they would never cover the ground. But just after nightfall they got in, and he was content to leave unharnessing the horses and baiting them to Simon, Mrs. Cork's son. His vixen was tired by then, as well as he, and they slept together, he in the bed and she under it, very contentedly.

The next morning he looked about him at the place and found the thing there that he most wanted, and that was a little walled-in garden where his wife could run in freedom and yet be in safety.

After they had had breakfast she was wild to go out into the snow. So they went out together, and he had never seen such a mad creature in all his life as his wife was then. For she ran to and fro as if she were crazy, biting at the snow and rolling in it, and round and round in circles and rushed back at him fiercely as if she meant to bite him. He joined her in the frolic, and began snowballing her till she was so wild that it was all he could do to quiet her again and bring her indoors for luncheon. Indeed with her gambollings she tracked the whole garden over with her feet; he could see where she had rolled in the snow and where she had danced in it, and looking at those prints of her feet as they went in, made his heart ache, he knew not why.

They passed the first day at old Nanny's cottage happily enough, without their usual bickerings, and this because of the novelty of the snow which had diverted them. In the afternoon he first showed his wife to little Polly, who eyed her very curiously but hung back shyly and seemed a good deal afraid of the fox. But Mr. Tebrick took up a book and let them get acquainted by themselves, and presently looking up saw that they had come together and Polly was stroking his wife, patting her and running her fingers through her fur. Presently she began talking to the fox, and then brought her doll in to show her so that very soon they were very good playmates together. Watching the two gave Mr. Tebrick great delight, and in particular when he noticed that there was something very motherly in his vixen. She was indeed far above the child in intelligence and restrained herself too from any hasty action. But while she seemed to wait on Polly's pleasure yet she managed to give a twist to the game, whatever it was, that never failed to delight the little girl. In short, in a very little while, Polly was so taken with her new playmate that she cried when she was parted from her and wanted her always with her. This disposition of Mrs. Tebrick's made Mrs. Cork more agreeable than she had been lately either to the husband or the wife.

Three days after they had come to the cottage the weather changed, and they woke up one morning to find the snow gone, and the wind in the south, and the sun shining, so that it was like the first beginning of spring.

Mr. Tebrick let his vixen out into the garden after breakfast, stayed with her awhile, and then went indoors to write some letters.

When he got out again he could see no sign of her anywhere, so that he ran about bewildered, calling to her. At last he spied a mound of fresh earth by the wall in one corner of the garden and running thither found that there was a hole freshly dug seeming to go under the wall. On this he ran out of the garden quickly till he came to the other side of the wall, but there was no hole there, so he concluded that she was not yet got through. So it proved to be, for reaching down into the hole he felt her brush with his hand, and could hear her distinctly working away with her claws. He called to her then, saying: "Silvia, Silvia, why do you do this? Are you trying to escape from me? I am your husband, and if I keep you confined it is to protect you, not to let you run into danger. Show me how I can make you happy and I will do it, but do not try to escape from me. I love you, Silvia; is it because of that that you want to fly from me to go into the world where you will be in danger of your life always? There are dogs everywhere and they all would kill you if it were not for me. Come out, Silvia, come out."

But Silvia would not listen to him, so he waited there silent. Then he spoke to her in a different way, asking her had she forgot the bargain she made with him that she would not go out alone, but now when she had all the liberty of a garden to herself would she wantonly break her word? And he asked her, were they not married? And had she not always found him a good husband to her? But she heeded this neither until presently his temper getting somewhat out of hand he cursed her obstinancy and told her if she would be a damned fox she was welcome to it, for his part he could get his own way. She had not escaped yet. He would dig her out for he still had time, and if she struggled put her in a bag.

These words brought her forth instantly and she looked at him with as much astonishment as if she knew not what could have made him angry. Yes, she even fawned on him, but in a good-natured kind of way, as if she were a very good wife putting up wonderfully with her husband's temper.

These airs of hers made the poor gentleman (so simple was he) repent his outburst and feel most ashamed.

But for all that when she was out of the hole he filled it up with great stones and beat them in with a crowbar so she should find her work at that point harder than before if she was tempted to begin it again.

In the afternoon he let her go again into the garden but sent little Polly with her to keep her company. But presently on looking out he saw his vixen had climbed up into the limbs of an old pear tree and was looking over the wall, and was not so far from it but she might jump over it if she could get a little further.

Mr. Tebrick ran out into the garden as quick as he could, and when his wife saw him it seemed she was startled and made a false

spring at the wall, so that she missed reaching it and fell back
heavily to the ground and lay there insensible. When Mr. Tebrick
got up to her he found her head was twisted under her by her fall and
the neck seemed to be broken. The shock was so great to him that
for some time he could not do anything, but knelt beside her turning
her limp body stupidly in his hands. At length he recognised that
she was indeed dead, and beginning to consider what dreadful afflic-
tions God had visited him with, he blasphemed horribly and called
on God to strike him dead, or give his wife back to him.

"Is it not enough," he cried, adding a foul blasphemous oath, "that
you should rob me of my dear wife, making her a fox, but now you
must rob me of that fox too, that has been my only solace and comfort in this affliction?"

Then he burst into tears and began wringing his hands and continued there in such an extremity of grief for half-an-hour that he
cared nothing, neither what he was doing, nor what would become
of him in the future, but only knew that his life was ended now and
he would not live any longer than he could help.

All this while the little girl Polly stood by, first staring, then asking him what had happened, and lastly crying with fear, but he
never heeded her nor looked at her but only tore his hair, sometimes
shouted at God, or shook his fist at Heaven. So in a fright Polly
opened the door and ran out of the garden.

At length worn out, and as it were all numb with his loss, Mr.
Tebrick got up and went within doors, leaving his dear fox lying
near where she had fallen.

He stayed indoors only two minutes and then came out again
with a razor in his hand intending to cut his own throat, for he was
out of his senses in this first paroxysm of grief.

But his vixen was gone, at which he looked about for a moment
bewildered, and then enraged, thinking that somebody must have
taken the body.

The door of the garden being open he ran straight through it.
Now this door, which had been left ajar by Polly when she ran
off, opened into a little courtyard where the fowls were shut in
at night; the wood-house and the privy also stood there. On the far
side of it from the garden gate were two large wooden doors big

enough when open to let a cart enter, and high enough to keep a man from looking over into the yard.

When Mr. Tebrick got into the yard he found his vixen leaping up at these doors, and wild with terror, but as lively as ever he saw her in his life. He ran up to her but she shrank away from him, and would then have dodged him too, but he caught hold of her. She bared her teeth at him but he paid no heed to that, only picked her straight up into his arms and took her so indoors. Yet all the while he could scarce believe his eyes to see her living, and felt her all over very carefully to find if she had not some bones broken. But no, he could find none. Indeed it was some hours before this poor silly gentleman began to suspect the truth, which was that his vixen had practised a deception upon him, and all the time he was bemoaning his loss in such heartrending terms, she was only shamming death to run away directly she was able. If it had not been that the yard gates were shut, which was a mere chance, she had got her liberty by that trick. And that this was only a trick of hers to sham dead was plain when he had thought it over. Indeed it is an old and time-honoured trick of the fox. It is in Æsop and a hundred other writers have confirmed it since. But so thoroughly had he been deceived by her, that at first he was as much overcome with joy at his wife still being alive, as he had been with grief a little while before, thinking her dead.

He took her in his arms, hugging her to him and thanking God a dozen times for her preservation. But his kissing and fondling her had very little effect now, for she did not answer him by licking or soft looks, but stayed huddled up and sullen, with her hair bristling on her neck and her ears laid back every time he touched her. At first he thought this might be because he had touched some broken bone or tender place where she had been hurt, but at last the truth came to him.

Thus he was again to suffer, and though the pain of knowing her treachery to him was nothing to the grief of losing her, yet it was more insidious and lasting. At first, from a mere nothing, this pain grew gradually until it was a torture to him. If he had been one of your stock ordinary husbands, such a one who by experience has learnt never to enquire too closely into his wife's doings, her comings or goings, and never to ask her, "How she has spent the day?" for fear he should be made the more of a fool, had Mr. Tebrick been such a one he had been luckier, and his pain would have been almost nothing. But you must consider that he had never been deceived once by his wife in the course of their married life. No, she had never told him as much as one white lie, but had always been frank, open and ingenuous as if she and her husband were not husband and wife, or indeed of opposite sexes. Yet we must rate him as very foolish, that living thus with a fox, which beast has the same reputation for deceitfulness, craft and cunning, in all countries, all ages, and amongst all races of mankind, he should expect this fox to be as candid and honest with him in all things as the country girl he had married.

His wife's sullenness and bad temper continued that day, for she cowered away from him and hid under the sofa, nor could he persuade her to come out from there. Even when it was her dinner time she stayed, refusing resolutely to be tempted out with food, and lying so quiet that he heard nothing from her for hours. At night he carried her up to the bedroom, but she was still sullen and refused to eat a morsel, though she drank a little water during the night, when she fancied he was asleep.

The next morning was the same, and by now Mr. Tebrick had been through all the agonies of wounded self-esteem, disillusionment and despair that a man can suffer. But though his emotions rose up in his heart and nearly stifled him he showed no sign of them to her, neither did he abate one jot his tenderness and consideration for his vixen. At breakfast he tempted her with a freshly killed young pullet. It hurt him to make this advance to her, for hitherto he had kept her strictly on cooked meats, but the pain of seeing her refuse it was harder still for him to bear. Added to this was now an anxiety lest she should starve herself to death rather than stay with him any longer.

All that morning he kept her close, but in the afternoon let her loose again in the garden after he had lopped the pear tree so that she could not repeat her performance of climbing.

But seeing how disgustedly she looked while he was by, never offering to run or to play as she was used, but only standing stock still with her tail between her legs, her ears flattened, and the hair

bristling on her shoulders, seeing this he left her to herself out of mere humanity.

When he came out after half-an-hour he found that she was gone, but there was a fair sized hole by the wall, and she just buried all but her brush, digging desperately to get under the wall and make her escape.

He ran up to the hole, and put his arm in after her and called to her to come out, but she would not. So at first he began pulling her out by the shoulder, then his hold slipping, by the hind legs. As soon as he had drawn her forth she whipped round and snapped at his hand and bit it through near the joint of the thumb, but let it go instantly.

They stayed there for a minute facing each other, he on his knees and she facing him the picture of unrepentant wickedness and fury. Being thus on his knees, Mr. Tebrick was down on her level very nearly, and her muzzle was thrust almost into his face. Her ears lay flat on her head, her gums were bared in a silent snarl, and all her beautiful teeth threatening him that she would bite him again. Her back too was half-arched, all her hair bristling and her brush held drooping. But it was her eyes that held his, with their slit pupils looking at him with savage desperation and rage.

The blood ran very freely from his hand but he never noticed that or the pain of it either, for all his thoughts were for his wife.

"What is this, Silvia?" he said very quietly, "what is this? Why are you so savage now? If I stand between you and your freedom it is because I love you. Is it such torment to be with me?" But Silvia never stirred a muscle.

"You would not do this if you were not in anguish, poor beast, you want your freedom. I cannot keep you, I cannot hold you to vows made when you were a woman. Why, you have forgotten who I am."

The tears then began running down his cheeks, he sobbed, and said to her:

"Go—I shall not keep you. Poor beast, poor beast, I love you, I love you. Go if you want to. But if you remember me come back. I shall never keep you against your will. Go—go. But kiss me now."

He leant forward then and put his lips to her snarling fangs, but though she kept snarling she did not bite him. Then he got up quickly and went to the door of the garden that opened into a little paddock against a wood.

When he opened it she went through it like an arrow, crossed the paddock like a puff of smoke and in a moment was gone from his sight. Then, suddenly finding himself alone, Mr. Tebrick came as it were to himself and ran after her, calling her by name and shouting to her, and so went plunging into the wood, and through it for about a mile, running almost blindly.

At last when he was worn out he sat down, seeing that she had gone beyond recovery and it was already night. Then, rising, he walked slowly homewards, wearied and spent in spirit. As he went he bound up his hand that was still running with blood. His coat was torn, his hat lost, and his face scratched right across with briars. Now in cold blood he began to reflect on what he had done and to repent bitterly having set his wife free. He had betrayed her so that now, from his act, she must lead the life of a wild fox for ever, and must undergo all the rigours and hardships of the climate, and all the hazards of a hunted creature. When Mr. Tebrick got back to the cottage he found Mrs. Cork was sitting up for him. It was already late.

"What have you done with Mrs. Tebrick, sir? I missed her, and I missed you, and I have not known what to do, expecting something dreadful had happened. I have been sitting up for you half the night. And where is she now, sir?"

She accosted him so vigorously that Mr. Tebrick stood silent. At length he said: "I have let her go. She has run away."

"Poor Miss Silvia!" cried the old woman. "Poor creature! You ought to be ashamed, sir! Let her go indeed! Poor lady, is that the way for her husband to talk! It is a disgrace. But I saw it coming from the first."

The old woman was white with fury, she did not mind what she said, but Mr. Tebrick was not listening to her. At last he looked at her and saw that she had just begun to cry, so he went out of the room and up to bed, and lay down as he was, in his clothes, utterly exhausted, and fell into a dog's sleep, starting up every now and then with horror, and then falling back with fatigue. It was late when he woke up, but cold and raw, and he felt cramped in all his limbs. As he lay he heard again the noise which had woken him—the trotting of several horses, and the voice of men riding by the house. Mr. Tebrick jumped up and ran to the window and then looked out, and the first thing that he saw was a gentleman in a pink coat riding at a walk down the lane. At this sight Mr. Tebrick waited no longer, but pulling on his boots in mad haste, ran out instantly, meaning to say that they must not hunt, and how his wife was escaped and they might kill her.

But when he found himself outside the cottage words failed him and fury took possession of him, so that he could only cry out:

"How dare you, you damned blackguard?"

And so, with a stick in his hand, he threw himself on the gentleman in the pink coat and seized his horse's rein, and catching the gentleman by the leg was trying to throw him. But really it is impossible to say what Mr. Tebrick intended by his behaviour or what he would have done, for the gentleman, finding himself suddenly assaulted in so unexpected a fashion by so strange a touzled and dishevelled figure, clubbed his hunting crop and dealt him a blow on the temple so that he fell insensible.

Another gentleman rode up at this moment and they were civil enough to dismount and carry Mr. Tebrick into the cottage, where they were met by old Nanny who kept wringing her hands and told them Mr. Tebrick's wife had run away and she was a vixen, and that was the cause that Mr. Tebrick had run out and assaulted them.

The two gentlemen could not help laughing at this, and mounting their horses rode on without delay, after telling each other that Mr. Tebrick, whoever he was, was certainly a madman, and the old woman seemed as mad as her master.

This story, however, went the rounds of the gentry in those parts and perfectly confirmed everyone in their previous opinion, namely that Mr. Tebrick was mad and his wife had run away from him. The part about her being a vixen was laughed at by the few that heard it, but was soon left out as immaterial to the story, and incredible in itself, though afterwards it came to be remembered and its significance to be understood.

When Mr. Tebrick came to himself it was past noon, and his head was aching so painfully that he could only call to mind in a confused way what had happened.

However, he sent off Mrs. Cork's son directly on one of his horses to enquire about the hunt.

At the same time he gave orders to old Nanny that she was to put out food and water for her mistress, on the chance that she might yet be in the neighbourhood.

By nightfall Simon was back with the news that the hunt had had a very long run but had lost one fox, then, drawing a covert, had chopped an old dog fox, and so ended the day's sport.

This put poor Mr. Tebrick in some hopes again, and he rose at once from his bed, and went out to the wood and began calling his wife, but was overcome with faintness, and lay down and so passed the night in the open, from mere weakness.

In the morning he got back again to the cottage but he had taken a chill, and so had to keep his bed for three or four days after.

All this time he had food put out for her every night, but though rats came to it and ate of it, there were never any prints of a fox.

At last his anxiety began working another way, that is he came to think it possible that his vixen would have gone back to Stokoe, so he had his horses harnessed in the dogcart and brought to the door and then drove over to Rylands, though he was still in a fever, and with a heavy cold upon him.

After that he lived always solitary, keeping away from his fellows and only seeing one man, called Askew, who had been brought up a jockey at Wantage, but was grown too big for his profession. He mounted this loafing fellow on one of his horses three days a week and had him follow the hunt and report to him whenever they killed, and if he could view the fox so much the better, and then he made him describe it minutely, so he should know if it were his Silvia. But he dared not trust himself to go himself, lest his passion should master him and he might commit a murder.

Every time there was a hunt in the neighbourhood he set the gates wide open at Rylands and the house doors also, and taking his gun stood sentinel in the hope that his wife would run in if she were pressed by the hounds, and so he could save her. But only once a hunt came near, when two foxhounds that had lost the main pack strayed on to his land and he shot them instantly and buried them afterwards himself.

It was not long now to the end of the season, as it was the middle of March.

But living as he did at this time, Mr. Tebrick grew more and more to be a true misanthrope. He denied admittance to any that came to visit him, and rarely showed himself to his fellows, but went out chiefly in the early mornings before people were about, in the hope of seeing his beloved fox. Indeed it was only this hope that he would see her again that kept him alive, for he had become so careless of his own comfort in every way that he very seldom ate a proper meal, taking no more than a crust of bread with a morsel of cheese in the whole day, though sometimes he would drink half a bottle of whisky to drown his sorrow and to get off to sleep, for sleep fled from him, and no sooner did he begin dozing but he awoke with a start thinking he had heard something. He let his beard grow too, and though he had always been very particular in his person before, he now was utterly careless of it, gave up washing himself for a week or two at a stretch, and if there was dirt under his finger nails let it stop there.

All this disorder fed a malignant pleasure in him. For by now he had come to hate his fellow men and was embittered against all human decencies and decorum. For strange to tell he never once in these months regretted his dear wife whom he had so much loved. No, all that he grieved for now was his departed vixen. He was haunted all this time not by the memory of a sweet and gentle woman, but by the recollection of an animal; a beast it is true that could sit at table and play piquet when it would, but for all that nothing really but a wild beast. His one hope now was the recovery of this beast, and of this he dreamed continually. Likewise both waking and sleeping he was visited by visions of her; her mask, her full white-tagged brush, white throat, and the thick fur in her ears all haunted him.

Every one of her foxey ways was now so absolutely precious to him that I believe that if he had known for certain she was dead, and had thoughts of marrying a second time, he would never have been happy with a woman. No, indeed, he would have been more tempted to get himself a tame fox, and would have counted that as good a marriage as he could make.

Yet this all proceeded one may say from a passion, and a true conjugal fidelity, that it would be hard to find matched in this world. And though we may think him a fool, almost a madman, we must, when we look closer, find much to respect in his extraordinary devotion. How different indeed was he from those who, if their wives go mad, shut them in madhouses and give themselves up to concubinage, and nay, what is more, there are many who extenuate such conduct too. But Mr. Tebrick was of a very different temper, and though his wife was now nothing but a hunted beast, cared for no one in the world but her.

But this devouring love ate into him like a consumption, so that by sleepless nights, and not caring for his person, in a few months he was worn to the shadow of himself. His cheeks were sunk in, his eyes hollow but excessively brilliant, and his whole body had lost flesh, so that looking at him the wonder was that he was still alive.

Now that the hunting season was over he had less anxiety for her, yet even so he was not positive that the hounds had not got her. For between the time of his setting her free, and the end of the hunting season (just after Easter), there were but three vixens killed near. Of those three one was a half-blind or wall-eyed, and one was a very grey dull-coloured beast. The third answered more to the description of his wife, but that it had not much black on the legs, whereas in her the blackness of the legs was very plain to be noticed. But yet his fear made him think that perhaps she had got mired in running and the legs being muddy were not remarked on as black.

One morning the first week in May, about four o'clock, when he was out waiting in the little copse, he sat down for a while on a tree stump, and when he looked up saw a fox coming towards him over the ploughed field. It was carrying a hare over its shoulder so that it was nearly all hidden from him. At last, when it was not twenty yards from him, it crossed over, going into the copse, when Mr. Tebrick stood up and cried out, "Silvia, Silvia, is it you?"

The fox dropped the hare out of his mouth and stood looking at him, and then our gentleman saw at the first glance that this was not his wife. For whereas Mrs. Tebrick had been of a very bright red, this was a swarthier duller beast altogether, moreover it was a good deal larger and higher at the shoulder and had a great white tag to his brush. But the fox after the first instant did not stand for his portrait you may be sure, but picked up his hare and made off like an arrow.

Then Mr. Tebrick cried out to himself: "Indeed I am crazy now! My affliction has made me lose what little reason I ever had. Here am I taking every fox I see to be my wife. My neighbours call me a madman and now I see that they are right. Look at me now, oh, God! How foul a creature I am. I hate my fellows. I am thin and wasted by this consuming passion, my reason is gone and I feed myself on dreams. Recall me to my duty, bring me back to decency, let me not become a beast likewise, but restore me and forgive me, oh, my Lord."

With that he burst into scalding tears and knelt down and prayed, a thing he had not done for many weeks.

When he rose up he walked back feeling giddy and exceedingly weak, but with a contrite heart, and then washed himself thoroughly and changed his clothes, but his weakness increasing he lay down for the rest of the day, but read in the Book of Job and was much comforted.

For several days after this he lived very soberly, for his weakness continued, but every day he read in the Bible, and prayed earnestly, so that his resolution was so much strengthened that he determined to overcome his folly, or his passion, if he could, and at any rate to live the rest of his life very religiously. So strong was this desire in him to amend his ways that he considered if he should not go to spread the Gospel abroad, for the Bible Society, and so spend the rest of his days.

Indeed he began a letter to his wife's uncle, the canon, and he was writing this when he was startled by hearing a fox bark.

Yet so great was this new turn he had taken that he did not rush out at once, as he would have done before, but stayed where he was and finished his letter.

Afterwards he said to himself that it was only a wild fox and sent by the devil to mock him, and that madness lay that way if he should listen. But on the other hand he could not deny to himself that it might have been his wife, and that he ought to welcome the prodigal. Thus he was torn between these two thoughts, neither of which did he completely believe. He stayed thus tormented with doubts and fears all night.

The next morning he woke suddenly with a start and on the instant heard a fox bark once more. At that he pulled on his clothes and ran out as fast as he could to the garden gate. The sun was not yet high, the dew thick everywhere, and for a minute or two everything was very silent. He looked about him eagerly but could see no fox, yet there was already joy in his heart.

Then while he looked up and down the road, he saw his vixen step out of the copse about thirty yards away. He called to her at once.

"My dearest wife! Oh, Silvia! You are come back!" and at the sound of his voice he saw her wag her tail, which set his last doubts at rest.

But then though he called her again, she stepped into the copse once more though she looked back at him over her shoulder as she went. At this he ran after her, but softly and not too fast lest he should frighten her away, and then looked about for her again and called to her when he saw her among the trees still keeping her distance from him. He followed her then, and as he approached so she retreated from him, yet always looking back at him several times.

He followed after her through the underwood up the side of the hill, when suddenly she disappeared from his sight, behind some bracken.

When he got there he could see her nowhere, but looking about him found a fox's earth, but so well hidden that he might have passed it by a thousand times and would never have found it unless he had made particular search at that spot.

But now, though he went on his hands and knees, he could see nothing of his vixen, so that he waited a little while wondering.

Presently he heard a noise of something moving in the earth, and so waited silently, then saw something which pushed itself into sight. It was a small sooty black beast, like a puppy. There came another behind it, then another and so on till there were five of them. Lastly there came his vixen pushing her litter before her, and while he looked at her silently, a prey to his confused and unhappy emotions, he saw that her eyes were shining with pride and happiness.

She picked up one of her youngsters then, in her mouth, and

brought it to him and laid it in front of him, and then looked up at him very excited, or so it seemed.

Mr. Tebrick took the cub in his hands, stroked it and put it against his cheek. It was a little fellow with a smutty face and paws, with staring vacant eyes of a brilliant electric blue and a little tail like a carrot. When he was put down he took a step towards his mother and then sat down very comically.

Mr. Tebrick looked at his wife again and spoke to her, calling her a good creature. Already he was resigned and now, indeed, for the first time he thoroughly understood what had happened to her, and how far apart they were now. But looking first at one cub, then at another, and having them sprawling over his lap, he forgot himself, only watching the pretty scene, and taking pleasure in it. Now and then he would stroke his vixen and kiss her, liberties which she freely allowed him. He marvelled more than ever now at her beauty; for her gentleness with the cubs and the extreme delight she took in them seemed to him then to make her more lovely than before. Thus lying amongst them at the mouth of the earth he idled away the whole of the morning.

First he would play with one, then with another, rolling them over and tickling them, but they were too young yet to lend themselves to any other more active sport than this. Every now and then he would stroke his vixen, or look at her, and thus the time slipped away quite fast and he was surprised when she gathered her cubs together and pushed them before her into the earth, then coming back to him once or twice very humanly bid him "Good-bye and that she hoped she would see him soon again, now he had found out the way."

So admirably did she express her meaning that it would have been superfluous for her to have spoken had she been able, and Mr. Tebrick, who was used to her, got up at once and went home.

But now that he was alone, all the feelings which he had not troubled himself with when he was with her, but had, as it were, put aside till after his innocent pleasures were over, all these came swarming back to assail him in a hundred tormenting ways.

Firstly he asked himself: Was not his wife unfaithful to him, had she not prostituted herself to a beast? Could he still love her after that? But this did not trouble him so much as it might have done. For now he was convinced inwardly that she could no longer in fairness be judged as a woman, but as a fox only. And as a fox she had done no more than other foxes, indeed in having cubs and tending them with love, she had done well.

Whether in this conclusion Mr. Tebrick was in the right or not, is not for us here to consider. But I would only say to those who would censure him for a too lenient view of the religious side of the matter, that we have not seen the thing as he did, and perhaps if it were displayed before our eyes we might be led to the same conclusions.

This was, however, not a tenth part of the trouble in which Mr. Tebrick found himself. For he asked himself also: "Was he not jealous?" And looking into his heart he found that he was indeed jealous, yes, and angry too, that now he must share his vixen with wild foxes. Then he questioned himself if it were not dishonourable to do so, and whether he should not utterly forget her and follow his original intention of retiring from the world, and see her no more.

Thus he tormented himself for the rest of that day, and by evening he had resolved never to see her again.

But in the middle of the night he woke up with his head very clear, and said to himself in wonder, "Am I not a madman? I torment myself foolishly with fantastic notions. Can a man have his honour sullied by a beast? I am a man, I am immeasurably superior to the animals. Can my dignity allow of my being jealous of a beast? A thousand times no. Were I to lust after a vixen, I were a criminal indeed. I can be happy in seeing my vixen, for I love her, but she does right to be happy according to the laws of her being."

Lastly, he said to himself what was, he felt, the truth of this whole matter:

"When I am with her I am happy. But now I distort what is simple and drive myself crazy with false reasoning upon it."

Yet before he slept again he prayed, but though he had thought first to pray for guidance, in reality he prayed only that on the morrow he would see his vixen again and that God would preserve her, and her cubs too, from all dangers, and would allow him to see them often, so that he might come to love them for her sake as if he were their father, and that if this were a sin he might be forgiven, for he sinned in ignorance.

The next day or two he saw vixen and cubs again, though his visits were cut shorter, and these visits gave him such an innocent pleasure that very soon his notions of honour, duty and so on, were entirely forgotten, and his jealousy lulled asleep.

One day he tried taking with him the stereoscope and a pack of cards.

But though his Silvia was affectionate and amiable enough to let him put the stereoscope over her muzzle, yet she would not look through it, but kept turning her head to lick his hand, and it was plain to him that now she had quite forgotten the use of the instrument. It was the same too with the cards. For with them she was pleased enough, but only delighting to bite at them, and flip them about with her paws, and never considering for a moment whether they were diamonds or clubs, or hearts, or spades or whether the card was an ace or not. So it was evident that she had forgotten the nature of cards too.

Thereafter he only brought them things which she could better enjoy, that is sugar, grapes, raisins, and butcher's meat.

Bye-and-bye, as the summer wore on, the cubs came to know him, and he them, so that he was able to tell them easily apart, and then he christened them. For this purpose he brought a little bowl of water, sprinkled them as if in baptism and told them he was their godfather and gave each of them a name, calling them Sorel, Kasper, Selwyn, Esther, and Angelica.

Sorel was a clumsy little beast of a cheery and indeed puppyish disposition; Kasper was fierce, the largest of the five, even in his play he would always bite, and gave his godfather many a sharp nip as time went on. Esther was of a dark complexion, a true brunette and very sturdy; Angelica the brightest red and the most exactly like her mother; while Selwyn was the smallest cub, of a very prying, inquisitive and cunning temper, but delicate and undersized.

Thus Mr. Tebrick had a whole family now to occupy him, and, indeed, came to love them with very much of a father's love and partiality.

His favourite was Angelica (who reminded him so much of her mother in her pretty ways) because of a gentleness which was lack-

ing in the others, even in their play. After her in his affections came
Selwyn, whom he soon saw was the most intelligent of the whole
litter. Indeed he was so much more quick-witted than the rest that
Mr. Tebrick was led into speculating as to whether he had not in-
herited something of the human from his dam. Thus very early he
learnt to know his name and would come when he was called, and
what was stranger still, he learnt the names of his brothers and
sisters before they came to do so themselves.

Besides all this he was something of a young philosopher, for
though his brother Kasper tyrannized over him he put up with it all
with an unruffled temper. He was not, however, above playing tricks
on the others, and one day when Mr. Tebrick was by, he made believe that there was a mouse in a hole some little way off. Very soon
he was joined by Sorel, and presently by Kasper and Esther. When
he had got them all digging, it was easy for him to slip away, and
then he came to his godfather with a sly look, sat down before him,
and smiled and then jerked his head over towards the others and
smiled again and wrinkled his brows so that Mr. Tebrick knew
as well as if he had spoken that the youngster was saying, "Have I
not made fools of them all?"

He was the only one that was curious about Mr. Tebrick; he
made him take out his watch, put his ear to it, considered it and
wrinkled up his brows in perplexity. On the next visit it was the
same thing. He must see the watch again, and again think over it.
But clever as he was, little Selwyn could never understand it, and if
his mother remembered anything about watches it was a subject
which she never attempted to explain to her children.

One day Mr. Tebrick left the earth as usual and ran down the
slope to the road, when he was surprised to find a carriage waiting
before his house and a coachman walking about near his gate. Mr.
Tebrick went in and found that his visitor was waiting for him. It
was his wife's uncle.

They shook hands, though the Rev. Canon Fox did not recognise
him immediately, and Mr. Tebrick led him into the house.

The clergyman looked about him a good deal, at the dirty and
disorderly rooms, and when Mr. Tebrick took him into the drawing
room it was evident that it had been unused for several months, the
dust lay so thickly on all the furniture.

After some conversation on indifferent topics Canon Fox said to him:

"I have called really to ask about my niece."

Mr. Tebrick was silent for some time and then said:

"She is quite happy now."

"Ah—indeed. I have heard she is not living with you any longer."

"No. She is not living with me. She is not far away. I see her every day now."

"Indeed. Where does she live?"

"In the woods with her children. I ought to tell you that she has changed her shape. She is a fox."

The Rev. Canon Fox got up; he was alarmed, and everything Mr. Tebrick said confirmed what he had been led to expect he would find at Rylands. When he was outside, however, he asked Mr. Tebrick:

"You don't have many visitors now, eh?"

"No—I never see anyone if I can avoid it. You are the first person I have spoken to for months."

"Quite right, too, my dear fellow. I quite understand—in the circumstances." Then the cleric shook him by the hand, got into his carriage and drove away.

"At any rate," he said to himself, "there will be no scandal." He was relieved also because Mr. Tebrick had said nothing about going abroad to disseminate the Gospel. Canon Fox had been alarmed by the letter, had not answered it, and thought that it was always better to let things be, and never to refer to anything unpleasant. He did not at all want to recommend Mr. Tebrick to the Bible Society if he were mad. His eccentricities would never be noticed at Stokoe. Besides that, Mr. Tebrick had said he was happy.

He was sorry for Mr. Tebrick too, and he said to himself that the queer girl, his niece, must have married him because he was the first man she had met. He reflected also that he was never likely to see her again and said aloud, when he had driven some little way:

"Not an affectionate disposition," then to his coachman: "No, that's all right. Drive on, Hopkins."

When Mr. Tebrick was alone he rejoiced exceedingly in his solitary life. He understood, or so he fancied, what it was to be happy, and that he had found complete happiness now, living from day to

day, careless of the future, surrounded every morning by playful
and affectionate little creatures whom he loved tenderly, and sitting
beside their mother, whose simple happiness was the source of his
own.

"True happiness," he said to himself, "is to be found in bestowing
love; there is no such happiness as that of the mother for her babe,
unless I have attained it in mine for my vixen and her children."

With these feelings he waited impatiently for the hour on the
morrow when he might hasten to them once more.

When, however, he had toiled up the hillside, to the earth, taking
infinite precaution not to tread down the bracken, or make a beaten
path which might lead others to that secret spot, he found to his surprise that Silvia was not there and that there were no cubs to be
seen either. He called to them, but it was in vain, and at last he laid
himself on the mossy bank beside the earth and waited.

For a long while, as it seemed to him, he lay very still, with closed
eyes, straining his ears to hear every rustle among the leaves, or any
sound that might be the cubs stirring in the earth.

At last he must have dropped asleep, for he woke suddenly with
all his senses alert, and opening his eyes found a full-grown fox
within six feet of him sitting on its haunches like a dog and watching
his face with curiosity. Mr. Tebrick saw instantly that it was not
Silvia. When he moved the fox got up and shifted his eyes, but still
stood his ground, and Mr. Tebrick recognised him then for the dog-
fox he had seen once before carrying a hare. It was the same dark
beast with a large white tag to his brush. Now the secret was out
and Mr. Tebrick could see his rival before him. Here was the real
father of his godchildren, who could be certain of their taking after
him, and leading over again his wild and rakish life. Mr. Tebrick
stared for a long time at the handsome rogue, who glanced back at
him with distrust and watchfulness patent in his face, but not without defiance too, and it seemed to Mr. Tebrick as if there was also
a touch of cynical humour in his look, as if he said:

"By Gad! we two have been strangely brought together!"

And to the man, at any rate, it seemed strange that they were
thus linked, and he wondered if the love his rival there bare to his
vixen and his cubs were the same thing in kind as his own.

"We would both of us give our lives for theirs," he said to himself as he reasoned upon it, "we both of us are happy chiefly in their company. What pride this fellow must feel to have such a wife, and such children taking after him. And has he not reason for his pride? He lives in a world where he is beset with a thousand dangers. For half the year he is hunted, everywhere dogs pursue him, men lay traps for him or menace him. He owes nothing to another."

But he did not speak, knowing that his words would only alarm the fox; then in a few minutes he saw the dog-fox look over his shoulder, and then he trotted off as lightly as a gossamer veil blown in the wind, and, in a minute or two more, back he comes with his vixen and the cubs all around him. Seeing the dog-fox thus surrounded by vixen and cubs was too much for Mr. Tebrick; in spite of all his philosophy a pang of jealousy shot through him. He could see that Silvia had been hunting with her cubs, and also that she had forgotten that he would come that morning, for she started when she saw him, and though she carelessly licked his hand, he could see that her thoughts were not with him.

Very soon she led her cubs into the earth, the dog-fox had vanished and Mr. Tebrick was again alone. He did not wait longer but went home.

Now was his peace of mind all gone, the happiness which he had flattered himself the night before he knew so well how to enjoy, seemed now but a fool's paradise in which he had been living. A hundred times this poor gentleman bit his lip, drew down his torvous brows, and stamped his foot, and cursed himself bitterly, or called his lady bitch. He could not forgive himself either, that he had not thought of the damned dog-fox before, but all the while had let the cubs frisk round him, each one a proof that a dog-fox had been at work with his vixen. Yes, jealousy was now in the wind, and every circumstance which had been a reason for his felicity the night before was now turned into a monstrous feature of his nightmare. With all this Mr. Tebrick so worked upon himself that for the time being he had lost his reason. Black was white and white black, and he was resolved that on the morrow he would dig the vile brood of foxes out and shoot them, and so free himself at last from this hellish plague.

All that night he was in this mood, and in agony, as if he had broken in the crown of a tooth and bitten on the nerve. But as all

things will have an ending so at last Mr. Tebrick, worn out and
wearied by this loathed passion of jealousy, fell into an uneasy and
tormented sleep.

After an hour or two the procession of confused and jumbled
images which first assailed him passed away and subsided into one
clear and powerful dream. His wife was with him in her own proper
shape, walking as they had been on that fatal day before her transformation. Yet she was changed too, for in her face there were visible
tokens of unhappiness, her face swollen with crying, pale and down-
cast, her hair hanging in disorder, her damp hands wringing a small
handkerchief into a ball, her whole body shaken with sobs, and an
air of long neglect about her person. Between her sobs she was con-
fessing to him some crime which she had committed, but he did not
catch her broken words, nor did he wish to hear them, for he was
dulled by her sorrow. So they continued walking together in sadness as it were for ever, he with his arm about her waist, she turning
her head to him and often casting her eyes down in distress.

At last they sat down, and he spoke, saying: "I know they are not
my children, but I shall not use them barbarously because of that.
You are still my wife. I swear to you they shall never be neglected.
I will pay for their education."

Then he began turning over the names of schools in his mind.
Eton would not do, nor Harrow, nor Winchester, nor Rugby. . . .
But he could not tell why these schools would not do for these
children of hers, he only knew that every school he thought of was
impossible, but surely one could be found. So turning over the
names of schools he sat for a long while holding his dear wife's
hand, till at length, still weeping, she got up and went away and
then slowly he awoke.

But even when he had opened his eyes and looked about him he
was thinking of schools, saying to himself that he must send them
to a private academy or even at the worst engage a tutor. "Why,
yes," he said to himself, putting one foot out of bed, "that is what
it must be, a tutor, though even then there will be a difficulty at
first."

At those words he wondered what difficulty there would be and
recollected that they were not ordinary children. No, they were
foxes—mere foxes. When poor Mr. Tebrick had remembered this

he was, as it were, dazed or stunned by the fact, and for a long time he could understand nothing, but at last burst into a flood of tears compassionating them and himself too. The awfulness of the fact itself, that his dear wife should have foxes instead of children, filled him with an agony of pity, and, at length, when he recollected the cause of their being foxes, that is that his wife was a fox also, his tears broke out anew, and he could bear it no longer but began calling out in his anguish, and beat his head once or twice against the wall, and then cast himself down on his bed again and wept and wept, sometimes tearing the sheets asunder with his teeth.

The whole of that day, for he was not to go to the earth till evening, he went about sorrowfully, torn by true pity for his poor vixen and her children.

At last when the time came he went again up to the earth, which he found deserted, but hearing his voice, out came Esther. But though he called the others by their names there was no answer, and something in the way the cub greeted him made him fancy she was indeed alone. She was truly rejoiced to see him, and scrambled up into his arms, and thence to his shoulder, kissing him, which was unusual in her (though natural enough in her sister Angelica). He sat down a little way from the earth fondling her, and fed her with some fish he had brought for her mother, which she ate so ravenously that he concluded she must have been short of food that day and probably alone for some time.

At last while he was sitting there Esther pricked up her ears, started up, and presently Mr. Tebrick saw his vixen come towards them. She greeted him very affectionately but it was plain had not much time to spare, for she soon started back whence she had come with Esther at her side. When they had gone about a rod the cub hung back and kept stopping and looked back to the earth, but at last turned and ran back home. But her mother was not to be fobbed off so, for she quickly overtook her child and gripping her by the scruff began to drag her along with her.

Mr. Tebrick, seeing then how matters stood, spoke to her, telling her he would carry Esther if she would lead, so after a little while Silvia gave her over, and then they set out on their strange journey.

Silvia went running on a little before while Mr. Tebrick followed after with Esther in his arms whimpering and struggling now to be free, and indeed, once she gave him a nip with her teeth. This was not so strange a thing to him now, and he knew the remedy for it, which is much the same as with others whose tempers run too high, that is a taste of it themselves. Mr. Tebrick shook her and gave her a smart little cuff after which, though she sulked, she stopped her biting.

They went thus above a mile, circling his house and crossing the highway until they gained a small covert that lay with some waste fields adjacent to it. And by this time it was so dark that it was all Mr. Tebrick could do to pick his way, for it was not always easy for him to follow where his vixen found a big enough road for herself.

But at length they came to another earth, and by the starlight Mr. Tebrick could just make out the other cubs skylarking in the shadows.

Now he was tired, but he was happy and laughed softly for joy, and presently his vixen, coming to him, put her feet upon his shoulders as he sat on the ground, and licked him, and he kissed her back on the muzzle and gathered her in his arms and rolled her in his jacket and then laughed and wept by turns in the excess of his joy.

All his jealousies of the night before were forgotten now. All his desperate sorrow of the morning and the horror of his dream were gone. What if they were foxes? Mr. Tebrick found that he could be happy with them. As the weather was hot he lay out there all the night, first playing hide and seek with them in the dark till, missing his vixen and the cubs proving obstreperous, he lay down and was soon asleep.

He was woken up soon after dawn by one of the cubs tugging at his shoelaces in play. When he sat up he saw two of the cubs standing near him on their hind legs, wrestling with each other, the other two were playing hide and seek round a tree trunk, and now Angelica let go his laces and came romping into his arms to kiss him and say "Good morning" to him, then worrying the points of his waistcoat a little shyly after the warmth of his embrace.

That moment of awakening was very sweet to him. The freshness of the morning, the scent of everything at the day's rebirth, the first beams of the sun upon a tree-top near, and a pigeon rising into the air suddenly, all delighted him. Even the rough scent of the body of the cub in his arms seemed to him delicious.

At that moment all human customs and institutions seemed to him nothing but folly; for said he, "I would exchange all my life as a man for my happiness now, and even now I retain almost all of the ridiculous conceptions of a man. The beasts are happier and I will deserve that happiness as best I can."

After he had looked at the cubs playing merrily, how, with soft stealth, one would creep behind another to bounce out and startle him, a thought came into Mr. Tebrick's head, and that was that these cubs were innocent, they were as stainless snow, they could not sin, for God had created them to be thus and they could break none of His commandments. And he fancied also that men sin because they cannot be as the animals.

Presently he got up full of happiness, and began making his way home when suddenly he came to a full stop and asked himself: "What is going to happen to them?"

This question rooted him stockishly in a cold and deadly fear as if he had seen a snake before him. At last he shook his head and hurried on his path. Aye, indeed, what would become of his vixen and her children?

This thought put him into such a fever of apprehension that he did his best not to think of it any more, but yet it stayed with him all that day and for weeks after, at the back of his mind, so that he was not careless in his happiness as before, but as it were trying continually to escape his own thoughts.

This made him also anxious to pass all the time he could with his dear Silvia, and, therefore, he began going out to them for more of the daytime, and then he would sleep the night in the woods also as he had done that night; and so he passed several weeks, only returning to his house occasionally to get himself a fresh provision of food. But after a week or ten days at the new earth both his vixen and the cubs, too, got a new habit of roaming. For a long while back, as he knew, his vixen had been lying out alone most of the day, and now the cubs were all for doing the same thing. The earth, in short, had served its purpose and was now distasteful to them, and they would not enter it unless pressed with fear.

This new manner of their lives was an added grief to Mr. Tebrick, for sometimes he missed them for hours together, or for the whole day even, and not knowing where they might be was lonely and anxious. Yet his Silvia was thoughtful for him too and would often send Angelica or another of the cubs to fetch him to their new lair, or come herself if she could spare the time. For now they were all perfectly accustomed to his presence, and had come to look on him as their natural companion, and although he was in many ways irksome to them by scaring rabbits, yet they always rejoiced to see him when they had been parted from him. This friendliness of theirs was, you may be sure, the source of most of Mr. Tebrick's happiness at this time. Indeed he lived now for nothing but his foxes, his love for his vixen had extended itself insensibly to include her cubs, and these were now his daily payments so that he knew them as well as if they had been his own children. With Selwyn and Angelica indeed he was always happy; and they never so much as when they were with him. He was not stiff in his behaviour either, but had learnt by this time as much from his foxes as they had from him. Indeed never was there a more curious alliance than this or one with stranger effects upon both of the parties.

Mr. Tebrick now could follow after them anywhere and keep up with them too, and could go through a wood as silently as a deer. He learnt to conceal himself if ever a labourer passed by so that he was rarely seen, and never but once in their company. But what was most strange of all, he had got a way of going doubled up, often almost on all fours with his hands touching the ground every now and then, particularly when he went uphill.

He hunted with them too sometimes, chiefly by coming up and scaring rabbits towards where the cubs lay ambushed, so that the bunnies ran straight into their jaws.

He was useful to them in other ways, climbing up and robbing pigeons' nests for the eggs which they relished exceedingly, or by occasionally dispatching a hedgehog for them so they did not get the prickles in their mouths. But while on his part he thus altered his conduct, they on their side were not behindhand, but learnt a dozen human tricks from him that are ordinarily wanting in Reynard's education.

One evening he went to a cottager who had a row of skeps, and bought one of them, just as it was after the man had smothered the bees. This he carried to the foxes that they might taste the honey, for he had seen them dig out wild bees' nests often enough. The skep full was indeed a wonderful feast for them, they bit greedily into the heavy scented comb, their jaws were drowned in the sticky flood of sweetness, and they gorged themselves on it without restraint. When they had crunched up the last morsel they tore the skep in pieces, and for hours afterwards they were happily employed in licking themselves clean.

That night he slept near their lair, but they left him and went hunting. In the morning when he woke he was quite numb with cold, and faint with hunger. A white mist hung over everything and the wood smelt of autumn.

He got up and stretched his cramped limbs and then walked homewards. The summer was over and Mr. Tebrick noticed this now for the first time and was astonished. He reflected that the cubs were fast growing up, they were foxes at all points, and yet when he thought of the time when they had been sooty and had blue eyes it seemed to him only yesterday. From that he passed to thinking of the future, asking himself as he had done once before what would become of his vixen and her children. Before the winter he must tempt them into the security of his garden, and fortify it against all the dangers that threatened them.

But though he tried to allay his fear with such resolutions he remained uneasy all that day. When he went out to them that afternoon he found only his wife Silvia there and it was plain to him that she too was alarmed, but alas, poor creature, she could tell him nothing, only lick his hands and face, and turn about pricking her ears at every sound.

"Where are your children, Silvia?" he asked her several times, but she was impatient of his questions, but at last sprang into his arms, flattened herself upon his breast and kissed him gently, so that when he departed his heart was lighter because he knew that she still loved him.

That night he slept indoors, but in the morning early he was awoken by the sound of trotting horses, and running to the window

saw a farmer riding by very sprucely dressed. Could they be hunting so soon, he wondered, but presently reassured himself that it
could not be a hunt already.

He heard no other sound till eleven o'clock in the morning when
suddenly there was the clamour of hounds giving tongue and not
so far off either. At this Mr. Tebrick ran out of his house distracted
and set open the gates of his garden, but with iron bars and wire at
the top so the huntsmen could not follow. There was silence again;
it seems the fox must have turned away, for there was no other sound
of the hunt. Mr. Tebrick was now like one helpless with fear, he
dared not go out, yet could not stay still at home. There was nothing
that he could do, yet he would not admit this, so he busied himself
in making holes in the hedges, so that Silvia (or her cubs) could
enter from whatever side she came.

At last he forced himself to go indoors and sit down and drink
some tea. While he was there he fancied he heard the hounds again;
it was but a faint ghostly echo of their music, yet when he ran out
of the house it was already close at hand in the copse above.

Now it was that poor Mr. Tebrick made his great mistake, for
hearing the hounds almost outside the gate he ran to meet them,
whereas rightly he should have run back to the house. As soon as he
reached the gate he saw his wife Silvia coming towards him but very
tired with running and just upon her the hounds. The horror of that
sight pierced him, for ever afterwards he was haunted by those
hounds—their eagerness, their desperate efforts to gain on her, and
their blind lust for her came at odd moments to frighten him all his
life. Now he should have run back, though it was already late, but
instead he cried out to her, and she ran straight through the open
gate to him. What followed was all over in a flash, but it was seen
by many witnesses.

The side of Mr. Tebrick's garden there is bounded by a wall,
about six feet high and curving round, so that the huntsmen could
see over this wall inside. One of them indeed put his horse at it very
boldly, which was risking his neck, and although he got over safe
was too late to be of much assistance.

His vixen had at once sprung into Mr. Tebrick's arms, and before he could turn back the hounds were upon them and had pulled

them down. Then at that moment there was a scream of despair heard by all the field that had come up, which they declared afterwards was more like a woman's voice than a man's. But yet there was no clear proof whether it was Mr. Tebrick or his wife who had suddenly regained her voice. When the huntsman who had leapt the wall got to them and had whipped off the hounds Mr. Tebrick had been terribly mauled and was bleeding from twenty wounds. As for his vixen she was dead, though he was still clasping her dead body in his arms.

Mr. Tebrick was carried into the house at once and assistance sent for, but there was no doubt now about his neighbours being in the right when they called him mad.

For a long while his life was despaired of, but at last he rallied, and in the end he recovered his reason and lived to be a great age, for that matter he is still alive.

The Rubáiyát of a Persian Kitten

by OLIVER HERFORD

Those who have read The Rubáiyát of Omar Khay-
yám lately will particularly enjoy these charming verses.

Wake! for the Golden Cat has put to flight
The Mouse of Darkness with his Paw of Light:
    Which means, in Plain and simple every-day
Unoriental Speech—The Dawn is bright.

They say the Early Bird the Worm shall taste.
Then rise, O kitten! Wherefore, sleeping, waste
    The fruits of Virtue? Quick! the Early Bird
Will soon be on the flutter—O make haste!

The Early Bird has gone, and with him ta'en
The Early Worm—Alas! the Moral's plain,
    O Senseless Worm! Thus, thus we are repaid
For Early Rising—I shall doze again.

The Mouse makes merry 'mid the Larder Shelves,
The Bird for Dinner in the Garden delves.
    I often wonder what the creatures eat
One half so toothsome as they are Themselves.

And that Inverted Bowl of Skyblue Delf
That helpless lies upon the Pantry Shelf—
    Lift not your eyes to It for help, for It
Is quite as empty as you are yourself.

The Ball no question makes of Ayes or Noes,
But right or left, as strikes the Kitten, goes;

Yet why, altho' I toss it far Afield,
It still returneth—Goodness only knows!

A Secret Presence that my likeness feigns,
And yet, quicksilver-like, eludes my pains—
    In vain I look for Him behind the glass;
He is not there, and yet He still remains.

I sometimes think the Pussy-Willows grey
Are Angel Kittens who have lost their way,
    And every Bulrush on the river bank
A Cat-Tail from some lovely Cat astray.

Sometimes I think perchance that Allah may,
When he created Cats, have thrown away
    The Tails He marred in making, and they grew
To Cat-Tails and to Pussy-Willows grey.

And lately, when I was not feeling fit,
Bereft alike of Piety and Wit,
    There came an Angel Shape and offered me
A fragrant Plant, and bid me taste of it.

'Twas that reviving herb, that Spicy Weed,
The Cat-Nip. Tho' 'tis good in time of need,
    Ah, feed upon it lightly, for who knows
To what unlovely antics it may lead.

They say the Lion and the Lizard keep
The Courts where Jamshýd gloried and drank deep.
    The Lion is my cousin; I don't know
Who Jamshýd is—nor shall it break my sleep.

Impotent glimpses of the Game displayed
Upon the Counter—temptingly arrayed;
    Hither and thither moved or checked or weighed,
And one by one back in the Ice Chest laid.

What if the Sole could fling the Ice aside,
And with me to some Area's haven glide—

Were't not a Shame, were't not a shame for it
In this Cold Prison crippled to abide?

Some for the Glories of the Sole, and Some
Mew for the proper Bowl of Milk to come.
　　Ah, take the fish and let your Credit go,
And plead the rumble of an empty Tum.

One thing is certain: tho' this Stolen Bite
Should be my last and Wrath consume me quite,
　　One taste of It within the Area caught
Better than at the Table lost outright.

Indeed, indeed Repentance oft before
I swore, but was I hungry when I swore?
　　And then and then came Cook—with Hose in hand—
And drowned my glory in a sorry pour.

What without asking hither harried whence,
And without asking whither harried hence—
　　O, many a taste of that forbidden Sole
Must drown the memory of that Insolence.

Heaven but the vision of a flowing Bowl;
And Hell, the sizzle of a frying Sole
　　Heard in the hungry Darkness, where Myself,
So rudely cast, must impotently roll.

Myself when young did eagerly frequent
The Backyard fence and heard great Argument
　　About it, and About, yet evermore
Came out with fewer fur than in I went.

Tho' Two and Two make four by rule of line,
Or they make Twenty-two by Logic fine,
　　Of all the figures one may fathom, I
Shall ne'er be floored by anything but Nine.

And fear not lest Existence shut the Door
On You and Me, to open it no more.

The Cream of Life from out your Bowl shall pour
Nine times—ere it lie broken on the floor.

So, if the fish you Steal—the Cream you drink—
Ends in what all begins and ends in, Think,
  Unless the Stern Recorder points to Nine,
Tho' They would drown you—still you shall not sink.

The Capture of the Great White Whale

by HERMAN MELVILLE

Melville, one of the strange geniuses which the American scene has produced, wrote the novel "Moby Dick" from which this extract is taken, superficially, about a ~reat white whale; it is generally agreed that Melville ~s less concerned with the monster than with what he symbolised to the soul of man. At any rate, it ranks extremely high among stories of adventures on the seas.

THAT night, in the mid-watch, when the old man—as was his wont at intervals—stepped forth from the scuttle in which he leaned, and went to his pivothole, he suddenly thrust out his face fiercely, snuffing up the sea air as a sagacious ship's dog will, in drawing nigh to some barbarous isle. He declared that a whale must be near. Soon that peculiar odor, sometimes to a great distance given forth by the living sperm whale, was palpable to all the watch; nor was any mariner surprised when, after inspecting the compass, and then the dogvane, and then ascertaining the precise bearing of the odor as nearly as possible, Ahab rapidly ordered the ship's course to be slightly altered, and the sail to be shortened.

The acute policy dictating these movements was sufficiently vindicated at daybreak, by the sight of a long sleek on the sea directly and lengthwise ahead, smooth as oil, and resembling in the pleated watery wrinkles bordering it, the polished metallic-like marks of some swift tide-rip, at the mouth of a deep, rapid stream.

"Man the mast-heads! Call all hands!"

Thundering with the butts of three clubbed handspikes on the forecastle deck, Daggoo roused the sleepers with such judgment claps that they seemed to exhale from the scuttle, so instantaneously did they appear with their clothes in their hands.

"What d'ye see?" cried Ahab, flattening his face to the sky.

"Nothing, nothing, sir!" was the sound hailing down in reply.

"T'gallant sails!—stunsails! alow and aloft, and on both sides!"

All sail being set, he now cast loose the life-line, reserved for swaying him to the main royal-mast head; and in a few moments they were hoisting him thither, when, while but two-thirds of the way aloft, and while peering ahead through the horizontal vacancy between the main-top-sail and top-gallant-sail, he raised a gull-like cry in the air, "There she blows!—there she blows! A hump like a snow-hill! It is Moby Dick!"

Fired by the cry which seemed simultaneously taken up by the three look-outs, the men on deck rushed to the rigging to behold the famous whale they had so long been pursuing. Ahab had now gained his final perch, some feet above the other lookouts, Tashtego standing just beneath him on the cap of the top-gallant-mast, so that the Indian's head was almost on a level with Ahab's heel. From this height the whale was now seen some mile or so ahead, at every roll of the sea revealing his high sparkling hump, and regularly jetting his silent spout into the air. To the credulous mariners it seemed the same silent spout they had so long ago beheld in the moonlit Atlantic and Indian Oceans.

"And did none of ye see it before?" cried Ahab, hailing the perched men all around him.

"I saw him almost that same instant, sir, that Captain Ahab did, and I cried out," said Tashtego.

"Not the same instant; not the same—no, the doubloon is mine, Fate reserved the doubloon for me. *I* only; none of ye could have raised the White Whale first. There she blows! there she blows!—there she blows! There again—there again!" he cried, in long-drawn, lingering, methodic tones, attuned to the gradual prolongings of the whale's visible jets. "He's going to sound! In stunsails! Down top-gallant-sails! Stand by three boats. Mr. Starbuck, remember, stay on board, and keep the ship. Helm there! Luff, luff a point! So; steady, man, steady! There go flukes! No, no; only black water! All ready the boats there? Stand by, stand by! Lower me, Mr. Starbuck; lower, lower,—quick, quicker!" and he slid through the air to the deck.

"He is heading straight to leeward, sir," cried Stubb, "right away from us; cannot have seen the ship yet."

"Be dumb, man! Stand by the braces! Hard down them helm!—brace up! Shiver her!—shiver her! So; well that! Boats, boats!"

Soon all the boats but Starbuck's were dropped; all the boatsails set—all the paddles plying; with rippling swiftness, shooting to leeward; and Ahab heading the onset. A pale, death-glimmer lit up Fedallah's sunken eyes; a hideous motion gnawed his mouth.

Like noiseless nautilus shells, their light prows sped through the sea; but only slowly they neared the foe. As they neared him, the ocean grew still more smooth; seemed drawing a carpet over its waves; seemed a noon-meadow, so serenely it spread. At length the breathless hunter came so nigh his seemingly unsuspecting prey, that his entire dazzling hump was distinctly visible, sliding along the sea as if an isolated thing, and continually set in a revolving ring of finest, fleecy, greenish foam. He saw the vast, involved wrinkles of the slightly projecting head beyond. Before it, far out on the soft Turkish-rugged waters, went the glistening white shadow from his broad, milky forehead, a musical rippling playfully accompanying the shade; and behind, the blue waters interchangeably flowed over into the moving valley of his steady wake; and on either hand bright bubbles arose and danced by his side. But these were broken again by the light toes of hundreds of gay fowl softly feathering the sea, alternate with their fitful flight; and like to some flagstaff rising from the painted hull of an argosy, the tall but shattered pole of a recent lance projected from the white whale's back; and at intervals one of the cloud of soft-toed fowls hovering, and to and fro skimming like a canopy over the fish, silently perched and rocked on this pole, the long tail feathers streaming like pennons.

A gentle joyousness—a mighty mildness of repose in swiftness, invested the gliding whale. Not the white bull Jupiter swimming away with ravished Europa clinging to his graceful horns; his lovely, leering eyes sideways intent upon the maid; with smooth bewitching fleetness, rippling straight for the nuptial bower in Crete; not Jove, not that great majesty Supreme! did surpass the glorified White Whale as he so divinely swam.

On each soft side—coincident with the parted swell, that but
once leaving him, then flowed so wide away—on each bright side,
the whale shed off enticings. No wonder there had been some among
the hunters who namelessly transported and allured by all this
serenity, had ventured to assail it; but had fatally found that quietude
but the vesture of tornadoes. Yet calm, enticing calm, oh, whale!
thou glidest on, to all who for the first time eye thee, no matter
how many in that same way thou may'st have bejuggled and destroyed before.

And thus, through the serene tranquillities of the tropical sea,
among waves whose hand-clappings were suspended by exceeding
rapture, Moby Dick moved on, still withholding from sight the
full terrors of his submerged trunk, entirely hiding the wrenched
hideousness of his jaw. But soon the fore part of him slowly rose
from the water; for an instant his whole marbleized body formed a
high arch, like Virginia's Natural Bridge, and warningly waving his
bannered flukes in the air, the grand god revealed himself, sounded,
and went out of sight. Hoveringly, halted, and dipping on the wing,
the white sea-fowls longingly lingered over the agitated pool that
he left.

With oars apeak, and paddles down, the sheets of their sails adrift,
the three boats now stilly floated, awaiting Moby Dick's reappear-
ance.

"An hour," said Ahab, standing rooted in his boat's stern; and he
gazed beyond the whale's place, toward the dim blue spaces and
wide wooing vacancies to leeward. It was only an instant; for again
his eyes seemed whirling round in his head as he swept the watery
circle. The breeze now freshened; the sea began to swell.

"The birds!—the birds!" cried Tashtego.

In long Indian file, as when herons take wing, the white birds were
now all flying towards Ahab's boat; and when within a few yards
began fluttering over the water there, wheeling round and round,
with joyous, expectant cries. Their vision was keener than man's;
Ahab could discover no sign in the sea. But suddenly as he peered
down and down into its depths, he profoundly saw a white living
spot no bigger than a white weasel, with wonderful celerity uprising, and magnifying as it rose, till it turned, and then there were
plainly revealed two long crooked rows of white, glistening teeth,

floating up from the undiscoverable bottom. It was Moby Dick's open mouth and scrolled jaw; his vast, shadowed bulk still half blending with the blue of the sea. The glittering mouth yawned beneath the boat like an open-doored marble tomb; and giving one sidelong sweep with his steering oar, Ahab whirled the craft aside from this tremendous apparition. Then, calling upon Fedallah to change places with him, went forward to the bows, and seizing Perth's harpoon, commanded his crew to grasp their oars and stand by to stern.

Now, by reason of this timely spinning round the boat upon its axis, its bow, by anticipation, was made to face the whale's head while yet under water. But as if perceiving this stratagem, Moby Dick, with that malicious intelligence ascribed to him, sidelingly transplanted himself, as it were, in an instant, shooting his pleated head lengthwise beneath the boat.

Through and through; through every plank and each rib, it thrilled for an instant, the whale obliquely lying on his back, in the manner of a biting shark, slowly and feelingly taking its bows full within his mouth, so that the long, narrow, scrolled lower jaw curled high up into the open air, and one of the teeth caught in a row-lock. The bluish pearl-white of the inside of the jaw was within six inches of Ahab's head, and reached higher than that. In this attitude the White Whale now shook the slight cedar as a mildly cruel cat her mouse. With unastonished eyes Fedallah gazed, and crossed his arms; but the tiger-yellow crew were tumbling over each other's heads to gain the uttermost stern.

And now, while both elastic gunwales were springing in and out, as the whale dallied with the doomed craft in this devilish way; and from his body being submerged beneath the boat, he could not be darted at from the bows, for the bows were almost inside of him, as it were; and while the other boats involuntarily paused, as before a quick crisis impossible to withstand, then it was that monomaniac Ahab, furious with this tantalizing vicinity of his foe, which placed him all alive and helpless in the very jaws he hated; frenzied with all this, he seized the long bone with his naked hands, and wildly strove to wrench it from its gripe. As now he thus vainly strove, the jaw slipped from him; the frail gunwales bent in, collapsed, and snapped, as both jaws, like an enormous shears, sliding further aft, bit the craft completely in twain, and locked themselves fast again in the sea, midway between the two floating wrecks. These floated aside, the broken ends drooping, the crew at the stern-wreck clinging to the gunwales, and striving to hold fast to the oars to lash them across.

At that preluding moment, ere the boat was yet snapped, Ahab, the first to perceive the whale's intent, by the crafty upraising of his head, a movement that loosed his hold for the time; at that moment his hand had made one final effort to push the boat out of the bite. But only slipping further into the whale's mouth, and tilting over sideways as it slipped, the boat had shaken off his hold on the jaw; spilled him out of it, as he leaned to the push; and so he fell flat-faced upon the sea.

Rippingly withdrawing from his prey, Moby Dick now lay at a little distance, vertically thrusting his oblong white head up and down in the billows; and at the same time slowly revolving his whole spindled body; so that when his vast wrinkled forehead rose—some twenty or more feet out of the water—the now rising swells, with all their confident waves, dazzlingly broke against it; vindictively tossing their shivered spray still higher into the air.[1] So, in a gale, the but half baffled Channel billows only recoil from the base of the Eddy-stone, triumphantly to overleap its summit with their scud.

But soon resuming his horizontal attitude, Moby Dick swam swiftly round and round the wrecked crew; sideways churning the water in his vengeful wake, as if lashing himself up to still another and more deadly assault. The sight of the splintered boat seemed to madden him, as the blood of grapes and mulberries cast before Antiochus's elephants in the book of Maccabees. Meanwhile Ahab half smothered in the foam of the whale's insolent tail, and too much of a cripple to swim,—though he could still keep afloat, even in the heart of such a whirlpool as that; helpless Ahab's head was seen, like a tossed bubble which the least chance shock might burst. From the boat's fragmentary stern, Fedallah incuriously and mildly eyed him; the clinging crew, at the other drifting end, could

---

[1] This motion is peculiar to the sperm whale. It receives its designation (pitchpoling) from its being likened to that preliminary up-and-down poise of the whale-lance, in the exercise called pitchpoling previously described. By this motion the whale must best and most comprehensively view whatever objects may be encircling him.

not succor him; more than enough was it to look to themselves. For so revolvingly appalling was the White Whale's aspect, and so planetarily swift the ever-contracting circles he made, that he seemed horizontally swooping upon them. And though the other boats unharmed, still hovered hard by; still they dared not pull into the eddy to strike, lest that should be the signal for the instant destruction of the jeopardized castaways, Ahab and all; nor in that case could they themselves hope to escape. With straining eyes, then, they remained on the outer edge of the direful zone, whose centre had now become the old man's head.

Meantime, from the beginning all this had been descried from the ship's mast heads; and squaring her yards, she had borne down upon the scene; and was now so nigh, that Ahab in the water hailed her:— "Sail on the"—but that moment a breaking sea dashed on him from Moby Dick, and whelmed him for the time. But struggling out of it again, and chancing to rise on a towering crest, he shouted,—"Sail on the whale!—Drive him off!"

The *Pequod's* prows were pointed; and breaking up the charmed circle, she effectually parted the whale from his victim. As he suddenly swam off, the boats flew to the rescue.

Dragged into Stubb's boat with blood-shot, blinded eyes, the white brine caking in his wrinkles; the long tension of Ahab's bodily strength did crack, and helplessly he yielded to his body's doom: for a long time, lying all crushed in the bottom of Stubb's boat, like one trodden under foot of herds of elephants. Far inland, nameless wails came from him, as desolate sounds from out ravines.

But this intensity of his physical prostration did but so much the more abbreviate it. In an instant's compass, great hearts sometimes condense to one deep pang, the sum total of those shallow pains kindly diffused through feebler men's whole lives. And so, such hearts, though summary in each one suffering; still, if the gods decree it, in their life-time aggregate a whole age of woe, wholly made up of instantaneous intensities; for even in their pointless centres, those noble natures contain the entire circumferences of inferior souls.

"The harpoon," said Ahab, half way rising, and draggingly leaning on one bended arm—"is it safe!"

"Aye, sir, for it was not darted; this is it," said Stubb, showing it.

"Lay it before me;—any missing men!"

"One, two, three, four, five;—there were five oars, sir, and here are five men."

"That's good.—Help me, man; I wish to stand. So, so, I see him! there! there! going to leeward still; what a leaping spout!—Hands off from me! The eternal sap runs up in Ahab's bones again! Set the sail; out oars; the helm!"

It is often the case that when a boat is stove, its crew, being picked up by another boat, help to work that second boat; and the chase is thus continued with what is called double-banked oars. It was thus now. But the added power of the boat did not equal the added power of the whale, for he seemed to have treble-banked his every fin; swimming with a velocity which plainly showed, that if now, under these circumstances, pushed on, the chase would prove an indefinitely prolonged, if not a hopeless one; nor could any crew endure for so long a period, such an unintermitted, intense straining at the oar; a thing barely tolerable only in some one brief vicissitude. The ship itself, then, as it sometimes happens, offered the most promising intermediate means of overtaking the chase. Accordingly, the boats now made for her, and were soon swayed up to their cranes—the two parts of the wrecked boat having been previously secured by her—and then hoisting everything to her side, and stacking her canvas high up, and sideways outstretching it with stun-sails, like the double-jointed wings of an albatross; the *Pequod* bore down in the leeward wake of Moby Dick. At the well known, methodic intervals, the whale's glittering spout was regularly announced from the manned mast-heads; and when he would be reported as just gone down, Ahab would take the time, and then pacing the deck, binnacle-watch in hand, so soon as the last second of the allotted hour expired, his voice was heard.—"Whose is the doubloon now? D'ye see him?" and if the reply was, No, sir! straightway he commanded them to lift him to his perch. In this way the day wore on; Ahab, now aloft and motionless; anon, unrestingly pacing the planks.

As he was thus walking, uttering no sound, except to hail the men aloft, or to bid them hoist a sail still higher, or to spread one to a still greater breadth—thus to and fro pacing, beneath his slouched hat, at every turn he passed his own wrecked boat, which had been dropped upon the quarter-deck, and lay there reversed; broken bow to shattered stern. At last he paused before it; and as in an already over-clouded sky fresh troops of clouds will sometimes sail across, so over the old man's face there now stole some such added gloom as this.

Stubb saw him pause; and perhaps intending, not vainly, though, to evince his own unabated fortitude, and thus keep up a valiant place in his Captain's mind, he advanced, and eyeing the wreck exclaimed—"The thistle the ass refused; it pricked his mouth too keenly, sir; ha! ha!"

"What soulless thing is this that laughs before a wreck? Man, man! did I not know thee brave as fearless fire (and as mechanical) I could swear thou wert a poltroon. Groan nor laugh should be heard before a wreck."

"Aye, sir," said Starbuck drawing near, " 'tis a solemn sight; an omen, and an ill one."

"Omen? omen?—the dictionary! If the gods think to speak outright to man, they will honorably speak outright; not shake their heads, and give an old wives' darkling hint.—Begone! Ye two are the opposite poles of one thing; Starbuck is Stubb reversed, and Stubb is Starbuck; and ye two are all mankind; and Ahab stands alone among the millions of the peopled earth, nor gods nor men his neighbors! Cold, cold—I shiver!—How now? Aloft there! D'ye see him? Sing out for every spout, though he spout ten times a second!"

The day was nearly done; only the hem of his golden robe was rustling. Soon, it was almost dark, but the look-out men still remained unset.

"Can't see the spout now, sir;—too dark"—cried a voice from the air.

"How heading when last seen?"

"As before, sir,—straight to leeward."

"Good! he will travel slower now 'tis night. Down royals and top-gallant stun-sails, Mr. Starbuck. We must not run over him before morning; he's making a passage now, and may heave-to a while. Helm there! keep her full before the wind!—Aloft! come down!—Mr. Stubb, send a fresh hand to the foremast head, and see it manned till morning."—Then advancing towards the doubloon in the main-mast—"Men, this gold is mine, for I earned it; but I shall let it abide here till the White Whale is dead; and then, whosoever of ye first raises him, upon the day he shall be killed, this gold is that man's; and if on that day I shall again raise him, then, ten times its sum shall be divided among all of ye! Away now!—the deck is thine, sir."

And so saying, he placed himself half way within the scuttle, and slouching his hat, stood there till dawn, except when at intervals rousing himself to see how the night wore on.

SECOND DAY

At day-break, the three mast-heads were punctually manned afresh.

"D'ye see him?" cried Ahab, after allowing a little space for the light to spread.

"See nothing, sir."

"Turn up all hands and make sail! he travels faster than I thought for;—the top-gallant sails!—aye, they should have been kept on her all night. But no matter—'tis but resting for the rush."

Here be it said, that this pertinacious pursuit of one particular whale, continued through day into night, and through night into day, is a thing by no means unprecedented in the South Sea fishery. For such is the wonderful skill, prescience of experience, and invincible confidence acquired by some great natural geniuses among the Nantucket commanders; that from the simple observation of a whale when last descried, they will, under certain given circumstances, pretty accurately foretell both the direction in which he will continue to swim for a time, while out of sight, as well as his probable rate of progression during that period. And, in these cases, somewhat as a pilot, when about losing sight of a coast, whose general trending he well knows, and which he desires shortly to return to again, but at some further point; like as this pilot stands by his compass, and takes the precise bearing of the cape at present visible, in order the more certainly to hit aright the remote, unseen headland, eventually to be visited: so does the fisherman, at his compass, with the whale; for after being chased, and diligently marked, through several hours of daylight, then, when night obscures the fish, the creature's future wake through the darkness is almost as established to the sagacious mind of the hunter, as the pilot's coast is to him. So that to this hunter's wondrous skill, the proverbial evanescence of a thing writ in water, a wake, is to all desired purposes well-nigh as reliable as the steadfast land. And as the mighty iron Leviathan of the modern railway is so familiarly known in its every pace, that, with watches in their hands, men time his rate, as doctors that of a baby's pulse; and lightly say of it, the up train or the down train will reach such or such a spot, at such or such an hour; even so, almost, there are occasions when these Nantucketers time that other Leviathan of the deep, according to the observed humor of his speed; and say to themselves, so many hours hence this whale will have gone two hundred miles, will have about reached this or that degree of latitude or longitude. But to render this acuteness at all successful in the end, the wind and the sea must be the whaleman's allies; for of what present avail to the becalmed or windbound mariner is the skill that assures him he is exactly ninety-three leagues and a quarter from his port? Inferable from these statements, are many collateral subtile matters touching the chase of whales.

The ship tore on; leaving such a furrow in the sea as when a cannon-ball, missent, becomes a ploughshare and turns up the level field.

"By salt and hemp!" cried Stubb, "but this swift motion of the deck creeps up one's legs and tingles at the heart. This ship and I are two brave fellows!—Ha! ha! Some one take me up, and launch me, spine-wise, on the sea,—for by live-oaks! my spine's a keel. Ha, ha! we go the gait that leaves no dust behind!"

"There she blows—she blows!—she blows!—right ahead!" was now the mast-head cry.

"Aye, ave!" cried Stubb, "I knew it—ye can't escape—blow on and split your spout, O whale! the mad fiend himself is after ye! blow your trump—blister your lungs!—Ahab will dam off your blood, as a miller shuts his water-gate upon the stream!"

And Stubb did but speak out for well-nigh all that crew. The frenzies of the chase had by this time worked them bubblingly up, like old wine worked anew. Whatever pale fears and forebodings some of them might have felt before; these were not only now kept out of sight through the growing awe of Ahab, but they were broken up, and on all sides routed, as timid prairie hares that scatter before the bounding bison. The hand of Fate had snatched all their souls;

and by the stirring perils of the previous day; the rack of the past night's suspense; the fixed, unfearing, blind, reckless way in which their wild craft went plunging towards its flying mark; by all these things, their hearts were bowled along. The wind that made great bellies of their sails, and rushed the vessel on by arms invisible as irresistible; this seemed the symbol of that unseen agency which so enslaved them to the race.

They were one man, not thirty. For as the one ship that held them all; though it was put together of all contrasting things—oak, and maple, and pine wood; iron, and pitch, and hemp—yet all these ran into each other in the one concrete hull, which shot on its way, both balanced and directed by the long central keel; even so, all the individualities of the crew, this man's valor, that man's fear; guilt and guiltiness, all varieties were welded into oneness, and were all directed to that fatal goal which Ahab their one lord and keel did point to.

The rigging lived. The mast-heads, like the tops of tall palms, were outspreadingly tufted with arms and legs. Clinging to a spar with one hand, some reached forth the other with impatient wavings; others, shading their eyes from the vivid sunlight, sat far out on the rocking yards; all the spars in full bearing of mortals, ready and ripe for their fate. Ah! how they still strove through that infinite blueness to seek out the thing that might destroy them!

"Why sing ye not out for him, if ye see him?" cried Ahab, when, after the lapse of some minutes since the first cry, no more had been heard. "Sway me up, men; ye have been deceived; not Moby Dick casts one odd jet that way, and then disappears."

It was even so; in their headlong eagerness, the men had mistaken some other thing for the whale-spout, as the event itself soon proved; for hardly had Ahab reached his perch; hardly was the rope belayed to its pin on deck, when he struck the keynote to an orchestra, that made the air vibrate as with the combined discharge of rifles. The triumphant halloo of thirty buckskin lungs was heard, as—much nearer to the ship than the place of the imaginary jet, less than a mile ahead—Moby Dick bodily burst into view! For not by any calm and indolent spoutings! not by the peaceable gush of that mystic fountain in his head, did the White Whale now reveal his vicinity; but by the far more wondrous phenomenon of breaching. Rising with his utmost velocity from the furthest depths, the Sperm Whale thus booms his entire bulk into the pure element of air, and piling up a mountain of dazzling foam, shows his place to the distance of seven miles and more. In those moments, the torn, enraged waves he shakes off, seem his mane; in some cases, this breaching is his act of defiance.

"There she breaches! there she breaches!" was the cry, as in his immeasurable bravadoes the White Whale tossed himself salmon-like to Heaven. So suddenly seen in the blue plain of the sea, and relieved against the still bluer margin of the sky, the spray that he raised, for the moment, intolerably glittered and glared like a glacier; and stood there gradually fading and fading away from its first sparkling intensity, to the dim mistiness of an advancing shower in a vale.

"Aye, breach your last to the sun, Moby Dick!" cried Ahab, "thy hour and thy harpoon are at hand!—Down! down all of ye, but one man at the fore. The boats!—stand by!"

Unmindful of the tedious rope-ladders of the shrouds, the men, like shooting stars, slid to the deck, by the isolated backstays and halyards; while Ahab, less dartingly, but still rapidly was dropped from his perch.

"Lower away," he cried, so soon as he had reached his boat—a spare one, rigged the afternoon previous. "Mr. Starbuck, the ship is thine—keep away from the boats, but keep near them. Lower, all!"

As if to strike a quick terror into them, by this time being the first assailant himself, Moby Dick had turned, and was now coming for the three crews. Ahab's boat was central; and cheering his men, he told them he would take the whale head-and-head,—that is, pull straight up to his forehead,—a not uncommon thing; for when within a certain limit, such a course excludes the coming onset from the whale's sidelong vision. But ere that close limit was gained, and while yet all three boats were plain as the ship's three masts to his eye; the White Whale churning himself into furious speed, almost in an instant as it were, rushing among the boats with open jaws, and a lashing tail, offered appalling battle on every side; and heedless of the irons darted at him from every boat, seemed only intent on annihilating each separate plank of which those boats were made.

But skillfully manoeuvred, incessantly wheeling like trained charges in the field; the boats for a while eluded him; though, at times, but by a plank's breadth; while all the time, Ahab's unearthly slogan tore every other cry but his to shreds.

But at last in his untraceable evolutions, the White Whale so crossed and recrossed, and in a thousand ways entangled the clack of the three lines now fast to him, that they foreshortened, and, of themselves, warped the devoted boats towards the planted irons in him; though now for a moment the whale drew aside a little, as if to rally for a more tremendous charge. Seizing that opportunity, Ahab first paid out more line: and then was rapidly hauling and jerking in upon it again—hoping that way to disencumber it of some snarls —when lo!—a sight more savage than the embattled teeth of sharks!

Caught and twisted—corkscrewed in the mazes of the line, loose harpoons and lances, with all their bristling barbs and points, came flashing and dripping up to the chocks in the bows of Ahab's boat. Only one thing could be done. Seizing the boatknife, he critically reached within—through—and then, without—the rays of steel; dragged in the line beyond, passed it inboard, to the bowsman, and then, twice sundering the rope near the chocks—dropped the intercepted fagot of steel into the sea; and was all fast again. That instant, the White Whale made a sudden rush among the remaining tangles of the other lines; by so doing, irresistibly dragged the more involved boats of Stubb and Flask towards his flukes; dashed them together like two rolling husks on a surf-beaten beach, and then, diving down into the sea, disappeared in a boiling maelstrom, in which, for a space, the odorous cedar chips of the wrecks danced round and round, like grated nutmeg in a swiftly stirred bowl of punch.

While the two crews were yet circling in the waters, reaching out after the revolving line-tubs, oars, and other floating furniture, while aslope little Flask bobbed up and down like an empty vial, twitching his legs upwards to escape the dreaded jaws of sharks; and Stubb was lustily singing out for some one to ladle him up; and while the old man's line—now parting—admitted of his pulling into the creamy pool to rescue whom he could;—in that wild simultaneousness of a thousand concreted perils,—Ahab's yet unstricken boat seemed drawn up towards Heaven by invisible wires,—as, arrow-like, shooting perpendicularly from the sea, the white whale dashed his broad forehead against its bottom, and sent it, turning over and over, into the air; till it fell again—gunwale downwards—and Ahab and his men struggled out from under it, like seals from a sea-side cave.

The first uprising momentum of the whale—modifying its direction as he struck the surface—involuntarily launched him along it, to a little distance from the centre of the destruction he had made; and with his back to it, he now lay for a moment slowly feeling with his flukes from side to side; and whenever a stray oar, bit of plank, the least chip or crumb of the boats touched his skin, his tail swiftly drew back, and came sideways smiting the sea. But soon, as if satisfied that his work for that time was done, he pushed his pleated forehead through the ocean, and trailing after him the intertangled lines, continued his leeward way at a traveller's methodic pace.

As before, the attentive ship having descried the whole fight, again came bearing down to the rescue, and dropping a boat, picked up the floating mariners, tubs, oars, and whatever else could be caught at, and safely landed them on her decks. Some sprained shoulders, wrists, and ankles; livid contusions; wrenched harpoons and lances; inextricable intricacies of rope; shattered oars and planks; all these were there; but no fatal or even serious ill seemed to have befallen any one. As with Fedallah the day before, so Ahab was now found grimly clinging to his boat's broken half, which afforded a comparatively easy float; nor did it so exhaust him as the previous day's mishap.

But when he was helped to the deck, all eyes were fastened upon him; as instead of standing by himself he still half-hung upon the shoulder of Starbuck, who had thus far been the foremost to assist him. His ivory leg had been snapped off, leaving but one short sharp splinter.

"Aye, aye, Starbuck, 'tis sweet to lean sometimes, be the leaner who he will; and would old Ahab had leaned oftener than he has."

"The ferrule has not stood, sir," said the carpenter, now coming up; "I put good work into that leg."

"But no bones broken, sir, I hope," said Stubb with true concern.

"Aye! and all splintered to pieces, Stubb!—d'ye see it.—But even with a broken bone, old Ahab is untouched; and I account no living bone of mine one jot more me, than this dead one that's lost. Nor white whale, nor man, nor fiend, can so much as graze old Ahab in his own proper and inaccessible being. Can any lead touch yonder floor, any mast scrape yonder roof?—Aloft there! which way?"

"Dead to leeward, sir."

"Up helm, then; pile on the sail again, ship keepers! Down the rest of the spare boats and rig them—Mr. Starbuck away, and muster the boat's crews."

"Let me first help thee towards the bulwarks, sir."

"Oh, oh, oh! how this splinter gores me now! Accursed fate! that the unconquerable captain in the soul should have such a craven mate!"

"Sir?"

"My body, man, not thee. Give me something for a cane—there, that shivered lance will do. Muster the men. Surely I have not seen him yet. By heaven it cannot be!—missing?—quick! call them all."

The old man's hinted thought was true. Upon mustering the company, the Parsee was not there.

"The Parsee!" cried Stubb—"he must have been caught in—"

"The black vomit wrench thee!—run all of ye above, alow, cabin, forecastle—find him—not gone—not gone!"

But quickly they returned to him with the tidings that the Parsee was nowhere to be found.

"Aye, sir," said Stubb—"caught among the tangles of your line —I thought I saw him dragging under."

"*My* line! my line? Gone?—gone? What means that little word? —What death-knell rings in it, that old Ahab shakes as if he were the belfry. The harpoon, too!—toss over the litter there,—d'ye see it?—the forged iron, men, the white whale's—no, no, no,—blistered fool! this hand did dart it!—'tis in the fish!—Aloft there! Keep him nailed—Quick!—all hands to the rigging of the boats—collect the oars—harpooners! the irons, the irons! hoist the royals higher—a pull on all the sheets! helm there! steady, steady for your life! I'll ten-times girdle the unmeasured globe; yea and dive straight through it, but I'll slay him yet!"

"Great God! but for one single instant show thyself," cried Starbuck; "never, never wilt thou capture him, old man—In Jesus' name no more of this, that's worse than devil's madness. Two days chased; twice stove to splinters; thy very leg once more snatched from under thee; thy evil shadow gone—all good angels mobbing thee with warnings:—what more wouldst thou have?—Shall we keep chasing this murderous fish till he swamps the last man? Shall we be dragged by him to the bottom of the sea? Shall we be towed by him to the infernal world? Oh, oh,—impiety and blasphemy to hunt him more!"

"Starbuck, of late I've felt strangely moved to thee; ever since that hour we both saw—thou know'st what, in one another's eyes. But in this matter of the whale, be the front of thy face to me as the palm of this hand—a lipless, unfeatured blank. Ahab is for ever Ahab, man. This whole act's immutably decreed. 'Twas rehearsed by thee and me a billion years before this ocean rolled. Fool! I am the Fates' lieutenant; I act under orders. Look thou, underling! that thou obeyest mine.—Stand round me, men. Ye see an old man cut down to the stump; leaning on a shivered lance; propped up on a lonely foot. 'Tis Ahab—his body's part; but Ahab's soul's a centipede, that moves upon a hundred legs. I feel strained, half-stranded, as ropes that tow dismasted frigates in a gale; and I may look so. But ere I break, ye'll hear me crack; and till ye hear *that*, know that Ahab's hawser tows his purpose yet. Believe ye, men, in the things called omens? Then laugh aloud, and cry encore! For ere they drown, drowning things will twice rise to the surface; then rise again, to sink for evermore. So with Moby Dick—two days he's floated—to-morrow will be the third. Aye, men, he'll rise once more,—but only to spout his last! D'ye feel brave, men, brave?"

"As fearless fire," cried Stubb.

"And as mechanical," muttered Ahab. Then as the men went forward, he muttered on:—"The things called omens! And yesterday I talked the same to Starbuck there, concerning my broken boat. Oh! how valiantly I seek to drive out of others' hearts what's clinched so fast in mine!—The Parsee—the Parsee!—gone, gone? and he was to go before:—but still was to be seen again ere I could perish—How's that?—There's a riddle now might baffle all the lawyers backed by the ghosts of the whole line of judges:—like a hawk's beak it pecks my brain. *I'll, I'll* solve it, though!"

When dusk descended, the whale was still in sight to leeward.

So once more the sail was shortened, and everything passed nearly as on the previous night; only, the sound of hammers, and the hum of the grindstone was heard till nearly daylight, as the men toiled

by lanterns in the complete and careful rigging of the spare boats
and sharpening their fresh weapons for the morrow. Meantime, of
the broken keel of Ahab's wrecked craft the carpenter made him another leg; while still as on the night before, slouched Ahab stood
fixed within his scuttle; his hid, heliotrope glance anticipatingly gone
backward on its dial; sat due eastward for the earliest sun.

THIRD DAY

The morning of the third day dawned fair and fresh, and once
more the solitary night-man at the fore-mast-head was relieved by
crowds of the daylight lookouts, who dotted every mast and almost
every spar.

"D'ye see him?" cried Ahab; but the whale was not yet in sight.

"In his infallible wake, though; but follow that wake, that's all.
Helm there; steady, as thou goest, and hast been going. What a
lovely day again! were it a new-made world, and made for a summer-
house to the angels, and this morning the first of its throwing open
to them, a fairer day could not dawn upon that world. Here's food
for thought, had Ahab time to think; but Ahab never thinks; he
only feels, feels, feels; *that's* tingling enough for mortal man! to
think's audacity. God only has that right and privilege. Thinking is,
or ought to be, a coolness and a calmness; and our poor hearts throb,
and our poor brains beat too much for that. And yet, I've sometimes
thought my brain was very calm—frozen calm, this old skull cracks
so, like a glass in which the contents turned to ice, and shiver it. And
still this hair is growing now; this moment growing, and the heat
must breed it; but no, it's like that sort of common grass that will
grow anywhere, between earthly clefts of Greenland ice or in Vesu-
vius lava. How the wild winds blow; they whip about me as the torn
shreds of split sails lash the tossed ship they cling to. A vile wind
that has no doubt blown ere this through prison corridors and cells,
and wards of hospitals, and ventilated them, and now comes blowing
hither as innocent as fleeces. Out upon it!—it's tainted. Were I the
wind, I'd blow no more on such a wicked, miserable world. I'd
crawl somewhere to a cave, and slink there. And yet, 'tis a noble and
heroic thing, the wind! who ever conquered it? In every fight it has
the last and bitterest blow. Run tilting at it, and you but run through
it. Ha! a coward wind that strikes stark naked men, but will not

stand to receive a single blow. Even Ahab is a braver thing—a nobler thing than *that*. Would now the wind but had a body; but all the things that most exasperate and outrage mortal man, all these things are bodiless, but only bodiless as objects, not as agents. There's a most special, a most cunning, oh, a most malicious difference! And yet, I say again, and swear it now, that there's something all glorious and gracious in the wind. These warm Trade Winds, at least, that in the clear heavens blow straight on, in strong and steadfast, vigorous mildness; and veer not from their mark, however the baser currents of the sea may turn and tack, and mightiest Mississippis of the land swift and swerve about, uncertain where to go at last. And by the eternal Poles! these same Trades that so directly blow my good ship on; these Trades, or something like them—something so unchangeable, and full as strong, blow my keeled soul along! To it! Aloft there! What d'ye see?"

"Nothing, sir."

"Nothing! and noon at hand! The doubloon goes a-begging! See the sun! Aye, aye, it must be so. I've oversailed him. How, got the start? Aye, he's chasing *me* now; not I, *him*—that's bad; I might have known it, too. Fool! the lines—the harpoons he's towing. Aye, aye, I have run him by last night. About! about! Come down, all of ye, but the regular lookouts! Man the braces!"

Steering as she had done, the wind had been somewhat on the *Pequod's* quarter, so that now being pointed in the reverse direction, the braced ship sailed hard upon the breeze as she rechurned the cream in her own white wake.

"Against the wind he now steers for the open jaw," murmured Starbuck to himself, as he coiled the new-hauled mainbrace upon the rail. "God keep us, but already my bones feel damp within me, and from the inside wet my flesh. I misdoubt me that I disobey my God in obeying him!"

"Stand by to sway me up!" cried Ahab, advancing to the hempen basket. "We should meet him soon."

"Aye, aye, sir," and straightway Starbuck did Ahab's bidding, and once more Ahab swung on high.

A whole hour now passed; gold-beaten out to ages. Time itself now held long breaths with keen suspense. But at last, some three points off the weather bow, Ahab descried the spout again, and instantly from the three mast-heads three shrieks went up as if the tongues of fire had voiced it.

"Forehead to forehead I meet thee, this third time, Moby Dick! On deck there!—brace sharper up; crowd her into the wind's eye. He's too far off to lower yet, Mr. Starbuck. The sails shake! Stand over that helmsman with a top-maul! So, so; he travels fast, and I must down. But let me have one more good round look aloft here at the sea; there's time for that. An old, old sight, and yet somehow so young; aye, and not changed a wink since I first saw it, a boy, from the sand-hills of Nantucket! The same!—the same!—the same to Noah as to me. There's a soft shower to leeward. Such lovely lee-wardings! They must lead somewhere—to something else than common land, more palmy than the palms. Leeward! the white whale goes that way; look to windward, then; the better if the bitterer quarter. But good bye, good bye, old mast-head! What's this?—green? aye, tiny mosses in these warped cracks. No such green weather stains on Ahab's head! There's the difference now between man's old age and matter's. But aye, old mast, we both grow old together; sound in our hulls, though, are we not my ship? Aye, minus a leg, that's all. By heaven this dead wood has the better of my live flesh every way. I can't compare with it; and I've known some ships made of dead trees outlast the lives of men made of the most vital stuff of vital fathers. What's that he said? he should still go before me, my pilot; and yet to be seen again? But where? Will I have eyes at the bottom of the sea, supposing I descend those endless stairs? and all night I've been sailing from him, wherever he did sink to. Aye, aye, like many more thou told'st direful truth as touching thyself, O Parsee; but, Ahab, there thy shot fell short. Good bye, masthead— keep a good eye upon the whale, the while I'm gone. We'll talk to-morrow, nay, to-night, when the white whale lies down there, tied by head and tail."

He gave the word! and still gazing round him, was steadily lowered through the cloven blue air to the deck.

In due time the boats were lowered; but as standing in his shallop's stern, Ahab just hovered upon the point of the descent, he waved to the mate,—who held one of the tackle-ropes on deck—and bade him pause.

"Starbuck!"

"Sir?"

"For the third time my soul's ship starts upon this voyage, Starbuck."

"Aye, sir, thou wilt have it so."

"Some ships sail from their ports, and ever afterwards are missing, Starbuck!"

"Truth, sir: saddest truth."

"Some men die at ebb tide; some at low water; some at the full of the flood;—and I feel now like a billow that's all one crested comb, Starbuck. I am old;—shake hands with me, man."

Their hands met; their eyes fastened; Starbuck's tears the glue.

"Oh, my captain, my captain!—noble heart—go not—go not!—see, it's a brave man that weeps; how great the agony of the persuasion then!"

"Lower away!"—cried Ahab, tossing the mate's arm from him. "Stand by the crew!"

In an instant the boat was pulling round close under the stern.

"The sharks! the sharks!" cried a voice from the low cabin-window there; "O master, my master, come back!"

But Ahab heard nothing; for his own voice was high-lifted then; and the boat leaped on.

Yet the voice spake true; for scarce had he pushed from the ship, when numbers of sharks, seemingly rising from out the dark waters beneath the hull, maliciously snapped at the blades of the oars, every time they dipped in the water; and in this way accompanied the boat with their bites. It is a thing not uncommonly happening to the whale-boats in those swarming seas; the sharks at times apparently following them in the same prescient way that vultures hover over the banners of marching regiments in the east. But these were the first sharks that had been observed by the *Pequod* since the White Whale had been first descried; and whether it was that Ahab's crew were all such tiger-yellow barbarians, and therefore their flesh more musky to the senses of the sharks—a matter sometimes well known to affect them, however it was, they seemed to follow that one boat without molesting the others.

"Heart of wrought steel!" murmured Starbuck, gazing over the side and following with his eyes the receding boat—"canst thou yet ring boldly to that sight?—lowering thy keel among ravening sharks, and followed by them, open-mouthed to the chase; and this the critical third day?—For when three days flow together in one continuous intense pursuit; be sure the first is the morning, the second the noon, and the third the evening and the end of that thing—be that end what it may. Oh! my God! what is this that shoots through me, and leaves me so deadly calm, yet expectant,—fixed at the top of a shudder! Future things swim before me, as in empty outlines and skeletons; all the past is somehow grown dim. Mary, girl! thou fadest in pale glories behind me; boy! I seem to see but thy eyes grown wondrous blue. Strangest problems of life seem clearing; but clouds sweep between— Is my journey's end coming? My legs feel faint; like his who has footed it all day. Feel thy heart,—beats it yet?—Stir thyself, Starbuck!—stave it off—move, move! speak aloud!—Mast-head there. See ye my boy's hand on the hill?—Crazed;—aloft there!—keep thy keenest eye upon the boats:—mark well the whale!—Ho! again!—drive off that hawk! see! he pecks—he tears the vane"—pointing to the red flag flying at the main-truck— "Ha! he soars away with it!—Where's the old man now? see'st thou that sight, oh Ahab!—shudder, shudder!"

The boats had not gone very far, when by a signal from the mast-heads—a downward pointed arm, Ahab knew that the whale had sounded; but intending to be near him at the next rising, he held on his way a little sideways from the vessel; the becharmed crew maintaining the profoundest silence, as the head-beat waves hammered and hammered against the opposing bow.

"Drive, drive in your nails, oh ye waves! to their uttermost heads drive them in! ye but strike a thing without a lid; and no coffin and no hearse can be mine:—and hemp only can kill me! Ha! ha!"

Suddenly the waters around them slowly swelled in broad circles; then quickly upheaved, as if sideways sliding from a submerged berg of ice, swiftly rising to the surface. A low rumbling sound was heard; a subterraneous hum; and then all held their breaths; as bedraggled with trailing ropes, and harpoons, and lances, a vast form shot lengthwise, but obliquely from the sea. Shrouded in a thin drooping veil of mist, it hovered for a moment in the rainbowed air; and then fell swamping back into the deep. Crushed thirty feet upwards, the waters flashed for an instant like heaps of fountains, then brokenly sank in a shower of flakes, leaving the circling surface creamed like new milk round the marble trunk of the whale.

"Give way!" cried Ahab to the oarsmen, and the boats darted forward to the attack; but maddened by yesterday's fresh irons that corroded in him, Moby Dick seemed combinedly possessed by all the angels that fell from heaven. The wide tiers of welded tendons overspreading his broad white forehead, beneath the transparent skin, looked knitted together; as head on, he came churning his tail among the boats; and once more flailed them apart; spilling out the irons and lances from the two mates' boats, and dashing in one side of the upper part of their bows, but leaving Ahab's almost without a scar.

While Daggoo and Queequeg were stopping the strained planks; and as the whale swimming out from them, turned, and showed one entire flank as he shot by them again; at that moment a quick cry went up. Lashed round and round to the fish's back; pinioned in the turns upon turns in which, during the past night, the whale had reeled the involutions of the lines around him, the half torn body of the Parsee was seen; his sable raiment frayed to shreds; his distended eyes turned full upon old Ahab.

The harpoon dropped from his hand.

"Befooled, befooled!"—drawing in a long lean breath—"Aye, Parsee! I see thee again.—Aye, and thou goest before; and this, *this* then is the hearse that thou didst promise. But I hold thee to the last letter of thy word. Where is the second hearse? Away, mates, to the ship! those boats are useless now; repair them if ye can in time, and return to me; if not, Ahab is enough to die— Down, men! the first thing that but offers to jump from this boat I stand in, that thing I harpoon. Ye are not other men, but my arms and my legs; and so obey me.—Where's the whale? gone down again?"

But he looked too nigh the boat; for as if bent upon escaping with the corpse he bore, and as if the particular place of the last encounter had been but a stage in his leeward voyage, Moby Dick was now again steadily swimming forward; and had almost passed the ship,—which thus far had been sailing in the contrary direction to him, though for the present her headway had been stopped. He seemed swimming with his utmost velocity, and now only intent upon pursuing his own straight path in the sea.

"Oh! Ahab," cried Starbuck, "not too late is it, even now, the third day, to desist. See! Moby Dick seeks thee not. It is thou, thou, that madly seekest him!"

Setting sail to the rising wind, the lonely boat was swiftly impelled to leeward, by both oars and canvas. And at last when Ahab was sliding by the vessel, so near as plainly to distinguish Starbuck's face as he leaned over the rail, he hailed him to turn the vessel about, and follow him, not too swiftly, at a judicious interval. Glancing upwards, he saw Tashtego, Queequeg, and Daggoo, eagerly mounting to the three mast-heads; while the oarsmen were rocking in the two staved boats which had but just been hoisted to the side, and were busily at work in repairing them. One after the other, through the portholes, as he sped, he also caught flying glimpses of Stubb and Flack, busying themselves on deck among bundles of new irons and lances. As he saw all this; as he heard the hammers in the broken boats; far other hammers seemed driving a nail into his heart. But he rallied. And now marking that the vane or flag was gone from the main-mast-head, he shouted to Tashtego, who had just gained that perch, to descend again for another flag, and a hammer and nails, and so nail it to the mast.

Whether fagged by the three days' running chase, and the resistance to his swimming in the knotted hamper he bore; or whether it was some latent deceitfulness and malice in him: whichever was true, the White Whale's way now began to abate, as it seemed, from the boat so rapidly nearing him once more; though indeed the whale's last start had not been so long a one as before. And still as Ahab glided over the waves the unpitying sharks accompanied him; and so pertinaciously stuck to the boat; and so continually bit at the plying oars, that the blades became jagged and crunched, and left small splinters in the sea, at almost every dip.

"Heed them not! those teeth but give new rowlocks to your oars. Pull on! 'tis the better rest, the shark's jaw than the yielding water."

"But at every bite, sir, the thin blades grow smaller and smaller!"

"They will last long enough! pull on!—But who can tell"—he muttered—"whether these sharks swim to feast on the whale or on Ahab?—But pull on! Aye, all alive, now—we near him. The helm! take the helm; let me pass,"—and so saying, two of the oarsmen helped him forward to the bows of the still flying boat.

At length as the craft was cast to one side, and ran ranging along with the White Whale's flank, he seemed strangely oblivious of its advance—as the whale sometimes will—and Ahab was fairly within the smoky mountain mist, which, thrown off from the whale's spout, curled round his great, Monadnock rump; he was even thus close to him; when, with body arched back, and both arms lengthwise high-lifted to the poise, he darted his fierce iron, and his far fiercer curse into the hated whale. As both steel and curse sank to the socket, as if sucked into a morass, Moby Dick sideways writhed; spasmodically rolled his nigh flank against the bow, and, without staving a hole in it, so suddenly canted the boat over, that had it not been for the elevated part of the gunwale to which he then clung, Ahab would once more have been tossed into the sea. As it was, three of the oars-men—who foreknew not the precise instant of the dart, and were therefore unprepared for its effects—these were flung out; but so fell, that, in an instant two of them clutched the gunwale again, and rising to its level on a combining wave, hurled themselves bodily in-board again; the third man helplessly dropping astern, but still afloat and swimming.

Almost simultaneously, with a mighty volition of ungraduated, instantaneous swiftness, the White Whale darted through the welter-ing sea. But when Ahab cried out to the steersman to take new turns with the line, and hold it so; and commanded the crew to turn round on their seats, and tow the boat up to the mark; the moment the treacherous line felt that double strain and tug, it snapped in the empty air!

"What breaks in me? Some sinew cracks!—'tis whole again; oars! oars! Burst in upon him!"

Hearing the tremendous rush of the sea-crashing boat, the whale wheeled round to present his blank forehead at bay; but in that evolu-tion, catching sight of the nearing black hull of the ship; seemingly seeing in it the source of all his persecutions; bethinking it—it may be—a larger and nobler foe; of a sudden, he bore down upon its ad-vancing prow, smiting his jaws amid fiery showers of foam.

Ahab staggered; his hand smote his forehead. "I grow blind; hands! stretch out before me that I may yet grope my way. Is't night?"

"The whale! The ship!" cried the cringing oarsmen.

"Oars! oars! Slope downwards to thy depths, O sea, that ere it be forever too late, Ahab may slide this last, last time upon his mark! I see: the ship! the ship! Dash on, my men! Will ye not save my ship?"

But as the oarsmen violently forced their boat through the sledge-hammering seas, the before whale-smitten bow-ends of two planks burst through, and in an instant almost, the temporarily disabled boat lay nearly level with the waves; its half-wading, splashing crew, trying hard to stop the gap and bale out the pouring water.

Meantime, for that one beholding instant, Tashtego's masthead hammer remained suspended in his hand; and the red flag, half-wrapping him as with a plaid, then streamed itself straight out from him, as his own forward-flowing heart; while Starbuck and Stubb, standing upon the bowsprit beneath, caught sight of the down-coming monster just as soon as he.

"The whale, the whale! Up helm, up helm! Oh, all ye sweet powers of air, now hug me close! Let not Starbuck die, if die he must, in a woman's fainting fit. Up helm, I say—ye fools, the jaw! the jaw! Is this the end of all my bursting prayers? all my life-long fidelities? Oh, Ahab, Ahab, lo, thy work. Steady! helmsman, steady. Nay, nay! Up helm again! He turns to meet us! Oh, his unappeasable brow drives on towards one, whose duty tells him he cannot depart. My God, stand by me now!"

"Stand not by me, but stand under me, whoever you are that will now help Stubb; for Stubb, too, sticks here. I grin at thee, thou grinning whale! Who ever helped Stubb, or kept Stubb awake, but Stubb's own unwinking eye? And now poor Stubb goes to bed upon a mattress that is all too soft; would it were stuffed with brush-wood! I grin at thee, thou grinning whale! Look ye, sun, moon, and stars! I call ye assassins of as good a fellow as ever spouted up his ghost. For all that, I would yet ring glasses with ye, would ye but hand the cup! Oh, oh! oh, oh! thou grinning whale, but there'll be plenty of gulping soon! Why fly ye not, O Ahab! For me, off shoes and jacket to it; let Stubb die in his drawers! A most mouldy and over-salted death, though;—cherries! cherries! cherries! Oh, Flask, for one red cherry ere we die!"

"Cherries? I only wish that we were where they grow. Oh, Stubb, I hope my poor mother's drawn my part-pay ere this; if not, few coppers will now come to her, for the voyage is up."

From the ship's bows, nearly all the seamen now hung inactive; hammers, bits of plank, lances, and harpoons, mechanically retained in their hands, just as they had darted from their various employments; all their enchanted eyes intent upon the whale, which from side to side strangely vibrating his predestinating head, sent a broad band of overspreading semicircular foam before him as he rushed. Retribution, swift vengeance, eternal malice were in his whole aspect, and spite of all that mortal man could do, the solid white buttress of his forehead smote the ship's starboard bow, till men and timbers reeled. Some fell flat upon their faces. Like dislodged trucks, the heads of the harpooners aloft shook on their bull-like necks. Through the breach, they heard the waters pour, as mountain torrents down a flume.

"The ship! The hearse!—the second hearse!" cried Ahab from the boat; "its wood could only be American!"

Diving beneath the settling ship, the whale ran quivering along its keel; but turning under water, swiftly shot to the surface again, far off the other bow, but within a few yards of Ahab's boat, where, for a time, he lay quiescent.

"I turn my body from the sun. What ho, Tashtego! let me hear thy hammer. Oh! ye three unsurrendered spires of mine; thou uncracked keel; and only god-bullied hull; thou firm deck, and haughty helm, and Pole-pointed prow,—death-glorious ship! must ye then perish, and without me? Am I cut off from the last fond pride of meanest shipwrecked captains? Oh, lonely death on lonely life! Oh, now I feel my topmost greatness lies in my topmost grief. Ho, ho! from all your furthest bounds, pour ye now in, ye bold billows of my whole foregone life, and top this one piled comber of my death! Towards thee I roll, thou all-destroying but unconquering whale; to the last I grapple with thee; from hell's heart I stab at thee; for hate's sake I spit my last breath at thee. Sink all coffins and all hearses to one common pool! and since neither can be mine, let me then tow to pieces, while still chasing thee, though tied to thee, thou damned whale! *Thus*, I give up the spear!"

The harpoon was darted; the stricken whale flew forward; with igniting velocity the line ran through the groove;—ran foul. Ahab stooped to clear it; he did clear it! but the flying turn caught him round the neck, and voicelessly as Turkish mutes bowstring their victim, he was shot out of the boat, ere the crew knew he was gone. Next instant, the heavy eye-splice in the rope's final end flew out of the stark-empty tub, knocked down an oarsman, and smiting the sea, disappeared in its depths.

For an instant, the tranced boat's crew stood still; then turned. "The ship! Great God, where is the ship?" Soon they through dim, bewildering mediums saw her sidelong fading phantom, as in the gaseous *Fata Morgana;* only the uppermost masts out of water; while fixed by infatuation, or fidelity, or fate, to their once lofty perches, the pagan harpooners still maintained their sinking lookouts on the sea. And now, concentric circles seized the lone boat itself, and all its crew, and each floating oar, and every lance-pole, and spinning, animate and inanimate, all round and round in one vortex, carried the smallest chip of the *Pequod* out of sight.

But as the last whelmings intermixingly poured themselves over the sunken head of the Indian at the main-mast, leaving a few inches of the erect spar yet visible, together with long streaming yards of the flag, which calmly undulated, with ironical coincidings, over the destroying billows they almost touched;—at that instant, a red arm and a hammer hovered backwardly uplifted in the open air, in the act of nailing the flag faster and yet faster to the subsiding spar. A sky-hawk that tauntingly had followed the main-truck downwards from its natural home among the stars, pecking at the flag, and incommoding Tashtego there; this bird now chanced to intercept its broad fluttering wing between the hammer and the wood; and simultaneously feeling that ethereal thrill, the submerged savage beneath, in his death-gasp, kept his hammer frozen there; and so the bird of heaven, with arch-angelic shrieks, and his imperial beak thrusts upwards, and his whole captive form folded in the flag of Ahab, went down with his ship, which, like Satan, would not sink to hell till she had dragged a living part of heaven along with her, and helmeted herself with it.

Now small fowls flew screaming over the yet yawning gulf; a sullen white surf beat against its steep sides; then all collapsed, and the great shroud of the sea rolled on as it rolled five thousand years ago.

Rab and His Friends

by JOHN BROWN, M.D.

John Brown, M.D., of Edinburgh, wrote little because he subjected all his work to the severest self-criticism. He is one of the few minor writers of the last century whose work has survived: this story of a dog is marked by his characteristic tenderness.

FOUR-AND-THIRTY years ago, Bob Ainslie and I were coming up Infirmary Street from the Edinburgh High School, our heads together, and our arms intertwisted, as only lovers and boys know how, or why.

When we got to the top of the street, and turned north, we espied a crowd at the Tron Church. "A dog-fight!" shouted Bob, and was off; and so was I, both of us all but praying that it might not be over before we got up! And is not this boy-nature? and human nature too? and don't we all wish a house on fire not to be out before we see it? Dogs like fighting; old Isaac says they "delight" in it, and for the best of all reasons; and boys are not cruel because they like to see the fight. They see three of the great cardinal virtues of dog or man—courage, endurance, and skill—in intense action. This is very different from a love of making dogs fight, and enjoying, and aggravating, and making gain by their pluck. A boy—be he ever so fond himself of fighting, if he be a good boy, hates and despises all this, but he would run off with Bob and me fast enough: it is a natural, and not wicked interest, that all boys and men have in witnessing intense energy in action.

Does any curious and finely-ignorant woman wish to know how Bob's eye at a glance announced a dog-fight to his brain? He did not, he could not see the dogs fighting; it was a flash of an inference, a rapid induction. The crowd round a couple of dogs fighting, is a crowd masculine mainly, with an occasional active, compassionate woman, fluttering wildly round the outside, and using her tongue and her hands freely upon the men, as so many "brutes"; it is a crowd annular, compact, and mobile; a crowd centripetal, having its eyes and its heads all bent downwards and inwards, to one common focus.

Well, Bob and I are up, and find it is not over: a small thorough-bred, white bull-terrier, is busy throttling a large shepherd's dog, un-accustomed to war, but not to be trifled with. They are hard at it; the scientific little fellow doing his work in great style, his pastoral enemy fighting wildly, but with the sharpest of teeth and a great courage. Science and breeding, however, soon had their own; the Game Chicken, as the premature Bob called him, working his way up, took his final grip of poor Yarrow's throat—and he lay gasping and done for. His master, a brown, handsome, big young shepherd from Tweedsmuir, would have liked to have knocked down any man, would "drink up Esil, or eat a crocodile," for that part, if he had a chance: it was no use kicking the little dog; that would only make him hold the closer. Many were the means shouted out in mouthfuls, of the best possible ways of ending it. "Water!" but there was none near, and many cried for it who might have got it from the well at Blackfriars Wynd. "Bite the tail!" and a large, vague, benevolent, middle-aged man, more desirous than wise, with some struggle got the bushy end of *Yarrow's* tail into his ample mouth, and bit it with all his might. This was more than enough for the much-enduring, much-perspiring shepherd, who, with a gleam of joy over his broad visage, delivered a terrific facer upon our large, vague, benevolent, middle-aged friend—who went down like a shot.

Still the Chicken holds; death not far off. "Snuff! a pinch of snuff!" observed a calm, highly-dressed young buck, with an eye-glass in his eye. "Snuff, indeed!" growled the angry crowd, affronted and glaring. "Snuff! a pinch of snuff!" again observes the buck but with more urgency; whereon were produced several open boxes, and from a mull which may have been at Culloden, he took a pinch, knelt down, and presented it to the nose of the Chicken. The laws of physiology and of snuff take their course; the Chicken sneezes, and Yarrow is free!

The young pastoral giant stalks off with Yarrow in his arms—comforting him.

But the Bull Terrier's blood is up, and his soul unsatisfied; he grips the first dog he meets, and discovering she is not a dog, in Homeric phrase, he makes a brief sort of *amende*, and is off. The boys, with Bob and me at their head, are after him: down Niddry Street he goes, bent on mischief; up the Cowgate like an arrow—Bob and I, and our small men, panting behind.

There, under the single arch of the South Bridge, is a huge mastiff, sauntering down the middle of the causeway, as if with his hands in his pockets: he is old, gray, brindled, as big as a little Highland bull, and has the Shakespearean dewlaps shaking as he goes.

The Chicken makes straight at him, and fastens on his throat. To our astonishment, the great creature does nothing but stand still, hold himself up, and roar—yes, roar; a long, serious, remonstrative roar. How is this? Bob and I are up to them. *He is muzzled!* The bailies had proclaimed a general muzzling, and his master, studying strength and economy mainly, had encompassed his huge jaws in a home-made apparatus, constructed out of the leather of some ancient *breechin*. His mouth was open as far as it could; his lips curled up in rage—a sort of terrible grin; his teeth gleaming, ready, from out the darkness, the strap across his mouth tense as a bowstring; his whole frame stiff with indignation and surprise; his roar asking us all round, "Did you ever see the like of this?" He looked a statue of anger and astonishment, done in Aberdeen granite.

We soon had a crowd: the Chicken held on. "A knife!" cried Bob; and a cobbler gave him his knife: you know the kind of knife, worn away obliquely to a point, and always keen. I put its edge to the tense leather; it ran before it; and then!—one sudden jerk of that enormous head, a sort of dirty mist about his mouth, no noise—and the bright and fierce little fellow is dropped, limp, and dead. A solemn pause: this was more than any of us had bargained for. I turned the little fellow over, and saw he was quite dead; the mastiff had taken him by the small of the back like a rat, and broken it.

He looked down at his victim appeased, ashamed, and amazed; snuffed him all over, stared at him, and taking a sudden thought, turned round and trotted off. Bob took the dead dog up, and said, "John, we'll bury him after tea." "Yes," said I, and was off after the mastiff. He made up the Cowgate at a rapid swing; he had forgotten some engagement. He turned up the Candlemaker Row, and stopped at the Harrow Inn.

There was a carrier's cart ready to start, and a keen thin, impatient, black-a-vised little man, his hand at his gray horse's head, looking about angrily for something. "Rab, ye thief!" said he, aiming a kick at my great friend, who drew cringing up, and avoiding the heavy shoe with more agility than dignity, and watching his master's eye, slunk dismayed under the cart—his ears down, and as much as he had of tail down too.

What a man this must be—thought I—to whom my tremendous hero turns tail! The carrier saw the muzzle hanging, cut and useless, from his neck, and I eagerly told him the story, which Bob and I always thought, and still think, Homer, or King David, or Sir Walter alone were worthy to rehearse. The severe little man was mitigated, and condescended to say, "Rab, my man, puir Rabbie,"—whereupon the stump of a tail rose up, the ears were cocked, the eyes filled, and were comforted; the two friends were reconciled. "Hupp!" and a stroke of the whip were given to Jess; and off went the three.

Bob and I buried the Game Chicken that night (we had not much of a tea) in the back-green of his house in Melville Street, No. 17, with considerable gravity and silence; and being at the time in the Iliad, and, like all boys, Trojans, we called him Hector of course.

Six years have passed—a long time for a boy and a dog: Bob Ainslie is off to the wars; I am a medical student and clerk at Minto House Hospital.

Rab I saw almost every week, on the Wednesday and we had much pleasant intimacy. I found the way to his heart by frequent scratching of his huge head, and an occasional bone. When I did not notice him he would plant himself straight before me, and stand wagging that butt of a tail, and looking up, with his head a little to one side. His master I occasionally saw; he used to call me "Maister John," but was laconic as any Spartan.

One fine October afternoon, I was leaving the hospital, when

I saw the large gate open, and in walked Rab, with that great and easy saunter of his. He looked as if taking general possession of the place; like the Duke of Wellington entering a subdued city, satiated with victory and peace. After him came Jess, now white from age, with her cart; and in it a woman, carefully wrapped up—the carrier leading the horse anxiously, and looking back. When he saw me, James (for his name was James Noble) made a curt and grotesque "boo," and said, "Maister John, this is the mistress; she's got a trouble in her breest—some kind o' an income we're thinkin'."

By this time I saw the woman's face; she was sitting on a sack filled with straw, her husband's plaid round her, and his big-coat with its large white metal buttons over her feet.

I never saw a more unforgettable face—pale, serious, *lonely*, delicate, sweet, without being at all what we call fine. She looked sixty, and had on a mutch, white as snow, with its black ribbon; her silvery, smooth hair setting off her dark-gray eyes—eyes such as one sees only twice or thrice in a lifetime, full of suffering, full also of the overcoming of it: her eyebrows black and delicate, and her mouth firm, patient, and contented, which few mouths ever are.

As I have said, I never saw a more beautiful countenance, or one more subdued to settled quiet. "Ailie," said James, "this is Maister John, the young doctor; Rab's freend, ye ken. We often speak aboot you, doctor." She smiled, and made a movement, but said nothing; and prepared to come down, putting her plaid aside and rising. Had Solomon, in all his glory, been handing down the Queen of Sheba at his palace gate he could not have done it more daintily, more tenderly, more like a gentleman, than did James the Howgate carrier, when he lifted down Ailie his wife. The contrast of his small, swarthy, weather-beaten, keen, worldly face to hers—pale, subdued, and beautiful—was something wonderful. Rab looked on concerned and puzzled, but ready for anything that might turn up—were it to strangle the nurse, the porter, or even me. Ailie and he seemed great friends.

"As I was sayin' she's got a kind o' trouble in her breest, doctor; wull ye tak' a look at it?" We walked into the consulting-room, all four; Rab grim and comic, willing to be happy and confidential if cause could be shown, willing also to be the reverse, on the same terms. Ailie sat down, undid her open gown and her lawn handkerchief round her neck, and without a word, showed me her right breast. I looked at and examined it carefully—she and James watching me, and Rab eyeing all three. What could I say? there it was, that had once been so soft, so shapely, so white, so gracious and bountiful, so "full of all blessed conditions,"—hard as a stone, a centre of horrid pain, making that pale face with its gray, lucid, reasonable eyes, and its sweet resolved mouth, express the full measure of suffering overcome. Why was that gentle, modest, sweet woman, clean and lovable, condemned by God to bear such a burden?

I got her away to bed. "May Rab and me bide?" said James. "*You* may; and Rab, if he will behave himself." "I'se warrant he's do that, doctor;" and in slank the faithful beast. I wish you could have seen him. There are no such dogs now. He belonged to a lost tribe. As I have said, he was brindled and gray like Rubislaw granite; his hair short, hard, and close, like a lion's; his body thick set, like a little bull —a sort of compressed Hercules of a dog. He must have been ninety pounds' weight, at the least; he had a large blunt head; his muzzle black as night, his mouth blacker than any night, a tooth or two—being all he had—gleaming out of his jaws of darkness. His head was scarred with the records of old wounds, a sort of series of fields of battle all over it; one eye out, one ear cropped as close as was Archbishop Leighton's father's; the remaining eye had the power of two; and above it, and in constant communication with it, was a tattered rag of an ear, which was forever unfurling itself, like an old flag; and then that bud of a tail, about one inch long, if it could in any sense be said to be long, being as broad as long—the mobility, the instantaneousness of that bud were very funny and surprising, and its expressive twinklings and winkings, the intercommunications between the eye, the ear, and it, were of the oddest and swiftest.

Rab had the dignity and simplicity of great size; and having fought his way along the road to absolute supremacy, he was as mighty in his own line as Julius Caesar or the Duke of Wellington, and had the gravity of all great fighters.

You must have often observed the likeness of certain men to certain animals, and of certain dogs to men. Now, I never looked at Rab without thinking of the great Baptist preacher, Andrew Fuller. The same large, heavy, menacing, combative, sombre, honest countenance, the same deep inevitable eye, the same look—as of thunder asleep, but ready—neither a dog nor a man to be trifled with.

Next day, my master, the surgeon, examined Ailie. There was no doubt it must kill her, and soon. It could be removed—it might never return—it would give her speedy relief—she should have it done. She curtsied, looked at James, and said, "When?" "To-morrow," said the kind surgeon—a man of few words. She and James and Rab and I retired. I noticed that he and she spoke little, but seemed to anticipate everything in each other. The following day, at noon, the students came in, hurrying up the great stair. At the first landing-place, on a small well-known blackboard, was a bit of paper fastened by wafers, and many remains of old wafers beside it. On the paper were the words—"An operation to-day. J. B. *Clerk*."

Up ran the youths, eager to secure good places: in they crowded, full of interest and talk. "What's the case?" "Which side is it?"

Don't think them heartless; they are neither better nor worse than you or I; they get over their professional horrors, and into their proper work—and in them pity—as an *emotion*, ending in itself or at best in tears and a long-drawn breath, lessens, while pity as a *motive*, is quickened, and gains power and purpose. It is well for poor human nature that it is so.

The operating theatre is crowded; much talk and fun, and all the cordiality and stir of youth. The surgeon with his staff of assistants is there. In comes Ailie: one look at her quiets and abates the eager students. That beautiful old woman is too much for them; they sit down, and are dumb, and gaze at her. These rough boys feel the power of her presence. She walks in quickly, but without haste; dressed in her mutch, her neckerchief, her white dimity short-gown, her black bombazine petticoat, showing her white worsted stockings and her carpet-shoes. Behind her was James with Rab. James sat down in the distance, and took that huge and noble head between his knees. Rab looked perplexed and dangerous; forever cocking his ear and dropping it as fast.

Ailie stepped up on a seat, and laid herself on the table, as her friend the surgeon told her; arranged herself, gave a rapid look at James, shut her eyes, rested herself on me, and took my hand. The operation was at once begun; it was necessarily slow; and chloroform—one of God's best gifts to his suffering children—was then unknown. The surgeon did his work. The pale face showed its pain, but was still and silent. Rab's soul was working within him; he saw that something strange was going on—blood flowing from his mistress, and she suffering; his ragged ear was up, and importunate; he growled and gave now and then a sharp impatient yelp; he would have liked to have done something to that man. But James had him firm, and gave him a *glower* from time to time, and an intimation of a possible kick;—all the better for James, it kept his eye and his mind off Ailie.

It is over: she is dressed, steps gently and decently down from the table, looks for James; then, turning to the surgeon and the students, she curtsies—and in a low, clear voice, begs their pardon if she has behaved ill. The students—all of us—wept like children; the surgeon happed her up carefully—and, resting on James and me, Ailie went to her room, Rab following. We put her to bed. James took off his heavy shoes, crammed with tackets, heel-capt and toe-capt, and put them carefully under the table, saying, "Maister John, I'm for nane o'yer strynge nurse bodies for Ailie. I'll be her nurse, and I'll gang aboot on my stockin' soles as canny as pussy." And so he did; and handy and clever, and swift and tender as any woman, was that horny-handed, snell, peremptory little man. Everything she got he gave her: he seldom slept; and often I saw his small shrewd eyes out of the darkness, fixed on her. As before, they spoke little.

Rab behaved well, never moving, showing us how meek and gentle he could be, and occasionally, in his sleep, letting us know that he was demolishing some adversary. He took a walk with me every day, generally to the Candlemaker Row; but he was sombre and mild; declined doing battle, though some fit cases offered, and indeed submitted to sundry indignities; and was always very ready to turn, and came faster back, and trotted up the stair with much lightness, and went straight to that door.

Jess, the mare, had been sent, with her weather-worn cart, to Howgate, and had doubtless her own dim and placid meditations and confusions, on the absence of her master and Rab, and her unnatural freedom from the road and her cart.

For some days Ailie did well. The wound healed "by the first intention"; for as James said, "Oor Ailie's skin's ower clean to beil." The students came in quiet and anxious, and surrounded her bed.

She said she liked to see their young, honest faces. The surgeon dressed her, and spoke to her in his own short kind way, pitying her through his eyes, Rab and James outside the circle—Rab being now reconciled, and even cordial, and having made up his mind that as yet nobody required worrying, but, as you may suppose, *semper paratus.*

So far well: but, four days after the operation, my patient had a sudden and long shivering, a "groosin'," as she called it. I saw her soon after; her eyes were too bright, her cheek coloured; she was restless, and ashamed of being so; the balance was lost; mischief had begun. On looking at the wound, a blush of red told the secret: her pulse was rapid, her breathing anxious and quick, she wasn't herself, as she said, and was vexed at her restlessness. We tried what we could; James did everything, was everywhere; never in the way, never out of it; Rab subsided under the table into a dark place, and was motionless, all but his eye, which followed every one. Ailie got worse; began to wander in her mind, gently; was more demonstrative in her ways to James, rapid in her questions, and sharp at times. He was vexed, and said, "She was never that way afore; no, never." For a time she knew her head was wrong, and was always asking our pardon—the dear, gentle old woman: then delirium set in strong, without pause. Her brain gave way, and then came that terrible spectacle—

> "The intellectual power, through words and things,
>   Went sounding on its dim and perilous way."

she sang bits of old songs and Psalms, stopping suddenly, mingling the Psalms of David and the diviner words of his Son and Lord, with homely odds and ends and scraps of ballads.

Nothing more touching, or in a sense more strangely beautiful, did I ever witness. Her tremulous, rapid, affectionate, eager, Scotch voice—the swift, aimless, bewildered mind, the baffled utterance, the bright and perilous eye; some wild words, some household cares, something for James, the names of the dead, Rab called rapidly and in a "fremyt" voice, and he starting up surprised, and slinking off as if he were to blame somehow, or had been dreaming he heard; many eager questions and beseechings which James and I could make nothing of, and on which she seemed to set her all, and then sink back ununderstood. It was very sad, but better than many things that are not called sad. James hovered about, put out and miserable, but active and exact as ever; read to her when there was a lull, short bits from the Psalms, prose and metre, chanting the latter in his own rude and serious way, showing great knowledge of the fit words, bearing up like a man, and doating over her as his "ain Ailie." "Ailie, ma woman!" "Ma ain bonnie wee dawtie!"

The end was drawing on: the golden bowl was breaking; the silver cord was fast being loosed—that *animula blandula, vagula, hospes, comesque,* was about to flee. The body and the soul—companions for sixty years—were being sundered, and taking leave. She was walking alone, through the valley of that shadow, into which one day we must all enter—and yet she was not alone, for we know whose rod and staff were comforting her.

One night she had fallen quiet, and as we hoped, asleep; her eyes were shut. We put down the gas and sat watching her. Suddenly she sat up in bed, and taking a bed-gown which was lying on it rolled up, she held it eagerly to her breast—to the right side. We could see her eyes bright with a surprising tenderness and joy, bending over this bundle of clothes. She held it as a woman holds her sucking child; opening out her night-gown impatiently, and holding it close, and brooding over it, and murmuring foolish little words, as over one whom his mother comforteth, and who sucks and is satisfied. It was pitiful and strange to see her wasted dying look, keen and yet vague—her immense love.

"Preserve me!" groaned James, giving way. And then she rocked back and forward, as if to make it sleep, hushing it, and wasting on it her infinite fondness. "Wae's me, doctor; I declare she's thinkin' it's that bairn." "What bairn?" "The only bairn we ever had; our wee Mysie, and she's in the Kingdom, forty years and mair." It was plainly true: the pain in the breast, telling its urgent story to a bewildered, ruined brain, was misread and mistaken; it suggested to her the uneasiness of a breast full of milk and then the child; and so again once more they were together and she had her ain wee Mysie in her bosom.

This was the close. She sank rapidly: the delirium left her; but as, she whispered, she was "clean silly"; it was the lightning before

the final darkness. After having for some time lain still—her eyes
shut, she said "James!" He came close to her, and lifting up her calm,
clear, beautiful eyes, she gave him a long look, turned to me kindly
but shortly, looked for Rab but could not see him, then turned to
her husband again, as if she would never leave off looking, shut her
eyes, and composed herself. She lay for some time breathing quick,
and passed away so gently, that when we thought she was gone,
James, in his old-fashioned way, held the mirror to her face. After
a long pause, one small spot of dimness was breathed out; it vanished
away, and never returned, leaving the blank clear darkness of the
mirror without a stain. "What is our life? it is even a vapour, which
appeareth for a little time, and then vanisheth away."

Rab all this time had been full awake and motionless; he came
forward beside us: Ailie's hand, which James had held, was hanging
down, it was soaked with his tears; Rab licked it all over carefully,
looked at her, and returned to his place under the table.

James and I sat, I don't know how long, but for some time—
saying nothing: he started up abruptly, and with some noise went
to the table, and putting his right fore and middle fingers each into
a shoe, pulled them out, and put them on, breaking one of the leather
latchets, and muttering in anger, "I never did the like o' that afore!"

I believe he never did; nor after either. "Rab!" he said roughly,
and pointing with his thumb to the bottom of the bed. Rab leapt
up, and settled himself; his head and eye to the dead face. "Maister
John, ye'll wait for me," said the carrier; and disappeared in the
darkness, thundering downstairs in his heavy shoes. I ran to a front
window; there he was, already round the house, and out at the
gate, fleeing like a shadow.

I was afraid about him, and yet not afraid; so I sat down beside
Rab, and being wearied, fell asleep. I awoke from a sudden noise
outside. It was November, and there had been a heavy fall of snow.
Rab was *in statu quo;* he heard the noise too, and plainly knew it,
but never moved. I looked out; and there, at the gate, in the dim
morning—for the sun was not up—was Jess and the cart—a cloud
of steam rising from the old mare. I did not see James; he was already
at the door, and came up the stairs and met me. It was less than
three hours since he left, and he must have posted out—who knows
how?—to Howgate, full nine miles off; yoked Jess, and driven her

astonished into town. He had an armful of blankets and was streaming with perspiration. He nodded to me, spread out on the floor two
pairs of clean old blankets having at their corners, "A.G., 1794,"
in large letters in red worsted. These were the initials of Alison
Græme, and James may have looked in at her from without—
himself unseen but not unthought of—when he was "wat, wat, and
weary," and after having walked many a mile over the hills, may
have seen her sitting, while "a' the lave were sleepin' "; and by the
firelight working her name on the blankets, for her ain James's bed.

He motioned Rab down, and taking his wife in his arms, laid
her in the blankets, and happed her carefully and firmly up, leaving
the face uncovered; and then lifting her, he nodded again sharply
to me, and with a resolved but utterly miserable face, strode along the
passage, and downstairs, followed by Rab. I followed with a light;
but he didn't need it. I went out, holding stupidly the candle in
my hand in the calm frosty air; we were soon at the gate. I could
have helped him, but I saw he was not to be meddled with, and he
was strong, and did not need it. He laid her down as tenderly, as
safely, as he had lifted her out ten days before—as tenderly as when
he had her first in his arms when she was only "A.G."—sorted her,
leaving that beautiful sealed face open to the heavens; and then
taking Jess by the head, he moved away. He did not notice me,
neither did Rab, who presided behind the cart.

I stood till they passed through the long shadow of the College,
and turned up Nicholson Street. I heard the solitary cart sound
through the streets, and die away and come again; and I returned,
thinking of that company going up Libberton Brae, then along
Roslin Muir, the morning light touching the Pentlands and making
them like on-looking ghosts; then down the hill through Auchin-
dinny woods, past "haunted Woodhouselee"; and as daybreak
came sweeping up the bleak Lammermuirs, and fell on his own door,
the company would stop, and James would take the key, and lift
Ailie up again, laying her on her own bed, and, having put Jess up,
would return with Rab and shut the door.

James buried his wife, with his neighbours mourning, Rab inspecting the solemnity from a distance. It was snow, and that black
ragged hole would look strange in the midst of the swelling spotless
cushion of white. James looked after everything; then rather sud-

denly fell ill, and took to bed; was insensible when the doctor came, and soon died. A sort of low fever was prevailing in the village, and his want of sleep, his exhaustion, and his misery, made him apt to take it. The grave was not difficult to reopen. A fresh fall of snow had again made all things white and smooth; Rab once more looked on, and slunk home to the stable.

And what of Rab? I asked for him next week of the new carrier who got the goodwill of James's business, and was now master of Jess and her cart. "How's Rab?" He put me off, and said rather rudely, "What's *your* business wi' the dowg?" I was not to be put off. "Where's Rab?" He, getting confused and red, and intermeddling with his hair, said, " 'Deed, sir, Rab's deid." "Dead! what did he die of?" "Weel, sir," said he, getting redder, "he didna exactly dee; he was killed. I had to brain him wi' a rack-pin; there was nae doin' wi' him. He lay in the treviss wi' the mear, and wadna come oot. I tempit him wi' kail and meat, but he wad tak naething, and keepit me frae feedin' the beast, and he was aye gur gurrin', and grup gruppin' me by the legs. I was laith to make awa wi' the auld dowg, his like wasna atween this and Thornhill—but, 'deed, sir, I could do naething else." I believed him. Fit end for Rab, quick and complete. His teeth and his friends gone, why should he keep the peace, and be civil?

Mary

by JOHN COLLIER

This fantastic tale about a sophisticated pig from "Presenting Moonshine" by John Collier is marked by charm, irony, and lightness of touch.

THERE was in those days—I hope it is there still—a village called Ufferleigh, lying all among the hills and downs of North Hampshire. In every cottage garden there was a giant apple tree, and when these trees were hung red with fruit, and the newly lifted potatoes lay gleaming between bean-row and cabbage-patch, a young man walked into the village who had never been there before.

He stopped in the lane just under Mrs. Hedges's gate, and looked up into her garden. Rosie, who was picking the beans, heard his tentative cough, and turned and leaned over the hedge to hear what he wanted. "I was wondering," said he, "if there was anybody in the village who had a lodging to let."

He looked at Rosie, whose cheeks were redder than the apples, and whose hair was the softest yellow imaginable. "I was wondering," said he in amendment, "if *you* had."

Rosie looked back at him. He wore a blue jersey such as seafaring men wear, but he seemed hardly like a seafaring man. His face was brown and plain and pleasant, and his hair was black. He was shabby and he was shy, but there was something about him that made it very certain he was not just a tramp. "I'll ask," said Rosie.

With that she ran for her mother, and Mrs. Hedges came out to interview the young man. "I've got to be near Andover for a week," said he, "but somehow I didn't fancy staying right in the town."

"There's a bed," said Mrs. Hedges. "If you don't mind having your meals with us—"

611

"Why, surely, ma'am," said he. "There's nothing I'd like better."

Everything was speedily arranged; Rosie picked another handful of beans, and in an hour he was seated with them at supper. He told them his name was Fred Baker, but, apart from that, he was so polite that he could hardly speak, and in the end Mrs. Hedges had to ask him outright what his business was. "Why, ma'am," said he, looking her straight in the face, "I've done one thing and another ever since I was so high, but I heard an old proverb once, how to get on in the world. 'Feed 'em or amuse 'em,' it said. So that's what I do, ma'am. I travel with a pig."

Mrs. Hedges said she had never heard of such a thing.

"You surprise me," said he. "Why, there are some in London, they tell me, making fortunes on the halls. Spell, count, add up, answer questions, anything. But let them wait," said he, smiling, "till they see Mary."

"Is that the name of your pig?" asked Rosie.

"Well," said Fred, shyly, "it's what I call her just between ourselves like. To her public, she's Zola. Sort of Frenchified, I thought. Spicy, if you'll excuse the mention of it. But in the caravan I call her Mary."

"You live in a caravan?" cried Rosie, delighted by the doll's-house idea.

"We do," said he. "She has her bunk, and I have mine."

"I don't think I should like that," said Mrs. Hedges. "Not a pig. No."

"She's as clean," said he, "as a new-born babe. And as for company, well, you'd say she's human. All the same, it's a bit of a wandering life for her—up hill and down dale, as the saying goes. Between you and me I shan't be satisfied till I get her into one of these big London theatres. You can see us in the West End!"

"I should like the caravan best," said Rosie, who seemed to have a great deal to say for herself, all of a sudden.

"It's pretty," said Fred. "Curtains, you know. Pot of flowers. Little stove. Somehow I'm used to it. Can't hardly think of myself staying at one of them big hotels. Still, Mary's got her career to think of. I can't stand in the way of her talent, so that's that."

"Is she big?" asked Rosie.

"It's not her size," said he. "No more than Shirley Temple. It's her brains and personality. Clever as a wagonload of monkeys! You'd like her. She'd like you, I reckon. Yes, I reckon she would. Sometimes I'm afraid I'm a bit slow by way of company for her, never having had much to do with the ladies."

"Don't tell me," said Mrs. Hedges archly, as convention required.

" 'Tis so, ma'am," said he. "Always on the move, you see, ever since I was a nipper. Baskets and brooms, pots and pans, then some acrobat stuff, then Mary. Never two days in the same place. It don't give you the time to get acquainted."

"You're going to be here a whole week, though," said Rosie artlessly, but at once her red cheeks blushed a hundred times redder than before, for Mrs. Hedges gave her a sharp look, which made her see that her words might have been taken the wrong way.

Fred, however, had noticed nothing. "Yes," said he, "I shall be here a week. And why? Mary ran a nail in her foot in the marketplace, Andover. Finished her act—and collapsed. Now she's at the vet's, poor creature."

"Oh, poor thing!" cried Rosie.

"I was half afraid," said he, "it was going wrong on her. But it seems she'll pull round all right, and I took opportunity to have the van repaired a bit, and soon we'll be on the road again. I shall go in and see her tomorrow. Maybe I can find some blackberries to take her by way of a relish, so to speak."

"Colley Bottom," said Rosie. "That's the place where they grow big and juicy."

"Ah! If I knew where it was—" said Fred tentatively.

"Perhaps, in the morning, if she's got time, she'll show you," said Mrs. Hedges, who began to feel very kindly disposed towards the young man.

In the morning, surely enough, Rosie did have time, and she showed Fred the place, and helped him pick the berries. Returning from Andover, later in the day, Fred reported that Mary had tucked into them a fair treat, and he had little doubt that, if she could have spoken, she would have sent her special thanks. Nothing is more affecting than the gratitude of a dumb animal, and Rosie was impelled to go every morning with Fred to pick a few more berries for the invalid pig.

On these excursions Fred told her a great deal more about Mary, a bit about the caravan, and a little about himself. She saw that he was very bold and knowing in some ways, but incredibly simple and shy in others. This, she felt, showed he had a good heart.

The end of the week seemed to come very soon, and all at once they were coming back from Colley Bottom for the last time. Fred said he would never forget Ufferleigh, nor the nice time he had had there.

"You ought to send us a postcard when you're on your travels," said Rosie.

"Yes," he said. "That's an idea. I will."

"Yes, do," said Rosie.

"Yes," said he again. "I will. Do you know, I was altogether downhearted at going away, but now I'm half wishing I was on the road again already. So I could be sending that card right away," said he.

"At that rate," said Rosie, looking the other way, "you might as well make it a letter."

"Ah!" said he. "And do you know what I should feel like putting at the bottom of that letter? If you was my young lady, that is. Which, of course, you're not. Me never having had one."

"What?" said Rosie.

"A young lady," said he.

"But what would you put?" said she.

"Ah!" said he. "What I'd put. Do you know what I'd put? If— *if*, mind you—if you was my young lady?"

"No," said she, "what?"

"I don't hardly like to tell you," said he.

"Go on," she said. "You don't want to be afraid."

"All right," said he. "Only mind you, it's *if*." And with his stick he traced three crosses in the dust.

"If I was anybody's young lady," said Rosie, "I shouldn't see anything wrong in that. After all, you've got to move with the times."

Neither of them said another word, for two of the best reasons in the world. First, they were unable to; second, it was not necessary. They walked on with their faces as red as fire, in an agony of happiness.

Fred had a word with Mrs. Hedges, who had taken a fancy to him from the start. Not that she had not always looked down upon caravan people, and could have been knocked over with a feather, had anyone suggested, at any earlier date, that she would allow a daughter of hers to marry into such a company. But right was right: this Fred Baker was different, as anyone with half an eye could see. He had kept himself to himself, almost to a fault, for his conversation showed that he was as innocent as a new-born babe. Moreover, several knowledgeable people in the village had agreed that his ambitions for Mary, his pig, were in no way unjustified. Everyone had heard of such talented creatures, reclining on snowwhite sheets in the best hotels of the metropolis, drinking champagne like milk, and earning for their fortunate owners ten pounds, or even twenty pounds, a week.

So Mrs. Hedges smilingly gave her consent, and Rosie became Fred's real, genuine, proper young lady. He was to save all he could during the winter, and she to stitch and sing. In the spring, he would come back and they were to get married.

"At Easter," said he.

"No," said Mrs. Hedges, counting on her fingers. "In May. Then tongues can't wag, caravan or no caravan."

Fred had not the faintest idea what she was driving at, for he had lived so much alone that no one had told him certain things that every young man should know. However, he well realized that this was an unusually short engagement for Ufferleigh, and represented a great concession to the speed and dash of the entertainment industry, so he respectfully agreed, and set off on his travels.

My Darling Rosie,

Well here we are in Painswick having had a good night Saturday at Evesham. Mary cleverer than ever that goes without saying now spells four new words thirty-six in all and when I say now Mary how do you like Painswick or Evesham or wherever it is she picks FINE it goes down very well. She is in the best of health and hope you are the same. Seems to understand every word I say more like a human being every day. Well I suppose I must be getting our bit of supper ready she always sets up her cry for that specially when I am writing to you.

With true love
FRED XXX

In May the apple trees were all in bloom, so it was an apple-blossom wedding, which in those parts is held to be an assurance of flowery days. Afterwards they took the bus to the market town, to pick up the caravan, which stood in a stable yard. On the way Fred asked Rosie to wait a moment, and dived into a confectioner's shop. He came out with a huge box of chocolates. Rosie smiled all over her face with joy. "For me?" she said.

"Yes," said he. "To give to her as soon as she claps eyes on you. They're her weakness. I want you two to be real pals."

"All right," said Rosie, who was the best-hearted girl in the world.

The next moment they turned into the yard: there was the caravan. "Oh, it's lovely!" cried Rosie.

"Now you'll see her," said Fred.

At the sound of his voice a falsetto squeal rose from within.

"Here we are, old lady," said Fred, opening the door. "Here's a friend of mine come to help look after you. Look, she's brought you something you'll fancy."

Rosie saw a middle-sized pig, flesh-coloured, neat, and with a smart collar. It had a small and rather calculating eye. Rosie offered the chocolates: they were accepted without any very effusive acknowledgment.

Fred put the old horse in, and soon they were off, jogging up the long hills to the west. Rosie sat beside Fred on the driving seat; Mary took her afternoon nap. Soon the sky began to redden where the road divided the woods on the far hill-top. Fred turned into a green lane, and they made their camp.

He lit the stove, and Rosie put on the potatoes. They took a lot of peeling, for it seemed that Mary ate with gusto. Rosie put a gigantic rice pudding into the oven, and soon had the rest of the meal prepared.

Fred set the table. He laid three places.

"I say," said Rosie.

"What?" said Fred.

"Does she eat along with us?" said Rosie. "A pig?"

Fred turned quite pale. He beckoned her outside the caravan. "Don't say a thing like that," said he. "She won't never take to you if you say a thing like that. Didn't you see her give you a look?"

"Yes, I did," said Rosie. "All the same— Well, never mind, Fred. I don't care, really. I just thought I did."

"You wait," said Fred. "You're thinking of ordinary pigs. Mary's different."

Certainly Mary seemed a comparatively tidy eater. All the same, she gave Rosie one or two very odd glances from under her silky straw-coloured lashes. She seemed to hock her rice pudding about a bit with the end of her nose.

"What's up, old girl?" said Fred. "Didn't she put enough sugar in the pudden? Never mind—can't get everything right first time."

Mary, with a rather cross hiccup, settled herself on her bunk. "Let's go out," said Rosie, "and have a look at the moon."

"I suppose we might," said Fred. "Shan't be long, Mary. Just going about as far as that gate down the lane." Mary grunted morosely and turned her face to the wall.

Rosie and Fred went out and leaned over the gate. The moon, at least, was all that it should be.

"Seems funny, being married and all," said Rosie softly.

"Seems all right to me," said Fred.

"Remember them crosses you drew in the dirt in the road that day?" said Rosie.

"That I do," said Fred.

"And all them you put in the letters?" said Rosie.

"All of 'em," said Fred.

"Kisses, that's what they're supposed to stand for," said Rosie.

"So they say," said Fred.

"You haven't given me one, not since we was married," said Rosie. "Don't you like it?"

"That I do," said Fred. "Only, I don't know—"

"What?" said Rosie.

"It makes me feel all queer," said Fred, "when I kiss you. As if I wanted—"

"What?" said Rosie.

"I dunno," said Fred. "I don't know if it's I want to eat you all up, or what."

"Try and find out, they say," said Rosie.

A delicious moment followed. In the very middle of it a piercing squeal rose from the caravan. Fred jumped as if he were shot.

"Oh, dear," he cried. "She's wondering what's up. Here I come, old girl! Here I come! It's her bed-time, you see. Here I come to tuck you in!"

Mary, with an air of some petulance, permitted this process. Rosie stood by. "I suppose we'd better make it lights out," said Fred. "She likes a lot of sleep, you see, being a brain worker."

"Where do *we* sleep?" said Rosie.

"I made the bunk all nice for you this morning," said Fred. "Me, I'm going to doss below. A sack full of straw, I've got."

"But—" said Rosie. "But—"

"But what?" said he.

"Nothing," said she. "Nothing."

They turned in. Rosie lay for an hour or two, thinking what thoughts I don't know. Perhaps she thought how charming it was that Fred should have lived so simple and shy and secluded all these years, and yet be so knowing about so many things, and yet be so innocent, and never have been mixed up in bad company— It is impossible to say what she thought.

In the end she dozed off, only to be wakened by a sound like the bagpipes of the devil himself. She sat up, terrified. It was Mary.

"What's up? What's up?" Fred's voice came like the ghost's in *Hamlet* from under the floor. "Give her some milk," he said.

Rosie poured out a bowl of milk. Mary ceased her fiendish racket while she drank, but the moment Rosie had blown out the light, and got into bed again, she began a hundred times worse than before.

There were rumblings under the caravan. Fred appeared in the doorway, half dressed and with a straw in his hair.

"She *will* have me," he said, in great distress.

"Can't you— Can't you lie down here?" said Rosie.

"What? And you sleep below?" said Fred, astounded.

"Yes," said Rosie, after a rather long pause. "And me sleep below."

Fred was overwhelmed with gratitude and remorse. Rosie couldn't help feeling sorry for him. She even managed to give him a smile before she went down to get what rest she could on the sack of straw.

In the morning, she woke feeling rather dejected. There was a mighty breakfast to be prepared for Mary; afterwards Fred drew her aside.

"Look here," he said. "This won't do. I can't have you sleeping on the ground, worse than a gippo. I'll tell you what I'm going to do. I'm going to get up my acrobat stuff again. I used to make a lot that way, and I liked it fine. Hand springs, double somersaults, bit of conjuring: it went down well. Only I didn't have time to keep in practice with Mary to look after. But if you'd do the looking after her, we'd make it a double turn, and soon we'd have a good bit of cash. And then—"

"Yes?" said Rosie.

"Then," said Fred, "I could buy you a trailer."

"All right," said Rosie, and turned away. Suddenly she turned back with her face flaming. "You may know a lot about pigs," she said bitterly. "And about somersaults, and conjuring and baskets and brooms and I don't know what-all. But there's *one* thing you *don't* know." And with that she went off and cried behind a hedge.

After a while she got the upper hand of it, and came back to the caravan. Fred showed her how to give Mary her morning bath, then the depilatory—that was very hard on the hands—then the rubbing with Cleopatra Face Cream—and not on her face merely—then the powdering, then the manicuring and polishing of her trotters.

Rosie, resolved to make the best of it, conquered her repugnance, and soon mastered these handmaidenly duties. She was relieved at first that the spoiled pig accepted her ministrations without protest. Then she noticed the gloating look in its eye.

However, there was no time to brood about that. No sooner was the toilet finished than it was time to prepare the enormous lunch. After lunch Mary had her little walk, except on Saturdays when there was an afternoon show, then she took her rest. Fred explained that during this period she liked to be talked to, and have her back scratched a bit. Mary had quite clearly decided that in future she was going to have it scratched a lot. Then she had her massage. Then tea, then another little walk, or the evening show, according to where they were, and then it was time to prepare dinner. At the end of the day Rosie was thankful to curl up on her poor sack of straw.

When she thought of the bunk above, and Fred, and his simplicity, her heart was fit to break. The only thing was, she loved him dearly, and she felt that if they could soon snatch an hour alone together, they might kiss a little more, and a ray of light might dispel the darkness of excessive innocence.

Each new day she watched for that hour, but it didn't come. Mary saw to that. Once or twice Rosie suggested a little stroll, but at once the hateful pig grumbled some demand or other that kept her hard at work till it was too late. Fred, on his side, was busy enough with his practicing. He meant it so well, and worked so hard—but what did it lead to? A trailer!

As the days went by, she found herself more and more the slave of this arrogant grunter. Her back ached, her hands got chapped and red, she never had a moment to make herself look nice, and never a moment alone with her beloved. Her dress was spotted and spoiled, her smile was gone, her temper was going. Her pretty hair fell in elf locks and tangles, and she had neither time nor heart to comb it.

She tried to come to an explanation with Fred, but it was nothing but cross purposes and then cross words. He tried in a score of little ways to show that he loved her: these seemed to her a mere mockery, and she gave him short answers. Then he stopped, and she thought he loved her no longer. Even worse, she felt she no longer loved him.

So the whole summer went by, and things got worse and worse, and you would have taken her for a gipsy indeed.

The blackberries were ripe again; she found a whole brake of them. When she tasted one, all sorts of memories flooded into her heart: she went and found Fred. "Fred," she said, "the blackberries are ripe again. I've brought you one or two." She held out some in her grubby hand. Fred took them and tasted them; she watched to see what the result would be.

"Yes," said he, "they're ripe. They won't gripe her. Take her and pick her some this afternoon."

Rosie turned away without a word, and in the afternoon she took Mary across the stubbles to where the ripe berries grew. Mary, when she saw them, dispensed for once with dainty service, and began to help herself very liberally. Rosie, finding she had nothing more urgent to attend to, sat down on a bank and sobbed bitterly.

In the middle of it all she heard a voice asking what was the matter.

She looked up and there was a fat, shrewd, jolly-looking farmer. "What is it, my girl?" said he. "Are you hungry?"

"No," said she, "I'm fed up."

"What with?" said he.

"A pig!" said she, with a gulp.

"You've got no call to bawl and cry," said he. "There's nothing like a bit of pork. I'd have the indigestion for that, any day."

"It's not pork," she said. "It's a pig. A live pig."

"Have you lost it?" said he.

"I wish I had," said she. "I'm that miserable I don't know what to do."

"Tell me your troubles," said he. "There's no harm in a bit of sympathy."

So Rosie told him about Fred, and about Mary, and what hopes she'd had and what they'd all come to, and how she was the slave of this insolent, spoiled, jealous pig, and in fact she told him everything except one little matter which she could hardly bring herself to repeat, even to the most sympathetic of fat farmers.

The farmer, pushing his hat over his eyes, scratched his head very thoughtfully. "Really," said he. "I can't hardly believe it."

"It's true," said Rosie, "every word."

"I mean," said the farmer. "A young man—a young gal—the young gal sleeping down on a sack of straw—a pretty young gal like you. Properly married and all. Not to put too fine a point on it, young missus, aren't the bunks wide enough, or what?"

"He doesn't know," sobbed Rosie. "He just doesn't know no more'n a baby. And she won't let us ever be alone a minute. So he'd find out."

The farmer scratched his head more furiously than ever. Looking at her tear-stained face, he found it hard to doubt her. On the other hand it seemed impossible that a pig should know so much and a young man should know so little. But at that moment Mary came trotting through the bushes, with an egoistical look on her face, which was well besmeared with the juice of the ripe berries.

"Is this your pig?" said the farmer.

"Well," said Rosie, "I'm just taking her for a walk."

The shrewd farmer was quick to notice the look that Rosie got from the haughty grunter when it heard the expression "your pig." This, and Rosie's hurried, nervous disclaimer, convinced the worthy man that the story he had heard was well founded.

"You're taking her for a walk?" said he musingly. "Well! Well! Well! I'll tell you what. If you'd ha' been here this time tomorrow you'd have met *me* taking a walk, with a number of very dear young friends of mine, all very much like her. You might have come along. Two young sows, beautiful creatures, though maybe not so beautiful as that one. Three young boars, in the prime of their health and handsomeness. Though I say it as shouldn't, him that's unattached— he's a prince. Oh, what a beautiful young boar that young boar really is!"

"You don't say?" said Rosie.

"For looks and pedigree both," said the farmer, "he's a prince. The fact is, it's their birthday, and I'm taking 'em over to the village for a little bit of a celebration. I suppose this young lady has some other engagement tomorrow."

"She has to have her sleep just about this time," said Rosie, ignoring Mary's angry grunt.

"Pity!" said the farmer. "She'd have just made up the party. Such fun they'll have! Such refreshments! Sweet apples, cakes, biscuits, a bushel of chocolate creams. Everything most refined, of course, but plenty. You know what I mean—plenty. And that young boar —you know what I mean. If she *should* be walking by—"

"I'm afraid not," said Rosie.

"Pity!" said the farmer. "Ah, well. I must be moving along."

With that, he bade them good afternoon, raising his hat very politely to Mary, who looked after him for a long time, and then walked sulkily home, gobbling to herself all the way.

The next afternoon Mary seemed eager to stretch out on her bunk, and, for once, instead of requiring the usual number of little attentions from Rosie, she closed her eyes in sleep. Rosie took the opportunity to pick up a pail and go off to buy the evening ration of fresh milk. When she got back Fred was still at his practice by the wayside, and Rosie went round to the back of the caravan, and the door was swinging open, and the bunk was empty.

She called Fred. They sought high and low. They went along the roads, fearing she might have been knocked over by a motor car. They went calling through the woods, hoping she had fallen asleep under a tree. They looked in ponds and ditches, behind haystacks, under bridges, everywhere. Rosie thought of the farmer's joking talk, but she hardly liked to say anything about it to Fred.

They called and called all night, scarcely stopping to rest. They sought all the next day. It grew dark, and Fred gave up hope. They plodded silently back to the caravan.

He sat on a bunk, with his head in his hand.

"I shall never see her again," he said. "Been pinched, that's what she's been.

"When I think," he said, "of all the hopes I had for that pig—

"When I think," he said, "of all you've done for her! And what it's meant to you—

"I know she had some faults in her nature," he said. "But that was artistic. Temperament, it was. When you got a talent like that—

"And now she's gone!" he said. With that he burst into tears.

"Oh, Fred!" cried Rosie. "Don't!"

Suddenly she found she loved him just as much as ever, more than ever. She sat down beside him and put her arms round his neck. "Darling Fred, don't cry!" she said again.

"It's been rough on you, I know," said Fred. "I didn't ever mean it to be."

"There! There," said Rosie. She gave him a kiss, and then she gave him another. It was a long time since they had been as close as this. There was nothing but the two of them and the caravan; the tiny lamp, and darkness all round; their kisses, and grief all round. "Don't let go," said Fred. "It makes it better."

"I'm not letting go," she said.

"Rosie," said Fred. "I feel— Do you know how I feel?"

"I know," she said. "Don't talk."

"Rosie," said Fred, but this was some time later. "Who'd have thought it?"

"Ah! Who would, indeed?" said Rosie.

"Why didn't you tell me?" said Fred.

"How could I tell you?" said she.

"You know," said he. "We might never have found out—never! —if she hadn't been pinched."

"Don't talk about her," said Rosie.

"I can't help it," said Fred. "Wicked or not, I can't help it—I'm glad she's gone. It's worth it. I'll make enough on the acrobat stuff. I'll make brooms as well. Pots and pans, too."

"Yes," said Rosie. "But look! It's morning. I reckon you're tired, Fred—running up hill and down dale all day yesterday. You lie abed now, and I'll go down to the village and get you something good for breakfast."

"All right," said Fred. "And tomorrow I'll get yours."

So Rosie went down to the village, and bought the milk and the bread and so forth. As she passed the butcher's shop she saw some new-made pork sausages of a singularly fresh, plump, and appetizing appearance. So she bought some, and very good they smelled while they were cooking.

"That's another thing we couldn't have while she was here," said Fred, as he finished his plateful. "Never no pork sausages, on account of her feelings. I never thought to see the day I'd be glad she was pinched. I only hope she's gone to someone who appreciates her."

"I'm sure she has," said Rosie. "Have some more."

"I will," said he. "I don't know if it's the novelty, or the way you cooked 'em, or what. I never ate a better sausage in my life. If we'd gone up to London with her, best hotels and all, I doubt if ever we'd have had as sweet a sausage as these here."